"WHY ARE

Tess considered refusing to answer but Bahktiian was a dangerous man. It was better to choose her words carefully. "I am here to travel with the priest and his party."

"I do not think that they want you to travel with them."

"But I will travel with them nevertheless. Do you intend to make me leave the tribe?"

"I have never had any such intention. I don't have time now to get you back to the port from which you can sail to Jeds. You will be safe with the tribe until we return."

"Until who returns?"

"Ah. You thought the khepelli party was to be escorted by the entire tribe. But it is many months' journey to the shrine of Morava, where these holy men hope to find enlightenment. My jahar, my riders, will be their sole escort. We can move faster, and if there is trouble, well then, we are better able to deal with it. You, of course, will stay with the women."

As if that settled the entire thing, Bahktiian nodded and excused himself.

Standing alone in unknown surroundings, Tess suddenly felt scared, a solitary and untried force against whatever convoluted plans the Chapalii had made, were making even now, against her brother. Yet she had no choice but to stay with them until she learned what they were plotting, until she could find a way of getting a warning back to her brother, a warning she prayed would not come too late . . .

JARAN

KATE ELLIOTT

DAW BOOKS, INC.
DONALD A. WOLLHEIM, FOUNDER
375 Hudson Street, New York, NY 10014

ELIZABETH R. WOLLHEIM
SHEILA E. GILBERT
PUBLISHERS

ACKNOWLEDGMENTS

The epigraphs by Empedocles of Agragas (Chapters 1, 18, 20, 24, and 26), Democritus of Abdera (Chapters 2, 6, 10, 12, 13, 23, and 27), Xenophanes of Colophon (Chapters 3 and 11), Musaeus (Chapter 4), Heracleitus of Ephesus (Chapters 5, 9, 14, 19, and 28), Epicharmus of Syracuse (Chapters 7, 15, and 22), Parmenides of Elea (Chapter 8), Antiphon the Sophist (Chapter 16 and 29), Pherecydes of Syros (Chapter 17), Prodicus of Ceas (Chapter 21), and Critias of Athens (Chapter 25) are reprinted by permission of the publisher, Harvard University Press, from *Ancilla to The Pre-Socratic Philosophers*, A complete translation of the Fragments in Diels by Kathleen Freeman. Copyright © 1966 by Harvard University Press.

Sappho, lines from "poem 2," which appear on page 336, are reprinted by permission of the publisher, The University of Chicago, from *Greek Lyrics* translated by Richmond Lattimore, Second Edition, revised and enlarged; copyright © 1960, A Phoenix Book published by the University of Chicago Press.

First Printing, June 1992
1 2 3 4 5 6 7 8 9

For my parents,
who made it all possible,

and for Carol Wolf
who, against all my protests,
made me do it right.

ACKNOWLEDGMENTS

This is a very long list, and I am sure I have forgotten some names. It took me long enough from first draft to finished draft that it would be amazing if I *hadn't* forgotten someone. All of them contributed in some way to making this book.

Sandy Campbell, wherever she may be; Dawn Hilton; Dr. Charles Sullivan III; Dr. Edward Milowicki and Dr. Elizabeth Pope; Steve Henderson, Hilary Powers, Bill Jouris, and the rest of the Orcs; Masae Kubota; Lorna Brown; Frank Berry; Greg Armbruster (for first suggesting we see more of Charles, even though I didn't listen to him at the time); Neile Whitney (for reminding me that women are not girls), Melissa Forbes-Nicoll, and my other Wales buddies; Jane Butler, my agent; Dr. Judith Tarr (who, among many many many other things, valiantly corrected my horse mistakes—any bits that strike you right are hers, the faults are incontestably mine); my writers' group, who shall go nameless because they know who they are; Jay Silverstein and his wonderful family; Brandon Chamberlain (for tactical advice); Kit Brahtin (for not letting me give up); Tad Williams (for much the same reason); Alis Rasmussen (for generously letting me borrow a corner of her universe); Raven Gildea; Ingrid Baber; Amy Conner (for the warp and weft); Dianne Boatwright; my dear cousin Eric Elliott; Todd and Barbara Craig (because it was always their favorite); Dr. John W. Bernhardt (for reading the penultimate draft); to Sibling Units One, Two, and Three, who have always been so supportive; and, of course, to my editor Sheila Gilbert, who made me make one damned last revision, and believe me I hated every minute of it, but she was right.

And last, but never least, to Jane Austen.

AUTHOR'S NOTE

Jaran names have been transliterated into their Earth equivalencies. For instance, *U'rhyinhias* (pronounced You-rye-EEN-yas) has been simplified into *Yurinya* (pronounced You-RHEEN-ya or YOU-rhee). This has proved easier on the eye for those inexperienced in Xenolinguistics, as well as lending a certain flavor to the jaran culture because of this superficial similarity to a well-known archaic Earth language.

"Bodies attract each other with a force
that varies directly as the product of
their masses and inversely as the square
of the distance between them."

—ISAAC NEWTON

Earth, Nairobi Port
A.L.C. 261 month 5 day 3
Terese Soerensen to Charles Soerensen

Dear Charles,
  Please don't think I'm running away. I really did mean, when I decided to go to Dao Cee system, to visit you on Odys—but I need to be by myself right now, without you trying to give me well-meant advice or telling me that being your heir is just a technicality and that it doesn't mean that much. Because it's not true.
  Charles, I didn't tell you that I got engaged six months ago. He insisted that we keep it a secret, and now I know why. Obviously he figured you would see through his "love" for me to his real motives. I made the mistake of telling him that under Chapaliian law a sister loses all right to her brother's [INSERT: or her father's] goods and titles upon marriage—that she assumes, totally, her husband's position. That was one month ago.
  One month ago I was still engaged, and I didn't know that humiliation could help a person do six month's work in five weeks. I feel sick. I hate myself for being so stupid. And I can't even tell you his name, because he's studying Xenodiplomacy at the Sorbonne, and I'm afraid he'll think I sabotaged his career. He's one of those men who think women have no honor. Can *you* understand how I fell in love with him? Because I can't.
  I thought that I had the courage to tell you to your face

that I don't want to be your heir, that I'm sick and tired of people implying that my success at Univerzita Karlova is due to your position and not to my talent, that I'm never seen as myself but only as an extension of you. Can't I just abdicate being your sister and let you adopt? Or is it only death or marriage that will remove me from your title? Not, of course, that I'm likely to find either situation appealing. God, Charles, I feel like I have no direction, that I can't trust my own judgment, that I've been abandoned in the middle of nowhere. And I hate being melodramatic.

[ERASE DOCUMENT]

Earth, Nairobi Port
A.L.C. 261 .5.3
Terese Soerensen to Charles Soerensen

Dear Charles,

   I finished my thesis early (with honors, by the way) and Univerzita Karlova agreed to give me a leave of absence. I've let out my flat in Prague and I'm going to visit Dr. Hierakis at the palace in Jeds. I know I don't have an official clearance for Rhui, but I do have a copy of the preserve regulations, and you know how well I speak Rhuian. I'm going to appropriate a place on the Rhuian cargo shuttle of the next ship headed to the Dao Cee system. I'm thinking of doing my dissertation on one of the Rhuian languages, so I'll be researching as well. I'm not sure how soon I'll get to Odys.

Your loving sister,
Tess

CHAPTER ONE

"I wept and I wailed
when I saw the unfamiliar land."
—EMPEDOCLES OF AGRAGAS

A spark flew, spiraling upward from the massive frame of
the new Port Authority building. Its fiery light winked out
against the heavy glastic pane that separated the deep pit of
the construction bay from the temporary spaceport offices.

Two young women sat on a padded bench by the huge
overlook. One, black-skinned and black-haired, watched the
work below. The second, looking pale and light-haired
mostly in contrast to her companion, studied the words she
had just typed into her hand-held computer slate. She
frowned.

"What are you writing, Tess?" asked the first, turning
back to her friend. Then she grinned. "Sweet Goddess, what
language is that in?"

Tess tapped *save* and *clear* and the words vanished. "Just
practicing." She shrugged. "That was late American En-
glish. It's only about 300 years old, so you could probably
puzzle it out given time. I built in a translation program.
Here's how the same thing would look in classical Latin."
Words appeared again. "Ophiuchi-Sei." The letters shifted
to a fluid script. "And here's court Chapalii. Formal Chapalii. And colloquial enscribed Chapalii. You'll notice how
the glyphs differ in written form only in the tails and in the
angling of the curve—"

"You *are* nervous, aren't you? What if the captain refuses
you passage?"

"He won't refuse," muttered Tess. She brushed her hand
across the screen, clearing it. "And steward class Chapalii
of course has no enscribed counterpart at all, so I've tran-

scribed it into Anglais characters. What do you think, Soje? It's an act of rebellion, you know, for stewards to write.''

Sojourner lifted her brows questioningly and glanced out at the new port building rising behind them along alien lines. Along Chapalii lines. ''Is that why the chameleons think we humans are barbarians? Because we allow everyone to write?''

Tess laughed. ''That doesn't help. No, because our spoken tongue and written tongue are the same, and a standard. Because we're too egalitarian. Because we're so young, as a species, as a culture, compared to them.''

''Because our physiological system is so inefficient, compared to theirs?'' Sojourner waved toward the building behind them. ''Just like our technology is primitive? I hate them.'' She glanced around the waiting chamber. The walls, a muted orange in the fading daylight, curved in at the top; their dullness diminished the thirty meters between the ends of the room. The air smelled of heat and spices: cinnamon, cloves, and cardamom. It was an alien room, designed for the taste of Chapalii, not humans. ''No. I don't hate them. They've proven neither cruel nor harsh as our masters.''

''Their grip is soft,'' said Tess in an undertone.

Sojourner gave her a sharp glance. ''But it chafes,'' she replied, quieter still. ''Tess, are you sure you really *want* to go see your brother? Jacques isn't worth this. He was a spoiled, pretty rich kid who wanted to get ahead without working for it. He's not worth your running away—''

Tess winced. ''I'm not running away. I finished my thesis. I've got obligations to Charles now.''

''What about your research? I *know* you don't want to follow in Charles's footsteps. Why go now?''

''Soje, *leave be.*'' The force of her comment silenced both of them. ''As if I could follow in his footsteps anyway,'' Tess murmured finally.

Sojourner lifted up her hands in defeat. ''Goddess, you're stubborn. Go. Be miserable. Just remember I told you so. You've always hated Odys. You always say so, and that one time I went there with you, I can't say as I blame you. Ugly planet.''

''It wasn't before the Chapalii got through with it,'' said Tess so softly that Sojourner did not hear her.

A chime rang through the room. A seam opened out of orange wall to reveal a nondescript man in police blues. His shoulders shrugged in an exaggerated sigh when he saw them.

"Office is closed," he said, obviously used to saying that phrase frequently. "And it's off limits to humans at all times, except for the midday hour *if* you've got a dispensation." He regarded them, measuring. What he saw, Tess could well imagine: two young women, only a single valise between them, dressed without any particular style that might mark them out as rich enough or important enough to rate a dispensation or otherwise be allowed entrance into the private corridors of humanity's alien masters.

"If you'll allow me to escort you out," he said, firmly but kindly.

Sojourner looked at Tess expectantly. Tess felt frozen. Again it came down to this: retreat with meek dignity, as any other human on Earth would have to, or use her brother's name like a weapon. How she hated that, having a name that meant something in four languages. Having a name that, through no work of her own, had become so identified with humanity's one great rebellion against the Chapaliian Empire that the name was now synonymous with that rebellion. Charles had come so early to a realization of what he had to do in his life that surely he could never comprehend her struggle. But she had backed herself into a corner and had no choice but to go forward.

"You *must* leave," he said, coming briskly toward them.

"My name is Terese Soerensen," she said, despising herself as she said it. "My companion is Sojourner King Bakundi."

The second name did not even register. He stopped stockstill. His face changed. *"The* Soerensen? You're his sister?" He hesitated. Then, of course, he looked both abashed and eager. "It is an honor. An honor, to meet you." She extended her hand and he flushed, pleased, and shook it. "I have a cousin. She fought at Sirin Wild, with the last fleet, on the *Jerusalem*. She was lucky enough to escape the decompression."

"I'm glad," said Tess sincerely. "Where is she now?"

He grinned. "She's a netcaster now. Ferreting information. For the long haul."

"For the long haul," echoed Tess fiercely.

Sojourner murmured, *"Amandla."*

A hum signaled a new parting of the wall. The guard,

startled, spun to look. One of the ubiquitous Chapalii stewards entered the room. Like all the Chapalii serving class, he wore long, thick pants and a heavy tunic belted at his narrow waist. A hint of green colored the pale skin of his face—a sign of disapproval.

"What is this intrusion?" he demanded. He spoke in the clean, clipped Anglais that those few stewards assigned to direct intercourse with humans used. "I insist these offices be cleared." His gaze skipped from the guard to Sojourner. "Of these *females*."

Tess stood up. The Chapalii steward looked at her. Like an indrawn breath, the pause that followed was full of anticipated release.

The green cast to his white skin shaded into blue distress. His thin, alien frame bent in the stiff bow Chapalii accorded only and always to the members of their highest aristocracy.

"Lady Terese," the steward said in the proper formal Chapalii. "I beg you will forgive my rash entrance and my rasher words."

Unable to trust her voice for a moment, Tess simply folded her hands together in her human approximation of that arrangement of hands called Imperial Clemency. The steward's complexion faded from distress to blessed neutrality again, white and even. Sojourner rose to stand next to Tess.

"I am here," said Tess in strict formal Chapalii, high rank to low, "to advise the captain of the *Oshaki* that I will board his vessel and depart with it so far as my brother's fief of Dao Cee."

He bowed again, obedient. "You would honor me, Lady Terese, if you granted me the privilege of showing you in to see Hao Yakii Tarimin."

"Await me beyond." Tess waved toward the still open seam in the wall. The steward bowed to the exact degree proper and retreated. The wall shut behind him.

"God, but it gives me pleasure to see them ordered around for a change," muttered the guard. Tess flushed, and the man looked uncomfortable, as if he was afraid he had offended her.

"Are they difficult to work for?" asked Sojourner quickly.

"Nay. Not if you do the work you're hired to do. They're the best employers I've had, really." He lifted his hands, palms up. "Which is ironic. Say, did you say Sojourner *King?*"

Sojourner chuckled, and Tess watched, envying her friend's easy geniality. "Yes. I was named after my great-grandmother, *that* Captain Sojourner King of the first L.S. *Jerusalem.*" She intoned the words with relish, able to laugh at her inherited fame in a way Tess had never managed. Then she sobered and turned to Tess. "I guess we part here, Tess. Take this, for luck." She took an ankh necklace from around her neck and handed it to Tess. "Keep well."

"Oh, Soje. I'll miss you." Tess hugged her, hard and quickly, to get it over with, shook the hand of the guard, picked up her valise, and walked across the room. The wall opened before her, admitting her to forbidden precincts.

"And don't you dare forget to send me a message from Odys," Sojourner called after her.

Tess lifted a hand in final farewell as the wall seamed shut, sealing her in to the corridor with the silent, patient steward. He bowed again, took her valise, and turned to lead her through the branching corridors. His lank hair and achromatic clothing lent the monotonous bleached-orange walls color in contrast, or at least to Tess's sight they did. She did not know what the walls looked like to his vision: like so much else, that was information not granted to humans.

It was hot, so hot that she immediately broke out in a sweat. Her hand clenched the computer slate. She felt like a traitor. Because she had no intention of going to Odys. She was afraid to go there, afraid to tell her own and only sibling that she could not carry on in his place, that she did not want the honor or the responsibility—that she did not know what she wanted, not at all. She did not even have the courage to tell a good friend. And Sojourner had been a good friend to her, these past years.

In the suite reserved for the captain, three Chapalii stood as she entered, bowed in by the steward. He hung back, retraining his hold on her exalted valise, as the wall closed between them. Tess surveyed her audience with dismay. To interview the captain was bad enough. To face three of them. . . .

She refused to give in to *this* kind of fear. The captain, thank God, was easy to recognize, because he wore the alloy elbow clip that marked his authority as a ship's master.

She drew in her breath, lifted her chin, and inclined her head with the exact degree of condescension that a duke's heir might grant a mere ship's captain.

Before the captain could bow, one of the other Chapalii stepped forward. "Who has allowed this interruption?" he demanded in formal Chapalii. "Our business here is private, Hao Yakii." The Chapalii turned his gaze on Tess, but she knew her ground here; indeed, conduct was so strictly regulated in Chapalii culture that she usually had a limited number of responses. It made life much easier. Knowing *he* was at fault, she could regard him evenly in return. As he realized that the captain, and, belatedly, the other Chapalii, were bowing deeply to her, his skin hazed from white to blue.

"I am honored," said the captain, straightening, "to be the recipient of your attention, Lady Terese. May I be given permission to hope that your brother the duke is in good health and that his endeavors are all flourishing and productive?"

"You may."

The slightest reddish tinge of satisfaction flushed the captain's face. He bowed in acknowledgment and gestured to his companions, introducing them in the formal, long-winded Chapalii style, not only their names but their house and affiliation and title and station and level of affluence: Cha Ishii Hokokul, younger son of the younger son of a great lord, no longer well off, traveling back to the home world; Hon Echido Keinaba, a fabulously wealthy merchant traveling to Odys to negotiate several deals with the merchants of the esteemed Tai-en Soerensen's household. Hon Echido bowed a second time, skin white, secure in his quick recognition of the duke's sister and doubtless hoping that his acumen here would stand him in good stead in the haggling to come. Cha Ishii bowed as well, but it was not nearly as deep a bow as a duke's heir merited.

Tess acknowledged them and nodded again at the captain. "Hao Yakii. I desire passage on your ship, to the Dao Cee system."

He did not hesitate. Of course, he could not. "It is yours, Lady Terese. You honor me and my family with your presence."

Before she could reply, Cha Ishii compounded his first offense by addressing the captain in court Chapalii. "Hao

Yakii, this is impossible that a Mushai's relative should be allowed on this run. You must prevent it.''

Hao Yakii went violet with mortification, whether at Ishii's effrontery or at some mistake he had just realized. Hon Echido watched, neutral, unreadable, and doubtless unsure whether any human could actually understand the intricacies of court Chapalii.

But Tess's dismay had evaporated, drawn off by her irritation at Ishii's assumption that she could not understand him, and by sheer human curiosity at the mention of that name, *Mushai*. "You refer, I believe," she said directly to Ishii in court Chapalii, thus indirectly insulting him, "to the *Tai-en Mushai*. Was he not a duke who rebelled against one of your ancient emperors?"

Ishii blushed violet.

Violet and pink warred in the captain's face. Approval won. "Lady Terese, it is, as you would call it—" A long pause. "A fable. A legend. Do you not have legends of ages past when your lands ran with precious metals and all people of proper rank had sufficient wealth to maintain their position, and then a traitor who would not adhere to right conduct brought ruin to everyone by his selfish actions?"

Tess almost laughed. How often as a child had she and her classmates been told of that time a mere two centuries ago when a consortium of five solar systems bound by inexplicably close genetic ties and the enthusiasm of newly-discovered interstellar flight had invested their League Concordance as law? A brief golden age, they called it, before the Chapaliian Empire, in its relentless expansion, had absorbed the League within its imperial confines.

"Yes. Yes, we do," she replied. She felt a fierce exultation in confronting these Chapaliians whom she now outranked, thinking of her brother's failed rebellion against the Empire, ten years before her birth, because he was not a traitor to *his* kind, to humankind, but a hero. Even now, when the Chapalii, for reasons only Chapalii understood, had ennobled him. Even now, made a duke—the only human granted any real status within their intricate hierarchy of power, given a solar system as his fief, endowed with fabulous wealth—Charles Soerensen simply bided his time, and the Chapalii seemed not to suspect.

"The honored duke will be pleased to see his heir on Odys," said Hon Echido.

His colorless words shattered her thoughts, exposing her to her own bitter judgment: that she was afraid, that her life lay in chaos around her, and that even what little her brother asked of her she could not grant. She wanted only to retreat to the quiet, isolated haven of the palace in Jeds and be left alone, with no one expecting anything of her. Suddenly she felt oppressed by these Chapalii watching and measuring her. She felt short and grossly heavy next to the gaunt delicacy that swathes of fabric and flowing robes could not disguise. Ishii's skin bore a blended shade that she could not recognize nor interpret. Yakii seemed torn between addressing a duke's heir and Ishii's demands.

"Lady Terese," said Hon Echido, either sensitive to these currents or else simply pressing his advantage, as a canny merchant must, "it would be a great compliment to my house if you would allow me to escort you personally to the *Oshaki*. With Hao Yakii's permission, of course." He bowed to her and acknowledged the captain with that arrangement of hands known as Merchant's Favor.

With mutual consent, the parting went swiftly. Tess left Yakii and Ishii to their debate, and walked to the shuttle with Hon Echido in attendance, the steward carrying her valise five paces behind. There would be time enough to arrange with Hao Yakii that she was going to Rhui, not to Odys. Both planets, being neighbors in the Dao Cee system, were on the *Oshaki*'s scheduled run.

Hon Echido proved a pleasant and undemanding companion. His concerns were material, his conversation pragmatic, and he seemed determined to treat her as he would any duke's heir, despite the fact that she was both human and female.

"May we be given to understand, Lady Terese," he asked as the shuttle lifted away from Earth and out toward the *Oshaki*'s orbit, "that the more frequent cargo runs to Rhui indicate that the duke will soon be opening that planet up to exploitation as he has the planet Odys?"

"No. Its designation as a natural preserve under the Interdiction Code protects it for at least a century. My brother desires to preserve the native cultures for as long as possible."

"Lady Terese, certainly the natives are quite primitive. Not equal to the worth to our societies of Rhui's magnificent natural resources."

"Ah, Hon Echido, but is it not here that our valuations of worth differ? While to you they are merely a less important part of Rhui's other natural resources, to us they are cousins."

Echido stroked his mauve robes. "More than cousins, surely. Are you not, in virtually every particular, identical species?"

If it was meant to be an insult, it was smooth. Tess could not refrain from smiling, but the expression was completely lost on the Chapalii. "Yes, we are both *Homo sapiens*. That is why you Chapalii cannot be allowed on the planet. However primitive the Rhuian natives might be, some of them *are* intelligent enough to question those characteristics by which the Chapalii differ from humans."

"Are they truly so intelligent?" he asked without a trace of irony. "How can you know, Lady Terese?"

"Because I lived on Rhui for three years, in a city called Jeds. That was about ten years ago, when I was a child. My brother allows limited contact between humans in his employ and the natives, for research purposes."

Echido settled his hands into that arrangement known as Merchant's Accord. "Certainly the duke is wise to ascertain the extent and disposition of Rhui's resources before exploiting them. It is a rich planet. My family can only hope that we will be allowed the privilege of bidding on any expedition once the interdict is lifted from the planet."

"I assure you, Hon Echido, that should it come to that, I will put in a good word for you with my brother."

He was delighted. It struck Tess that the mauve of his robes and the reddish tint of satisfaction that flushed his skin did not remotely match. God, but she was tired.

Stewards met them at the *Oshaki*'s lock and vied for the honor of showing her to a suite of rooms suitable for a passenger of her eminence. The original steward kept his grip on her valise. It was a relief to be left alone in the suite. The solitude was palpable. It was also hot.

She developed a routine quickly as the *Oshaki* left Earth orbit and began its run to Dao Cee and thence to the home worlds. She slept and washed, and ate her meals alone in her rooms. She wanted to wallow in depression. All the anger and frustration and the caustic wound of Jacques's rejection of her had room to swell up and fill her until she mostly just lay on her bed and stared at the ceiling. She could not manage tears: she wanted them too badly.

But when, one half day out from Rhui, yet another begging invitation from Hao Yakii that she dine at his table came in, she felt guilty. She owed it to Charles. He would expect her to dine, to converse, to glean any slightest bit of information that might be valuable to the cause. And she needed to tell Hao Yakii that she was going to Rhui, not to Odys.

The ship was large, and a steward appeared to escort her to the captain's dining hall. The dining hall itself was as big as her flat in Prague. Hao Yakii rose at her entrance. Five other Chapalii rose, bowing. She acknowledged, in formal Chapalii, the two she recognized: Cha Ishii Hokokul and Hon Echido Keinaba. The others were introduced: minor lords and merchants. Somehow, Echido managed to sit beside her, and his presence acted as a buffer because he was so good at keeping the conversation on a technical, commonplace level. To her relief, the dinner went smoothly.

She rose finally. Echido begged leave to escort her to her suite. At the door, she paused: She had not told Hao Yakii about her true destination. It was so hard, in front of these strangers. She hesitated, struggling with herself. She could simply send him a message through the comm, but God, she was damned if she'd be that cowardly.

Behind her, in court Chapalii, one of the merchants said to the captain: "Will the Tai-endi be confined to her suite until you leave Rhui orbit?"

The captain flushed green, glancing toward the door. Cha Ishii flushed blue, though he did not look toward her, and a moment later, the merchant flushed violet, mortified.

"Hon Echido," said Tess in clear, formal Chapalii, "you did not tell me if Keinaba has already opened negotiations with the Tai-en?" A quick glance back as they left showed her that the captain's flush had faded to white.

Echido was tinged blue along the jawline, a faint line of distress. "We have not, Lady Terese. Unforeseen events have brought us to Dao Cee." Then, smoothly, he took the subject off on another tangent.

Alone in her suite, Tess sat down on her bed and pondered. Why should the captain confine her to quarters? He could not, in any case. Becoming fluent in the language had not given her, or any human, much insight into the Chapalii mind. That someone of lower rank should presume to prohibit their superior any place whatsoever was inconceivable to the Chapalii. On a Chapalii starship, whose highest official was a captain she outranked, she could go anywhere he could go. To suggest confining her, then—the implications of that were staggering.

They were hiding something. They must be. Something to do with Rhui, or the cargo shuttle. What unforeseen events had Hon Echido been talking about? Perhaps it was a good thing she was here, after all.

She opened her valise and changed into the clothing she had brought, clothing that could pass as native on Rhui: light undergarments, special thermal cloth cut into tunics that layered over trousers, and leather boots. The cut and texture of the clothes felt strange. At least the thermal cloth insulated her from both heat and cold.

A pouch hung from the belt she put on. She filled it: Jedan coins, mostly, a handkerchief, gloves, the old Egyptian ankh necklace given to her by Sojourner, unremarkable odds and ends for hygiene, a volume of philosophic essays from the university in Jeds. Anything else she needed she could get once she arrived at the palace in Jeds.

She laid the computer slate down on a table and reread her letter. The sentence about her dissertation she erased, and in its place she wrote: *I have reason to be suspicious of this cargo run. I'll keep my eyes open.* She locked the slate's memory. A looped message on the screen instructed that the slate be taken to her brother. On impulse, she keyed the *cosmetic* function and ran a hand over the screen. It darkened to a reflective surface, mirroring her. Light brown hair—some called it auburn. Not slim, though her former fiancé had constantly reminded her that she could be. She only resembled her brother in her deep-set eyes, her high cheekbones, and in a certain grace of form lent by the co-ordination of parts and an evenly proportioned body. Perhaps it would be best just to go on to Odys. God, though, she did not want to face Charles.

Even as she thought it, the captain's intercom, which she had left on, chimed to announce that the cargo shuttle would depart in one Chapalii hour. She slapped the reflective screen off, not even wanting to face herself, and left the suite. She was doing her duty to Charles, going to Rhui on this shuttle.

A steward waited outside. She waved him off and headed alone by lifts and passageways down to docking. Her retinal-ident scan gave her access to the entire ship. As she passed, stewards bowed and got out of her way. She cycled through the decontamination threshold and crossed the transom to the feeder that snaked out to the waiting shuttle. In the holding room off to one side, Hao Yakii, elbow clip gleaming, stood speaking with a cluster of Chapalii.

Tess hesitated. No one, not even a steward, blocked the feeder. Doubtless cargo was being transferred into the shuttle farther down. To go over to Hao Yakii demanded that she change her direction, announce her arrival in another room, and inform him of her change of plans in front of an audience. A real investigator would just go on, not asking for permission. She barely slackened her steps as she walked up the feeder and on to the shuttle.

Was she being bold, or simply cowardly? Tears stung her eyes, and she wiped them away impatiently. A bubble lift gave access onto the control bulb, and through its open tube she heard the pilot conversing with some merchant about their cargo. *Horses?* The lift must be distorting his words. Ahead, an elaborate glyph marked a contained storage hold. She could either ride down in there or confront the pilot now. She had lifted up her hand before she even realized she'd made the decision. The wall seamed away from the entrance to the hold. She took one step in. Stopped, amazed, and then shook herself and slipped inside as the wall closed behind her.

Horses!

She had expected sundry bags of trading goods for the handful of Earth merchants and anthropologists who lived, disguised, among the native populations, or possibly even boxes within boxes of laboratory or communications equipment for the hidden rooms in the palace at Jeds. She had certainly not expected horses.

The animals breathed and shifted around her. Their scent lay heavy and overwhelming in the confined space. A quivering hum stirred the shuttle. The horses moved restlessly, and Tess felt the floor shift, a nauseating distortion, and they were free of the *Oshaki*. She settled back into a shadowed corner to wait.

The hold's walls gave off enough light that she could extract the book of essays from the pouch and read aloud to

herself, practicing the language which had gone on to give
its name to the planet. It was the language spoken in Jeds,
where Charles had established a native provenance for himself, and a role, as the prince of that city, through which he
could keep track of his interdicted planet.

A loud snort startled her from her book. High vibrations
shook through the floor—the landing engines. She had
thought the *Oshaki* to be above the northernmost reaches of
the Jedan continent; it had been a remarkably fast trip. The
shuttle jerked and shuddered, then stilled. They had landed.

Silence, broken by the nervous shifting of the horses.
With a sharp crack, the hull opened. Light poured in. Tess
flung one hand up over her eyes to protect them. Didn't the
shuttles land on their off-shore island spaceport at night, to
minimize the risk of being seen? Perhaps the routine had
changed.

From the outer stalls, horses were herded out. Someone
counted down a list in Chapalii: thirty-two, forty-five, fifty-
six. Hooves rang on the ramp. Two Chapalii discussed grass
and manure in neutral, colorless voices. Finally, their boots
sounded dully, fading, on the metal ramp as they left. In
the distance, a horse neighed. Someone shouted in Chapalii. Saddles? The word was unfamiliar.

Tess rose, put away the book, and walked to the ramp to
look outside. She saw grass, sloping up to the ring of low
hills that surrounded this tiny valley. About fifty yards away
a clump of broken boulders littered the grass. Around the
shuttle to her left she heard the horses, and other sounds—
unloading on the primary ramp, the cargo master going over
lists with the League agents who channeled the trade between the island and Jeds.

She half slid down the ramp, hopping to the ground. Thick
grass cushioned her landing. The air was sharper, fresher,
colder than she remembered.

With a burst of movement, horses emerged from behind
the shuttle, herded by eleven riders dressed in native clothing. The riders looked strange; in fact, all of this looked a
little strange. She did not recall the shuttle valley to be a
land with so little variety: the sky such a monotone of deep
blue, cloudless, the land a gentle incline to the heights,
covered with an unbroken layer of grass and patches of un-
melted snow. The riders paused at the crest. A few looked
back before the entire group rode out of sight.

The riders were Chapalii. And they were wearing native clothing. Charles would never countenance this. She ran out to see where they were going, to find whomever of Charles's people was letting this violation of the interdiction take place.

A high hum warned her. She threw herself down on the ground. A gust of heat roiled over her and faded. She rose to her knees, lifting her hand to alert them that she was here. But the shuttle had already taken off. She stared, astounded. The blast of a human ship would have killed her, this close. She watched the sleek smoothness of its upward path, hearing only the wind against her ears, like the faint echo of the lengthening of its arc. They had not had time to unload the entire cargo. There was a last wink of silver and then only the violet-blue of the sky. If she had not known what to look for, she would never have seen it.

This was insane. She dusted herself off, flicked a stem of grass away from her mouth, and walked back to the charred site of the shuttle's landing. Such a faint scar, to mark its having been here. The breeze cooled her cheeks as she strode along the trail of beaten-down grass left by the horses. Snow patched the shadows, but her clothes adjusted their temperature accordingly. She did not bother to pull on her gloves. After all, she would catch up with the Chapalii soon enough. The island on which Charles's engineer had disguised his spaceport was tiny; every hill overlooked the sea. Off-world women and men in Charles's employ lived in the island's only village. There, Tess could find a galley sailing the rest of the way across the vast bay, to the harbor at Jeds. There was no other way off the island.

By the sun, she guessed that her trail led east. Climbing, she felt invigorated, enjoying the sweet pungency of the air, the untainted crispness of the wind. She came to the crest of the nearest hill quickly, her cheeks warm with the effort.

There was no ocean. There was nothing except grass and snow and broken forest straggling along the march of hills. As she stared out at the unvarying expanse, dwarfed by the huge bowl of the sky and the wide stretch of hills, she knew that she had never seen this place before. This was not an island.

"Oh, my God." Empty space swallowed her words. Her legs gave out, and she dropped to her knees. The air had a sweet, alien odor. A bug crawled up her thumb. She shook it off, cursing. No wonder the Chapalii had left so quickly. Trespassing—such a flagrant act of contempt for her brother's authority that they must have some reason to risk a conviction of Imperial censure which would strip them of all rank. But there was nothing on Rhui worth *that* to a Chapalii.

For a long moment she did not move. What if there was?

Hills hid the Chapalii riders, but they had left a trail. She followed it. At the base of the hill it veered south. Wind brushed through the grass, lifting trampled stalks. Tess fished in her pouch, found the necklace and put it on, and pulled on her gloves. Then she walked.

The trail proved inconstant, but even when it faded, she could always find it fifty meters on. At first she was optimistic.

That evening it was the cold and her thirst that plagued her. But sheltering in a miserable patch of trees, with her cloak wrapped around her head and body, her clothing kept her just barely warm enough to doze. In the morning she melted snow in her bare hands and drank, and melted more, until her hands grew so stiff that she had to put her gloves back on. At least she would not die of thirst. But during the day the trail got worse.

Half the time she walked by instinct, following the curve of the hills, the snow-laden shadows, as if this Chapaliian violation of her brother's edict left an invisible line that she, the avenging representative, could stalk. They should not be here—had never been here. What if they knew that Charles was biding his time, consolidating his power until he could successfully free humanity from their grip? What if their purpose all along had been to put him in a position within their hierarchy from which they could easily ruin him? And now, stupidly, she had gotten herself lost. He could not adopt a new heir unless she was certified dead. He would not know where to look for her—somewhere near Jeds—of course, the Chapalii would cover up their unauthorized landing. And she was the only one who knew they were here.

That night it was hunger more than the cold. Small plants grew under the grove of scrub trees she sheltered amidst, but she dared not try to eat them. In the darkness, as she stared up at the sky through a gap in the branches, none of the stars seemed familiar. She had known the night sky of Jeds well. It took her a long time to go to sleep.

The third day. It was harder to keep a steady pace. A thin cut on her upper lip stung constantly. She believed she was still following a trail—she had to believe it. In the afternoon, when she stumbled across a small water hole bordered by a ring of trees, she broke the crust of ice with one boot and drank until she was bloated. Then she fell asleep, exhausted.

Jacques was laughing at her. Her faithless lover was laughing. She had taken him once to her folk-dance club, where she went with her friends. He thought dancing silly. "Flying," he said, "is a man's sport." So she said, "I'll race you on the Everest Loop." But she beat him, beat the president of the Sorbonne flying club. Bright, popular, magnetic, he was so much that she wasn't. It had been a terrible mistake to beat him.

Until she found herself in the same class, Diplomacy and Chapalii Culture, and he had honored her with his laughter again. "You speak Chapalii so well," he said. Withdrawn, uncomfortable with most people, she was flattered when he asked her to be in his study group. Later, somehow, he discovered she was the heir to the admired Soerensen, freedom fighter, duke in the Empire, champion of Earth and the League. That summer he asked her to marry him.

"No," she said. She woke up, shivering.

Night. Late. Without thinking, her eyes focused on a formation of stars. She recognized the constellation. In Jeds, the Horseman rose high in the sky, sword leading. Here he hugged the hills, and by the angle of his sword she knew she was very far north, a thousand times farther north than she could possibly walk. She knew the map of the Jedan continent. Its northern mass was taken up by vast plains, broad as Siberia. She might as well attempt to walk from Mongolia to Venice. And she did not know whether winter was ending or just coming on. *Oh God,* she thought, *don't let me be there: I can't be there.*

When she slept again she dreamed that her bones lay, white, laced with the flowering vines of spring, on a golden, infinite hillside.

The rising sun woke her. Her left hand ached, the cloth of her cloak clutched in its fist. Shaking with cold, she pried it open with her other hand, and rose and drank and looked around. There was no trail. No sign that anyone had passed here, nothing, no life at all, except her. But south was surely that way, south to Jeds. She had a duty to Charles. However she had failed him before, she could not fail him now.

Strangely, the walking seemed easier, but she was very light-headed. Her eyesight grew unclear at intervals. When she picked up her feet, they seemed to fall from a great distance before they struck the ground. The sun rose high and cold above her.

Rounding the steep end of a small rise, she saw before her trampled grass, scattered ashes, and one long thin strip of worn leather. She was in the middle of it before she realized it was an abandoned camp. Her knees collapsed under her and she sat. She covered her face with her hands, not knowing whether to laugh or to cry. It was recent, yes, alien and primitive, and there was a trail leading away, a trail she could follow.

She set off immediately. Ran sometimes, thinking she had seen something, stumbling, falling once into a freezing hard layer of snow, walked again, catching her breath and rubbing her cold cheeks with her bare hands. But as midday passed into afternoon, the grass thickened and lengthened, the hills ended abruptly, and the trail disappeared.

She stood silent on the edge of a vast plain. At first she merely stared. Nothing but grass, and grass and sky met in a thin line far in the distance, surrounding her, enclosing her in their vast monotony.

The wind scoured patterns in the greening grass. A single patch of flowers mottled a blazing scarlet through the high stems. A body could lie a hundred years in such space and never be found. In a hundred years her brother would be dead.

Her throat felt constricted. Tears rose, filling her eyes. But this was not the time to cry—think, *think*. She coughed several times, eyes shut. That, perhaps, was why she did not notice his approach.

A stream of words, incomprehensible, delivered in a steady, commanding voice.

She whirled. A man stood on the slope above her. He had dark hair, cut short, a trim dark beard, and the look of a man hardened by many years of difficult life, yet he had no coarseness. He waited patiently. His shirt was scarlet and full, his trousers black; his high boots were tanned leather and fit closely to his ankle and calf. A long, curving blade hung from his belt. He took one step toward her and asked another question in the same incomprehensible tongue.

She held her ground and replied in Rhuian. ''Who may you be, good man?'' she asked, remembering formality somehow, perhaps only because it was all that was left her. Here, not even her brother's name mattered, except as a courtesy. ''I am Terese Soerensen. I have nothing in my possession that could harm either you or your people.''

His unreadable expression did not change. He spoke a third time in his strange tongue, motioned to her, and turned to walk up the hill. She hesitated the barest second. Then she followed him.

CHAPTER TWO

"Speech is the shadow of action."
—DEMOCRITUS OF ABDERA

He waited for her just over the crest of the hill, one hand loosely grasping his horse's reins. Compared to the horses she had traveled downside with, this was a stocky animal, with no beauty whatsoever; its legs were thick, its neck short and powerful. Its thin mane straggled over a dense coat, and its muzzle had a blunt shape that gave it the look of some prehistoric creature. Against its imperfections, the man standing at its head looked faultless: His red shirt was brilliant against the dull grass, his posture utterly assured, his eyes a deep, rich brown, his face—

Too hard. There was too little kindness in his face. Wind stirred Tess's hair and a bird called in the distance, a raucous cry. The man's eyes as he examined her in his turn were intelligent. She recalled her conversation with the merchant: intelligent enough to suspect her off-world origins? How could he, when Jeds itself—thousands of miles away but at least still *on* his planet—was likely a meaningless word to him? When Rhui was interdicted, protected from the knowledge of the space-faring civilizations that surrounded it? Without realizing she was doing it, she shook her head. The movement made her dizzy. Her hunger and thirst flooded in on her, and she stumbled.

She did not even see him move, but his hands were under her elbow, pulling her up. She jerked away from him.

"Damn it," she said, ashamed of her weakness. "I suppose it was too much to hope that you would speak Rhuian." He stood very still, watching her. "God-damned native wildlife," she added in Anglais, just to make herself feel better, but even her tone made no dent in his impassivity. He simply retreated to his horse, returning to her side a moment later with a hard, flat square of bread and a damp leather pouch filled with water.

She ate the bread, but drank only enough water to slake her thirst, and offered the pouch back to him. After he had tied it to his saddle, he mounted and held out one hand for her to swing on behind him. The strength of his pull surprised her; she had to grab at his shoulder to keep from falling over the other side. What he said under his breath did not sound like commendation.

Tess bit at her lip. She put one hand on each side of his waist, the cloth of his shirt fluid and smooth under her hands. Ahead, a wind moved in the grass. He glanced back at her, moved her arms so that they circled his waist entirely, and gave a terse command—even without knowing the language, she could translate the tone of voice. She took in a deep breath and held it, because her instinct was to tears. His legs moved against hers. The horse started forward.

His entire back was in contact with her. She turned her face to one side. Her cheek pressed against the back of his neck. The ends of his dark hair tickled her eye. His back was warm, and under her hands, held open and flat on his middle, she could feel every movement of the hard muscles in his stomach, his slow, controlled breathing. She closed her hands into fists.

They rode down onto the plain. Here, away from the hills, the sky seemed even larger, as if some giant hand had pushed the horizon down to reveal more blue. They seemed so small, the three of them alone in such an expanse, invisible, surely, to any eye looking down from above, yet his sense of purpose and direction gave them significance.

She could not judge time, but soon her thighs began to ache. After an eternity she began to believe that there had indeed been some change in the sun's position. The grass continued on around them without a break. Snow glittered in occasional patches. The man in front of her neither spoke nor moved appreciably, except for the finest shifts to adjust for the horse.

A flash of brilliance sparked on a far rise, vanished, only to appear again closer: another rider in scarlet and black. This one had a second horse on a lead line, trailing behind him. Quickly, more quickly than Tess expected, the two riders met, slowed, and halted their horses.

The newcomer was a young man with bright blond hair and a cheerful smile. The smile emerged as he met them, fading into astonishment as he looked at Tess. He spoke in a flood of words, to which the dark man replied curtly. Unabashed, the younger man swung down from his horse and came over to stand below Tess. He blushed a little—easy to see on his fair skin—and lifted his arms up to her.

She flushed with embarrassed anger—he was helping her down as if she were a child. But her eyes met his, and there was something in his gaze, something utterly good-natured, that made her smile slightly, at which he blushed a deeper shade of pink and lowered his gaze. At least he was as embarrassed about this as she was. She let herself be helped down. He let go of her instantly, and for a moment she stood next to him under the censorious gaze of the dark man and felt allied with the young blond against a force impatient with both of them. Without a word, the dark man reined his horse around and left them standing there together while he rode back the way he and Tess had come.

She gaped, she was so surprised at this desertion. Beside her, the young man laughed.

"Not worry," he said in perfectly horrible Rhuian. "Ilya is always angry."

"I beg your pardon!"

He repeated the words, slower this time, so that she caught them all. "I beg pardon for my tongue," he added, not looking very sorry about it. "It is not so good."

"How did you learn Rhuian?" she demanded.

He shrugged. "I study in Jeds."

She felt herself gaping again: this young native—nondescript except for the merry cast of his face, arrayed as barbarically as any savage, living out on a trackless plain—had studied in Jeds.

Under her stare, he dropped his gaze shyly. "I apologize. Forgive me. I have not given you my name. I am Yurinya Orzhekov." Long lashes shaded his blue eyes. "But perhaps you will call me Yuri." He hesitated, as if this request were a liberty.

Tess began to feel dizzy again and, leaning forward, she put her hand on the first thing within reach: his horse.

"Are you well? We go to camp now. Ilya says you were walking many days."

"Yes, I . . ." In a moment her head cleared. "I'm Tess. Terese Soerensen, that is. But Tess, that is what my friends call me."

"Ah," he said wisely. "Can you mount?"

Under his stare, not intimidating at all, she felt it possible to be truthful. "The last time I rode a horse was, oh, ten years ago."

"Well, then, I will keep the lead, and you hold on. Can you manage that?"

By this time she had adjusted for his atrocious accent—his vocabulary was decent enough. "Yes," she replied gratefully, "I think I can manage that."

He helped her mount, mounted himself, and led the way forward at a sedate walk. After he saw that she could manage that much, he let his horse ease back beside hers. "You are from Jeds?"

"Ah . . . yes."

"It is a very long way. Many months' journey."

"Yes, I suppose it is." She hesitated to question him further on geography, for fear of revealing the wrong sort of ignorance. Instead, she chose silence.

"Ah, you are tired. I will not bother you." He lapsed into a silence of his own, but a rather companionable one, for all that.

She let it go because she was exhausted, still hungry, still dizzy on and off. When at long, long last they topped a low rise and she saw below a perfectly haphazard collection of about four dozen vividly colored tents, she felt only relief, not apprehension. A rider some hundred meters distant hailed them with a shout and a wave, and Yurinya waved back and led Tess down into a swirl of activity.

Their arrival brought a crowd of people to stare, mostly women and children, and soon after a woman whose broad, merry face bespoke a blood relationship to Yuri. She held a child in one arm, balanced on her hip, but when Yuri spoke briefly to her in their language, she handed the child over to another woman and crossed to stand next to Tess. She called out to the crowd, and it quickly dissipated, except, of course, for a score of curious, staring children.

She looked up at Tess and smiled. It was like water in the desert. Tess smiled back.

"I am Sonia Orzhekov," said the young woman. "I am Yuri's sister, so he has properly brought you to me."

"You speak Rhuian." Tess stared at her, at her blonde hair secured in four braids, her head capped by a fine headpiece of colored beads and leather; she wore a long blue tunic studded with gold trim that ended at her knees, and belled blue trousers beneath that, tucked into soft leather boots. An object shaped like a hand mirror hung from her belt. "I suppose you studied in Jeds, too."

Sonia laughed. "Here, Yuri." Her accent was far better than her brother's, and she spoke with very little hesitation. "We'll walk the rest of the way." She lifted up her arms and helped Tess down. "There. Men can never talk to any end, sitting up so high all the time. Yuri, you may go, if you'd like." Although couched politely, the words were plainly a command. Yuri glanced once at Tess, smiled shyly, and left with the two horses.

"But did you?" Tess persisted. "Study in Jeds, I mean."

"You are surprised." Sonia grinned at Tess's discomfiture. "Is Jeds your home?"

"Yes." The lie came easier to her, now that she realized it was the best one she had, and not entirely untrue.

"So you do not expect to see such as we studying in the university in Jeds. Well." Sonia shrugged. The blue in her tunic was not more intense than the fine bright blue of her eyes. "You are right. *Jaran* do not normally study in Jeds. Only Yuri and I, and Dina now, because Ilya did, and he thought it would be—" Her grin was as much full of mischief as laughter. "—*good* for us. Poor Yuri. I suppose he was miserable the entire time, though he will never say so much to me, even if I am his sister. And never ever would he say it to Ilya."

"Who is Ilya, and why was *he* studying in Jeds?"

"Ilya Bakhtiian? He is my cousin, first, and also the *dyan* of our tribe's *jahar.*. You would say in Rhuian, perhaps, the leader of our riders. Why he went to Jeds? You will have to ask him. He's the one who found you, if Yuri did not say."

Tess, remembering that dark, aloof, censorious man, and their ride together, flushed a furious red.

Sonia merely laid a soft but entirely reassuring hand on Tess's arm, guiding her, supporting her. "Come, you're tired. Eat and sleep first. Then we can talk."

So Tess did as she was told, and was relieved to be treated

both kindly and firmly. Sonia took her to a huge, round tent, gave her warm stew and hot tea to drink, chased four inquisitive children out of the curtained back alcove of the tent, and helped Tess out of her boots and clothing. Then, giving Tess a yellow silk shift to wear, she pointed to a pile of furs and left, returning once with a small bronze oven filled with hot coals. Tess lay down. The furs were soft enough, but they smelled—not bad, precisely, but musky, an exotic, overpowering scent. Outside, children laughed and called in some game. A woman chuckled. Pots chimed against each other in the breeze. More distantly, a man shouted, and animals bleated and cried in soothing unison. A bird's looping whistle trilled over and over and over again. Tess slept.

* * *

Charles Soerensen sat at his desk, staring out at the mud flats of Odys Massif that stretched for endless miles, as far as one could see from this tower and farther yet. While his companion spoke, Soerensen sat perfectly still, engrossed in the scene beyond. But Marco Burckhardt knew that Charles Soerensen listened closely and keenly to everything he had to report.

". . . and while I was in Jeds, Dr. Hierakis isolated another of the antigenic enzymes in the native population that has been puzzling her. Which reminds me, this lingering illness that the Prince of Jeds is suffering is either going to have to get better or you're going to have to kill yourself off and let your sister take over, or some invented son, once she can be fetched back from whichever damned place overseas you supposedly sent her to study. It's been over two years since you've appeared publicly in Jeds, or even been downside at all."

Charles reached out and with one finger rotated the globe of Earth suspended to the right of his desk a quarter-turn, revealing the Pacific Ocean. "Eighteen months. And in any case, I just inherited twenty years ago. We've got a while before we need a new prince down there."

"If you say so. I think I'll sail the coast up north from Jeds next. Northeast, that is, up the inland sea."

A soft click sounded, barely audible, but both men stilled, and Marco turned expectantly toward the tiled wall opposite the huge open balcony that looked out over the tidal flats.

A seam opened. A woman dressed in an approximation of Chapalii steward's garb appeared.

"Visitors," she said, low, and quickly. "The *Oshaki,* in from Earth. Hao Yakii Tarimin."

Charles nodded. He did not stand, but Marco did. The woman backed out of the room. A moment later, Hao Yakii entered and paused on the threshold. Marco gestured for him to enter, and Yakii came forward and with a precise, deep bow, presented himself to Charles.

"Tai Charles," he said in formal Chapalii. "I am thrice honored to be allowed into your presence, and I beg leave to thank you again for your generosity in letting my ship transport cargo and passengers through your demesne."

Charles inclined his head the merest degree. He folded his hands together, one atop the other.

Marco echoed the folded hands. "The Tai-en accepts your thanks. Is there any news to report? Have you your manifest for the Rhui cargo?"

Yakii produced a palm-thin slate and offered it to Marco, and bowed again to Charles, retreating a step.

Marco studied it, puzzling out the letters of formal merchanter's Chapalii. "Laboratory equipment," he said in Anglais. "The usual kit for the good doctor. Forty boxes of bound paperbooks for dissemination. Silk bolts. Iron ingots. Spices. Some luxuries from home for the personnel. Pretty sparse for a cargo, I must say." He glanced up. Charles rubbed his chin with his left forefinger. "Nothing missing that I can see," Marco added in Ophiuchi-Sei, the only human language they were fairly sure the Chapalii had not learned, since its structure and cadences were decidedly and pointedly egalitarian.

Charles returned his gaze to the monotonous gray-green flats and stared, as if he saw something out there Marco did not. Yakii waited with Chapaliian patience for the duke to acknowledge the manifest or dismiss him. Finally, Charles reached out and turned the globe again, and rested his right forefinger lightly in the middle of eastern Europe.

"Is there also a message," asked Marco in his painstaking but rather rough formal Chapalii, "from the Tai-endi Terese Soerensen?"

Marco saw the faint flush, the quiet creep of blue onto Hao Yakii's skin before it melted and blended back into white. Whether Charles could detect the color shift in the reflection of the glastic pane he could not be sure.

"I received no message," said Hao Yakii in a colorless voice, "from the Tai-endi Terese Soerensen to convey to the duke."

Charles's eyes narrowed slightly, scarcely noticeable, unless one knew him as well as Marco did.

"You may go, Hao Yakii," said Marco.

Yakii bowed to the correct degree and retreated out of the room. Charles stood up.

"Get Suzanne," he said. "I want her to take the next ship back to Earth."

"Aren't you overreacting?"

"Tess sends a message by every ship that comes through here via Earth. We agreed on that when she decided to study at Prague."

"Still, Charles." Marco walked to the desk and laid his palms flat on the satiny surface. "Wasn't she in the last throes of writing her thesis? Damned linguists. I've studied Chapalii since before she was born, and she still speaks it ten times better than I do."

Charles had pale blue eyes, deceptively mild eyes except when their full force was turned on an adversary. "When I have every reason to suspect that Chapalii Protocol officers arranged the accident that killed my parents? I don't think I'm overreacting."

Marco shrugged. "I'll go."

Charles considered. "No. Suzanne can handle this. I'll have her send a bullet back to us from Earth once she's there."

"That's pretty damned expensive."

Charles laid a hand on the north pole of the Earth, gently, reverently. "Why the hell do you think I accepted this honor? She's my only heir, and you know damned well we're the only toehold humanity's got to the chameleons' power structure. Now." He removed his hand from the globe, and his tone altered, softened, as he sat down again. "Is there anyone else from the *Oshaki* I am meant to see?"

Marco pushed off the desk and went to the transparent wall. The tide was coming in, a low, steady swell that overtook islands of reeds and swallowed them. On the horizon, the towers of Odys Port winked in the light of the setting sun. "The merchant, Keinaba."

With a soft click, a door opened in the back wall. The woman came in and walked straight up to the desk.

"Curiouser and curiouser," she said. "Marco, haven't I told you that turquoise blue is *not* your color?"

"You're welcome to undress me, my love," said Marco with a grin, "and show me something more appropriate to wear."

"Fat chance, sweetheart. Here, Charles, this is from the *Oshaki*." She dropped a thin slate down on the desktop. "No sooner did the captain hie himself out of here but his steward comes in with this message from the Chapalii merchant. Hao Yakii and house Keinaba's regrets, but Hon Echido Keinaba has been unavoidably detained and will continue with the *Oshaki* to Chapal system. I can't believe that anything in this galaxy would drag a merchant from that house off the chance we offered them to tie in with our trade and our metals foundries."

Charles steepled his fingers and rested his chin on them. He did not look at the formal Chapalii script inscribed on the slate's screen. The tide lapped at the wooden docks built below, stirring a rowboat and a gross of lobster cages tied to the pilings. "Let's not take offense yet," he said slowly. "Let's keep channels open with the Keinaba house." He glanced up, first at Marco and then at the woman. "Suzanne, I need you to go to Earth and find out why Tess didn't send her usual message. What's the next ship heading out that way? On second thought, commandeer one. Not the *Oshaki*, I think."

Suzanne picked up the slate and keyed in a few quick commands. "Five days would be easy. But if you really want to pull rank, I can leave tomorrow."

Charles nodded at the flats, shimmering, stilling as the tide settled and the last glow of the sun scattered out across the dull water. "Tomorrow," he said.

* * *

Tess woke abruptly, to silence. She did not know how long she had slept. She sat up. Suddenly she heard two men arguing, fluid, foreign words, and a woman weeping, a constant undercurrent to their angry exchange. The conversation ended abruptly, but the weeping kept on, fading at last as if the woman had walked out of reach of Tess's hearing. It was utterly, unnaturally quiet.

Tess groped forward and opened the flap that led into the

front half of the tent. Light streamed in here, dappling her clothing, which was neatly folded next to a pouch of food and a tin pot of water. Quickly, she dressed, drank, and ate, and then ventured outside.

The sun lay low along the far rise, but she could tell by the quality of light that it was morning. The camp was empty. Tent flaps stirred in the dawn breeze, but not one single figure moved along the trails beaten down in the grass between the tents. Movement caught her eye, up along the rise, and she saw two figures disappear over the height, edged by the glare of the rising sun. She followed them.

The tribe had gathered in the shallow valley on the other side of the rise. They stood in shadow, the sun's light creeping down toward them, and Tess stopped at the height, staring down, aware that some alien, serious ritual was taking place. To her left, she saw another solitary figure crest the rise into sunlight and then descend again into shadow. She recognized him by his walk, and the dark line of his beard: the man who had found her—Bakhtiian. The air, heavy with dew, felt soft and cold on her cheeks. She watched him descend, for a moment seduced from her other thoughts by the grace of his walk and bearing. Then she winced and went down to the right, where she could see and hear the proceedings but not be part of them.

The tribe stood silently in a rough semicircle. A baby cried and was hushed. One man, fair-haired, middle-aged, dressed in black, stood by himself beyond the crowd. He stared straight ahead—although the sun rose directly into his eyes—and his stance was stiff.

The crowd parted soundlessly to let Bakhtiian through their ranks. His stride was unhurried and smooth. Drops of dew glistened on the tops of his boots and on the hilt of his saber. He halted in front of the single figure.

The silence spread beyond them so that Tess was not aware even of the birds calling or the wind's slow breath on her cheeks. Bakhtiian spoke. What he said had a rhythmic quality, like a spell or a poem, and it wrapped around Tess like a snake so that when he ceased speaking she pulled her arms close in against her chest. A single voice, unsure and weak in the silence left by his speech, answered him, followed by several more in a set way that made her realize that this *was* some kind of ceremony.

Bakhtiian addressed the man standing apart. He responded with one word. A second question, another single word. A third; the same word again. He was a pale figure, this man, alone against the blank sky and the endless grass. No one spoke. A high call came from above, and a lone bird swooped low, rose into the wind, and flew toward the sun.

Bakhtiian moved slightly, drawing his saber. A sigh spread through the crowd as though strewn by the wind. The point of the blade rested on the man's forehead. The world seemed to stop, its only motion the movements of Bakhtiian. Tess could not look away. He looked to the sky and spoke a short invocation to the expanse above. Something awful was about to happen, but it was too late to run away.

In a kind of ghastly slow motion, the more terrible for the effortless beauty of his movement, he drew his saber up to his left shoulder, stepped left, and cut back to the right. Without meaning to, Tess clapped her hands over her eyes. Forced them down, only to see the man, covered with his own blood, collapse into a grotesque heap on the ground. Bakhtiian stepped forward, dropped the saber on the man's body, and turned away and walked, without a word, back toward the camp.

There was a brief, horrified hush. People moved back to let him through and stared after him, hands hiding the sudden buzz of whispering.

Not even aware of her path, Tess fled—from the camp, the crowd, the dead man. She huddled in a little hollow, unable to weep or retch or rail, unable to do anything but bury her head against her knees and shudder, over and over, her arms clenching her knees so tightly that it felt as if bone was touching bone. How long she stayed like this she did not know.

After a time she began taking deep breaths and letting them out slowly, inhaling the musty sweetness of the grass. She rocked back and forth, relaxing her clenched muscles one by one until at last she could shut away the ghastly picture of the man collapsing, of his blood staining the grass—

She took another breath, let it out. Her neck ached. She lifted her head carefully, as if it were so delicate that the slightest jar would break it, and almost screamed. Bakhtiian stood not twenty paces away, watching her.

CHAPTER THREE

"If God had not created yellow honey,
they would say that figs were far sweeter."
—Xenophanes of Colophon

Far above, a bird dove toward the earth, a bundle thrown
from some high spot to be dashed to pieces against the
ground. Abruptly it broke its plummet and jerked upward,
wings spread. Tess's hand was on her throat.

Bakhtiian walked toward her, slowly, each step measured
and even. A saber swayed at his hip.

Tess forced herself to lower her hand and, knowing that
it is always best to face your fears directly, she stood up—
slowly, so as not to startle him—and looked him straight in
the eye. He looked away; that fast, like a wild creature bolt-
ing; then, deliberately, he returned her gaze. His hesitancy
gave her courage, and she found that her heart was no longer
beating so erratically.

"I suppose you think us savage," he said in a low voice.

He spoke such faultless Rhuian, enhanced rather than
marred by a melodious accent, that it took her some full,
drawn-out moments to even wonder why it ought to matter
to him. "My God." It was the only response that came to
hand.

"Sonia says you come from Jeds." She simply stared at
him; when she did not reply, he went on. "I studied there
myself, at the university, some fifteen years ago. I was very
young." He paused. "But even then I thought the architecture of the university, set out around such a fine square, was
particularly remarkable." The wind stirred the scarlet silk
of his shirt. It reminded her of blood.

"*Savage* is too kind," she said hoarsely. Then, realizing
that she had just insulted a man who could kill her as easily

as he had his previous victim, she cast round desperately for a safer haven. "Anyone who's been in Jeds knows that the university is unique because its buildings are set in the round."

His expression, unrevealing, did not change. "I've seen men killed in more brutal ways in Jeds. And for less compelling reasons. You're pale. You shouldn't be alone."

"Go away." She deliberately turned her back on him. Five breaths later, she realized what she had done, and she whirled back. But he was gone.

"Tess."

She bolted right into Yuri.

"Tess. Don't be scared of me."

She could not help herself. She gripped his shirt in her fists and sobbed onto his shoulder. He stood very still. After a bit she stopped crying and stepped a half pace away. She dried her eyes on her hand, feeling like a fool, and looked at him. "Your shirt is all wet."

"I don't mind." He stared at her so earnestly that she looked away. "You are sad."

"Oh, Yuri, that was awful."

"It's true that he got a more merciful death than he deserved. My mother and the other—elders—will be angry with Ilya now, I can tell you that."

"Good Lord," she murmured, utterly bewildered. "How could that be called merciful? How was he supposed to die? No, don't tell me that." She lapsed into silence.

"Tess, he had to die. He had broken the gods' law. Otherwise his—crime, is that the word?—would have made the whole tribe suffer."

"What did he do?"

Yuri looked shamed, and he hesitated, as if he was afraid to confess the magnitude of the man's wrongdoing. "He shot a whistler."

"A whistler?"

"It's a bird." Wrung from him, the admission seemed both anguished and, to Tess, utterly incongruous.

"A bird." What kind of people had she fallen in with?

"He shouldn't have been out hunting with women's weapons anyway, and he was three times a fool to shoot into a thicket. He should have flushed out the game." Yuri shrugged. "But it's done now. The gods must have guided his hand. It was a just execution."

He spoke so matter-of-factly that Tess was appalled, and not a little frightened. "Yuri. You'll tell me, won't you, if I'm about to do something that would offend, that would break your gods' law?"

Now he looked shocked. "You don't think we punish children? Or those who act in ignorance? We're not savages!"

"No, no, of course not. I'm sorry. I didn't mean—" But Yuri could not maintain outrage for longer than a moment. He grinned at her consternation. "Well," said Tess, "I appreciate you coming to find me. Did Bakhtiian send you?"

"Ilya? Why would he send me? No, Sonia did." Abruptly he blushed. "She thought, if you were upset, that you might want—a man's comfort." The constrained tone of his voice left no question as to what Sonia meant by a man's comfort.

For an instant, unable to look at Yuri, Tess was too embarrassed to speak. But then, glancing up at him, she realized that Yuri was far more embarrassed than she was. Their gazes met. Yuri covered his mouth with his hand, and they both laughed.

When Tess tentatively laid a hand on his arm, they sobered. "I don't—I don't need a lover, Yuri. Not right now. But a brother . . ." Had Charles received her computer slate already? Only to send a message to Jeds and find that she had never arrived? "I could use a brother, right now."

He smiled, looking both relieved and honestly pleased, and grasped her hand with his. "Then I will be your brother, Tess. I would far rather be your brother, because a woman's lovers come and go, but her brother she keeps always." He studied her a moment, serious. "But you'd better wash your face. I'll take you to the stream."

They walked back through camp. Yuri led them wide around his family's cluster of tents, where Tess could see a little gathering: Bakhtiian, standing as if he was on trial in front of a half circle of older women and men. On the far side of camp, they followed a stream past a low rise. The stream slipped down a smooth ladder of rocks and broadened into a pool. Yuri left her at the top of the rise, and Tess picked her way down the slope alone. Sonia, standing with a group of young women, saw her and waved.

"Tess." She came to greet her. "Perhaps my brother does not interest you." About twenty young women gathered around. They were not shy at all; they pointed to Tess's clothing and even touched her brown hair, exclaiming over its color—theirs was either blonde or black, with no shade in between.

Under their scrutiny, Tess was amazed she could keep her composure. "No. No, I like him very much. But I am not looking for a lover."

"Ah." Sonia shooed the other women away and immediately began to undress. "Your heart has been broken. I can see it in your face." She stripped down to a thin white shift. Around them, the other young women, naked now, plunged gasping and laughing into the pool. "A man has treated you badly. Here, let me help you take those off."

Tess was not entirely sure she wanted to strip naked in what was after all no more than an early spring day, however fine, and swim in a stream that looked bitterly cold, but after the execution, she did not want to refuse. "Yes," she agreed, to both statements.

"What fine undergarments you wear." Sonia examined Tess's underclothes without the least sign of self-consciousness. "Perhaps you can show us how to fashion some. Here, Elena, Marya—" Several of them splashed right out of the pool to exclaim over this new discovery, and when they had tired of that, they bullied Tess into stripping completely and coming back into the water with them.

It was like ice. But the company, and the energy with which they all splashed about, soon made her forget her goose bumps. Only Sonia spoke Rhuian; the others addressed her cheerfully in their own language and she quickly learned names and a few words. About half the women had scars on their left cheeks.

"So you are not married?" Sonia asked. "No? How old are you? Twenty-three? A widow, perhaps?"

"No. I . . . I was to be married, but . . ."

"Ah. This is the man who has broken your heart. Well." Sonia dismissed the betrayer with a blithe wave of one hand, and a retaliatory splash in the direction of the gray-eyed, blonde girl she called Elena. "In Jeds the customs are different. I did not like them. We have many young men here who are polite as well as handsome."

Tess could not help but laugh. "When I'm ready for a lover, I'll ask your help in picking one out."

"I sent you my brother. But perhaps—" She laughed. Her laugh gave color to the air and sparked her eyes and wrinkled up her nose. "When I know you better, Tess, then I can help you choose. But I think it is time you got a husband, for I see that you have no—what is it to say in Rhuian?—none of the Mother's threads on your belly. As old as you are. I am twenty-four, and I have three children. You must not wait too long. Everyone knows the story of Agrafena's aunt."

The story of Agrafena's aunt was not, it transpired, about anyone living in the tribe, but an old tale. Giggling and shivering, everyone hurried out of the pool, dried off, and dressed. They sat farther up on the slope, the pool dappled by shadows below, an untidy collection of bodies sprawled in the sun with Sonia and Tess at their center. By turns two or three of the young women took clothing to a stretch of flat stones below the pool and beat them clean in the water. As Sonia told the story, it took a fair while to tell, alternately in Rhuian and in *khush*. It was about a woman who waited so long to have children that when at last she married and wanted them, she was barren—having offended the spirits of earth and water by her stubbornness—and so had to send her niece on a long journey in order to find the holy woman who could restore her to favor.

Poor Agrafena had not yet found the holy woman when a little girl raced down from the direction of the camp and delivered a message to the group. Sonia rose and reached down to help Tess up. "The men are coming."

Slinging the damp clothes over their shoulders, the women walked in a straggling group back to camp. A path had been beaten down through the coarse grass, winding around the base of the hills, and they followed this. Elena, at the head of the line, whistled suddenly. The whole group quieted. A young man, then another, and another, came around a rise— the men going to the pool. All the girls straightened their shoulders, swaying their hips as the men did when they were wearing their sabers, and when the first of them passed the first young man, the entire group broke into song. The men, all young, stared silently at the ground; many were grinning. One had flushed a desperate, flaming red; another hid his eyes with his hands. Toward the end of the line, a young man with reddish-blond hair looked up as he passed Sonia and Tess, and winked. He had piercingly blue eyes. Sonia gasped, laughing, and looked back at Tess.

"Did you see that? Did you? *Trust* Kirill!" The last of

the men passed them. All the women were laughing now, breaking off their song. "Did you see?" Sonia addressed the whole group. "I want you all to know—" first in khush, then in Rhuian "—I want you all to know. He winked."

"Who?" called Elena from the front.

"Who do you *think?*"

A chorus, up and down the line, answered her. "Kirill!"

"You see." Sonia turned back to Tess again. "He's terribly forward. He has no shame at all."

"I'm not sure I understand what happened."

Sonia swung her wet burden out in front of her and, with a quick turn of the wrist, made it snap in the air. Faint drops of water sprayed. "We sang a man's song at them, which reminds them of the order of things. If a woman sings a man's song, it makes fun of men, you see."

Tess did not see, but she was saved from having to answer by their arrival in camp. Whatever other consequences the execution might have had, it had no effect on the daily round of life: at dawn, the camp had been empty. Now it bustled with activity. A fair-haired young woman, weaving at a loom fastened at one end around her waist and at the other to an awning corner pole, paused in her work and smiled at Tess. At another tent, an elderly woman simply stopped scouring out a pot and stared at Tess. She called a question to Sonia, which the younger woman answered with a few words. The two toddlers at her skirts stared, wide-eyed but unafraid. Three men, standing next to hides pegged out over the ground, glanced up quickly at her and away before she could meet their eyes. Farther out, beyond the tents, children raced in from the fringes of the herds to stare at Tess and were chased back to shepherd again.

Sonia's tent was not actually Sonia's tent, but the one belonging to her mother. The smaller tents that Mother Orzhekov had gifted each of her four daughters with lay pitched around the large tent. Tess helped Sonia hang the wet clothes up along the tent-lines to dry and then was given a board and a knife and a slab of meat to cut into strips for stew. Yuri strolled up with a baby on his hip and with a look of relief deposited the child on Sonia's lap and turned to sit down beside Tess. He looked around rather furtively and, seeing no other young men in sight, drew his knife and helped her cut up the meat. Sonia took the baby away, and Tess and Yuri sat for some time in companionable silence.

Occasionally young men passed by, and Yuri would hide his knife under his leg and lean back as if he were relaxing.

"I do appreciate it, Yuri, but you don't have to help me," said Tess after the third time he had hidden the knife. "I wouldn't want you to get into trouble."

"Oh, I don't mind. Now that I'm a rider it's supposed to be beneath my dignity to do anything but practice saber and whatever work Uncle Yakhov needs done with the herds."

"But you helped Sonia with the baby."

"Everyone cares for the children. And, of course, a man does what his family asks of him."

"But I see men working at many things besides those who are out with the herds. Don't those men fight?"

"Every man can fight, Tess, but not every man rides in jahar. We're almost done anyway." Three men appeared suddenly from around the back of the tent, but after one startled glance, Yuri simply returned to slicing meat. One was Bakhtiian. Beside him walked an older, silver-haired man, and two steps behind followed a fair, pretty young man who wore a profusion of necklaces in a multitude of colors that clashed with the garish embroidery decorating the sleeves and yoke of his scarlet shirt. Tassels of gold and silver braid hung from his boot tops. Tess could not help but stare. Except for a brief, piercing glance, Bakhtiian ignored them. The young man copied Bakhtiian. But the older man met Tess's eyes and inclined his head with a friendly smile before accompanying Bakhtiian on into camp.

"Who was that?" Tess asked.

"Who? Niko? Nikolai Sibirin. He's the eldest rider in jahar. You'll like him."

"Who was the other one?"

"The other one? Oh." Yuri shrugged dismissively. "Vladimir. He isn't anybody. He's an orphan that Ilya took in, because he had a good hand for the saber."

"He dresses—" She faltered.

"He'd like to be noticed. I suppose women might find him attractive." By his tone, Tess could tell that if women did, their taste was inexplicable to Yuri. "Sonia said that I should teach you khush, if you'd like."

"Yes, I would," Tess replied, realizing that Vladimir was a subject completely uninteresting to Yuri.

"Well, then, let's start with naming things. Damn." He hid the knife.

Tess looked up. A young man sauntered toward them, saber swaying at his hips. He had blond hair, shot through with the red-gold of flames, and a light mustache above full lips. For an instant their gazes met. His head tilted to one side and, with the barest grin, he winked at her before looking as quickly away in a move both shy and flirtatious. Tess flushed.

"Trust Kirill," said Yuri under his breath. He stood up. "What do you want?"

"Really, Yurinya." Kirill halted before them, not at all abashed by Yuri's tone. "Don't you know Mikhal's waiting for you to relieve him?" With another sidewise glance at Tess, he spun and almost too casually strolled away.

Yuri squinted at the sun. "Not yet, he isn't," he muttered. He grinned suddenly, looking down at Tess. "He did that just to get a close look at you."

"I guess I'll take that as a compliment."

"Kirill has no shame at all. If any other man were so forward, he would be run out of camp. I don't know how Kirill gets away with it."

Tess bit down on her grin, hiding it. "He's not unhandsome."

"I suppose not," Yuri agreed glumly. "And he knows it." Then his expression lightened. "But Maryeshka Kolenin showed him, though, when he tried to marry her."

Before Tess could ask for details of this intriguing event, Sonia came around the corner with the baby on one hip and a little girl holding on to her opposite hand. "Yuri! Are you still here? Misha must be waiting for you to relieve him."

"Not *yet*," exclaimed Yuri, completely exasperated now.

"Do you want me to come with you?" Tess asked.

The casual question brought much more of a reaction than she expected. Yuri blushed. "No. You can't—"

"Yuri." Sonia set the baby down on the rug and let go of the girl.

Yuri said nothing.

"I can't what?" Tess asked.

"Ilya said not to tell her—"

"Yuri," said Sonia. She let out a sigh and dumped the cut meat into a gleaming copper pot. "You might as well say. I never thought it was right not to tell Tess, and you've said too much as it is." She exchanged a glance with Tess and set a woven bag filled with wet tubers down next to the rug, taking the board from Tess. Then she and her daughter turned their backs on Tess and Yuri and with a fresh knife cut up the vegetables, although the little girl peeked back frequently.

"What is it you weren't supposed to tell me?"

Yuri hesitated, glancing to the right, to the left, at Sonia, and finally back at Tess. "About the *khepelli.*"

"The khepelli?" Tess felt like all the heat had flooded out of her body into the ground and the air. The late afternoon breeze was chill and damp, presaging rain.

"They say you were on the same ship with them," Yuri continued, apparently oblivious to her expression. "When Ilya told them you were following us, they were very surprised. They said you must have followed them from the coast. They said that you were a—a spy—is that the right word?"

"You *knew* I was following your trail? And the Chapalii—khepelli—" The word, in his tongue, sounded strange and dangerous to her ears. "—they knew, too?"

Yuri's cheeks flushed pink.

Pretending not to listen, Sonia nevertheless said in a low voice, "I call it dishonorable to leave a woman walking so long. How she made it alone from the coast I can't imagine. She might have died. It's a disgrace. And I told Ilya so myself."

Yuri grinned, glancing up from under long lashes at Tess. "She did, by the gods. You should have heard it."

Tess was too coldly furious to respond to the grin. "And just what do these khepelli say they're doing here, that I should want to spy on them? And risk my life like that while I'm at it?" Abruptly, before Yuri could answer, she stood up and wiped her hands on her trousers. "No, don't bother to answer. Just take me to them."

"I can't. Ilya would. . . ." He trailed off, unable to express what Ilya would do.

"He wouldn't—it isn't—" Tess realized suddenly that she knew nothing at all about this culture, except that they practiced summary execution. "He wouldn't *kill* you?"

Yuri sighed. "Killing would probably be a mercy, compared to what he would say to me," he replied, evidently having already forgotten the horrible act committed in front of his eyes that very morning. "Ah, Tess, you've never been on the sharp end of his tongue."

"Well, then, Sonia, will you take me?"

Without hesitation, Sonia met her gaze. "I can't, Tess. This is men's business, not mine. But Yuri, on the other hand, *ought to* take you. Isn't that so, Yuri?"

Yuri sheathed his knife, adjusted the position of his saber on his belt, and ran a hand down the black and gold embroidered pattern that decorated the sleeves of his red shirt.

"Yuri."

"Yes, Sonia. Come on, Tess." He led Tess off in silence, but as soon as they were away from the camp, out walking up a rise, the grass dragging at their knees and thighs, he was voluble enough. "It isn't fair, having four sisters, and all of them older than you. Well, three, since Anna died with the baby. But it's always, Yuri do this and Yuri do that, and what am I to say? *They* don't have to face Bakhtiian. He would never dare raise his voice to *them,* and if he ever did—although I can't imagine him ever trying to—then Mother would find out, and *then* Ilya would hear about it." He looked suddenly pleased with the image brought to him by this hypothetical turn of events. "I'd like to hear *that.* But then," and he looked at Tess with an impish smile, "Ilya never makes mistakes, so it will never happen."

"Yuri, I promise you, if Bakhtiian tries to blame you for bringing me with you, *I'll* deal with him."

Yuri regarded her skeptically but did not reply.

It was a shorter walk than Tess expected to the huddle of tents standing next to a makeshift corral of banked earth, stakes, and ropes. Far enough away from the main camp to give privacy to the foreigners, but close enough, Tess judged, for easy access. She recognized the tall, thin silhouettes of the Chapalii immediately. They wore plain brown tunics and trousers, but as always, the clothing could not disguise their gauntness or their pallor. There were other men as well, men of the tribe, but by and large those men were engaged in riding and currying and otherwise examining—horses.

"Horses." The word gusted out of her in a sharp breath. She stopped stock-still far enough away from the tents that no Chapalii ought to recognize her. These were nothing like the horses that Bakhtiian and Yuri, and she herself, had ridden. She knew without question, with that instinct carried down over millennia of Earth generations, that these were Earth horses. The horses from the shuttle's hold.

"They're very fine, aren't they?" said Yuri enthusiastically. "They are a breed called—*khuhaylan*. When Ilya saw the first one, two years back, and the khepelli traders told him that he could have a hundred more just for helping them search for the lost haven of their god, of course he agreed. They're much stronger than they look. With such horses—" He went pale. "There he is. He's seen us."

"Chapalii," said Tess in Anglais, watching one dark figure detach itself from a cluster of men and start with a determined and menacing stride toward them, "don't believe in a god. Just in commerce and rank."

"I beg your pardon?"

"Come on, Yuri." She started for the nearest tent, where a lone Chapalii had stopped to stare at them.

"But Ilya—" He trailed after her, glancing over his shoulder at the approach of his cousin.

"I have business with these Chapalii, Yuri, not with Bakhtiian, who, need I remind you, let me walk for three days without food or water, and then—by God!—then the first time he spoke to me in Rhuian, asked me trick questions to see if I was really from Jeds."

Yuri murmured something indistinguishable behind her. Tess did not bother to ask him what it was.

CHAPTER FOUR

"Art is ever far better than strength."
—MUSAEUS

"I greet you with good favor, Cha Ishii Hokokul." Tess halted in front of the Chapalii, whom she recognized as the one who had protested so vehemently against her presence on the *Oshaki*. A sickly shade of blue gave color to his face as he stared at her. Belatedly, he remembered to bow. Tess smiled. She was so angry at seeing him here, and at knowing that he had known all along of her plight, that she did not mind watching him squirm.

Eventually he found his voice. "May I be allowed to offer good greetings on my part, Lady Terese," he said, his voice as expressionless as any well-trained Chapalii's had to be, but the hint of blue in his cheeks betrayed his consternation.

"You may." For a moment she let her anger get the better of her, and she lapsed out of Chapalii and into Anglais. "Just what the hell do you think you're doing on an Interdicted planet? Where your species is very specifically prohibited?"

He regarded her blankly. Of course, as a member of the ruling culture, he had no reason to learn *her* language. "Cha Ishii, I feel sure that you are well aware that you and whatever people are with you are violating the duke's Interdiction order covering this planet. I think you must also be aware that *I* can have you stripped of all your wealth for this infraction."

But his color faded, and he regained his pallor. "You are also in violation of this edict, Lady Terese."

"I am heir to this system. If I choose to journey through my brother's demesne, I do not need *your* permission."

He flushed violet and then, looking up, went pale again. "But I comprehend, Lady Terese, that we are here now, and to reveal us for what we are to these natives—if indeed they could understand it in any case—would be an even greater violation of your brother's edict."

"Tess." Yuri sounded nervous as he glanced from Tess to Cha Ishii and then behind her. She turned. Bakhtiian came up, looking grim, with Nikolai Sibirin in tow. He stopped equidistant from both Tess and Ishii.

"Evidently you know one another," he said in Rhuian. He did not sound pleased. His gaze settled for one uncomfortable moment on Yuri, who looked distinctly anxious, and then flicked back to Tess and on to Ishii.

"Why, yes," said Tess sweetly. "We do. I was hired to act as an interpreter for their party. How unfortunate that we became separated. I am sure Cha Ishii will agree with me." She added, in court Chapalii, "You will, of course, agree, Cha Ishii. Do you require my efforts to translate for you?"

"I am not unprepared, Lady Terese. I speak some Rhuian." He twisted to address Bakhtiian in that language. "Certainly it was unfortunate." Tess was stricken to silence by astonishment at his knowing such a primitive tongue. His command of the language was rough, but serviceable. "I apologize for any inconvenience this oversight may have caused you."

"No inconvenience at all," replied Bakhtiian. Tess did not know him well enough to be sure if he meant the remark to be as sarcastic as it sounded to her. "Had you mentioned her before, I might have been able to reunite you sooner."

"But Ilya," said Yuri, "you knew someone was following them before we even met them at the lakeshore."

"Yuri. The horses need water."

Yuri reddened from neck to brow and mumbled something in khush, glancing back at Tess as he left.

His summary dismissal did not improve Tess's mood. "I confess myself curious to know why I was left to walk that long when you knew I was following you." She stared straight at Bakhtiian. "But I now need to speak with Cha Ishii. Alone."

Something subtle shifted in Bakhtiian's already severe expression, a narrowing of the eyes, a tenseness in his lips. "Indeed," he said, scrupulously formal. "You introduced yourself to me before, Terese Soerensen.'' He did not stumble, only slowed, over the awkward syllables. "But I have never introduced myself. I am Ilyakoria Bakhtiian.'' He gave a polite bow, like those Tess remembered from the court at Jeds, but she felt it was as much mocking as respectful. She returned it, mimicking him exactly. He did not smile. "If you will excuse me.''

Someone, off in the group of men clustered around the corral, laughed, choked it back, and there was a murmur of voices that quieted abruptly as Bakhtiian turned away from Tess and returned to the horses. The older man lingered.

His short, light silvering hair and weathered face and hands offered Tess abundant signs of the natural aging that did not show in his posture. "If I may interrupt a moment,'' he said in heavily accented Rhuian. He inclined his head in a brief nod of greeting, not really waiting for their assent. "We have not met. I am Nikolai Sibirin.''

Despite his sober expression, some light in his eyes made her want to smile at him. "I am honored,'' she replied, when she saw that his introduction was meant for her. Ishii, as attuned to nuances of hierarchy as all Chapalii must be, stepped back to afford them privacy for their conversation.

Sibirin hesitated, mulling over words. "While I do not, by any means, recommend unquestioning deference to Ilyakoria's leadership in these matters, I do find it inadvisable to provoke him deliberately.''

Tess recalled the execution in vivid detail. "Yes, I see. Thank you.''

"Well,'' said Sibirin apologetically, watching her closely, "perhaps you do and perhaps you don't. He's not usually so volatile, but when he is, one steps carefully and rides with a light hand on the reins.'' Then, to take the sting out of the words, he smiled. By the lines in his face, she could see that he smiled a great deal.

"I have been known to have a quick temper. And I'm grateful for your people's hospitality.'' He nodded, satisfied, and she could not resist a question. "Did you learn Rhuian in Jeds, too?''

"No, no. Only Ilyakoria and three of his kin have traveled so far. But I have always liked other tongues, and I try to learn as many as I can. Most jaran speak only khush.''

"Then I shall have to learn khush.'' Having said it, she felt a sudden consanguinity, not so much that feeling of having known someone before but rather of being certain that she would like him very well, and he, her. He smiled and excused himself, leaving her with Ishii.

Three other Chapalii had appeared from inside their tents. They merely stood at the entrance flaps and watched as Ishii bowed again, acknowledging that her attention had returned to him.

"Well," said Tess to herself in Anglais. Her initial flood of anger had dissipated with Sibirin's gentle words and she was better off for it, able now to measure with a cooler heart what she said. "Cha Ishii. You will understand very well that I am shocked and disappointed that you and your party, with the connivance of Hao Yakii and unknown others, have willfully chosen to violate the Interdiction of this planet by the duke. But perhaps your explanation will bring matters into a more positive perspective." She folded her hands in front of herself in that arrangement, palm to palm, fingers of the right hand concealing the left thumb, known as Imperial Judgment.

A hint of violet colored Ishii's face, but it was only a suggestion, paling to white. "We are pilgrims, Lady Terese."

"Chapalii have no God."

A swell of color flooded their faces. One of the Chapalii back by the tent put his hand on his belt. It was a threatening gesture, although there was no obvious weapon there. Cha Ishii raised a hand, and the other turned and went back into a tent.

"You gain nothing by insulting us, Lady Terese. I compliment you on your impressive and scholarly command of our language, but you cannot comprehend all of our culture. And whatever you may choose to believe about us, we have told these natives that we are a priest and his pious followers. It is a currency that they understand."

"Pilgrims engage in pilgrimages. Where are you going on an unmapped, primitive planet?"

"The duke has satellite maps."

"Geological maps, not geographical."

"May I remind you again, Lady Terese, that if you endeavor to expose us to these natives, you will be forced to utterly overturn the duke's Interdiction and meddle irreparably with their cultural development. We have merely asked for guidance and protection, offering horses as coinage, leaving no other trace of ourselves or our culture but our brief presence here. They believe us to be from an empire over the sea. It is a sufficient fiction to leave them unsuspecting. Any other, and you risk obliterating all the protections the duke has put in place.''

Instead of replying, she found herself listening. It was a quiet land; the noises of the horses and the hushed voices of the men tending them, a soft scraping sound coming from inside one of the Chapalii tents, and the high whistle of a bird, that was all—no background noise at all, except the whisper of the breeze through the tall grass. Ishii had her, of course, had the right of it. She could not compound their transgression with a worse one of her own. Perhaps they could manage an entire journey and scarcely mark the cultures through which they traveled. It was possible.

''As well, Lady Terese,'' he added softly, and presumptuously, hearing some kind of submission—or admission—in her silence, ''I am aware, as you must be, that the duke has had a handful of men traveling and mapping this world for the last twenty years, for what you call anthropological reasons, and certainly for future resource exploitation, when such times come, as they undoubtedly will. One cannot sit forever on such wealth as this planet holds.''

Faced with her brother's flouting of his own rules, she could scarcely claim to be righteous—after all, she had come to Rhui, and to this pass, with no one's permission but her own. ''Very well, Cha Ishii. There is some justice in your claims, although you will understand that I must report this infraction. Nevertheless, since I will be journeying with you, if you and your party behave appropriately, I will ask that the penalties be softened.''

''You are most gracious, Lady Terese.'' He inclined his head to signal his obedience. She could read neither his tone nor his skin to give her a clue as to what he was thinking now. ''If I may ask your indulgence, I have ablutions to perform.''

''You may.'' She watched him bow and back away into the tent, followed by the two remaining Chapalii, and then she turned and walked back toward camp. His quick acquiescence made her uneasy, but what could he do now that she was here? Kill her? She dismissed the idea as quickly as it occurred—it was simply too alien and revolutionary an idea to the chapalii psyche as she knew it. Hierarchy was too ingrained for one of lower rank to consider doing harm to any person above him. She had only to wait and watch, listen and be patient. Eventually they would betray their true purpose for being here.

At the top of the rise she paused to look back, at the round, tall white tents of the Chapalii and then at the men examining the horses. She could not be sure any of them was Yuri. One man detached himself from the group. By his walk and his dark hair and by the single-minded purpose of his stride, she guessed it was Bakhtiian—coming to talk to her. She started forward as fast as she could at a walk, not wanting to seem to run. She had no desire whatsoever to talk with Bakhtiian, not yet. She had a story to get straight, facts to invent. More than anything, she had to absorb the Chapalii's presence here and what this meant to herself and to her brother. If Charles were here, he would know what to do. But Charles wasn't here. It was up to her. *And I'm not the right person to be his heir.* She wanted to glance back to see how close Bakhtiian was but she refused to let him know that she knew he was following her. *Why can't Charles see that? I don't want this work.*

Then what do you want? It was a mocking question, thought at herself, but the answer appeared unexpectedly, although it was the answer to a different question. Tess saw Sonia, walking at the edge of camp with a boy, midway in age between the babe-in-arms and the older girl, in reluctant tow. She saw Tess and halted, smiled, and then, looking past Tess, smiled broadly.

"Tess." As soon as Tess was close enough, Sonia took the boy's dirty hand and pressed it into Tess's.

The boy, who had been wailing insincerely a moment before, snapped his mouth shut and gazed up in awe at Tess with eyes as blue as the summer sky. "You're tall," he said. "You're as tall as my papa."

Sonia chuckled. "Vania, your manners. Tess, is that Ilya I see? He looks quite angry." She seemed quite cheerful. Tess did not have the nerve to turn around enough to see the contrast between Sonia's fair, blonde prettiness and her cousin's harsh, dark features.

"I don't suppose you can hide me? I don't want to talk to him right now."

Sonia's eyes widened in surprise. "Then don't talk to him.

But here, you just stay quiet." Tess took a step back, turning, as Bakhtiian came up to them.

"I would like—" he began without preamble, ignoring Sonia.

"Well, Ilya, what is it you would like?" The curtness in Sonia's tone shocked Tess. Yuri had practically slunk away from Bakhtiian's anger.

Bakhtiian himself ceased speaking for three whole breaths together. "I beg your pardon, Sonia," he said in a softer tone. "Cousin, perhaps you would allow me to speak with your companion, Terese Soerensen?"

"Well, Ilya, really, now that Mama has taken her in, you must approach Mama with that request, I think. Although Mama *is* out with the younger Kolenin girls today, since there was a herd of *grazel* seen by the scouts, so she'll be gone until dark. But there will be supper in any case. Mama may be back by then."

It was not difficult, Tess reflected, to see that Bakhtiian was seething with fury, having had something he wanted denied him. She tried very hard not to smile. Sonia was being very earnest, but a mocking and almost scolding tone still crept through.

"As you say, Sonia." He gave a brusque bow. "Excuse me." He left.

"But, Sonia," said Tess when she realized she was still breathing, "he just ordered Yuri to do what he wanted him to do."

"Yuri is a man. He cannot be so free with you."

"Are there people I should not talk with? Or approach? I hope you will be honest with me, Sonia. I would not want to—offend—anyone."

Sonia looked puzzled a moment, but then her expression cleared. "Of course, even while I speak Rhuian I forget you are of Jeds. Though Vania is right. You are taller than any woman of the tribes. You must remember that here, with us, because you are a woman you may speak with whomever you please. Now, *kriye,*" she said to her son, who had watched the proceedings with unblinking interest, "you will behave yourself with Tess." He nodded and gripped his grimy hand more tightly around Tess's fingers. "I wish he were always so well-behaved, but I am afraid that he takes after his uncle. But come, you will meet my sisters, and then this evening Mama will receive you into the family.

Katerina and Stassia made welcome cakes just for the occasion.''

She led Tess away into the haven of women's company, a haven that was comprehensive in providing both companionship and work. Sonia's mother arrived with a pair of adolescent identical twin girls with bronze-gold hair. The girls struggled along in her wake, each with a slender antelope slung over her shoulders and a bow and quiver of arrows strapped onto her belt. Mother Orzhekov was a small, thin woman of vast energy, whose features were easily as stern as her nephew's. She welcomed Tess with sober grace and invested her into the family, all without a particle of discomfiture at their lack of any common language. But by the end of the evening, Tess had learned perhaps fifty words of khush and could thank the matriarch in her own tongue, a feat which pleased the entire family immensely: Mother Orzhekov, her three grown daughters and their husbands and ten children, her dead daughter's husband and two children, and her son, Yuri, two great-nephews, three grand-nieces and a half dozen assorted other family members.

Once accepted into the Orzhekov tent, Tess discovered quickly enough that her place in the tribe itself was established and unshakable. There was plenty of work for the women, but never too much because it was shared. If the men treated her with distant interest and an intense reserve, the women shamelessly enjoyed her company and monopolized her time. The children, of course, were always underfoot. Tess never had to be alone and never asked to be. However solitary she had lived at Univerzita Karlova in Prague, she had imposed it on herself because of her brother's name and reputation. But what was the Chapaliian Empire to these people? They did not even know it existed. The Prince of Jeds was just a name; that Bakhtiian, Yuri, and Sonia had been to Jeds mattered little to anyone else, except as a curiosity. She felt free.

Seven days after her arrival she felt confident enough with her khush to venture out alone at dusk. She first took the short side trip to survey the Chapalii tents. The Chapalii stayed inside, mostly, and she did not yet want to attempt to bully her way into their most intimate territory—after seven days with the jaran, she had come to have a great respect for the sanctity of tent and family. But the corral with the Earth horses was close enough to serve as a good observation post, and it gave her a legitimate destination. The man on watch was Sonia's husband Mikhal. He acknowledged her with a shy nod and strolled away, leaving her.

Tess leaned against the high side of one of the pair of wagons that formed the barrier and stared over it at the animals. She found it easy to pick out the Earth horses from the handful of native animals. What was the khush word for horse? *Tarpan*, that was it. The Kuhaylan Arabians were beautiful creatures by any measure, small, certainly, with delicate heads, huge eyes, and small, mobile ears, but there was strength in their line, in the elegant arch of their tails, and intelligence in their broad foreheads. No wonder these riders desired such stock.

The sun sank below the horizon and one bright star appeared in the darkening sky: the planet Odys. Charles was there, deeply involved in his work, ignorant of this trespass. She alone could warn him that Chapalii had invaded Rhui, yet there was so very much space between them. Surely he had gotten her letter, and had put in a message to Dr. Hierakis at the palace in Jeds—put in a message, only to discover that she had not arrived in Jeds. Her disappearance would simply be another burden laid on him.

The horses were quiet, but their movements spoke. They swished their tails. One stamped. Another snapped at a fly. Dappling the hillside beyond the corral, the mass of goatlike herd animals that provided milk and wool and meat for the tribe blanketed the grass. Something scuffed the ground behind her. She whirled.

"I beg your pardon," said Bakhtiian. He did not look very sorry. The wind stirred his hair and rustled the folds of his shirt, more gray than red in the half light.

"You didn't waste any time," she replied, emboldened by seven days among forthright women. "This is the first time I've been alone."

"Indeed."

"Was there something you wanted to know?" Seeing his expression, she could not restrain a smile. "No, I don't mean that as facetiously as it sounds. They are beautiful animals, aren't they?"

"Yes, they are," he said fervently, distracted by this comment. He leaned against the wagon an arm's length away from her and gazed with rapt intensity at the horses. "See the stallion—the gray—there. He alone is priceless. The black stallion is picketed out—" He gestured with a turn of his head. "And mares—thirty-six here, another hundred at journey's end. It is not so long to travel, to receive such a prize."

"How long a journey is it?"

He smiled, not at her. When he turned to look at her, the smile faded. "Your employers have not kept you very well informed, I see. It seems of a piece with so negligently leaving you behind at the port. And being surprised that you had followed them so far."

"Ah, well," said Tess in khush, using a phrase she had learned from Yuri, "the wind has a careless heart."

"You learn quickly."

"I like languages. What will you use these horses for?" It was a casual question, thrown out to distract him, so she was not prepared for the sudden change in his expression.

"To make war." He did not smile. "Now. You are no interpreter. Why are you here?"

She considered refusing to answer, but he was a dangerous man. It was better to choose her words carefully. "I am here to travel with the priest and his party."

"I do not think that they want you to travel with them."

"But I will travel with them nevertheless. Do you intend to make me leave the tribe?"

"I have never had any such intention. I don't have time, now, to get you back to the port from which you can sail to Jeds. You will be safe with the tribe until we return."

The implication of this reply took a moment to sink in. The breeze shifted, bringing the rich, musty scent of horses directly to her. "Until who returns?"

"Ah. You thought the khepelli party was to be escorted by the entire tribe. But it is many months' journey to the shrine of Morava, where these holy men hope to find enlightenment. My jahar, my riders, will be their sole escort. We can move faster, and if there is trouble—Well, then, we are better able to deal with it. You, of course, will stay with the women."

As if that settled the entire thing, he nodded and excused himself. He faded into the darkness, but she heard him exchange words with Mikhal a moment later, and then there was silence. She pushed away from the corral and walked lowly over to stare from a safe distance at the Chapalii ents. Two were dark, but one had a light on inside, a steady glow that she recognized as artificial. What other technology had they brought with them? She had not even brought an emergency transmitter, knowing she could rely on Dr. Hierakis once she reached Jeds.

She stood awhile, as the night air cooled around her, chilling her neck, and watched, until the light flicked out with unnatural suddenness. An animal chittered in the grass. Above, a brilliant spray of stars littered the night sky. She felt scared, suddenly, standing alone in unknown surroundings, caught out on a trackless plain, a solitary and untried force against whatever convoluted plans the Chapalii had made, were making even now, against her brother. The breeze tickled her cheeks. She sighed and walked back to camp, to the bright sanctuary of Sonia and her family.

CHAPTER FIVE

"Harmony consists of opposing tension."
—HERACLEITUS OF EPHESUS

Tess followed Yuri out of the corral the next morning and walked with him behind the herd of horses as they were driven down to water at a pool. There was a skirmish, biting, a kick, and then the horses at the fore settled down to drink. Watchful young men patrolled the fringe of the herd mounted on sturdy tarpans.

"It looks like they're fighting over precedence," Tess said, "but I suppose that's just me wanting to make them like people. Or Chapalii," she added to herself in Anglais.

Yuri glanced at her. "You don't know much about horses, do you?"

"They have four legs, two ears, and a tail. That about covers it. Surely these aren't all the horses your tribe owns?"

"Of course not. We keep the herd out on the grass. But we'll keep the khuhaylans in close so that they can get to know us and trust us." He called a greeting to an adolescent boy who rode by, and then turned and started back to camp.

"Yuri," said Tess as she walked beside him, "can you teach me to ride?"

"Why?"

"Because I'm coming with you, when you leave."

Now he lifted his head to stare at her. "But Tess, women don't ride. I mean, not that women can't ride horses, of course. They often ride out to hunt, but they never ride with the jahar."

"I have to get to Jeds. I have to travel with the pilgrims."

He examined her. Unlike the other young men, he was

not shy with her, because of his status as her adopted
brother. His expression was always a mirror of his thoughts,
and right now he was troubled and thinking hard. "Are you
a spy, as the priest Ishii says you are?" he asked finally.

"No, I'm not."

"I believe you, Tess, but you must tell Ilya something
convincing in order to get him to change his mind about
letting you go with the jahar. It's a very serious matter,
riding. Ilya has enemies."

"If Cha Ishii requests that I accompany you, then surely
Ilya must agree."

"I don't think the priest Ishii wants you to go."

"He doesn't, but he will do as I say."

"I think Ilya will be very curious to know why the priest
will do as you say, Tess. You are alone, you have no saber,
no horse, no tent, no family. Why should the priest obey
you when he does not want to?"

Over the last seven days, Tess had developed a story, of
sorts, to satisfy the women's interest in her past. Now
seemed the appropriate time to spin it further. "You know
my brother is a merchant, Yuri. But I haven't said—he has
trade agreements, treaties, with the khepellis, and has recently suspected that they are not adhering to these treaties.
So he sent me to their empire, their lands, to discover—
well, I followed this party, I came over the seas with them,
on the same ship. According to these treaties, they ought
not to be here, and—and I need to know what they are
looking for."

Yuri rubbed his lower lip with one finger. "I never liked
Jeds," he said at last. "I never understood it. This is not
Jeds, and this is not the land where the khepellis come from.
So how can you have a treaty that says which of you may
travel here?"

The question took Tess aback for a moment, but her training in Chapalii culture—more mercantile even than Earth's—
saved her. "Trade rights. Who gets to trade where."

The answer evidently satisfied Yuri. "Well, I suppose
Mama can spare you from the work for some time each day.
If she agrees, then I will teach you."

"And Bakhtiian?"

"If my mother gives you permission, then there is no
reason for him to object. Why should he anyway? You'll

need to know how to ride whether you travel with the tribe
or the jahar.''

"How many days will I have?''

"To learn? Until Eva Kolenin's baby comes, I think. Ten
days, perhaps, or twelve. But I warn you, Tess, no matter
how well you can ride, you will have a hard time convincing
Ilya.''

"Bakhtiian won't have a choice. I'm going, Yuri.''

Yuri simply shook his head and refrained from comment.

Mother Orzhekov proved amenable, as long as Tess did
her share of the work. It had not taken Tess many days to
discover that there was leisure as well as work in this culture, and that a handful of women washing clothes were as
likely to pause for an hour to gossip or play with the children as to work straight through and hurry on to another
task. No one hurried except Bakhtiian, who was commonly
said to have breathed too much southern air than was good
for him when he had left, seventeen years ago, an impetuous, serious child of sixteen, and returned from Jeds five
years later, just as serious and not one whit less impetuous.
That journey had made him hasty and reckless, although
Mother Orzhekov could be heard to mutter that Ilyakoria
had always been hasty and reckless. But even she treated
him with a respect that no thirty-three-year-old man, that
not even Nikolai Sibirin, twenty years his senior and a healer
as well, came close to receiving. He was a visionary—he
was *their* visionary. Bakhtiian had great plans, and the tribe
would follow him, even to the ends of the earth. The name
he had earned on that trip—*bakh-tiian*, he-who-has-traveled-
far—was as much a mystical as a physical appellation, and
it now superseded his own deceased mother's name of Orzhekov, which by birth he ought to be called.

And when Eva Kolenin went into labor and all the men
were chased out of camp until the babe was safely born, for
fear their presence might attract malignant spirits, Bakhtiian
went only as far as his own small tent, set somewhat in back
of the cluster that marked his aunt's family.

Sent to get water from the stream, Tess and Sonia and
Elena, the handsome gray-eyed girl who was still somehow
unmarried, walked through the camp. Tent awnings flapped
over empty ground cloths; men's work, a shirt half-
embroidered, a knife getting a new hilt, a saddle half made,
lay abandoned, left in neat piles. The low trembling of

drums accompanied their walk. A lulling chant rose and fell
in time with the rhythm. A group of children ran by, giggling. They hushed suddenly, overborne by a swell in the
chanting, and escaped in a rush out into the high grass.
Alone at this end of camp, Bakhtiian sat in front of his tent,
stitching at a pair of boots. He glanced up as the three
women passed. Elena smiled at him, but his impassive eyes
swept across them without pausing before he went back to
his work. Elena frowned. Tess looked back and saw that he
had, for a moment, looked after them.

"Why may he stay in camp?" she asked, slowly, in
khush.

"You've the ending wrong," said Sonia, correcting her.
Her baby, Kolia, was asleep in a sling on her back. "This
way." She repeated it twice, and then went on. "Bakhtiian
has his own tent, so there is no one to make him leave."

Elena glanced back, and when she spoke, she measured
her words carefully so that Tess could understand most of
them. "They say that in some tribes, by the settled lands,
the men own the tents. Do you suppose that is true? I would
not want to live in such a tribe."

"But not every woman has a tent," said Tess.

"No." said Sonia. "A woman who is marked for marriage is gifted a tent by her mother or her aunt."

"Marked for marriage?"

Sonia lifted one hand to brush at the diagonal scar that
ran from her cheekbone to her jawline. "When a man
chooses to marry you, he marks you."

"He *marks* you—with *what?*"

Sonia and Elena looked at each other. Elena had no scar.
"With his saber," said Sonia, as if it ought to be obvious.

Tess was appalled. She could not imagine Sonia allowing
a man to mutilate her like that. But she was not about to
say so. "And—ah—is that the only way to be married? To
be—marked?"

"Yes," said Elena.

"No." Sonia shrugged. Grass dragged against the hems
of their bright tunics. "There is another. 'The long road to
the setting sun, the binding of the four arches.' But that is
a path held by the gods. Few people wish—or dare—to ride
it."

Elena sniffed. "Better marked than bound."

"I see," said Tess, not understanding at all. She hesitated. "Does it hurt?"

Sonia smiled. "Yes. At first. But it is not a very deep cut. Bearing a child hurts far more. The small pain prepares you for the larger one."

They reached the stream and began to fill the large leather pouches with cold water. "I'm not sure I would choose to marry, if I had to get such a scar," said Tess carefully.

Elena turned sullen abruptly, hands caught in the rushing water. "What choice does a woman have in marriage?"

"Elena," said Sonia. "Everyone knows Vladimir prefers you to all the other girls. Mikhal said that Vladi refused Lila's and Marya's advances, all because he's trying to work up enough courage to mark you."

"A kinless orphan! What woman would want that kind of husband?" Elena leaned forward, her hands in fists, her pale eyes fixed on Sonia. "I won't let him get close enough to mark me. He's fine as a lover, but I won't have him as a husband." Tears filled her eyes, and she jumped up and ran off.

Sonia deftly extracted from the rushing stream the two half-full pouches that Elena had dropped. "She's always wished that Ilya would mark her, but it's a vain hope, I fear."

"Do you really have no choice in marriage?"

"In the choosing? No. You must see, Tess, that men have no power over us at all when we're unmarried, but a man who is married can command his wife in certain things, or has at least some power over her that he has over no other woman."

"Then why do you marry?"

The sun shone full on Sonia's face and fair hair, casting a glow on her cheeks. "Sometimes a man has that look in his eye that is hard to resist. You have forgotten, Tess, because I think your heart still aches."

Tess was silent. The wind blew tiny ripples across a shallow backwater.

"It is no shame," said Sonia softly. "We have all hurt for a man who did not love us."

"I tried so hard."

"Perhaps that is why you failed."

Tess put her hands full into the stream. The cold water dragged at her fingers. "Jacques wanted something he thought I had, that I could give him—power and wealth. Something he was too lazy to earn for himself. When he found out I couldn't give it to him, he left. He never loved me at all. I was such a fool.'' She pulled her hands out of the water. They were already so chilled it was difficult to bend them, but she forced them slowly into fists.

"When you have a full and eager heart in you, you must not go to the man whose heart is empty and weak.''

"I don't know if I can judge anymore.'' Tess sat silent for a long moment, watching the light move from ripple to ripple on the stream. "I'm afraid to try.''

"Fear is a poor teacher. But now you have friends. We will help you. It would be best, I think, if you did not approach any of the married men to begin with. One must be discreet, especially in the camp. It is terribly impolite, especially in front of the wife, to flaunt such a thing. But no matter. We have many fine unmarried men to choose from. Vladimir—no, too vain. Kirill—too forward. Yuri—''

Tess laughed. It seemed very natural to speak of affairs so intensely personal, here, with Sonia, in the warming spring sun, the drums a quiet drone in the distance. "Yuri is my brother.''

"Yes. A brother is of far greater value than a husband or a lover. They are much easier to order around. Come, we ought to go back.'' She rose and, grasping Tess's hand, helped her to her feet. They distributed the extra pouches around their shoulders and walked back to camp. Kolia slept on. A striped tent flap, untied, fluttered in the breeze, one bright end snapping up and down. Pots dangled from side ropes, striking a high tinny accompaniment to the resonant pulse of the women's voices beyond. When they passed Bakhtiian this time, he did not even look up. He had one hand tucked inside the boot, the needle pulling in and out in an even stitch. Sonia's daughter Katerina crouched beside him, intently watching him work.

"Why did he go to Jeds?'' Tess asked. "Why would he even have thought of it? Had you ever heard of Jeds before? Had any other jaran ever gone?''

"No, Ilya was the first. I suppose he heard of it when he was a boy. Jaran often trade at ports along the coast. Even so far east as we are now, Jeds is known at every port. I don't know why he went. He was only sixteen. Mama once

said there was something to do with his sister, that when
she married, he was very angry, but Ilya has always looked
farther than others do. I remember when he came back. He
told us that if the jaran were one people, and not many
tribes, then we would never have to fear the *khaja,* the settled people, who build their stone tents farther out each year
on the plains that the gods meant for our home.''

''Are there many tribes?''

''There are a thousand tribes, and a thousand thousand
families. We are as plentiful as the birds, and as swift as
our horses, and as strong—as strong as a woman avenging
her child. So Ilya began to weave a great tapestry, and the
Elders of many tribes offered to be the warp in his loom,
and the dyans of many jahars offered themselves and their
riders as the weft. So the pattern grew. He made enemies.
And—oh, it was seven years ago, now—those enemies rode
into camp one night when he was away and killed his sister
and his mother and father and his sister's five-year-old son.''

They had reached the far end of camp and just as they
handed the water over to Sonia's mother, the chanting
stopped abruptly, pierced by the high wail of a baby. Immediately, singing broke out. A girl ran off to find the father. Kolia snuffled and yawned and opened his eyes.

Sonia set him on the rug under the eye of his grandmother
and tugged Tess away. ''We'll go start supper. The men will
be hungry.''

''But then what happened?'' Tess glanced back at the tent
where the birth had taken place. The infant cried in bursts.
Suddenly there was silence, and the midwife stuck her head
outside the tent and called: ''He's already suckling.''
Women crowded in to greet the mother.

''What happened? Oh, with Ilya? He went on. What else
could he do? But he has never loved anyone since, except—''
Her lips tugged in an involuntary grimace. ''Well, he cannot care too deeply now, for fear he may lose more. But
he listens to no one. He's made all the jaran his, almost,
and when he gets the rest of these khuhaylan horses from
across the sea, he'll breed them and then lead the jaran
against the khaja, and the name of our people will be on
the lips of every person in every land there is, because those
lands will be ours. Oh, good. Stassia found *dhal* roots. Katerina, you little imp, what have you done to your shift?''
She gathered her daughter into her arms and gave her a kiss,

apparently oblivious to the incongruity of Bakhtiian's great plan for conquest set hard against her sister's plans for supper.

The next morning, Yuri met her for the riding lesson. He was flushed as he jogged up to her. He did not wait to catch his breath before addressing her.

"Tess. We leave day after tomorrow. Ilya would have liked to leave tomorrow, I think, but he could not deny Konstans the celebration for his first child."

Tess's breathing constricted with excitement and apprehension. "But is it too soon? Can I ride well enough?"

He shrugged. "You could travel with the tribe this year. They'll be riding southwest, behind us. Perhaps you could find another tribe going east or north, who could take you to a port this spring. Or wait for us. We won't be gone over a year."

"A *year*? How far are you going?"

"To the shrine of Morava. And then on to the western sea where the khepelli will sail back to their own lands."

The western sea? Tess dug in her memory, seeing the huge inland sea whose northeastern reaches bordered the southern edge of the vast bulk of the northern continent—these plains. And southward, far south on a bay protected by a minor archipelago, lay Jeds. "No, Yuri, I have to go with you. If the khepelli can sail out from the western ports, then I can as easily sail south to Jeds from there. I'll go speak with Ishii now, and then talk to Bakhtiian. There's no point in waiting."

"Tess." He laid a staying hand on her arm. "At least wait until morning. There's no point in spoiling the dance. Ilya gets in a foul mood when things don't go as he wants them to. Men are riding in from another tribe. A scout brought the word. You won't get a chance to speak with Ilya today in any case."

Tess acquiesced and went to help the women prepare for the dance. Any celebration was a great occasion. The arrival of a dozen men from another tribe could only add to the excitement. Indeed, most of the tribe had gathered at one end of the camp to greet the visitors. Tess found a spot next to Elena and Sonia and watched as the ten men rode in, dismounted at a prudent distance, and were escorted into the bounds of the camp itself by Niko Sibirin and another older rider. There, they waited for Bakhtiian to arrive.

The men of Bakhtiian's jahar filtered over in twos and threes to engage in that easy, informal flow of talk carried on between acquaintances who have the same complaint in life. Boys peered at them from behind tents; little girls clustered in packs and stared. The old women ignored them; the married women looked at them from the corners of their eyes; and Marya Kolenin, who wore bracelets around her ankles to show how many lovers she had and who had once kicked a man as hard as she could in the groin to stop him putting the mark of betrothal on her, went right up to them and pulled the eldest's silver-flecked beard. Everyone laughed, including the visitors.

"There he comes," breathed Elena, distracted from this interplay.

Bakhtiian was walking down the rise toward them, the sun bright on his face, his scarlet shirt catching points of light. He had a way of walking that drew the eye to him, that made his surroundings seem merely a stage for himself. He had a great deal of grace, but for the first time Tess realized that not all of it was unconscious. He was purposefully making an entrance. She laughed.

He glanced at her and then away.

Elena elbowed her. "Why are you laughing?"

"I remembered a thing said by an ancient poet of my people," said Tess, "that my brother used to say to me, about the name of vanity being man."

Elena put her hand on her necklaces. "What made you think of that?"

Sonia saved Tess from having to reply. "Come, Tess. They will go on all day with men's talk, which is far more boring to listen to than to watch. We'll go clear a dance circle, and then I think you ought to wear one of my tunics, just for tonight, to please Mama."

It took most of the day to collect enough fuel for as great a fire as the celebration warranted, and the rest of the day for each woman to dress out her one fine tunic with elaborate braids and headpieces and gold and jade earrings. They polished their hand mirrors and traced their eyes with dark kohl. Even the men brought out their best embroidered shirts and fastened tufted and beaded epaulets to their shoulders. Sonia put on six fine necklaces on each arm, and, a thick copper bracelet incised with a spiral pattern, and she wove green ribbons through the two chains that strung her mirror onto her belt.

Food was shared out at every tent. The entire holiday atmosphere was intensified by the brief appearance of the young mother and infant, escorted by the proud father once through camp. Then the musicians settled down by the dance circle, the fire was lit, and the music began.

Nikolai Sibirin, as the eldest rider in jahar, led out his wife. Other married couples joined in, and the unmarried women solicited the unattached men. Light illuminated bits of body and face, changing as the dancers turned. The first ring of watchers was shadowed. Beyond, all was darkness. Tess watched until Yuri came up to her.

"Really," he whispered, "the women are supposed to ask, but since we're kin of a sort perhaps you'll dance with me."

"Yuri, I don't know any of your dances."

"Well," he said, much struck by this, "that's true."

"You go on. I'm happy just to watch."

He left. Tess faded back into the farthest ring of light. The drums were heavy, a strong, rhythmic pulse, the lutes a thick texture through the middle with the pipes shrilling a high, exuberant melody harmonized in fifths and octaves over the rest. Though she enjoyed watching, she found herself longing to dance, but she did not have quite enough courage to put herself forward. The steps they danced were not so different from patterns she already knew, and she grew so interested in analyzing them, even in trying a few surreptitiously, that Cha Ishii's sudden appearance at her side took her entirely by surprise.

"Lady Terese." He bowed. She started. In the darkness, he had her completely at a disadvantage because she could not see the fine shades of color on his skin. "If I may speak?"

"Cha Ishii." To regain her composure, she took a moment to give permission. "You may. I am surprised to see you here."

"It is indeed a primitive display. But I will be brief. We leave day after tomorrow. I wish you to know that once we return to space, we will see to it that the duke is made aware of your presence out here. To that end, I can supply you with a ring-shaped beacon of human manufacture that we will activate once we have returned to the *Oshaki.*"

Thereby, Tess thought, *leaving it to be your word against mine that you were ever here in the first place.* She shook her head. "No, Cha Ishii, that will not be necessary."

"But you have no such technology with you. Our instruments showed—" He broke off, and Tess wished dearly that she could see what emotion he was feeling now.

"What instruments do you mean?"

"Those aboard the *Oshaki,* of course. A slip of the tongue, Lady Terese. Forgive me for disturbing you with my hasty temper."

"Of course. There is no need, Cha Ishii, for a beacon because I am coming with you."

The music stopped. After laughter and applause, the lutes began a slow melody accompanied by a sinuous line dance.

"It is too dangerous a journey, Lady Terese. I strongly advise against it."

"With you to look out for my interests, Cha Ishii, I have absolutely no doubt that I will arrive safely, with you, in Jeds."

The implication of that comment left him without a reply for a long moment as the dance shuffled on behind them. "I cannot allow this," he said at last.

"Do you have something to hide? Surely not, Cha Ishii."

"We have nothing to hide."

"Then you can have no objection to my coming."

"Bakhtiian will not let you go."

"You are paying him. If you request that I go with you, then he cannot refuse."

He pressed his hand together, palms touching, to convey his disapproval of this scheme. His voice remained expressionless. "Lady Terese, I must strongly object—"

She set her hands, fist to palm, in that arrangement known as Imperial Command. "Cha Ishii, I am the heir to this dukedom. You cannot object."

He lowered his hands. "I obey," he said finally, bowing to the precise degree due her rank. "If you wish, I will inform Bakhtiian of my decision now."

"Now?" She looked to her left, around the circle made by those of the tribe who weren't dancing, and saw Bakhtiian standing nearby, watching them. She sucked in a big breath, blew it out through full cheeks. "Very well. We may as well settle it now."

Ishii bowed again and walked over to Bakhtiian. They conferred together. Standing next to Bakhtiian, Ishii looked angular and stiff; Bakhtiian had tilted his head at such an angle that he did not appear to be looking up.

"Tess! Are you sure you don't want to dance? This next one is very easy, really—" Yuri stopped beside her and followed the direction of her gaze. "What's that all about?"

"Ishii is asking that I come along."

"Oh," said Yuri, sounding apprehensive as Ishii took his leave of Bakhtiian and disappeared into the gloom. Tess grinned at Yuri, but a moment later Bakhtiian walked across and halted beside them. He looked as if he was quite angry but trying very very hard to pretend that he was not.

"Terese Soerensen. When we first met some days past I formed the impression that you had no experience riding horses. You cannot travel with us if you cannot ride."

Tess found that she had enough malice in her soul to enjoy a slow smile at his expense. "But I can ride. Surely Mother Orzhekov told you that Yuri has been giving me lessons. I'm no master of the art, but I can stay on a horse well enough to travel with your jahar, I believe."

"She can, Ilya," said Yuri impulsively. "She's very quick."

Ilya glanced, quick as lightning, at Yuri. "Then I congratulate you," he said to Tess, "although I won't presume to guess how you persuaded the priest to request that you come with us. I don't think you made a friend by doing it."

"Do you mean yourself?"

"I was speaking of the priest," he said impassively. "I have never found it advisable to offend those who are under the special protection of the gods."

"On that count I have no fears."

A high voice broke into their circle. Little Katerina ran up to Bakhtiian, laughing, wanting to tell him something. He crouched beside her, whispered in her ear, and she looked wide-eyed up at Tess and ran away again. The music wound to a close and there was much laughter and a round of singing as the musicians broke off to rest.

"We shall see." Bakhtiian stood up. "It is against my instinct and all my better judgment, but this is the priest's choice, not mine." A single gold necklace shone at his throat, winking in the inconstant firelight as he turned to regard Yuri. "Yurinya. You will see that Terese Soerensen takes proper care of her horse, that she eats, is warm, and is always ready to ride. Do you understand?" It sounded more like a threat than a request.

"Yes, Ilya. Of course, Ilya."

"Terese Soerensen, until such time as we arrive at a port and can put you on a ship, you will abide by my decisions and my orders. You don't know this land. I do. You will ride with me and at other times will stay with Yurinya. If for some reason you can't ride with me, you'll ride with Nikolai Sibirin. Do you understand?"

"Yes. I know I'm inexperienced, but I'll learn."

"You'll have to. Yuri, come with me. Excuse us." He took Yuri by the wrist, as if he was a child, and dragged him away so fast that Yuri stumbled over his own feet and could only manage a brief, despairing glance at Tess before he vanished with Ilya into the darkness of the camp.

Tess had a sudden premonition that Yuri was in for a bad time. She circled the crowd, seeking Sonia, and found her talking easily with one of the men who had ridden in that day. Sonia had laid a hand on the man's arm as casually as if he were her husband, and their heads were close enough together as they spoke that it gave them an intimate appearance. When Tess hesitated, unsure whether to interrupt, Sonia glanced up, saw her, and excused herself immediately.

"What is it?"

Tess told her.

"Ah. You were right to come to me. Ilya will be furious at being outmaneuvered. You wait here."

"No, I ought to come with you."

"As you wish, but stay in the shadows. It will be better for Yuri if Ilya does not know you fetched me."

Tess followed Sonia into camp. Tents surrounded them, cutting off the distant glow of the great fire. There was no sound, no movement, except for the wailing of a child that faltered and stilled. Tess had to move slowly, hands out to either side, fingers occasionally brushing the coarse fabric of a tent wall. Sonia had lost her, but as the music started up again behind, she heard voices ahead, a quiet counterpoint to the distant melody of celebration. She stumbled over a guy-rope and froze, stopped by the voices coming from right around the edge of the tent.

"You deliberately used my aunt's authority to undercut mine." Bakhtiian's tone was so cutting that Tess instantly regretted ever asking Yuri for help. "Of course I would not object, since I did not suspect what you and she were planning."

"I didn't think—"

"Obviously you didn't think, Yuri. Women don't ride with the jahar. Her inexperience will slow us down and could be dangerous."

"But that's why I gave her the lessons."

"If she couldn't ride, there would be no question of her traveling with us, would there?"

"But you just said yourself that—"

"Have you ever bothered to ask yourself why she is here? Or wonder why the priest says she is a spy—"

"You don't really believe—"

"Had I finished speaking?"

The pause that followed was both heavy and uncomfortable. Into it, the distant music metamorphosed from a slow, pacing number into a frantic tune.

"Well, Ilya," said Sonia, walking into their silence with all the aplomb of an angry and protective older sister. When Sonia spoke, clear and carrying, Tess abruptly realized that they were all speaking in Rhuian, a family quarrel that no one else could understand. "Have you finished bullying Yuri now? Or shall I leave until you are done?"

"This is men's business, Sonia."

"Is it, indeed? When two men meet in the dark to discuss a woman, I call that women's business. Yuri, you may go."

"I haven't given him permission—"

"Ilya. Must I speak to Mama about your manners?"

"Go on, Yuri," he said curtly.

Tess, standing frozen behind the dark wall of a tent, did not see in which direction Yuri fled.

"You have made your point, Sonia," said Bakhtiian coldly. "Have I your permission to leave?"

"Certainly, Ilyakoria. But I am curious as to why you were so insistent that Nadine and I travel the long path to Jeds, alone, need I add, where we might have encountered any danger, and in lands where you know very well how they treat women. We cannot even be sure we will ever see Dina again."

"Knowing Dina, we will undoubtedly receive an envoy

from the Prince of Jeds himself requesting that we remove her before she destroys the entire city.''

Sonia chuckled, despite herself. ''That is very probably true. Don't distract me. What I mean to say is, if you risked us, then whatever excuse you give Yuri about Tess not going because she is a woman is the most ridiculous nonsense I have ever heard.''

''Do you suppose she can use a saber?''

''I suppose she can learn, well enough to defend herself, at least. I do not expect her to become such a paragon of saber fighting as Vladimir, or yourself, dear cousin. And I will give her my own bow and arrows, since a woman can use them to protect herself without any shame. What is your real reason?''

''I don't trust her. There are great things in front of us, in front of our massed armies, if we can get so far. I must rid myself of those last few riders who don't understand that we must unite, that the old ways no longer protect us. And I need those horses. What if she acts to harm the priest, to disrupt this journey, to ruin all the work I've done so far?''

''Why should she care? She is a merchant's sister, traveling home to Jeds. She says herself that it was a foolish impulse that led her to follow the priest off the ship, that she only meant to protect her brother's trading rights.''

''Do you believe this story?''

''I trust Tess.''

He did not reply immediately. ''She lied to us once. She is not their interpreter. She's still lying, Sonia.''

''How can you know?''

''I feel it in my gut.''

''And you're never wrong.'' Sonia's voice came cold and flat and sarcastic. ''Never you. Never Bakhtiian. You never listen to anyone else.''

''I would listen to others if they had anything worthwhile to say.''

''If you'd listened to others, Natalia and Timofey and your parents would still be alive.''

The tension was so palpable that Tess felt it as loudly as any words. Bakhtiian made a sound, like the beginning of speech, and then fell silent, as if he were so furious that he could not even talk. She took a step back, suddenly sure that her presence here would do Sonia no good if it were discovered.

"Come out," said Bakhtiian, as if her thoughts alone had alerted him.

"Ilya—" Sonia began, protesting.

"Whom are you protecting?" he snapped.

Tess knew that however much she did not want to walk around the tent and see either of them, in such a mood, she could not leave Sonia to end this conversation alone.

So she joined them. Sonia stood, hands drawn up into fists on either side of her waist, pale, facing Bakhtiian. He had heard the scuff on the grass and he turned; instantaneously took a step back away from Tess, surprised to see *her*. He froze, as though touched by some stilling hand.

"Excuse me," she said, and heard the betraying quaver in her voice. "I was looking for Sonia."

His gaze had the cutting edge of a knife. Tess tensed, knowing for that instant that he was about to say something so vicious that it could never be forgiven. Sonia moved, stepping toward Tess as if she meant to shield her.

Bakhtiian caught his breath and whirled and strode away into the darkness.

Distant voices rose to accompany some melody. Tess put her hands to her face. Against her cold palms, her cheeks felt flushed and hot. Sonia came over to her and grasped her wrists. A moment later, they were laughing and crying all at once.

"Gods," said Sonia at last, letting go of Tess. "It's no wonder that there are men out riding just to kill him."

Tess brushed a wisp of grass from her lips. It was true enough what Bakhtiian had said, that she was lying. But how much could she tell them? How much would be right? How much would be fair? How much could they even believe? She did not know. "Poor Yuri," she said, to say something. "It's just as well I'm going, Sonia. He needs someone to protect him."

"That's right." Sonia leaned forward and kissed Tess on the cheek. "But Tess, however hard it may be, try not to lose your temper with Ilya. It's easy enough to do, but gods, it makes you say the most awful things."

"It is true, Sonia? What you said about his family?"

"I don't know. Other people warned him that there had been threats, but he never would listen. But I shouldn't have said it to him. Harsh words won't bring them back." The high, brisk sound of claps underlaid by muffled stamping reached them, sharp in the clear air, followed by cheers, encouragement to some solo dancer. "Listen to us! This is supposed to be a celebration. We'll wash our faces and run back. The men are showing off. We don't want to miss that." She grabbed Tess's hand, and they went together.

In the morning, Yuri waylaid her as soon as she woke. He looked anxious.

"What's wrong?" she asked.

"We have to choose you a horse. I think the little bay. You'll need a saber, a knife. . . . Did I say clothing? A blanket!" He broke off when Tess laughed at his expression. "I would never have believed that Bakhtiian would agree to take you, but you weren't afraid, and so you got what you were reaching for. We call that *korokh,* one who reaches for the wind. They are few and always brave. The gods favor them."

"I'll need it." And she wondered, suddenly, finally, what she had gotten herself into.

"There's Sonia. She'll help us."

By judicious application to various members of their family, Sonia and Yuri acquired all the articles that they thought Tess would need on the journey. It did not come to much, since it all had to be carried, but to Tess it seemed like riches: a saber, a knife, an extra set of clothing down to gloves and belt, a thick blanket and light sleeping mat, a bone comb carved in arborescent detail, a lump of soap, and beaded leather strips to braid in her hair as it grew out. Stassia gave her two bracelets, and her youngest son, barely five, insisted that she take his stamped leather flask. After all this, Sonia led her aside to where her mother sat weaving.

"You will be the only woman," said Mother Orzhekov. Her strong hands did not falter, feeding out thread, pulling the shuttle across. "You must have your own tent. Sonia, you know the one. And her mirror. No woman ought to be without a mirror." She dismissed them before Tess could thank her.

"You must thank her," said Sonia as they left, "by behaving in a manner that will make her proud. Words are only words, after all. It is easy enough for me to call you sister, but by the gift of this tent and the mirror, she has made you her daughter in truth."

"She has honored me." Tess wiped a tear from one cheek. The tent and hand mirror she received had belonged to Anna, the sister who had died in childbirth. The tent was beautifully woven, the pattern of stripes, gold, orange, and green as befitted a young woman. On the tent flap a spiral of interlocking, thin-limbed beasts curled infinitely around themselves, and this same spiral of beasts was carved into the wooden handle and back of the mirror. "My parents died when I was ten years old. My brother is the only family I have left."

"Now you have us as well," said Sonia.

They walked on for a time in silence, companionable, going nowhere. Tess stroked her mirror where it now hung from her belt, the grooved handle and the embossed leather case with its cloisonne clasps that protected the mirror's face. Horses whinnied beyond. Wind sounded faintly in the sparse trees.

Two women and a child knelt at a long, flat loom. Stassia's husband Pavel worked, sweating, at his forge. An ancient withered woman tenderly dabbed steaming water spiced with the sweet scent of herbs from a copper pot onto a rash of red sores that blistered a child's back. A girl sang, pounding out meal. Two old men chattered together while they worked at embroidery. A young man sat holding a mass of wool for a girl Tess knew to be unmarried. He smiled as he looked at the ground, up at her as she spun the wool out on her spindle, and down again.

"I'll see a whole land," Tess said. "More than I've seen in my entire life." A life spent within buildings, parks, cities—here it would be all sky, huge, unknown; dangerous, yes, but also new. "I want you to have something, Sonia, to remember me by." She reached into her pouch and drew out the little book of essays from the University in Jeds. "It's all I have, really. And at least you can read them."

Sonia's eyes widened. She reached out and touched the tiny leather volume with reverence. "A book. A real book." Taking it, she held it to her chest. "Oh, Tess." And then, without more thought than that, she hugged her.

"Mama! Mama!" Sonia's little Ivan ran up to them. Sonia released Tess, tucked the book carefully into her belt, and squatted beside him. He put a crude carved figure into her hands. A horse. She smiled, cheeks dimpling, her eyes mirroring his innocent joy, his spontaneous, unreserved expression of love. She looked up, drawing Tess down, laughing together, sharing it with her. Ivan quickly grew tired of their praise and ran away to show his father.

"Wasn't it awful?" said Sonia as they rose. "But so wonderful."

Tess put a hand to one eye and found tears. "I'm sorry to be leaving you, Sonia."

Sonia took both Tess's hands in hers. "You'll come back to us."

Tess smiled. "Can you see the future?"

"No," said Sonia, "but I can see something else, and that will bring you back."

CHAPTER SIX

"It is better to deliberate before action
than to repent afterwards."
—DEMOCRITUS OF ABDERA

They started auspiciously enough. Tess readied her pack the night before. Indeed, sleep eluded her until the stars had wheeled halfway around the Wagon's Axle, late, late into the night. But in the morning, Sonia brought her yoghurt and bread and Yuri saddled her horse as well as his own, so she made her good-byes without much trepidation and followed close behind Yuri as the jahar, escorting the Chapalii, rode out of camp. Women waved, wiping away tears. A pack of children raced after them, clustering on the top of a rise from which they watched as their fathers and brothers and uncles and cousins disappeared onto the vast emptiness of the plains.

At first Tess concentrated simply on riding, on staying on the bay mare and finding some accommodation with this animal. She knew that it ought to be possible to ride as one with the horse, who was amiable enough though strong, but she lacked some trick or understanding of the art. After a time, the duration of which she could not guess, she risked looking beyond her hands and Yuri's back at the group around her. The jahar rode in a V-formation, like birds flocking, with the remounts and pack ponies herded in a clump at the broad base of the V. Besides Yuri and Cha Ishii, Tess recognized Niko Sibirin and a few of the younger men: Sonia's husband Mikhal, Konstans, father of the new baby, and Kirill. Kirill was watching her. For an instant their eyes met. His head tilted to one side, his lips parting, and he smiled at her. Tess looked away. Yuri muttered a word under his breath that Tess did not know.

"Yurinya." Bakhtiian rode smoothly past Tess, so at one with his mount that they seemed almost one creature. "You will ride scout with Fedya."

Yuri flushed at his cousin's curt tone of voice, but he nodded his head obediently. "But Ilya, who will Tess ride with?"

Something smug in Bakhtiian's expression made Tess instantly suspicious. "She will ride with me."

"But you always ride rear scout. Tess can't keep up with—" Yuri faltered, blushed from his chin to the tips of his ears, and with a despairing glance at Tess, reined his horse abruptly away from them and rode off. Bakhtiian watched him depart without any expression at all.

Tess drew in a deep breath. Can't keep up with you, he had been about to say. Suddenly she knew what Bakhtiian was about.

"We are not so far from camp yet," said Bakhtiian, "that I cannot have one of my riders escort you back to the tribe, if you wish."

Tess met his gaze squarely and had the satisfaction of seeing him look away. "You won't be rid of me so easily," she replied. Her mare took a rough patch of ground, hard, and Tess clutched at the high front of the saddle to keep her seat.

Bakhtiian did not exactly smile, but he looked satisfied. "Follow me." He reined his horse toward the back of the group. Tess followed awkwardly, and she felt rather than saw that many in the group watched her go, though whether with sympathy or malice she could not be sure. Cha Ishii's white face flashed past, and she had the momentary pleasure of seeing that the Chapalii's seat was no steadier than her own. Then, as they separated from the last wings of the V, she had no luxury for any thought but staying on her horse.

Bakhtiian did not wait for her. The entire day blurred before her as she tried to catch up with him. He always rode just ahead, changing direction and speed capriciously, stopping abruptly to stare at the ground or at the horizon, but always, before she reached him, riding on.

By the time they reunited with the main group at dusk, she hurt everywhere. Everywhere, intensely, and her inner thighs and knees felt rubbed raw. She was too exhausted to dismount, so she simply remained slumped in the saddle.

She wanted nothing more than to cry, but she was damned if she would.

Bakhtiian had already dismounted. He paused beside her as he led his horse toward the others. "She needs to be unsaddled and brushed down." Then he was gone.

Beyond, in the inconstant glare of the fire, she saw the four conical tents of the Chapalii, already set up, but no other tents. Dark figures stood in clusters around the fire, warming themselves. She sat alone beyond its warmth. At least the mare was content to stand for now.

"Tess." Out of the darkness Yuri appeared. "Here is food. Something to drink."

"I'm not hungry," she said, and was surprised to hear how dry and cracked her voice sounded.

"No, Tess. You must eat. I'll take care of your horse." He set down his bundle and reached up to pull her off. She could not resist him, but God, it hurt to move. He gave her a hunk of flat bread and a pouch of yoghurt, and she drank from her own waterskin. He led the mare away.

Tess collapsed. She almost cried out as her muscles cramped agonizingly. In the distance, angry words were exchanged, but they faded away. After a time Yuri returned with her bedroll and half carried her out where she could have some privacy, and left her. She rolled up in her blanket and slept.

* * *

Very few people knew it, but Charles Soerensen spent most of his time in the spartan office that looked out over the mud flats of Odys Massif. To the right, concealed behind the flat-screen wall that projected two-dees on its surface or holos out into the room, lay a small bedroom and washroom, equally spartan. In the central tower of the great palace lay the official ducal state suite: sleeping chamber, efficiency, sitting room, receiving room, and the border room whose high, rib-vaulted aisles gave onto the arcade that led to the female tower, untenanted and unused. If a visitor of sufficient importance came to Odys, Charles used the state suite. Otherwise, he lived in his office.

Marco found Charles sitting at his desk. Its lights were up, projecting first flat text, then numbers, then graphs, then virtual representations in three dimensions over the smooth surface of the desk. Charles sat straight in his chair. Now and then he keyed in commands on his keypad. Now and then he spoke a word or two and the holo changed or dissipated to flat text and numbers again.

Marco stood by the door and watched. It was the same program. It was always the same program.

The fledgling League, composed of the planets colonized by the human populations of Earth and their human cousins of Ophiuchi-Sei-ah-nai, explores slowly outward and meets the alien Chapalii. The benign but powerful Chapalii gift this young race with many technological presents: increased youth and vigor to the full span of 120 human years; their own, impossible brand of interstellar spaceflight; other trivial or incredible miracles. But soon enough, Chapalii gifts turn to outright co-option, and the Chapaliian Empire absorbs the entire League into its massive bureaucracy. What choice does the League have but to accept absorption and the rule of the emperor? The Empire outweighs them in size (vastly), in technological expertise (vastly), and in sheer, inhuman patience and attention to detail.

Their grip is soft. But it chafes. A young man named Charles Soerensen, only child of a lab technician and a teacher, studies revolution. He puts a revolt together, slowly, secretly, and when the time is right, humanity rises up to cast off the yoke of the oppressor.

The rebellion fails. Very few humans are punished: only those who broke Chapalii laws and taboos already in place. The Chapalii do not seem overly concerned; they seem more paternalistic, as if at an adolescent's wild behavior before she grows older and returns to the fold. For the ringleader: well, Earth mourns, Ophiuchi-Sei-ah-nai mourns, the colonized worlds mourn, expecting his execution.

But the Chapalii do not think as humans think. They are alien, and because their form is humanlike, though their skin changes color, it is easy to forget that. They ennoble Charles Soerensen. They raise him to their highest noble class, short of their princes and emperor. They make him Tai-en, a duke, and grant him a fief: two systems, the one known to humans as Tau Ceti, which has long since been colonized and is a rich source of mineral wealth, and Delta Pavonis, only recently "discovered," mapped, and marked by the League's Exploratory Survey. Dao Cee, the Chapalii call this fief, for Chapalii reasons, inexplicable to humans.

Marco walked farther into the room. He had the skill of entering and exiting silently, a skill honed in travels on the surface of Rhui, visiting queendoms and kingdoms and other more primitive lands where a false step meant death in a barbaric and doubtlessly excruciatingly painful manner. On Odys, where he knew quite well where he stood, he was bored and restless.

"What did I do wrong?" Charles asked the air, not of Marco so much as of the demon that drove him. "What weakness didn't we exploit? The entire rebellion was planned, timed, and executed perfectly. What have they hidden from us?"

"Everything?" Marco sat on one corner of the desk, one booted leg dangling down, one braced on the floor, as he studied the graph floating in the air at his eye level. "We don't even know how long this empire of theirs has been around. Five hundred years? Ten thousand? One hundred thousand? Nothing in their language reveals it, or at least, nothing in their language that *I* can comprehend. We haven't any access to their histories, if they even write histories."

"Is an empire capable of being stable for so long?"

Marco laughed. "A human empire? I don't think so. But after forty years under their rule, I'd believe anything about them. They value stability and order over everything else. That's my observation, for what it's worth. You did well against them."

"Not well enough." Soerensen tapped another command into the keypad, and the graph twisted and melted and reformed as a miniature star chart. Blue pinpricks of light marked the systems known by the League to be colonized, exploited, or ruled by the Chapalii Empire. It was a considerable expanse, enhanced by the newly won human systems. One light blinked red, out past Sirius, a system mapped and marked by the League Exploratory Survey but not yet reported to the Chapalii. A little victory, worth not more than the knowledge that for a short time humanity could conceal information from its masters.

"We need more knowledge. Once Tess is done with her thesis, I'll send her to Chapal. They'll have to let her go there. Only the emperor could forbid it. With her linguistic skills, she should be able to gain solid data that we haven't had access to before."

"But she's female."

"She's my heir. Legitimized by the emperor. He probably thought it was an amusingly eccentric quirk in his token human duke. So they can't sequester her.''

"Charles." Marco hesitated. Not because he was afraid of Soerensen's power, of his temper, of losing his friendship by speaking his mind, but because he knew how useless it was to attempt to steer Charles in any direction but the one he had already decided to go.

"Charles. The few times I've spoken with her, I didn't get the impression Tess wanted to use her language skills in such a way. I'm not sure she's ready to be involved in building the next—" But here, by unspoken consent, he halted.

The star chart vanished, and the stars outside bathed the bleak mud flats in their pale light. The bright tails of flitterbugs wove aimless patterns among the tules.

"It doesn't matter what Tess wants." Charles said it matter-of-factly, without rancor, without exasperation, in that same level voice he always used, quiet and commanding. "Through no fault of her own, she was conceived because my parents wanted a child who was theirs alone. Except, of course, they no longer could have a child who was anything but my sibling.''

"Poor thing. And so much younger than you, too."

"Nevertheless, it doesn't matter what Tess wants. She is my heir, and as such, she has a duty to me. And more important, a duty to humanity. We will not remain slaves." He flipped the holo back on and started the program again, searching for flaws, for the hidden key that would make the next rebellion succeed.

"Nevertheless," muttered Marco, knowing very well that Charles would not hear him. "Poor thing."

* * *

Yuri shook Tess awake. She ached all over. She brushed grass from her face and sneezed. Pain woke and shot like fire through her arms. It was chilly, and cold damp seeped through and stiffened her muscles. The sun nosed at the horizon. Light spread out along the grass tips, gilding their green shoots golden. Tess shivered and yawned.

"Hurry, Tess. I saddled a horse, and here is some bread—"

Behind, a figure loomed, Bakhtiian on his horse. In the distance, Tess heard men talking and horses snorting and blowing. She struggled to her feet. Her legs and thighs were in spasms. She leaned to bend, to roll up her blanket, and could not, simply could not. The pain brought tears to her eyes. Yuri knelt and rolled up the blanket, handing it to her.

"Yurinya," said Bakhtiian, "Fedya has already left. You were to be with him."

Yuri touched Tess on the arm and palmed a stick of dried meat into her hand. He handed her the reins of a horse, one of the stocky tarpans, then mounted and rode away.

"This isn't my bay." Tess regarded the restless tarpan with suspicion.

"You can't ride the same horse day after day," said Bakhtiian, "unless you want to ruin it. I'm leaving now."

She did not reply. Tying the bedroll on to the back of the saddle hurt. Her back was sore, her shoulders ached. Biting her lip, she lifted her left foot to the stirrup. Tears streamed down her face. Beyond, Bakhtiian had paused to watch her. She swore under her breath and pushed off. Every muscle screamed. But she refused to give up now. Grimly, she rode after Bakhtiian.

This day passed much the same as the one before. But at dusk, when they arrived in camp, Yuri brought her food and Mikhal cared for her horse. Niko gave her a salve for her chafed skin. In the morning the bay mare was already saddled. That night, Kirill took the horse when she rode in, and the next night, Konstans shyly brought her yoghurt and cheese and fresh, sweet roots to eat. The fifth morning she saddled her bay mare with Yuri's help. Though she was still sore everywhere, it was an ache and not outright pain.

On the sixth day she managed to ride beside Bakhtiian, not behind him, for most of the day. Yuri and Mikhal and Kirill and Konstans met her when she rode in, and a few new faces, young men she barely knew by name, joined the group as well. The Chapalii remained in their tents. She had not spoken to Cha Ishii in days. What Bakhtiian thought of her partisans she could not tell; in six days she had exchanged perhaps ten sentences with him, and his overwhelming attitude seemed to her to be one of annoyance that she had gotten so far. On the eighth night she unsaddled and brushed down her horse by herself and had enough energy left to ask Yuri for a lesson in khush.

But on the tenth morning, setting out with the sun on their left, she found herself examining the grass, the tiny nuggets of grain piled one atop the other, the leaves as broad as a finger touched with green, the reed-thin stalks golden, and glimpses of earth, as brown as Bakhtiian's eyes, in worn patches. She no longer felt that riding was merely a battle between her muscles and the horse. The grass barely touched her boots. When she had been walking, starved and thirsty, it had dragged constantly at her calves and thighs. She laughed aloud at the sheer joy of it and felt a shift of tension between her and the bay, the mare in that instant responding to her as if they had come to know one another. She leaned down to kiss its silky neck, its clean scent faint in her nostrils, thought through all the words of khush Yuri had taught her and christened the horse—her witnesses the sun and the wind and the unending grass—*myshla,* which in that tongue meant "freed of the earth."

To her surprise, at midday they circled in to take the break with the main group. She was happy to stand for a bit, stretching out her muscles. When Bakhtiian dismounted next to her, she turned from checking Myshla's hooves to look at him. Behind them, the horses, alone or in pairs, had scattered across the grass, their riders in small groups between them like the bright centers of flowers.

Bakhtiian watched her sidelong for an uncomfortable moment, but then, with decision, he looked at her directly. "The spirit has found you." He lifted a hand to trace a brief figure in the air. A wind touched her face, as if echoing his gesture.

"Is that meant to be a compliment?" she asked, a little sarcastically, and regretted it instantly. He turned and with that breathtaking sweep of grace mounted and cantered away to speak to Niko Sibirin.

Later, when the call came to ride, in khush, she understood it, mounting before it was repeated in Rhuian for the Chapalii. She fell in beside Bakhtiian.

"You learn our tongue," he said in khush.

"Only a small portion," she replied in the same. "Only a gentle breeze yet." She smiled, loving language and the way in which each language grew out of its environment.

"You learn," said Bakhtiian.

That afternoon when they paused just below the top of a rise and Bakhtiian simply sat, staring at the expanse of grass and sky that surrounded them, Tess grew impatient with his silence.

"What do you see?"

He looked at her. "What do you see?"

Tess laughed, unable not to in acknowledgment of her own ignorance. "I see grass, and more grass, a few low rises but mostly flat land, and a very blue, almost purple-blue sky. And the sun."

"What about the clouds, there?"

"There at the edge of the horizon? Yes, those, too."

"Clouds can mean rain."

She refused to take his bait. "I suppose they can, if you know what kind of clouds bring rain, and how fast the wind is traveling, and in what direction. I don't know those things."

His lips tugged upward slightly, but he did not smile. "A jahar, about twelve men, passed this way two days ago. They camped down below us. Do you see how the grass hasn't yet risen to its full height there? A piece of leather was left behind. No fire. They're riding for speed or secrecy."

Tess stared down, but she could not see any of these signs. Except—perhaps—she could see the slight depression in the tall grass, grass that, in a rough semicircle, was not quite as high as the surrounding stems.

"There," he continued, "you see that khoen."

"Khoen?"

"The rocks at the top of the rise."

She looked again, and there, now that she was looking, she saw a pile of rocks half hidden by the grass. Such a structure could not be natural, three flat rocks arranged in a triangle, with six smaller stones, chipped into rough shapes, placed in a cross pattern in the center. "What is it?"

"The passing jaran build these, to mark their way for themselves and to record their passing for others. This one—" He hesitated. Tess waited. His mouth turned down, giving him a severe, stubborn expression. "We'd better return to the jahar."

"Why?"

For an instant she thought he meant to chastise her for questioning his orders, but he was merely leaning forward to stare at the sky where a flock of birds wheeled and drove, chattering, for the sun. His lips moved. She knew enough khush to recognize that he was counting under his breath. "There is a dyan called Doroskayev," he said aloud, settling back into his saddle and starting forward. "He wants to prevent me from uniting the jaran. This was his jahar, or part of his jahar, that rode this way. That means we are near each other. I had hoped to avoid anyone so far north this early in the year."

Tess urged Myshla after him. "If you meet him, what will happen?"

"We will fight, his riders and mine."

He said it matter-of-factly. Tess felt as if a stone had dropped into her stomach. They would fight—and where would she be? Lord, and what would Cha Ishii do, faced with such a battle? "I've been a fool," she muttered under her breath.

"I beg your pardon?"

"I just wondered," she said quickly. "You said before that you'd gotten these horses to make war. Is this the war you meant?"

"Not at all. Doroskayev, and a few other men, are simply obstacles in my path." The flock of birds, still screaming, swept back over them, low, their tiny shadows dotting the earth. His eyes followed them again, and he smiled to himself. "My war is against all the khaja. All the settled people. I mean to sweep them off the plains forever. And once they are driven off the plains, once all the khaja lands bordering the plains are subject to us, then we need fear the khaja no more."

"Do you fear them now?"

"My people fear them." He glanced at her. "But I do not. I have been to Jeds, and I have seen that even the best and the wisest of the khaja are no different than us. What they have, we can have as well."

That night no fire was built, and double guards were posted. Tess and Yuri watched the Chapalii putting up their tents, and caught the tail end of an exchange in which Bakhtiian attempted to convince Ishii that speed and stealth necessitated no tents at all. The tents went up, but when Bakhtiian left, Tess thought he looked more thoughtful than annoyed. She strolled over and greeted Ishii in formal Chapalii. Yuri tagged at her heels.

Ishii bowed. "Your endurance is commendable, Lady Terese."

"I welcome your compliments, Cha Ishii. But I am surprised that you set your tents under such circumstances."

He bowed again. "We cannot sleep in this open air, Lady Terese. Surely you appreciate the physiological differences that demand we maintain some period of rest in atmospheres altered to suit our metabolism."

"Within those tents?" Tess asked, suddenly acutely curious to go inside one. The four tents looked common enough—a heavy cotton or canvas, something unremarkable to the natives—but what had the Chapalii built into them?

It was too dark to see what color his skin flushed, though she thought it changed slightly. His voice continued imperturbably. "We have mechanisms, Lady Terese."

"What if this other party attacks? Are you not concerned for your life and the lives of your party, Cha Ishii?"

"I am not concerned, Lady Terese. If I may be excused?"

She nodded. He beat a strategic retreat into the nearest tent. One Chapalii stood outside the second tent, watching her attentively. He was clearly not of the steward class; their deference to her was so complete as to render them almost invisible. Then, bowing directly to her—a slightly arrogant breach of manners, since she had not formally recognized him—he, too, turned and vanished into his tent.

"Why do they bow to you?" Yuri asked. "I never saw people bow except in Jeds, when what they called—what is that word?—the nobility went past."

"I think that Bakhtiian would like to be bowed to."

Yuri grinned. "I'll just bet he would." Then, either distracted from his question or letting it go, he changed the subject. "We should start teaching you to use that saber. Just in case. Kirill will help. He's a good teacher, though he doesn't act it. And Mikhal and Konstans and Nikita and Fedya. I suppose we ought to ask Vladimir to join, too." He took her over to where the youngest men in the jahar had gathered, and they showed her how to hold and balance her saber, and how to take simple backward and forward cuts.

In the morning, Niko Sibirin rode out to scout with Bakhtiian and Tess. For a while, he and Bakhtiian spoke rapidly together in khush. Tess caught the name Doroskayev many times, and other words and phrases in bits and pieces, but not enough to string together into understanding. Then Bakhtiian rode off by himself, leaving Tess with Niko.

"How are you getting on?" Sibirin asked in Rhuian.

"I'm still here."

"Yes. I'm glad to see it. I've seen others fail this test."

"Does he do this to every new rider?"

Niko chuckled. The lines on his face softened when he smiled, gentling the sharpness of his eyes. "Oh, no, my dear. Only those he does not trust yet for one reason or another. Poor Vladi had enough trouble from the young men when Ilyakoria took him in to foster so that he took it doubly hard when he was run into the ground his first ride out. I suppose he thought that Bakhtiian taking him in assured him a place. It did not."

"He must have passed the test."

"Well enough." He glanced to his right. A moment later Bakhtiian appeared around the low swell of a rise. Here the plains still rose and fell like waves, slopes that hid the near ground but revealed what was in the distance.

"Nothing," said Bakhtiian in Rhuian, sounding disgusted. "So you studied at the University in Jeds?"

The sudden question took Tess by surprise. "Why, ah, no, I never did. I was too young, and then my brother sent me overseas to study. He wanted me to learn languages that would benefit him in his trading. So he couldn't be cheated, or sold bad goods." It was close enough. Charles had never possessed a knack for the Chapalii language. That his sister proved adept at languages had been an unlooked-for advantage to his plans. All the more reason that her loss would hurt him badly. Where was Charles now? Did he think she was lost? Kidnapped? Dead? She pressed her lips together, feeling ashamed that she had brought this problem upon Charles, with everything else he had to worry about. Sibirin and Bakhtiian were watching her, Sibirin with interest, Bakhtiian with—? She could not be sure.

"Still, perhaps you came across the works of Iban Khaldun?" Bakhtiian concealed his thoughts with these innocuous words. "The great historian? His works came to Jeds from overseas."

Tess choked back an exclamation. It turned into a cough. "Yes," she said cautiously. "I've heard of him. Didn't he write about cycles of conquest and civilization?"

To her surprise, Bakhtiian launched into an explication of

Iban Khaldun's work leavened by frequent questions to her and to Niko—for it quickly became apparent that Niko had somehow or other also been introduced to these writings—about their opinions and arguments. They talked in this vein until midday, when they joined up with the jahar. For the first time, Bakhtiian ordered both Tess and Yuri to ride with the main group.

"Is he protecting me?" Tess asked as Bakhtiian left again with Niko, back out to scout.

"Not really. You're a—a burden, Tess. If he's caught in the open with you, and Doroskayev and his riders appear, he'll have to defend you rather than get away." He sighed. "It will be easier when you've learned khush."

"What? For me to scout?"

"No, for me to talk with you. I don't speak Rhuian well."

"You speak it well enough. Although your pronunciation isn't very good."

"Tess, you speak khush better already after six hands of days than I did Rhuian after a year in Jeds. And Ilya and Sonia had taught me some ahead of time. Ilya still makes me speak it when he wants to talk to us so that others can't understand what we're saying. It's the only reason I remember any, except now, of course, because I speak it with you."

"Why is Doroskayev trying to find us?"

"To kill Ilya." Yuri grinned. "Can you blame him?"

"And if he kills Ilya?"

"Then all the tribes go back to warring among themselves like they did when Ilya was a child. And the khaja move farther out onto the plains each spring. You see, in the long ago days, before the *rhan*—the tribes—had horses, the khaja took tribute from us. Then a girl was taken from the tribes as a portion of the tribute, but with the help of He-Who-Runs-With-The-Wind, she stole horses from the khaja and gave them to her people, and He took her to His Mother's Tent in exchange and granted us freedom. That is why we are jaran, the people of the wind."

"So the jaran are one people?"

"One people, many tribes, if that is what you mean. Josef Raevsky, there, the older rider, came from a different tribe to ride with Ilya."

"But he is also jaran."

"Yes. Look, Tess, whistlers." He pointed up. A dark

patch of birds skittered and flew far above them. "That is an auspicious sign, to see them this far north so early in the year." He began to count. Tess could scarcely see them except as a blot against the deep blue bowl of the sky, much less discern any individual birds.

"How much do you travel? Each year?"

Yuri shrugged as if he did not understand her question. "We always travel. North in the spring, south in the fall."

"Isn't it hard, moving so much?"

He laughed. "But I love to ride, just as—as fire loves to burn. I love to see the mountains in the winter, the sea and the northern hills in the summer. Would you live forever in one place, never seeing another?"

Tess laughed, echoing him. "No, I wouldn't." She glanced around and caught Kirill, who was riding point, looking back at her. He waved. To her left, Vladimir stared sullenly forward, looking at no one. His necklaces jostled as he rode, slapping his chest, and the tassels on his boots swayed with the movement of his horse. None of the other men wore such finery, not now, at any rate.

To her right, the Chapalii rode in their stiff, stubborn fashion. Cha Ishii's gaze seemed fixed on his horse, but one of the other Chapalii looked across at Tess. She was sure this was the same one who had bowed to her before. What did he want of her? What did he know? She met his gaze, and he inclined his head, as much of a bow as he could manage on horseback. She did not acknowledge him.

CHAPTER SEVEN

"If you seek something wise,
reflect during the night."
—EPICHARMUS OF SYRACUSE

At the late afternoon when they halted for the night, Fedya rode in from scouting with an antelopelike creature sprawled across the neck of his horse. He had shot it, and now took a good deal of teasing from the other men because of his prowess with a woman's weapon. Bakhtiian let the young men build a fire and agreed that those who wished to could pitch their tents as well. Tess and Yuri put up her tent and then returned to the fire. They watched while Nikita and Konstans disemboweled and skinned the dead animal, peeling the pelt whole from the pink flesh. The scent of bowels and blood flooded the air and blended with the must of grass. Pavel took the fat away to feed the horses. Tess left when they cracked open the skull. Yuri followed her, and a moment later, Kirill joined them.

"Tess. If Doroskayev's riders are coming, we'd better teach you some more about saber." Kirill grinned at her. What little diffidence he possessed had vanished after they had left the tribe. Tess sighed. Kirill lifted a hand to his chest, mocking her sigh. "The saber will keep you alive. You can't enjoy lovers if you're dead."

"Kirill!" Yuri exclaimed.

Tess flushed, and was glad of the opportune appearance of Fedya. "We're practicing over by the horses," Fedya said, as if answering a question. "Konstans and Mitenka are waiting."

"Thank you, Fedya," said Tess, and he smiled at her, as if knowing full well that she was thanking him for his intervention not the invitation. His smile had a wraithlike quality, shadowed by some unknown sorrow.

They were camped in a spring-fed hollow in the low hills through which they rode. They came now into sight of the scatter of tents pitched outside a grove of scrub trees and beyond that the huddle of horses. Bakhtiian stood talking to Konstans and Mitenka. He looked up as the others arrived and moved to intercept Tess. Kirill paused deliberately as Bakhtiian approached them, but Yuri nudged him from behind and Fedya brushed his elbow and led him on over to Konstans.

"I was wondering," said Bakhtiian to Tess when the others were out of earshot, "about something you said today, when we were discussing the view held by the Gallio school that words can give no true account of the past."

"Bakhtiian, could we discuss this after dark?"

"Of course. 'The day for action; the night for contemplation,' " He nodded to her and left.

"The Gallio school?" Yuri asked. "It must be something he learned at Jeds. I thought you scouted."

"Niko was with us. We talked about history."

"History?"

"Niko is very knowledgeable."

"Niko reads books when he can get them. Ilya and Sonia brought books back with them from Jeds. Well, I did, too, but only because they wrote me a list."

"Ah. That explains Niko. He and I agreed, but Bakhtiian didn't." She chuckled. "We almost got into an argument."

"Who won?"

"Yuri, no one wins that kind of argument."

Yuri rubbed one hand over his eyes. Smoke and the sweet scent of meat cooking carried to them on the breeze. "I never understood what they taught at University. Hah!" He whirled, saber out and up before he had completely turned to meet Konstans' charge. The two sabers met and sounded, a crisp ring. Tess drew her saber.

Laughing, Kirill walked over to her. "That's right. Don't retreat. But you're too close to Yuri." He put one hand lightly on her hip and gently pushed her two steps over. And grinned, near enough that she could see how very very blue his eyes were.

"Thank you," she said dryly, and shifted so that his hand slipped off her hip.

"This much room," he continued, unrepentant. "And cover—Fedya! Now if Fedya was to come in from this direction, you'd have to cover two angles." Fedya, coming in from that direction, showed her how to parry a side-sweep. Beyond him, outside the ring formed by their little group, a lonely figure adorned with elaborate embroidered sleeves and draped with ornate necklaces watched the practice but did not join in.

When the light faded, they went back to the fire. Dusk made shadows of the tents. The fire outlined groups of sitting and standing men. Sibirin waved to Tess, and she sat down beside him and rested her arms on her bent knees. Yuri brought her meat hot from the fire. She savored it, licking the juice from her fingers when she was done.

"Sibirin, I believe that you promised today to tell me something of your youth, what life was like when you were a boy."

"Do you expect a man of my years to remember that far back?"

"Yes, Sibirin, I do."

"Come now, girl. If I'm going to reveal my youth to you, you had better call me by my youthful name."

"Did you have a different name when you were young? Or did they speak a different language then, if it was so long ago?"

He laughed, revealing deep lines at the corners of his eyes. "No. I'm not so old that I recall the time before we had horses. But you call the young men by their given names. If I tell you of the times when I was that age, then you must call me Niko."

"So if I was to tell you of how it might be for me when I'm older, could you call me Tess?"

"Most things are possible if one decides they are."

"Please, no more philosophy. Tell me a story of adventure."

The smell of burning leather hung in the air and, above it, the faint, sweet odor of flowers. "Shall I tell you how I won my wife? She was niece of the *etsana* and sister to the *dyan* of another tribe. In those days the jaran were divided."

"Yes. Before—"

"May I join you?" Bakhtiian stood before them, lit by

the glow of the fire behind him. Somewhere, a horse whickered.

"Niko is telling me how he won his wife. Now, Bakhtiian, we'll see if his words give a true account of the past."

"But neither you nor I can judge that. We weren't there."

Niko laughed. "Has the argument moved to a new discipline?"

"It was not an argument, Niko. It was a discussion." Bakhtiian settled into the usual seat of the jaran men: one leg bent and flat on the ground, the other perpendicular to the first and also bent, so that the arm could rest on the knee. He smiled at Sibirin. His smile was a rare thing, like the moon on a cloudy night. Tess had seen that he favored Niko alone with it with any regularity, but even with Niko he smiled infrequently. The smile faded slowly and Bakhtiian glanced at Tess. She looked quickly away.

Niko smiled. "Yes, Juli was willful. By the gods, she still is. She was the youngest child in her family, which accounts for it."

Across the fire Mikhal picked out a tune on his lute. Bakhtiian laid a hand on Niko's arm. "Fedya is singing."

Fedya's high, sweet voice rose with the melody. The song matched his looks: sorrowing, mournful, arcane. No one spoke while he sang. After he finished, the lute kept up with cheerful tunes, and talk resumed.

"Fedya always seems so sad," said Tess in a quiet voice.

"His wife died of a fever, two years ago—as did Kirill's— but Fedya still mourns." Niko glanced at Bakhtiian, who gazed, unmoving, toward Fedya.

"So he hasn't married again? Kirill has, hasn't he?"

"Not exactly. He tried to mark Maryeshka Kolenin."

Tess giggled. "Was he the one she—?"

"Yes," said Niko quickly. "But I expect Kirill will mark her next spring. She'll want children soon. But Fedya, no. Women aren't interested in a man who is sad."

"Why not?" Tess glanced to where Fedya sat with the younger men, part of the group but not of the conversation. His air of sadness made him somehow more attractive to her, just as, she thought, she trusted Yuri because he had been shy at first.

"There's no profit in being sad. Life is hard enough. Why lessen its joys by dwelling on its sorrows?"

"The jaran fight against everything," said Bakhtiian, surprising Tess because she had not thought he was listening. "Against each other, against the khaja, against the land, and their final fight is against death. Battle against death, but if the black wind blows up inside and one can no longer fight, then die honorably. Honor alone is worth winning. That alone denies death Her final victory."

"I wouldn't want my entire life to rest solely on the way I died," said Tess.

"How else can you measure it?" Bakhtiian stared into the fire, his face illuminated by its light. "A man's life has no sum until he is dead. He must make what he can while he lives, and he must live every moment as if he were to die the next."

"But isn't it in how you live that you measure your life?" Tess said. "By doing everything as well as it can be done? By striving to find—to find excellence? Then life derives its own worth apart from death. Then you can transcend the routine of existence by living superbly."

Niko stroked his silvering beard and shook his head. "Both of you ride the same path. Seeking honor is no different from striving for excellence. You are looking for something you can never quite find." He held out his hands to catch the warmth of the fire. "What would you say if I told you that of all things given to us, love alone is worth having?"

"That makes you dependent on others," said Tess.

"Each of us must struggle alone," said Bakhtiian.

Niko drew his hands back. "Should all people live as hermits, then?"

"Niko, don't misunderstand me," said Bakhtiian. "Affection for others is a part of life, just as riding and breathing are a part of life."

"But no greater or lesser than these? That is cold, Ilyakoria."

"It's too inconstant." Tess wrapped her arms around her bent knees and gazed into the fire. "Duty is constant, not love."

"I did not claim that love is constant, or free of pain," said Niko with a smile. "That is the risk you take."

"I no longer gamble," said Bakhtiian, almost inaudibly.

"If you believe that, Ilya, then you do not know yourself. You need only look at what you've done. Do you gamble, Tess?"

"It depends on the game."

"All games are the same."

"No, they're not."

"Hmph." Sibirin rubbed a knee with one palm. Across the fire, Kirill and Mikhal and Fedya stood and left. "I was twenty when I met Juli. There was a gathering of tribes that year, but as usual, instead of binding ourselves together, the tribes only sought new feuds."

Bakhtiian looked up sharply. "I ended that. What a waste. It was an affront to the gods who gave us freedom."

"Well, I can't disagree with that. Juli was seventeen. She had more bracelets on her ankles than any other girl in all the tribes, and she made sure everyone knew it. She was vain."

"Then why did you marry her?" Tess asked.

"She was a beautiful girl."

"She is a beautiful woman," said Bakhtiian.

Niko brushed a strand of grass from one boot, but he smiled. "There was a dance. Of course, I was simply one face out of many, but she was, perhaps, bored with the lovers she had and she saw me: a new face, a face, I flatter myself, not altogether unappealing."

Tess laughed. "I expect you were quite handsome, Niko."

"Be careful, young woman. I'll think you're making up to me."

"I could never be so presumptuous. And anyway, I like your wife."

"What does that have to do with it?" asked Bakhtiian.

"Oh, why, nothing." The heat of the fire scalded her face. "In my country, a man and a woman who marry, marry with the understanding that they'll be for each other—that they will never—that they'll remain faithful—"

"Faithful? What is that?"

"That they will never lie with anyone else."

Niko and Bakhtiian exchanged glances. "How barbaric," said Niko.

Tess flushed and looked down at her feet.

Niko coughed. "Yes. The dance. Juli came up to me, and we danced, and she took me aside. She assumed that I would become her lover. Who could refuse her? It angered me to be just one more man counted on her bracelets. Well, I was almost as proud as Ilya in those days." Bakhtiian frowned, studying the fire. "Of course I wanted her. I had to choose, to walk away or to go with her, and I became so infuriated because each moment I desired her more and each moment I felt more humiliated that I drew my saber—without thinking—and marked her. We were both so surprised that at first we just stared. Then she beat me."

Tess gasped, half in laughter, her fingers touching her lips. "She did what?"

"She beat me. Gave me two black eyes, cut my upper lip, and almost broke my arm."

"You can't mean it. She can't have been stronger than you?"

"You don't think I would raise my hand against a woman, do you?" He looked affronted, but at her shamefaced expression, he settled down. "But the mark can never be removed from a woman's face. Ten days later they set the bans over us. She could have broken it then."

"Yes." It was very still, with only the light of stars above, the low rustle of the horses beyond, and the thin, hard lines of grass beneath her. "Once the bans are set, you can't break certain rules for nine days, and if you do, the marriage isn't binding."

"And you may never see that person again," added Niko. "We don't enter into marriage lightly in the jaran. But Juli was too proud to be known as a girl who had broken the bans."

"So that is how you won her."

"Oh, no, child. That is how I married her. Winning her was an altogether different thing, and that took several years."

"Bakhtiian!" A rider called from the edge of the firelight.

Bakhtiian stood. "Excuse me." He vanished into the night.

"Won her love, you mean?" Tess asked. "That took several years?"

"Winning the love of a stubborn, proud woman, or man, can be as hard as winning fame or living superbly, and it is far more rewarding."

Tess looked away from him into the fire, but the fire only showed her Jacques's arrogant, handsome face as he told her that their engagement was ended. "Is it? Then you're only living your life for someone else."

"So young to be so bitter. My child, one can have both."

"Is that possible?"

"Most things are possible, if one decides they are."

She rose. "I think I'll go to bed." Yuri was gone, so she strolled over to her tent, but the thought of crawling inside that closed space bothered her. She stared up. There were no clouds, and the moon had set. Stars burned above. Where Charles and her duty lived. The camp was silent. No light at all shone from the Chapalii tents. Somewhere an animal called and was answered. Tess stood still, breathing. The air smelled of grass and soil, and a breeze stirred her hair. Hills, low and dim, rose on all sides.

She walked past the trees and up the near slope, disturbing a few insects. At the crest, she pressed down the knee-high grass and sat, staring up at the brilliant, familiar patterns above. She traced constellations, cluttered with fainter stars never seen from Earth's bright skies, and then picked out the constellations Yuri had taught her: the Wagon's Axle, the Horseman, the Tent.

A slight noise interrupted the murmur of night sounds. Tess looked around. Nothing. Several insects chirruped, braving the silence. A sound, and the insects stopped again. She moved away from camp, crawling on her hands and knees back over the crest toward a cluster of rocks below. The sharp ends of grass poked into her palms and knees. Another noise. Breaking for the rocks, she ran right into him.

He grabbed her and pulled her down behind the rocks, one hand over her mouth, the other pinning her arms to her stomach. "Damn it. What are you doing out here?"

All her breath came out in a quick sigh. It was Bakhtiian.

"Well?" His hand fell from her mouth.

"Looking at the stars. 'The night for contemplation.' "

He said nothing, finally releasing her and rising to his knees. "Stay here. Don't move or speak until I tell you. Do you understand?"

"Yes. What's wrong?"

He was already gone.

After a time, she began to think she was alone on the slope, but she did not move. How little she knew of these wild, alien plains. How blithely she assumed that she was

safe here, fearing the Chapalii more than the barbarian lands
themselves. She cupped her hands over her mouth and nose
to muffle the sound of her breathing, feeling scared and
foolish all at once: *Like the maenads I've drunk the wine,
and now I have to accept the madness.*

Chill settled into her flesh. Her sheathed saber pressed
awkwardly against her thigh. A cold wind blew down from
the higher lands, the *ayakhov,* the wind of the deep night.
She shuddered, froze.

Someone approached.

A shadow appeared, pausing by the rocks. It must be
Bakhtiian. She hardly dared look up, as if the white of her
eyes would give her away. The shadow moved. It was not
Bakhtiian. It was too graceless, too thick. Tall but not lean,
and all the tall riders in Bakhtiian's jahar were, like Bakhtiian, slender. He had said his enemies were following them.
What an idiot she had been, not to appreciate what that
meant.

She held her breath, her nose pressed against the cloth of
her glove. Feet scraped on the pebbled dirt between the
rocks, hesitant steps, careful of the ground. A boot struck
her leg. Her heart pounded wildly, but she did not move.

"What?" This in khush.

She barely had time to draw her knife and begin to roll
before his full weight pinned her to the ground. The knife
spun away, lost. He pressed a hand down hard over her
mouth. The point of his saber pricked her calf. With his
free hand he briefly explored her chest. She swore and tried
to kick him.

"By the gods," he whispered. "Has Bakhtiian come to
this? A woman!"

Tess's fingers, reaching, brushed the hilt of her knife. He
relaxed, staring down at her in the dim light. She took a
deep breath, held it.

Exhaled. She heaved her left hip up, and at the same
moment bit his arm. He started back. Her fingers closed on
her knife, and as he shoved her back down, she thrust. The
blade bit into his shoulder. With a curse, he wrenched the
knife from her hand, twisting her wrist until she gasped at
the pain.

He called her a name, but she did not understand the
word, only the intent. His weight on her stomach seemed
enormous. She could barely see his face, could not make

out his features except for some obstruction, a darkness at one eye. "But don't worry about your good name," he said contemptuously. "Having had Bakhtiian will just make you twice as popular."

He jumped up and ran off, holding his shoulder, making no attempt to conceal himself. Tess was halfway to her feet, hand on her saber, before she remembered Bakhtiian's warning. She swore and dropped back down to the ground. Lord, did she really think she could use a saber against one of these men? She shook with adrenaline.

After a time the trembling stopped. She was unharmed. She lifted her head to look around. A shape fled against the landscape, catching her eye. Two hunched figures ran up the far slope to disappear over the crest. Three forms detached themselves from the hill, just below the far crest, and ran down. From a trench in the dip, five figures rose to intercept them. A flash of metal, so brief that she was not sure she had seen it, and the sight of struggling, the more eerie for its quiet: a pained grunt, the thud of a weight hitting the ground, the thin, distinct tone of sabers touching now and now and—a pause—now.

Eight forms moved, but three were constrained and one limped. Silence descended for a time, overruled once by the sound of running feet and again by an assembly of sabers talking all at once, out of her sight, seeming sentient in the way their conversation varied, first fast, then slow, then a flurry and, last, a silence when the conversation ended. A quick staccato of words penetrated the stillness, then suddenly cut off.

Nothing stirred. Her back prickled as if several thousand insects crawled up and down it. She forced herself to breath slowly, in and out, in and out. *Don't think about it. Don't be scared.* There was only the hushed wind and the mute stars and the coarse dust harsh against her skin.

She felt him there before she saw him, flat on his stomach where he slid in beside her. She gasped. Her hands clutched pebbles.

"Oh, God." She shut her eyes and opened her hands. "You scared me."

"By the gods. You stabbed him. You can sit up if you want to. We captured them all."

"What did they want?"

"To kill me, of course." Bakhtiian's voice was calm.

She remembered, suddenly, violently, the man in his own tribe whom he had executed. "Are you going to kill them?" she asked, in a whisper, and she felt sick with apprehensive horror as she said it.

"Not this time. They'll serve my cause better alive. For now. We'll tie them up and leave them here." He was still lying on his stomach. "Except Doroskayev." He chuckled. "He's the one you stabbed."

"That's a funny name. 'Scar-sight'?"

"He got a bad wound some years ago to his right eye. Never forgave me for it." Bakhtiian laughed. "A pretty piece of work with your knife. Yuri got it back for you."

"I'm not hurt," said Tess stiffly.

"Of course not. No jaran man would harm a woman. What a thought. I know they do in Jeds."

"Oh, no. In Jeds, jaran men don't hurt women either."

Bakhtiian laughed again. Tess had never seen him so jolly. It made her nervous. There was a moment's silence before he jumped to his feet. "By the gods, I'm tired."

"Was anyone hurt, of ours?"

"Ours?" She could not see his face but felt his grin. "Ours, indeed." He put out a hand and, when she took it, pulled her to her feet. She dropped his hand and brushed off her clothing. "Josef Raevsky got a wound in the thigh, but it isn't serious. Kirill got a cut across the arm. By the gods, why are we standing here, woman?"

He set off for camp, Tess walking beside him.

"Bakhtiian." They reached the crest and started down into the little camp, where a number of men lay tied up near the campfire, Bakhtiian's riders clustered around them. Gazing down at the prisoners, Bakhtiian had the grin of a satisfied and well-fed predator. He looked at her. "What does this mean?" She said the name Doroskayev had called her.

He stopped quite short, and finally made a slight, coughing sound. "Forgive me. No man will ever explain that to you."

"My God." She smiled. "Then I'll have to ask Sonia."

"No woman ought to know that word," said Bakhtiian sternly, "but if one does, then doubtless that one is Sonia." They both laughed.

Descending to the camp, he guided her directly to her tent, avoiding the captives. "It will be better if those men never know you are with us. My riders will say nothing."

"But Doroskayev saw me."

"One does not always believe what Doroskayev says. And perhaps you now understand why you must always wear your saber, and keep it by your side when you sleep. Now, if you will excuse me." He gave her a curt bow, but the gesture was not entirely mocking.

She watched him fade into the night, and then knelt to enter her tent. A closed, private refuge seemed suddenly desirable, and safe. A foot scuffed the grass. She jumped back and whirled. A Chapalii stood behind her, not five paces from her. He bowed, formal.

"Cha Ishii," she began, and then realized abruptly that this was not Ishii at all.

"Lady Terese. I beg your pardon for this rash intrusion. Perhaps you will condescend to allow me to introduce myself."

She stared for a moment, amazed by his audacity. By his inflections, he ranked as a merchant's offspring, of that class one step below the nobility. Why had he come with Cha Ishii's expedition? The last dregs of fear and adrenaline from the skirmish melted away, seared into oblivion by her need to know what Ishii was doing here, and what it meant to her brother. "You may." She set her hands together, palm over palm, in that arrangement known as Imperial Patience.

He bowed, acknowledging her generosity. "I am Hon Garii Takokan. I beg your indulgence." She waited, curious. "I was distraught to discover that these savages with whom we ride were to engage in violence this very night, but far more was I distressed to know that you, Lady Terese, perforce must face such dangers unarmed."

"You are well spoken, for a merchant's son, Hon Garii."

"I have studied to improve myself, Lady Terese," he answered, slipping in two inflections that skirted the bounds of impropriety, hinting that he had, perhaps, some connection with noble blood in him. "If I may be allowed to say as much."

"You may."

"Therefore." He stopped short, glancing furtively behind and to each side. "If you will condescend to permit me to present you with this gift."

Tess considered. Giving gifts in the Chapalii culture was a gesture loaded with implied obligations and serious consequences. But her curiosity got the better of her, so she held out her hand to receive it.

He handed her a knife, bowed, and slipped quickly away, not even waiting for her thanks. She held it up. And stared.

This was not a knife. Certainly, it looked like a knife; it had a hilt and a blade. But twin points of light peeped from the crosshilts, and when she held the blade, it felt warm to her touch. This was something more, far more. That this was Chapalii-manufactured, a Chapalii weapon made to look like a native thing, she did not doubt for an instant. Like the tents. It took no great leap of imagination to guess that this was some kind of energy gun. No wonder Ishii was not concerned about these savages' petty little wars. With such a weapon, one person standing alone could obliterate Bakhtiian's jahar before they got close enough to put her in danger.

"But I wonder," she said to herself, tucking the knife into her belt and crawling into the sanctity of her tent, "I wonder if Ishii knows that Garii has given this to me." It disturbed her very much to suspect that he did not.

CHAPTER EIGHT

"Thou shalt inquire into everything."
—PARMENIDES OF ELEA

Two days later they deposited Doroskayev in the middle of a stretch of featureless flat lands, the hills a dark billow to the northeast. Tess and Bakhtiian tracked him that afternoon as he walked back toward his comrades, who had been trussed and tied and left by the water hole to wait in sullen expectation for their release. Finally, Bakhtiian reined in his horse on a rise. Tess stared down at the solitary figure, whose face was indeed disfigured by an ugly scar over his right eye. It seemed a short enough time ago that she had stumbled, alone and scared and determined, through grass that scraped constantly at her legs. Now it merely brushed the soles of her boots. They turned their horses southwest and caught up with the jahar by evening.

It might have been dull, this riding day after day, week after week, across a land as routine as their daily tasks, but it was spring, and spring was a joy, and the life itself was new, like a language that needed learning. Tess could never resist the lure of an unknown tongue. The sky lifted far above. The land slipped by beneath horses' hooves. It rained once or twice, but it was no more than an inconvenience. Huge herds of antelopelike animals passed them, heading north in a frenzy of bawling and mewling, and on many days Fedya brought in a fresh kill. The other riders foraged for *modhal,* a tuber they mashed and shared equally between men and horses, and *nekhal,* a reedy grass whose shoots were edible. They mixed these with mare's milk and with the hard bread and dried meat brought from the tribe.

The Chapalii ate sparingly of this diet, and if they ate anything else in their tents at night, Tess was none the wiser.

So it was that when, one afternoon as Tess and Bakhtiian scouted the wake of a passing herd, they saw five women riding southward with their day's catch, Bakhtiian hailed the hunters and spoke with them while Tess hung back and watched.

"I know this tribe," he said when he returned. "We'll stop a few days with them."

They returned immediately to the jahar. At the first good campsite, a small lake ringed with scrubby trees and a profusion of flowering bushes, Bakhtiian called a halt for the night.

"Why don't we just go on today if this tribe is so close?" Tess asked Yuri as they walked to the lake's edge. She batted away a swarm of insects, ducked her head as they returned, and retreated from the reedy shore.

Yuri laughed at her and strolled on. It had become the jahar witticism to call them dhal and khal, the twins, because they spent so much time together. Tess liked it because she saw in it an acceptance of her place in the jahar: she was one of them, not one of the pilgrims.

"There are courtesies," Yuri explained when she caught up with him, "when one tribe comes upon another. Some people might not observe them, but Bakhtiian is very traditional. Now they have warning to know we are coming." He grinned. "And Vladimir can polish his stones so his necklaces can gleam brighter and impress the young women."

"Poor Vladimir."

Yuri looked at her consideringly. "Have you ever really spoken with Vladimir?"

"No. I think he avoids me. But then, you and Kirill and the others scarcely make him welcome."

"A horse ridden too hard," said Yuri in khush, "is a horse ruined." He added, in Rhuian, "If Vladimir is not welcome, look to him, not to us. We'd better teach you to dance, Tess. There's sure to be a dance in Bakhtiian's honor. It would look odd if we kept you to ourselves. Though how much we can teach you in one afternoon. . . ."

"I've danced before," said Tess, but the image that came to her, thinking of her folk dancing club at the university, was unwelcome: that night, when Jacques—so cowardly that he had to choose a public place, where pride constrained her from reacting with real emotion—had told her their engagement was over, broken, while they were dancing the last waltz of the evening.

"Are you all right?" Yuri touched her on the arm.

"No, I'm fine. Just hungry. Fedya didn't bring in a kill today, did he? He shouldn't be the only one who hunts. I want to practice archery while it's light. We can dance with a fire. I'm going to get good enough with the bow to do some hunting."

Yuri laughed at her vehemence. "You'll ruin my good name. Very well. But you have to get Sonia's bow. Meet me over there."

The minutes she spent fetching the bow and arrows gave her time to regain her composure. Damn Jacques, anyway; he wasn't worth agonizing over. But her anger carried over into her first course, and she shot poorly. Yuri sighed, fetched the arrows and readjusted the four ribbons tied for the target at varying heights around the tree trunk.

"You did better than that with Sonia," he chided.

While he shot, Tess watched the water birds as they paddled aimlessly back and forth on the pond and with no warning upended and dove under the surface, vanishing, without even a ripple, for so long that one's breath stopped until they suddenly resurfaced in a flurry of wings and water somewhere else. Submerged—that was the word that haunted her. She had been submerged in Charles's life since the day she was born. She had never been herself, but always his sister, his heir, doing his work.

"Three out of five," said Yuri proudly. "Let's see you match that." Returning with the arrows, he handed the bow to her. She aimed and hit.

"There. Is Doroskayev the only dyan riding against Bakhtiian?"

"He's one of the few left. Roskhel is dead now. Veselov—Ilya won him over. Zukhov, Boradin, Makhov. They're all dead, too. Boradin and Makhov died in the battle at the *khayan-sarmiia.* Ilya shouldn't have won that battle because they outnumbered him, but he did. Doroskayev only hates Ilya because he hates Ilya, if you see what I mean. But his tribe is small. There is one dyan left, Dmitri Mikhailov, who commands a jahar large enough and dangerous enough to threaten us. But we haven't seen him for two summers. I think he's given up.''

Tess nocked another arrow and drew. ''What about the tribal Elders? The women?''

''War is men's business.''

''Meaning women are left to clean up.'' She shot, missing the tree entirely.

''It's your concentration.'' Yuri rested one hand on the back of his neck. She drew again, steadying herself. ''Ilya could never have united the jaran without the approval of the Elders. After all, his own mother was the first Elder he had to convince, and if he could convince her, he could convince anyone.'' Tess shot and hit. ''Do you know,'' Yuri added, ''when a person stands so still, you see them best. Like your eyes. I never knew eyes could be the color of *gorad* leaves. Such a green.''

Her fourth and fifth arrows hit true. Yuri shot and hit five times along the length of the tree. ''You're better at this than you think,'' she said when he returned with the arrows.

''For a man. It comes of having four sisters. But I always liked archery better than saber.''

''What's wrong with that?''

''Yuri!'' Kirill called to them from the shore of the lake. He strode over and stopped to stare at the younger man. ''You're not actually practicing that, are you?''

Yuri hastily handed the bow to Tess, who turned to face Kirill with one hand on her hip. ''If you practiced, we might eat fresh meat more often.''

Kirill had a careless air about him that belied his authority among the younger men. ''It isn't a man's weapon, but it's true, on such a long trip, we would eat better. I know.'' He smiled. ''We'll have a contest.''

''I don't like this,'' muttered Yuri.

But the young riders took quickly to the idea: ten shots each. Mikhal immediately took the lead, with seven midhits, but this was blamed on his willingness when courting Sonia to go hunting with her.

Eventually Bakhtiian came up. Tess, finishing, found herself with five mid-hits, third behind Mikhal and Yuri. ''Do you want a turn?'' she asked Bakhtiian, made bold by her success.

''Gods, contest with the rest of us, and with a woman's weapon?'' asked Kirill.

Bakhtiian's face shuttered as he looked past Tess at Kirill. Birds landed on the lake, wings skittering. Kirill returned Bakhtiian's scrutiny with an even gaze. No one spoke.

"Very well." Bakhtiian accepted the bow from Tess. "I would never disparage a woman's prowess in archery, especially not if she had bow in hand. Not unless I had a very long head start."

Everyone laughed except Kirill, who turned and left. Tess felt tension that she had not known was there leave her throat. Bakhtiian stood perfectly still, entirely concentrated. The dark waves of his hair matched his intense eyes and severe expression. With his arm drawn back, the curve of the bow framing him, he could have been the god of the hunt, caught forever in the instant before death. All ten shots hit between the middle ribbons.

Kirill returned, and he brought Fedya with him. Fedya was neither for nor against joining the contest. Kirill insisted.

"You don't have to," said Tess.

Fedya shrugged. "I don't have the energy to refuse." He was one of the shorter riders, stocky without stoutness, with long blond hair caught back in a single braid. Alone among the men he wore a second braid, a horse-tail pinned into his hair. He also habitually wore an expression that suggested that he knew the one, awful secret of man's doom but was kind enough to hide it from everyone else. "I don't mind. After all, I'm the only one here who can outshoot Bakhtiian." The look he gave Kirill was ironic. But he also hit ten mid-shots.

It was growing dark. Tasha, at the fire, called to them that the food was ready. Tess did not follow the others, and Yuri sat with her, finding pebbles to toss into the pond.

"I like it here," Tess said finally, watching the birds dive.

Yuri glanced at her but did not reply. The shifting greens and yellows of leaves stirred in the twilight breeze. Several birds flapped their wings, spraying water, and then settled.

"Fedya's as good as some of the women. I thought men never practiced archery."

"Fedya doesn't need to practice. He sings to the bow, and it responds."

"He looks as if he knows the wrongs of the world."

"Fedya was touched by the gods as a child. What he knows, he'll never tell."

They rose and walked slowly toward the fire. This close, the breeze brought the spicy scent of Tasha's vegetable stew to her. Stars bloomed one by one in the darkening sky. "Do you mean to say . . ." Tess hesitated, then began again in a lower voice. "That Fedya never boasts, or—"

"If you mean, does he talk about his lovers, no, he doesn't. For all anyone knows, he hasn't gone off with a woman since his wife died. If you made up to him, no one would ever find out through him."

Tess halted, flushing. "You go so fast from start to finish."

"Tess." Yuri laid a hand on her shoulder. The ring of firelight faded into darkness a few meters in front of them, framing the men around the fire. "You're having a hard time of it because of things inside you, and here you are, alone with twenty-seven men. I don't count the pilgrims, you understand. It isn't healthy."

There was a silence.

"Forgive me." Yuri removed his hand. "I didn't mean to offend. As your brother I thought—"

Tess began to laugh. "Healthy!"

"Well, I don't see what's so funny. It's true."

"Oh, Yuri. I'm not laughing at you."

"You'll see I'm right." He headed toward the fire.

"It's when you're being smug," replied Tess, following him, "that I can really see the family resemblance between you and Bakhtiian."

"I beg your pardon!"

Tess grinned. "Now, didn't you say you would teach me some of your dances?"

"There." Yuri pointed. The morning sun shone down on the spread of tents laid in neat lines beyond the edge of a narrow river. "I remember this tribe. Sakhalin is etsana here, and her sister's son the dyan of their jahar. I was only a boy when we met with them last, but they are friends of our tribe. Bakhtiian says we will stay four nights with them."

At the jahar's appearance on the rise, two men and two women detached themselves from the camp and walked up to them. Bakhtiian and Niko dismounted and strode forward to meet them halfway. After what seemed to Tess a long, drawn-out conversation punctuated with elaborate gesturing, Bakhtiian returned, leaving Nito to walk back into camp with them.

Now Bakhtiian spoke with Ishii, and Tess noted with interest that Ishii's face bore a green cast—he was displeased. But when Bakhtiian nodded and retreated from his side, Ishii sent his horse forward, down to the camp. The other Chapalii followed. Tess found Hon Garii easily enough. He rode beside another Chapalii, just behind Ishii, and behind them, the other eight rode in a mob that shifted precedence daily. In the clear light of early morning, she could discern on each of these eight the faint tattoo on the jaw beneath the right earlobe that marked these Chapalii as stewards. Born to serve, certainly, but not the lowest class by any means. Stewards alone served the nobility and had, in their turn, servants as well. That stewards made up the rest of the party, that they did work normally left to lesser castes, simply proved to Tess the importance of this expedition. Now that she had settled in with the riding, it was time to investigate, slowly, circumspectly. She had time.

She laid a hand on the knife thrust between her trousers and her belt. As if the gesture had caught his eye, Ishii glanced back at her, and she removed her hand guiltily. But he looked away again, directing his people down and to one side of the tribe's camp.

"We will stay four nights," Bakhtiian was saying to the jahar. "You will comport yourselves in a respectful and modest manner." He looked at Kirill as he said this. Kirill returned his gaze blandly. With Vladimir riding just behind him, Bakhtiian led the jahar down into camp.

As Tess dismounted, an elderly woman with a baby in a sling at her hip walked up to her. "Ah, my dear girl, I am Elizaveta Sakhalin. You are Terese Soerensen. Is that it?" She spoke khush slowly so that Tess could follow her words.

"Tess, if you will." Tess felt comfortable with her at once.

"Yes, you will want to be with women again. My daughter—here, Konstantina!"

A young blonde woman with an unattractive face but sharp and friendly eyes came over. "But, Mama," she said forthrightly, "Tsara and I and the others are to go out to hunt today. There is that great—" The word was lost on Tess. "—just beyond the ford."

"Konstantina. A guest! Your manners."

"But perhaps, Mother Sakhalin," Tess began hastily, using the only honorific she knew for a tribal etsana, and seeing immediately that Sakhalin and her daughter approved of it. "If your daughter does not—will not mind—I hunt, go hunting, with her."

Konstantina brightened. "Yes, Mama. You are good with the bow?"

Tess smiled. "No. Not at all. So I am tired of no fresh meat. Traveling with men."

Enlightenment blossomed on both women's faces. "Of course. Such a long journey and no herds. You will go with Konstantina. She will teach you. Then you can hunt for the jahar."

Konstantina hustled Tess off as quickly as if she feared that her mother would change her mind, given a moment to reconsider. And into the company of women Tess was welcomed without reservation. She strode along, finding it difficult to keep up with their pace, and was given a lecture on the behavior of herds, animals, and shooting that she understood perhaps half of. The actual hunt proved more instructive. A huge herd of bovine grazing beasts milled along the river's edge. Tess crouched, and watched, and stalked, and waited, and was even allowed to shoot a few times, although none of her shots brought down any game. Of the seven women with her, six brought down kills, and three of those brought down two. Konstantina allowed her to drag in one of her kills, and with the slender, musty-smelling calf draped across her shoulders, Tess trudged the long walk back to camp and was grateful to collapse in the shade of Mother Sakhalin's great tent.

"Tomorrow," said Konstantina, crouching beside her while they watched her brothers skin the kills, "we will have a dance. So." She grinned slyly. Next to her, her cousin, Tsara, a pretty, dark-haired girl, dimpled and whispered into Konstantina's ear. "Tsara wishes to know which of these riders is the best lover."

Tess blushed. "I don't know."

"You don't know! Surely—how long have you traveled with them?"

"Six hands of days, now." Seeing that Konstantina regarded her suspiciously out of those piercing blue eyes, Tess felt constrained to add, "In my land, it is different between men and women."

"Of course. You are a foreigner. I had almost forgotten."

Tsara sighed. "But so many of them are good-looking. And they are only here four nights. How will I choose?"

Studying Tsara, whose cheek was clear of the scar of marriage, Tess reflected that such a pretty girl would have no trouble attracting lovers. "Well, Kirill," said Tess, and flushed, wondering why he had come first to her mind.

"Aha," said Konstantina, watching Tess's face. "A good recommendation, I think."

"Mikhal is quiet and still in love with his wife. Yuri is sweet."

"He is Bakhtiian's cousin, is he not?"

"Yes, and Fedya—"

"The Singer? But who wants a sad man?"

"He sings very sweetly," said Tess defensively. "He has a beautiful voice."

"And what," asked Tsara, "about the one with the necklaces? He is very pretty."

"He's an orphan." Then, seeing their faces, she was sorry she had said it.

Konstantina waved one hand dismissively. "An orphan. What about the others?"

"What about Bakhtiian?" Tsara asked in a low voice.

Bakhtiian. Tess's vocabulary failed her utterly. What about Bakhtiian?

But Konstantina, either oblivious to Tess's sudden silence, or sympathetic to it, shook her head decisively. "Tsara, men like Bakhtiian are not for girls like us. You see who comes out of Nadezhda Martov's tent in the morning."

"Oh." Tsara's eyes went very round.

"Who is Nadezhda Martov?" Tess asked, feeling a little disgruntled.

"She is the finest weaver in all the tribes," said Konstantina proudly. "She is my mother's cousin's cousin's daughter, though she's rather older than you or I. You'll see."

But Tess, going back to her own tent that night, where Yuri had pitched it for her back behind the Sakhalin tents, saw Bakhtiian sitting beside Niko and some of the men from the tribe around a distant fire, talking intently. Later, dozing, she heard him speaking with Vladimir, and she peeked outside to see him crawl, alone, into his own tent.

She spent the next day with Konstantina and Tsara and

some of the other Sakhalin cousins, preparing a flat ground for dancing. Children raced around, some helping, some playing. Tess let Tsara fit a sling to her and carried around an amiable infant until it got hungry. In the afternoon, the young women lent her women's clothing, insisting that no woman ought to attend a dance dressed as she was. They braided her hair properly, and Tsara lent her one of her beaded headpieces to cap her hair and drew kohl around her eyes to highlight them. Tess felt terribly embarrassed, walking at dusk to where the bonfire had just been lit, with the accustomed weight of her mirror, free of its case this night, but without her saber. But the riders of Bakhtiian's jahar had well and truly blended into the mass of riders from this tribe, and she did not have to face their scrutiny up close. Ensconced among the women, Tess found it easy to take refuge in their confidence.

The music, as it began, sounded familiar and exciting. Tess recognized a dance Yuri had taught her, but as the women around her filtered away, seeking partners, she did not have the courage to go seek one of her own. She stood in the shadows and watched until Yuri came up to her.

"Well." Yuri examined her. Tess blushed. "Sonia would approve." He left it at that. "Would you like to dance?"

"Yes!"

Yuri caught her up, pulling her around, and her feet moved into the pulse of their own accord. Faces, muted in the firelight, flashed past. She loved dancing perhaps more than anything except for flying, was good at it, and this firelit stage, a hall enclosed by dark, with sound echoing in the air, voices singing with pipes, bodies, skirted tunics, brushing past her, the fine taste of grass and dust on her tongue, all heightened her senses so that the steps seemed as natural as breathing.

After two dances, Konstantina took Yuri away from her. Tess wandered to stand near the musicians, looking for a familiar face, but it seemed to her that all the men she knew were out dancing. She rubbed her hands together, feeling a little stupid. Vladimir came up to her. He smiled, looking straight at her.

"Oh, hello, Vladimir," she said, feeling even more stupid. If she had exchanged twenty words with him on this journey, she would have been surprised.

He laid a hand on his necklaces, stones that winked and

gleamed in the firelight. He wore bracelets on each wrist, rings on four fingers, and his eyes were unusually dark, startling against the blondness of his hair. "Neither you nor I have partners."

Tess lowered her gaze. She knew this dance all too well; it reminded her of Jacques. "No," she replied faintly.

He put out his hand, palm up.

Flushing, she put her hand on his and let him lead her out to the circle. He was her height, slim-waisted, and he danced gracefully enough that he easily covered the mistakes she made. He did not speak much, either. She danced with him again and again. Then, catching sight of Bakhtiian to one side, he excused himself hurriedly and walked away.

Left alone, she put her hands, warm from him, on her cold cheeks. A drum pounded out a slow, elegant rhythm, and Tsara ran up to lead her out into a line dance for women. Pipes serenaded them as they swept through the measures, the bright bells on their trousers and the brilliant headpieces of gold flashing against the firelight. But they abandoned her ruthlessly when it came time to dance with the men again— not, Tess thought, out of any selfishness, but simply because they seemed to think she could fend for herself. If only she had their confidence.

And Vladimir came up and asked her to dance again. They stood in the farthest ring of light after the dance ended, sleeves touching, the hem of her long tunic brushing the tasseled tops of his boots, and she felt in charity with Vladi for keeping her company. Glancing at him, she caught him looking at her speculatively. She flushed again, and cursed herself silently for flushing. *I'm terrible at this,* she thought. *I ought to just—* He watched her steadily, and he smiled, as if he was aware of the way her thoughts were tending. *I ought to just get it over with. God knows, he's pretty enough.*

He laid his hand on her arm, light but intimate.

"Why aren't any of the other women dancing with you?" she asked.

His hand tightened on her sleeve. "Someone said something. Kirill. I'd wager. He never has liked me."

"Vladimir," she began, suddenly guilty, knowing it was herself who had spoiled his chances, and somehow they had taken a step back, out of the last ring of light, and now they stood in shadow.

"Tess!" It was Yuri. Vladimir whirled and vanished into the darkness.

"What is it?" Tess asked a little peevishly, as Yuri halted next to her.

He didn't answer for a moment, looking past her into the dark where Vladimir had disappeared. The music ended. "The next dance. The one I taught you that you liked so much. Come on." He took her hand, hesitated. "It isn't so bad for me to dance with you because everyone knows that by giving you my sister's tent my mother sealed us brother and sister by every claim but blood. It's all right for a brother to ask his sister to dance."

"Are you trying to tell me something?" Oh, God, she'd done something wrong. As always, with men; as always.

"We'd better hurry. They're forming up." He dragged her into the circle and placed her so that her back was to the fire and he faced her. "Now don't forget: step, behind, step, behind, step, then turn, and you've got the quick step-hop. And don't forget to switch partners. But when the hold is called, you're to stay with that partner until you've missed a step. That's the contest. But don't worry. No one will be watching you anyway."

The drums began, a slow, straight beat in four. Tess did not worry. Identical sets, the music starting slow and getting faster and faster, and the switch of partners; if they wanted to make this a contest—where those who made mistakes dropped out and the last pair without mistakes won—she was happy just to dance it, because she loved its complexity. No man, faced with this foreigner when the drummer called "hold," would expect her to dance without error.

The pipes came in with the melody. She danced the set twice with Yuri and on a double clap and turn moved right to a new partner. Spins and high steps, stamps that sounded hollow and muffled on the ground, a strong arm pulling her around, laughter across the fire. A man whistled. She loved it. She had that sense of dancing that anticipates the rhythm and so is exact, the ability to duplicate the melody in the steps. She danced, spun to a new partner, danced, moved.

The high melody, faster now, pierced through the thick sound of feet, of breath expelled and drawn in, of the snap of fire and the slap of clothing. The lutes took up a counter-melody and the drums added an off beat. The women's long tunics swelled out on the turns, sinking back in, swirling around legs. Tess stamped and twirled and came to Niko. He grinned, breathing hard from exertion, and swung her around. As the dance went faster, it became somehow easier for her as she lost her self-consciousness in her absorption in the music. Low drums came in, the high ones pounding out patterns above, matching the pipes. She danced, kick-hop, slide step away, clap and return, moved to the next partner, danced, stamped, and whirled into the arms of Bakhtiian.

"Hold!" yelled the drummer: hold to this partner. The contest had begun.

Bakhtiian glared at her, but pulled her in, and they pivoted. Where she pulled out, she felt an exact counterweight against her. His hand on her lower back signaled her steps, and when he had to turn her so fast that she got dizzy, his other arm steadied her, strong at her waist, until she got her balance back. By the end of the first set, they understood each other. By the end of the second, they could no longer tell if the music was speeding up.

Tess laughed. Step-behind and five stamps, five stamps. She felt as if her soul were flowing out through her limbs, her fingers and her toes, her eyes and her lips. His face seemed luminous, as though sparks of fire had caught it and then spread down to burn in flashes on his shirt; he was not smiling. He spun, and she spun—the drummer called out, "To end!"—and she and Bakhtiian pivoted ten times and came to a perfect halt, stock-still and panting and exactly placed in the circle.

Except there was no circle. They had won.

"Oh, God," said Tess in Anglais.

"You're a good dancer," said Bakhtiian, releasing her and bowing as they did at the court in Jeds. His hair seemed thicker, fluffed into a luxuriant disarray by the activity, touched with moisture on the ends. For an instant she had the urge to touch it. He straightened.

Yuri stood beyond, laughing. Beside him, Kirill had his arms crossed on his chest, grinning. Tsara stood next to him with one hand draped possessively over his arm. Konstantina clapped and cheered, egging on those around her. Niko and Mother Sakhalin stood together, smiling. Vladimir stood off to one side, alone, and he looked furious.

"Thank you," Tess said. Words deserted her. She stared

blankly at him, and he averted his eyes. "Ah, yes," she
went on, stumbling, mortified. "You understand."

"Understand what?"

"Dancing." She felt as if she were about to dive into a
deep pool of murky water; something lay in the depths, and
she did not know what it was. "Some people move their
feet while there is music, some move their feet with the
music."

He smiled, swiftly, like the sight of a wild animal in flight:
a moment's brilliant grace and an unfulfilled suggestion of
beauty. "What you found in riding, you already knew in
dancing."

Tess could think of nothing to say and was beginning to
feel stupid again when Yuri came up.

"Tess, I had no idea you could dance so well. Everyone
knows that Ilya can dance like the grass, but he never does.
I don't know why."

"Yuri," said Bakhtiian.

"I think that was a warning," said Tess to Yuri.

"Excuse me," said Bakhtiian curtly, and left them.

Yuri took Tess's elbow and guided her past couples forming for the next dance, past the ring of watchers, some of
whom congratulated her in low voices, to the shadowy edge
of the firelight. His lips were pressed together into a thin
line, and his shoulders trembled with suppressed laughter.
Behind them, the lutes began a slow melody, accompanied
by the shuffle and drag of feet.

"No one . . . no one ever says things like that to Bakhtiian."

"Why not? It was a warning. I remember when he told
you to go look after the horses. I'd never seen anything so
rude."

"Oh, Tess. The look—on his face when you said it." He
bit at his hand to stop himself from giggling.

"I didn't see it."

"Oh, oh." Tears sparkled on his cheeks. He was still
laughing, one hand pressed to his abdomen. "Oh, Tess,
make me stop laughing. My stomach hurts."

Tess began to wipe at her eyes, recalled the kohl, and
stopped. "Listen, Yuri. I need your advice. About Vladimir."

Yuri stopped laughing.

"I've done something wrong, haven't I?" she whispered. From the fire came a swell of laughter.

"No." He reached for her. She avoided his hand. "Vladimir's behavior—as if anyone could blame you—"

"Oh, Lord." She broke past him and ran away, skirting the clusters of tents, until she found her own, pitched in solitary splendor at the very edge of camp. She flung herself down, crawled inside, and covered her face with her hands.

Once again, she had made a fool of herself with a man. She never knew what to do. She always did it wrong. She snuffled into her palms but could not force tears. Voices, angry voices, interrupted her, and she froze, scarcely breathing.

"By the gods," said Bakhtiian. He sounded furious beyond measure. "If I ever see such an exhibition as that again, Vladimir, then you will leave my jahar. Perhaps Elena Sobelov might keep you as her lover, a kinless man without even a dyan to call loyalty to, but her brothers will kill you if you ever try to mark her."

"I didn't do anything wrong." Vladimir's voice was sullen.

Tess squirmed forward and peered out the front flap of her tent. She could see neither of them.

"Not even Kirill would flaunt himself like that in front of a woman. Not even Kirill, by the gods, would put himself forward so, without any shame at all, and as a guest in this tribe. I expect my riders to behave as men, not as khaja savages."

Out a little farther, and she could see them, standing by the glow of the fire around which Bakhtiian and Niko had spoken with men from this tribe the night before. Bakhtiian stood stiff and straight, anger in every line of his body. Before him, bowed down by his bitterly harsh words, Vladimir stood hunched, cowed. Tess felt sorry for him suddenly, the recipient of Bakhtiian's ill humor.

"She's just a khaja bitch," said Vladimir petulantly. "She doesn't matter."

Bakhtiian slapped him. Vladimir gasped. Tess flinched.

"Never speak of women that way." Bakhtiian's voice was low but his words burned with intensity. "Have you no shame? To throw yourself at her, there at the dance? What do you think Sakhalin must think of me, of our jahar? That we are so immodest that we make advances to women?"

A muffled noise had started that Tess could not immediately identify. The shadowy figure that was Vladimir lifted a hand to his face. He was crying.

"None of the women, none of them . . . came up to me. . . ." He faltered. "She is khaja. I thought it wouldn't matter."

"Oh, gods, Vladi," said Bakhtiian awkwardly, his voice softening. "Go to bed."

Vladimir turned and fled into the safe arms of the night. Bakhtiian sighed ostentatiously and kicked at the fire, scattering its coals. The last flames highlighted his fine-boned face.

"Ah, Bakhtiian." The woman's voice was low and pleasant. She strode into the fire's glow with confidence. "I was looking for you, Ilyakoria."

He glanced up at her and looked down again. "Nadezhda. We have had so little time to talk since I arrived."

"To talk?" She turned to rest a hand on his sleeve. She was older, a handsome woman dressed in long skirts and belled trousers washed gray by the night. "Talk is not precisely what I had in mind."

He shifted so that his arm brushed hers, but still he did not look at her. "You flatter me." She laughed, low and throaty, and lifted a hand to touch his face.

His diffidence astonished Tess and she felt suddenly like a voyeur, spying on a scene not meant for her eyes and ears. She shimmied backward into the tent, covered her ears with her hands, and curled up in her blankets. Eventually, she even went to sleep.

* * *

Light shimmered through the crystal panes that roofed and walled the Tai-en's reception hall. Rainbows painted the air in delicate patterns, shifting as the sun peaked and began its slow fall toward evening.

Marco sat on a living bench, grown from polished *ralewood*, growing still, shaded by vines. He watched as Charles Soerensen moved through the crowd. Worked the crowd, really; Marco had always liked that use of the word. Each new cluster of Chapalii bowed to the same precise degree at Charles's presence. The humans shook his hand, except for the Ophiuchi-Sei, who met him with a palm set against his palm, their traditional greeting. A handful of individuals from alien species under Chapalii rule also graced the reception, but Charles was always armed with interpreters of some kind, and he had the innate ability to never insult anyone unknowingly. Marco studied the crowd, measuring its tone, measuring individuals and family affiliations among the mass of Chapalii honored enough to receive this invitation, enjoying the consternation in the Chapalii ranks at the carousing of a score of human miners in from the edge of the system on holiday, marveling for the hundredth time over how the Chapalii architect responsible for this chamber had managed to coordinate the intricate pattern of the mosaic floor with the shifting rainbows decorating the loft of air above.

At the far end of the hall, under the twin barrel vaults that led out into the stone garden, Suzanne appeared.

Marco did not jump to his feet. He never did anything hastily or blindly, except for that one time in the frozen wastelands far to the south of Jeds, when he had run for his life with a spear through his shoulder, an arrow through his neck, and his dead guide left behind in a spreading pool of blood.

Suzanne did not move from the entrance. She merely stood to one side, shadowed by a pillar, and waited. After a few minutes, Marco rose and strolled aimlessly through the crowd, making his spiral way toward Charles. When he at last touched the sleeve of Charles's shirt, he noted that Suzanne had vanished from the hall. Charles shook the hand of a ship's master, exchanged a few easy words with her mate, and followed Marco out through the narrow side corridor that led to the efficiency and thence through a nondescript door to a hall that circled back and led out onto a secluded corner of the stone garden.

Suzanne waited there, standing under the shade of a granite arch cut into a lacework of stone above. A Chapalii waited with her. Seeing Charles, he bowed to the precise degree.

"Charles," said Suzanne, "this is Hon Echido Keinaba. He has come to Odys on behalf of his family to negotiate shipping and mineral rights. I hope you will be able to find time to discuss this matter in detail with him tomorrow." Then she repeated her speech in halting formal Chapalii, for Keinaba.

Charles nodded.

Keinaba bowed, his skin flushed red with satisfaction.

"Tai Charles," he said, speaking slowly, more as if he were choosing his words carefully than making sure the duke could understand him, "I am overwhelmed by your generosity to me and to Keinaba in this matter. I was most gratified to meet and converse with your esteemed heir the Tai-endi Terese on the shuttle from Earth up to the *Oshaki*, and I can only hope that her influence has helped bring your favor onto our family." He bowed again, hands in that arrangement known as Merchant's Bounty.

Charles did not move or show any emotion on his face. He simply nodded again.

"Perhaps, Hon Echido," said Suzanne, "you would like to see the reception hall."

"It is my fervent desire," replied Echido. He bowed again and retreated.

"Where the hell did he come from?" asked Charles. "When did you get back?"

"One hour past, on the same ship as Echido. I rather like him, as much as I like any of them. Charles, Tess has vanished."

"Explain."

"The reason I came back in person instead of sending a bullet is that it only took me one day to establish without any doubt in my own mind that Tess finished her thesis, left Prague, and boarded the *Oshaki* with the intent to come to Odys. I have a holo interview with her friend Sojourner, with a security police officer from Nairobi Port, with a Port Authority steward, and a confirmed retinal print from the boarding access tunnel on Lagrange Wheel."

"And?"

Suzanne shrugged. She slipped her hand into an inner pocket on her tunic and handed a thick, palm-sized disk to Charles. "My feeling? Sojourner had the distinct impression Tess didn't want to come to Odys, but that she was running from an unhappy love affair."

"Lord," said Marco.

"Don't kid yourself, Burckhardt. She evidently thought the boy was in love with her, but he was in love with her position and what she was and dumped her when he found out about the inheritance laws."

"Do you mean to say," Charles asked quietly, "that Tess was planning on getting married?"

"Looks like it."

Charles's eyes narrowed ever so slightly. "She didn't tell me. And then?"

"No other ports of call, according to Echido, except Rhui and Odys. I picked him up on Earth. He did not in fact go back to Chapal, despite what that message said. He debarked from the *Oshaki* at Hydri and went back to Earth to get a ship back here. But he was very clear that he had met Tess. He said they talked about Rhui and the interdiction and Rhui's rich resources."

Charles considered the pattern of subtly shaded stones set in linked chevrons between twisting statues carved from black rock. "Suzanne, you will follow the trail of the *Oshaki,* as far as Chapal, if need be. Marco, to Jeds."

Suzanne nodded. "I've already made arrangements for the *Lumiere* to run a shipment of musical instruments to Paladia Major. We can leave in two hours."

Charles held out the disk. "This is a full report?"

"Of course."

"Then go." Suzanne said nothing more, but simply left, walking briskly on the path. Pebbles whispered under her shoes.

Marco coughed into his fist. "Charles, what if she doesn't want to be found? What if she needs some time alone, to be away from you, from—from everything? You ride her pretty damned hard."

"She would have sent me a message." Charles turned the disk in his hand over, and over again. "In any case, she and I haven't the luxury of time away. It's hard, but that's where it stands. Tess must be found. Do you really suppose that I trust the Chapalii in a matter like this? The captain of the *Oshaki* lied to me. He knew she was on his ship. Even if he colluded with her, if her intent was to hide on Rhui, still . . . still . . . she's leverage over me, and they know it."

"They made you a duke."

"And we still don't understand how their damned alien minds work. Start in Jeds, Marco. You or Suzanne *will* find her."

Marco watched Soerensen walk away, back to his duties at the reception which he would perform without the slightest visible sign that he had just discovered that his only sibling, his heir, had disappeared. Charles was about as yielding as the stone in this garden. Sun dappled the path where it wound underneath the granite arch, cut by the lacy filigree into twisting and subtly chaotic patterns that blended with the shapes of the pebbles. Perhaps the stone was more flexible. If Tess was missing by some machination of the Chapalii, there would be hell to pay, although Marco could not for the moment imagine what Charles could actually do about it. Chapalii did not harm their superiors, and very few Chapalii outranked Tess. She would be in no physical danger, at least, however small a consolation that was. And if Tess had run, and was hiding, and he found her and brought her back where she did not want to be: well, that might be worse.

* * *

Cloth brushed her back, and Tess started awake and lay still, cursing herself for her dreams. Jacques again, damn him. She felt flushed all along her skin, up and down her body, and she sighed, resigned, recalling the dream more clearly now. Jacques's presence had not been the important element in this dream; what they were doing together was.

Outside, bells jingled softly, muffled by distance, and one of the herd beasts lowed, sounding more like a cow than the goat it resembled. A bird trilled once, twice, and then ceased. It must be nearly dawn. Yuri had taught her that trillers heralded dawn, whistlers noon, and hooters dusk.

"This isn't his tent," said a man, his voice pitched so low that Tess would not have heard him if he hadn't been standing a hand's breadth away from her, separated from her only by the cloth of her tent. "This is a woman's pattern."

A foot dragged along the fabric, pushing the wall in ever so slightly. Grass rustled, the barest sound, as he crept away. A word exhaled, farther away, so she heard the breath but not the meaning. She reached to pull her tent flap aside to look out.

"Stahar linaya!"

The force of the words—Battle! Night! Treachery!—ringing out in—in Fedya's voice?—sent her forward without thinking, responding to his piercing cry for help. She tumbled out of her tent and ran right into a body crouched outside. The figure stumbled forward, reaching for his saber. She caught a flash of white face as she reached for her own saber, only to recall that she was in women's clothing. The man took off running.

A confusion of figures clustered around Bakhtiian's solitary tent. A man screamed in rage. Suddenly, sabers winked pale in the hazy predawn dimness.

Two men—Vladimir and Fedya—faced off against three, their shapes shifting in a delicate dance around Bakhtiian's tent.

"Get back, Tess!" A hand pressed her back against her tent, and she looked up to see Kirill beside her. He clutched a blanket around his waist with one hand. His torso was utterly naked, and for a wildly improbable moment, she simply stared, at his arms, at the pale down of fine hair on his chest—

"—your saber!" he hissed urgently.

She swallowed hard and reached back into her tent and pulled out her saber. He grabbed it from her one-handed, slipping the blade free with a deft twist, and ran forward into the fight. "Vladi! Disarm him now! Fedya, to me. Yuri, Konstans, to their backs."

With a blur of strokes, Vladimir disarmed one man and then without pausing flung himself on the other and wrestled him to the ground. Faced with Fedya and Kirill, and the appearance of several other men in various stages of undress, the third man threw down his saber. Yuri darted forward and picked up the three sabers. He wore only trousers and no boots. A man cried out in pain, and then Bakhtiian appeared at the same moment as the first swell of light, the disk of the sun cresting the horizon, flooded the scene with dawn's pale light. He was, of course, impeccably dressed, shirt tucked in, trousers straight, saber held with light command in his right hand—but he was barefoot.

"Vladi," he said in a calm voice that carried easily in the hush of the moment, "let him up."

Vladi sat atop the second man, knife pressed against the edge of the man's eye. Blood welled and trickled down the man's cheek, and he whimpered in fear. Some of the older riders had taken over, holding the other two men captive. Now many of the tribe filtered in to form a rough circle around this altercation. Vladi sat back reluctantly and withdrew his knife. The man did not move from the ground, but he lifted a hand to cover his eye.

"What is this?" Elizaveta Sakhalin and her nephew arrived. "What men have breached the peace of this tribe?"

Niko and Josef yanked the man from the ground and hustled him over to stand by his compatriots. In the light, the raiders looked a sorry bunch, ill-fed, sallow, and peevish.

"I don't recognize them," said Bakhtiian.

One man lifted his head and spat in Bakhtiian's direction. "I'm only sorry we didn't kill you."

"You will be sorrier when we are done with you," said Elizaveta Sakhalin, favoring the three captives with a withering stare.

"This is men's business," the bold one snapped.

"Conducted within our tents? I think not. Yaroslav." She nodded to her nephew. "You will confine them until the Elders have discussed their fate."

"There," said Konstantina, startling Tess by coming up quietly beside her. "You see, Tsara." She angled her neck to include her cousin, who had trailed after her, both hands holding a blanket demurely around herself. "I was right. There is Nadezhda Martov."

Tess was distracted from watching the captives being led away by the sight of Martov arriving some steps behind Bakhtiian, decently dressed in a shift and skirt. Bakhtiian glanced back at her, aware of her presence, and then moved forward to speak with Niko and Fedya and Vladimir.

"And get some clothes on," he said to the other men.

Konstantina chuckled. "You see. All the women have arrived to take a look."

Glancing around, Tess realized that a disproportionate number of the younger women of the tribe had arrived. A few whistled as Kirill came back over to her tent. His eyes were lowered in a becoming fashion, but there was no doubting the slight sauntering display in his walk.

"You, too, Kirill," said Bakhtiian. "Fedya, was it you caught the intruders? I thought as much. And you did well, Vladi."

"Thank you," said Kirill as he returned Tess's saber. Tsara laid a hand on his arm and led him away, looking smug.

"What will happen to the captives?" Tess asked Konstantina, who still hovered at her elbow. Sakhalin and her nephew reappeared to consult with Bakhtiian.

"Oh, I should think that we'll leave them for the birds. Ah, there he is. If you'll excuse me." Konstantina strode away straight toward Yuri, Tess noted with interest, as he retreated hastily from the fray.

"No," Bakhtiian was saying, "I take full responsibility for this act. Had I not been here, this would never have happened. I do not want to bring further trouble for your tribe, Mother Sakhalin. We will leave today."

Sakhalin considered and spoke with her nephew, and then they all walked off together. Vladimir trailed in their wake. Only Fedya remained, standing quite still, head tilted slightly, as if he was trying to hear or taste something on the wind. He turned slowly and walked off, toward Tess at first, and then veering away toward the edge of camp, tracking some unseen path.

"It is a beautiful tent." Tess looked round to see Nadezhda Martov standing four paces away from her.

"It is," agreed Tess cautiously. "It was gifted me by Mother Orzhekov. It used to be her daughter's."

"Then you are, by her decree, Ilyakoria Bakhtiian's cousin," said the woman pleasantly. "Mother Orzhekov is a renowned weaver. Her niece wove the finest patterns I have ever seen."

"Her niece?"

"Bakhtiian's elder sister. I knew her before she died."

"Ah," said Tess, not knowing what else to say.

"You are from—a long ways away?"

"I am from a—city—a place of many stone tents—Jeds. . . ."

"Yes, I have heard of it. Ilyakoria speaks of it."

For an instant, Tess had an uncomfortably vivid image of just when he spoke of such things to Nadezhda Martov. She suppressed it and smiled instead.

"Those are borrowed clothes, are they not?" asked Martov. When Tess nodded, she nodded in return. "Come. Though you must ride in men's clothing, I think you will benefit from having women's clothing of your own, as well. And with your coloring—" A gleam of challenge lit her eyes. "I know just what will suit you."

They did not leave until midday. Bakhtiian gave them one of his khuhaylan mares, and most of the tarpans were exchanged for fresh mounts. Tess was forced to consult with Yuri on how to add her burgeoning possessions to her saddle roll: a fine suit of women's clothing gathered by Martov from women throughout the tribe. Tsara gave Tess a fine silver bracelet. Yuri managed to fit the roll of clothing on to one of the ten horses now burdened with the generous provisions given to the jahar by the women of the tribe.

"So, Yuri," asked Tess as they rode out of the tribe, "how did you find Konstantina Sakhalin?"

Yuri blushed crimson.

"Poor Kirill. He's sorry to be going." Kirill was half turned in his saddle, gazing back at the cluster of women who had gathered to bid them heartfelt farewells. "Are you?"

Yuri set his lips and refused to be drawn.

"Soerensen." Bakhtiian pulled in beside them. He did not glance back at the tribe. "We'll be riding forward scout."

Tess laughed.

"Why are you laughing?" he asked suspiciously.

"I don't know," she said truthfully, but she whistled as she urged Myshla forward to ride out with him.

CHAPTER NINE

"The eyes are more exact witnesses
than the ears."
—HERACLEITUS OF EPHESUS

The sweep of grass, the clear air, the high sun; these were her day. Summer surprised them. Now the plain flowered a second time, the stalks of the flowering plants hidden, engulfed in the grass, only the petals showing like brilliant spots of emerald and turquoise, ruby and amethyst. Occasionally it rained. Herds of *khey,* deerlike animals that proved more placid than the migrating antelopes, provided meat.

One day, when they stopped early to take advantage of a good campsite, Tess convinced Fedya to take her hunting and was rewarded with her first kill, though she made Fedya cut its throat once she had brought it down. Together they brought back her kill and the one Fedya brought down, and so great a fuss was made over her that Tess finally escaped all the attention by going to pitch her tent with Yuri, an act no man but a brother would ever suggest overseeing.

"Fedya is almost as good a hunter as the women," Tess said as she rolled out her tent. "Is that why he rides scout so often? Even Bakhtiian doesn't ride scout every day."

Yuri shrugged. "He likes to be alone. And he has sharp eyes."

"Yes." Tess paused in her work to gaze at the distant fire and the figures gathered around it. "He's so melancholy, but not sorry for himself. And he's kind."

Yuri smiled but said nothing.

Bakhtiian now spoke very little Rhuian with her as they rode scout, using khush almost exclusively. But when they talked about Jeds and the disciplines studied at the University there, he lapsed back into Rhuian. Tess began to appreciate the breadth of his learning: conversant with all the things a jaran man must know, he had also taken full advantage of his three years at the University in Jeds. Gallio and Oleana, Narronias and the great legalist, Sister Casiara of Jedina Cloister, these Tess knew because she had read their works on Earth in order to keep her Rhuian fresh. But Bakhtiian's knowledge took surprising turns at times.

"Aristotle!"

"Well, you pronounce it rather differently. Surely you've read his works on natural history?"

"I suppose you've read Plato, too?"

"Pla—? Oh, yes, Playtok. But I never found his arguments convincing. I find his dialogue form too self-conscious."

"Ah," said Tess wisely, beginning to wonder what her brother had been up to these past ten years since she had last set foot on Rhui. But then, she had been too young those three years she had spent in Jeds with Charles and Dr. Hierakis, too shocked by the death of her parents, to be aware of what they might have been doing in the midst of the burgeoning renaissance of the city.

"But perhaps . . ." He hesitated, and then, decisively, he reached into his saddlebag and withdrew a leather-bound volume and opened it. "Perhaps you can help me understand this." He read aloud. " 'Every body perseveres in its state of rest, or of uniform motion in a right line, unless it is compelled to change that state—' "

"Let me see that," she demanded, and he handed the book to her without a word. "My God. This is Newton's *Principia.*"

"So you have heard of him."

"Ah, yes, I have. I suppose you have a volume of Descartes back there as well."

"Dhaykhart? No, I have not heard of this philosopher."

"Thank God. Where did you get this?" She gave the book back to him, and he tucked it neatly back into his pouch.

"I have a—a friend in Jeds. We arranged, before I left, that this friend would send books to a certain port and a certain inn proprietor. Every other year or so, we journey near that port—this year, we will put the khepelli to ship there—and then I collect the books.''

"Oh. I wondered how you and Niko got books. But where did that book come from, the Newton?"

He shrugged, mystified by the intent of her question. "One of the printing houses in Jeds. I have only had it one year. My friend writes that this Newton lives overseas, but Jedan traders have brought in many new philosophic volumes to the University in recent years."

"Overseas," muttered Tess. "Of course."

"I beg your pardon?"

"No, I was merely surprised because I studied overseas near . . . where this man lives—"

"Have you met him?"

"Ah, no, no, but I was simply surprised because his works were so swiftly translated and sent to Jeds."

"Perhaps your brother was the one responsible," said Bakhtiian, watching her far too closely. "Soerensen . . . the name is familiar, but I can't place it. He must trade extensively to have chosen to send his only sister so far away to study."

"Perhaps he was," said Tess, not liking the measuring way in which Bakhtiian examined her. It was easy enough to forget that the Chapalii had accused her of spying, and that Bakhtiian had told Sonia he thought Tess was lying about herself, about her merchant brother and her reasons for being here, about how much else, she could not guess. "But," she added a little sharply, "he is not the only man to have sent his relatives a great distance to go to a university."

And Bakhtiian remembered that he was, after all, speaking with a woman, and he looked away from her to scan the level plain and the arching sky.

"Look," said Tess suddenly, "look there! A khoen."

"You are learning to use your eyes." They brought their horses up next to it, a small mound layered with an elaborate arrangement of rocks, mostly hidden in the grass. He stared down. His shoulders tensed and his lips thinned. "Damn them," he said softly, followed by a word Tess did not know. He twisted his reins twice around one fist, unsheathed his knife, looked at it, sheathed it again. Tess waited. He untwisted the reins and his horse put its head down to graze. "So." He squinted briefly at the horizon.

"The last three dyans are combining forces against me. Now that I'm on a long journey with a small jahar, they think this time they can kill me because they know that once I have those horses, it will be too late. You chose a poor time to accompany us."

"Who's combining? Isn't Doroskayev's group behind us? Yuri says you still don't know which dyan those men call loyalty to, the ones who tried to kill you in Sakhalin's tribe. And how can you read all that from these rocks?"

"Why are women always so damnably curious?" asked Bakhtiian. He smiled.

"Because men keep everything from them, of course."

He laughed. "Very well. I relent. I'll show you." He glanced around before dismounting to explain the intricacies of this language of stone and stick and earth. When they were riding again, he said, "The jaran have no language that is set down, unlike Rhuian. Our poetry and songs live in all our memories. Only the stone mounds have meaning."

"No written language at all?"

"Some priests carve in stone, but few know the secret of that tongue."

"Do you?"

"I cannot say."

"Then you do."

"Perhaps. Perhaps not."

"Why are men always so damnably evasive?" asked Tess. She smiled.

"Because of women," said Bakhtiian.

For some reason, this produced a silence. A bird called loudly overhead. Tess gazed up at the sky. It had a slate color, a tinge of gray, as if one storm cloud had been ripped to pieces and mixed in with the blue. In Jeds it had the blue of turquoise, but in Jeds the other colors had not seemed so bright. A torn wisp of cloud clung to the horizon.

"Why did your brother send you overseas?" he asked.

She turned, astonished and irritated, to stare directly at him. "You don't trust me."

His lips tightened, and he reined his horse away from her so abruptly that it shied under the hard rein. He turned it downslope and let it have its head, Tess trailing behind.

She retreated immediately to the company of the young men that evening, and sat at the fire watching Mikhal and

Fedya across from her as they sang a riddle song to an appreciative audience.

"Yuri, I'm hungry," she said peevishly, still annoyed and troubled by her afternoon's conversation. "Why can't we eat?"

Yuri sat with his arms curled around his one upright knee, staring morosely into the fire. "Didn't Ilya tell you? Tomorrow we come to *zhapolaya,* the sacred hill. We have many laws that we must follow at a holy place."

"Including starving? Have the khepelli been out of their tents at all since you set up camp?"

"How should I know? Do you think I care?"

"Well at least you're hungry, too." Yuri made a face at her, but it was a half-hearted attempt. "What is this zhapolaya?"

"The stone that crowns the sacred hill. Something the gods left us."

"How nice of Bakhtiian to tell me," Tess muttered.

"What?"

"Is this one of the sacred places the khepelli want to see?"

"Yes. I think so."

"Wait. Are you saying that they knew it was here?"

"But everyone who knows this land knows of it. Why shouldn't they?"

Of course they would have asked Bakhtiian to direct them to holy sites. Something the gods had left. Could it be the relic of some star-faring civilization? But this planet had been discovered by the League Exploratory Survey, annexed at the same time the League had been annexed by the Chapalii Empire, and then deeded to her brother when the emperor had honored him with the dukedom. Perhaps some ancient Rhuian empire had laid tracks across this trackless plain and then vanished. Perhaps. It was the easiest explanation.

Tess followed the shifting red of flame up and across and found that her gaze had drawn and met Fedya's where he sat next to Mikhal. He smiled in return and looked away, the smile lingering on his face as if he had forgotten it. Tess ran her knuckles over her lips thoughtfully, focusing on the darkness beyond so that her knuckles separated into two exact duplicates, one solid, one shadow. She rose, bidding

Yuri good night, and wandered out toward the Chapalii tents.

But what if Yuri had meant his comment literally—what if the Chapalii had known exactly where they wanted to go and had chosen this way, riding cross-country, to get there as unobtrusively as possible?

The four tents stood isolated beyond the fire and the casual clutter of the jahar. Three stood dark against the night sky. In the second, the tent of Hon Garii and his companion, Hon Rakii Makokan, another son of a merchant house, a low gleam of steady light filtered from the tent. But shouldn't a light inside canvas reveal silhouettes? This one did not. She shook her head, impatient with herself. What could she do, alone on this journey, except keep an eye on them for Charles? Spy on them. She ought to at least use the correct word. Someone coughed nearby. She turned to see a figure standing about twenty paces from her, a tall, slender form traced dimly against the spread of stars. She knew that it was Bakhtiian. Watching her. Watching her spy.

"Damn him." She stalked off to bed.

In the morning, she felt nauseated with hunger. Bakhtiian's pace as they scouted only emphasized the hollow jolting, and now and then, when he wasn't looking, she would put her hand over her mouth. To her unspeakable relief, they reached the sacred hill in the early afternoon.

The hills they had seen on the horizon the day before now rose abruptly out of the plain as if the earth had frozen in the act of bubbling. The grass here, more brown than gold, grew sparsely enough that soil showed through in patches. The zhapolaya was distinguishable from its companions only by the standing stone at its peak, a dark rectangle whose angularity and solid mass looked unnatural against the fluid hills. A standing stone—some kind of marker, perhaps, like the milestones the Romans had used.

"There is a hollow for a camp," said Bakhtiian, and they found it out of sight of the sacred hill. These were weak-soiled, low hills, crumbled in spots from the winter rains. Several dry watercourses ran through the hollow, but there were no clouds, no danger of a washout.

"No storms. Not yet." Bakhtiian laughed. Some tone in his laugh caught at her, made her shiver all the way down her spine, made her warm. The jahar rode in and she watched them, acutely aware of the lines of their bodies, their movements as they dismounted and walked and stretched and glanced—one or two—at her, quickly and then away. She turned away to hide her blush, and she knew: the long drought had caught up with her at last. Some tone in his laugh: remembered pleasure, or anticipation. She dismounted, glad to unsaddle the horse.

She took as long as she could caring for Myshla, checked her hooves twice over, brushed her until her coat gleamed, talked to her. The Chapalii retired early to their tents. The jaran men settled down around the fire, their tents a close wall behind them. Tess walked over reluctantly and sat down beside Yuri, aware of their glances, their bodies, their presence. Niko scattered herbs over the flames, and a sweet, strangely harsh scent drifted out to them.

"What is that?" Tess asked, not sure that she liked the powerful tang.

"Ulyan," whispered Yuri. "All the men carry some." He shifted so that she could see a tiny pouch snuggled up against the hilt of his saber, looped to his belt.

"Why?"

"To greet the gods. A man who dies in battle, or a woman in childbirth, is welcomed to the gods' lands, and we burn ulyan with him on his pyre, so the gods' messengers will come to carry away his spirit. Jahar riders and pregnant women always keep a pouch of ulyan with them."

"I can't stand the scent. It's so strong. I'm going to take a walk."

Yuri patted her hand. "It also covers the smell."

Tess left, walking aimlessly out into the gathering darkness, the hollow lost behind her, the sacred hill hidden behind the hill to her right. She touched her belt in four places, a little ritual: saber, knife, mirror, and Chapalii knife. Covered the smell, he had said. *Of burning flesh? With any luck at all, I'll never find out.*

The moon, large and bright and not yet half full, rose like a cautious animal over the horizon and began its leisurely circuit of the sky. Stars appeared here and there.

Beneath her feet the ground sloped upward. Tess followed it, letting other forces dictate her movements. She came upon him unexpectedly, sitting on a rock embedded in an overhanging lip of hill. The view was of nothing, except the formless shape of hills. He was, perhaps, watching the moon.

"Hello, Fedya."

"He is happy tonight," he answered, by way of greeting. He did not look at her.

"Do you mean the moon?" She sat beside him, cross-legged, her hands on her knees.

"Of course." He looked at her fleetingly.

"Do you call the moon a man, a male, in the jaran?"

"What a strange question. Yes."

"In my land, we call her a maiden or, sometimes, an old woman."

"But the moon is not nearly as bright as the sun." Fedya considered the moon, tilting his head to one side. He had a soft profile, blurred by his mustache and thick lashes, and by the clean, round line of his jaw.

"Then what is the sun?"

"A woman." He looked at her, puzzled. "Of course."

She looked down. It smelled of soil here rather than grass, a heavy scent unstirred by wind. "There is so much that is different."

"Between a man and a woman, do you mean?"

"Yes."

Fedya shook his head. "There is nothing different."

"You haven't been in my land."

"What is a land but people? Your ways may be different, but people are the same."

"I don't know. I don't know if I believe you."

"How can you not believe me?" he asked, fixing her with a stare so intimate that she felt her face warm with a flush.

"Fedya, will you—do you want to—" She almost laughed, but it came out a half-strangled, tiny sound. "I don't know what to say, how to ask."

"You already have." He put his hand on her shoulder and drew it down, slow and caressing, down along her sleeve to her wrist. She had to hold her breath to stop from sighing, and she was suddenly aware of every inch of skin, tingling, aching. "Tess." His voice was gentle. "I must tell you this first. I can only think of my wife, or of what comfort there is in lying with a woman."

"But it's only—comfort I want. I can't—not men who want more—" Her hand lifted to touch her own lips, lowered. "—than I can give them. Than I have. I'm not explaining myself."

"But you are." His hand lay steady on hers. He looked

up at the moon. "The soul is cold and alone when darkness comes. It needs comfort. But the other things, possession, passion, love—ah, they bring hurt."

"Betrayal. Betraying the confidence you give, between a man and a woman."

"Betrayal," Fedya echoed. Her hand warmed now where his touched it. "Perhaps I felt she betrayed me when she died, like the sun, always deserting the moon to the darkness." The light of the moon shadowed his eyes.

"No confidences," said Tess. "Only comfort."

He lifted one hand to cup her face. "Below this rock it is dry."

He was gentle, and quiet, and he knew how to laugh when it was appropriate. He fell asleep afterward, half in her arms, and Tess saw that when he slept he looked much younger, almost as if he were a child again. The roughness of his cloak tickled her skin, but pleasantly, softly, as if it meant to remind her that contentment was all very well, but there was work still to be done. They lay in darkness, the moon far gone on his nightly path.

Something that had been kicking in her had calmed; another alarm now took its place. Work to be done. She slipped on her clothing and wrapped him in his cloak, carefully tucking the cloth around his feet. He did not wake. It was chilly. She reached the crest of the hill, yawning.

A light lit the sacred hill opposite. Shadowy forms, thin and awkward in their movements, clustered around the standing stone, limned by the glow. Tess dropped to her knees and waited and watched.

For a long time they simply stood there, as if they were examining the megalith. She surveyed the ground all around, but she could detect no other watchers. Just as she decided to make a careful circuit, to be sure that no one, especially not Bakhtiian, was also observing this scene, the light cut off.

She scuttled down the hill, keeping low, and at the base of the zhapolaya crouched and stared up. A rectangle of oblivion, drowning out the stars, marked the standing stone. She knew her eyes had adjusted, but she could see no one, no forms, no shapes, nothing but the stone, above her. The Chapalii could not have moved so fast and disappeared so utterly. On the dark face of the stone, a red light winked

and vanished. She ducked, expecting laser fire, but none
came. The light winked and vanished again, and she waited,
and it winked and vanished yet again. A signal.

She crept up the hill. No one shouted. Nothing moved.
The light blinked on and off, on and off, beckoning her.

A beacon. The thought struck her forcibly as she reached
the top and cautiously stood next to the stone. The megalith
dwarfed her, standing three times her width and twice her
height. Just above her eye level, embedded within the stone,
gleamed the blood-red point. She placed her hand on the
stone, next to it, and felt the roughened texture of rock on
her skin. But the rock was warm, and the barest pulse
throbbed through it, blending with the beat of her heart.
She slid her hand across its surface until she covered over
the tiny depression within which the point of light lay winking.

The stone gave off an exhalation, like an old woman's
tired sigh. Warm air brushed her face. She felt dizzy, disoriented, until she realized that the rock face was pulling
away from her, opening. The ground moved, and she stared
down into the earth, down a flight of stairs that led—

That led wherever the Chapalii had gone. A ghostly blue
light emanated up from the depths.

Tess put a foot on the first step. A hand closed on her
shoulder from behind, and she froze. A thin, hard hand,
preternaturally strong, and with it, the scent of cinnamon,
distinctive and strong. She knew it was a Chapalii before
she even attempted to turn.

From below, drifting on the warm draft that rode up the
stairs, she heard the low double chime of "signal received," Chapalii standard, and then a voice.

"Progress received. Continue observation of Soerensen.
Proceed with caution. Do not act rashly."

A shadow obscured the light from below. "Wa-sen. You
were ordered to eliminate intruders." The voice was harsh
but inflected as merchant to steward.

"Honorable. I beg to ask pardon, but—"

"Who is this?" The Chapalii halted three steps below
Tess and stared.

"Who is this?" asked Tess, coldly formal.

"I beg a thousand pardons, Lady Terese. A thousand,
thousand pardons. Your welfare alone precipitated my arrival. I beg you to allow me to escort you away before—"

"Garii? What is this commotion?"

Under his breath, Garii cursed.

"Move aside," said the third Chapalii, who could only be Ishii. Tess laid a hand over her Chapalii knife and backed up, forcing the steward behind her to back up as well, until all four of them stood in the chill air of midnight. The stone closed behind them as soon as they were free of the threshold.

"My God. This is a transmitting station. How did this get here?"

No one replied. The steward kept his hand on her shoulder. His sweet-smelling breath tickled her cheek. In the distance, a bird shrieked, and a rodent's squeal arced and cut off.

"Lady Terese," said Ishii. "I solicit your permission to speak."

"I want an explanation. When did you build this? Why is it here?"

"I regret that I am not at liberty to speak further on this matter, Lady Terese."

"You are not at liberty? I command you, Cha Ishii."

"I regret, Lady Terese, that I am commanded by a higher authority than your own on this matter."

"If that is so, then why did this higher authority not request permission of the duke to travel on this planet?"

"I submit, Lady Terese, that such permission would have been denied."

"If that is so, Cha Ishii, then why did this higher authority not command permission to travel?"

Another Chapalii appeared out of the dark. They surrounded her on all sides now. The hand gripping her shoulder relaxed and released her, but even standing without restraint, she knew they had her trapped.

"I regret, Lady Terese," replied Ishii, his tone so well-modulated that she could detect no emotion in it at all, "that I am unable to unravel the thinking of those who station outranks my own. I beg you to leave now, and to believe that both your suspicion and your fear of us remain unfounded, and to recall that your own actions brought you to this pass, not any act of ours. Perhaps you will permit Hon Garii to escort you back to the camp."

What could she do? Charge past them down the stairs? What if this confrontation had already attracted notice?

Rhui's interdiction was already breached. To draw the jahar's attention now was to compromise the interdiction even further, and in a more fundamental way. And what had Garii said, "to eliminate intruders?" What if Fedya came looking for her? If Yuri was on watch?

"I will go, Ishii." She dropped the honorific to let him know she was displeased. Lord, what choice did she have? His face was a pale shadow in front of her, the standing stone a huge blot behind him. All four Chapalii bore knives at their belts. Behind Ishii, the red light blinked on, and off, and on, and off—and did not come on again.

"Transmission has ceased," said a faint, disembodied voice that emanated from the stone itself.

"Hon Garii." Tess inclined her head, acknowledging him. The stewards retreated, and Ishii clasped his hands in front of himself in that arrangement known as Lord's Obedience.

She let Garii escort her to the base of the hill. "I will go alone," she said, not wanting to be seen with any Chapalii.

"Lady Terese." Garii hesitated. "I beg of you to let me offer you my thanks. Cha Ishii—" Hearing his hesitation, again, Tess wondered what color his face was, what emotion his level voice hid. "You concealed the knife."

"I did."

"My gratitude is yours, Lady Terese, if you will accept it. More than that—"

"Garii." From above, Ishii's voice called, carrying on the breeze.

"I accept," said Tess. Garii bowed and backed away up the hill. "I accept," Tess murmured, and wondered what it was she had accepted. "You speak the language well enough," she said to herself in Anglais, "but you don't understand a damned thing about their culture, not really."

A blue glow cast a faint nimbus of light around the stone, and then, like mist, dissipated into the cold darkness. Tess shivered. Would they really kill to protect their secrets? The knife felt warm against her fingers, storing energy within. The night was utterly still.

She skirted the hill, walked halfway around it, looking up, before she turned her steps back to camp. Darkness curled in around her, and she felt suddenly alone, isolated, lost beyond finding. It had stood before her, an illegal transmitter station built by the Chapalii on a planet on which they were prohibited from setting foot, a planet deeded to the human they could never trust. Some conspiracy against Charles—that must be their purpose here. But to what end? What did they hope to accomplish? And she had failed to investigate this transmitter, been caught at it like the merest amateur.

Why couldn't Charles understand? Why couldn't he adopt a new heir, someone suited to the task? The Chapalii recognized adoption; it was legal, it was binding. She would never shirk her duty. But surely there was some other way for her to serve the cause. Why couldn't he see how unsuited she was? What if she was forced to take over from him? She would destroy everything he had accomplished so far.

Around the curve of the next hill, with the megalith hidden behind her, the distant glint of the campfire drew her eye. Her feet caught on some imperfection of ground, and she stumbled.

The watcher rose from where he had been crouched, an abrupt shadow blocking her path. Startled, rising, she lost her balance again and caught herself on one hand and one knee on the ground, frozen, staring up, unable to catch her breath.

"We are going to have a talk," said Bakhtiian.

CHAPTER TEN

"The eagle has black bones."
—DEMOCRITUS OF ABDERA

A cloud, trailing up from the horizon, hid the moon. She could not see his face, only the shadowed opacity of his form and a slash of darkness swinging out from his hip—his saber. Behind him, remote shapes moved by the far gleam of campfire. Tess sat down so precipitously that he almost dived for her, checking his movement just in time to make him seem high-strung and timorous.

"What do you want?" she demanded, too angry at herself, at the Chapalii, at him for startling her, for following her, to care how her words sounded now. Leave diplomacy to Charles.

He sank down beside her. "I don't understand you," he said, more conversational than accusing. "How can you claim that you are not a spy, and then be caught by the khepelli in the act of spying on them?"

The absurdity of the situation struck her suddenly, sitting here, brushed by the soft night breeze, being cross-examined by the light of the stars and the moon. She chuckled. He said nothing. "Oh, all right," she said, tired of trying to play this game. "I was spying on them, but I'm not a *spy.*"

"I fail to see how you can make that distinction."

"Intent. I really did get lost. I really was on my way to Jeds. I really was surprised to find the khepelli with you."

"You were surprised that khepelli trade on these coasts, that we knew their name. I have reason to believe that you didn't even know how far it was to Jeds, or how to get there, and I must admit that your real ignorance inclined me to believe your professed ignorance."

"Thank you. May I go now?"

He shifted, slightly, but he did not rise. "You know very well that because you are a woman, you may go any time you like. But as leader of this jahar, I will simply find another time and another place to continue this conversation. I have men who are beholden to me, and whom I have put in danger because of their loyalty to myself and my plans. If you are a danger to the jaran, then I promise you that I will find out."

"What danger could I be?"

"If your brother is a merchant powerful enough to be making treaties with the khepelli over lands so distant from his home and theirs, then I want to know what he intends."

"What about what they intend? The khepelli?"

The clouds, drifting, let moonlight filter out into the night again. Bakhtiian had a slight smile on his face, but Tess did not find the expression reassuring.

"Be assured that I keep my eye on the khepelli as well. When this expedition was first offered me, I did not take it, because I had not yet peace enough within the jaran to risk such a long journey."

"What do you mean, when the expedition was first offered you?"

"Five years past, it was offered."

"Five years past! How long have the khepelli been trading on that coast?"

"You don't know?"

"I—" She stopped and clamped her mouth shut, realizing that to say anything now would be to risk too much. The wind, shifting, brought the faint, bittersweet perfume of ulyan.

"Cousin, you know too much about some things, and too little about others. I find that puzzling."

Tess wanted nothing more than to end this whole conversation now, because she knew that she was losing whatever skirmish was being fought here. But to go now was to acknowledge the rout. She would never do that. "Bakhtiian, you ought not to talk about people whose educations have been unusual."

He laughed. "You're trying to distract me. It's a good technique. Very well, I'll change the subject. I've heard stories that the khepelli control great powers, especially those like Ishii, who are priests. Do you believe they do?"

"No, I don't."

"Is it true?"

He had trapped her, and Tess cursed herself inwardly for letting him use language against her, of all people, who had been studying language all her life. But not studying war. And she knew she had no choice but to lie outright.

"Ah," said Bakhtiian, for whom her silence had been answer enough. "The dawn." He tilted his head, as if this new angle might allow him to understand her. "There are other stories, about a people who lived here long, long ago, who were driven away by war or by sickness or by drought, and fled under the hills, never to be seen again. *Zayinu,* the ancient ones. Why do the khepelli bow to you?"

Her heart skipped a beat. She swallowed her exclamation. He was a master at this game; she was far outmatched. "I must go." She stood hastily, choosing rout over surrender.

But he had stood. Before she could move away, he closed one hand around her right wrist and held her, not too tightly but firmly. "Oh, no," he said, the more powerful for his softness. "I will know this."

"Damn you. My brother is the Prince of Jeds."

Bakhtiian swore softly. "The Prince of Jeds. By the gods, I have seen him. You do not look alike. Why should I believe you?"

"Oh, for God's sake," she snapped, "because it is true."

"I rather think it is." He let her go. "Forgive me, I do not mean this as an insult, but you are not very skilled at dissembling."

"How can you be so sure?"

"You can't deceive me."

"Can anyone deceive you, Bakhtiian?"

He smiled softly. "I can't know that, can I?" In the distance, the campfire was doused suddenly, its broad glow shrinking to a few separate points of red.

"May I go now?" she asked sarcastically.

"Cousin, you don't need to ask my permission. Now, if you will excuse me." He gave her a curt, mocking bow and strode out into the darkness in the direction of the zhapolaya. For a vicious moment, Tess hoped one of the Chapalii would kill him as an intruder, but Bakhtiian would never be so clumsy as to let himself be seen, much less caught.

Unlike me. She emptied her lungs in a long sigh. A cool wind sprang up, and she shivered and rubbed at her eyes.

God, she was tired. How could the Chapalii have built a
transmitter in the middle of this wilderness? Been trading here
for at least five years, unnoticed, unseen? Yet on a primitive
planet much could go undetected from what limited surveillance Charles could use, by his own regulations. Undoubtedly the unscheduled and illegal shuttle landing that
had left her stranded had also been shielded from satellite
surveillance. But if Charles was disseminating Newton and
Aristotle, why should he shrink from breaking other regulations, as long as no one else knew about it? What if he
knew the Chapalii were here, and was playing his own game
with them in turn? What if Bakhtiian discovered too much?

"Lord, Tess," she muttered to herself, "there's nothing
you can do about it now. Go to bed."

* * *

On a windswept island in the archipelago that lies off the
coast from Jeds, a technician sat at her console and moni-
tored a conversation. She was deft. Filter here, delay there,
a tweak in the right place, and no one could overhear, not
even the Chapalii. Especially not the Chapalii. Luckily,
those conversing had agreed with her to dispense with holo.
She was not sure she could cover a holo transmission. Over
such a vast distance, from a back room in the palace in Jeds
to the wide chamber that Charles Soerensen used as his
office on Odys, the technician had advised that a simple
voice transmission, analog, with its delays and its static,
might be so primitive that the Chapalii would not notice it
at all. She watched three screens simultaneously, tweaked
the volume, and let the conversation flow past her.

"No," a woman was saying—that was Dr. Hierakis,
"Tess is not here. I received no message. Nothing. The
scheduled shuttle came as usual, though not all the equipment I expected arrived on that flight."

They waited long minutes; then the reply: "Anything
else?" That was Soerensen.

From the same pickup as the doctor came Marco Burckhardt's voice. "There was one discrepancy. Karima?"

The technician clicked her tongue against the roof of her
mouth, activating her voice pickup. With her left hand, she
pulled up a new screen, data, and a graph. "I ran back
every slightest bit of tape from the *Oshaki*'s visit, from the
moment it came into orbit until it left again. We do have a
trace of the cargo shuttle leaving the *Oshaki*, and the record

of its landing on the island. Considerably more time elapsed from leaving the ship until landing than was necessary for the distance traveled, and there were no atmospheric conditions to warrant the delay.''

A long delay. ''Any ideas?''

''No trace.'' Karima stared at the data from the shuttle's flight. ''As well as I could trace the flight pattern, it conformed to the default route, although given where it detached from the *Oshaki,* one could model any number of north-continent landing points given their usual flight patterns.''

''And they are so damned efficient,'' said Dr. Hierakis. ''Always the shortest line between two points. It's the national religion, I think. It must have been deliberate.''

Delay. ''Karima, any indications of unauthorized landing? Has the station picked up any planetside communications?''

''None. Off here.'' She clicked off her pickup and concentrated on scrambling.

''Which doesn't say a hell of a lot,'' said Marco.

''Thank you, Karima. I'll want a model of the most likely interim landing points if the shuttle did indeed make an unauthorized landing. It's true, we've suspected Chapalii incursions in the past but never been able to prove anything. Damned chameleons. Marco, you were talking before about taking ship northward, up the north coast and into the inland sea.''

''Yes. I haven't explored that way yet.''

''Make an itinerary that can overlap with points on Karima's model. Then hold tight. I'll be back to you. Cara, wasn't it the Keinaba trading consortium that the medical establishment first worked with on the aging breakthrough?''

''Yes, in fact, it was. Why do you mention that?''

Marco made some noise, but not speech.

''I've got a cat and mouse up here. Echido is clearly acting as emissary for his family, but he's being very circumspect. They want something, something very delicate.''

''Not just transport rights to Tau?'' Marco asked.

''Something much deeper. Something linked all the way back to Chapal, and possibly to the emperor himself.''

''Do you want me to come back?'' asked Marco.

''Not yet. Echido speaks Anglais.''

Marco whistled.

Dr. Hierakis said, "Damned right they want something badly if he's bothered to learn human talk."

Even Karima paused for an instant in her scrambling, astounded by the thought of a Chapalii not of the serving ranks speaking Anglais.

"Keep searching. No further transmissions until I get word from Suzanne. Soerensen off."

Karima spread a burst of static over the Odys line and shut it down. "What do you think, Marco?" asked Dr. Hierakis, and then Karima shut down the Jeds line as well and went back to the trace of the cargo shuttle, running the pattern again and again.

* * *

Crawling out of her tent in the morning, Tess was first distracted by the smell of food cooking, and then by the acute fear that everyone knew about her and Fedya. But she heard no whispered comments. Fedya passed her as she saddled her remount, but he merely smiled quickly and went on. Beyond, the short grass on the sacred hill shone white under the early sun. The standing stone hulked black against the pale blue of the morning sky. If Bakhtiian had seen anything after leaving her the night before, he showed no sign of it now, eating his stew with relish and chatting and laughing with Niko and Josef and Tasha. The Chapalii stewards rolled up and folded their tents under Rakii's supervision. Ishii reclined on the ground while Garii wrote laboriously with a stylus to Ishii's dictation. She was too far away to hear what they were saying, and this morning she could not summon up the stubbornness to break in on their business.

"Good morning, Tess." Yuri led his saddled horse up to her. "Have you eaten already?"

"Yuri." She folded her arms, considering him, as she recalled what Bakhtiian had said the night before. Yuri raised his eyebrows questioningly. "Have you ever repeated things I've said to you to Bakhtiian?"

Yuri flushed, but he did not look away from her. "The welfare of the jaran must be my first consideration. Surely you understand that."

"But if you told him things I said in confidence, things I might otherwise not have said—"

"Gods! You don't think I've repeated anything . . . inti-

mate that you said to me? Violated a sister's confidence!''
He looked disgusted. ''You'd think that of me?''

She laughed, and Yuri laughed with her. His flush faded.
''I'm sorry. That was stupid of me. Of course you didn't.''

''It's good to be stupid now and again. It isn't healthy to
be right all the time. That's why I worry about Ilya.''

''Easy enough. We'll have a contest to see who can catch
him out first.''

''What will be the prize?''

''Satisfaction, Yuri. Pure satisfaction.''

''Tess! You're wicked!''

''No, merely practical. He sets himself too high, our
Bakhtiian.'' And then, because she had been thinking about
it all morning, because she didn't want anyone to know but
had to tell someone, she hesitated. ''There's something else.
A secret.'' She crouched down. Following her lead, he knelt
beside her, so close their sleeves and thighs brushed. The
horses grazed placidly behind them. He put his hand to her
knee. ''About Fedya.'' Her voice slipped to a murmur.

''Tess! You didn't. You did! Hah!''

''Shh! Yuri!''

He lifted one hand to yank playfully at her braid. ''By
the gods, we'll make you jaran yet. Sonia said we would.''

''Did she? When was this?''

An approaching horse interrupted them. ''We are leaving,'' said Bakhtiian, far above them, his face and hair
framed by the sky. Tess and Yuri stood hastily, brushing off
their clothing. They exchanged furtive looks, stifled gig-
gles, and Tess went with Bakhtiian.

Much later, they paused to water the horses.

''They had a light,'' said Bakhtiian. ''Neither a torch or
a candle. Can you explain this?''

''No,'' said Tess truthfully, meeting his gaze.

''I think they were worshiping the stone, or its god. I
couldn't make out their rituals. It was too dark.'' An animal
rustled through the grass. ''I wouldn't care to be a god
confined in a rock. Do you know if that is what they worship?''

''I don't know. But I do know that people worship many
strange things in many strange ways. There is a people in
my land—''

''In Jeds?''

"No, in the land overseas where I studied. They worship their god by abstaining from all earthly pleasures."

"All of them?" Bakhtiian looked like a boy being told a tale he did not believe but could not disbelieve. "Wouldn't they starve, or die of thirst?"

Tess looked away to hide her smile. "They eat and drink enough to stay alive, of course."

"Of course. Undoubtedly." He looked at her, eyes widening. Tess grinned. "You don't mean to say they don't— By the gods, what insanity."

"No." She blinked, straight-faced. "They are filled with the passion of God's divinity."

"But how tedious." They both laughed and, quite suddenly, he blushed and looked away from her. They rode on, but later he demanded that she explain how such a religion could exist after one generation.

Two days and four days and six and eight, and then, to vary it, she counted in threes: three days and six days and nine and twelve. It grew warmer and windy. The Chapalii remained polite, and she left them alone, for the moment. They set up their tents every night and packed them up at dawn, all as they had done before, but now the stewards occasionally unbent so far as to gamble with the riders: they taught each other a few simple games and played for ridiculous stakes—beads, needles, necklaces, trinkets. Tess could not see that one or the other ever had the advantage. However technologically superior the Chapalii might be, in these gambling games wit and luck were all that counted. Niko learned how to say 'good morning' and 'good evening' and 'the weather is fine today' in formal Chapalii, but when Garii requested that he be allowed to give Sibirin further lessons, Ishii refused, just as he refused when Garii asked to be allowed to scout with Bakhtiian and Tess.

And all the Chapalii came to listen when, for ten evenings running, Fedya sang for them the long epic tale of the first dyan Yuri Sakhalin and his feud with the demons of the hills and his love for the sun's daughter.

Tess now spoke khush with little hesitation. To relieve the monotony, Kirill pretended to be in love with her, which made everyone laugh; even the Chapalii could appreciate the humor of frustrated passion. Tess marveled that no one suspected her and Fedya. Yuri said simply, "Why should they look? Who would care, anyway?"

Bakhtiian told her more ancient stories: the coming of the people to the plains; the birth of the moon and the sun and the clouds and the wind. How mother sun and father wind gave birth to daughter earth and brother sky, to sister tent and son river. How aunt cloud and uncle moon gave birth to cousin grass and cousin rain. And they discussed Newton's universal theory of gravitation.

Tess wondered what Charles thought he was doing. She remembered his last visit to Earth, five years ago—and wasn't it five years ago that Bakhtiian claimed to have first met the Chapalii? She had been eighteen, Charles fifty-eight, looking no older than Bakhtiian did now. She took him to her favorite outdoor café; it was summer in Prague, hot, but he drank coffee so she did as well, though she had never liked its bitter taste, though she wanted something cool. He sat across from her at the little café table, well-groomed, neatly dressed. She tended toward a diffident, sloppy casualness, and she sat warily, nervous, wondering if anyone would recognize them, dreading that always. Charles simply held his cup and mused, looking supremely relaxed. Though she was his only sister, though her first memory was of him taking her for a flitter ride, still she could never read past his surface, know his thoughts, tell his fears or his doubts, if indeed he had any. He spoke that day of his work in the Delta Pavonis system, of his efforts to keep Rhui preserved.

"I've seen records of too many civilizations ruined because a stronger, more forceful civilization swept in and destroyed them. Sometimes inadvertently. Sometimes on purpose. It's easy enough for us to say that the Rhuian natives are primitive, that it is our duty to raise them up to our level. But without respect for what they are, we *will* destroy them. That's the Chapaliian way, the paternalistic way they treat all of their client states. Like us." His voice was calm and serious, never intense or passionate, but always forceful. "When the Chapalii modernized Odys, they completely wiped out the old indigenous culture. Accidentally, of course. A by-product of civilization. All of the indigenes died."

"Aren't there some *onasiu* left?" she asked, eager to show off her knowledge.

"In arcologies. That doesn't count."

"No. No, of course not." She flushed and took a sip of the now lukewarm coffee to cover it.

"I won't let that happen to Rhui. Odys can remain my proper ducal capital, as the Office of Protocol once reminded me was necessary to a duke—" His grin was ironic. "—of my station." His sand-colored beard, trimmed almost to a point at the chin, emphasized the hollows of his cheeks. "How can I complain?"

"You're still alive," Tess said, because she knew he liked her sardonic sense of humor.

He laughed. "Yes, and in such a beautiful, modern, expensive place. But I wonder what Odysian mythology was like. They had no moon. Imagine that. Sun for god, and only the light of the stars at night." If one looked, this close, when he sat this still and in the glaring light of the summer sun, one could see faint lines at the corners of his gray-blue eyes. "How I wonder."

Then, of course, a journalist had found them, and they had been forced to retreat from such a public stage. Or had that been the time the proprietor had hidden them in the kitchens and, when the media had been sent away on a false trail, ensconced them merrily at his tables once again? "Whatever I can do for the next rebellion, for the long haul," the proprietor had said, and he was only half joking.

"But however much I loved the learning there," Bakhtiian was saying, "I never thought to stay there."

"To stay—in Jeds?" Tess stammered, caught out by her thoughts, unsure of what Bakhtiian had been saying before, of where this conversation had come from and where it was leading. They rode slowly, following the curve of the hills.

"There was too much to be done on the plains."

"With the jaran?"

"A people poor in reputation, unknown. How strange that I never knew that until I went so far away, and the people whom I met on my travels did not know who I was or from whence I came. Not a soul knew of the jaran." Watching him as he stared raptly out at the far horizon, at the sweep of grass and the soft curve of the land, Tess realized that however much Bakhtiian was like Charles in being a leader, he was utterly unlike him. Where Charles concealed his strength and his power, working quietly and in tiny steps, Bakhtiian radiated his. Where Charles masked his feelings so completely that no one, not even his sister, could read him, Bakhtiian projected all of his; even when you could not tell what he was thinking, you knew it was because he wanted you not to be able to tell what he was thinking.

"But they will know," Bakhtiian said at last, slowly, imbuing each word with potency. "Soon we will be spoken of even in Jeds." He glanced at her, gauging her reaction. "We are only now coming into our time of greatness."

"Measured against—?" It came out before she thought, but of course he did not—could not—understand her meaning: that measured against the vast reach of the Chapalii Empire, against the slow progress of Charles's plans, his campaign was trivial.

"How does one measure the good against the bad? My sister and her child died because of me. My parents died because of me. I know well enough that more of my people will die."

Tess gazed at the horizon of green grass and blue sky, so like Earth and yet so unlike, a subtle shifting of color and shade. She felt abashed. Of course his campaign was not trivial, not to him. Not to the people who would die.

"But still you persist," she said at last, thinking of Charles.

"Still."

They rode on in silence.

That night at campfire Fedya persuaded Bahktiian to sing. He was slightly embarrassed but not ill at ease. He sang without accompaniment. He had a clear baritone and he sang a man's song: days of riding, little rest, the hope of a woman's smile. He knew what suited his voice and kept to it. When he finished, he grinned and began another song. The men chuckled. This was a maiden's song, and a man of the jaran who sang a maiden's song did it to mock women, maidens in particular. He sang it well. Men laughed, wiping at their eyes. Tess hid her grin, glad she sat in the shadow.

"This is the night for the quiet ones to sing," said Yuri, looking at her.

"Yuri, you don't think I'm going to—"

"Of course, you must sing for us."

"Good Lord." Tess frowned at Yuri. "You'll be sorry for this." She stood up. "This is the only song in khush that Yuri has taught me," she lied. It was a man's song, about none of the women wanting to go off with him. She sang it straight-faced, managing to finish that way despite the laughter that erupted all around the fire.

"By the gods," said Yuri proudly, "you sang that well. You should sing more often."

"You should teach me suitable songs." She sat down.

Niko came over to them and crouched, still chuckling. "You are undoubtedly gifted, child. But I'm surprised at Yuri."

"At me?"

"At you, Yurinya. To teach a woman such a song—" He clucked disapprovingly. "Such indelicacy in a youth shocks me."

"But, Niko, I have four sisters."

"That is true," replied Niko sagely. "We cannot fight the gods, or women." He and Yuri sighed together.

"Of course," said Tess. "Blame it on the women." She glanced up to find Bakhtiian standing behind Niko. He caught Tess's eye, and he smiled. If it had not been so dark, she would have sworn he winked. "I suppose next you'll be saying that Sonia taught you that song and encouraged you to teach it to me."

"But she did," Yuri said guilelessly.

Tess laughed, and Yuri, who could never help but laugh with her, covered his face with his hands.

Niko contrived to look offended for a moment. "You see, I am vindicated."

Smiling, Bakhtiian crouched down between Niko and Tess. "I would be honored, Cousin, if you would agree to teach me some of the songs you know, from Jeds and other lands."

Tess caught in her breath, but she smiled at him. "Only if you will teach me jaran songs."

For an instant, she thought he drew back slightly, but then he shrugged and relaxed. "That could be arranged."

"I meant, of course," she added hastily, "only songs that it is appropriate for a man to teach a woman."

All four laughed, Yuri lowering his hands and cuffing Tess on the neck.

"Now, Tess," said a voice above them, "you don't suppose that Bakhtiian would ever do anything inappropriate, do you?"

All four looked up, startled. Kirill had surely chosen that direction to approach them from because the fire, behind

him, made a halo about his form. The glow lit red highlights
in the thick waves of his fair hair, shone through the angles
of his elbows where they stood away from his body, and
outlined his stance, easy, a little arrogant. He had his head
cocked to the right and he smiled down at her. Nature had,
unfortunately, endowed him with a smile as sweet as a girl's,
one much at variance with the impudence in his eyes and
his demeanor.

Bakhtiian stood up. He was no longer smiling.

"Hello, Kirill,' said Tess, because no one else was saying
anything.

"I thought you were supposed to be on watch," said Yuri.

"Well, Yuri, you must have been mistaken."

The big fire sparked, flaming until a rider stamped it down
to coals. "As I remember—" Bakhtiian folded his arms on
his chest.

"Fedya!" called Niko.

Fedya wandered over. His glance went first to Bakhtiian
before skipping briefly back to Kirill. He gave them all his
quick, unpretentious smile as a greeting. "Tess," he said
in a quiet voice, "I admired your singing."

"Thank you, Fedya."

"I admired your singing, too," said Kirill. "As well as
the rest of you."

Tess flushed.

"Kirill." The lowness of Bakhtiian's voice made it more
threatening. Yuri scrambled hastily to his feet.

"But it's true." Kirill spread his palms upward in front
of himself with such an expression of innocence in the face
of false accusation that Tess could not help but giggle. Niko
coughed.

"The men in my jahar have manners, Kirill."

"Are you saying I don't, Bakhtiian?"

Bakhtiian's left hand moved to his saber hilt. Kirill's right
hand brushed the sheath of his knife. Tess, caught in the
middle, pushed herself back.

"You know, Ilya," said Niko quickly, "Fedya escaped
without having to sing tonight."

For a moment, all movement stopped. Bakhtiian's gaze
moved to Niko. Some look Tess could not interpret passed
between the two men.

"That is true, Niko." Bakhtiian settled back on his heels,
his left hand dropping to hang by his thigh, and he trans-

ferred his gaze smoothly to Fedya. "You promised me once to teach me some more of your songs."

Kirill was playing with the embroidery on one of his sleeves, his fingers pale in the dim light.

"Did I?" Fedya asked. "I'm not sure I agreed to give them up so easily." His audacity amazed Tess.

"Well, I don't intend to start pleading," said Bakhtiian.

Fedya smiled. "My lute is over by the small fire. We could go now."

"Yes. If you will excuse us." Bakhtiian nodded briefly at Tess, and he and Fedya left together. Tess sat forward with a long sigh, brushing off her palms.

Yuri rounded on Kirill. "You don't have any manners."

"Aren't you a little young to lecture me, Yuri?"

Yuri stiffened.

"I am not too young to lecture you," said Niko. "You provoke him deliberately."

"What of it?"

"Kirill, I will not bother to answer that question. But I will say that your conduct is not always well considered."

Kirill shrugged. "We're well away from the sacred hill. I have nothing to fear here."

"What does that have to do with it?" Tess asked, annoyed because there was some long-standing enmity here that she did not understand. Kirill and Bakhtiian were only five years apart in age, yet Kirill was clearly included with the youngest men of the jahar.

"On holy ground," said Niko, "the slightest misstep or misconduct, even accidental, may bring the wrath of the gods upon you. Even the khaja know this to be true. It is desecration."

"The priests scared me enough when I was little. I'm not going near such places," Kirill said, and he grinned when Niko chuckled. "Yes, I know, and you'd advise me not to, for my own safety."

"But what would happen?" asked Tess.

"It would be sacrilege," said Niko.

Tess did not reply. The big fire burned down to coals, a dull red speckled with black.

"Kirill! Ho!" Konstans strolled up. "Think to escape from your watch, do you? Nikita sent me. You're to relieve him."

Kirill gave Tess a long-suffering look as if in apology and left.

"I thought so," muttered Yuri.

"Niko." Tess lifted her hands to blow on them and then lowered them to her lap. "It isn't only misconduct at a holy place, is it?"

His hair seemed cast of starlight, a finer light than the coarse red of flames. "Sacrilege away from holy places is limited to those few actions that are repulsive to the gods and which flout without shame their few direct prohibitions. But at a holy place, many things we do gladly in normal life are offensive to the gods."

"At all holy places?"

"Not all. Only those the gods have left quiet. The shrine of Morava, for instance, is not quiet at all, and priests live there."

"What do you mean by quiet?"

"Left to the birds and the animals."

"The birds. Niko, what happened to the three men who tried to kill Bakhtiian at Sakhalin's tribe?"

"They were left for the birds."

"Ah." Tess decided she didn't really want to know. "So some things, like the man in your tribe who killed a bird, those things are always sacrilege?"

Niko considered her. "That shocks you." He nodded. "We have a story, Tess, of a hawk that warned the first tribe of jaran, who were camped against the mountains, of an avalanche, and saved them, and so saved the people."

"That's in the tale Fedya sang about the first dyan."

"Yes. Because of that hawk, all birds, who fly above and can therefore see farther, are sacred to the gods."

"Do you believe that story?"

"My child." Someone stirred the fire, covering most of the coals, killing their light. "If the people did not believe in one way, then there would be no jaran."

Tess could find nothing to say to that. The three of them sat in silence for a time. Tess finally rose and excused herself.

Her path led her near a small fire removed from the rest of the camp. She paused in the dark beyond it. Fedya and Bakhtiian sat there together, the light on their faces, Fedya bent over his lute. As she stood silently, watching, she heard Fedya sing a line and Bakhtiian sing it back to him. And she wondered, for there was something in this music not quite like the usual songs the jaran sang by the fire at night or with their tasks during the day. And she wondered at Bakhtiian, for his bearing as he sat beside Fedya gave to the younger man the status of an elder; she had seen Bakhtiian command the respectful attention of women and men twice his age. She stood for a long time, listening to the two voices, one a high, sweet tenor, one rich and full, but she did not approach them. It was late when she went to bed.

CHAPTER ELEVEN

"Also, in certain caves, water drips down."
—XENOPHANES OF COLOPHON

Twelve days later they reached another holy place, the site of a crumbling temple called *zhastoynaya*. Tess and Bakhtiian reached it first.

"It's beautiful," said Tess.

The temple lay at the base of an escarpment. The cliffs had crumbled away here and there to obliterate much of the back half of the ruins. Behind them lay a river, shallow, sluggish, and muddy, which they had forded to reach the temple grounds. The water somehow signaled the limit of the plain, separating that mortal place from this retreat of the gods, which seemed greener, richer, quieter than the lands humans haunted. A spring bubbled from the ground in the center of the ruins and coursed down, a fluid line shot through with sunlight, to stream silver into the river and then, a meter out, mingle and lose itself in the brown waters.

They let the horses stand and wandered up through the temple. In this land where a tent was the largest shelter, the ruins—no more than three fallen buildings—seemed enormous. Most of the central columns still stood like two lines of soldiers at attention, fluted, wider at the base and top and chipped all along their length, worn away by the wind and the rain. There was no roof. Two buildings flanked the first, one a low line of stone, the other an outline of waist-high walls and stone lintels without doors.

Bakhtiian led her up to the spring and knelt beside it. The water gushed up from an invisible source, filled a stone basin to the rim, and sluiced down between parallel columns half in and half out of a stone trough that had been sunk into the ground to guide it down to the river.

"It is said that a person who drinks from this spring will gain courage and wit and the respect of those worth being respected by." He looked up at her. "Will you drink?"

She gazed at the spring: clear water, without a doubt cold and satisfying. "Who says that?"

"It is an old legend, left here by the gods."

"Then I will drink."

"Drink your fill."

The water was so cold it made her gasp; it took only a little to satisfy her. "Don't you drink, Bakhtiian?"

"Drinking once gives you the favor of the gods. Drinking twice . . . only a greedy man drinks twice."

They wandered down the avenue of columns and, at Tess's insistence, explored a bit more. He drew the line at climbing the cliff, so Tess climbed one of the taller walls—chest-height—and sat on it, letting her heels drum the stone as she gazed out beyond the river, watching for the arrival of the jahar. Bakhtiian leaned against the wall beside her. He took out his knife and his hands played with it absently as he, too, studied the distant swell of golden plain. A wind bent the grass tips down, sending fluid patterns of light across the land. Tess would have known this place was a temple even without being told. The touch of the gods lay on it, deep, heavy, eternal. A few birds whistled above. Insects droned dreamlike in the grass. The sun beat warmly on her face, and she sighed and closed her eyes.

And thought of the Chapalii.

"Does this temple belong to one of your gods?" she asked.

The knife lay still in his hands. "The jaran have no temples. Our gods are as restless as we are, although there is One you can petition in the dark, in the night, if you are in desperate need. But the gods have touched this place, so we honor it."

"You don't know who it was built for? Who built it?"

"Does it matter? Winds blow from all directions."

"What if it's important what direction it blows from?"

The corners of his lips twitched up. "Ah, yes. Will it be a cold wind or a warm one? Fierce or gentle?" He lapsed into Rhuian. "One that will guide a ship into port or break it on the rocks? That, of course, would be a Jedan analogy.

No. I don't know who built this place. Perhaps the khepelli do.''

"That's what I'm afraid of," Tess muttered under her breath. But this place was so old, ruined—and the transmitting station was functional. She could not link the two.

"I beg your pardon?"

"I just—I would have thought that the jaran would be more—more jealous of their own gods.''

He considered this a moment. "But they aren't jealous of us. When I was in Jeds, I read of a land across the seas where they worship five underground pools and think their Lady resides within. At the zhapolaya, the khepelli worshiped the stone as if their god lived there. And you spoke of a people who abstain from pleasure and fill themselves instead with their god's passion. They are all gods. That they are different, and so many, does not lessen them. I would never presume to say that my particular gods are worthy of a temple, and not any others.''

The wind moved in her hair. "And yet you killed a man for your gods. Are other gods as worthy?''

"I remember. But I have learned that the world is a delicate thing, and the gods—all gods—are as one with it, are the keepers of that balance. And since the world is within me as well as outside of me, if the balance is disturbed and not righted then I am also left in discord, and if I do nothing to correct this imbalance, then we, the world and I, shall never return to harmony. And if this is true for me alone, how much more true it is for an entire people.''

"But Yuri said that—" she hesitated— "that you gave him a merciful death, compared to what—what he was meant to receive.''

Bakhtiian looked away from her, his expression shuttered. "I am not a savage," he said almost inaudibly.

Tess fell silent. The wind brought to her a sharp, rich fragrance, like vanilla. "It's true," she said finally, "that the world forces us to make bitter choices. I suppose that makes it hard to search for the truth, especially if we believe that truth can only be found along the path that is familiar to us.''

He tossed his knife up. It caught the sunlight and flashed. For that instant, as he watched the knife reach its peak and begin to fall again, his face opened somehow, giving her a glimpse of the boy, twenty years ago, who had played with such dangerous toys with the same unself-conscious joy and absorption with which a child plays with building blocks. Then the knife fell, and he caught it.

"God, isn't that dangerous?"

He laughed. "Of course." He sheathed the knife. "How can any one of us claim to know which paths the gods walk? How can we hope to walk on their path at all? Except for philosophers like Newton, of course."

"Newton walked many strange paths. I have to suppose that all paths have gods of one kind or another. But I think we are responsible for finding our own way."

"We must do what we can with what we have?"

Tess pushed herself to the edge of the wall and jumped down. Bakhtiian put out a hand to steady her landing, a momentary touch, no more. "Is that what you believe?"

"What I believe?" Leaning back against the wall, he folded his arms over his belt. Wind caught a strand of his hair and blew it up away from his forehead. "I don't know where the sun and the moon came from, how the grass and the hills came to be. I suppose they came by themselves. But I believe that there is truth to be found, and I'm not always certain that it is only to be found in the gods. Or in what we call the gods."

"You've been reading too much philosophy."

He smiled. "Is philosophy dangerous?"

"Very dangerous."

"What do you believe, then?"

"I believe that there is truth to be found inside every person, but that very few people find it because it is dark inside, and deeply hidden, and the trees grow thickly."

"But you forget, there are always springs one can drink from." He looked toward the plains. "Ah, there are our fellow mortals."

"Come to bask in the fragrance of immortality, however fleeting?"

"Bask in the fragrance? I think you mean bask in the warmth."

They walked down to the grazing horses to wait for the approaching riders. The jahar splashed over the ford and halted beside them. Most of the riders wandered aimlessly around the ruins, curious. A few drank at the spring. Ishii and Garii and Rakii made the most cursory of inspections before returning to their horses.

Ishii came up to Bakhtiian. "We have seen what we need here. We can go on."

If this surprised Bakhtiian, he concealed it very well. The entire company set off westward, Tess and Bakhtiian waiting till the rest had gone.

"So it is a temple. I knew it."

"I beg your pardon?"

"The khepelli asked to see the zhapolaya, didn't they? Did they ask to see this place as well?"

He blinked. "I am beginning to think the prince has curious concerns. What do you mean?"

"Oh, hell," she said under her breath, but she had no one else to ask and she needed to know. "Specifically, by name."

"Ah," said Bakhtiian, meaning by that breath of a comment nothing Tess could fathom. "Yes, they did. Why do you ask?"

She grinned. "I'm searching for the truth."

He smiled. "Have it your way. For now. I'm patient, and our journey is a long one." He reined his horse out, over the ford.

Tess lingered a moment, staring up at the cliffs. The touch of the gods. She was glad that this place had nothing to do with the Chapalii, that it did indeed have gods, that it existed for itself alone. And she was relieved that the Chapalii didn't know everything there was to know about Rhui, that they had believed these ruins might be of interest to them. In which case, did that mean they had known that the transmitter was a transmitter, or not? Neither prospect was reassuring. She sighed and followed Bakhtiian.

They rode southwest through low hills. In the early afternoon the ground broke under them, the uniformity of the plain disturbed as abruptly as a pebble breaks the still surface of a pond. At first, steep hillocks and low sheer slopes radiated out, and then the earth itself fell away on either side, a few rivulets descending past curves, lost to her sight. Coming around the last of the little hills, they pulled up.

Tess saw the lake first, a pale jewel at the center, before her gaze fanned out to the huge basin that cradled this circle of blue. It was an ancient crater; nothing else could form such a distinctive shape, could be so unnaturally round. Or could account for the strange hills, flung out like debris from some massive impact. A meteor, surely—and then

Myshla shied away from the bright wink of sunlight, glancing off a smooth surface embedded in the ground. Bakhtiian, ahead of her, had not noticed.

Tess pulled up Myshla and stared down. Dirt had eroded away from a plate of metal. It gleamed, uncorroded. A shock of grass obscured most of the plate. In days, Tess thought, the entire patch would be grown over. She dismounted and tried to pry it out, but it was too thick. Where the grass ended, the plate disappeared back under earth. She drew her knife and dug down, working quickly. A third of a meter down there was still no break. This was not the artifact of a primitive culture. Bakhtiian called back to her, and she mounted and urged Myshla forward to catch up with him.

Staring around at the steep slope of the crater, down to the flat-bottomed basin below, she wondered how big a ship, crashing or purposefully blown up, would make such a mark in its leave-taking.

At the same time, she realized that it was not the deepness of the crater but the pall of smoke over the land below that gave the bottom an indistinct tinge. She saw neatly laid out fields, some still green. Others looked strangely altered, as if they had been trampled.

It was the town that was on fire, flames licking up from some of the houses huddled inside the earth wall that from this height seemed pitifully insignificant. In another quarter, a whole street lay blackened, smoking like cold breath on an icy afternoon. Figures ran and labored under the sun. A broken line extended out to the lake, a tenuous string to the water.

"Curse them," said Bakhtiian. "Come on." He turned his horse to ride along the edge of the crater.

"We're not going down there, are we? I didn't know there were settlements out here. What do you think happened?"

"I don't know." His voice, like his shoulders, was as taut as a strung bow. "But see, there are vultures."

She saw the birds, circling near a few squat trees. Below, none of the hurried figures took any notice of the pair far above them.

"I'm sorry," said Bakhtiian suddenly, "that you have to see this."

They weren't trees. They were posts, driven into the ground. Six posts stood in a semicircle just above the well-

trodden path, marked by a solitary seventh post, that led
down into the valley. The birds cried out raucously and
flapped away as Tess and Bakhtiian approached. The stench
hit, fetid, overwhelming.

Three jaran men, clad in red shirts and black trousers,
had been tied to the posts. All three were dead, and while
one, perhaps, had died naturally of his wounds, the manner
of execution of the other two was quite obvious.

"They may have been my enemies," said Bakhtiian quietly, "but I can only hope that they were dead when that
was done to them."

A bird, emboldened by their stillness, settled onto the
slumped head of the farthest body.

"Go away!" Tess kicked Myshla forward. The bird
squawked and fluttered away. She found herself on top of
the scattered and half-eaten entrails that littered the ground
in front of the men. Insects swarmed over the remains. Jerking Myshla hard to the left, she pulled away, gagging, to
halt in front of the solitary post that marked the descent of
the trail.

"Look here," she said quickly, desperate to stop her gagging, to not have to look behind her and see the burnt-out,
bloody eye sockets, the gaping abdomens— "There's writing posted here, but I can't read—here at the bottom it's a
bit like Rhuian. I think that's a 'b' there and some vowel, I
think an 'o' maybe, and I'm sure that's a 'c' but it would
be a hard 'c' if it was related to the northern dialect that
the sailors in Jeds spoke and then that must be—my God!
It's your name." She put one hand over her mouth.

"It was the obvious choice," said Bakhtiian, so close
behind her that her startled gasp almost made her retch.
"Don't be too proud to be sick if you have to," he added,
more gently.

"Not as long as I don't have to touch them. Can you read
what it says?"

"A little. Evidently a jahar attacked and set fire to this
settlement. I suppose their goal was to blame the attack on
me, and thus make the khaja hatred for me greater than it
already is. My enemies have done this before."

"Do you know who they are?"

"Oh, yes. They're Doroskayev's men. You never saw
them."

"No," she said faintly.

''We'd better go.'' He reined his horse around. ''Look. They've seen us.''

''Bakhtiian!'' In her outrage, turning Myshla after him, her gaze flashed past the three strung-up bodies to follow his back. ''Aren't you even going to bury them?''

He kept riding. ''*Bury* them? You'd condemn them to burial for raiding a village?''

She came up beside him as they rounded the curve of a steep hillock, the crater and the site of execution shut out by the slope. ''Condemn? I don't understand.''

''Let's get away from here.'' He urged his horse to a canter. Emerging onto the plain, rolling here toward a range of low hills, they slowed the horses to a walk.

''Forgive me if I was hasty,'' he said after a silence. ''Burial is the worst thing that could happen to the jaran. But perhaps in other places that isn't—'' he shuddered— ''true.''

''It isn't. Why is it so bad?''

He turned his head to stare at her, amazed. ''To be *trapped* beneath the earth, forever separated from the sky, never again to live where the wind can touch you? That is only for the sacrilegious.''

''Is it better to be torn to pieces by the animals?''

''But they are the gods' creatures, scattering our bodies back to the wind. And the wind gathers us up and pours our spirit into the womb of a woman ripe for conception, and the world receives us back again.''

Tess was silent, staring out at the wide stretch of plain, that sudden sink of land lost behind them like a dream. Around them the grass seemed empty of any life but the wind's. ''But I thought you burned the dead.''

''That privilege is only given to those who die in battle, men in honorable war, women in childbirth. The fire releases you from all bonds to the earth, and the gods, alerted to your coming by the bitter herb ulyan, welcome you to the heavens. And your spirit is free forever from this world.''

''And everyone else. . . .''

Bakhtiian said nothing for a moment. ''It is also an honorable death. Many choose it.''

''How can you choose to be left lying on the ground?''

''Old people, ill ones, those who can no longer keep up, often stay behind of their own choosing, knowing that their time has come.''

"You abandon them?" She had such a horrible vision of sitting alone among the grass and insects, figures growing smaller, gone, finally, the sun silent above, that for one wild instant she thought all this the dream and herself still far north, lost forever in grass.

"We move, always. We cannot wait." His eyes, his whole expression, seemed remote, staring at something she could not see. "That is how I intend to die, when the time comes, not seeking to prolong it."

"You have no intention of dying in battle?"

"None at all."

"But you carry ulyan."

Now his gaze focused on her, but it made her feel quite isolated. "But I don't. I want to come back."

They rode the rest of the way in silence. The three men, hung out like leavings for the birds, and the half-buried plate of metal ran like loops through her mind, first one, then the other, then the first again, until she wished she could simply stop thinking. Bakhtiian planning war against the khaja; his enemies trying to start that war early to disrupt his plans. Or simply trying, one way or the other, to get him killed? Or simply enamored of killing—how was she to know? The moon was up when, having been challenged by three separate sentries, she and Bakhtiian trotted over a low hill and down into the scatter of tents.

Niko jogged up to them immediately and took the reins of Ilya's horse. "So many sentries?" Bakhtiian asked.

"Tasha spotted a scout this morning and held on, but the fellow veered east. Josef got a glimpse of him this afternoon, but he slanted off again. Josef thinks he's solo."

Bakhtiian nodded as he bent to check his mount's left foreleg. "See here. It's swollen and hot." Niko frowned with concern and examined the stallion's leg while Ilya watched. "Let's see if we can lure this scout in tonight and capture him. I wonder if Mikhailov has at last picked up our trail or even joined up with Doroskayev? Gods, I can't believe Mikhailov would stoop so low."

"Couldn't it be one of Doroskayev's men?" Niko asked.

Bakhtiian smiled slightly and, glancing up at Tess, moved decisively to hold Myshla's bridle so that she, too, could dismount. "But we have news," he said as Tess swung down, "that will put things in quite a different light. As-

semble the riders. Single sentry should be sufficient for
now.'' Niko nodded and went off.

"Do I have to hear this?" Tess asked.

"No. Yuri will have put up your tent." He led the black
away.

Finding herself alone in the gloom, Tess allowed the tears
to come, but the force of them overwhelmed her and she
shut her eyes, leaning against the comforting bulk of Myshla.
The image of the three mutilated bodies flared so vividly in
her mind that she gasped.

"Tess?" She put out her hand and grasped substance, an
arm, the silken sleeve of a shirt, ridged with embroidery.

"Fedya." She opened her eyes.

"It will only be a short assembly."

"Yes." Her fingers slipped down his arm to grasp his
hand. "Afterward."

"Past the horses is a spring and past that a copse." He
squeezed her hand, so gentle a pressure that the feeling it
left vanished as quickly as he did, gone after Bakhtiian.

She unsaddled Myshla, checked her hooves doubly carefully, groomed her and hobbled her and set her out with the
other horses under Pavel's care. Pavel nodded at her but he
was busy plastering a cold compress of herbs on the foreleg
of Bakhtiian's black, the fine khuhaylan stallion that no one
wanted to lose to lameness. The saddle was an easier burden
than her thoughts as Tess walked through camp, past the
assembly to the very edge of the tents, where Yuri had
pitched hers.

As she knelt to dump the saddle on the ground, she saw
four Chapalii walk out over a low rise into the darkness.
Making a quick tour back through camp, she realized there
were no Chapalii anywhere, unless the rest were all in their
tents. Surely they could not intend to trek all the way back
to the crater by night? A ship, blowing up. . . . What if it
had been a Chapalii ship? But that was impossible. Whatever impact had made that crater had occurred millennia
ago. Had there been an alien empire before the Chapalii? A
greater one than theirs? A hundred possibilities presented
themselves. She circled around toward the spring, passing
Nikita on sentry duty, and then she was alone again.

She found the Chapalii past the copse, hidden by a rise.
They had gathered in a tight clump in the declivity made by
the joining of two rises. On her hands and knees, pausing

just behind the crest, she could make out all eleven figures, shadowed by the moon. A tiny blue-white light gleamed softly from within their ranks. The night lay still around her. No breeze stirred the air. Voices drifted up to her, phrases broken by pauses and replies.

". . . identified two previous . . . unsure whether the duke . . . Keinaba . . . constant surveillance . . . insufficient evidence to believe . . ."

A communication. They were communicating—with whom? A Chapalii ship? But none stayed in orbit around Rhui. How far *could* they transmit? How far did this conspiracy reach? She pulled the little knife Garii had given her from her belt, and hunkered down even more to conceal herself from them as she stared at it. White lights speckled the hilt. She hadn't a clue how to operate it, and either Garii had purposefully left her ignorant or he had simply not thought he needed to tell her. Tess stuck it back in her belt and lifted herself up carefully to watch again. The scene had not changed.

Wind moved the grass above them. Startled, Tess looked in that direction. In the instant before she really saw, she realized that a man was creeping down on them, was halfway down the hill opposite. Light-haired? Had Nikita followed her? But this man was stocky. *My God!* She stood up. Fedya must have come after her.

At that same moment one of the Chapalii said something, a slight cry. As if in sudden panic, another of the aliens whirled and crouched. Light streaked out soundlessly toward the man on the hill. He seemed to leap backward, half-rising. The thin line of light cut out through the night again, and the man fell, tumbling down the slope to land at the feet of the aliens. Tess cried out and ran down to him.

Ishii's voice. "Do not shoot her, you imbeciles."

She stopped short, facing four knives. Red beads of light shone sharply at their hilts. Armed. Lethal.

"Let me go to him." Her voice broke on the edge of a sob.

"Let her go," said Ishii. A path formed for her.

She stumbled past them, collapsing on her knees beside the body. The second shot had opened up his abdomen, a cleaner cut than those endured by Doroskayev's men, half cauterized by heat. Blood seeped onto the grass. "Oh, God, Fedya," she cried, reaching out to touch his shoulder.

Her touch jostled his head, and it rolled, back, staring at her, one eye strangely shut. One eye scarred shut. It was not Fedya at all, but Doroskayev. She jerked her hands back. The Chapalii clustered around her.

Ishii stood above her, seeming almost to touch the sky. "How fortunate that it is not one of Bakhtiian's men. For a moment I feared that my man's rashness would be irreparable, but now I see he may have done Bakhtiian a service." Tess stood up slowly, still shaking. "Excuse my impertinence in speaking without your leave, Lady Terese, but I saw that this situation needed a male's firmness. Please allow me to assure you again that we have never wished to do you any harm. You have only to say the word, and the suspicions that have grown between us shall be laid to rest." He clasped his hands in that arrangement known as Lord's Supplication.

Tess stared at him. She shook. She did not dare look down at the body. She had not the slightest idea what to do with her hands. Ishii could have let his men kill her, could have buried her, and who would have known? Standing alone among them, their only witness the moon and the stars, she could not imagine any human set against her in such a delicate dance showing such forbearance. She outranked him; she was heir to a Chapalii dukedom; she was sacrosanct. Ishii gazed back at her. The moon washed his face so pale it seemed almost translucent. Like the plains beyond, the Chapalii mind had many aspects that seemed unchanging to an alien. Lost in that careful game of diplomacy and treachery that Charles and the Chapalii played with each other; lost on these uncharted plains of Rhui; the two circumstances of her life seemed very similar right now.

"Truce," she said.

"You honor us, Lady Terese." He bowed, and the others echoed the bow as befitted their stations. Straightening, he turned to his men. "Cut away the sod carefully. We must inter him so that there is no trace. Perhaps, Lady Terese, you will indulge us by identifying this man. He was, I think, one of Bakhtiian's enemies?"

"Yes."

Emboldened by her passivity, Ishii went on. "Perhaps you will permit me to allow Hon Garii to escort you back to camp? You need not stay for the interment. I understand very well that females have heightened sensibilities."

They moved away from her, preparing a grave. Trapped beneath the earth. Had Doroskayev deserved such a fate? She walked past them, stumbling slightly in the darkness. Garii followed her, unasked. At the base of the hill, she stopped. He stopped behind her. Without turning around she put her hand on her knife.

"How do I use this?" she whispered.

He did not reply immediately. When she tilted her hand to see him, she saw that he had glanced back to where dark figures worked just beyond the crest of the rise.

"If I may be permitted to speak, I have attuned it to human use, Lady Terese," he said at last. "The heat of your thumb, pressed over the third and second lights, causes the beam to activate. Forgive me. A thousand thousand pardons be granted me that I did not realize you needed instruction in this gift."

"You are pardoned," she said automatically.

"I am yours, Tai-endi," he said, the formal response, and he bowed, as liegeman to his liege.

"Go," she said hastily, abruptly afraid that she had acknowledged something far deeper than she realized. "Ishii will be watching."

"As you command." He retreated back up the hill.

I am yours. Lord, Tess, you've gotten yourself into it now. The wording had been precise and formal: the bond of servant to master, not any slight thing bound by a wage or a common goal, but true fealty. Surely Garii was already bonded to Ishii's family, and such bonds lasted until death, and beyond death into the next generations.

Light flashed, a brief, searing pulse, and she started and hurried away toward the copse and the spring. Bodies on grass. They should leave him to rot. She would have been left out there, months ago, walking on the plains. A body could lie a hundred years in such space—

By the spring, someone waited for her, sitting on a low rock. She broke into a jog, remembering how she thought they had killed him.

"Fedya," she said. Stopped. It was Bakhtiian. A blanket and his cloak lay, folded neatly, on the rock beside him.

"Did you catch a glimpse of our mysterious escort?" he said with a slight smile, but his tone was serious and his eyes met hers. One of his hands rested casually on his blanket. "But if he eluded Josef, he could elude anyone."

For a long moment she could not speak. "I'm sorry," she said finally. "I just had to be alone. I'm modest."

"All good women are."

"And good men?"

"Even more so," he answered, not a trace of humor in his voice. There was a pause. "We're extending our sentry ring tonight," he said at last. "If you feel crowded in your tent, it would be safe, tonight, for you to sleep outside of camp."

"I know."

Blanket and cloak tucked under one arm, he stood up so that they faced one another on a level. "I understand that you have sustained a shock."

"Oh, hell," said Tess under her breath, putting one hand to her face to stop the sudden flow of tears. Bakhtiian took one step toward her. Footsteps rustled in the grass.

"Tess?" He came up beside her, bedroll in one hand, cloak slung over his shoulders. "Ilya!" Now he was startled.

There was a very long silence.

"Excuse me," said Bakhtiian abruptly, and he left.

"Tess." Fedya reached up and gently drew her hand down from her face. "In the morning, it will not seem so terrible."

And in the morning, it did not.

In the morning, Niko rode out with her and Bakhtiian. They circled back but found nothing, from which both men concluded that the trailing scout had veered off. Around noon, coming back to the copse and spring they had left that morning, they spotted the jahar away to their left where, Tess thought, they surely should not be. The range of hills dwindled away in front to the familiar flatness of plain. The three of them dismounted and crouched on the height, the horses downslope behind them.

Tess saw their jahar out on the plain. But the riders still in the hills—another jahar. Closing quickly, too quickly, with their position.

"Niko," said Bakhtiian crisply. "Get our jahar to cover. I'll delay them. We're not ready for a battle, not yet." But Niko did not answer, was already on his horse and riding.

"How long until they reach the spring?" Tess asked.

"Not long enough, although they may stop to water the

horses. That can't be Doroskayev. They can't know we're so close, or they'd not be pacing themselves. . . . Why are you still here?'' He stared at her as if he had just seen her. ''Follow Niko.''

''What are you going to do?''

''Decoy them back the way they've come.''

''But once they see you, they'll know your jahar is near. How many will bother to follow a lone man?''

''If that man is Ilyakoria Bakhtiian, quite a few.''

She glanced to where his remount stood, a stocky tarpan. ''They'll catch you.''

''I'll ride Myshla. They won't catch us. Now, woman. Go.''

Tess jumped up and ran back to the horses, grabbed the tarpan's reins, and mounted Myshla, kicking the mare even before her seat was stable.

''Damn it,'' Bakhtiian yelled, rising. ''Get back here!''

''I suggest you get down in that copse and hide. And hurry.''

He took two stiff steps toward her. ''Damn you, Soerensen. This doesn't concern you. I *said*—''

''You're wrong. I need to get to Jeds, urgently. If you stay there, they'll run you down.'' She reined Myshla farther away. ''You'd better go. We haven't got much time. Trust me.''

She turned Myshla and cantered down the slope to the copse, the remounts trailing behind. *How to throw them off the scent, how?* She tethered the two horses securely to a tree and pulled off the distinctive jahar saddles, obscuring them with the saddlebags. She ripped open her saddlebags, cursing under her breath; everything was jaran, everything. Why hadn't she even brought a change of clothing from the ship?

''Oh, God, Tess, you're in for it now.'' What was it she had once said about maenads and madness? Sometimes you had to choose all or nothing. And sometimes your weakness became your strength. All at once she knew what to do.

She strewed all her belongings about, piling them into disarray so that their provenance might be concealed. She took her blanket and ran back into the nearest screen of trees and awkwardly—for who knew where Bakhtiian was now—took off her tunic and trousers and wrapped herself in her cloak. It was difficult enough to go out there clad in her underclothes, underneath the cloak, but she had to trust what she knew of jaran culture. The white blouse Nadezhda Martov had given her was generic enough, seen from a distance, so she drenched it in the spring and dampened her Earth-made tunic and trousers and retreated to the edge of the trees, hanging the clothing over bushes to dry. She unlaced her boots and left them by the clothes, but not before stuffing her bracelets inside them; hid the saber and knife under the saddles, but kept the Chapalii knife with her, and finally rolled out her bedroll at the edge of the screen of trees and sat down on it. Nervously she fingered her necklace, the pewter ankh from Sojourner.

The branches of one lopsided tree scraped incessantly against the trunk of another. On the other side of the water hole, the low rock Bakhtiian had sat on last night lay naked and dark in the midday sun. There was no sign of him. She prayed that he had taken refuge deep in the farthest screen of trees. She touched the hilt of the knife and withdrew her hand. Her palms were slick with sweat.

Then came the sound of hooves, pounding along the earth.

There were at least forty of them, scarlet shirts with low collars and banded cuffs, black trousers cut fuller than those of Bakhtiian's men but clearly jaran. They pulled up, undeniably amazed. She leapt to her feet with a cry of surprise, managing to almost let her cloak fall without actually revealing anything.

By the looks on their faces when the cloak slipped, she knew she would succeed.

CHAPTER TWELVE

"Of pleasures, those that come most rarely
give the greatest enjoyment."
—DEMOCRITUS OF ABDERA

"Why have you come back?" she cried in Rhuian. She
clutched her cloak with both hands, pinning it closed at her
chest. "You said you were going to the great temple of the
goddess. You cannot have gotten there and back so soon."

A good three dozen or more men stared at her, and she
suddenly doubted herself. She was utterly vulnerable to them
except for the Chapalii knife belted over her underclothes,
a weapon she had never used and was not certain she could
use. How could she be sure Garii was the least bit trustworthy? Wind pulled up one corner of her cloak, revealing
a glimpse of knee. As if it were a signal, the men's gazes
flicked away one by one, and most of them colored as they
looked at anything but her. Her hands gripped the cloth
more tightly and she forced herself to breathe slowly. It had
to work, it could still work, and yet it all rested on this:
manners, custom.

A hurried consultation began among the leading rank of
riders. She used its cover to look them over as surreptitiously as possible: like all jaran, most of these riders were
light-haired and fair-complexioned with a sprinkling of
darker ones throughout, but she recognized none of them,
only the characteristic scarlet shirts boasting embroidered
sleeves and collars and black trousers and boots that proclaimed these to be jahar riders.

Finally three of the men dismounted and walked slowly
toward her. They kept their eyes averted. The grass made a
low whispering sound as they passed through it. The first,
a man of Bakhtiian's age, tall and very fair and unusually

handsome even for a man of the jaran, glanced at her frequently but did not meet her gaze. The other two men were older. The man on the right had a sullen, angry expression, and he regarded her with the most direct gaze, suspicious of her. He looked like the kind of man who is suspicious of all people. The third man, in the middle, was the oldest, his fair hair silvering, his shoulders bowed, his expression that of a man harassed beyond all bearing. When the other two halted a decent two body-lengths from her, he came forward another three steps and stopped.

"Do you speak khush?" he asked.

Tess shrank back a step, feigning confusion.

"What is a woman doing out here on her own?" said the sullen man. "Do you think she's from that khaja town? She may recognize us."

The middle-aged man hunched his shoulders even more, frowning. "She may recognize *you*, Leotich. My men had nothing to do with that idiotic raid. Could you understand what she said, Vasil?" This to the blond.

An auspicious time to break in. "Who are you?" Tess asked in Rhuian. "You are not the men I talked to before."

Vasil tilted his head, thinking hard. "Something about men. But she speaks too quickly."

"But it is this—*Rhu-an?*"

"I think so."

Tess shrank further into her cloak and spoke very slowly and with precise enunciation. "Can you understand me?"

Vasil smiled suddenly. It lit his face like fire, and Tess caught herself staring at him even as he looked right at her, and he flushed and shifted his gaze. His eyes were a vivid, fiery blue. "I speak," he said hesitantly. "Little."

"Only a little?" She emphasized the disappointment in her tone, and then wondered if she was overdoing it. "The other man spoke Rhuian very well."

"Man?" Unconsciously, Vasil leaned toward her. Necklaces swung forward from his chest. "Other man? He speak?"

"Yes. He spoke like a native but he wore much the same clothes as you do. Is he one of you? Is he here with you?"

"I'm sure of it, Dmitri." Vasil looked triumphant. "A man who spoke with her in Rhuian. It has to be Bakhtiian." Leotich glared at her obliquely, lips tight.

"What else did she say?"

"I don't know."

Tess lowered her eyes, not wanting to seem too interested in a conversation she ought not to understand. She resisted the urge to glance at her belongings, at the copse behind, wondering if it all concealed her true purpose as well as she hoped. Wondering if it concealed Bakhtiian.

"I'll try again," said Vasil to Dmitri. He coughed, hesitated again. "Man," he said. "Other man." He sighed, frowned, concentrated, and then when she glanced up at him, he gave up and pointed to his scarlet shirt. "Is?"

"Yes, yes." Tess let her hold on her cloak slacken slightly. "Such clothes, red shirt, black trousers." She let one arm emerge to point at their clothing and then did risk a half turn to look behind her, where her traveling clothes—obviously foreign—lay drying on the bushes. The white-barked trees beyond stood stark, barely clothed with scant green in the sunlight. When she looked back, all three men were looking not at her, or her clothes, but at each other.

"It has to have been Ilya," said Vasil in a fierce undertone, almost exultant. "It has to."

"Don't get too excited," said Leotich to Vasil.

Vasil's head jerked back, one hand brushing his knife hilt. "Don't tempt me," he muttered.

"Vasil!" Standing between them, Dmitri lifted his chin, and that gesture alone convinced Tess that he was the man to be reckoned with. "Find out which direction."

Vasil returned his attention to the ground on Tess' left. "Other men. Where?"

"Other men! Yes, there were many others, and they were going, like me, to the great temple, but they would not take me with them."

"Many? Temple? Temple!" He grasped Dmitri by one arm. "Many of them, going to the old temple near the town."

"But Doroskayev said they were behind us." Leotich's frown made his eyes pinch together with suspicion. "How could they have gotten ahead of us? Why would they turn back?"

"Gods, man," said Dmitri. "Who knows *why* Bakhtiian does what he does? He may have gone past the temple and then gone back. He's a far more religious man than you are."

Leotich snorted in disgust.

"And since I obviously must remind you, he is escorting a party of khaja pilgrims. There is a reason to return to the temple. Perhaps he was forced to avoid it in the first place because of Doroskayev's idiocy."

Leotich's pale eyes focused on the other man, and he kicked at the grass, tearing a thin scar in the ground. "Doroskayev is the only one with any kind of plan. Whatever you may think of his raids, he always leaves Bakhtiian's name. Even if Bakhtiian eludes us, someday he'll come too close to khaja lands and they'll kill him for us, for revenge."

"Doroskayev is a fool." Dmitri's voice, sharp as the winter wind, froze them all. "He has played into Bakhtiian's hands, and I, by the gods, intend to tell him so when we meet up with his jahar. Bakhtiian says the khaja are a threat. Doroskayev will stir up a war and then they will be a threat. Don't you see? Now Bakhtiian can justify his work. Fool and idiot twice over."

Leotich's frown had turned into a scowl. "Doroskayev said Bakhtiian had a woman with him. How do we know she isn't some trick of Bakhtiian's, left here to throw us off the scent?"

Vasil flushed with anger. "You're no better than a khaja pig, Leotich. Bakhtiian would never put a woman in such danger."

"You'd know, wouldn't you," snarled Leotich.

Vasil put his hand on his saber. Leotich grinned, almost feral.

"Stop quarreling!" Dmitri's voice cracked over them. Tess huddled backward, cringing away from their angry voices, not entirely pretending fear. "Doroskayev!" His disgust for his ally was all too evident in his tone. "Since when do we believe everything Doroskayev says? None of his men saw a woman. Whatever else you may think, Leotich, I've studied Bakhtiian for years. I know him as I know my own brother, as only one enemy can know another. Bakhtiian would never devise such a ploy as this. Gods, Vasil, see if you can make the woman understand we mean her no harm."

"Why would a woman be out here alone?" Leotich put in, uncowed by Dmitri's speech.

"Vasil?"

Vasil sighed, facing Tess again. "Temple," he said

slowly, as if he knew that his pronunciation was terrible. "Men—temple. You—see?"

Tess untwisted one hand from her cloak, realizing that this was at last the real test: knowing nothing about khaja culture, she had to hope they knew even less. "I go to the temple." She pulled out her ankh necklace, holding it by the chain and displaying it to them as if it ought to mean something to them. Then, dropping it, she crossed herself, because it was the most pious gesture she could think of. More by accident than design, her cloak slipped again to reveal one pale thigh. With an exclamation, she yanked it tightly around her. The three men looked away.

"She's going to the temple," said Vasil in a low voice to Dmitri. He looked sidewise toward Tess. "You go? Temple?"

"Yes. Yes."

"Men? Men go?"

"Men go to temple. Men go. To temple. To temple."

"I take it," said Dmitri dryly, "that they were going to the temple."

"Think straight, Mikhailov," snarled Leotich, jerking his head to one side. "It doesn't add up. How did they get ahead of us? How do we know it's the same group? And what about her? Why is she here?"

"You saw her necklace, the sign she made." Vasil took one step toward Leotich. The top of his saber pushed down the grass beside him. "She must be a pilgrim."

"Bakhtiian has pilgrims with him. She could be one of them."

"Why are you talking for so long?" asked Tess in a high, hurried voice that she did not have to feign. "Why don't you leave me and go on your way? Is it not penance enough that I must travel this barbaric land alone? Must I be threatened with savages as well?"

"You're frightening her," said Vasil.

"Frightening her!" Leotich took one aggressive step toward Tess. "Greater things are at stake here, Veselov. Doroskayev said—"

"I'm beginning to suspect you're a fool, too." Dmitri reached out and took hold of Leotich's sleeve with enough pressure that the man had no choice but to step back. "Karol Arkhanov saw those pilgrims. Eleven, he said, tall and very pale, all men. His word is good enough for me."

"My clothes are there," Tess broke in, desperate now for them to leave. Vasil, glancing at her, blushed and looked away when her gaze met his. "And here I am, surrounded by men." She took out her necklace again. "I am a pilgrim, a holy woman. What do you mean to do?"

"Come on," said Vasil. "We've frightened her enough. Let's go."

"I don't believe it," said Leotich. "I want to see what she's got on underneath that cloak." He put his hand on his knife and strode forward before the other men could react. Tess jerked back, twisting free of his grasping hand, and an involuntary cry escaped her. She stumbled back and fell to her knees.

Dmitri grabbed Leotich and yanked him up short. Vasil had his knife out, but he sheathed it again. Behind, the men in the jahar murmured, a swell of disbelief that faded as Leotich stood stiff and angry in Dmitri's grasp.

"Gods, man," said Dmitri. "You'll get a reputation no man could live down."

Tess sank down into the most abject huddle she could make, kneeling, and fumbled inside her cloak for the knife, palming it.

"No." Leotich wrenched free of Dmitri. "Maybe Doroskayev was mistaken. Maybe Bakhtiian didn't have a woman with his jahar. But let's ask Vasil. After all, he knows better than anyone else whether Bakhtiian would have any use for a woman."

Vasil backhanded him, hard. Leotich lunged at Vasil, but the younger man caught his blow on an arm and slugged him. Dmitri stepped between them and grappled for their arms. The scuffle neared Tess, and she scuttled backward, hand clutching her knife beneath her cloak.

The movement brought them all up short, as if it had suddenly reminded them of her presence. Dmitri now had both of Leotich's wrists in his hands. "Sometimes I don't know what I brought you for." His voice was tight with contempt.

Leotich glared at him, pulling back. "We could at least split up. One to check out her story, the other to go on."

Dmitri let him go with a snort of disgust. "Splitting up is the stupidest thing a jahar can do. We'll catch him. Now get back to your horse." However nondescript a man he might appear, he had command. Leotich sulked away.

"So." He let his gaze come to rest on Vasil, and Tess could not interpret the expression with which he viewed the younger man. Vasil met his gaze without shame, but it was obvious that the younger man was still angry. "So, Vasil," Dmitri continued, "I believe it was agreed that you might ride with my jahar if you kept your grievances to yourself."

"It will not happen again."

"Well, then, can you make her understand that we mean her no harm?"

Vasil glanced at Tess and lowered his eyes, a lock of pale hair falling carelessly across his cheek. Tess wondered, quite at random, what it would be like to push that lock of hair aside, what he, the sum of his particular pleasing parts, would be like as a lover. Lord, she was beginning to think like a jaran woman! He took one tentative step toward her.

"Go away! Go away!" she cried, shrinking back.

Vasil shrugged and looked at Dmitri.

"So be it. At least we can track Bakhtiian now. Come on." Dmitri turned away and walked back to the jahar. Vasil hesitated. He removed a necklace from around his neck and, crouching, laid it on the ground as slowly as if she were a wild animal.

"For you," he said in Rhuian. He mounted and they all left, riding back the way they had come, northeast, back toward the temple.

Her heart beat as hard as if she had been running all this time instead of talking. When they disappeared from view, she sank back on her heels. All of her breath gusted out. Her hand still gripped the knife. After a bit, she uncurled her fingers and sheathed it. They would never meet with Doroskayev, and suddenly she felt glad that the Chapalii had killed him. She moved forward and picked up the necklace, draping it across her palm, amberlike stones strung on bronze links. It lay cool and smooth in her hand. Rare. She smiled. A gift from a renegade.

"Although," she said aloud, "I suppose that depends on your point of view."

Then she realized that she was still half-naked, and that Bakhtiian was hidden somewhere behind her. She got up hastily and went back to her clothing. It was dry enough. She felt like an idiot, shielding herself with a tree trunk, wrestling her trousers and tunic on under her cloak, but at last she was dressed and could venture out without embarrassment. The grass by the water hole, where she knelt to drink, was brilliantly green, short and slippery and cool to the touch. Last night, she thought, smiling, it had seemed warm. The shifting leaves made patterns of light on her arms. She washed her face, put on her jewelry, and laced on her boots. She hesitated. *What if they returned?* She glanced across the copse of trees but she saw no sign of Bakhtiian. Surely he'd chosen to be as cautious as she had. Adjusting her tunic and her weapons, she hiked to the top of the rise.

The sun beat warmly on her face. At the top, she surveyed the plains around her. There, in the distance, riding northeast, was the enemy jahar. Out on the flat beyond she saw no sign at all of Bakhtiian's jahar. She seated herself on an outcropping of rock and waited, watching, until the enemy jahar vanished entirely from her sight. Then she walked down again.

Halfway down, she spied movement. Bakhtiian appeared, leading out the two horses. He saddled Myshla, and she reached him as he finished the last cinch and turned to saddle his own horse.

He looked up as she approached, pausing with one hand on the saddle. "By the gods, that was Dmitri Mikhailov's jahar."

"You should be furious," said Tess, trying to sound contrite when she really felt like grinning. "I took a great chance."

"There are no chances." He favored her again with that unreadable look. "You succeed or you fail. Battles are not won by men who refuse to take risks." It was quiet. Only the rustle of an animal in the undergrowth disturbed the sighing of the wind through the leaves. He returned to cinching up the saddle, the tarpan patient under his hands.

"Do you know, Bakhtiian, they were all good men."

He glanced at her. "How do you mean?"

"They were all modest." Now she grinned. She simply could not resist the urge.

His head tilted to one side and one eye narrowed, giving him a quizzical look. "Do you mean you—" He straightened, putting his hands on his hips. "The cloak, the clothes, a female alone. You did it all on purpose. You meant all along to embarrass them." He burst out laughing, full laughter, without restraint and yet not uncontrolled. Tess suddenly felt extremely flattered. He stopped laughing and favored her with a smile. "Gods, you're a dangerous woman. Using our own customs against us."

"No more dangerous than you, Bakhtiian."

"Perhaps." He finished with his horse while she packed up her saddlebags and tied her belongings on to Myshla. "So they're going back to the temple."

"How did you know?"

"I deduced it." He grinned. "Penance, indeed. I was also close enough to hear."

"I never saw you!"

He blinked, guileless. "You weren't supposed to. Do I really speak Rhuian like a native?"

"You have an accent," she admitted, "but you speak Rhuian very, very well."

"Thank you," he said, and she thought the comment sincere. "We should go." But he paused with one hand on the saddle. "Vasil left something for you."

"Do you know them *all?* All the men who are riding against you?"

"Not all of them. Just the important ones, the ones whose grudge against me is so deep that they will not give it up unless they are dead." He waited.

She took off the necklace and handed it to him. He looked almost discomposed as he took it from her.

"This is precious." He turned the stones over in his hands, slipped them through his fingers as if their touch communicated some message to him. "Very rare. The stone comes from a princedom south of Jeds, and it is crafted by a master jewel-smith in the Tradesmen's Quarter."

"In Jeds? How would a jahar rider get a necklace from Jeds?"

But Bakhtiian's face had shuttered, and he gave her back the necklace without a word and mounted his horse. "We must go." He rode off without waiting for her, and she hastened to follow. They paused at the crest to gaze north and south, but there was no sign of men or horses, only the smooth, golden flow of grass spreading out on all sides. Tess gazed, watching ripples of wind stir the blanketing gold, and she felt—happy. Somehow, somewhere, she had developed an affection for this peculiarly same yet diverse land. Some movement of Bakhtiian's made her glance at him. He was watching her. When she met his gaze, he did not look away, but stranger still, he seemed, for an instant, shy.

"Will you call me Ilya?" His hands lay still on his horse's neck. His voice sounded as studied and calm as ever. She might have hallucinated that glimpse of shyness.

"If you will call me Tess."

"Perhaps—" He hesitated again, slowly put out a hand. "Clasp friends?"

"I'm not sure I understand."

"It is a mark of friendship. I give my honor into your hands, and you may call on it if you are in need. And your honor into my hands, the same. But it is not a gift to be lightly given or lightly used."

"No," she breathed, staring at him. Here, now, he was asking her to be not only his friend but his equal. "Of course." Her voice shook slightly. "Of course I will clasp friends with you. Ilya." She took his hand in hers.

"I am honored. Tess."

By evening, when they caught up with the others, she felt so pleased with herself that she engaged Cha Ishii in the meaningless, polite, but deviously complex formalities of Chapalii dinner conversation just to test her adroitness. When she tired of that, she collected her blankets and sat out alone, just breathing in the cool air and watching the moon. Behind she could hear the riders laughing, pausing, and laughing again as Bakhtiian told the story of her encounter, no doubt embellishing it with a great deal of exaggeration. After a bit they quieted, and she guessed that a serious council was taking place.

Sometime later Fedya found her. "Tess." He chuckled. "You're a marvel." She could see only the pale oval of his face in the moonlight as he settled down to sit beside her. The night bled all color from his shirt. "To fool Mikhailov. That is the marvel."

"Fedya, how well does Bakhtiian know these men?"

He shrugged. "Mikhailov has been riding against Ilya for years."

"What will they do next?"

He shrugged again, but it was a fatalistic gesture this time. "They'll find out you sent them wrong. We have to prepare."

An insect ran up her hand. She started, shuddering, and shook it off. "Prepare for what?" But even as she said it, she knew what he would reply. If Bakhtiian respected Mikhailov so much, then any battle against him would not fall out as easily as that night skirmish against Doroskayev and his men had. People died in real battles.

"They outnumber us, but we know where they are. We'll choose the ground and ambush them." Perhaps Fedya felt her shiver, though they were not touching. He put his hand on hers, a comforting gesture, but his skin felt cold. "Don't worry," he said softly. "*You'll* be safe. I promise it."

"Safe," she murmured, and she kissed him, wanting more comfort than that.

CHAPTER THIRTEEN

"Courage minimizes difficulties."
—DEMOCRITUS OF ABDERA

They rode for six days, until they came to a range of rugged hills that severed the flat monotony of the plains like a knife. Here they halted, setting up the jahar's tents at the mouth of a canyon and the Chapalii tents what Tess judged to be about a kilometer away in a sheltered hollow. For two nights the riders slept in their tents. On the third, they slept in the scrub. Late on the afternoon of the fourth day, Fedya asked Tess if she would like to go hunting, and Tess, feeling nervous and jumpy, and knowing full well that she had seen no game in these hills, understood the invitation to be a smoke screen for his real intentions. She strapped on her quiver and rode out with him.

Their trail soon led to a rocky overhang close by, but well-hidden from, the Chapalii camp. Bushes and vines screened off the entrance from the casual eye. He pushed them aside and, ducking under the overhanging lip, she went in. Light filtered through the leaves, dappling the bed of moss and grass he had laid for them on the earth. The gesture was so touching and so intimate that she felt embarrassed suddenly, afraid that her feelings for him—tenderness and liking crossed with simple desire—might prove inadequate for his toward her. What if he loved her? She halted on her knees beside the little bed, hands buried in soft moss, knowing that she could never really *love* him, not as more than a friend and bedmate, not with her entire being. She was not sure anymore if she could love anyone in that way, the way she had thought she had loved Jacques.

Fedya stood just behind her. He laid a hand tenderly on

her shoulder. "I made you a song, Anya," he said softly, and then he chuckled, because he had just called her by his wife's name. "Forgive me, Tess. I have not made a song since she died."

Tess caught her breath, relieved and touched at the same time. "I am honored, Fedya," she said, equally softly, and she felt a sudden warmth toward him, unrelated to their friendship, to their lovemaking, because that inadvertent slip made the truth so evident that she could not believe she had not seen it until now: she had never loved Jacques, just as he had never loved her. She had been infatuated with him, certainly, but love—Fedya had *loved* his wife. She did not feel diminished because he loved Anya still, though his Anya was dead and he stood here with a different woman. "I hope you will sing it for me."

"For what other reason would I make it, if not to sing it for you?" He knelt across from her, head slightly bowed by the slope of the overhang, and he sang. It was a song about the legendary dyan Yuri Sakhalin who, wounded unto death, had come to beg healing from the daughter of the sun.

Tess stretched out and leaned on her elbows, cushioned by the moss and his blanket, and watched him, transfixed. Singing, he was entirely with her and yet entirely away from her, so that she could really look at him, at his face, his shock of pale hair and the curve of his mouth, the elaborate design of birds embroidered into the sleeves and collar of his shirt, the fine spiraling patterns worked into his leather belt, his saber, lying parallel to his legs where he sat. In a more luxurious land he would have tended to plumpness, but this land had made him lean and tough, hardened with the riding. Yet his voice was sweet, as fragile as a budding flower. And when he finished, silence lay on him as naturally as song had.

"It's beautiful, Fedya," she said, a little in awe. "Thank you." She kissed him.

"Remember it. Remember this place."

Tess let her face slide in against his neck. His hair brushed her eyes. "He's chosen this place for the ambush," she said, because for four days no one, not even Yuri, had spoken a word to her about fighting.

He slipped his hand down to her back, holding her against him. "The plains are wide, but when men travel on a set

path, they are very small, indeed.'' His fingers found her
waist and explored it to the clasp of her belt.

''Too small to run?'' His hair smelled of grass. ''Too
small to avoid—your pursuer?''

''Tess,'' he said. ''There are better things to think of,
this night, than war and death.''

She woke with a start. Someone in her dream had been
calling her name insistently, unable to reach her.

''Tess. Tess.'' The voice was wrong. That voice and her
name did not belong together in waking life. Therefore, she
was still asleep. But as she opened her eyes, she knew the
voice for Bakhtiian's. She reached out her hand—

Fedya was gone.

''Tess.''

Light infiltrated their bower. It had been dark when she
had fallen asleep. Her clothes lay in a heap at her feet, so
tangled that she had to pull them apart and set them in a
neat row before she could put them on. Her hands shook.
She tried to tuck in her shirt with one hand and comb her
hair with the other, gave it up, and tucked her trousers into
her boots instead. Crawling on her hands and knees to the
entrance, pushing through leaves, untangling a vine from
her hair, she stood up just outside. His back was to her.

''Ilya?'' Morning sun shone brightly in her eyes. She had
to squint, and still she could not make him out clearly. He
turned. She saw, with a shock, the streak of blood down his
face, and then, like a rush of sick trembling, she realized
that it was not his blood at all but someone else's. ''The
blood,'' she gasped.

His hand lifted and explored his cheek. He looked surprised, as if he had not noticed it before. ''I must have been
too close when I killed him,'' he said conversationally. His
body was tense with controlled energy: nervousness or perhaps exhilaration. She shuddered. What had he said?

''Killed who?'' Her hand rose to touch, on her own face,
the area the blood covered on his.

''I don't know,'' he said cheerfully. ''He was about to
gut Niko. By the gods, woman, I couldn't let a man do that
to my oldest friend.'' He sat down abruptly and his expression changed so completely that it frightened her. ''Listen,
Tess. I have to tell you something.''

The world was silent, waiting on his words. They were

too far from the jahar camp, even from the Chapalii camp, to hear—anything—and there was not even wind to rustle the grass. The sun simply shone, painfully bright as it crested the hills. "What happened? Damn it. Tell me."

"No one told— He didn't— Oh, gods." He ripped up a handful of grass and wiped the blood from his cheek. Pale streaks remained, striping his skin.

Tess knew what had happened. She hadn't even said good night to Yuri yesterday afternoon; she'd been in such a hurry to go off with Fedya— She couldn't even picture where she'd left him, last seen him. She sank down onto her knees.

"Who was killed?" she whispered. She almost reached out to touch him.

He looked away, troubled.

"Ilya," she said, his name strange on her lips.

"Fedya."

Tess merely stared at him, caught between relief and disbelief. She had been with Fedya only a few hours past; he was simply gone away for a bit. But Yuri— All her breath sighed out of her and she slumped forward, catching herself on her hands.

"Yuri is alive? Where is he? I want to see him." Fright made her childish. She was horrified that she had slept while blood was shed.

"You can't see him."

"Why not? Why not! He's dead. Just tell me he's dead!"

"Don't go hysterical on me." His voice shook and he leaned toward her, one hand jerking out as if to steady her.

She drew back. "I never faint. Where is Yuri?"

"I sent him with Niko to help the khepelli break their camp and move out. We must travel as far from here as possible today."

"Let me go to him."

"Yes. But after you come with me."

She simply sat, unable to absorb the tone of his voice—implacable or entreating, she could not tell. He frowned, angry or impatient, and took hold of her arm and pulled her to her feet. A kind of haze descended on her. She let him lead her, as if he were afraid she would bolt given the chance, and they walked and walked, grass dragging at their boots. He talked as they went, his voice a level monotone.

"Seven of our riders were injured, but all will live. Eight of the horses, but we'll have to kill three of them, may the gods grant them peace. Six of Mikhaillov's men I know we killed, and at least twelve were hurt, perhaps more. It isn't that we're such better fighters, even though they outnumbered us. We had the advantage. I chose the ground carefully and we ambushed them, forced them to split into two groups. Vasil. . . . The one who gave you the necklace fought well. He got away unhurt.''

He led her down to a place she never had any clear idea of, only glimpses: three men building a fire, the bittersweet smell of ulyan sifting into the air; a bird hovering high above, wings unfolded in some updraft; a dead horse being flayed and its flesh cut into strips for provisions; and beyond it—

"Who was killed?" She would have run, but Bakhtiian held her arm and she knew, anyway, who had been killed. In a way, she had known even before he told her. Bakhtiian waited until they were close to the body before he let her go.

She took one step, and a second, and then stopped. *Fedya.* A blanket lay over him, stained reddish-brown at the chest. He could have been asleep; there was nothing but peace in his face. He looked young, relaxed, unguarded. She moved to kneel by him and glanced up.

They were all turning away, averting their faces, offering her privacy for her grief as the only consolation they could give. Everyone had known, everyone. Yuri had lied to her when he said that no one knew. He had lied to spare her, perhaps to spare Fedya, though surely Fedya had had no illusions about the secrecy of their affair. Lord, had she really thought such a thing could be kept secret?

She stared at his quiet face, and she reached out to touch, briefly, his slack body. She smelled blood and grass, that was all. She should have stayed with the tribe, should have stayed on Earth. And she was afraid because as she gazed at the dead man she felt no grief for him, torn so abruptly and horribly from life, only affection for what he had given her, as if her living, her memory of him, made up for his death. Why had he sung her that beautiful song last night of all nights? How could she have slept through the battle, fought so close, paid for so dearly? How could she not have known and acted to prevent it? Surely there was something she could have done.

"He knew he was going to die," she said aloud, trying

to absolve herself, but all the riders had moved away. She shuddered, drawing her hands in to her chest.

"There are some who seek release from the burdens of earth." It was Bakhtiian's voice, not too close, but low and gentle.

She stood and turned to him. The tears in her eyes blurred his form. "He was protecting me, wasn't he?" she demanded, suddenly furious. "He took me out there to make sure I stayed away from the battle." As if, if he had not, he might still be alive. She walked away from all of them, found her way to the shaded, empty overhang, and wept.

The sun, bright and silent, viewed the earth from her high seat and found nothing there worth mentioning, not even the stretch of ground where so short a time ago two bands had met and struggled and come to a temporary decision. Now the field of battle lay empty, yet from such a height it looked the same whether peopled by fifty or one.

Or two. These two were dark and fair, night and day, maturity and youth. They lay without moving on the slope, watching their horses, watching the vacant plain, watching the last flames of the pyre.

"Ilya?" Vladimir sat up. "Will it storm soon?"

Bakhtiian did not move. "Yes."

"Down from the mountains." Something lit in the eyes of the younger man. "When will we reach the mountains?"

"You should be able to work that out for yourself. Forty days."

Vladimir took a breath, hesitated. "When we get back to our tribe, would you object if—if I marked Elena?"

"Why should I object, Vladi?"

"Why should—?" Vladimir swung his head around so fast that his hair caught for an instant in his eyes. "Don't be coy, damn you. It's common knowledge that she makes up to you every chance she gets."

"Is it?"

"You're laughing at me." He jumped up and began to pace. "You always laugh at me when I talk about this. I know very well you've got no eye for her, but so much is said and— and it's true I've nothing to bring her, being an orphan—and I never know what she thinks, and the gods know I want your approval." He stopped in front of Bakhtiian.

"Vladi, it isn't my approval you need. You'd best discuss this with my aunt. Or Niko's wife, perhaps."

"That's not what I meant."

"I know what you meant. If you worry a bit more about what people are saying or thinking about you, then you'll be almost as unsure of yourself as I was at your age. In this matter, my opinion isn't important."

"It is to me. . . ." Vladimir's comment trailed off into silence. He sat down.

"Vladi, who do you suppose built that temple?" Ilya picked a blade of grass and chewed at it halfheartedly, gazing out over the plain, half watching, half waiting.

"I don't know. The gods did."

"I don't think the gods build in that manner." He traced the curve of his lips with the rough, broken end of the stem. "It must have been long ago. What people could they have been?"

"What were the khaja doing so far out on the plain?"

Bakhtiian curled the stem around one finger and snapped the finger up, splitting the fibers. "I was also wondering that." He touched his tongue to the moisture left on his finger. "I wonder who built the shrine."

"Which shrine?"

"The shrine of Morava. I wonder who she thinks built it."

Vladimir grimaced. "I'm glad I don't have to go to this Uynervirsite in Jheds that everyone talks about. It's madness, wondering so much."

"It might be, at that," said Ilya, sitting straighter and staring at something in the distance. "But don't be so sure you won't have to go."

"Ilya! You wouldn't. Here I've finally got a place and—oh, damn you. I never know when you're joking. Is that Yuri and Niko? Why did you tell the others to send them back?"

Ilya stood and walked down the slope to meet them. They pulled up and dismounted, the horses snuffling and blowing.

"Mikhailov's jahar?" asked Niko.

"Josef and Kirill are still tracking them. Tasha brought me the last report. I think we're rid of them. For now."

Yuri had been looking about. "Ilya, you've got Myshla. Where is Tess?"

"Get her and bring her to the new camp. She's up—" He motioned.

"I know." Yuri led his horse over to Myshla and then, taking both leads in his hands, walked away up into the hills.

"She's been up there all this time?" Niko demanded. "After she saw Fedya? Damn it, Ilya! You know better. Why didn't you go up?"

Bakhtiian looked up at the sky, down at the ground, and, finally, out of the corners of his eyes at the old man. "Because I'm a damned coward."

"Ilya."

Bakhtiian colored, turning quickly to walk over to Vladimir. "Ah, thank you, Vladi." He took the reins Vladimir offered him. "Shall we go?"

Tess watched silently as Yuri left the horses below and climbed the rocky slope. She did not rise as he reached her, but when, wordlessly, he put out a hand, she gave him hers and let him pull her to her feet. They paused a moment, frozen there.

"Oh, Tess," he said, the barest whisper, but his eyes held a grief surely greater than her own. She turned in to him, hugged him for a timeless while. He was alive, he was here with her, solid and comforting. She did not want to think, but her thoughts wound around viciously nonetheless: what if she had been given the choice, to save Yuri or Fedya? Was it wrong of her to be glad that Yuri was alive? Not glad that Fedya was dead, never that, but she could not help but feel that her preference for Yuri, given the inevitability of the death of someone she cared for, had somehow influenced the outcome.

Moisture cooled her face. She pulled back to look at him; tears wet his cheeks. He wiped at them quickly, the movement made jerky by his embarrassment. "Don't tell anyone," he said in a low voice that caught even as he spoke.

"Oh, Yuri, I'm sorry. You knew him better than I did."

He shook his head, unable to reply. In the sun, his hair had the same dull gold cast as the grass.

His sorrow so eclipsed hers as to make her ashamed, and doubly ashamed that where she might be allowed her grief, he must hide his. "Oh, God," she said, directing her shame into self-loathing, "I slept through it. How can anyone sleep while someone else dies?"

"Gods. Tess. I hope you never see battle."

"No. I'd rather have seen it. He was here, and then I woke up, and he'll never come back. I don't want to live like that. I want to see the things affecting me."

"You don't want to see that."

But I do, she thought, but she did not say it. Yuri's face was white and strained. Below, Myshla pawed restlessly at the ground and pulled at the tether. "Where is everyone else?" she asked.

"They've gone on to the new camp."

"Do you mean Bakhtiian has entrusted me to you?"

He rallied. "Just for the afternoon, dear Sister. And we've got a long ride to camp. If we don't get there before dark, Bakhtiian will skin me and use my hide for a tent."

"How revolting, Yuri. And what did the Chapalii think of all this?"

He shrugged, clearly not much interested in the Chapalii. "Lord Ishii is as cold as a stone in winter. He's never the least bit afraid. But the younger one, Garii—he offered to Niko to help him tend the wounded."

"Garii offered to help tend the wounded?"

Yuri nodded.

"And Ishii did not forbid it?"

"Why should he forbid it, Tess? If Garii has some knowledge of healing. . . . Any man would do the same."

"Any *man,*" Tess muttered under her breath, wondering what game Garii was playing now. "Come on." She took two steps down the slope, heading for the horses.

"What's wrong?" he asked when she paused.

"Wait." She hesitated, turning back to regard the entrance to the overhang. With resolve, she crawled back inside where the blanket still lay. She brought it back out, shook it as Yuri stared, and rolled it up neatly. "It's Fedya's blanket," she said at last, when he still did not speak.

"He has a sister," he said finally.

A sister who would mourn him. A sister who did not even know yet that he was dead. Tears filled her eyes, and she wiped at them impatiently, as if that would make them stop.

Yuri took her hand. "Come, Tess," he said softly. They went down together.

CHAPTER FOURTEEN

"The best men choose one thing above all else:
everlasting fame among mortal men."
—HERACLEITUS OF EPHESUS

If they treated Tess more and more like one of their own, she scarcely noticed it because it seemed to flow naturally from her time among them. The ways of the jaran lay in her hands: she examined each one and let it settle within her until her strange hybrid of customs grew so complex and interwoven that, at odd moments, she forgot where one left off and the other began. The days removed her from Fedya's death; he became increasingly the inhabitant of a sequestered dream.

For months now she had become accustomed to the swell and flow of the plain, a grand monotony alleviated by hills and the occasional watercourse slicing through it. But the plains do not continue forever, just as happiness and sorrow both eventually come to an end. Their first hint of the highlands was a rough stretch of land pitted with gorges and rugged valleys that were barren of cover and composed of rock as stubborn and sharp and unyielding as a saint. The jaran playfully called it *krinye-tom*, the little mountains; Tess called it hell and wondered what the big mountains were like.

They slowed their pace to a crawl and ranged wide to find enough fodder for the horses. The dirt clung to Tess. The heat baked the walls of hard stone, and sweat plastered her shirt to her back. The men veiled their heads in cloth to protect themselves from the sun. Tess's scalp itched, but she did not dare undo her braided hair, having no water to wash it in. The horses got the greatest share of the water. Was there a point past which one could not become clean again?

She dreamed of showers. At least the others looked as filthy as she felt, and they joked about it constantly, liking it as little as she did. Only the Chapalii, who did not appear to sweat at all, appeared unaffected; Tess knew that this heat was doubtless a relief to them, being closer to their natural climate.

At long last, they came out onto the watershed of the mountains, grass and shrubs and a scattering of trees on level land. Not a lush land, by any means—that would be far far south, across the great range—but a breeze cooled her cheeks and her shirt dried. They came to an isolated khaja village, and Bakhtiian traded gold trinkets and two tarpans for grain.

Two days' ride out from the village, Bakhtiian called an entire day's halt when they came to a deep-bedded stream. Tess found a pool upstream from the horses, stripped, and washed herself and her hair—that twice—and every piece of clothing in her possession, for the dirt had contaminated even the saddlebags. Surely this stream of all streams was blessed by the gods, for the clearness of its water and the lazy trickle of its flow. She spread her damp blanket over a smooth-surfaced rock and, naked, stretched out on it to dry.

Pulling her mirror case free of her gear, she undid its clasps and slid the mirror out. Her face surprised her, she had not seen it in so long: the blunt chin, the high cheekbones, the deep green of her eyes. Not a bad face, after all, though the green eyes seemed out of place; she kept thinking they ought to be blue or brown. She had grown lean. Streaks of gold lightened her hair. Her hands were strong. She felt—content.

Except for Charles. Somewhere, Charles was worrying about her, searching for her. At least she was headed in the right direction. Yet at this moment, Jeds seemed like a goal too distant to agonize over. Turning over to let her back dry, she rested her chin on her laced fingers and stared at the rippling water. Light sparked off it, ever-changing, a constant, inexorable flux.

Her privacy was assured, a privilege, not a prison, conferred on her because she was female, and that was a thing she had never known on Earth, where locked doors bought privacy and privacy could be violated by crime or, for those unlucky enough to be related to the most influential human in the Chapalii Empire, by the media and the ubiquitous

Protocol Office. Only the most degraded of outcasts would assault her here and, as for the Chapalii, she outranked them. In this land, a person's fortune could be measured in sun and sweet wind and kinship with other people. Material possessions became, in the end, a burden; what you possessed of the spirit was far more valuable. Gloom was disdained: in a world of fighters it was a hindrance; to a people beside whom freedom ran like a hound, it was absurd.

Except for Fedya. But for Fedya, it had proved fatal. With a sigh, Tess sat up. She braided her hair, pinned the braid atop her head, and went swimming. The water felt cool and soft against her skin. The sun warmed her face. She did not go back to camp until evening.

In the morning she rode out with Bakhtiian. Ahead, dark stained the land, and she asked him what it was.

"*Don-usbekh.* The dark wood. Days of it, east and west, and south to the mountains. The khaja say it is haunted." He smiled, looking at her to see what her reaction would be.

"Haunted by what?" she asked, not quite laughing.

He shrugged. "The khaja fear many things, not least their own nightmares. I do not know."

"Do you think it is haunted?"

"I think that no khaja will live there. But there's an old road that runs through it, so once people must not have feared it as they do now."

An old road. "Will we follow this old road?"

"It's the only track through. See there—that broken pillar. We'll follow the road from there."

But despite her fears—or hopes—the old road proved to be just that—an old road. Ancient, stone paved, half grown over in spots, it looked exactly like what she guessed it must be: some relic from an old empire, thrown across the vast land.

"Perhaps the people who built this also built the great temple on the plains," she said to Bakhtiian as they waited in the first outlying tendril of the forest for the jahar to catch up with them.

"Perhaps they did."

She spotted the first ranks of the jahar in the distance, tiny figures moving closer. "Bakhtiian, if Mikhailov's men could find you on the plain, aren't you worried that they might find you more easily on a road like this? We'll be trapped on it, on a single road surrounded by trees.''

"Mikhailov, whatever else he may be, is not fool enough to follow us into khaja lands. For that is what lies beyond the don-usbekh.''

"Then why are we going?''

Bakhtiian's stallion shifted beneath him. Bakhtiian stroked the black's neck with affection. "For more of these horses, I would risk much more than this.''

And one hundred more of these horses he would have, should they reach the end of this journey. "Well,'' said Tess, but nothing more. The jahar arrived then. Bakhtiian sent Josef and Tasha and Niko back to cover their rear, and he rode ahead with Tess, leaving the main group to ride at their leisure in between.

Soon enough the close ranks of trees began to seem oppressive to her even while she told herself that this forest was far more open than many. A dank, rotting scent hung in the air. So much vegetation, falling in and covering itself, and no wind to sweep the air clear. Even the colors turned somber and dense. Now and then an animal that had ventured too close to the road would flee into the forest, a trail of sound marking its path. It was never entirely still. Noise scattered out from the undergrowth, and rodents chittered and birds called from the branches above. The light bled down in patches and stripes so that day never came completely and night came without even the grace of stars.

That night a storm blew down from the mountains. The constant drumming of rain and the patter of falling leaves and twigs disturbed her sleep as she tried to make herself comfortable inside her tent. It was a relief to ride the next morning, although the trees dripped on them all that day and the day after. By the third morning, the forest had leached itself dry in the warm summer air, though the undergrowth looked greener for the drenching. They rode on, having to cut away growth in some places to clear the road, and Tess began to wonder if the forest would ever end.

"I've never seen Ilya so cheerful,'' said Yuri one evening as he helped Tess set up her tent. Because the trees grew up to the very edge of the road, indeed overgrew the road in many areas, the jahar set up camp on the road itself at night. "He must smile once a day now, and he never smiled

but once a month before. What do you two *do* while you're
riding?"

"We *talk,* Yuri."

He chuckled and sat down next to her tent, fishing in his
saddlebags for his spare shirt and his embroidery needles
and thread. "Do you want to try again?"

"And ruin your shirt? No, thank you."

"Well, it's true women have little hand for embroidery.
But you've taken to saber well enough." He threaded a needle with a thick golden thread and began to embroider
golden spirals through the thick black pattern that textured
his sleeves. "I thought you might take to this if you tried it
again."

"Yuri, I'm sore from my saber lesson tonight. May I just
lie here for a while and watch you?"

"If you think this stone is a comfortable bed, then please,
lie there as long as you wish."

She laughed. It was not quite dark yet, and a fire built
within a ring of stones some ten paces away gave light as
well. Here, in this deserted place, game was plentiful and
easy to kill, and deadwood for smoking the meat was in vast
supply. Bakhtiian had decided to halt for a few days, to
hunt, to graze the horses in nearby meadows, to rest. "I'm
teaching him some of the songs I know," Tess said at last.

"Who? Oh, Ilya."

"And he's teaching me jaran songs. Only decent ones, of
course."

"My dear sister," said Yuri primly, "Bakhtiian would
never think to teach a woman any songs but those that it is
decent for her to know."

"Unlike some I know."

Instead of replying, he squinted at his work in the inadequate light. Kirill and Mikhal and a few of the other young
men were gambling. Farther on, the conical tents of the
Chapalii thrust up among the trees, like pale ghosts lost in
the leaves.

"And Newton," she said.

"Newton? Who is Newton?"

"Oh, a philosopher. Not just him, but Casiara and Narronias and—and the work of many others."

"Gods. Sometimes I'm amazed that Ilya ever came back
from Jeds. How he loves khaja learning."

"You're right," she said, realizing that it was true. "I

hadn't thought of it that way.'' It had not occurred to her before that there might be some link between his relentless ambitions and the constant, restless inquisitiveness of his mind. Just as she could not resist a new language, he could not resist a new philosopher. If she mentioned a name he did not know, he demanded that she recite every scrap of writing she could remember, a feat she usually accomplished by broad paraphrasing since she had not his training in wholesale memorization. He loved to quibble over the smallest point and discuss the large ones to the finest detail. The scope of her knowledge, fostered by a decade in the schools of a stellar empire, was balanced by his experience, his impressive memory, his capacity to assimilate new information, and his astuteness; she always had to be careful of what she said. ''I guess I always thought,'' she said, discovering that Yuri was watching her curiously, as if wondering where she had gone, ''that a man with ambitions of conquest would be too single-minded to aspire to be a philosopher as well.''

''Oh, I don't think Ilya wants to be a philosopher,'' said Yuri lightly. He yawned, laying down his shirt, and let a hand rest on Tess's back. ''He just doesn't like other people knowing something he doesn't.''

Tess laughed. ''That's unkind, Yuri.''

''Do you think so? I don't. Ilya has no one to answer to. That means he must know *everything*. It would be enough to drive me mad. I think it's the reason Ilya is so harsh.''

''Harsh? Maybe at first, but not lately—'' She grinned. ''With Kirill, yes.''

''Well, Kirill deserves it.''

''No, he doesn't!'' She laughed again. ''Maybe. But *I* like him. He's—he's *Kirill*. And you must admit that he's the only one of you who has the courage to make fun of Ilya at all.''

''He's the only one stupid enough to do it in front of him.''

''He's the only one who doesn't take Ilya as seriously as Ilya takes himself.''

Yuri picked up his embroidery. ''I resent that. You never saw Ilya at his worst. When the mood was on him, he would come into camp and, like that, everyone walked everywhere on their toes to avoid his notice.''

Tess giggled.

"He hasn't been bad at all this trip. I think he likes you."

"Likes me?" She found a perceptible crack in the stone fitting and traced it out as far as her hand could reach.

Yuri rubbed the light shadow of beard on his chin. "Did I leave my razor with you?" he asked, and then he went on, not waiting for her reply. "He likes Niko. I think he likes Vladimir, or at least is fond of him, and I know he likes Josef and Tasha and my mother, and Sonia, although he would never admit he likes Sonia. But you can never be sure who else he likes. I don't even know if he likes me, but I think he likes you."

"Oh." Tess brushed dirt out of the crack with her middle finger. "I like him. He's easy to talk to."

Now Yuri laughed. "If I'd heard anyone say that a year ago, I would have thought they were as mad as Yevich the Weaver."

"Who is Yevich the Weaver?"

"You don't know the story of Yevich the Weaver? By the gods, that will have to be settled."

The story of Yevich the Weaver took four evenings to tell as told by Josef, the best tale-teller in the jahar now that they no longer had Fedya to sing tales for them. By the time Yevich had gone mad twice and finally settled his score with the wind-maiden and her four brothers, they had ample provisions. They rode on and passed out of the tangled dark wood and into the feet of the mountains.

They traveled for a day up a series of terraces of scrubby grass linked by ridges of rock. The road had vanished entirely, and the ridges proved so devoid of paths that the riders were forced to dismount and lead their horses up each one. Now and again a drying riverbed offered easier passage and even water as they climbed from level to level through the ridges, until the last terrace spread out like a sea before them, a broad plateau brought up short by the mountains.

Tess stared. The air was so clear that it seemed only a thin sheet of glass between her and the mountains, which were surely close enough for her to touch, and yet so distant, lacking any detail, that their size alone awed her.

"Those are the children," said Bakhtiian, watching her. "The grandparents are farther in. It's said they are so high that one cannot see their tops."

"That would depend on where you were standing." She grinned. "Rather like a man's reputation, don't you think?"

"So awesome from a distance, so meager up close?"

"I thought it was the other way around. Small and insignificant from far off, but massive at its base."

"Weighed down by its own importance."

"A heavy burden," said Tess.

"Only to the man who has had it forced on him," said Bakhtiian, suddenly serious. "Fame is a light and welcome burden to the man who picks it up of his own will."

"I don't agree. Fame becomes a heavy burden either way."

Bakhtiian raised one hand, like a teacher making a point. "But by *choosing* to carry it— Dismount!" She dismounted almost as quickly as he did. "Damn," he said to himself, and then to Tess, "Follow." A spur of rock jutted up, a solitary sentinel of the ridges that fell away behind it. Bushes and clinging grass patched the dark surface. They halted at its base. "Stir up the ground."

He took the horses around the rock while Tess trampled grass and scuffed dirt. "Good enough," he said, returning without the horses. He studied the spur for a moment and, choosing a path, began to climb.

Tess scrambled after him, her feet slipping on loose pebbles, her hands grabbing bare knobs of stone and long, sinuous roots. He halted at a small ledge, screened by bushes, and pulled Tess up after him, leaving his hand on her arm when she stood beside him. She could feel every point of pressure, however light, where his fingers touched her skin.

"You may as well sit, if you wish," he said. "They may not have seen us, but I know they saw the horses. This rock is the only cover, unless we wanted to risk breaking our necks by running down into the rough. Two against—I'd guess forty-two. We should go to ground."

She took the hint and sat. His hand released her, leaving a lingering tingle on her arm where he had held her. He remained standing.

"Who?" Tess asked. "Another jahar? I didn't see them."

"Another jahar, yes—" He hesitated, absently staring at his hand. "And no."

"If you thought these men really wanted to kill you, we wouldn't be sitting here."

Bakhtiian transferred his attention from his hand to the plateau. Grass and mountains, nothing else. "I just want to look at them before we exchange pleasantries."

"The weather is fine today, and my what a lovely horse that is?"

He looked down at her and smiled, a smile that lit the corners of his eyes. "The jaran have a tale of a woman who brought misfortune to her tribe because she was too curious."

She tilted her head. "Is that so? We have a story something like that."

"If two old moral tales won't teach you, I'll never be able to. What was the woman's name?"

"Pandora."

"Pandora. That's prettier than the woman's name in our story: Vlatagrebi."

"Poor thing, saddled with a bad reputation and a name like that."

"Then you'd rather be called Pandora than Vlatagrebi?"

"By whom?"

Bakhtiian leaned back against the rock face. A spray of dirt skidded down the face to settle behind his boots. He folded his arms over his chest. "By me. It's only fitting."

"We have a saying in our land: 'the pot calling the kettle black.' "

"The pot calls— Shameless woman. If I were a brave man I'd—" He checked himself.

"You'd what?"

"I take it back. I wouldn't."

"Who are they, Ilya?"

It took him a moment to answer because the smile that crept onto his face was the kind that arrives slowly and leaves reluctantly. "I surrender." He put his hands against the rock by his shoulders, palms up and open. *"Arenabekh.* The black riders."

"I saw nothing."

"You weren't looking. You were staring at the mountains."

"How could you tell they were these—arenabekh?"

"All in black."

"Is this a particular tribe?"

The wind rolled a single wilted leaf past his boot. "They have no tribe."

"No tribe? And they're riding, so they must all be men."

"They have renounced tribe, kin, women, any ties to order or custom or family."

"I thought my abstainers were severe."

"They don't necessarily abstain."

"They take lovers amongst themselves?"

He colored slightly. "This is not a fit subject for a man and a woman to discuss."

"But I'm khaja. And fully as curious as you are."

He smiled. "So you are. Well, then, some do. Not all. Some believe that our life now is not the life the gods gave us to live, so they live as it is said jaran lived in the early days."

"Without women? How could there be jaran now if that was so?"

"Exactly. And how are we to know how the jaran lived in the early days, having only old stories to tell us, which may have been changed in the telling? Do you see them now? Don't shift forward. They're sharp-eyed, these demons."

The screen of bushes and hedge concealed them, but eventually she got a view of the approaching riders through a gap in the shrubbery. Bakhtiian hummed something under his breath, fingering the hilt of his saber. She felt his excitement, and it made her nervous; she had seen that same excitement in him before—for battle.

She wished now that she was not sitting because it made her feel vulnerable, unable to move quickly, but she could not stand up now. The black riders rode straight for the spur of rock.

"God," whispered Tess as they neared. "They look grimmer than you ever did." Because she had not meant to say it aloud, she looked up. He glanced down, a glint of amusement in his eyes, and put two fingers to his lips.

They pulled up a stone's toss away, suspicious and watchful. The dull coats of their horses, the dourness of their expressions and, most of all, the unvarying black of their dress made them cheerless and forbidding. No embroidery decorated their shirts. None wore jewelry.

"A quick night's camp," said one in a strong dialect.

If Tess had thought the jaran men of her acquaintance hard, she had no word for these. One had no right arm, only a loose, empty sleeve that stirred restlessly in the breeze. Next to him a younger man, beardless and rosy-cheeked, examined the rock with one clear eye; his other eye was scarred shut, puckered and white. These men hunted, they had their quarry trapped, and they knew it. She bit her lip to stop herself breathing through her mouth, as if even that faint sound might alert them to her presence.

"The fox has gone to the hill," said a bearded fellow with a haughty forehead and cruel eyes. His blond hair fell in a long braid to his waist.

"Patience, Sergi," said the one with the dialect, a black-haired man who had possibly been given a frown at birth and had been unable to remove it. A tic, almost hidden in his rough beard, disturbed his right cheek. "You three check around the rock."

The three brought back the two horses. Tess saw how all the riders stared at the stallion and the mare, two creatures so obviously superior in line and breeding to their own animals that it was rather like standing a man of the jaran dressed in all his finery next to an ape dressed in skins. Bakhtiian stood utterly still, his eyes narrowed, his expression more anticipatory than apprehensive. How easily he could blend into the group of men below. Then, startling her with the suddenness of his movement, he stepped out from behind the screen of bushes to stand in full view of the jahar below, but he glanced once swiftly back at her as he did so.

"They are beautiful, aren't they?" he asked. He froze, almost as if he were posing for the benefit of his audience, with one hand on his saber hilt and the other resting on the hilt of his dagger. He looked dangerous.

"By the gods, Bakhtiian!" said the bearded Sergi. "Come here, you ill-favored son of the cold winds, and I'll show you the special trick I've learned with the saber just for you."

"You flatter me." Bakhtiian did not move. Leaves brushed at his boots.

"And bring your treasure down, too, the one you're hiding. Is it some handsome lad you're afraid we'll spirit off?"

Bakhtiian caught Tess's eye and lifted his chin. She stood up and came two steps forward. Even as she halted next to Ilya, about ten men turned their horses away and rode off to one side, backs to her, heads lowered. More than half of those left averted their faces, so as not to look at her, but the rest examined her with cold, inquisitorial interest.

"Gods!" cried Sergi. "It's a damned woman! Who would ever have thought it!"

"Shut up, Sergi," said the one with the pronounced dialect.

"Shall I come down?" asked Bakhtiian with all the familiar pleasantry of a venomous snake.

"Please do," said Sergi. "But keep the woman up on the ledge. Some of our men haven't seen a woman in five years, and I can't answer for them if they catch her scent."

Tess straightened her shoulders, met his eye, and held it. "They wouldn't dare touch me." She laid one hand on her saber hilt, though she had no illusions about her ability to use it against any of these men.

Sergi let out a whoop. "A khaja with spirit, and listen how she talks. They won't touch you. Certainly not if you're Bakhtiian's."

Bakhtiian, descending with composed dignity, stopped dead. One of his feet slipped on the incline and pebbles skittered out and rattled down to the base of the rock.

Tess drew her dagger, tossed it up into the air, and caught it. "You've got it half right, Sergi. They won't touch me. I don't know what Bakhtiian has to do with it."

Bakhtiian, regaining his balance, resumed his descent as if nothing had happened.

"Sergi, shut up," said another man. His face bore a broad, ugly white scar that stretched from forehead to chin, puckering one side of his face into a permanent leer. "You can only keep your mouth shut for as long as it takes a horse to shit."

On the pretext of sheathing her knife, Tess looked away. The jaran men she knew never swore in that way—or at least, not in front of her.

"So, you are Ilyakoria Bakhtiian," said the man with the dialect, and suddenly all attention focused on him, though he had made no obvious effort to attract it. "I am Keregin. You seem a little short for a man with such a tall reputation."

"That depends on where you're standing," said Bakhtiian, looking as though his greatest concern was the fit of his clothing.

"Choose your man," said Keregin. "I want to see if you deserve your reputation. Bakhtiian." He savored the flow of the syllables. "What kind of luck got you a name of your own?"

"Luck is only my lover, not my wife," replied Bakhtiian easily. He drew his saber. "If ever I wed, it will be skill and intelligence."

"Tedious bedfellows," said Sergi.

"Shut up," said the scarred man.

"Choose," said Keregin.

Bakhtiian looked over the arenabekh one by one, his gaze measuring and keen but never quite insulting. Watching him, Tess realized she had clenched her hands into fists without realizing it. This was to be a real fight, a real duel. What if Keregin meant it to be to the death?

"He has too heavy a hand," said Bakhtiian, "and that one, no instinct."

"Got you there, Vlacov," said Sergi.

But Bakhtiian appeared not to hear the comment and the low mutter of laughter it produced. He examined a man far to the side whose light eyes were shadowed by dark circles beneath and whose nose was broken. "He's too angry. There, too unsteady a hand, and that one, he drinks too much khaja wine." He paused, then pointed with his saber at a particularly unprepossessing man of middle years, a remarkably unkempt fellow whose only conspicuous features were a long nose and brilliant blue eyes. "That man."

Keregin laughed. "We'll concede your eye for flesh. Tobay, fight him."

"What will we do with the woman after Tobay kills him?" asked Sergi. "None of us has any use for such a thing."

"Sergi, if you can't keep your mouth shut while they fight, we'll bury your head in the ground and stuff your saber up—"

"Silence!" shouted Keregin. "Move back. Now, Bakhtiian. Make us remember you." The lanky Tobay dismounted and came forward, holding his saber as if he did not know he had it in his hand. "Left-handed," added Keregin. "Or I might get bored."

With no change of expression, Bakhtiian switched hands and circled left, measuring his opponent. Tobay stared dumbly at him as if he had not a wit in the world. Bakhtiian had moved about a quarter of a circle when Tobay suddenly stepped left and cut in with a broad sweep toward Bakhtiian's right shoulder. Bakhtiian parried, stepping in to the blow, and there was a moment of suspension, metal pressed against metal, and then both men fell back unmarked.

"A greeting in passing," said Sergi.

Bakhtiian edged back toward the rock. He lunged forward suddenly to Tobay's right, cutting low. There was a quick exchange: low, low, and high; then low, and Bakhtiian came out to the open space with Tobay backed against the cliff.

"An exchange of kisses," said Sergi. "How passionate."

Tobay's face and demeanor changed utterly, as if, Tess thought with sudden fear, a light had been turned on inside him. He moved back until less than a meter separated him from the rough wall of rock. With his right hand he reached back to brush the rock with his fingers, and the angle of his saber changed ever so slightly. Bakhtiian circled in, trying to push Tobay completely against the rock, feinting high but striking low again. But Tobay's saber swept the cut aside and went on sweeping for Bakhtiian's head.

Tess gasped, breath suspended. Bakhtiian fell to his knees, saber barely catching the blow. For an instant the tableau held and then Bakhtiian twisted Tobay's saber around, cut free from a flurry of blows, and leapt backward, regaining his feet.

"A conversation," said Sergi. "About the weather."

But Bakhtiian was wounded. Tess stared. Blood welled and, welling to fullness, bled off a cut on Bakhtiian's wrist. She breathed again. Not deep enough to be fatal, or even perhaps, debilitating. And yet, what if Tobay was only playing with him?

They moved away from the rock. Their exchanges grew more complex. Tess saw only a mix of high and low, wide and close, movements begun in one place that ended in another until she could not recognize where one began and the other left off. And all the time, the slow drip of blood from Bakhtiian's wrist tracked his movements over the ground. She could not move. They both feinted, and feinted again, their sabers never touching. Every second she expected to see Tobay kill Bakhtiian. Every second Bakhtiian escaped.

Tobay fenced him against a slab of rock and went for his face, angled the slice into an arc that would open his stomach. Somehow Bakhtiian twisted the blade and was still whole and moving. He parried and pressed, made a bid for open ground, and gained it. They backed off, eyeing each other, breathing fast and hard. Bakhtiian's face shone with intensity. *My God,* she thought, watching him as he circled slowly, so concentrated that it seemed his entire being had caught fire: *if he ever looks at me like that, I'll last about as long as tinder under a glass.*

And she suffered an instant of stark fear, wondering what such a blaze would do to her.

"Right hands," said Keregin.

Tess watched the rest of the fight in a haze. Somehow, now that they were right-handed, they seemed more evenly matched, but still she knew that she ought to fear more for Bakhtiian than for Tobay. Until, in a furious exchange, Tobay wrenched himself free and slapped his left hand over his right arm. Blood leaked out between his fingers. He grinned.

"Enough!" yelled Keregin, dismounting.

"The woman didn't bolt," said Sergi. "I'm more impressed with her than with Bakhtiian."

Keregin strode over to Bakhtiian, who stood breathing deeply to regain his wind.

"By the gods," Keregin squinted down at him. "Maybe there's something to your reputation after all. Tobay, put up and go." Tobay sheathed his saber, looking again half-witted and lifeless. Many of the men, who had looked up to watch the fight, turned their heads away again. "Tobay's got no interest in life but saber. He prefers fighting two or three men, since one is too easy. He wasn't going for the kill."

"I know." Blood still dripped from Bakhtiian's wrist.

Keregin laughed. "And not too proud to admit it." His expression changed. "You've got foreigners with you."

Bakhtiian shrugged. Tess crouched, balancing herself with a touch of one hand on the pebbles that littered the ledge.

"I know the ruins up in these mountains. A place to inspire the gods in you if nothing else might, but I warn you, Bakhtiian, to reach them you've got to ride through khaja lands. There have been jahar raids into khaja towns, and your name linked to them. I won't lift a hand against you, but there's been mischief done. Is it yours?"

"No."

Keregin lifted his right hand to flick a piece of grass off his beard. His little finger was missing. "I believe you. But

remember, the khaja know your name now. They blame
you. They are like us in one way, Bakhtiian, if not in any
other: They seek revenge.''

"I'll scarcely bend a blade of grass as I go.''

"One blade might be too many. Well, then, can you
promise me one thing?''

"How can I know until you ask?''

Keregin smiled. "I admire your companion, who wears
a man's clothes with a woman's courage, who is foreign and
yet speaks our tongue. Don't let her get into their hands.
I've seen khaja do things to their women that made me
cringe, and I'm not an easy man to sicken.''

Bakhtiian's head moved slightly, as if he began to look
back up at Tess and then chose not to. "That I can promise
you, Keregin. No woman for whom I have accepted responsibility will ever fall into khaja hands. Don't forget that I
have also seen how khaja treat their women.''

'' 'He who has traveled far,' '' Keregin mused. "I begin
to think you might even deserve it.''

Bakhtiian sketched him the merest trifle of a bow, half
respectful, not quite mocking. "You honor me.''

Keregin chuckled. "Do I, indeed? I'd offer you a place
with us, but I don't think you'd accept.''

"I wouldn't.'' He smiled. "I love women too well, Keregin, to give them up now.''

"Yet you've made no jaran woman your wife.'' Behind,
the other riders began turning their horses away. Keregin
angled his gaze toward the two horses standing quietly between them. "They're beautiful horses, Bakhtiian, as well
you know.'' He smiled, a little mocking in return, and
glanced once at Tess. "Breed strong stock if you can. I wish
you luck.''

He mounted without waiting for the reply that Bakhtiian
seemed unlikely to give in any case, and reined his horse
away from them. The rest of the arenabekh followed, not
even glancing back as they galloped off. The sound of
hooves drummed away, fading into silence in the clear air.

When they were out of sight, Bakhtiian sat down and
rested his head in his hands. Tess scrambled down from the
rock.

"Ilya, are you hurt?''

He lifted his head to give her a wan smile. "Just regaining my composure.''

"I'll get the horses."

"Thank you," he said into his hands.

She busied herself with the horses, recovering her own composure. Eventually he appeared and took the black's reins from her.

"Thank you," he repeated. He rubbed his horse's nose and talked nonsense to it for a bit, slapped its neck, and mounted. Tess, who had been repelling Myshla's attempts to chew off her ear, quickly followed suit. "A congenial group," he said.

"Keregin offered you a place. Would you ever have gone with them?"

"I thought of it once, a long time ago. For them, it is the only life." He shook his head. "It can't be mine."

"I didn't like them."

He smiled and brought his left wrist up to his mouth, touching partially congealed blood to his lips. "And blood is sweet, but life is sweeter." He urged the black forward and they walked the horses parallel to the ridge. "Tobay is better than I am. Much better."

Wind touched her throat and her eyes. She blinked. "Because fighting is his whole life?"

"He could have killed me." He lowered his hand, turning it slowly, eyes on the cut, its slow well of blood almost stopped now. "He chose not to."

She put a hand on her stomach. "Good Lord." He turned his hand over; the cut no longer showed. "But Keregin was impressed."

Bakhtiian flicked several bits of grass off the knee of his trousers. "Tobay can kill any of them, too, if I'm any judge of saber. I did well. With more experience, Vladimir would give him a fight."

Silence followed for a moment, which Tess broke. "Keregin mentioned ruins. Are we near the shrine of Morava?"

"No. The shrine is farther south. This is another temple. I would rather pass it by, but the pilgrims have insisted on seeing every one. What Keregin said about the khaja—well, I shall have to discuss this with Ishii."

He did discuss it with Ishii, that night at the campfire. Bakhtiian flanked by Niko and Josef and Tasha, Ishii by Garii and Rakii.

"Because the shrine of Morava lies still on the plains, some days north of the *don-tepes*, the great forest, no for-

eign towns rest nearby and no foreign people come there
but the occasional pilgrims,'' Bakhtiian was saying as Tess
settled in next to Yuri, far enough away that she could pretend to be listening to Mikhal strum his lute, but close
enough to overhear. "But this temple, the *zhai'aya-tom,*
rests in the mountains themselves, Cha Ishii, and to reach
it we must pass by a city with walls and ride up into the
mountains, and thereby make ourselves vulnerable to their
attack, should the war leader of this city choose to pursue
us. And then we must ride back the same way. It will be
very dangerous. It might mean a battle, and we are too few,
and the mountains themselves too great a disadvantage to
the way we jaran fight, that I can offer you with any surety
what the outcome of such a battle might be.''

Ishii sat with perfect impassivity, hands clasped in front
of him in that arrangement known as Lord's Patience, and
listened. When, after a moment, he accepted that Bakhtiian
had said as much as he meant to say, he nodded. "We appreciate your concerns, Bakhtiian, but our god protects us.
We fear no battle.''

Tess lifted her gaze from a close examination of the knives
at their belts to see Bakhtiian's face tighten in exasperation.

"Neither do I *fear* a battle, but it is folly to ride into a
trap when the trap is there to see. It is only one temple.
Cha Ishii. I promise you that the shrine of Morava is by any
account the greatest temple in these northern lands. It will
not disappoint you.''

Ishii inclined his head. "All the temples or none. I believe, Bakhtiian, that we made this agreement.''

Bakhtiian did not reply, merely giving Ishii a curt nod,
and he turned away to walk out into the night, Niko and
Josef and Tasha following him. The three Chapalii shifted
as if with one thought to look at Tess, and she hurriedly
evinced an overwhelming interest in Yuri's embroidery.

In the morning, they rode across the plateau. Fields appeared, then settlements, each one a handful of cottages
surrounded by stockades of varying height and strength but
all showing signs of frequent and recent repair. That first
day, riding wide around these hamlets, Tess saw them as
ugly squares intruding on the landscape like sores on otherwise healthy skin, their inhabitants forever bound and im-
prisoned by the protecting walls. The idea of defending one
place seemed preposterous, until her settled sensibilities

took over and the idea of always fading into the brush and never making a stand suddenly seemed cowardly. It was hardly surprising that these people, settled and wandering, could not trust each other.

Bakhtiian led them through without stopping. No one harassed them. Indeed, they saw no one at all. But at every stockaded village they passed, Tess felt, knew, that they were being watched. They halted late that night, kept a triple watch—sleeping in shifts—and rose before dawn to ride on. Somehow word had passed on ahead of them. Empty fields ripe for harvest lay quiet in the sun. No one walked the trails linking the hamlets. Every stockade gate stood shut. Now and again, they glimpsed faces, peering over the walls. Another day passed.

The next morning Bakhtiian gathered them all together.

"Today we reach the mountains. The ruins are at the head of a gorge. To reach it we must pass close beneath a city." There was little color this early. He looked mostly gray, shaded dark and light. "We'll ride fast. Expect attack but do not provoke it. They may ignore us."

The Chapalii waited, patient, unafraid. As they mounted, Garii hung back as if his horse was balking and hissed softly between his teeth as Tess went by.

"Lady Terese, I beg pardon for my presumption," he said quickly, not even looking up to see if she was slowing her horse to hear him—which she was—"but I implore you to have a care for the gift which you were so magnanimous as to accept from me." Glancing down, she saw he had a hand on his knife.

"Garii?" Ahead, Ishii had turned and was staring back at them.

"Yuri," Tess said, riding on as if no exchange had taken place, "how long until we enter the mountains?" She kept going, not even waiting to hear Yuri's reply.

At noon the scouts, hardly more than a shout away, came back from all sides. The mountains loomed before them, huge and impenetrable. But there, like a scar, a great valley slashed through the wall. Where the valley opened onto the plateau, a city rose, hard against the eastern heights of the mountain. A fortress, heavy with stone; high, castellated walls weighted it to the earth. Fields and hovels sprawled out from it like so much debris. A narrow river pushed past, curving east. The valley opened before them and then they rode up between the high sides of the mountains.

They galloped past the town, Bakhtiian leading them as far against the western heights as he could. Small figures gestured atop the stone walls, but they were too far away to attack. The jahar rode on, up the broad valley, and soon enough they left the fortress behind. The last traces of fields merged into the wild scrub of the narrowing gorge. Bakhtiian signaled a halt, and everyone dismounted, walking their horses to cool them.

It was a brief halt. They mounted again and went on. Tess stared at the sheer dark cliff faces, veined with white, that rose like an iron stockade to her left, at the rocky defiles that climbed up and up to her right. Ahead, the gorge ascended toward the white-topped peaks in a gentle but narrowing incline, colored in greens and grays and dry golds. Tess urged Myshla up to ride next to Bakhtiian. He had a slight smile on his face that disturbed her.

"What if they do pursue us?" she asked.

He laughed. "They can't catch us, not on foot. Certainly not on horses. Khaja don't know how to ride."

Tess began to make a comment about how *she* was a khaja, and then thought better of it. "But Ilya, even if they don't catch us, we're going to run into the peaks eventually. And then we'll have to ride out this way again. They can simply wait for us."

"They can wait," he agreed. He did not glance back. "But I have heard there is another path out of this gorge, a rough trail, but better, I think, than returning the way we came."

Tess chuckled. "Yes. Nature is so much safer than men are."

"Is she?" A cold wind stirred her sleeves, chilling her fingers. "I wonder."

"How far to the ruins?"

"Two days."

"But look how close the mountains are. We'll run into them before then."

His mount shied. A small rodent ran chittering off the trail to disappear under rock and moss. He pulled the black in, undisturbed. "The mountains have as many twists and turns as a devious man."

"As many as you, Bakhtiian?"

"Oh, far more."

She smiled, and then sobered, glancing back. "But what if they follow us? What happens then? I don't think these khaja like the jaran."

"Neither do I." He did not answer her question.

CHAPTER FIFTEEN

"I thought in a dream that I was dead."
—EPICHARMUS OF SYRACUSE

Yuri told her that it was autumn, by their reckoning, and she looked for signs of the change of season. It was bitter cold at night, but that could have been the altitude. Streams spilling down from the heights fed the gorge, feeding green to the thickets and the meadows of thin grass. Smaller plants that neither she nor any of the jaran had a name for grew abundantly. Colors she never saw on the plains, crimson and olive and mustard, dappled the rocks, growing sparser the higher they rode. And yet the eye quickly grew accustomed to the variety. How monotonous the plains were in comparison.

The first night they rode until the moon set, changing mounts as the horses tired, slept in shifts, tentless, fireless. Not even the Chapalii demurred. Even the thermals in her Earth clothing barely kept Tess warm. The gorge angled right, a narrow scar that cut up into the mountains as though some long-dead giant had left this furrow in the wake of his planting. It was cool and damp between the high walls of stone, moss and orange-gray lichens everywhere. They did not see the sun until mid-morning. A stream rushed down one side of the defile, more white than water. It was shockingly cold to the touch.

They followed a road littered with rocks, but a road for all that. Paving stones showed here and there under lichens; tufts of grass sprouted in lines too straight to be natural. The gorge narrowed until they could ride only three abreast, then two, then single file. The hooves of the horses echoed strangely in the enclosed spaces. Just when Tess knew they could not possibly ride any farther, the gorge opened out abruptly into a secret glen. They had reached the ruins.

"That was never a temple." Tess moved her mount up beside Bakhtiian as she gazed out and up at the little valley, a large, open area of grass and ruins, sprinkled through with a profusion of tiny white flowers. "That was a fortress."

"That's what I'm counting on," said Bakhtiian.

Except for the defile through which they had ridden, they were surrounded on all sides by the mountains. An avalanche had obliterated the leftmost portion of the ruins. The back of the vale ended in a sheer cliff face that rose cleanly into the mountains for about twenty meters before beginning to climb in stair steps to the huge, snow-capped peak towering behind.

The glen itself rose in three broad stair steps to the cliff face: directly in front of them, a bluff—not quite the height of two men—ran the entire length of the shallow meadow that the neck of the gorge emptied into. A stone wall rose flush from its edge, so that from where Tess and Bakhtiian sat below, they could see only the suggestion of another wall, above and beyond, that marked a higher level. Here and there the bluff had eroded away and a stone tumbled down into the meadow. The remains of the road continued along the base of the bluff to its lowest point, where it snaked up through a stone gate that had once, perhaps, borne a lintel over the two pillars that flanked it.

They guided their horses around stray rocks, along the road to the gate, but in the end they had to lead their horses up the bluff where the last slice of road, badly fallen away, gave access to the next level.

Here, in front and to the left, the ground was littered with the remains of old buildings. To the right the land rose again in an escarpment, ending in that other wall: the second line of defense. Behind it the ground seemed level and empty for a space, and behind that Tess saw the line of escape: a trail twisting upward into the heights, disappearing behind a huge outcropping of veined rock.

Dusk came sooner here, hedged in as they were by rock. Bakhtiian sent them all up to the level area behind the second wall, and put four men on watch below. He even allowed fires. The Chapalii stood huddled beyond the horses, conversing earnestly among themselves. Tess walked to the wall and stared down at the ruins below, and the long line of wall that edged the bluff below them.

Had men or nature destroyed these? On the one side, certainly, the avalanche had been the culprit. But as she studied the ground below, she could not imagine how any army could take this ground; if the defenders had enough people and missile weapons, their position would be virtually unassailable. Surely no human attack could have ruined these buildings—or was it just one huge rambling building?—so thoroughly. Only time, working with storms and harsh winters, could wreak so much havoc. How many thousands of years old must these ruins be to be so extensive and so wracked?

And yet the surface of this wall, chest high and a meter wide, was as smooth as obsidian. She ran her right hand along it, out away from herself and back again. Scars marred it, chips gone, a runnel scored across it in one place, but otherwise cool and even, like a polished stone. She ran her left hand out—and stopped. And stared down.

Symbols, letters, had been traced into the surface. She ran her finger along them, feeling the dust and debris of long years caught in their track, feeling the eroded edges, blurred by time and wind and rain. The first two, partially eaten away by erosion, she did not recognize. The third she did. The Chapalii glyph for ''tai.'' *Duke.* She stood frozen for a long moment. The murmur of voices drifted to her on the cold air of evening. Kirill, telling a ribald story about a man who crept into the wrong woman's tent one night. One of the stewards, complaining about not being able to set up the tents. A lower voice, Pavel's, talking about storms.

Breath stuck in her throat, she traced out the fourth symbol with her middle finger. And laughed. The fourth letter was a ''w.'' Or two ''v's'' linked in the middle. Or the archaic Chapalii glyph for mountains. And the first, going back to it: with a little imagination and a tiny bit of allowance for erosion and time could be the Maya symbol for nought.

''Lord, Tess,'' she muttered under her breath. ''You'll be finding the Rosetta Stone next. There're only so many shapes can be chiseled into stone.'' Maybe it was cuneiform. She sighed at her own folly and returned to the fire.

Yuri was on watch so she joined Niko and Bakhtiian where they sat together in the half light of one of the fires, arguing good-naturedly about the defensibility of the ruins. Niko smiled as she sat down, but Bakhtiian only glanced at her and continued speaking.

"I can't agree that rain or storm gives the defenders the greatest advantage. Certainly, it ruins footing, but for both the hunter and the hunted. The loss of visibility is a far greater disadvantage for the defender than the attacker."

"What do you think, Tess?" asked Niko politely.

"I think," said Tess cheerfully, "that this is a terrible place to be holed up in. I feel like a pig trussed up and left in a pen for slaughter. Although I can see that the defending party does have the advantage of fortification and that narrow approach. Especially if they're using spears or bows."

"A jaran man never uses a bow in battle," said Bakhtiian stiffly.

"Good Lord, I wasn't talking about jaran. Sabers alone can't hold this kind of position. I thought that was obvious."

Bakhtiian stood. "Excuse me." He left.

Tess stared after him. "Excuse me! I thought this was a theoretical discussion. Or was it presumptuous of me to have an opinion?"

"My dear girl." Niko laid a hand on her shoulder, a fatherly gesture. "First of all, this is a holy place, and to liken it to a place where one would butcher animals is rather—shall we say—irreverent. Second, you might consider that Bakhtiian was the one who made the decision to lead us all here."

She shut her eyes, wincing. "Oh, God. That was a stupid thing for me to have said." She looked up at Niko. "I suppose I could just as well have said I thought he was a fool for bringing us here."

"Be assured," said Niko softly, "that he is wondering that himself." Then, unexpectedly, he chuckled. "But few people admit their mistakes as readily as you do, my dear."

"I wouldn't learn anything if I always thought I was right. But I will say that he was awfully quick to get angry."

"He has a heavy burden on him, Tess, and you must remember that."

"I suppose I must. Can you entertain yourself here?"

"Don't mind an old, frail, friendless man. I'll manage."

Tess laughed at him and left. She found Bakhtiian leaning against the wall, staring down at the ruins and beyond them to the neck of the gorge. His form seemed merely an extension of the shadows.

"Ilya?" He didn't move. She put her elbows on that uncannily smooth wall and leaned out, staring down. The wall below stood like a purplish line against a darker background. "I'm sorry. I didn't think."

"No. The things you said were true enough. The khaja will not scruple to use bows against us, when we ride into their lands. And here . . . well, no man likes to be told something he already knows and doesn't want to hear."

She shifted her elbows to fit into two hollows that marred the level surface of the wall. "And not when he could already be trapped."

"Tess." He turned his head enough to see her. "You have a habit of choosing unfortunate words."

"What—oh, you mean 'trapped'?"

"Among others. I don't—" He reconsidered. "When you return to Jeds, you'll have to be more careful. In khaja lands, people veil their true opinions in a layer of false words."

"Oh, yes." Tess leaned her chin on her intertwined fingers and stared morosely out at the moonlit outlines of the vale. The white ruins looked like a litter of bones on the dark ground. "When I return to Jeds—" She contemplated this event, amazed at her own lack of eagerness. When she returned to Jeds, when she returned to Odys, to be trapped once again by her duty to Charles. She pushed the traitorous thought away. "Why did you agree to bring me along?"

"You're not going to admit that I was right all along?"

"You weren't."

"And you're not going to tell me that now we've been run into a trap worthy of the fire-keeper's daughter herself that you're sorry you came?" He was, she realized, laughing at her.

"No." She found she was blushing. "I'm glad I came," she said softly, looking up at a bright star that shone above the gorge, glittering in the cold air.

"Yes," he said, as if to himself. "Even for this short time." He blinked, as if he had just realized where he was, and moved his elbows to a different place on the wall. "Of course you would be glad. Yuri and—and Fedya, and the others."

"Yes. Yuri and Fedya and the others. It will be hard to board that ship."

"It is always hard to board ships."

"You haven't answered my question."

"No, I haven't. I should have known better than to try to avoid it. Ishii insisted, finally. I'll always wonder what you said to him."

"But you're too polite to ask."

"That may be." He smiled. "I also admired your spirit."

"Now there's a very handsome way of telling me that I was a nuisance."

"You were. Jaran women are much better behaved."

"I don't believe that for an instant, Ilya." She laughed. "Are you telling me now that you're sorry I came?"

"Tess." In the silence she heard, far away, the low cry of an animal, followed by a slide of rock, distant and muted. "Tomorrow morning you'll see an army in that gorge."

"What do you mean?"

"They did pursue us. At least one hundred soldiers."

"Oh, God, Ilya. And I said—" He was staring down, his hair and body dark, blending into cliff and wall, his face and hands starkly contrasting with the darkness. "Can you forgive me? I can't believe I said—"

"Stop it, Tess."

She swallowed. "How long have you known?" she asked in something resembling a normal tone of voice.

"Last night I went back down the gorge."

"You might have been caught!"

"I doubt it. They have no more night wit than a crying infant."

"One hundred soldiers." She gazed down at the shadowed gorge. From the rocks came a bird's cry, deep and wailing, like an owl's hoot or a woman's mourning. "The khaja must hate the jaran more than I thought."

"This is their holy place as well. For us to be here no doubt defiles it in their eyes. And jaran have raided a town. Many towns. What did Keregin say? They are like us in that they seek revenge."

"And yet—" She turned her head to look at him. "Yet you rode through their lands and into—into this? Why?"

The dim illumination made his complexion ashen and bloodless except for the shaded hollows of his eyes. "It's a kind of madness," he said, as softly as the merest brush of wind.

"No," she said, equally quietly, because she felt impelled to reassure him. But she knew that to be the kind of man he was, doing what he meant to do, he had indeed to be infected with a kind of madness, a fire that would burn inward and outward until, in the end, he would be consumed and his people transformed on the anvil of change. "No, it's a kind of honor."

He turned his head slowly and met her eyes. "Do you think so?"

"Yes."

"Death should not be unwelcome to the honorable man."

Tess felt her insides tighten. She found it difficult to speak. "You once told me you had no intention of dying in battle." He gazed at her, the two of them oblivious for that instant to all that surrounded them. *Not me,* she thought, *I'm not going to get burnt in that fire.* And then shook her head, disgusted at her own train of thought.

He shook himself as well and smiled, straightening his back. "Did I mention dying?" he asked, his tone light.

Tess attempted a laugh.

"I sent Josef up the back trail," he continued conversationally, "to discover if it can indeed take us out. The pilgrims can look at the site tonight. In the morning, if the trail is good, we'll ride out that way, though I'll have to leave four archers behind to cover our retreat."

"Who will you leave?"

"Mikhal, Tadheus, Konstans—"

"I'm better than Konstans."

"You're not included."

"Who's the fourth?"

"I am."

"Of course," she said softly. "Where did you learn to shoot so well?"

"In Jeds. I know how to shoot to kill a man. May the gods forgive me."

"Why don't jaran men use bows and arrows in battle?"

"Arrows in battle. That's a grim thought." Below, at the neck of the gorge, there was a slight movement. Stillness, a flash of light hair. Bakhtiian began to speak again. "The plains are as wide as you can see, and there is space to run. There is nothing to defend, except your kin and your honor, and honor rests in facing your opponent in a land where you could just as well flee."

"In this land, between these walls, you'll be dead before you can reach the man you're trying to kill."

"Do you wonder at our enmity?"

"No. I don't wonder."

"Look. The pilgrims have gone down. Just as I suggested to them. A surprise, don't you agree?"

She looked down to the right, where a light moved among the ruins on the far side, against the slide, dipping up and down. They were looking for something.

"Good God." She felt blood drain from her face. What if the symbols on the wall *were* Chapalii, worn away by time—but they could not have been here that long—worn away by some inexplicable confrontation, then. She had seen, she had touched, their transmitter with her own hands. She had found a fragment of a metallurgy too sophisticated for Rhuian development. What if the transmitter wasn't a single anomaly set up in the last five years to prepare for this expedition? A whole cluster, perhaps dating from the first years after the League's discovery of the planet, or from immediately after Charles's ennobling and his receipt of the system. Set up to monitor him. And if he was disseminating the odd volume of Newton and Aristotle, what else might he be surreptitiously doing that violated his own interdiction order? What if the Chapalii had set up monitoring positions to incriminate him? It made sense.

She needed proof.

"I have to go," she said, staring down at the light. She took one step away.

"No." He stopped her with his voice alone. "Don't go. Please."

She turned back slowly, her throat tight, flushing along her neck and cheeks. She could just make out his face in the moonlight as he watched her, and she trembled, sure that he was afraid that this might be his last night on earth. What would she do if he asked her to spend it with him? *God knows, he's attractive enough,* she thought; *men like him always are.*

"If you don't disturb them now," he continued, "then there will be no trouble about leaving before dawn tomorrow. But if you interrupt them, what will I do to convince them to go?"

She recovered her normal breathing, sure that it was fear that made her overreact in this way, cursing herself inwardly for forgetting everything she knew about jaran men. About this man in particular. "Surely when you tell them about this army, they'll agree to run," she said, knowing that the Chapalii could easily defend themselves against a hundred men, that they would, without hesitation. Missile weapons. She did not know whether to laugh or cry, thinking of it. And which would hurt Charles more—that she not investigate here now, or that she let the confrontation come and force the Chapalii to reveal what kind of magic, what kind of utterly superior weaponry, they possessed?

Bakhtiian stared beyond her at the disembodied, flameless light moving below them. "It has been said before that the khepellis control great powers. Magical powers. I have no use for magic." He broke off. "Not any more. Can't you wait until the shrine of Morava? We'll be there for a hand of days. Enough time for spying, I should think." But it was said without heat or accusation.

Enough time for spying. In a way, it was almost as if he knew what she was thinking, as if he were offering her a way out, an excuse to follow his lead and exercise restraint now for the promise of a later chance. And she found that against his asking, she could not refuse. "If we get that far," she said, though she knew the very words sealed the agreement, that she would not disturb the Chapalii, not at this time and in this place.

"Be assured," said Bakhtiian coolly, "that I do not intend to die here." He turned away from her to return to the fires, *as if*, she thought with sudden bitterness, *now that he has what he wants, the conversation no longer interests him.*

Yuri woke her. It was quiet, damp, cold, and still dark. She lay still for a moment, hearing the soft sound of whispers, and horses, and of leather creaking and rustling against cloth.

"Get up, Tess," Yuri said in a low but urgent voice. "We have to get the horses saddled."

"Are we leaving now? There's barely enough light to see by."

"When Josef gets back."

"Yuri, what if that trail is a dead end?"

"It can't be. It just can't be. Come on, you're one of the last."

"The khepelli?"

"They're ready. I don't even think they slept. Niko has them." He pointed, and Tess could faintly make out a group of men saddling horses, all gray and dim. Then he grabbed her hand and pulled her roughly to her feet. "Tess! Don't you understand? A khaja army is down there, waiting to kill us."

"Are they already attacking?" The last dregs of sleep vanished, obliterated by adrenaline.

"No." He looked back, but all was silence and darkness below. "Not until daybreak. They hate us, but they also fear us. It's bad enough having to come up that path one by one, without it being dark as well. Ilya has fifteen men along the lower wall with him. The rest of us will go when Josef returns, then the fifteen from below—"

"And last the four archers?"

"Yes. Last." A horse whinnied softly. "I'm a better archer than Konstans. But *he* says I'm to go with you and Niko."

Tess thought, *he's doing that for me.* She said, "If only you had bows for everyone. If only you could all shoot well."

"It isn't honorable," Yuri began, but he hesitated. "They are only khaja, after all." He put out a hand and Tess took it and laid it on her cheek. It was cold. "I don't know what we'll do if we lose Bakhtiian."

"Neither do I," she replied. They saddled their horses in silence and herded the rest to the base of the trail. The khepellis assembled behind them.

It grew light as they finished, Niko saddling one of the tarpans for Bakhtiian.

"Why isn't he riding his black?" Tess asked.

Niko looked up at her, eyes dark. "He wants it to go with the herd." He stood and laid a hand on the horse's withers. "Headstrong idiot," he muttered, and then, "Well, this is all we can do. Damn it, where is Josef? He knows our situation. Something must have happened to him." And then, as if appalled that he had said it, he lapsed into angry silence.

From her position at the base of the trail, Tess could see the neck of the gorge and the first level of wall, gray now, lightening. She glanced at the Chapalii; they looked completely undisturbed, pallid and colorless. Yuri put a hand on her shoulder.

The night retreated as the sun rose. The fifteen men were ranged along the wall below. One of them detached himself from the line and ran up toward them: Bakhtiian. Tess and Yuri gave their reins to Nikita and walked over to Niko, who had gone to the upper wall. Bakhtiian scrambled up the escarpment and pulled himself up to sit on the wall, one leg dangling, the other flat against the stone.

"Josef?" If he was breathing quickly, it was from excitement not from his short run.

"No sign," said Niko.

"I've changed my mind. You'll go up the trail now. We'll follow as soon as we confuse them enough to set them back a bit."

"How are you going to do that?" Tess asked.

He did not even look at her, his attention on the narrow gorge. Movement flashed and vanished. "You mustn't hasten the game."

"What if the trail is a dead end?" Niko asked.

"Then we're dead either way. Let us hope the gods favor us today."

Movement again at the neck of the gorge. Bakhtiian stood up on the wall. White flashed, and then a white cloth tied to a spear appeared.

"So they want to talk to a priest," said Bakhtiian. "I hope I'll do."

A man appeared, holding the spear aloft. The white cloth shuddered and danced in the breeze. The man halted and placed the spear butt on the ground: parley. Nothing moved. Deep shadows surrounded him. The man shifted nervously and then threw back his head.

"We have no quarrel with jharan," he shouted.

"Jharan jharan," the echoes returned. "He speaks khush!" Tess whispered to Yuri.

"A similar tongue."

"Give us Boctiyan!" the man cried. "The others may go free." His accent was atrocious.

Tess looked up. Bakhtiian was smiling. "What do you want with Bakhtiian?" he shouted down.

"Boctiyan—he has burnt town, killed children, forced women. He is an evil man, cruel, a demon sent by—" He

lasped into a description of something, or someone, that
sounded horrible but which Tess could not follow.

"I have gotten a reputation," said Ilya. "Of the unsavory
kind."

"That," said Tess, "is an understatement."

The man, silent now, stared up at Bakhtiian, a figure
lighter than anything below, the wind moving in his hair
and flaring the loose sleeves of his blood-red shirt as he
stood, unmoving, on the high wall.

"Do you suppose they think I'm mad?" he asked. He
grinned, looking like an uncomfortable blend of beauty and
menace: the bright child gone evil.

"You are mad," Tess muttered, wondering if he had already forgotten what he had said last night. And then, because he was looking down at her, she went on hastily.
"They probably scare their children into bed at night by
telling them stories about you."

He laughed. "Gods. I'm still young. I'll end up by giving
myself nightmares." He stared down at the man below. "He
must be a priest. Don't khaja priests wear that cut of tunic
and those thick—what are they called?" He switched to
Rhuian briefly. "Baldrics." He lifted his chin and shouted
again. "What will you do with Bakhtiian?"

"He has offended our god by killing our holy brothers in
Eratia and Tiarton. We of Tialla Great Walls are doubly
stricken, for he has fouled our sacred temple by setting his
cursed feet in it. Our god must have revenge."

"Niko!" His gaze remained on the priest below. *"This*
temple?"

"I know of no other near here."

"These khaja are a religious people."

"Devout. Fanatic. Their god offends easily, if the death
of a holy brother is of greater account than that of a child."

"Keregin of the arenabekh says that they treat their
women particularly badly here. Would lying with a woman
in here offend them, do you think?"

"Ilya!"

"Damn it, Niko, would it? We need time. Would they try
to stop it? Or retreat?"

That hushed sound, Tess thought. *It must be the stream.*

"Damn you, Ilya. I talked with a khaja once years ago,
a man from hereabouts. We were trading."

"Niko."

"He said that to murder or to rape in a temple brought the anger of the god, and—gods! Yes, I remember. Or to see it done!"

"Ha! Priest! Priest!" He shouted, one hand moving to his saber. "So you think *I* foul your temple."

The priest dropped the spear, grabbed it. "Black demon!" he cried. Two men helmeted with leather coifs appeared and then vanished back into the gorge behind him.

"So your god is offended!" shouted Ilya. "Niko," he said, not turning his head. "Everyone mounted." Niko moved back, Tess and Yuri following. "No," said Bakhtiian. He reached down, glancing back, and grabbed Tess's wrist. "Up." His pull was so strong that instead of coming up to her feet on the wall she lost her balance, boots skidding on the smooth stone, and fell to her knees on the wall. She stared up at Bakhtiian; the priest stared at her. Bakhtiian reached down and tugged at her braid. Her hair fell loose around her. "Priest!" he shouted. "Since you offend me, I'll defile your temple."

The priest wailed a protest, incoherent at this distance.

"Fight me," Bakhtiian demanded, jerking her up. She twisted away from him and kicked out, half slipping again. He reacted so instinctively that he wrenched her arm and she gasped in pain. "I'm sorry," he whispered.

"No!" cried the priest. "Do not defile the temple!"

She was caught, bent backward, half balanced on one hand and half held up by Bakhtiian's arm behind her back. The sky had a transparent quality; the peaks shimmered. "Scream," he said. He put his free hand to the top of her tunic.

"I've never screamed in my life,' she said, paling. "I don't know how."

"Scream, damn it!"

Tess screamed.

"No," cried the priest. Men appeared, armed, bows ready, spears leveled. "No!" he yelled, desperate. "Stay back. Do not compound the offense. Stay back!" The men retreated. The priest fell to his knees and covered his eyes, calling once, twice, to his god, entreating His aid.

Bakhtiian's glance shifted, and he lifted his chin, signaling to the men stationed along the wall below. Then he glanced back. "Yuri. Tell the others to go. We can't wait for Josef. You wait with Tess's horse.'' He looked down at Tess. ''Do you have anything on under this?''

''Yes.''

From above, they heard noises, the beginning of the retreat. The priest looked up. Bakhtiian ripped off her tunic. The priest shrieked and covered his face. At the wall, the fifteen riders leapt up and ran for the escarpment.

''That's Nadezhda Martov's pattern,'' said Bakhtiian, looking bemusedly at the collar of the white blouse she wore under her now-ripped tunic.

''Stay back! Stay back!'' the priest was crying. ''We must not compound the crime with offense of our own.''

The fifteen men reached the upper wall and scrambled over it to land panting on the packed earth behind.

''Everyone go except the archers,'' said Bakhtiian.

''But—''

At the sudden silence, the priest ceased wailing and lowered his hands from his face.

''Go!''

Twelve left. Tess saw them, quiet and swift, and heard their horses pounding away up the trail. The priest looked up, confused. Then he stood, dropping the spear, and the white cloth fluttered to the ground.

Bakhtiian closed his hand on the thin white fabric of her blouse. And hesitated. ''I can't do this.''

''Damned male.'' Tess kicked him, swung with an arm, and squirmed for the edge of the wall. The priest hid his eyes and yelled again at the soldiers behind him to stay back, adding a string of incomprehensible, hysterical words.

Tess's legs lay half off the wall on the upper side, Yuri crouched beneath her. Bakhtiian lay half across her chest, his left arm pinning her to the rock. Cold edges thrust into her back. His head rested two hands above hers, shading her from the sun. He was not looking at her, but staring down at the priest, a small figure in white and blue far below. She noticed how the waves of his dark hair flowed in patterns that had the same sweep and curve and richness as rose petals. A breeze cooled her cheek.

''Now what?'' she asked.

Bakhtiian looked down at her. His mouth twitched. ''I think I'm going to start laughing.''

Tess shut her eyes and choked back a giggle, gulping in the thin air. Six of them left. Someone was not going to make it up that trail. "How long do you think they're going to believe this?" she cried, not at him really but at the fate that had brought them here. She pushed at him, trying to get free. "Yuri!" yelled Bakhtiian. "Get her out of here." To the others: "Ready!"

Yuri hauled her off the wall. Bakhtiian jumped down after. Faintly, she heard yelling from the priest, orders being given. Tears blurred her sight. Yuri dragged her away toward the horses.

"We can't leave them!" Tess pulled away from him. An arrow struck the ground and skittered to a stop a meter from her. Yuri grabbed her at the elbow and yanked her forward, shoving her into Myshla.

"Mount!" he yelled, as if she were deaf. She swung up reflexively. More arrows peppered the packed dirt, too spent to penetrate. "Come on, Tess."

Far below, a man cried out in pain.

"Ilya got one. Damn it, Tess. Ride." He wheeled his horse back and slapped Myshla on the rump. Four arrows hit, and one stuck in the earth. Myshla moved, ears cocked forward. Tess urged her to a trot, hearing the swell of shouts and cries from below. She looked back: four jaran men crouched behind the upper wall, their shirts like blood against the black stone, shooting.

"Yuri!" She waved frantically at him. "They can't hold them!" She reined Myshla back.

"Ride, Tess!" He reined his horse in, waiting for her, impatient, angry, scared. The horses sidestepped, catching their fear. Myshla neighed, calling to those left behind.

"Mikhal. Konstans. Go." Bakhtiian's voice carried easily in the clear air. Bent low, the two men ran for their horses and started after Tess and Yuri. Behind, the last mounts shifted nervously.

"What if they bolt?" she yelled.

"Then they're dead. Damn it, Tess. Damn it. Ride!" He came close enough finally to grab Myshla's bridle and start dragging her. Tess still stared behind. They came to the head of the trail, where it wound up between rocks until a sharp corner hid its path.

"Go!" Yuri waved her ahead. Mikhal and Konstans neared, cantering. She could not see the stretch of wall that sheltered Bakhtiian and Tadheus, only the high, impenetrable barrier of mountain and a tuft of grass fallen, its brown, withering roots exposed, onto a jagged ledge. She kicked Myshla and rounded the corner.

"Yuri!" she screamed.

Black, all in black, like the avenging spirits of the gods. How she turned Myshla and thrust her back through the others to the ruins she never knew. The arenabekh spilled out behind her, out over the cleared area and scrambling down the escarpment to the ruins below. Curses and shouts of fear came from below, and from above, from a man not twenty feet from her, a yell like the scream of a carnivore after blood. The riderless horses bolted but one of the arenabekh caught them and led them over to Bakhtiian and Tadheus. Tasha's shirt bore a wet stain: blood. A broken arrow lay at his feet, its shaft striped with scarlet. The black riders arrayed themselves over the slopes, utter black against gray and gold and green. Like the obsidian walls, they reflected nothing but darkness. From below came only silence. Except for one body lying prone in a shadow, the khaja soldiers had retreated back into the gorge.

Bakhtiian stood and turned. "My own demons from the mountains."

Keregin rode over to Bakhtiian. "Your sweethearts are no longer so eager."

Bakhtiian looked down at the mouth of the gorge. A few shadows still overlay it, but light descended steadily, and soon enough it would lie fully lit in the glare of the sun. "They don't approve of my relations."

"They'll get over it. Do you want us to entertain them when they return?" Keregin grinned, peering through half-closed, heavy-lidded eyes.

"You have no obligation to take on my quarrels."

"The gods have touched your head, Bakhtiian. You send away your jahar to make the odds interesting, and then, because that isn't enough, you send away the last four, so that you can impress the world by beating off—how many?"

"One hundred and seven."

"One hundred and seven! Ah, Bakhtiian, you've taken our fighting from us by uniting the jaran. Whom can we hire ourselves to now? Give us this. Don't be greedy."

"You are only forty riders."

Keregin laughed. "Rather unfair odds against those khaja bastards, don't you think? If we'd wanted to live forever, we'd have married and gotten children. No, let us do this. This day's work alone will make your reputation.''

Bakhtiian smiled slightly. ''Make my reputation what?''

''Something for you to live with and live up to. And yet, I still have no good idea of your height.'' He grinned, purposely insulting. ''From up here, you still don't seem that impressive.''

''I improve as one gets closer.''

''Oh, I like you, Bakhtiian.'' Keregin slapped his thigh. The sound reverberated through the vale, and he chuckled. ''If only I were a younger, handsomer man—but no, you wouldn't make that choice, would you? Ho, there, Sergi!'' he yelled down to one of the lead riders. ''What are our sweethearts up to down there?''

''Cowering,'' replied the distant man. ''Afraid of love, the fools.''

''Love!'' shouted Keregin. ''No. Passion.'' His shout echoed back at him.

''Keregin, I've never before let others do my work for me.''

''If you plan to lead the jaran, Bakhtiian, you'd best get used to it. Other men have made you a devil to our friends below. Why shouldn't you leave us to make you an atrocity that will terrify them for generations?''

''Damn you. Leave a few alive to tell the tale.''

The wind was rising. ''We'll tell them you called us up from the very depths of your fire-scorched heart.''

Tadheus had mounted. Bakhtiian paused, as if to say something, but swung up on his horse without a word. He sat there a moment, while he and Keregin simply looked at one another.

Abruptly, Keregin reined his horse downward and yelled at his riders. They all left the upper level, scattering down into the ruins, and those in the forefront started down to the gate that led onto the meadow and from there to the neck of the gorge. A volley of arrows sprayed out from the gorge. Tess caught her breath, but no one fell.

Not yet. The riders shouted insults at each other, arguing among themselves over who would get to lead the charge. Until Keregin, shouting, ''Move aside!'' sent his horse down in front, thrusting past the others, through the gate, and plunged down onto the meadow, the rest crowding behind.

Soldiers burst out of the gorge, swords out. Arrows flew.

Two of the riders fell, but four khaja were struck down by the sabers that flashed in the sun. The khaja soldiers retreated in great disorder back into the gorge, and Keregin, to Tess's horror, charged down the neck of the gorge after them, shouting, all in black, like the shadow of death against rock. The rest of the arenabekh followed him, one by one. Shrieks of agony and shrill, exultant cries echoed through the vale.

"Tess!" A touch on her arm. Yuri. Tadheus, Mikhal, and Konstans had already gone, vanished up the trail. Bakhtiian, like her, had been watching. Now he rode up beside her.

"Go on, Tess. Haven't you had enough excitement?"

"I don't call that excitement," she muttered, but neither man heard her, Yuri riding in front, Bakhtiian behind, as they followed the trail up into the mountains, the vale and the sounds of fighting lost in the towering rocks they left behind. Her last glimpse: fair-haired Sergi, thick braid dangling to his waist, saber raised, horse half rearing as he drove it down into the gorge. *Someday,* she thought, *a great avalanche will cover it all up.*

Yuri paused at the switchback to glance back at her. He grinned. Tess pulled the last of her ruined tunic free and tossed it away, letting it fall where it would. The sun warmed her back where it penetrated the delicate weave of her blouse. Ahead, a bird trilled.

"I'll get you a new shirt," shouted Bakhtiian from below. Tess laughed. "By the gods," he said, coming up beside her, "we'll give you a red one."

CHAPTER SIXTEEN

"When therefore in the air
there occurs a clash of contrary winds and showers."
—ANTIPHON THE SOPHIST

They followed the narrow trail all day, hemmed in by high rock, then dismounted and walked their horses until the moon set. Tess slept huddled in her cloak, shivering, starting awake at intervals, but even so, Yuri woke her all too soon. The flush of dawn stained the sky, softening the darkness, and they went on.

The path curled through the heights, ascending and descending by turns. For one interminable stretch a fall of rock half obliterated the trail, and they dismounted and picked their way over the gray slivers that littered the ground. At midday Bakhtiian stopped them at a waterfall that fed a lawn of lush grass; the horses drank and grazed. Tess slumped against a rock, chewing on a strip of dry meat. She was glad of the rest at first, but as it stretched out she became afraid. What if the khaja soldiers were behind them? What if Keregin's men hadn't killed them all? What if more khaja had come hunting them? At last Bakhtiian called to them to mount, and they continued on. Still, they saw no sign of their jahar.

"Niko's driving them," said Bakhtiian when they halted by yet another stream. They rode again until the moon was gone, shadows staggering over the ground. Yuri's Kuhaylan mare went lame with a stone in its hoof. Mikhal's chestnut tarpan began to cough and wheeze.

Tess slept badly. When she woke at dawn, one of her calves had cramped. Her back ached. She limped. The path worsened and their pace slowed. Bakhtiian stopped them again at midday to water and graze the horses; Tess ate her food mechanically, without hunger. The shock she had had in the vale, the sudden appreciation of death, had drained her; she kept going now only because Myshla followed the other horses.

In the late afternoon they halted to let the horses breathe, a rough, tearing sound in the stillness. Tadheus, white-faced and sweating, was too exhausted to dismount by himself, but at least his wound was no longer bleeding. Konstans sat hunched and shaking on the ground. After a bit he rose and checked all the horses' hooves with unnerving thoroughness. Then he argued with Mikhal and Bakhtiian over whether to kill the chestnut, who was lagging badly. They decided to kill it.

Tess leaned against Myshla, not wanting to watch. She breathed in the mare's hot, dry smell as if it were tenacity. No matter how much of the thin air she gulped down, it was never enough.

"Here, Tess." It was Yuri, holding a cup of blood, still warm. "Drink."

Tess clutched Myshla's mane, feeling dizzy with revulsion. "I can't."

"Drink it."

Because it was an order, she obeyed.

"Thank the gods, Myshla and Khani are holding up so well," said Yuri, taking the empty cup from her. He rubbed Myshla's nose affectionately. "Ilya says he's never seen horses with the stamina of these khuhaylans. The khepellis must be the finest breeders of horses in all the lands. Come, Tess. We need your help." He left.

Tess went to relieve Mikhal, who was watching the horses, so he could go help with the slaughter. The horses stood, heads drooping, exhausted. Tasha dozed on the ground. Yuri's words bothered her: the Chapalii—and the Arabians they had given to Bakhtiian—who should have been doing the worst on this journey, were doing the best. Chapalii efficiency. The horses had to have been altered somehow. Yuri brought more blood, and she lifted Tasha up and helped him drink. After an interminable time, the men finished their work. They went on, leaving the chestnut's carcass to rot on the path behind. Yuri and Konstans stank of blood.

The moon rose, bright, throwing hallucinatory shadows on the rock walls that surrounded them. Tess held onto

Myshla's reins and stumbled along in Yuri's wake. This went on forever.

Eventually the path narrowed. Directly ahead rose a blind wall of stone blocking their trail. Somewhere in the rocks an animal called, mocking them. A shout carried back from Konstans, who rode at the fore. She could not see him. The sheer cliff loomed before her, impassable, huge, and she began to rein Myshla aside, for surely they must halt here, having no farther to go. But the path twisted sharply to the right between two hulking black boulders, angled back to the left, and she heard a laugh above her and looked up.

"Kirill!" At that moment she could have seen nothing more pleasing.

He stood on a small ledge, looking more then usually self-satisfied. "Tess. I could have spitted your four companions as they rode past, but I thought that if I did, I'd block the path with bodies and then *you* couldn't get through."

Tess laughed, spirits already lighter. "You're too good to me, Kirill. Where can I find a space large enough to sleep?"

"At my breast," said Kirill cheerfully, aware that Bakhtiian had come up behind her and was listening.

"Wanton," said Tess.

"If you go on," he added, not a bit contrite, "it opens up and we've made a little camp."

She walked on. The path remained an arm's span wide for about one hundred paces. Shadowy forms, concealed at strategic intervals, greeted her. Where the path widened, Niko was waiting. He took Myshla's reins.

"Yuri says you're tired, child. Let me take the horse."

She merely stood after he left, her eyelids fluttering, her head sinking. A low humming filled her ears.

"Tess." Yuri took hold of her hand and led her to a small space away from the path. "Sleep." He dumped her blanket and cloak on the ground and left. She slept.

The sun woke her. Its warmth on her face felt like the stroke of a hand, soft and comforting. Until it occurred to her that in this ravine the sun had to be very high to shine down on her; that they should still be here at this late hour of the morning was impossible. She sat up.

"I thought you'd never wake up."

Looking up, she saw Yuri smiling at her from where he perched on top of the boulder against which she slept.

"Why are we still here?" She got hastily to her feet and blinked in the brightness. Ahead, she saw the camp—the four Chapalii tents and one fire crowded in between the high walls. One scrubby, yellow-barked tree shaded the fire, and a few bushes clung to the slopes. "It must be midday."

"Ah, Tess," he said in Rhuian, "your perspicacity amazes me."

"Why, Yuri, your vocabulary is finally improving."

He grinned, then lifted his head and looked around, so remarkably like a lizard that Tess laughed. He slid down the rock to stand beside her, lowering his voice. "Ilya and Niko had a terrible argument last night. You were already asleep. Ilya was furious with himself for not sending everyone ahead up the trail to begin with, but Niko told Ilya that only a damn fool sent horsemen ahead on a trail that hadn't been scouted and that other circumstances had forced his hand. Well, it was a good thing the arenabekh came along when they did."

Tess nodded.

"But now we can rest and take an easy pace to our next camp. You looked just awful last night though you look fine this morning."

"How you flatter me."

"It comes naturally from having four sisters. One learns how to keep on their good side."

"Where is our next camp?"

"The first good site with forage we come to. We have to wait for Ilya."

"Where did he go?"

"Back to the temple."

A cloud shaded the sun. She shivered. "You can't mean it."

"What do you mean, I can't mean it? He took fresh horses and left as soon as he saw that Niko had everything in order. After they had argued, of course. Niko thought Josef should go back."

"Last night? But we'd been riding for two and a half days."

"Don't you think I know that? If Khani wasn't so damned stubborn she'd have gone dead lame from that stone, and we'd have killed her. Pavel say she'll be fine. But the chestnut—" He shook his head. "Still, I could hardly keep my eyes open. Surely you know that Bakhtiian has nothing in common with such weak stuff as you or me. So off he went, fresh as a spring breeze, singing—'' Tess giggled. ''Very well. He wasn't singing. You must want something to eat.''

''I'm starving.''

Yuri laid a hand on her shoulder before she could leave the shelter of the rock. ''Niko is going to give you a red shirt. I wasn't supposed to tell you, but I thought you'd rather be warned.''

Her face suddenly felt hot and it was not just due to the sun emerging from the clouds.

''I don't remember any woman being given a red shirt. It makes you—this story will be told everywhere, even after you—''

''After I what?''

He hung his head. ''After you leave us,'' he said softly, but, being Yuri, he brightened immediately. ''That's so much later I can't even think of it.''

''Good. I don't know what you're talking about.'' She took a step and paused, not quite willing yet to be fussed over—for knowing these riders, fussing it would be. The conical white tents caught her eye. Ishii sat outside one, alone. Rakii and Garii reclined on the rocks above, gambling to pass the time. Meanwhile all eight stewards were busy saddling horses and taking down the first two of the tents.

Had she really feared them so much? Like the khaja priest's terror at the possibility of sacrilege in the temple, the Chapalii's adherence to custom and hierarchy had protected her all along. She could spy on them because of her rank. Ishii would keep secrets from her because his mysterious liege outranked her. But Garii's allegiance puzzled her. Clearly he must be pledged to Ishii's house to have come on this expedition. As clearly, he had pledged himself personally to her in direct violation of his previous pledge, a breach of Chapalii custom that ought to brand him as something lower than a serial killer in her eyes. And yet, as a human, she wondered if perhaps he was just trying to better himself, hoping to attach himself to the household of a lord who outranked Ishii.

''Tess? Are you coming?''

She sighed and transferred her gaze from the Chapalii to the riders, who gathered in anticipation of her arrival. After staring death in the face, she could not imagine why she had ever really feared the Chapalii. Truly, they posed no greater threat than the threat this little presentation posed to her composure: it was her own resources being challenged. Death—real, stark, painful death, that Fedya had faced without flinching—was something else again.

"Tess." Niko came forward to lead her over to the fire. "We have something to present to you, which you have fairly earned." Somehow Kirill had got hold of the shirt so that *he* got to give it to her along with a kiss on the cheek. Despite all this, she still found that she could receive it without blushing. Until Yuri said, "But, Tess, that's exactly your color!" and everyone laughed. The sound echoed round the little vale, and she blushed and smiled and knew suddenly that she had gained a whole family of cousins and uncles—that gifted one tent and one mirror and one shirt, she now had a tribe, a place where she belonged simply for herself.

Unexpectedly, in the chaos that attended leaving, Garii brought her saddled tarpan.

"Lady Terese. Please allow me to offer you this service," he said colorlessly, offering her the reins.

"I thank you, Hon Garii," she said, accepting them. He flushed pink.

"If I may be permitted to ask a question?" She nodded again. "These men have given you a shirt. Although my understanding may be incomplete, the gift itself seems to act as a symbol of your acceptance into their bonding unit. Perhaps you will be generous enough, Lady Terese, to enlighten me on this."

"No, it is true enough, what you surmise."

"And yet," he hesitated, colors chasing themselves across his cheeks in a brief, muted display, "they have offered you this not because you are Tai-endi, the heir of a duke, but because of acts you have yourself accomplished."

"That is also true, Hon Garii."

"This culture," he said, "is very different from my own." He bowed, glanced back to where the Chapalii were readying their horses, and looked again at Tess. "My family of Takokan has been pledged to that of the Hokokul lordship for only five hundred of your years, a great dishonor to my clan, for we had an impetuous ancestor who transferred his pledge away from the Warakul lordship when that lord used my ancestor's wife and daughters in an impolite fashion."

"Hon Garii, why are you telling me this?"

For the first time, he looked her straight in the eye, without arrogance and yet without any shame either. "Lady Terese, what has passed between us—has passed between us. I withhold from you none of my family's disgrace. I trust you to judge fairly." He bowed and retreated, walking back to Cha Ishii and the other Chapalii.

What had passed between them? He could be referring to nothing but his offer of personal loyalty to her the night Doroskayev had died. An offer that would make him a pariah in his own culture should it become public. But given the protection of a duke's heir, would being a pariah even matter? No wonder opportunism was so reprehensible a trait in a culture whose hierarchy had not changed in centuries.

She sighed and rubbed her finger along the smooth red silk of her new shirt. Not even the Chapalii could ruin this day. She grinned and mounted and rode with Yuri. They took a slower pace for the sake of the horses, and it was fine weather for the sake of her equally fine mood.

At dusk on the second day they camped in a small, high-sided valley tinted with green, the ghost of summer still resisting autumn's pull. From one of the containing ridges the plateau could be seen, flat and yellowing. The sight of it was welcome. Two days passed uneventfully. In the early afternoon of the third, the watch on the trail let out a shrill yell, and soon Bakhtiian could be seen, slowly leading a string of fifteen horses, his black at the forefront, along the valley to the camp.

He looked terrible. The stallion no longer had any trace of glossy sheen to its coat, but it held its head up. A number of men ran to care for the horses. Vladimir took the black. Ilya washed first, and he went from there directly to his tent. That was the last anyone saw of him until morning. Everyone rose early the next day and lavished their energy on the horses, these relics of the arenabekh, yet always they kept an eye on Bakhtiian's tent. When he finally emerged, however, Niko and Josef and Tadheus greeted him first. Tess and Yuri sat on some boulders a bit above the camp, tossing stones at a cleft in the rock, watching the four men as they talked.

"How does he keep his looks?" Tess asked.

Yuri grinned and began to laugh, an infectious and utterly irresistible influence. "I dare you to ask him that."

Tess swallowed a giggle. "Don't, Yuri. I will."

Yuri put a hand over his mouth. Below, the stream shone, sparkling in the sunlight. "I don't believe it."

"Bakhtiian!" yelled Tess.

Yuri choked and held his stomach. "Tess!" he squeaked.

Bakhtiian said something to his companions, detached himself, and walked toward them, his boots light on the moss and low grass. Yuri shook in silent mirth, tears seeping from his eyes.

"We were just wondering," said Tess as Bakhtiian came up to them, "how you manage to keep your looks, running around at the pace you do." She had so far managed some semblance of seriousness, but a giggle escaped from Yuri and she had to cough violently to stop herself from laughing. Bakhtiian stared at them for a moment, as if puzzled. He drew himself up very straight and advanced on them sternly. Yuri's glee vanished like a flake of snow on fire.

"Oh," he said, eyes widening. "I take it all back, Tess."

"All of it?" Bakhtiian halted in front of the young man, arms crossed.

"Help!" said Yuri faintly, but Tess started to laugh. Yuri stared at her in horror. Bakhtiian climbed up to sit on the rock, with Yuri between him and Tess. He wiped dust from his hands.

"Well," he said to Yuri, "it is my experience that when a woman shows interest in a man's looks, he'd best begin to pay attention."

"What!" Tess's laughter vanished. "I deny everything." She blushed.

"I keep my looks," said Bakhtiian with dignity, still looking at Yuri, "by not indulging in frivolity."

"He must have been a dull child," said Tess to Yuri.

"And a dull youth," said Yuri.

"And I fear he's becoming a dull man," finished Tess. She glanced surreptitiously at Bakhtiian. It might have been that he was blushing slightly, or perhaps only the brisk wind on his cheeks, but in any case he had found something in the camp that attracted his gaze.

"I don't really believe it," said Yuri to Bakhtiian. "You must have been the boy in the middle a hundred times before you were twenty."

"At the risk of destroying your very gratifying faith in me, Yuri, I must be honest with you. It pains me even now to remember how very thoroughly I was ignored by the girls when I was young."

"I don't believe it," said Yuri.

"It might even have partially influenced my decision to go to Jeds. And of course there was—" He paused and seemed to change his mind about something. "Nataliia," he finished.

"Of course." Yuri stared at Bakhtiian as though he had never seen him before. "Ilya, I—" He flushed. "I didn't mean to. . . ."

Bakhtiian's gaze flashed past Yuri to Tess and immediately returned to Yuri. Tess suddenly got the impression that this entire conversation was between her and Bakhtiian, with Yuri serving simply as the intermediary. A small, rodentlike animal rushed across rock, paused to look at them, and ran on, disappearing into the tiny crevasse.

"Your sister Nataliia?" Tess asked.

"Yes," he answered, still looking at Yuri. He smiled slightly. "Growing the beard may have helped." He stroked the dark line of his beard absently.

"Men! You're all of you vain."

"We have to be," said Yuri, turning to Tess. "Since we live every moment of our lives subject to the whims of women."

"Do you?"

"Yes," said Yuri and Bakhtiian at the same moment.

Tess opened her mouth to reply, closed it, and shrugged.

"Ilya," said Yuri. "What did you find at the temple?"

Bakhtiian shut his eyes. The high ring of sabers startled Tess. Down in the camp, several men were practicing. "Nothing that I ever want you to see, Yurinya. So. We ride at dawn tomorrow."

"That bad?" asked Yuri.

"Autumn also brings the early storms, here by the mountains. We're ten or fifteen days now from the shrine of Morava. We have to reach the port before the ships stop sailing for the winter months."

"It must have been terrible," said Yuri to Tess.

"I brought you something," said Bakhtiian. A flat tone of metal from below, a curse, and laughter. "A gift from the dead. Run down to my tent and bring me the long leather sack. There is something for Tess, too."

"Of course!" Yuri scrambled off the rocks, dust spraying down after him, and ran down into camp.

"Where I come from," said Tess, resting her elbow on one knee and turning her head to look directly at Bakhtiian, "we call that contriving to get rid of someone without insulting them."

Bakhtiian smiled. "I believe it's called much the same thing everywhere. I want to apologize to you."

"For what?"

He stared down at his hands. Eyes lowered, he looked so incongruously modest that she had to smile. "At the temple. My behavior was . . . inexcusable. For a man to behave toward a woman in such a fashion is . . . shameful."

"Ilya! We did that to save lives."

He did not look up. The brown rodent ran out from the crevasse and halted on the next rock, its bright eyes fixed on them. "Please believe that I would never have done such a thing if I'd been thinking clearly, but I never think clearly when I'm in battle."

"No, you think quickly, and that is why you're a good commander."

He glanced up at her. "You don't hold it against me?"

"Bakhtiian!" She slapped a hand down on her thigh. The little animal scrambled away. "Did you ever see a play in Jeds?" He nodded. "We were acting. It was a scene played out for that moment, nothing else."

"I learned well enough in Jeds how lightly they hold such violence." He studied his palms where they lay open in his lap. "This is not a thing that is ever spoken of between men and women, but should a jaran man ever try—may the gods forgive me for even thinking of such a thing—to force a woman, he would be dead the next instant. And no man would lift a hand to stop the women from executing their justice."

"There are many things I admire about the jaran, and that is one of them." She lowered her voice. "Ilya, you and I understand why it was done. Every man in this jahar understands." Reflexively, she smoothed the silky soft sleeve of the red shirt she now wore.

He shrugged conciliatorily and at last met her eyes. "You don't think I'm a demon?"

"No." She could not resist smiling. "Though I liked Keregin's suggestion that you called the arenabekh from—

what did he say?—from the depths of your fire-scorched
heart. Did they all die?''

"I hope so, since those who did not would have been
taken prisoner by the khaja.''

"And the horses?''

"Those too badly injured I killed. The others—'' He gestured below. ''—as you see, though not all will be able to
keep our pace. Here is Yuri.'' And it occurred to Tess that
Bakhtiian's own remount had not come back with him.

Bakhtiian jumped down from the rocks, took the bag from
Yuri and, rolling down the edges, carefully lifted sabers out
and placed them side by side on the ground.

"Gods!'' exclaimed Yuri. Tess merely gaped. Light
flashed from the blades.

"Spoils,'' said Ilya. ''I thought they would rather we had
them than the khaja. I couldn't carry many, so I took the
ten best. And an eleventh, for myself.'' He looked at Tess.
''Tobay. Do you remember? His saber is as good as his
arm.'' He reached down. ''Here, Yuri. This one for you.''

"But, Ilya, it's beautiful.'' Yuri tested it, turning his arm,
feeling its weight. ''I can't possibly deserve it.''

"Perhaps it will inspire you to practice as often as you
should. This for Mikhal. Oh—'' He laughed, picking up
another by its ornate, jeweled hilt. ''This for Vladi, of
course.'' He replaced them one by one in the bag until there
was only one left: a delicately curved thing that rang when
he struck the blade with his nail. ''Cousin,'' he said to Tess.
''Our kinsman Yurinya did very poorly for you when he got
you a saber. He must have applied to his most miserly cousin
who could scarcely bring himself to begrudge you his third
blade, and only a few men have two. That you have any
aptitude for saber at all is incredible, considering how ill-
balanced and ill-wrought that thing is. I suggest you take it
off, cast it in the dirt, and forget you ever knew it.'' He
held out the saber. She stared at it. When he put it into her
hands, the metal cold on her fingers, she merely continued
to stare, until she saw the mark.

"This is Keregin's saber. I remember this mark. Is it a
rune? I can't take this.''

"I think he would have been pleased to know you inherited it. It was the finest blade on the field. Yes, that is a
rune on the hilt.''

"What does it mean?''

Bakhtiian frowned. "It can't be explained in one word. It means, the soul that finds the wind that will bear it the highest and does not shrink from being borne. The soul that does not fear being swept up into the heavens. The soul kissed by the gods that rejoices in their cares. That hardly does it justice. Words are too poor."

"Excuse me," said Tess in a small voice. She turned and walked away from them, cradling the saber against her like a baby.

Bakhtiian stared after her, motionless, his back to the sun, his face shadowed.

"Ilya," said Yuri, "that was your old saber you gave me for Tess when we left the tribe."

Bakhtiian started and bent to hoist the bag, his face lit now as he turned into the sun. "Let's take these down," he said.

Tess spent the rest of the day with her saber, sharpening it, polishing it, turning it so that it flashed in the sun, convincing now this man, now that, to give her a short lesson in fighting. She slept with it that night and welcomed the dawn and their early departure because there was nothing more glorious to her at that moment than the feeling of her saber resting on her hip as she rode.

"I'd have brought you another," said Bakhtiian, "if I'd known you'd be so pleased with this one."

Tess reined Myshla past a slight irregularity of ground and laughed. "Gods! What would I do with two? There's enough to learn with one."

Bakhtiian smiled. "Watch yourself, or your brother won't recognize you when you reach Jeds."

"Why not?"

"You've begun to swear in khush. The outer trappings of an alien culture are easily assumed, but when the inner workings begin to touch your own, then you're in danger."

"In danger of what? Being consumed? Amnesia?"

"What is *amnhesia?*"

"Forgetting who you are."

He considered. Tumbled boulders obscured the sides of the path. Plants thrust up from every cleft and crack in the stone, reaching for the light. "There were times, in my three years in Jeds, when I felt confused as to who I was, but I was never in any danger of succumbing to *that* culture. I'm not very adaptable.''

"But that's not true, Ilya. You are.''

"Being able to understand alien ways, being able to accept the fact of them, is not necessarily adaptability. I am jaran heart and soul. Nothing will change that.''

The path snaked up to the top of a ridge, where they halted. Far below Tess saw the golden sheet of the plateau. They sat for a moment in silence and simply looked. He had killed a man—long ago it seemed now—for transgressing the code of jaran religion, for nothing more than killing a bird, and yet he struggled to understand Newton and was compelled to ask what amnesia was, hearing it mentioned. It was as if half of him questioned incessantly and the other half never questioned at all.

"Perhaps,'' she replied at last. "But many people would not be able to understand enough of the inner workings of another people to know that, say, the religious strictures of the khaja would be strong enough to stop them at the temple when—''

"Please.'' Bakhtiian turned away from her, urging his black down the slope. "It is my disgrace that I acted as I did. It is also improper for a man and a woman to speak of such a thing.''

"Forgive me,'' said Tess coldly, but the comment was addressed to his back. She followed him as they descended into a long valley. A thin layer of clouds trailed along the horizon. A snake moved sluggishly off the white-soiled path, leaving an elegant line in the dust. Here, deep in the valley, there were few sounds.

After a long while, he spoke. "Those clouds are no threat, but here in the hills, the weather can change very quickly.''

Tess, still angry at his rejection of her and feeling humiliated that she had stupidly broached a subject that offended him, did not reply. Instead, she pretended she was studying the lay of the land. The trail forked below where a huge rock outcropping thrust up from the ground. One path ran on toward the plateau, but the other ran up the opposite ridge and disappeared over its crest. Even so, she was surprised when he pulled up next to the split in the path. In the shadow of the rock lay a dead shrub, scattered and brittle. Bakhtiian dismounted and stacked a triangular pile of rocks on an area of flat ground to one side of the fork.

"What message are you leaving?" she asked, irritated that he had not volunteered the information.

He glanced up at her. "These trails are too well worn. If the arenabekh knew about them, surely the khaja do, too. I want to scout the upper trail, see where it leads. But the jahar should go down. If we're attacked, better for us that we be in the open." He hesitated, frowned, and looked away. "We'll join them at nightfall. Of course."

"Of course." The sunlight stung her eyes. She shaded them with one hand.

"You can wait, if you wish, and ride with the jahar."

"No," said Tess, sure that he only wanted to be rid of her. "I'm curious to see where the trail leads."

He shrugged, and they went on. For a time they saw the second trail like a thread winding away beneath them before they topped the ridge. Beyond, the path dipped into a shallow, rocky canyon, climbing up the canyon's far slope in a series of gradual switchbacks. The sun rose steadily as they rode up to the far crest. Below them now lay a forested valley. Trees, touched orange and yellow on their leaves, stood in thick copses that thinned and dissipated into meadows and rock-littered open areas. Flashes of gray sheets of water showed here and there, streams and pools. It was nearing midday. In the distance, at the far end of the valley, smoke rose.

"Khaja," said Bakhtiian. "Some kind of settlement. Come on." They rode down. The light, broken by leaves and branches, made patterns on their faces and hands. Reaching the valley floor, they found a thick grove of trees and dismounted and led their horses in. Tess tied them on long reins to a sturdy pair of trees within reach of grass and water. Bakhtiian left.

So much vegetation. Scents blended here, damped down by shadow. Moss hung from branches.

He reappeared presently, surprising her, his approach had been so quiet. "I don't know. No doubt we'd be better off leaving, but I'd like to scout out that settlement. I can get there and back by mid-afternoon. We can still catch the jahar before the moon sets."

"*You* can get there and back?" Water pooled and murmured near her feet, slipping in and out of light as leaves swayed in the breeze. "I'm not staying here by myself."

"Soerensen, I gave you the option of riding with the jahar. Now you can stay here with the horses. The settlement is at the other end of the valley, and not large, by the signs. You won't be found here.''

''Did Keregin say something about how the khaja hereabout treat their women? How do you suppose they would treat me, Bakhtiian, if they found me here alone?''

He flushed and looked away from her. ''Very well,'' he said in a tight voice. ''The horses can protect themselves.'' He began to walk away, halted, and glanced back at her as she followed him. ''But when we get close to the village, you'll stop where and when I tell you.''

''Agreed.''

But they had not gotten even a third of the way up the valley when Bakhtiian froze suddenly. Despite her efforts to move just as he did, Tess still made twice as much noise, shifting at the wrong moment, getting her hair caught in branches. When he stopped abruptly and put his hand back to warn her, she stiffened to a halt: following the line of his gaze, she saw the hunter.

The hunter could not have seen them yet, but he had certainly heard something. He turned his head this way and that, listening for further noise. Through the brown branches and fading green and yellow thickets their scarlet shirts would betray them. She dared not stir. She wanted to sneeze.

The hunter moved, shoulders twisting as he turned half round to look behind him. In a single movement, Bakhtiian stepped backward and pushed Tess down. She caught her weight on her hands and lowered herself to lie full on the ground. The leaves and moss smelled of moisture and rich soil. Bakhtiian lay beside her, barely breathing. His arm still lay across her back. His hand rested on her far shoulder. Her other shoulder pressed against his, her hand caught under his chest, party to the movement of his lungs, her hip and thigh warmed by his, her foot captured under his ankle.

The hunter whirled back, hearing the rustle. He checked his knife, drew an arrow from his quiver, and fitted it to his bow.

Bakhtiian's hand tightened on her shoulder, his thumb tracing the line of her shoulder blade through her shirt, up and down. A strange double awareness descended on her, an instant drawn out into eternity: the man tracking them; the weight of Ilya's arm on her back, the pressure of his fingers, the unintentional caress. Death stalked her in the guise of a black-haired, middle-aged khaja hunter. Desire had already trapped her, how long ago she did not know, only knowing now that her heart pounded so fiercely not just because she was afraid of being killed. If they had been alone, and this had been Fedya, the cushioning leaves would have been invitation enough—but Fedya had understood that some expressions could be left pure, that they need not become entangled in deeper concerns. Fedya had perhaps been a simpler man. Certainly his needs had been simple, and they had accorded with hers.

Nothing with Bakhtiian would be simple. Imagine that restless, penetrating intelligence focused on her. Imagine *him,* compulsively ambitious, driven, obsessed with conquest, discovering that the sister and heir of the Prince of Jeds—the greatest city he knew of—was interested, attracted, drawn to him.

The children of different worlds, there were so many things between them that could never be resolved. She had a duty to Charles, she had to leave, she could never tell Bakhtiian where she really came from, and she would live—however primitive Dr. Hierakis might claim the longevity treatments were—she would long outlive him. But they could be friends, surely, and to let the vagaries of physical attraction, the insidious compulsion of the loins, ruin that, ruin everything— Never! *If I once gave way to him, I would burn like straw.* She would not accept it. In that instant of drawn-out time, fear fought desire and won, and she fled, internally, seeking refuge with cold Reason, a friend of little comfort but great constitution.

Time started again. His hand moved, as cautious as the hunter, wandering to her neck. His fingers, light, smooth, brushed her skin. The hunter paused; Tess's hands tightened into fists; Bakhtiian drew his breath in sharply.

He rolled away from her, leapt to his feet, and dodged left through the undergrowth, making a great deal of noise.

The hunter dashed forward, pulled back his bow, and stopped. Nothing moved. Silence had fallen like a sudden fog. The hunter stared fixedly in the direction Bakhtiian had run. A twig snapped to Tess's right. The hunter's gaze swung around, exploring. She saw Bakhtiian moving up behind him. The hunter began to swing back. Her hand found a pebble. She flung it as far as she could to her right. It clacked against twigs. A bird fluttered noisily up into the trees. The hunter whipped back, taking a step toward her. The rocky ground of a little meadow lay behind him. Bakhtiian moved to the edge of the trees.

The hunter took another step toward her, eyeing the trees above. She drew the Chapalii knife—but no, Ilya would see. She had to save it as a last resort. She found another rock and flipped it away. A dull *thup* as it struck the leaves of a nearby bush. The hunter's gaze shifted down, and down. Bakhtiian pushed himself away from the trees, sprinting for the hunter's back.

Stumbled. Fell, landing on one knee, his head thrown back. The hunter, bow drawn, whirled and aimed.

Tess jumped up, shouting, and dove for him, hand slipping on the knife. Twisting back, he shot at her. As she threw herself flat, conscious in a detached way of the nearness of the bow, the notched arrow, the jolt up her arms as she struck the earth, she saw a flash, heard a gasp of pain and, a second later, a grunt.

For a long moment she lay perfectly still. The heavy scent of moss and leaves drowned her. Dampness seeped into her palms and through the cloth of her trousers at her knees. Finally she raised her head slightly. The arrow lay a body's length away, its point slid under a clump of yellow lichen. There was no sound at all from the two men. She rolled onto her side and pushed herself up with one arm.

Bakhtiian stood in front of her, his face white, his saber bloody. Something in his stance was peculiar. He looked fierce, wild, with his hair mussed and his empty hand in a fist, but she was not scared. Instead she stared up at him, a sudden sinking in her heart, knowing without knowing why that the easy, cheerful friendship she had with Yuri was a thing she could never have with Bakhtiian. Something else waited; she felt it like a force between them. Behind him, leaves drifted down from the trees, shaken loose by the wind.

"If you've killed him," she said, "we'd better go."

He stared at her. "You could have been killed!" His eyes seemed black with anger, focused on her face.

"By God, Bakhtiian!" She could have struck him for belittling her in such a way. "I did what had to be done." He did not hold out a hand to help her up. She would not have taken it in any case.

She did not want to see the body. As she stood, she
sheathed the knife and turned away, to go back the way they
had come, to return to the horses, to leave this valley. A
soft noise behind her stopped her.

"I can't walk." His voice was strained and thin.

She turned back, recognizing all at once the whiteness in
his cheeks and the pinched line of his mouth: he was in
pain. He was standing on one leg.

"My knee." It was hardly more than a whisper. His eyes
shut. Shadow grew on the meadow. "I have to sit down,"
he said, almost apologetically.

She put out a hand and, using it for leverage, he lowered
himself without putting any pressure on his injured knee,
but he winced as he touched the ground. Beyond him, she
saw the bloody corpse. A line of sunlight illuminated the
open, staring eyes.

"Oh, God," said Tess.

CHAPTER SEVENTEEN

"Hollows, ditches, caves and gates."
—PHERECYDES OF SYROS

It was very still, as if all the animals had fled, only the whispering lilt of a distant stream like a muted counterpoint to the undertone of his ragged breathing. Branches clicked together in a rustle of wind. He sat against a slim tree trunk, eyes shut, face ashen. She collapsed to her knees beside him.

"Ilya?" Her voice shook.

For a long moment, as the vibration of her spoken word disappeared into the stillness, he did not move. Finally, he pulled his trouser leg out of his boots and probed his knee, his fingers as careful as an artist's. The blood drained from his face. He was so obviously on the edge of agony that it hurt her to watch him. His breath shuddered, stopped, and began again with forced evenness, but he finished and at last lifted his hands away and opened his eyes. They had a vacant, unseeing cast.

"Not broken." Each syllable was distinct, as though it were hard for him to form them.

"Oh, Lord." It came out of her like a sigh.

Abruptly his gaze sharpened on her. "Can't you do *anything?*"

He might as well have slapped her. She stood up, spun away from him, and walked, hands clenched, over to the dead hunter.

The hunter could have been asleep on his side except for the spray of blood that spread out from his neck, soaking into dirt and moss. A tiny black bug crawled across one of his open eyes. She pressed the heels of her palms across her eyes. Bile rose in her throat.

She picked up all his weapons—bow, arrows, dagger— and set them down beside Bakhtiian. Took in a full breath and walked back to the hunter. First she stripped him of what clothing was not too drenched in blood to be unusable. Then she grabbed his ankles—almost dropped them because they were still warm, the skin soft, yielding under her fingers. She gagged, clenched her lips together. His toes were white; hair grew below the first joint, but the nails were reddish-brown and dirty, as if they were already decaying.

She dragged him downslope over the rough ground and into a dense thicket. Branches stung her back and head and arms. She shoved him down an incline, and he rolled farther into the vegetation, twigs snapping under his weight. Retreating, she did what she could to cover his path, picking up dead branches and sweeping the trail the body had left until she came back to the congealing blood and scattered clothes at the beginning. Dirt stuck to the soles of her boots. The heavy scent of blood permeated the air. She put her hand to her throat, swallowed once, and turned and ran upslope, sound scattering out from her feet, until she was out of earshot. Then she dropped to her knees and was sick.

The stream murmured nearby. Its gentle chorus brought her back to herself, and she rose, still trembling, and explored until she found it. The shock of bitterly cold water on her face made her think again.

She ran back to the clearing.

Bakhtiian had not moved. She gathered up the dead man's trousers and two tunics, shook them off, and went over to Bakhtiian.

"Ilya. Put these on."

He looked up at her. Only a thin line of iris gave color to his eyes. His gaze strayed past her to the clearing. "He's gone."

"Yes. What happened to your knee?"

His gaze did not light on any one thing. "It went backward. I went forward."

"Hyperextended, probably." She offered him the clothing. "Do you need help?"

"I have clothes on."

"Damn it! You have to stay warm. *Over* yours." She

tossed the clothing in his lap. "Let me see what I can do about your knee."

Just beyond the path of blood that stained the center of the clearing lay the dead hunter's sandals and heavy leggings. A yellowing undershirt lay draped across them, half covering a small, hollowed-out animal horn tied to a thong, the last of his possessions. She grabbed the undershirt and walked back to the stream.

It was like encasing her fingers in ice, but she grimly soaked the cloth and ran back to Bakhtiian. He had gotten both tunics on and was cleaning his saber on the hunter's trousers, slowly and with a kind of desperate concentration. "I told you to put those on." She crouched next to him. If he heard her, he gave no reply. "Ice the injury," she said, feeling as if she were talking to herself. "Isn't that what you're supposed to do first?" She pulled up his trouser leg, and winced. Already the knee was swollen. Discoloration mottled the skin. He paused in cleaning the blade, and his eyes shifted to her. In a swift, careful move, she wrapped the cold cloth around his knee.

Suddenly, his hands relaxed their grip on his saber, his lips parted slightly. He shut his eyes and leaned his head back against the tree. Tess finished cleaning his saber with two smooth strokes. Then she set to work again. She found a walking stick and two straight branches for a splint, then eased off his boot—already it was tight at the top as the swelling increased—and bound his calf in the leggings. The blood that lay like rust on the rocks and lichen in the middle of the clearing could be disguised for the time by spreading it out with branches, sprinkling dirt over it, ripping up long swatches of moss and draping them across stained rock. She broke up this activity with trips to the stream, to resoak the shirt and bind his knee. Last, she threw the little animal horn into the same thicket that held the body. *Like a grave offering,* she thought, hearing the light thud as it struck dirt. Then there was only silence. It was almost as if the hunter had never existed. Almost.

"Can you walk yet?" she asked, going back to Ilya.

His eyes were still shut. "Yes."

"We've got the hunter's belt and some rope from the quiver, for the splint."

He opened his eyes. "Very well."

After a time they managed something marginally effective. He grasped the heavy walking stick with one hand, bent his good leg under him, and pushed off. Halfway up his bad leg shifted, pressing into the ground. He gasped. Before he could fall, Tess grabbed him by the waist and pulled him up. He swayed. When she let him go, he staggered back a step. His free arm circled the tree he had been sitting against. He rested his head against the bark. All was quiet, except for the *tik tik* of an insect and the uneven flow of his breathing. Finally he opened his eyes and thrust himself away from the tree. Without a word, Tess slung all the extra gear over her shoulders, waiting for him to set the pace.

Watching Bakhtiian as he hobbled back along the valley toward the horses was a lesson in something; Tess wasn't sure what. After every ten steps, he halted. After the space of time to take ten steps had elapsed, he started again. His eyes, his whole face, were glazed with pain. Sometimes Tess spoke, to break the silence. He never answered. Once, when she made a bad joke, she thought he smiled slightly.

Finally, seeing that his progress was slowing perceptibly, she redirected their course toward the hills, hoping to find and follow a stream back to the end of the valley. When she heard the soft rush of water nearby, she left Bakhtiian where he had halted yet again and went ahead with the undershirt.

The stream pooled just below a ridge of rock over which Tess could see the slope of the nearest hill. After slipping down five shale steps, it trailed back into the forest. She knelt, plunging the shirt into the water, gasping from the cold.

A note rose high on the breeze, low and trembling. At first she thought it was an animal, but as the sound arced to a peak and cut off she knew suddenly that it was close by, far too close, and that it was a horn. She looked up. Froze, hands still in the water.

The man stood not twenty paces from her. He stared, as surprised as she was. He raised a hand, taking in her scarlet jaran shirt, her saber, and—she could see it by the widening of his eyes—her feminine form and face. She kept her hands below the surface of the water, terrified all at once that he would see his dead companion's shirt. How could she have forgotten? No one hunted alone.

He drew an arrow and nocked it, but he did not immediately let fly. Instead, he stared. She lifted her right hand from the water. It ached with cold. It hurt to curl her fingers around the hilt of her Chapalii knife, but she did so, watching him. He grinned and said something, foreign words. She drew the dagger. He raised the bow and said something more, clearly a threat. What had Garii said? Thumb over the third and second lights. The world slowed. She slid her thumb along the smooth hilt. The hunter drew the bowstring back and aimed and spoke—

Light streaked out. A flush of heat. He fell. She gasped audibly, jumped to her feet, and ran to him. He lay motionless on the ground. He stank, but it was an honest smell: dirt and onions and too many months without washing. He was still breathing.

For a long moment she simply gaped. How could he not be dead? One side of his face was flushed red. Daring much, she bent to touch it—it was warm, unnaturally so, but not burned. Stunned, not dead.

She lifted a hand to wipe at her face. She had broken out in a sweat. She felt hot under her clothes though the autumn air had a chill snap to it. *Stunned not dead!* Garii had given her a knife set to stun. So it couldn't be used against him? Against any Chapalii?

What the hell did it matter anyway? She ran back to the pool and fished out the wet shirt, wrung it out, swore, and ran back to the hunter and took all his weapons. Raced into the woods, stopping before she reached Bakhtiian. How could she explain these weapons? Her saber was not even bloodied. She ought to go back and kill the hunter while he was unconscious, but she knew she could never do it. She sawed the bowstring into thirds and then dumped the weapons into the densest clump of undergrowth she could find, and ran on.

When Bakhtiian saw her, he sheathed his saber. "How many?"

"One." She wrapped the wet shirt around his knee, which was by now so swollen that she couldn't even make out the shape of the patella.

"Did he see you?"

"Yes." She hesitated. He held onto a low-hanging branch and waited. "We just have to move fast. I'd suggest trying to follow the stream."

"We'll leave a clear trail."

"He has no weapons. He'll have to go back and get help.

If we follow the stream, we can keep the swelling down.'' She tied the shirt at his knee into knots, securing it to the splint. "And hope they don't find the dead man until tomorrow."

"That's the only thing that helps," he said.

"Besides your stubbornness."

There was silence, except for a few birds calling and the distant spill of water. "You'd better go. Find the jahar."

She slung the gear onto her back and handed him the walking stick. "Come on."

"Did you mention stubbornness?" He pushed himself away from the tree. "I mistakenly thought you referred to me."

She angled their path to avoid the pool. This time they made it all the way to the stream before he had to stop. While he rested, she wrapped his knee again, then scouted ahead a ways, but she heard nothing, saw nothing. Shadows stretched out around them. The bottom rim of the sun touched the blurred line of trees at the height of the hills, casting a deep red glow like blood against the low advance of clouds. Bakhtiian coughed, and she glanced over at him. The last of the sunlight cast gold across his face. It highlighted his cheekbones so that the skin seemed taut across them, in sharp relief like the face of a man who is starving or near death.

Eyes shut, he said, "Don't be an idiot. Go on without me."

"Bakhtiian, did it ever occur to you that I probably can't find the horses, much less the jahar, by myself?"

He was silent.

"By God. Now that's a compliment."

One corner of his mouth tugged upward. He opened his eyes. "You're right." He coughed again, but it was a trembling sound. "I don't know how I could have thought that." They both laughed.

And, eyes meeting, cut off their laughter abruptly. Silence. A bird sang in the distance, a little five-note figure over and over. Bakhtiian grasped his walking stick and pushed himself up. He winced, took a step, winced, took another. They went on.

His pace was so slow that night made no difference to their progress. Animals accompanied their retreat: noises fading out into the brush, drawing closer when they halted, a snuffling once, that skittered away when she threw a rock in its direction.

Each time they halted he counted. Each time, he reached a higher number before he rose and struggled on. Now and then she had to help him over a fallen log, through a thick scattering of rocks, past a screen of branches. Wet vegetation slapped her face. Vines caught at her legs or brushed, slippery and damp, across her hand. Once she fell asleep balanced on a log, but when Ilya rose the log shifted under her and she woke, startled. Dawn came before they reached the end of the valley. It was another hour at least before they staggered into the copse where the horses were tethered.

Ilya sank down onto the ground. Deep circles smudged his eyes. "I can't go on right now." He covered his face with his hands and slumped forward.

"You have to eat." She brought him food from their bags.

He took the food but did nothing with it. "You should sleep," he said. "I'll wake you."

"*You* should sleep."

"I can't sleep. I'll watch." He shut his eyes again and leaned back, resting against a tree trunk.

Tess rubbed her face. She checked the horses, forced herself to eat, forced herself to refill the water flasks before she allowed herself the luxury of lying down on her cloak three meters behind Bakhtiian, facing the high screen of bushes. Here, in the close wood, the leaves were the brightest green at the tops of the bushes, lit by the sun, shading down to a dark green near the earth, where shadows obscured most of the ground. Encased in gloves, her hands felt almost warm. She fell asleep.

* * *

The palace in Jeds looked out over the sea, over the wide mouth of the bay, out toward the islands littering the horizon like so much flotsam cast back to drift. Marco Burckhardt stood alone on the sea wall, watching the waves slide in along the strand and murmur through the hedge of rocks scattered at the base of the wall. Spray lifted in the wind and misted his face. To his left lay the crowded harbor, sailing ships anchored out in the bay, galleys and boats moored to the docks; beyond it, crawling up and down the hills, the fetid sprawl of Jeds itself. And to his right, set a little away from the city in the midst of neat fields, the university, established at least a century ago but transplanted to its new grounds twenty years past by the first prince of the new line in Jeds.

"Admiring your handiwork?" Cara Hierakis came up beside him and slipped a hand into the crook of his elbow. The wind blew the curls of her black hair away from her face.

"My great masterpiece." Marco grinned.

"I hate to remind you, my dear, but the new buildings were actually built after you died and Charles inherited."

"I meant my death. I think I engineered it very well, dedicating the grounds and then being crushed under stones in that horrible accident."

"Yes, you do like coming close to death, don't you?"

"It's how I know I'm alive. Although an engineered accident does lack something, especially that *frisson* of risk. The best part of it was getting to become a new man afterward, with a new face and a new name."

"Marco, have you ever considered psychoanalysis?"

"Isn't that outdated?"

"Of all the inhabited planets you could spend your time on, which do you choose? It's only fitting."

They stood awhile in silence, watching Jeds.

"I love this city," said Marco at last. "Because I found it. And don't tell me the Jedans already knew it was here. You know what I mean."

"Yes, it was convenient of old Prince Casimund to be on his deathbed and with no immediate heirs but nephews whose mothers had married lords in the other city-states. You never told me how you convinced him you were one of those nephews and the true heir to the princedom."

"And I never will. You wouldn't approve. I only did it for Charles, my love." Cara laughed. Marco looked offended. "You know very well that I didn't want the position for myself. But we had to get a toehold on the planet somehow. I grasped the opportunity where I found it."

"It's true it chafed you soon enough, all that responsibility."

"Your flattery is boundless, Dr. Hierakis. As well as your cynicism."

"A good scientist must be skeptical. It isn't the same."

The tide was coming in, swelling up under the distant docks. Men worked, tiny figures loading and unloading the ships and the galleys, tying Jeds in to the greater world of Rhui and feeding out goods and knowledge brought forth in the renaissance that gripped Jeds under the rule of Prince Charles the Second, ''son'' of the late and lamented Charles the First, whose reign had been short but merry.

''A message came in,'' said Cara. ''That's what I came out to tell you. Charles got a bullet from Suzanne, from Paladia Major. The *Oshaki* put in at Paladia Minor and hasn't stirred for a month. She found no indication that Tess disembarked at Minor.''

''Could she still be onboard the *Oshaki?* Where do you think she is?''

''I think Charles expects her to be like him, but she isn't. You can't make silk out of a sow's ear. Which is not to compare Tess to a sow's ear, though pigs are certainly my favorite domestic animals. But I think you grasp the analogy.''

''You didn't answer my question.''

''I don't have enough evidence to make a guess. Where is Tess? Why is a high-ranking merchant of the obscenely wealthy Keinaba house loitering on Odys, frittering away his valuable time in endless discussions about the hypothetical worth of Dao Cee's resources—and in Anglais at that? Why did that shuttle flight follow a most inefficient path? And I will not bore you with the number of questions I have about the human population on this planet, such as, why are they *homo sapiens*, how did they come to have better health than the humans of Earth's ancient past, and, if I can solve the antigen problem, can we interbreed?''

Marco stared out at the gray water and the white flash of sun on the distant isles. ''We already know that we can interbreed.'' His hands curled, gripping hard on the stone.

''I know, Marco,'' she said gently. ''I meant, without endangering the pregnant woman's life. But at least the baby lived. She would have, too, if I could have got to her in time.''

''Sweet Goddess, it was an easy enough delivery.''

''Marco, there was nothing you could have done. You didn't know about the reaction that set in.''

''I damn well could have not gotten her pregnant!''

''Yes, you could have. One can take this going native business too far.''

''Thank you, Cara. Your sympathy overwhelms me.''

"My sympathy rests with that poor girl. Where do you think Tess is?"

"I think she's on Rhui. Just a feeling I have."

"Then why didn't she come here? Where could she possibly be? Marco, can you imagine the kind of danger she could be in, if that's the case?"

Marco smiled, but mockingly, without any humor at all. "Yes, in fact, I can."

* * *

The horns woke Tess. She started awake, standing abruptly. A white rump flashed, an animal bounding away into the trees. Twigs snapped. A bird shrieked.

Bakhtiian woke just before she reached him, one hand on his saber hilt, the other open, out in front of him as if he were confused. Tess halted out of range of his saber.

"Bakhtiian?"

He pulled his hands in and looked up at the sky. His eyes followed the invisible trail of the sun to the rim of the western hills where clouds, a low gray sheet stretching halfway back across the sky, obscured its face. Shadows drew long lines across the meadow. "It's late."

"I'll go saddle the horses." She turned away.

"Tess." She turned back. "You'll have to ride Kriye. I can't handle him with one leg."

"Who?"

There was color in his cheeks, but that might only have been from his afternoon's rest. "My black," he said in a constrained voice.

Tess almost started laughing. *"Kriye.* That's what you call a very young boy. 'Little one,' but masculine?" He said nothing. "You must admit, Ilya, it's hardly what one would expect you to name a horse." Still he did not reply. "I don't think there's anything wrong with it," she added hastily. "I think it's sweet. But what if you can't ride at all?"

A withering leaf, blown up by an eddy of wind, rolled across his knees. He grabbed it, flinging it to one side. "I can ride."

"Fine. What do I do with an unconscious man?"

"I don't faint."

"Just like you don't sleep?" Then, seeing his face, she realized she had gone too far, and she quickly left.

Kriye remained placid for Tess. In the level valley, forced

to a slow walk by the dusk and the trees, and with the stirrup adjusted to hold his splinted leg pretty much in place, Bakhtiian managed Myshla, who was more amiable than the tarpan remounts. But they had barely started up the trail, Tess riding behind, when Myshla broke into a trot, and Bakhtiian acted instinctively to slow her. It was his curse more than any movement that alerted Tess; in the darkness she could see only shapes. She urged Kriye up beside him. He gripped the saddle in both hands, reins slack in his fingers. Tess pulled the reins from him and kept going.

Clouds scudded across the farther reaches of sky. The hooves of the horses rang like the echo of a bell on the hard trail. When the clouds reached the far horizon and covered the moon, she had to dismount and lead the horses.

The wind struck when she reached the crest. Her hair streamed back, caught in the flow. In the darkness, she felt as if she were on the edge of an abyss, the world falling away before and behind her. Dark masses of rock loomed around her, the suggestion of ages. She felt very old, knowing that as she stood here, with the wind's pull like the rush of the planet's rotation, she was as much a part of the scene as the wind itself.

Myshla shifted. Glancing back, she saw Bakhtiian sway in the saddle. She shook him. Finally he blinked and stared at her. His look of complete confusion frightened her.

"You can faint when we get to shelter," she snapped. "I could hold out longer than that. I could hold out twice as long."

"I doubt it," he whispered, but he pushed himself up.

The wind tore at her clothes as if it was trying to scatter her off the heights. She tugged the horses forward, stumbling down the path. Her boots slipped on pebbles. Kriye's breath warmed her neck. Her hands stiffened into a tight grip on the reins. Her toes ached with cold.

When the trail gave out on a broad ledge that angled up into a deep overhang, she realized that in the dark she had missed the switchback and taken an offshoot. As she moved forward she no longer felt the wind, only a still presence over her head. She halted and untied the blankets from Kriye's saddle.

"Where are we?"

"Shelter. For the rest of the night." She laid out the blankets by the far wall.

She had to help him off the horse. He slumped against her. She let him down very carefully onto the blankets and knelt beside him. She was shivering.

"Ilya?" There was no answer, no movement at all. "Oh Lord." She rested a hand on his chest. His breathing was regular and even. She sat back with a sigh. She cared for the horses first; afterward, taking two strips of meat, she settled down at the far edge of the overhang. Darkness surrounded her. Soon, she dozed.

A rush of sound startled her awake. It was raining. She sank back against the wall, tucking her hands under her cloak. For a time the rain kept her awake. Later, despite the cold, it lulled her to sleep.

She woke abruptly at dawn, chilled and shivering. Her cheeks and forehead felt warm. No wind penetrated the overhang, a shallow cave eroded from the hill by a millennia of storms. Outside the rain had stopped. Surely such rain would cover their tracks.

She stamped her feet and rubbed her hands together to try to bring some warmth into them. Turning, she caught Bakhtiian looking abruptly away from her. He was already sitting up. Dark circles set off his eyes. A smudge of dirt mottled one cheek. The night had tangled his hair and trapped a tiny yellow leaf in his beard. Unbelted, the tunics bunched and wrinkled at his waist. One sleeve of his red shirt, showing at a wrist, had twisted at the cuff.

"This is all very foolish," he said.

"You don't still think I should go on ahead, do you?" She offered him water and food.

"It's cold," he said.

She felt her heart race with fear. If he was getting ill from the shock—

"No," he said, reading her expression. "I'm not—I'm well enough. But the air. Can't you feel it? It's the ayakhov, the wind from the peaks. It brings the storms. This shelter can't possibly protect us." He halted, just breathing for a while, as if the effort of speaking so much had exhausted him.

"Can you go on? I'll saddle the horses."

He shook his head, a gesture compounded half of answer, half of pain. "No." She waited. "If we're caught in the open— These storms last days sometimes. You'll have to scout for better shelter. Even a deeper overhang where we can set up the tent. . . ." He trailed off.

"Yes," she said, not wanting to remind him that they had no tent with them. "I'll go now." She saddled Myshla and left. She rode down into the canyon and half up the other side before tethering Myshla and exploring. By the time she found a good cave, the wind had indeed blown up, cold enough that all her exertion did not keep her warm. She gathered all the brush she could find, arranging the softest into a couch set against the steep-sloping cave wall, and gathered scraps, everything she could find for fodder for the horses, and piled rocks for a corral in the dark recesses of the shelter.

He was asleep when she returned. She unsaddled Myshla and took all four horses out on a long lead, letting them graze and water behind her as she hiked up to the crest. As she had hoped, the rain had swept all traces of their passage from the rock-littered trail. At the height she tried to recapture that timelessness she had felt the night before. But the rocks looked drab, worn away by the weather and the years, and there were too many windblown plants clinging to their surface, a few wilted leaves holding tenuously to branches.

It was cold. Wind whipped the ends of her cloak around her knees. No one was following them. Surely the khaja had given up their search. Turning away, she saw a mass of thick clouds tipped with darkness, sweeping down, almost on her where she stood high and exposed on the ridge. Alarmed, she mounted Myshla bareback and rode back to the overhang.

She found Bakhtiian standing at the entrance, hands clutching his walking stick, staring at her as she dismounted and led the horses under the rock. If he could have looked anything but haggard, pained, and tired, she would have said he looked glad to see her. He had made some effort to tidy himself up. His face was clean, his hair combed, the hunter's tunics straight and neatly belted.

She chuckled, because the incongruity—of their desperate situation, of the approaching storm, of his appearance—was simply too much.

"Where were you?" he demanded.

"Scouting. I found shelter." She began immediately to saddle Kriye and Myshla. "The storm is coming."

"Why didn't we leave sooner?"

His bad temper irritated her. "You were asleep. And I must say you needed it."

"I am aware," said Bakhtiian slowly, "that I am not looking my best."

Tess laughed and stooped to pick up the blankets he had already rolled up and readied. "Do you know why I like you, Ilya?"

"I can't imagine."

She knew she should stop now, but the storm, the danger, his whole attitude, made her reckless. "Because you're vain."

He limped across to Myshla. "At least," he said, tying the blankets to the saddle with hard, efficient jerks, "I am not uncivil."

"No." Her whole face burned, with excitement, with fever, with anger—she could not be sure. *"That* fault will never tarnish your reputation." She turned back to Kriye and tightened the cinch of his saddle. "Do you need help to mount?"

He cursed, a phrase she did not recognize, and she started around to see that he had already mounted. He clutched the pommel, eyes shut. "Forgive me." Though his voice was scarcely more than a whisper, she knew he was in earnest. "My language."

Immediately she felt guilty. "No, I'm sorry. I have a terrible temper." When he did not reply, she judged it prudent simply to go.

She led the horses out. Drops of ice-tipped rain stung her face. She tucked her braid beneath her cloak and pulled her hood up over her head.

A gust of wind scattered leaves across the trail. Kriye whickered and tossed his head, and Tess moved her grip up closer to his mouth. The wind dragged at her, pulling her hood back off her head, so cold that it stiffened her joints even as she moved. The trail veered down around a boulder. Tess slipped on a damp stone; only Kriye's pulling back kept her from falling. Rain spattered her face. All color faded suddenly. She looked up to see the entire sky darken, curling down like a black glove from invisible heights.

"We've got to go faster!" she yelled. "Can you hold on?"

He was hunched so far over Myshla's neck that his hood

had not been blown back. "Yes." The word vanished on the wind.

She mounted Kriye. He sidestepped, taking her into a bush. Branches scraped her leg. She jerked him back onto the trail, driving him ahead. Myshla came forward, and the tarpans, nervous, hesitated and then followed the drag of their lead-lines. The wind swelled. Rain broke over them, hard as pellets, sounding like thunder on the rocks around them. Her head was soaked in an instant. Water blurred her vision.

Finally, finally, they reached the valley floor. She slowed to negotiate a litter of rocks. Water streamed away in little runnels between them. A leaf blew into her face, attaching itself like a damp tentacle. She flinched back, jerked the reins. Kriye shied. For an instant she had all that she could do to control him. A thick gust of rain drove into her from the side. A large branch tore loose from a tree behind them and crashed down onto the path. Myshla bolted.

The mare stumbled on the rough ground and fell, flipping over sideways. She pushed back up to her feet and then, unaccountably, she calmed.

"Ilya!" Tess scrambled down off Kriye, throwing the reins over the black's head. Rain drowned the landscape in gray. Bakhtiian lay half in a ditch at the side of the trail. Water eddied over his boots. She grabbed him under his arms and tugged him up onto the trail, and knelt by him, pulling him up into her arms. "Ilya!"

His eyelids wavered, opened. He had a cut below one eye, thin and jagged. The brown tunic was ripped. Blood welled up from a scrape on his palm. He mouthed something. She had to lean down. Rain drenched her neck, slipping under her cloak to run down the curve of her spine. She shuddered.

"Go on." He shut his eyes.

She eased him down on the trail. With both hands she smoothed his hood back away from his face. Then she took off one of her gloves and slapped him as hard as she could. He sat up. Rain and blood painted a broad red line down his cut cheek. He lifted a hand to his face. Blood dripped from his palm.

"Stand up, damn you!" She got behind him and lifted. He got his good leg under him and came up with such strength that she had to take a step backward to balance. He pushed her away with one arm and hobbled over to Myshla. Blood leaked from a gouge midway down Myshla's left foreleg.

"Oh, hell." Tears burned her eyes. "Ilya, you'll have to ride Kriye." He did not reply, but with a movement half extraordinary and half ungainly, he got himself on the stallion. Tess mounted her remount bareback, tying Myshla to Kriye's saddle. They went on.

Partway up the far slope, with wind and rain pouring against them, she had to dismount. Bakhtiian lay bent, almost hugging Kriye's neck. She tied her mount on behind, put her head down, and led them forward. Water gushed down the path in fresh trails. The hard surface had dissolved into mud. The rain soaked through her gloves, through her trousers. Rivulets trailed down her calves to pool in the toes of her boots.

The pile of stone marking the approach to the cave was half obliterated. Beyond it, rock fell in slick ledges down toward the bottom of the canyon that lay, dim and obscure, far below. Rain pelted at the low bushes, stripping them of their last leaves. Tess got a tighter hold on Kriye, up at his mouth, and started across.

That Kriye was surefooted was the best of her luck. In this direction, the wind whipped her cloak open. Rain drenched the front of her shirt. Convulsive shivers shook her every few steps. She picked her way across the pathless slope of loose rock, slipping once, knee jarring on stone, one hand plunged to above the wrist in a sink of icy water. Kriye held steady. Tess pushed herself up, slipping again, clutching the reins. A steep slope, its carpet of lichen torn into strips by the storm, a rubble-strewn ledge, and at last the broad entry and narrow doorway of the cave.

"The gates of paradise." Bakhtiian's voice, faint and far off behind her. Kriye nosed against her, recognizing shelter, and suddenly the rain no longer pounded furiously on her head.

CHAPTER EIGHTEEN

"We have come into this roofed cavern."
—EMPEDOCLES OF AGRAGAS

Somehow Bakhtiian got himself off Kriye. With cold-numbed fingers, Tess fumbled with the harness. Myshla's saddle slipped from her hands to land on her feet. Pain lanced up her leg. She led the horses into the rock corral and rubbed them down with the hunter's undershirt. The gouge on Myshla's leg did not look too deep. She put salve on it and wrapped it, and left the horses to their forage. There was still enough light to see. She thanked someone for this; whom, she was not sure. From inside, the high whistle of the wind and the rain's monotonous staccato sounded almost subdued.

Dizziness engulfed her. She sat down. She felt hot and cold together, and her head felt as if it was about to float to the ceiling. A low voice cursed in an undertone to her left. A spark caught, and then flame: Bakhtiian had started a fire. He rubbed at his eyes, pausing in the action to rest his forehead on a palm.

Tess stood, unsteadily, and gathered together the blankets—few enough with this bitter cold. "I'll make a bed for you," she said, and carried them over to the couch of branches she had laid earlier in the day.

He glared bleakly at her. "You'll have a fever by morning. Dry your clothes first."

She knelt by the fire. The heat steamed off her. A draft carried the smoke up and out, and the fuel burned merrily, snapping and crackling. Then she realized that he was taking his clothes off. She averted her gaze and stared at the horses.

"I *said* dry your clothes."

"I am." She peeled the cold, wet cloth of her red shirt away from her skin, but it reattached itself an instant later, and she flinched.

There was a silence. She did not look to see what his expression was. His red shirt lay on the ground next to the fire. A moment later, his right boot joined it, and then his trousers, laid out to absorb the heat.

"Soerensen." His voice was hoarse with pain or anger. "This is not a request. Take them off." A flutter in the air, and a blanket struck her on the side of her face. Forced to turn, she could not help but look at him. He was entirely covered, wrapped quite primly in a blanket, only his feet showing, where they were thrust out close to the flames. His face was white with exhaustion, but he also looked annoyed. Seeing her turn, he pulled an edge of the blanket deliberately across his face, so that he could not see her.

"Oh, God," sighed Tess. She stripped and wrapped the blanket around herself. It was damp but offered warmth despite that. After a time she actually felt her toes and fingers. The darkness deepened as night came on and the storm continued to rage outside. Inside, fire illuminated them. The gray rock walls of the cave curved up into darkness, their surface rippled and rough as though some ancient chill had frozen them in the midst of movement. The air seemed close and harsh against her throat. Smoke settled in her lungs. The part of her farthest from the fire felt perpetually chilled, so she shifted frequently. She yawned.

"At least they'll never follow us in this storm," she mumbled. She glanced up. Bakhtiian lay slumped over his knees.

She got on her trousers and shirt through a combination of habit and fear and circled the fire to kneel beside him. The blanket had fallen down, revealing the strong curve of his shoulders, and as she tugged it up with sudden prudishness, his eyes fluttered and opened. He stared at her, confused. His hands closed on her waist. The blanket slipped to reveal his naked torso. Tess jerked back.

He clutched the blanket and pulled it tight around his chest. "I passed out," he said.

"Your clothes are dry." She turned and walked across the cave to converse with the horses. Over the next several minutes he swore three times in a very low voice. The fire flared briefly. She heard him moving, but she did not look. Then it was quiet. Myshla nosed at her ear. She shivered. Rain drummed softly outside. Inside, it was freezing.

"Soerensen." His tone was sharp.

She turned. The fire was still bright enough that she could see Bakhtiian. He had taken the blankets and cloaks and the hunter's clothing and layered them on the couch of branches she had laid, and dragged himself on top of them.

He met her eyes. He was flushed, and his mouth was drawn in a severe line. "Come here."

She did not move. "If you give me the two cloaks, I'll be warm enough."

Bakhtiian swallowed. He looked as if his greatest desire at that moment was to pass out again. "I beg pardon for my immodesty, but in a storm like this, in our condition, we need the warmth."

Tess shivered and rubbed her hands along her arms. It was hard to speak, her lips were so cold. "You're right, of course. We don't have any other choice."

"I would never have said it otherwise," he replied with considerable reserve.

She kicked the coals of the fire into a smaller circle and stared at them. Finally she walked over to Ilya. "Well," she said.

He was already lying on his side, left leg resting on the uninjured one. "Share the blankets." He rested his head on a pillow of dry grass and shut his eyes. Gingerly, she settled down next to him. "No," he mumbled, "on your side. Back to me. There, so if I shift, my leg won't move."

She rolled up on her side, angling her legs so that they supported his. Yawning, blinking back sleep, she tucked the blankets around their legs.

"Lie against me," he whispered. "I'll get the last blankets. Gods, woman, you're shaking with the cold."

He had folded his arms tight between his chest and her back, but otherwise she lay against him. This couch of branches was not the most comfortable bed she had ever slept on, but *he* was warm. She heard, like a counterpoint to the furious storm, a distant slide of loose rock, the thin crack of breaking branches and, to her left, the slow drip of water pooling somewhere under the overhang. Heat crept into her shoulders and knees and hips. She slept.

Odys had no colors but brown and gray and the faded green of its reeds. It had no heights and no valleys, except in the archipelagoes where no one had any reason to live. It was a drowned world, the sea and the massif almost one, the mud flats interminable, stretching out in all directions from the only slab of ground that stood above the waves, the Oanao Plateau.

But the palace and the port and the city of Odys Central itself had heights and valleys in profusion. Perhaps the architecture here was deliberate, to provide contrast with the terrain; perhaps all Chapalii architecture was this way, on all imperial planets. No human survey had been allowed to ascertain which was true.

And there was color as well. Color especially in the vast greenhouse, acres broad, that jutted off the fourth spoke of the ducal palace. Charles stood among the irises, chatting amiably with his head gardener about economic theory in preindustrial Earth cultures as contrasted to the development of communal theory on pre-space Ophiuchi-Sei-ah-nai.

"Ah, there he is, Jamsetji," said Charles. "I must go. Come to dinner tonight, and we'll finish arguing this out."

Jamsetji tipped his cap back and glanced toward the gazebo half hidden by the wisteria and trailing roses. "That the merchant who speaks Anglais? Cursed trouble, if you ask me."

"Is this one of your hunches?"

"Might say it was. But that's not saying you don't want to get involved with it either."

"Or that I have any choice," added Charles. "Listen in." He strolled off down a winding turf path and came by a circular route to the little gazebo. Hon Echido sat on a wrought iron bench in the gazebo, directing two stewards in the placement of cups and saucers and a kettle and a pitcher on the little round table before him. He saw Charles and stood up, bowing to the precise degree.

Charles acknowledged him and entered, sitting down on the bench opposite. He dabbed sweat from his forehead and accepted a cool drink from one of the stewards. The stewards retreated out of earshot. "Please, Hon Echido, sit down."

Echido sat. Pink flushed his skin but quickly faded. "You

do me a great honor, to meet me here, Tai-en," he said in
Anglais.

"It is a beautiful spot." Charles gazed for a moment at
the far lines of vegetation: the clustering flowers nearby, the
vegetable flats, the grain fields, the tasseled rows of corn,
the orchards farther off, and the distant line of trees, de-
marking the park and exercise ground for those humans
serving voluntary exile on Odys with Soerensen. Scent hung
here like something one could touch, overpowering, yet at
the same time reassuring. "Although it's hot."

Swathed in robes, Echido looked comfortable. He sipped
from his cup, steaming liquid that smelled of cloves and
aniseed and tar. "The layout is from a human plan, I see.
There is a certain disorder, artful, indeed, but disorder all
the same that precludes these grounds being of Chapalii
design."

"You speak Anglais remarkably well, Hon Echido."

"Your praise is generous, Tai-en."

"As well as being perfectly true. I have enjoyed our discussions of the various trade and mineral rights available
for exploitation in my fief. Yet I feel that for the Keinaba
family, whose wealth and acumen is known and admired
throughout the Empire, to instruct one of their own to learn
Anglais, one as high-ranking, as valuable, and as perceptive
as yourself, Hon Echido, means that there is a more delicate
matter you wish to broach."

Echido arranged his hands in Merchant's Humility. "The
Tai-en honors us with his attention to such an insignificant
family as our own."

Since the Keinaba merchant house was one of the wealth-
iest merchant houses in an empire where wealth counted as
a marker of rank, Charles simply waited. In the distance,
he could hear Jamsetji singing an afternoon raga in a reedy
voice.

The merchant's skin shaded to violet, the color of mortification, and his fingers altered slightly to add the emphasis of Shame to the arrangement of Humility. "I beg of you,
Tai-en, to allow me to explain before you cast me out of
your presence, as any lord would feel every right, every
compulsion, to do. For time uncounted, for years beyond
years, Keinaba has served the *Yaotai* Kobara princely house
and the Tai Kaonobi dukes. We served well and faithfully,
as any merchant house ought."

The violet shade to his skin deepened. "Yet now we are shamed and utterly cast down. I do not presume to know the doings of the *Yaochalii-en,* may peace be with the Sun's Child, but the Kobara princely house and the Kaonobi ducal house are no more. Their names have been obliterated from the imperial view, and they are as if they had never been. With a full sense of our disgrace, I mention them now, but for the last time."

Charles arched one eyebrow. This was, perhaps, the most interesting news he had gotten out of the Chapalii since his own elevation to the nobility. "I am surprised, then, that the name of Keinaba may still be spoken."

Echido's skin was all violet by now: deep, and rather attractive against the white-washed lattice walls of the gazebo and the purple flowering wisteria trailing down to the ground. "The Yaochalii himself, may peace surround his name, conducted the investigation into the charges of conspiracy and breach of protocol against the prince whose name may no longer be heard, and although the Tai line was tainted by the stain, it was found that Keinaba had no part in this terrible offense against protocol. The Yaochalii himself, may his name endure forever, granted a dispensation from the rite of extinction to Keinaba, if we were able to find a new lord."

"Knowing full well no lord or duke would wish to take on the allegiance and obligation of a house so dishonored," said Charles.

Echido bowed his head in the deeply subservient fashion of the *ke,* the most menial of all Chapalii classes, who were not even granted the dignity of given or family names.

"Your command of Anglais is not just remarkable, Hon Echido," Charles continued. "It is astonishing. What offense did the princely house commit?"

Echido's skin lightened perceptibly to a pale violet. "I do not know. But always, the yaotai, the princes, struggle for the yaochalii's favor."

"And only one prince may become emperor."

"There are protocols to be observed. So there have been for time uncounted, for years beyond years. To stray from the path of right conduct is to dishonor oneself and one's family."

"Tell me, Hon Echido, are you certain that the Tai-endi Terese boarded the *Oshaki?*"

"Quite certain, Tai-en." Echido's skin paled to white. His hands shifted, and he regarded Soerensen evenly.

"Why did you not debark from the *Oshaki* when she reached Odys?"

"I was not allowed to, Tai-en, and when I protested, I was reminded of the disgrace of my family and our lords."

"Yet you disembarked at Hydri and made your way back to Earth."

Echido arranged his hands in a way Charles had not seen before. If only Suzanne, or Tess, were here to interpret. "Tai-en, you are the only lord with whom we of Keinaba have any hope of maintaining our house. If we must lose our name and become as the ke, then that is only just. But I told my elders that I would approach the *daiga*, the human Tai, and so determined, I have now done so. We await your judgment, Tai-en."

"The dispensation from the emperor?"

"I have a copy, Tai-en. The original rests in his hand, may it hold firm and bring peace to our lands."

Charles rose. Hon Echido rose like an echo. His skin was pale white, balanced with equal parts of hope and fear.

"Hon Echido." Charles put his hands together carefully into that arrangement known as Imperial Choice. Then he waited a moment while the scent of roses hung in the air and a bird called piercingly in the silence. "I take you in."

Echido flushed red first, shading away into the orange of peace. "Tai Charles." He bowed to the precise degree indicating the fullness of his loyalty. "I am yours."

"Deliver the dispensation to me tomorrow at the zenith. You may go, Hon Echido."

Still orange, Echido bowed again and retreated, his stewards flanking him three steps behind. Charles watched them go and then retraced his path. He found Jamsetji kneeling in the dirt, thinning irises.

"What do you think?" Charles asked.

"Cursed trouble, I think. But by damn, Charles, they're sharp, that merchant house. I think they'll be worth the trouble."

"I hope so. And what is the protocol involved in taking over a merchant house from a dishonored duke?"

"Wasn't done, I'd have thought."

"I'd have thought, too. This is the kind of thing we must learn."

"Good thing your sister speaks the language so well."

"A good thing, indeed. We learn as we go."

"Damned chameleons," said Jamsetji, without much heat.

"Dinner tonight, then? Good." Charles nodded at him and strolled away, taking his time, out through the greenhouse and into the palace, coming at last to his office. He sat down at his desk and considered the mud flats. Then he called up the models by the technician Karima and stared at them, at the lines tracing flight paths and potential landing sites, all in the northern mass of the continent on which Jeds lay far, far to the south and west. He smoothed a hand over the callpad on his desk.

"I want a message, scrambled, to Jeds. To Marco Burckhardt from Charles Soerensen. Marco, I have no further message from Suzanne. It is time to take action on Rhui. Take the emergency kit and the model of landing sites provided by Karima. Sail north. End of message."

* * *

Tess woke from a deep, soundless sleep into total darkness, her first impulse to snuggle back against the cushion of warmth behind her. Then she remembered where she was, and she became aware all at once of several things: his deep, steady breathing and the warmth of his breath on her neck; an arm flung around her, casual as a lover's embrace; the smell of sweat and horse and lingering blood. She felt unnaturally hot, except for the chill lingering in her toes. Cloth tickled her face. She searched upward with her hand, gently, not wanting to wake him, and found that they were completely covered, toe to head. The horses shifted without nervousness to one side. She heard the hush of rain and the low whine of the wind. She shifted slightly. His arm tightened around her as he sighed in his sleep. His face moved against her hair. She was far more comfortable than she wanted to be, far more comfortable. She fell asleep.

She woke briefly when he left her, woke enough to struggle to her feet and cross to the corral, to check the horses, to relieve herself. The gouge on Myshla's leg was swollen, huge. What if they had to kill her? Terrified, Tess collapsed back onto the couch, exhausted, cold and hot by turns, and slept. When she woke again at Ilya's return he had barely gotten settled before she sat up.

"Can't we get rid of these blankets?" The cold air caressed her cheeks. She pushed the blankets away and got to her knees.

He gripped her arm and stopped her from rising. "You've got a fever. Here, drink."

Her mouth was dry, her lips, her hands. The light hurt her eyes and made her temples ache. She drank eagerly, until he took the waterskin from her.

"Lie down."

"I'm hot. Why do I need blankets?"

"To burn your fever away."

"Who needs a fire?" she muttered, but she lay down and he tucked the blankets in around them. "Just stick my arm in kindling and it'll ignite. I hope I'm not being incoherent. How is your knee?"

"Rest is the best cure. I slept all night."

"Don't you usually?"

"Not often," he replied cryptically. He crossed his arms tight against his chest, an inoffensive barrier between them.

"I feel terrible. Tell me a story."

He laughed softly. "To make you fall asleep?"

"Yes. Rest is the best cure. I heard that once from a very warm man—I mean a very *wise* man."

One of his hands moved, bunching into a fist. He took in a deep breath and let it out slowly.

Tess giggled. "Freudian slip," she said in Anglais.

"What does that mean?"

"Can't explain. It's a medical term. What about Vlatagrebi?" A throb began between her eyes.

"Well," said Bakhtiian briskly. "If only Josef was here, but I'll do my best."

Partway through the story she fell asleep. She woke again, hot and aching. Pain lanced her eyes. Her pulse pounded incessantly through her ears. He gave her more water. She went back to sleep.

To wake again. And again. She was damp with sweat. She tossed fitfully, aching and miserable. He told her more of the story, or perhaps it was a different story, she could not be sure. The fire burned, as fitful as she was.

Day came, and with it light. Night followed. Finally the fever broke. She dozed calmly, waking at last when Bakhtiian moved.

"What happened?" She sat up. The unaccustomed light made her blink. She felt light-headed and tired but somehow cleansed. Then, seeing him standing, holding on to his walking stick, she rubbed her eyes. "What are you doing? Your knee."

"Is better. Possibly. I'm going outside."

"But the storm—"

"Cousin, we've been here a night and a day and a night, and most of this day. The storm has passed down the mountain. I expect we can leave in the morning."

Tess slowly unwound herself from the confusion of waking and looked up at him. "But your knee—Myshla! How is Myshla?"

"Still tender, but she's putting weight on the leg. She'll do. I need some fresh air and a chance to look at the weather. We also need more water. And I thought—" He hesitated. He had color in his face again, and this time she thought most of it natural. "I thought you might like some privacy to attend to yourself."

It was said so demurely that she had to laugh. "Your manners are impeccable, Bakhtiian," she said in Rhuian. "You have my permission to go."

After attending to herself and fussing over Myshla, she walked outside to comb her hair and to set the blankets out to air. She felt weak but not terribly so. A wind rose up from the plains, a touch of late-summer warmth in it. Sitting on a terraced boulder, she sang a jaran song. The sun warmed her hair and her face. Bakhtiian hobbled into view and sank down beside her on the boulder.

"You finally had such nice color in your face," she said, "but it's all gone again."

"It really is better. Can you take the horses out?" She nodded. "But do it quickly. There isn't much light left."

"Bakhtiian. Everything you say is true. Doesn't it wear on you?"

He stood up. "Cousin," he said, reserved, "I am not quite so good-natured as you think I might be."

"But, Cousin, I have hope that you could be," she said, laughing at him, and beat a hasty retreat to the horses.

She got back before the sun set, stabled the horses in their corner, and sat down by Bakhtiian's feet. "I couldn't find anything dry for the fire. Lord, I'm tired. I'm starving."

"We'll eat the last of the meat tonight." He parceled it out. "The weather should hold for two days yet. We'll catch the jahar by then."

"Can you ride?"

"I have to ride or we'll never get out of here."

"Well," said Tess, too cheerfully. "I remember sleeping in my brother's bed in Jeds when there were thunderstorms."

"Oh, yes. I shared a tent with Natalia for many years."

With these expression of sibling felicity, they felt able to resume the sleeping arrangements of the previous nights. In the morning, she saddled Kriye and Bakhtiian's remount. They were out of the valley and down to the fork by midmorning.

CHAPTER NINETEEN

"It is not possible to step into
the same river twice."
—HERACLEITUS OF EPHESUS

At the fork, Bakhtiian dismounted and rested his leg, his back against the thick-grained red rock, his bad knee propped upon the peeling trunk of the dead shrub. His breathing was shallow, but after a bit he mounted by himself and they went on. They emerged onto the plateau unexpectedly, rounding a corner into the midst of short, yellow grass. Behind rose the mountains. On the other three sides, only sky.

Tess turned to smile at Bakhtiian, blushing when she found his eyes on her. If he could still pass for an attractive man in her eyes after the past four days, as disheveled and worn as he was, with lines of pain enduring around his eyes and mouth, then she had only herself to blame. She remembered the feel of his face brushing her hair, his arm tightening around her—he had been asleep.

Kriye shied. Tess, calming him, felt hardly any transition from one state to the next as he settled.

"You're becoming a good rider," said Bakhtiian.

"Thank you."

"You have a hand for them. Your little mare is fond of you." He glanced back at Myshla as they rode out onto the plateau. His left hand gripped the pommel, white-knuckled. "She's a beautiful animal. Are you fond of her?"

Tess was inordinately fond of Myshla, a fondness intensified by Myshla's recognition that she, Tess, was her particular friend. But Tess thought of Jeds and looked away. "I am not in the habit," she said evenly, "of becoming fond of things I will shortly have to part from."

Silence, except for the constant drag of wind in grass.

"I understand you very well," said Bakhtiian finally.

There was no more conversation. Late in the afternoon they agreed to camp, halting at a brush-lined stream.

"It's much milder tonight," said Tess as she unsaddled Kriye.

"Yes. Here are your blankets."

She did not sleep very well, but perhaps that was because the ground was hard. She woke at dawn, stiff. Bakhtiian was already awake, saddling Kriye, forced to stand very curiously in order to favor his injured leg.

"*I'll* saddle the horses," said Tess, rolling up her blankets. He did not answer. She made a face at his back and went to wash in the stream. When she got back, he had saddled her remount as well. They mounted without speaking and rode on. Soon afterward they found a pyramid of flat-sided rocks, a khoen, at the crest of a rise.

"That's ours!"

Bakhtiian merely nodded. At midday they spotted a rider in red and black atop a far rise, and the rider saw them. It was Kirill. He cantered up and pulled his horse around to walk with theirs.

"I rescue you again, my heart." He winked at her and flamboyantly blew her a kiss. Kriye waltzed away from the sudden movement, but Tess reined him back.

"You're a shocking flirt," she said, laughing.

"Your manners, Kirill," said Bakhtiian. "Where are the others?"

Kirill grinned slyly at Tess and pulled his chin: old gray-beard. Tess giggled.

"*Well?*"

"Against the hills," said Kirill hastily. "How did you hurt your leg?"

Bakhtiian briefly described the nature and getting of the injury.

"Oh. So it was an injury. We thought—" He faltered. Tess, twisting one of her bracelets, stared at her wrist. Bakhtiian turned his head to stare directly at the younger man. "Ah, yes," Kirill finished quickly. "We thought you had gotten into trouble."

"I don't know what else would have kept us out in such weather," said Bakhtiian.

Kirill caught Tess's eye and mouthed the words, "I do."

Tess coughed, hiding her laughter, and then gave Kirill an abbreviated version of the last several days. Kirill engaged her in a lively discussion of how best to keep unconscious men on horses. Bakhtiian remained majestically silent.

"But Kirill, even tied to the saddle— Look! There it is!" She broke away from her two companions, Kriye stretching out into a gallop. The men gathered in the camp scattered, laughing, at her precipitous entrance. She rode almost through the camp before she got Kriye stopped. At first she was besieged by the curious, but Yuri finally escorted her away so that she could wash and change. Later, she walked with Yuri up the narrow valley at the mouth of which they were camped.

Tess took in a breath of cool air and pushed a branch away from her face. The sun shone overhead, though it was not a particularly warm day. "You wouldn't know, with the weather as it is now, that we almost froze to death up there."

"The worst of the storm went round us, but it was cold, and it rained. We had five fires. Tess." He stopped at the foot of a shallow escarpment. Tufts of coarse grass dangled from its lip above his head. "How did you manage not to freeze to death? I had your tent. Ilya mentioned a fire, but. . . ."

She blushed. "We managed," she said stiffly.

Yuri grinned. "How like Ilya you sound, Sister. He said exactly the same thing, and in much the same voice. Do you know, when you didn't come in that first night, we all assumed that the two of you had—"

"Don't be a fool, Yuri. Bakhtiian was injured."

"I rather liked the idea myself."

"Then you can learn to dislike it." She stepped sharply away from him, but the loose gravel, damp from rain, slipped away from under her feet. She slid down, one leg out, and had to throw an arm back to catch herself. Poised ungracefully on all fours, almost like some crustacean, she lowered herself to sit on the ground. Her frown dissolved and she laughed. "Gods, I've been in a bad temper these past few days. Listen, Yuri. If you tell anyone else, I'll skin you alive."

"I won't!" He collapsed backward to sit beside her.

"We had to share the blankets and the cloak."

"Oh," said Yuri wisely, "you slept together for warmth.

That probably did save you. I suppose, with his knee like that, you couldn't have—''

"Yuri!"

"I'm just teasing."

"Then stop teasing."

"Why? Was it that uncomfortable?"

"It was too damned comfortable!" She glanced around, suddenly conscious of the cool quiet of the afternoon and the heated loudness of her voice. There was a pause, as if to let her words dissipate into the calm.

"Do you know what I think?" said Yuri finally.

"I won't."

"Your words say you do not want him, but everything else, your face and your tone and the way you put your words together, says that you do."

"No."

"You lay with Fedya."

"Fedya never demanded anything. We shared—what we wanted to share, nothing more than that. More like friends than like lovers."

"Why can't you do that with Ilya?"

"Yuri, do you really suppose that it would be that easy with Ilya?"

He regarded her thoughtfully. "I don't know, Tess. It depends on what Ilya wants."

And what if Ilya decided that he wanted Jeds? But she could not say it aloud for fear of hurting Yuri's feelings. "It depends on what *I* want, and I don't want him. Don't look at me like that. Yes, I'll admit I find him attractive. I'll even admit he annoys me frequently, which I suppose is a bad sign. But all other things aside—I'm leaving.''

He laid a hand on her arm. "I'd forgotten."

She scooped up a handful of pebbles and let them dribble in ones and twos through her fingers. They landed on the other stones in a shower of snaps. "I have to return to Jeds."

"Do you want to?"

She stared at the ground. A single, fine strand of her hair was wound among the pebbles like a snake. "I have a duty to my brother. He must be worrying about me. He doesn't know where I am. I have to go back. Oh, let's talk about something else."

"We were talking about you and Ilya before."

"Were we? You see, I've already forgotten. Yuri, Fedya

loved his wife, and yet I always felt that it was somehow shameful that he did. Don't jaran believe in love?''

"Fedya never gave up his grief, Tess. There is a difference. Of course jaran love. Niko and his wife are as devoted as the rain and the grass. Mikhal loves Sonia.''

"What about Sonia?"

"Frankly, I think the attachment is stronger on his side. Oh, she's fond enough of him, and happy, but when she was younger, before Mikhal marked her, I think she lost her heart to a rider from another tribe.''

"Why didn't he marry her?"

"I heard that two years later he went off with the arenabekh. Some men dislike women that much. Some men love only other men. Some—I don't know why the others go. I'd never willingly give up the chance to marry.''

"Why, Yuri, do you have anyone in mind?'' To her surprise, he blushed. "You do! Who is it?''

With terribly casual nonchalance, he palmed a rock and flipped it up into the brush above them. The buzz of an unseen insect stopped, resuming a moment later. "Well. Maybe. Perhaps I'll mark Konstantina Sakhalin.''

"Konstantina Sakhalin! I didn't know you'd fallen in love with her. And in such a short time.''

"In love with her? I like her well enough—" He flushed again and could not disguise a satisfied smile. "But, Tess, surely you understand that it would be a good connection for our tribes. Not that I'm so valuable of myself, not like Sevyan and Pavel.''

"Why do you call them valuable? I thought they were important because they're married to Kira and Stassia. They don't ride in jahar.''

"Tess!'' Yuri blinked, looking astounded. "How can you say so? They're smiths, and very fine ones, too, for being— well, Sevyan's only forty, and Pavel's about Ilya's age. Mama was overjoyed when Mother Raevsky told her that Sevyan Lensky was interested in Kira. And it was sheer luck that his brother had also taken to the craft and that he and Stassi—'' He chuckled. "I was only six but I still remember how Mama and Mother Raevsky and the Elders of both tribes haggled for *ten days* over the wedding portions. Uncle Yakhov was wild when Mother Raevsky demanded the prize ram from the herds and half the female lambs from the next season. And the rest, which I can't recall now. But, of course, he saw that Sevyan and Pavel were worth it, when we only had old Vadim Gorelik for smithing, and he never better than a middling smith anyway. And then it helped him in the end, because when Mikhal fell in love with Sonia—oh, years later, of course—Mama simply looked the other way when Misha went to mark her, though he'd nothing really special to bring to the etsana's tent. No craft, and though he's got a good hand for the lute, he wasn't gifted by the gods for music like Fedya was. And he's not a remarkably handsome man either.''

"But he's very good-natured."

"Yes."

"But then, Yuri, I don't mean to sound—"

He laughed. "Why should Mother Sakhalin agree to *me*? Because I'm Bakhtiian's cousin. And my mother is etsana. Konstantina will be etsana someday, and I know exactly what is to be expected of an etsana's husband."

"Wouldn't Ilya be the best choice to marry an etsana?"

"Ilya?" He chuckled. "Ilya is exactly the last man any etsana would want to marry. She doesn't want a husband who will put himself forward, or who will quarrel with whichever cousin or nephew is dyan of her tribe's jahar. So you see, I am perfect." He preened a little, to make his point.

Tess laughed and draped an arm around his shoulders. "I always knew you were perfect, Yuri. But then who will Bakhtiian marry, if not an etsana's daughter?"

"I thought you said you weren't interested in him."

"I'm *curious*, damn you."

"Tess, Tess, no need to be snappish. How should I know, anyway? Why do you want to know?"

"Well, for one thing, he can't have children unless he's married, can he? He might have gotten a child on some woman but he wouldn't be considered its father."

"Yes, I remember in Jeds I was surprised how great a fuss those barbarians made over which man got which child on which woman. I only ever had *one* father, Tess."

"What if an unmarried girl gets pregnant, or if a child's mother dies?"

Yuri regarded her quizzically. "A child always stays with its mother, or with her kin if its mother dies. And, of course, you know about the herb girls use so they don't get pregnant. Only married women have children."

"Well, then, what about Vladimir? Didn't his mother have any kin to take him in?"

Yuri shook his head. "His parents were priests."

"They're dead?"

"No, given in service to the gods. Those few jaran who take the white robe break all ties with the tribes. A little like the arenabekh, but for different reasons. There are priests at the shrine of Morava. And they're both men and women, so, of course, sometimes there are children."

"But without kin. How did he come to ride in your jahar?"

"We found him at *jahar-ledest*. In Jeds you would call them schools, I suppose. There is one here in the west, and one in the east, where young men can train."

"You told me about them once." Above them, a few clouds floated like calm fish in untroubled waters. "Bakhtiian mentioned one once. Doesn't he know the man who trains there?"

"Kerchaniia Bakhalo. He rode with Ilya's father."

"Why do you have these 'schools'? The jaran wander."

"Oh, the influence of khaja, I suppose. Bakhalo made the first one, some twenty years back. I learned more there about fighting than I ever learned in the tribe because it's all you have to think about. Like the arenabekh, but temporary, thank the gods. You'd like it, Tess. Bakhalo has about forty young men at a time. He lives by a town near the coast. That put me off at first, to live in one place, but I'd just been in Jeds and, anyway, we lived in tents. The townspeople there are happy because with the jaran there the pirates don't bother them. It's a strange arrangement, but it works. I was never any good at saber until I went there."

"Why not?"

"I never bothered." He sighed ostentatiously. "That didn't make me any more popular among the girls. They like a boy who can flash his blade."

"I'll bet."

"Or one who has a reputation, like Ilya. They dangle like so much plump fruit in front of him, but really, when I think of it, he rarely picks from that tree."

"Why do you think he doesn't?"

"Are you sure you're not a little bit in love with him?"

A wind stirred through the brush. Twigs scraped softly against rock. "I think you should make up to him."

"And be left dangling like the rest of the ripe, or over-ripe, fruit? No thank you."

"Perhaps I chose an unfortunate expression."

"Very unfortunate."

"But, Tess, think of the rest of us. Haven't you ever no-ticed that the more Ilya denies himself, the worse of a mood he gets in? Niko once told me that he'd never known Ilya to sleep through the night except when he was with a woman."

She flushed scarlet. "Yuri! No."

He grinned, enjoying her discomfiture. "You're just stub-born."

"No, I'm protecting myself. He's very attractive."

"Then why don't you—" He broke off, laughing, to hug her. "It's much better having you for a sister than a lover, because I get you forever as a sister."

"Unless I kill you first."

"Tess," he scolded, "you'd never manage without me. Who got you through that first ten days? Who saddled Myshla for you and brought you food?"

"Definitely a brother. Only a sibling would hold *that* over my head." She hugged him suddenly and fiercely. "Yuri, I—" She broke off.

He pushed her back. "What's wrong? Don't cry!"

"My brother is so much older than me. I always wanted another brother, one close in age, so we could share—" She hesitated, went on awkwardly. "One I could love right here, next to my heart, instead of from far away."

Yuri's whole expression transformed, as if his heart, long buried, now shone from his face. Then, unaccountably, he lowered his eyes to stare at his hands. "I love you, too, Tess," he said in a low voice, as if afraid the admission would offend her.

"Well, you might at least look at me when you say it!" she demanded, suddenly embarrassed, and then she laughed because he was as flushed as she was.

"Of course, you know what this means." He looked up at her with a sly grin.

"What what means?"

"Siblings are bound by the oldest of customs to protect one another, even if it means death."

"Very well, Yuri. If Bakhtiian ever begins to scold you, I'll come to your rescue."

"It needn't go that far," said Yuri quickly. They both grinned and got up to return to camp, brushing dirt and withered blades of grass from their clothing. "We were worried though, Tess. Especially when that storm blew down and you hadn't gotten back yet." They walked slowly along the escarpment, boots scuffing through damp grass, content for the moment in each other's company.

"I'm surprised Niko didn't send Josef to look for us."

"He would have in another three nights."

"Yuri, we could have been dead by then."

"But Ilya left us a message that we shouldn't wait. How were we to know what that meant?"

Tess stopped, suddenly suspicious. "What did you think it meant?" Yuri knelt abruptly, turning his face away from her, and busied himself brushing imaginary grass from his boots. "Look at me. Why nine nights?"

He straightened, his flush fading to a slight pink tint along his high cheekbones. "It's just superstition."

"Yes, and?"

The flush rose a little high, creeping up to his ears, but he met her gaze. "I don't want to talk about it," he finished, his tone edged.

"You thought we— Never mind. I know what you thought. Everyone else evidently thought the same thing."

He smiled slightly, conciliatorily. "At least give us credit for thinking, Tess."

"Oh, Yuri," she said in disgust, "I'm hungry. Isn't there something hot to eat?"

Yuri's gaze shifted past her toward the camp. "The stew must be ready by now. I'll go check. I pitched your tent over there—" He nodded toward the opposite bluff. "All your gear is there."

"Thank you, Yuri. What would I possibly do without you?"

He gave her a sidewise look. "I'm used to older sisters, always ordering a man around and telling him what to do."

"Oh, go away," she said, as much with humor as with pique, and he grinned, happy to annoy her, and left.

She strolled slowly toward the opposite bluff, glad to be alone with her own thoughts. On a whim, she walked over to the four white tents of the Chapalii. None of them were outside, that she could see, so she simply stood for a moment and watched. Even in this weak sunlight, the white fabric of the tents shimmered, as if light was woven in with it. And perhaps it was—she knew there was more than cloth in their weaving. All plain white but for the lettering at their peaks that marked one as a lord's tent, one as a merchant's, and the other two for the lowly stewards. Even disguised, as they were in a fashion for this journey, they still must mark their rank for themselves.

The flap on the merchant's tent swept aside and Garii emerged, looking straight at her, as if he knew she was standing there. "Lady Terese! You have returned!" Colors flushed his face in a blur before he controlled himself and his skin faded to a neutral pallor. He bowed. "I beg your greatest indulgence for my outburst, Lady Terese. Only, I feared for you—" He broke off abruptly.

Ishii pushed out of his own tent and examined first Garii and then, bowing punctiliously, Tess. "Lady Terese. Please permit me to express how gratified I am to see you restored to our party. I hope there was no trouble."

Caught out, she thought fast. "Indeed, Cha Ishii, I accept your felicitations. I thought to inquire if you and your party have suffered through this difficult cold weather, knowing as I do that you are better adapted to heat."

"Your concern honors us." He inclined his head. Garii stood stiffly to one side, silent. "Indeed, we have been forced to remain within our tents for the most part of these past days, but as I understand that we will reach the shrine of Morava soon, we are able to endure such trials knowing that they will come to an end and that we shall return to more hospitable environments." He looked pointedly at Garii. Garii, caught looking at Tess, bowed abruptly and subserviently, and retreated into his tent.

"I feel sure," said Tess to cover the awkward silence, "that you anticipate with pleasure such a change in your circumstances."

"You are discerning, Lady Terese. I only wish all those of my party had so much discrimination as yourself, but I fear that low birth or unstable family often contributes to a lack of discretion or even to poor judgment." He bowed.

That he was warning her was clear. Unsure what to reply, she chose, like Garii, retreat. "You may return to your duties, Cha Ishii."

He bowed with exactly the correct measure of humility and pride, and went back into his tent.

She forced herself to get out of earshot before she allowed herself to swear, a single word, just to express her frustration. And she was then greeted by the sight of Bakhtiian, sitting on the lip of his tent, which some fool had pitched not thirty paces from her own. A leather pouch cradled his injured knee. He was very white-faced, talking—or arguing—with Niko while diligently keeping his attention on the shirt he was mending. Tess averted her gaze and passed them. In a moment, she felt someone come up behind her. It was Niko.

"Tess."

Tess did not stop until she reached her tent. Then she turned. "What do you want?"

"I do not appreciate being the recipient of your ill humor, my girl, having done nothing to deserve it."

"I'm sorry, Niko."

"You ought to be. Now what happened?"

"What happened where?"

"Tess, having just played this scene with Ilyakoria, I have no patience to repeat it with you."

"He hurt his knee. We had a very difficult six days getting back to you."

"All this is evident to the discerning man. Doubtless the days would not have been so trying if Bakhtiian did not think he has to endure twice what another man can." He rested his hand on her shoulder, a light touch but firm, so that she knew he meant her to look at him. He watched her intently, his eyes very bright against the weathered tan of his face. "Or would they have been? Do you know anything about this, young woman?"

"If I do, it's nothing I set out to do," she exclaimed, shaking loose from his hand.

Niko smiled. The wrinkles of old laughter showed at the corners of his eyes. "That answers my question. I won't trouble you further." He left.

"Why is everyone so annoying today?" Tess muttered. She ducked into her tent, but she had to rummage around for a bit, cursing under her breath, before she found her bowl.

Coming out of her tent, she saw Kirill walking toward her, his light step and red-gold hair making him seem like a shaft of barely controlled energy in the quiet of the afternoon. She hurried toward the fire.

"Tess!" he called.

"Damn," she said under her breath, but she halted.

"We should make all the women wear jahar dress. I've never seen such an appealing sight as you in red and black." She was thankful that they were so far from the main fire, and yet, truthfully, was happy to see him. His easygoing humor sparked in the air between them as he came up to her. Her gaze drifted briefly to one side. Bakhtiian's tent was no farther than twenty paces away now. His eyes had lifted from his shirt, although his hands kept to an even stitch, thread a thin line between his fingers. Kirill stopped two paces from her. Though his eyes were full of laughter, his expression was serious. "None of the men," he finished, "looks half so good."

"That depends on who is looking at them, Kirill," she replied, attempting dignity. "I prefer a man in red and black to a woman any time."

"Tess." He smiled. He had a sweet, charming smile, the kind that made it impossible to resist his impudence or even to hold it against him. "You never told me."

"You never asked." Absurdly, she felt herself drawn into the game. Whatever else Kirill might be, he was exceptionally easy to flirt with. "Which is exactly the kind of behavior any jaran woman would expect from a well-mannered man." She moved to circle him but he kept getting in her way.

"But you aren't jaran, my heart."

"Kirill!" The source and, more particularly, the tone surprised them both. Kirill paled slightly; he turned. Bakhtiian still sat by his tent, but his hands no longer worked at his half-mended shirt. His face was devoid of expression. "It is assumed that the men in my jahar have both manners and reputation. Take care that you don't lose your share in all three."

Kirill colored. "This is a private conversation."

"Conducted in so public a place and at such a level? It would in any case be doubly offensive if it were private."

Kirill crimsoned. He deliberately put a hand on the hilt of his saber. Bakhtiian merely watched him. Kirill paused, and Tess could see his expression change as he decided on something.

"Kirill," she began in a low voice, but he was not even aware of her.

He drew his saber. "Not if she were my wife."

If Bakhtiian had been pale before, he went dead white now. He threw the shirt down and began to push up to his feet.

"Sit down!" snapped Tess. She took a step toward Bakhtiian. Kirill's hand was clutched so tightly around the hilt that his tendons stood out. "Kirill. Put that thing away."

"No," said Kirill, still looking at Bakhtiian.

Bakhtiian had frozen, half up, looking as ungainly as he ever could. Eyes on Kirill, he slowly lowered himself back down. His arms stayed poised by his belt.

"Kirill," said Tess reasonably, moving to face the younger man, "Maryeshka Kolenin kicked you in a vulnerable spot once. I have a knife and a saber."

For a moment he still stared past her. When his eyes shifted to her, the line of his mouth softened abruptly. He sheathed his blade, a dull *shick,* and laughed. "And I taught you how to use them."

"That's better."

"I never meant to use it."

"That's good."

"I'm not really running after you as shamelessly as it may at times appear."

"Aren't you?"

He grinned, and added a judicious appendix. "But if you ever get cold some evening. . . ."

"If I get cold some evening, I'll borrow an extra blanket."

"Tess! Aren't I good-looking?"

"A man is only as handsome as his reputation, Kirill." He laughed. Tess glanced at Ilya. He had gone back to his mending. If his lips were pressed together in disapproval, his hands, at least, suffered from no unsteadiness. "Come here."

Kirill followed her out past the tents. Shadows spread out over this end of camp as the sun sank below the heights. Two of the riders, seated at one tent, sharpened their sabers. The harsh sound grated on her nerves, but she managed a polite reply to their greeting. When she could no longer hear the sound, she and Kirill had walked well beyond the camp, back up into the vale in the same direction—though not as far—as she and Yuri had come. It was very still, not even the noise of insects could be heard. She halted and rounded on him.

"Now. Just whose benefit was that display for? Mine, yours, or Bakhtiian's? I don't like being placed in that position."

"Listen, Tess." Kirill's hair had the color of burnished gold in the shadow. "It's true enough that I oughtn't to have made that scene, and I apologize to you most sincerely." Then, as if this earnestness had exhausted his supply, he offered her a sweetly mischievous grin. She could see faint laughter lines at his eyes. "I really just wanted to get a reaction from Ilyakoria."

"You can do that without me. You do it all the time."

He looked away from her. There was a muteness in the vale, almost a lull, as if the world was caught between day and night and could not quite forsake the one or gain the other. "I was fond of my wife before she died. But she thought she was in love with Bakhtiian." He lifted his gaze to her, pale lashes fringing the steady blue of his eyes. "They all do, don't you see? But you—you took Fedya! We were all waiting to see which one you would choose—well, I beg your pardon, but it's only the truth, Tess."

"I suppose," she said coolly, "that you even had a few wagers running on which one it would be, and how soon."

Kirill fought to suppress a grin and failed. "Well, Tess, one woman and twenty-seven men—I don't count the pilgrims, you understand—what do you expect? But no one expected Fedya."

"Yuri might have," she muttered.

"Yuri refused to wager."

"Good for Yuri," she said, and then she laughed. "Gods, how lowering. Did everyone know?"

"Tess, we're not stupid. Or blind." He smiled very sweetly, and she reflected that he was, after all, a good looking man, and well aware of it. "After all, my heart, some of us might have entertained hope for ourselves."

"Don't even try to kiss me, Kirill. I'm not in the mood."

Color infused his cheeks. "But, Tess—"

"What does all this have to do with Bakhtiian anyway? Or was everyone wagering on him?"

"Don't blame me. I didn't wager on him." He grew serious suddenly. "But the odds were overwhelmingly in his favor."

"Oh, Lord," Tess sighed.

"I've never seen a woman so impervious to Bakhtiian," he went on, "and certainly never an attractive woman, and every man, every man in the world, looks twice at the woman who doesn't look twice at him."

"So you wanted to show Bakhtiian that I was more interested in you than in him."

"Well." He straightened a sleeve that already lay perfectly in place and brushed a nonexistent strand of hair away from his cheek. "Yes."

Tess considered Kirill. He smiled, recognizing her scrutiny for what it was and, with that careless confidence that was a large part of his charm, not fearing her judgment. Yes, he would be very easy to take as a lover. And Bakhtiian would be furious. She laughed, knowing that to take him as a lover just to anger Bakhtiian was not only unfair to Kirill but all too revealing about how she might actually feel about Ilya.

"I hope," he said, a little on his dignity now, "that I am not *that* easy to laugh at."

"Why do you resent him? I can understand about your wife, but still, Yuri says that he rarely takes any woman up on her offer."

"That's true. It's no wonder he's so foul-tempered all the time. It isn't really about my wife." He considered her in his turn, but now as if deciding whether to really confide in her. "I'm only five years younger than he is. We grew up together, and I remember him as a child. He changed. At first, when he came back from Jheds, it was easy to believe in what he dreamed of. But he kept changing. He got harder and colder, and he shut out all of those who had once been his friends and companions until all he saw was the vision that leads him. Oh, I still believe in it. Never doubt that. But Bakhtiian is not the same man he was. I remember that day when he stood up in front of the assembled Elders of twenty tribes and told them that the path they had chosen for the tribes was the wrong one. Of course, they immediately agreed with him, *and apologized*, because he's always right."

"Yes, he is always right, isn't he? He has to be. I think you're the only one who understands."

"No, you're the only one who understands. Not even Niko—but I won't say a word against Sibirin. When you decided to come with us, Tess, I waited. I knew Ilya would run you into the ground and send you back to the tribe, but, by the gods, you kept riding. It had been years since I last saw him bested like that." He stood very still. The last light caught red streaks in his hair, like tiny fires in gold. "And I've been waiting ever since."

"Waiting for what?"

"He doesn't like to lose. And if there's anything I hate, it's a person who can't concede even one race, even if the other rider took the course fairly and rode the better race that one time. What does it matter anyway? One race?"

She stared at him as if his whole character had been illuminated for her in that instant. "Bakhtiian couldn't be who he is if it didn't matter to him," she replied, realizing it herself as she spoke.

"I suppose I feel sorry for him in a way. He'll always miss the best part of life for trying to grab hold of what's out of his reach."

Tess felt a sudden flood of warmth for Kirill, who trusted her enough now to reveal so much of his soul to her. "What is the best part of life, Kirill?" she asked softly.

He shrugged and looked suddenly and incongruously diffident.

She almost laughed, because without knowing it, he had chosen in that instant the surest way of winning her over. Instead, she placed her hands, palms open, on his chest, looking up into his face. His eyes were a deep, rich blue, like the late afternoon sky reflected in water. Solemn, his face had a kind of repose that suited his features unexpectedly better than the quicksilver smiles that usually characterized him. "I think it's going to be cold tonight." She kissed him on the mouth.

Quite abruptly, he flushed pink, and he lowered his gaze from hers. "Tess," he murmured. He glanced at her, and she saw to her great satisfaction that he was both surprised and elated.

"Well," she said, stepping back from him, "I'm hungry. Aren't we going to eat?"

He laughed. "How like a woman. Yes, Tasha made stew." They walked back together. She felt disgustingly pleased

with herself and would not have cared for the world if everyone knew—but Kirill acted with the greatest discretion,
not sitting with her, not treating her any differently than he
ever did, so that when she parted with Yuri to go to her tent,
Yuri did not even suspect.

Sitting on her blankets, listening to the mellow howl of
the wind while she took off her boots, shivering a little, she
began to wonder if he had changed his mind. But there was
a sudden, quiet scuff outside and then he tumbled in, laughing under his breath. She was so surprised she grabbed him,
and he, quick to take advantage, embraced her and buried
his face in her neck.

"Ah, gods," he murmured into her hair, "that damned
Bakhtiian is still awake. What a canny piece of tracking it
took to get in here unseen."

She began to laugh, because his excitement was infectious, and because he was very warm and very close.

"Shh, Tess." He laid a finger on her lips. "This is a
small camp. Do you want everyone to know?"

"Won't they know soon enough anyway?" she asked,
feeling a surge of recklessness, now that she had made her
choice.

She felt him grin against her cheek. "I'll wager you, my
heart. How many days—no, nights—do you think we can
keep this a secret?"

"What will the stakes be?"

"Why, kisses, of course."

"Just kisses? Surely we can risk higher stakes than that."

"Then name your stakes. By the way, here, I brought an
extra blanket for you to borrow. It is a cold night, after all."

"You're smug tonight, Kirill."

"Don't I have every reason to be?"

She did not bother to reply, at least not in words.

CHAPTER TWENTY

"Many fires burn below the surface."
—EMPEDOCLES OF AGRAGAS

Later in the night, it began to drizzle. Kirill stirred and sat up, waking her.

"Where are you going?" she whispered.

In the darkness, he had to struggle a bit to find and put on his clothing. "I'm leaving."

"But it's raining."

She felt him shrug. "What's a bit of rain? Tess, I am not so ill-bred as to flaunt my good fortune to the others by being found here in the morning."

"My, Kirill. Nobility suits you."

He leaned to kiss her. "Certainly it does. I also have to relieve Konstans on watch, my heart."

She laughed and let him leave.

In the morning, it continued to drizzle, but they rolled up their tents despite the damp and went on their way. Because Bakhtiian could not scout, Tess rode with Yuri at the fore of the main group, enjoying this novelty although not the rain.

" 'What's a bit of rain,' " she groused when they halted at midday. "How anyone can shrug off this miserable weather is beyond me."

"Why?" asked Yuri casually. "Did someone say that?"

She turned her head away to hide her expression from him. Behind them, Kirill was talking with Mikhal and seemed unaware of her. Composing her face, she said, "Yes, Kirill did."

Yuri wiped a bead of rain away from his right eye. "I've

never heard Kirill complain about any hardship Bakhtiian
has put us through."

"Just about Bakhtiian?" Tess glanced back to where
Bakhtiian rode next to Niko. Ilya was looking at her. She
jerked her gaze away and fixed it self-consciously on Yuri.
"But he follows him."

"I remember when I was a boy, and Kirill was just old
enough to ride in jahar, and Bakhtiian had started this great
ride of his—and Kirill clung as close to Bakhtiian as Vladimir does now. He admired him. But Ilya changed, and
Kirill grew up and became his own man. Somehow, I think
they never forgave each other."

"Forgave each other for what?"

"Kirill never forgave Ilya for casting aside all his old ties
of friendship, for giving up everything for the path he chose
to ride. Ilya never forgave Kirill for beginning to question
him."

"You're being very wise today, Yuri."

He grinned. "Am I? Was there something you wanted to
tell me, Tess? You have that look about you."

"No, I just hate this rain."

That he did not suspect was obvious. Yuri, of all people,
would not hesitate to either congratulate her for finally behaving as a jaran woman ought, or, she supposed, censure
her for heedlessly antagonizing Bakhtiian—not that it was
any business of Bakhtiian's who she slept with, by God.
And she had grown to know the riders in the jahar well
enough by now to recognize the little signs that would show
that they knew, and were amused, and teased Kirill. The
signs that, had she known them those months before, would
have shown her that the entire jahar knew about Fedya. Kirill, especially, would be teased relentlessly, in that subtle,
merciless, but discreet way the riders used when there were
women present. And Kirill, she realized with a sudden flash
of insight, was well enough liked and well enough respected
that no man in the jahar would begrudge him what he had
fairly gained: her regard. Or at least, no man possibly but
one.

Three days passed, riding. Three nights, she pitched her
tent so that its entrance faced away from the others, out at
the edge of the little camp, and Kirill crept in. Always in
the best of humor, despite the damned rain. As well he

might be. No one commented. It was beginning to look likely that he would win their wager.

"Gods," said Yuri to her as he helped her set up her tent that night, where they had camped at the edge of a range of hills. "If Bakhtiian has said ten words these past four days it's been out of my hearing."

"He's in pain. That he can ride all day amazes me."

"Does it? It shouldn't. He is Bakhtiian, after all. What he really needs is a woman to take pity on him and find a way to take his mind off that injured knee."

"Yuri. No, no, no, no, no."

"If you insist, but I still think—"

"Must we have this conversation every night? How did these damned blankets get damp?" She threw them inside and then thought of Kirill and smiled.

"What's wrong with you?" Yuri demanded. "You look awfully pleased with yourself."

"Oh, it's just the stars. I'd forgotten how I miss them at night, now that the clouds have cleared off and it's stopped raining." She stood up and stretched, relishing the delicate touch of the twilight air on her skin. "Niko says we've only a day's ride through these hills tomorrow and then we'll be back on the plains again."

"Yes." Yuri stood as well. "Gods, I'll be glad to be on the plains again." He hesitated and sighed. "Well, I'm off to set up Ilya's tent. Wish me luck."

"Can't Vladimir do it?"

"*I'm* Ilya's cousin, Tess. Mother would be furious if I let Vladimir interfere while Ilya can't do it himself."

"Well, then, Yuri, if you're so afraid of Ilya's bad temper, I'll go with you and help you."

"Oh, he won't say a word to me. That's why it's so bad. He just sits there. How he hates being beholden to others. Actually—" Yuri grinned— "I rather enjoy it in a way because he knows I know how he feels."

She laughed. "Why is it that the ones who look the sweetest hide the most malicious hearts?"

"Why, Sister, how should I know?"

He left, and she had a sudden urge to just walk, alone, and smell the air and gaze up at the sharp brilliance of stars above. She hiked up the nearby hill and settled herself on a rock that lay beneath three leafless trees grown up on the lee side of the hill. Rain, after all, wasn't such a bad thing

as long as one's feet stayed dry, and hers had. And it was
not so very rainy in this part of the world, or at least the
jaran knew where to ride so as to stay out of it.

Below her, a few fires lay strewn like a cache of untidy
jewels across a strip of land. She breathed in. Air like this
no longer existed on Earth. All of her life on that distant
planet seemed at that moment inconsequential. She had so
utterly lacked confidence that her slightest movement caused
her fear—that she was doing the wrong thing, that someone
was watching, that she only mattered because of who her
brother was; worst, that she would fail Charles somehow.
To be honest, about her feelings, about any action she took—
that was dangerous in the extreme. While here. . . .

Sonia's family, for no reward whatsoever, had taken her
in, had given her the initial mark of respectability that had
allowed her to build a place for herself within the jaran. For
she had built such a place. She knew the men of this jahar
respected her. She knew that she could expect the same
open friendship she had received from the women of both
the Orzhekov and the Sakhalin families at any tribe they
might meet, simply and purely because she was a woman.
She had a family. She had a lover—one, by God, she had
chosen herself, with confidence, with fondness, with a fair
measure of real, artless love.

Certainly their technology was primitive, but their spirit
was passionate and free. Bakhtiian claimed to be jaran to
the core; if that were so, then the jaran, like the wind, could
fill any form no matter its size and shape. They could adapt
and hold firm. They could revere the quiet heart of the gods'
mysteries on earth and still remain unquenchably curious.
Like Kirill, they could be brash and diffident together. She
smiled, then frowned, hearing familiar voices approaching
her sanctuary.

Like Bakhtiian, they could be enthralling and utterly per-
ilous. She shrank back into the protection of shadow and
held still.

"Damn it, Ilya," Yuri was saying, "you'll just ruin your
knee, walking around like this. You ought to be lying
down."

"I'm not sleepy."

"I'm sure Josef is in the mood to tell a good tale. He
always is. He knows a thousand we haven't heard yet."

"Yuri, leave me alone."

"I won't! Mother will have my head if I don't try to stop you hurting yourself for no good reason. What's wrong with you?"

Bakhtiian did not dignify this plea with a reply, but Tess heard his breathing, husky from pain, as he halted not ten paces from her on the other side of the trees.

"Very well, then, I'll tell you." Yuri's voice had a reckless tone to it that surprised her. "You won't admit to yourself that you're attracted to her. You certainly won't act on it."

"It is not a man's place to act."

"Yes, you'll hide behind that excuse, won't you, knowing very well that any man can find a hundred ways to let a woman know how he feels and win her over."

"As Kirill did?"

"Gods. Kirill is always flirting. You know it doesn't mean anything."

"How odd that I should then see him coming out of Soerensen's tent these four nights past."

Dead silence. "I don't believe you."

"I don't care whether you believe me or not."

"By the gods. Maybe I do believe you. I think you're jealous."

This silence was deeper and colder and lasted longer. "Yuri, leave me right now."

"No. You *are* attracted to her."

"Very well. It may be that I am suffering from certain desires that could, after all, be aroused by the close proximity of any woman. And satisfied by the same female, or another, whichever was closer."

Yuri gasped, a sound caught somewhere between horror and disbelief. His voice, when he finally spoke, had such a sarcastic edge to it that Tess flinched. "You bastard. But could a female satisfy them?"

"Yurinya." Bakhtiian's tone could have been chiseled, it was so hard. "I will thrash you to within a hand of your life if you ever say anything to me on that subject again."

Tess got an itch on her nose, stubborn and flaming, but she dared not move.

"Well, I say good for Kirill and be damned to you." Yuri strode away uphill, boots stamping through the grass. After a long pause, Bakhtiian began his slow, limping pace back down toward camp.

Tess lifted her hand slowly, rubbed her nose, and stood up. A breeze pushed through the trees and a few final drops of water scattered down from the branches onto her uncovered head. She ducked away, wiping at her hair with disgust. Heard footsteps. But it was only Yuri, returning.

"Yuri?"

"Tess! Where did you come from? Did you hear that?"

"Yes."

He came up beside her. "I'm sorry."

"Are you through matchmaking now? Maybe you've learned your lesson."

"I feel scorched," he replied. "Gods. Don't you start on me, too."

"Listen. Let's settle this right now. Of course I'm attracted to him. He's that kind of man. But he's a hard, cold, ambitious bastard—you said it yourself, so don't try to disagree with me now—and he'll never be able to care for anyone as much as he cares for himself and, well, to be fair, for this thing that drives him. He may well desire me. I have the honor, after all, of being the female in closest proximity to him."

"Tess. . . ."

"Let me finish. And, of course, I didn't succumb instantly to his charm, which doubtless gives me a little originality."

"You can spare me the sarcasm."

"What did you mean, anyway, about a female not—"

"Never mind. Forget I said it. Please. I thought you were going to finish."

She shrugged. "I'm done. Do you understand, Yuri? I would think you of all people would."

But Yuri's silence was mulish, not conciliatory in the least. "I know him better than you do," he said in a soft, troubled voice. "You think he isn't capable of really loving someone but he is. He's slow to trust because he's been hurt so badly before, because he's been responsible for people he loved dying—for his own sister and nephew and parents—and he can't forgive himself for it. Yet he can't stop what he has to do either. But if he ever gives his heart to a woman, he will give it absolutely."

"Then I wish her all my sympathy. He'll burn her alive."

"Not if she's strong. Tess—"

"You're damned stubborn, Yuri, and I'm not in a very good mood, or at least, I was, but I'm not anymore."

But Yuri plunged onward with remarkable obstinacy. "There are times a brother's advice is of uncounted value, my dear sister, however much their sisters dislike to hear it. Just ride carefully and, gods, don't antagonize him now. If he decides he wants you—"

"You mean if I antagonize him he'll decide he wants me in revenge? I don't call that giving one's heart absolutely."

"You're just not listening to me! It's all the same thing with him. Oh, never mind. Next time you're riding straight into an ambush don't bother to expect a warning from me." He whirled away from her and stalked down toward camp.

"Yuri!" She started after him. "Yuri." He halted. "I don't want to be angry with you."

"Oh, were you angry with me? I thought I was angry with you."

She put out her hand. "Truce?"

With reserve, he shook it. "Truce. Is it true about Kirill?"

"None of your business." She grinned. "What do you think?"

"I was wondering why he was so polite to Kirill these past three days." He laughed. "Kirill! Well, he did come in second in the—" He broke off.

"In the wagering?"

"How did you know?"

"Oh, I know a great many things. Actually, Kirill told me."

"He's subtle, is our Kirill. You'd never think it to watch him."

"*Subtle?* What does that mean?" That old, creeping, chittering fear that she had somehow done something stupid, that she had allowed herself to be taken advantage of, reared its ugly form again, and then, laughing, she neatly squelched it. "Well, Yuri," she said smugly, "subtle or not, I have no reason to complain."

"How like a woman," said Yuri with disgust, but they walked down to camp together quite companionably, and discussed whether Josef ought to be prevailed upon to tell a story or Mikhal to play his lute.

They rode through the hills the next day without incident. The next morning they came out onto the plain. Tess felt unburdened of a weight that she had not been aware she was carrying. She smiled at Bakhtiian, inquired politely about his injury, and was rewarded with a perfectly normal conversation about the recent debate in Jeds over the form of poetry most conducive to philosophy. Yuri was driven by this display of good fellowship to beg to be allowed to scout, if they meant to continue in this fashion. But once his reassuring presence vanished, they both grew self-conscious, and the dialogue trailed off into awkward sentences that even Niko's late arrival could not repair.

That night she sat and sat and sat in her tent, but Kirill did not arrive. At last she bundled up in her cold, empty blankets and forced herself to sleep. To be awakened very late by Kirill.

"Forgive me, Tess," he repeated at least three times as he stripped and snuggled in next to her. "Bakhtiian switched my and Mikhal's watch just as Mikhal was about to go out. Do you suppose he suspects?"

"Who, Mikhal?"

"You're teasing me."

"My sweet Kirill, would I tease you?" He only laughed and hugged her a little more tightly. "He's known all along."

"What? How do you know?"

"Yuri knows, too."

"Yuri! Begging your pardon, my heart, but Yuri is not my caliber at this business. I can't imagine how he would have known unless you told him."

"No, Bakhtiian told him. There's nothing for it, Kirill. I have won the wager."

"Well," he said, resigned, "so you have. I was hoping you might."

That morning it was a near thing that Kirill got out of her tent before the camp woke to dawn. And to unexpected news, as well. Yuri greeted her with it as she saddled Myshla.

"Tess! Tess! Have you heard? We've come across Veselov's tribe! Josef just rode in." His face shone with excitement.

"Veselov. Why is that name familiar?"

"The best of my friends from growing up is with Veselov

now,'' he rattled on, ignoring her comment. His voice rang clear in the still morning. ''I haven't seen Petya for two years.''

''For what possible reason would your Petya give up the opportunity to ride in Bakhtiian's jahar?''

''Oh, they'll all be Bakhtiian's jahars soon enough. But Petya left us to marry—'' He stopped abruptly and glanced uncertainly toward his cousin. Bakhtiian, who had evidently been looking at them, looked away. ''Well,'' Yuri continued in a lower voice, ''you'll meet her.''

They rode into the tribe itself at midday. It felt familiar, somehow, tents scattered haphazardly along the course of a shallow river. A goodly number of people had gathered just beyond the farthest rank of tents, and they waited, watching, as the jahar rode up. Bakhtiian halted them a hundred paces away, and they all dismounted.

''We wintered by them two years ago,'' Yuri whispered to Tess as the two groups appraised each other in a silence broken only by isolated comments passed murmuring from a handful of individuals. ''Tasha's sister's husband came from this tribe, and . . . and. . . .'' His color had gone high again as his eyes searched the gathered people. Their mood was, Tess thought, still one of measuring rather than welcome.

''Petya!'' Yuri shouted, forgetting all protocol and modesty in sheer excitement. ''Petya!''

He started forward suddenly. Like an echo, movement shifted as the tribe parted to let someone through. A young man burst out of the assembly and strode—half running—to meet Yuri right in the middle of the ground that separated the two groups. They hugged, two fair heads together, but where Yuri's had a pale, dull cast like winter grass, Petya's shone as brightly as if it had been gilded by the sun.

Some barrier dissolved between the groups. An older man stepped forward and hailed Bakhtiian. Ilya gave Kriye's reins to Vladimir and left the jahar, limping across the open space, Niko and Josef and Tadheus a few steps behind. His careful progress lent him dignity, though, Tess considered wryly, it was probably not entirely unconscious. Others filtered forward, men to greet acquaintances and friends amongst the riders, women to observe and draw whatever conclusions they wished.

And three women walked directly toward Tess. Tess had

time to examine them as they neared: one old; one young, dark, and pretty; and one—

Surely this was the "her" Yuri had spoken of.

She had that rare sum of parts that is called beauty. She was quite tall for a woman, almost as tall as Tess, and pleasantly slender. Her hair shone gold, and it hung to her waist, unbraided. She was cursed as well with truly blue eyes and full lips gracing an impossibly handsome face blemished only by the thin, white scar, running from cheekbone to jawbone, that was the mark of marriage. The three women halted in front of Tess, but it was the fair-haired beauty and Tess who did the assessing. Without rancor, both smiled.

"Welcome," said the beauty. "I am Vera Veselov."

"I'm Tess. Tess Soerensen." Tess hesitated and glanced at the older woman, sure that this must be the etsana.

"Yes," said Vera, as if this information was no surprise. "This is my aunt, Mother Veselov. Oh, and Arina, my cousin." Arina smiled tremulously, looking as if she might like to say something but did not dare to. "She will be fine with me now, Aunt," Vera finished, and thus dismissed, the etsana meekly withdrew, nodding once at Tess.

Arina loitered behind and, when Vera said nothing, ventured a few steps closer. But Vera was not actually paying any attention to Tess either. She was staring past Tess toward—Tess turned—Bakhtiian.

"He looks no different," said Vera softly. She glanced at her husband, who still stood talking eagerly and with all the enthusiasm of youth to Yuri. What lay in that glance Tess could not read for it lasted only a moment. Then Vera looked again toward Bakhtiian. He stood talking easily with the older man who had first hailed him.

"Well, Tess Soerensen," said Vera finally, breaking her gaze away from Bakhtiian. "You have ridden an unusual road for a woman."

"Yes, I suppose I have."

Vera smiled again and she had that rarest of things in a self-conscious beauty: a smile that enhanced her. "We will have a dance tonight. You must meet our young men." A glance here again for Bakhtiian. "And tell us about your own. Oh, are you still here, Arina? Why don't you take Tess along and have Petya take her horse and then show her where she can pitch her tent?" Without waiting for a reply, she nodded to Tess and walked away, straight across toward Bakhtiian and his companions.

Tess looked at Arina, who scarcely came up to her chin. Arina smiled. "Can you really use a saber?" Arina asked.

"A little."

"Oh," said Arina with such reserve that Tess wondered if she had offended her. "I always wanted to learn. I made my brother teach me when I was little, but then Vera said it was unbecoming in a woman to—" She flushed. "I beg your pardon. I didn't mean—"

"No, I know what you meant," said Tess kindly. "You are Mother Veselov's daughter, then?"

"Yes. Here is my brother Anton." She called to a burly, black-haired man who looked to be about twice her age. "*He* will take your horse." A brief exchange, and Anton took Myshla from Tess with the greatest courtesy. "Vera oughtn't to have offered Petya," Arina muttered darkly, "but then, she'll always do as *she* wishes, whether it is seemly or not." She shot an expressive glance toward her cousin, who had insinuated herself into the group surrounding Bakhtiian.

"Who is the older man?" Tess asked.

"Who? That is my uncle, of course, Sergei Veselov. Vera's father."

Tess was finding the undercurrents in this tribe more and more interesting. "I beg your pardon for seeming stupid, Arina, but if he is her father, how can he have the same name? Who is her mother? And isn't he—he must be the dyan of this tribe."

Arina sighed and led Tess out of the chaos attending the arrival, over to a quiet corner where she helped her set up her tent. A few young women strayed by, pausing hopefully to watch, but Arina gestured them away with more authority than Tess would ever have guessed she would have based on first impressions.

"Cousins, of the same grandmother, through sisters. Everyone knows they oughtn't to have married, but they never cared for anything but to please themselves. And they say," she added, lowering her voice ominously, "that the children of cousins possess all their worst traits twice over. Six children they had before she died bearing the last one, and only two are still alive today. And look at them."

"Ah," said Tess, feeling terribly embarrassed.

Arina looked up at her with unexpected and acute understanding. "I'm sorry." She smiled and again appeared like a perfectly harmless and unusually diffident young jaran woman, black-haired, petite, and charming. "What must you think of me? But I really hoped to get you aside to ask you about Kirill Zvertkov. I see he is with the jahar. Has he married again?"

Tess felt as if she had been slapped. She bent to busy herself unrolling her blankets, desperate to hide her reaction. "No." She stuck her head into the tent to at least attempt to disguise the sound of her voice. All the while, her thoughts raced wildly. *Hoist with your own petard, my heart*, she said to herself, *and not a damned thing you can do about it because it would be the worst of ill-bred behavior, and you're the guest here, not she.*

"Oh," said Arina, with a flash of that unexpected acuteness. "He's your lover."

Tess withdrew from the tent, blushing madly, and grasping for every shred of dignity and graciousness she could muster. "Well, yes," she admitted. "I beg your pardon. I know it isn't—isn't seemly to be—" She trailed off, feeling like an idiot.

Arina sighed and suddenly looked very sad. "Is he going to marry you, do you think?" she asked, without anger or jealousy.

"No," said Tess, feeling firm enough on that score. "I'm traveling south. I won't be here past the winter."

Arina brightened. "Oh, well, that's all right, then. I can speak with Mama, who can speak with Bakhtiian, who can speak with Kirill. And then when we meet up with them again. . . ." She hesitated. "If you'd rather I not approach him at all while you're here—"

"No, no," Tess lied, not wanting to get a bad reputation. "I couldn't possibly be so selfish." *Oh, yes, you could*, her heart muttered, but she found it impossible to dislike Arina Veselov, especially after her selfless offer to leave Kirill alone. Arina was playing fairly; by God, she would, too. After all, Kirill could damned well refuse her offer, couldn't he?

"Arina!" Vera marched up to them, leading a trail of young women like a host of worshipers in her wake. "Are you keeping our guest to yourself? For shame. Here, girls, you see, she does have *brown* hair. I beg your pardon,

Tess, but Aleksia refused to believe me. Come, we'll show you the camp." With no discernible expression on her face, Arina retreated to the background.

The time until supper had all the tranquillity of a wind-storm. They were a lively enough bunch and good company. They made sure that she was thoroughly bewildered as to what their names were, showed her the spot where they would hold the dancing, and besieged her with so many questions that she could only laugh. At last Vera took her to supper.

The estana's tent shared a fire with Vera's tent, and Tess saw immediately that the two tents were sited so as to receive equal standing. Indeed, it surprised her that so young a woman as Vera even possessed one of the great tents that usually housed a grandmother and her adult daughters and multitudinous kin. But Mother Veselov, though of the same fair-haired and slender stock as her cousin and niece, was utterly dwarfed by their personalities. She presided, as was proper, over the supper served by her daughter and son and his wife and assorted other relatives, but she never once spoke unless an opening was given her deliberately by Sergei Veselov or Vera. Besides three men who evidently acted as Veselov's lieutenants, and Tess, five of the men from Bakhtiian's jahar had been honored on this occasion. Bakhtiian, of course, and Niko and Josef—Tadheus having gone to his sister's husband's kin—and Yuri, because he was Bakhtiian's cousin. And Kirill, who had astonishingly, and to Tess's great dismay, been seated next to Mother Veselov. *The better to size him up,* Tess thought uncharitably, but she had to concede that given such blatant provocation, Kirill behaved circumspectly and Arina, moving around him frequently, did not flirt with him at all.

Bakhtiian and Veselov spoke together mostly. Tess, placed across the fire, could not join in but only listen. Vera had, of course, placed herself on the other side of Bakhtiian and banished her young husband to Yuri's company, next to Tess. Yuri and Petya were reminiscing, oblivious to the others and, for that matter, to her.

"You have not yet explained to me, Bakhtiian," Sergei Veselov was saying, "how you intend to feed so many jahars, all gathered into one army."

"A fair enough question, Veselov," replied Bakhtiian smoothly, letting the hostility in Veselov's voice slip off him, "and one which I will return to you. Let us assume the situation. What would you do?"

And so, deferring with strength, in the end he got Veselov to agree it could be done. Bakhtiian seemed different to her here. He showed none of that arrogance that came from having the assurance of admiration. He was tactful, respectful, even clever, slipping gracefully past a question meant, possibly, to offend him, making one grim fellow laugh, arguing carefully and with good humor to a conclusion favorable to himself. Perhaps charisma and craft, strength and obsession, were not all that made up a leader. Perhaps you could have all of these, and still lack the sheer instinct for leadership that made Bakhtiian—that made Charles—the kind of men they were.

"Yet you rode into khaja lands and came out unscathed," Veselov was saying. "I recall when Leo Vershinin took forty-five riders into those lands and—"

While Veselov went on, clearly beginning a long anecdote, Bakhtiian looked up across the fire directly at Tess, as if he had known she was watching him. Their eyes held a moment and dropped away together.

As soon as the anecdote ended, with Vershinin's jahar reduced to five men, Vera said, "Aunt?" Recalled to her duties, Mother Veselov excused all the women to prepare for the dance, now that twilight was lowering in on them. Arina approached Tess, but Vera swept her away and Arina retreated back to her mother's tent.

"Perhaps you would like to borrow some clothing?" Vera asked. "Some women's clothing, I mean."

"Oh, thank you. But I have some."

"Well, then, if you would like, I will walk you to your tent." Tess submitted to the escort and allowed Vera to lead her away to the other end of the camp, where her tent was pitched. "You know Bakhtiian well."

"We've ridden together a long way."

Vera put a long-fingered hand on Tess's forearm. It was dim enough that this gesture was neither public nor particularly intrusive. "You have also lain with him?"

Tess turned her head away, pretending to look at the distant field where a great fire was being prepared. Broad-skirted figures moved back and forth, snatches of singing and laughter and the high, unfamiliar music of women's voices punctuating the merriment within the camp. When she trusted herself, she turned back.

"No."

Vera's fingers lifted from her arm. "That's too bad. I would have liked to compare what you knew of him with what I know."

There was a pause, as if some reply was expected. Tess could not speak.

Vera brushed her thick hair back with one hand, a graceful, practiced gesture that drew the eye to the faultless line of her jaw and chin. "There are only three men I ever hoped would mark me. One is dead now, the second loved another, for which I cannot begrudge him his choice, but Bakhtiian—he knew he could have had me, but he stood by while that boy marked me."

"Perhaps," Tess began, faltering, almost stuttering, "perhaps he knew that Petya wanted you more."

"Petya," said his wife, uttering his name so dispassionately as to betray her complete disregard for her husband, "is a blind child. He is five years younger than I am."

"I don't understand. Women take lovers, but men take wives."

"That," said the beauty bitterly, "is the way of the jaran. I will kill the woman he marks."

"Do you really think he will ever marry?"

"If you had lain with him, you would know. He is *diarin.*"

"What is that?"

Vera looked back toward the main cluster of tents. The men had gathered in groups by small fires to await the dancing. Her nose, which in her father and aunt was merely thin, gave her an aristocratic look of one to whom the world should surely do some obeisance. "You have been with men," she replied, turning back to Tess. "This is a woman's word. *Diarin,* a man who dishevels a woman's hair. Passionate in bed. But perhaps Vasilley will kill him after all, and then he cannot marry."

"Vasilley?"

"My brother. He rides with Dmitri Mikhailov."

Vasil. Vera's brother. This was delicate ground indeed. "Ah," said Tess, playing for time while she gathered her wits, "Do you want him to kill Bakhtiian?"

"I'm married to a man I do not want, and I want a man I cannot have. Why should anyone else have him?"

"If Petya dies," said Tess ungraciously, "you could have him."

"When he stood by, *stood by,* while Petya did this to me?" Her fingers lifted to touch the white scar that marred the perfect beauty of her face.

"You would have the mark whether it was Bakhtiian or Petya or any man."

"No." The grip of Vera's fingers, closing on the sleeve of Tess's shirt, was strong. "There is one other way given to the jaran to marry, but it is only for the bravest, for the most exceptional." She tilted her head back to gaze up at the first spray of stars gracing the sky. *"Korokh."*

Korokh: one who reached for the wind, Yuri had said. Tess touched the priest-rune engraved on the hilt of her saber. It felt very cold. "For a man to choose a woman?"

"The quiet road," breathed Vera. Her lips stayed slightly parted. Her hair flowed down around her shoulders like strands of silk—she wore it as an unmarried girl might, not in the married woman's tight braids. "The four-times-covered road from tree to stone." Tess realized that it was very still, as if a hush had fallen in deference to Vera's show of passion. "I wanted that road. I wanted that, not this."

A sudden cheer and a swell of laughter interrupted them, the lighting of the great fire. Flames sparked up.

"But here, we'll be late. I'll let you go." She left.

Tess stared after her. A group of young men hurried past her toward the fire, laughing and jesting, and a musician began a racing beat on a drum.

Tess ran to her tent and debated, briefly, whether to give up this attempt to change in the dark, but change she did, feeling with peculiar hindsight that Nadezhda Martov had known quite well what she was about, gifting this foreign stranger with decent women's clothing. But whom was she trying to impress? That was the question that troubled her.

Coming out of her tent, she paused to try to get a glimpse of herself in her mirror. She was not sure that the beaded headdress over her braids was arranged correctly. She felt a presence come up beside her, and smelled a fleeting breath of cinnamon. She whirled.

"Cha Ishii!" He stood before her, straight, hands folded at his chest in 'Lord's Supplication.'

Unfolding his hands, he bowed. "Lady Terese, your most generous pardon, I beg of you, for this unexpected intrusion."

"You surprised me." She took one step back from him. "I did not expect to see you venturing out at this sort of—social occasion."

"Lady Terese." The color of his face was lost in darkness, no shade to his voice at all. "With greatest deference, I advise you to stay here with this tribe. Do not go with us in the morning. Please be so munificent as to believe me when I say I have no desire to see you come to any harm, even though you would have brought it on yourself should anything happen to you."

"What would happen? Why should I stay here? Cha Ishii!"

But he simply turned and walked away, to be hidden swiftly by the night. Tess gaped after him.

"Tess?" It was Arina, tentative as always. "I thought you might—oh, I don't know. Here, let me straighten that for you." She adjusted the headpiece. "There. Would you like company, to go out?"

"Yes, I would," said Tess, liking Arina very much, however much she wanted to dislike her.

It proved easy enough to lose herself in the festivities. She knew quite well that she ought not to dance more than the occasional dance with any of the riders of Bakhtiian's jahar, so she turned her attention to the riders of Veselov's tribe. She felt completely at ease as she flirted with them in the casual, straightforward manner that jaran women had. She danced twice with Petya because she felt sorry for him. Beneath the undeniably handsome exterior, beneath the self-effacing bashfulness devoid of conceit, beneath the quick, unpretentious smile and the delicate, pale blue of his eyes, Petya was desperately unhappy. She took Yuri aside to ask him about it.

"I think he knows she'll never love him," Tess said.

"Love him! She doesn't even like him." They walked together to the periphery of the light, choosing solitude for their conversation. "I doubt if she ever lets him forget it."

"Can she really be so cruel?"

"Cruel? I don't know if I would call Vera Veselov cruel. I think she is so blind to anything but what she wants that she cares not in the least if she hurts someone who has gotten in her way. That family is far too handsome for its own good.''

"Yes," said Tess, remembering Vasil. "And her brother is the most beautiful of the lot, if only because he isn't so arrogant.''

"Ah, yes, Vasil," Yuri muttered. "I never could dislike him. But he's as single-minded as the rest, and as selfish, in his own way.''

"Somehow I detect a long history of association between your tribe and this one.''

"Yes. It started in my great-grandmother's time when her uncle insulted the Veselov etsana by refusing to marry her sister. And then just when the feud was at its worst, his daughter and the sister's son ran off together, when it had all been arranged that they were to marry for alliances into other tribes.''

"Is this a long story?" Tess chuckled and, seeing Kirill strolling by, made eyes at him.

Kirill stopped dead, took her hand, and kissed it. "You are more beautiful than the stars, my heart." He grinned at Yuri. "I will retreat before the wrath of the brother." And did so.

"Tess, stop that. Do you want everyone to know?"

"Maybe I do. Oh, Yuri, you know very well that if Kirill was to stop flirting with me altogether that would be as good as shouting it to the world.''

"True enough. But I noticed he sat beside Mother Veselov tonight. Who has an unmarried daughter. Oho, Sister, what is this? You're jealous! Do you *love* Kirill?''

The question stopped her cold. She forgot to be angry or jealous. Did she love him? "Gods, Yuri," she said, and fell silent, unwilling to unravel the chaos that writhed through her heart.

"Yes," said Yuri finally, "it is a long story. And I'm sure that the Orzhekov tribe and the Veselov tribe have not done yet with hating and loving one another. Poor Petya.''

Poor Petya stood alone, watching as the dance swirled by him, never approached by any of the young women of his own tribe, though he was certainly one of the handsomest men there. "I've even heard her say *in front of him* that Ilya would have marked her if Petya hadn't charged in first.''

"That can't be true.''

"She doesn't care in the least how much she hurts him.''

"No, that Ilya would have marked her."

"Ilya's a damned idiot sometimes, but he's not *that* stupid."

"She told me that she had only ever wished to marry three men."

"Yes, that's something else she tells everyone. The first was Khara Roskhel. He was darker than Ilya, twice as proud, but mean with it. He had that cruelty in him that Nature is afraid to give out to more than one man in each generation. He had better hands for the saber than our Vladimir. He was a plain-looking man, but he had a pull about him that made him seem as handsome as—as Petya. He supported Ilya at first but then he turned against him. No one knows why. His men killed Ilya's father and nephew, but they always said that Roskhel himself murdered Ilya's mother and sister." He shuddered. "But it's bad luck to speak of it. It was an ill-omened thing, all of it, that year."

"Gods," said Tess. "What happened to him?"

"Ilya killed him. He strangled him."

A woman let out a shrill yell as she was tossed into the air in the dance and caught again. Three pipes pierced above the clapping. Tess rubbed her throat with one hand, feeling the smooth skin and, under that, the ridge of her windpipe.

"The year after his family died Ilya was more dangerous than the mountains in winter."

Tess made a sound imitating laughter. "I'll bet. And the other one?"

"The other one? Oh, Vera's other love." He laughed. The firelight gleamed in his eyes. "You're wearing his saber."

"Keregin? I don't believe you."

"What greater catch for a girl than the man who leads the arenabekh? But he fell in love with her brother. Only everyone knew that Vasil—well, Keregin didn't pursue it. But he certainly never had an eye for her."

A shout and cheering ended the dance. Tess saw a swirl of bright hair, and Vera entered, dressed in such finery as to put all the other women there to shame.

"How old is she?"

"Twenty-five. She put off everyone, you see, by one scheme or another and stayed unmarried until she was twenty-three. Petya got her because she wasn't looking."

"Poor Petya," Tess echoed.

"You ought to make up to him."

"Yuri! I don't even know him, except to sit beside at supper. And he spent the entire time talking with you."

"He's shy. He was so happy to see me. I'm not sure he's made many friends here."

Without really thinking about it, they both looked around the circle for Petya. Saw him in a gap out at the farthest edge of the dark: two familiar figures standing close together and yet, by the set of their shoulders, at a great distance. The poor child was speaking with his wife and it was not a happy interview.

"Yurinya Orzhekov. I don't suppose you remember me." A young woman strode up and planted herself in front of Yuri. Her dark braid hung casually over one blue-clad shoulder down to the swell of her full breasts.

"I should never forget you, Aleksia," said Yuri in a muted voice, his eyes lowered.

Aleksia glanced at Tess and winked. "Have you forgotten how to dance, then?" She took his hand and led him away into the crowd of gathering dancers. Yuri neither looked up nor back.

Tess smiled and settled back to watch. Yuri took his place in the circle meekly enough. There, Mikhal partnered a dark-haired woman, and Petre and Nikita and Konstans stood up as well with young women whose cheeks were unmarred by the scar of marriage. Even Josef, looking amused, was being teased by a girl half his age. Beyond the dancing, Sergei Veselov conversed with Niko and Tadheus and, of all people, Arina Veselov. Past them, Kirill regaled a group of impressionable-looking young men with some exaggerated story. On around the circle, strange faces blended together until, like a sudden beacon brilliantly illuminating a dark shore—

Ilya. Leaning forward, shoulders straight, he was explaining something with his habitual intensity to an elderly man. They sat together on a blanket, off to one side. Two older women came by and paused to join the conversation. When they left, smiling, the elderly man rose with a polite nod and went with them. A boy, barely in his teens, halted tentatively at the edge of the blanket. Ilya, seeing him, beckoned him closer. They spoke. Another boy came by, then a girl, and then they, too, left. Alone on the blanket, Ilya bent his head as if he were tired. With one hand he rubbed his injured knee. Tess smiled to herself, feeling foolishly sorry for him, and made her way over to him.

She came out of the crowd on his left and paused at the edge of his blanket. He was still staring down, the firelight a glow on his forehead and eyes. Abruptly he glanced up, straight at her. For an instant he seemed startled. Then he smiled.

Tess stepped onto the blanket and sat down beside him. "How you must hate being injured when you could be dancing."

He did not even look at the dancers but kept his gaze on her face. "I'm perfectly happy," he said quietly. "Now."

It was impossible not to know what he meant. He was flirting with her. *Flirting*—gods, did Bakhtiian even engage in such frivolous activities as flirting? She did not know whether to laugh hysterically or to run. Bakhtiian simply watched her, drawing whatever conclusions he might from the expressions chasing themselves across her face.

"Yes," she said, choosing to misunderstand him. "It must be satisfying to win over a tribe formerly so hostile to your own."

"It always is," he said tonelessly.

She dredged for a more neutral topic and grasped at the only one she could recall from supper. "You let Veselov work out how to supply an army. How do you intend to do it?"

He took the cue. Perhaps, explaining, he was more conscientiously serious with her than he usually was. She let it pass. What he said was interesting enough, though she was no student of war as he quite clearly was. Then with a word and a warning pattern on his drum, the head drummer called out the next dance.

"This is my favorite dance. Please excuse me, Ilya." She scrambled to her feet and stared about desperately for the nearest available man whom she knew was a good dancer. There was Vladimir, but . . . ah, well, he already had a partner.

"You mean you wouldn't rather sit and talk with me?" asked Bakhtiian, but although his voice had the inflection of humor, he was not smiling.

"Of course I would," she said absently, and then she smiled brilliantly, catching Kirill's eye before Arina Veselov, coming out of the crowd next to him, could catch him for herself. "But I *love* this dance. I'll come back." And she ran over to Kirill and led him out.

It was a long dance, and the next was a line dance for women into which she was seduced by the combined persuasion of Arina and Aleksia. But when she had finished that, she felt guilty for having left him so abruptly, so she threaded her way back through the crowd to where he sat. Partway around the circle, halted by a passing clump of children, she saw over their heads that Bakhtiian was not alone.

Vera had braided her hair for this occasion only so that she could wear the glittering headdress of onyx and amethyst beads that set off her fine features so admirably. That was Tess's first thought. Her tunic was cut unusually low, displaying a good deal of fine, white throat and slender shoulders. Somehow she had spread out the skirts of her tunic so that a fold fell possessively over one leg of his trousers. Lower, a slim ankle showed, bare and delicate, resting next to one of his boots. Leaning forward, Vera said something. Ilya smiled. Tess turned and, seeing Yuri, walked over to him and asked him to dance.

When the dance had finished, she could not help just one surreptitious glance toward Bakhtiian. But the blanket lay empty, abandoned, crumpled at the edges as people walked over it and pushed it into folds.

"Oh, gods," said Yuri, "is that Petya out there?" Petya stood in the same place where he had had the argument with his wife, far enough away from the main group that no one remarked on his bowed shoulders, on his solitude.

"Tess." Kirill joined them. "So you've seen him. Listen, Tess, you ought to make up to him."

"I ought to make up to him!"

"Yes," Kirill said without blinking. "Anton Veselov told me that his cousin slapped Aleksia Charnov and bullied her for months after Charnov lay once with Petya. And Veselov never even lets Petya in her tent, except—well, now and then, Anton says, begging your pardon, Tess. But Petya never deserved to be made miserable. But you could make up to him. Vera Veselov can't do anything to you, and perhaps if the other young women see your example, they'll defy her a little. Ordering her aunt around as if *she* were etsana, and not her!"

"But Kirill!" Tess felt as if she had been betrayed.

"What a fine idea, Kirill," said Yuri. "We'd best leave Tess to work out what comes next." He grabbed the other man's arm and pulled him away. Kirill, looking puzzled, let himself be led, glancing once back at Tess with a shrug and, God help her, a complicitous grin. He didn't even care if she slept with another man!

Of course he didn't care. Of course he thought she had every right to sleep with any damned man she wanted.

A fresh-faced boy suddenly came up to her out of the whirl. "I beg your pardon," he said shyly. "Is this yours?" He handed her Bakhtiian's blanket, shaken out and neatly folded.

"Thank you." Tess gave him a smile, at which, satisfied, he took himself off. Holding the blanket, Tess marched over to Petya and persuaded him to go for a walk with her along the river.

He did not take much persuading. At first, strolling through the pale grass, stars a net of brightness above, the river a melodiously soft accompaniment, neither of them spoke much, except about commonplaces.

"Yuri doesn't think you're happy here," said Tess finally, realizing that Petya, who was very sweet, would never confide in her without prompting. "I'm his sister, you know. Mother Orzhekov gifted me with Anna Orzhekov's tent."

"I always liked Anna," said Petya. They walked, and the river rolled on alongside them. Then, as if it was impossible to conceal secrets from Yuri's sister, he began to talk.

Petya, Tess realized, was indeed sweet, ingenuous, and shy, and he was also a little shallow, having none of Yuri's unexpected depth. He had fallen in love with Vera Veselov and had marked her, as a man ought. After two years, he had at last deduced that she was angry with him but for what reason he was still not entirely sure, although he did acknowledge that she might well love Ilyakoria Bakhtiian.

"But Bakhtiian would never have marked her," he said naively, "so I can't understand why she would be angry with me about that."

He had formed no lasting friendships. None of the women approached him. Vera admitted him to her tent if she pleased, and banished him therefrom if it suited her. Altogether, he was miserable.

"But, Petya," said Tess, exasperated, "it isn't your fault."

"But surely there's more I can do to win her over. To make her love me."

Tess sighed and spread out the blanket. "Petya, sit down." He sat. She sat beside him. The moon had risen. Its narrow silhouette lay tangled in the rushing water, breaking, re-forming, and breaking again. "Petya," she began, and stopped. It would do no good to criticize Vera. "Haven't you any friends here?" she asked instead.

"Anton Veselov has always been kind to me," he admitted.

"I think you'd do well to cultivate Anton and Arina Veselov. After all, Arina will be etsana someday, not Vera."

"Yes, and Vera hates her."

"No doubt. Petya. I think—" He looked up at her, trusting and, as Yuri had said when speaking of Petya's wife's family, too handsome for his own good. Tess thought that Petya had probably had things much too easy growing up, with a sweet face like that. He had probably been a gorgeous, indulged child. She took in a breath. "Petya, I think that Vera would respect you more if you took a—a firmer hand with her." She tried not to wince as she said it, unsure of what ground she was on here in the jaran. "For instance, if you will pardon a sister's confidence, she hadn't any right to punish Aleksia Charnov for making up to you." Petya was silent. "I am sure," Tess continued, seeing that he was receptive to this elder-sister tone of voice, "that a husband ought to expect the same respect from his wife as she expects from him."

"It is true," he said in a low voice, "that a wife has certain obligations to her husband that he may demand if she is unwilling to give them to him freely."

Tess decided that to inquire into the scope of these obligations would be treading on too thin ice. "Well, then, I think you ought to stand up for yourself. Otherwise she will never forgive you."

"She may never forgive me whatever I do."

"That is true. But it's yourself you have to respect most of all, Petya."

He smiled, utterly guileless. "I hadn't thought of it like that. And it wasn't right, about Aleksia. Anton tried to tell me but I wouldn't listen. I could have put a stop to it." This realization hit him with some force, and he stopped speaking.

"Yes," said Tess, feeling that Petya had as much to absorb as he was capable of for one evening. "It's so late. Shall we go back?"

They strolled back in good charity with each other, and Petya told her about the pranks he and Yuri had played on the older boys, growing up. He left her at the edge of camp, and she devoutly hoped that he was not so fired up that he would charge straight over to his wife's tent because she knew very well who was in there with her. *Bitch,* she said to herself, and wandered out to watch the last coals of the great fire burn themselves down.

A pair of figures had come there before her, and she paused. "Sibirin, he is no longer my son," Sergei Veselov was saying in a cold voice, "and when Dmitri Mikhailov took him in, that is when I broke with Mikhailov."

Tess retreated and wandered back through camp, tired but not quite sleepy. Only to see Kirill, with that wonderful, provocative chuckle he had, emerge from Arina Veselov's little tent, pitched far behind her mother's. She stared, too shocked to move, and then, recalling herself, began to hurry away. But he was too quick for her and far too good a scout.

"Tess," he called in a whisper, and he jogged after her. She had to stop. He came up to her and, glancing round once to see that no one else was about, flung his arms around her and kissed her, laughing.

She pushed him away.

"Tess, what's wrong?" He looked utterly bewildered and a little hurt.

"I'm just tired," she said crossly. "Good night." She walked back to her tent and burrowed in under her blankets, throwing Bakhtiian's blanket outside. Knowing that Kirill had behaved as a jaran man ought did not make it easier to forgive him. Then, chastised by her own sense of justice, she reached outside and pulled the blanket back in again.

In the morning, Petya had gained so much in spirits that Vera actually looked twice at him as he helped Tess saddle Myshla, a task Vera had probably not ordered him to do.

When the time came for them to leave, Tess deliberately waited until everyone else had mounted before calling Petya back and, in front of the assembled jahar and the tribe, giving him the beautiful amber-beaded necklace that Vasil had given her.

"For luck," she said softly, and kissed him on the cheek.

He flushed bright red but he looked delighted. Vera, caught in the crowd, looked furious. Arina Veselov was smiling with malicious pleasure. And then Tess mounted Myshla, blinking innocently under all their gazes, and drew Myshla into line next to Yuri's mount. For good measure she caught Cha Ishii's eye and acknowledged him with a cool, defiant nod. Bakhtiian made polite farewells, and they left, immediately driven by Bakhtiian's command to an unrelenting pace that kept up until midday.

"Tess, Tess," said Yuri as they started out at a pace more reasonable for the horses after the break. "You're wicked, my dear sister. Oh, her face, her face when you did it."

"Serves her right, the bitch."

"Well, she wasn't deserted last night, was she?" He screwed up his face, looking disgusted. "Gods, Ilya hasn't said a word since we left. I hope he and Sergei Veselov didn't argue. They've never been easy together."

"Perhaps he misses *her,* Yuri."

"Oho, you're being nasty today, aren't you? Is it Kirill you're mad at, or is it Ilya? Or both of them?"

"You've gotten full of yourself."

He laughed. "I had a pleasant night, Tess. But please, don't argue with me. Petya looked so much better this morning. I don't know what you did—"

"I only talked with him."

"Still—"

"Yuri." Bakhtiian drew up beside them. "North scout. You and Kirill." Yuri opened his mouth, shut it, and rode away. Bakhtiian kept his horse even with Tess's. He rode at one with the animal, as always, but his back was so stiff that a board could have been nailed there to hold the shape. There was a tight, drawn edge to his mouth, dark smudges of sleeplessness under his eyes. He neither spoke nor looked at her.

They rode on for some time in this manner. Clipped, drying grass rustled under their horses' hooves. A golden brown haze marked the distant hills. His eyes remained fixed on some unmoving point situated just in front of Kriye's head. Now and again an irregularity in the ground interrupted the black's steady pace and she would see Bakhtiian's eyes tighten at the corners and his lips pale from the pain. Still he said nothing.

"Nice day, isn't it?" she asked finally.

His head turned. He fixed her with a stare so turbulent that she almost reined in Myshla to get away from him. "When my aunt gave you that tent," he said, his voice so level that a brimful glass would not have spilled a drop if set upon it, "she expected you would behave properly. If you persist in flaunting your flirtations, especially with married men, so that you lose whatever reputation you have, you will no longer have the right to call it your own."

"What I'm wondering," said Tess, smiling, "is who got the beauty and who got the beast last night. Why don't you come back when you've got something civil to say to me?"

Kriye shifted pace with a slight jolt. Bakhtiian's eyes went almost vacant. The moment passed, and he stared straight at her again.

"This is advice," he said tonelessly, "that you had better heed."

"Had I?" She flipped her braid back over her shoulder with all the blithe unconcern of a very popular girl confronted with the plainest and least interesting of her rivals. "Forgive me if I choose to consult with Sonia about such matters first."

He continued to stare at her, his eyes fixed on her face with the intensity of a panther which, hidden in the grass, watches its prey.

"You'd better say what you want right now, Bakhtiian, because I'm going to go find more congenial company."

His right hand tightened. Slowly, he moved it so that it came to rest on the hilt of his saber.

Her hand was on hers in an instant.

He opened his hand and reclosed it finger by finger around the hilt. "I don't give advice lightly."

"No one ever does." She had tried to keep her tone light and sarcastic. Now she simply lost her temper. "And how do you—by God!—how do you intend to make me heed your advice?"

She regretted it immediately. The color banished from his cheeks by her comments, he regarded her with the expression of a man who has that instant conceived a diabolical plan. He took his hand off his saber. Fear, receiving no answer to its knock, opened the door and walked in.

"By the gods," said Ilya. "I will." He turned his horse and cantered to the back of the group.

CHAPTER TWENTY-ONE

"Desire when doubled is love,
love when doubled is madness."
—PRODICUS OF CEAS

She caught Kirill looking at her over the campfire that evening, and he smiled at her, but it was a serious smile and rather sober. She smiled back and *then* he looked like Kirill again, and he went back to his supper, satisfied. Tess ate slowly, ignoring the Chapalii. But when she rose and walked out onto the plain, she saw a tall, thin, angular form shadowing her far to her right. She went back into camp.

"Walk with me, Yuri," she said within Kirill's hearing.

Yuri obeyed. "We're being followed," he said as soon as they were out of sight of camp.

"I know." She turned.

"I should have known," said Yuri, seeing that it was Kirill coming up behind them. "Somehow, I think I'm wanted back in camp."

Kirill greeted him cheerfully as they passed. "I brought blankets," he said to Tess. Then, reconsidering his words, he hesitated. "I mean, if you're cold. . . . Do you want me to go away?"

"Oh, Kirill, I'm sorry. I have an awful temper."

"No, I'm sorry, Tess. I ought to have known better. It was an ill-bred thing to do. I'm no better than that loathsome Veselov woman. But then, I never have liked any of that family."

"You liked Arina Veselov well enough."

"She's a pretty enough woman. You took Petya, after all."

"Oho! You were jealous! But you encouraged me to make up to him."

"Doing what is right," said Kirill with dignity, "is not always easy."

Tess laughed and put her arms around him. It felt very good to hug him. "My sweet Kirill."

"Were you really jealous?" he asked in a low voice, as if he had no right to.

"Terribly."

"My heart," he said, and then nothing more.

In the morning, Yuri and Kirill were sent out to scout again. And again on the third morning. Bakhtiian did not so much not speak to her as ignore her with so much force that she knew the entire jahar was aware of it. How could she ever have thought he and Charles were men cut from the same cloth? Charles would never let his anger show. He would certainly never let the world know of his disapproval. That entire dinner party, soon after she had come to Jeds after her parents' death, still loomed large in her memory. She had been a reckless and troubled ten-year-old girl intent on ruining everything Charles had worked for on Rhui, that delicate balance of his off-world retinue and the Rhuian guests ignorant of his off-world origins. Charles had dealt with her all evening in a firm but pleasant manner. He had even warned Dr. Hierakis off when the doctor had rebuked her. Then, in the privacy of Tess's room, she had gotten the scolding. She could not now remember what he had said. But she remembered that he had never raised his voice. She had felt bitterly ashamed of herself. She had disappointed him. She had not lived up to his expectations. But that once, she had wished mightily that she could make him angry instead.

Well, Tess, just as well, she thought wryly, staring at Bakhtiian's profile as he rode five men over from her. The wind ruffled his dark hair. His lips were set together and he contemplated the horizon with that expression of preoccupied intensity that was habitual with him. Then he turned his head to meet her gaze and as deliberately looked away.

That afternoon, standing apart from the others as they watered their horses at a spring, she saw Niko break away from the group and walk across the grass to her. He let his hand rest on Myshla's withers as he considered Tess gravely. Tess crouched to look at herself in the smooth pond. The water reflected her face, the high cheekbones that sank into the deep hollows of her eyes. A single braid hung down over one shoulder, brown against the scarlet silk of her shirt. A pebble fell suddenly into the midst of the picture, dissolving her into ripples. She stood up.

"I'm not here to scold you, you know. But I think it's time you resolved your differences with Ilya. I will mediate, if you wish that protection."

"I have nothing to resolve with Ilya. My behavior has been unexceptionable."

"That may be, but when you stir up coals, you must be prepared for flames."

Tess glanced toward the jahar. They were ranged out in clusters, talking easily among themselves. Bakhtiian stood alone. Even at such a distance, she knew—she could *feel*—that he was watching her.

"I won't make up to him," she said stubbornly.

"I said nothing of that. Look to your own heart before you judge others. And never, never again take a lover away as blatantly as you did two nights past. It is bad manners, my girl, and you know better. For once in my life, I lay no blame on Kirill." She flushed, angry and embarrassed. "Don't make it worse. I know him very well. Remember that." With a terse nod, he left her. It took her a moment to realize that his final comments referred to Bakhtiian not to Kirill.

"Damn them all," she muttered. Then, because any excess of ill humor in herself disgusted and bored her, she decided to walk it off. She led Myshla the long way around the spring. A curtain of half-bare trees screened the far end, though incompletely. Damp leaves squelched under her boots, and a heavy odor rose from each measured step. Rounding a clump of evergreen shrubs, she almost ran into Hon Garii, who was crouching at the lip of the pond.

He started up. "Go back!" he whispered urgently.

She was too surprised to ignore the order. She jerked Myshla around and returned the way she had come. A moment later, she heard voices speaking in Chapalii, inaudible if she had not been listening for it.

"Have you obtained the water sample?"

"Assuredly, Cha Ishii, it has been done as you commanded."

Then she was too far away to hear more. *Go back.* Meant for that moment, or meant to reiterate the warning Cha Ishii had given her at Veselov's tribe? But there was nothing for it but to go on now, and she had never been one to be minded to turn back. Full speed ahead and damn the consequences. With a sigh, she returned to the jahar.

That evening Bakhtiian addressed a trivial comment to her. She was so shocked that she answered him.

As if encouraged by her reply, he paused beside her. "What do you expect the shrine to look like?"

"I have no idea, but I'll admit to curiosity."

He smiled, as if at a private joke. "I trust it will make an impression on you that you will never forget," he said with something resembling amiability.

Instantly suspicious, she was thwarted from further questioning because he excused himself and left. In the morning, she had scarcely gotten her tent rolled up when he limped over toward her, Niko dogging his tracks.

"You'll want to leave that with Yuri." He nodded to the tent. "We'll be riding forward scout today."

"Ilya," Niko said, "are you well enough to ride scout?"

"I know what I'm doing."

This had nothing to do with his knee. "I'll go saddle Myshla," Tess said, retreating from the fray. But whatever Niko said, it evidently came to nothing, and she and Bakhtiian rode out together. Without remounts.

It was a quiet ride. How he contrived to keep his seat on Kriye with such ease she could not imagine. Around midday, the ground began to slope and fold. By early afternoon they rode into uneven hills. Their pace did not slacken, except when it was necessary to rest the horses. They were not scouting, or at least not as she had grown used to it. When they passed a gathering of plump grazers, he neither noted them nor even suggested she try to kill one for supper. Their path veered up, away along a bare ridge, down through a hollow of high grass, and up a shallow stream until it disappeared into a chasm at the base of a hill.

Bakhtiian pulled up his horse. "Ah. The shrine."

Tess stared. Nothing but grass and the stream's underground escape. Bakhtiian rode on up the slope. She kicked Myshla to follow and came up beside him where he halted at the crest of the hill. They looked out over a long, deep valley that stretched westward, the shrine of Morava at its far end.

She had not expected a palace.

Long ago some wealthy noble from a far-flung empire must have taken these lands and built a home for herself befitting her exalted rank. When the empire shrank in the course of time, as empires do, the palace had been left as the last remnant of a great civilization in the wilds of the north. It could not have been that long ago.

It shone. From this distance, she could only guess that it was built of marble. A high dome graced the center. Two towers, filigreed with windows and carvings, stood on either side of the dome. Beyond them, squat towers marked the wings. Far to the left stretched a low wall. In the very middle lay a wide expanse of white stone stairs and a broad landing bounded on the side by thin, black pillars. From this distance it looked as if time and wind and rain had left it untouched. And when the jaran, freed by horses from the limits of the eastern plains, had found it, they had thought it a marvel and made it a shrine.

Already, he had ridden halfway down the slope. She hastened to follow him. At the base of the hill he waited for her, and they rode together into a line of trees that edged the valley floor. All of it planted, she guessed, as they rode out of the trees and into an overgrown but still patterned wilderness of shrubs and hedges and a few flowering bushes, and then back into a copse of trees, and out again. They followed a path, half concealed by grass and leaves, that led them alternately from the twilight of woods through sun-drenched glades and back again.

When they broke out of the woods for the last time, they reined in their horses at the base of a long, broad avenue that led in a direct line to the palace. The great building rose suddenly near. The setting sun streamed light across the pale stone surface of the avenue. It sank toward the low hills directly between the two high towers. Tess stared.

"There are few things in this land as beautiful as the shrine of Morava at sunset," said Ilya.

His voice startled her, and she looked at him. But he was gazing at her, not at the shrine, an odd, incandescent light in his eyes. He was complimenting her not the palace, but in that awkward, restrained, ponderous way that the very shyest or most conservative jaran men used when dealing with women. Rather than answer or acknowledge his gaze, she urged Myshla forward onto the avenue. He followed her.

Hooves rang muffled on the seamless white stone. Statues bounded the avenue, alien things, twisting, chaotic, but enticing to the eye nevertheless. Stone unlike any stone she knew: black as the void, some of them; others speckled like granite, encased in a glasslike shell; most were translucent. Their angles caught the sun, splintering delicate patterns of light out across the avenue.

An arch of tangled vines spanned the avenue, trailing striated leaves halfway down to the ground. She put up her hand to push through. Breaking past, she saw that the pavement of the avenue was now broken by chevrons chiseled into the stone.

" 'Like the very gods in my sight is he who sits where he can look in your eyes,' " said Ilya, " 'who listens close to you, to hear the soft voice, its sweetness murmur in love and laughter, all for him.' " Her cheeks burned with heat. His recitation did not falter. " 'But it breaks my spirit; underneath my breast all the heart is shaken. Let me only glance where you are, the voice dies, I can say nothing.' "

How could she help it? She turned her head to look at him. Only he was staring ahead at the bright disk of the sun, at the gleaming stone of the palace, so drawn in to himself that she could read nothing from his expression, nothing from his voice, except the evidence of his words.

" 'But my lips are stricken to silence, underneath my skin the tenuous flame suffuses; nothing shows in front of my eyes, my ears are muted in thunder. And the sweat breaks running upon me, fever shakes my body, paler I turn than grass.' " Here he faltered. Kriye paced on, eerily placid on the muffling stone. Still Ilya did not look at her, but his face bore the perplexity of a man struck by revelation. " 'I can feel that I have been changed, I feel that—' " He broke off and dropped his gaze to stare at his hands.

They passed under a second arch, a broad curve of translucent blue stone carved with intricately figured animals. Here the chevrons melded with circles no larger than the circumference of Myshla's hooves.

"Can you sing?" he asked in a muted voice, as if the request might somehow break the spell with which the air of this valley had gripped them, a place untouched by time, weighted with the silence of eternity.

All she could think of was "Greensleeves." Afraid not to, she sang it, but she refused to look at him as she did so, all that long, slow ride until finally a third arch bridged the avenue, shimmering and silver-toned. She faltered and broke off the song. As soon as they passed under the silver arch, the palace looming huge and intricate before them, Ilya began to sing.

Her breath caught in her throat. How could he have known? When could he have learned it? He sang the song Fedya had made for her, about the dyan and the daughter of the sun. With whatever uncanny genius Fedya had possessed, he had made that song for Ilya to sing to her, never for any other purpose. How could it be otherwise? Not wanting to look at him, she had to look at him.

He was completely involved in the song, his expression totally unguarded in a way Tess had never seen before, all the veils that concealed his soul blown up as if a wind had caught them, revealing his true face for an illicit moment: his beautiful eyes, scarred by sorrow, the strong, stubborn line of his mouth and chin, above everything the intensity of the passion that drove him, pervading his entire being.

I love him.

His eyes met hers. The song broke off mid-line as he stared, as they stared, and then, with an effort recalling himself, he haltingly picked up the thread of the song once more.

This was the pyre of immolation. She knew it now for what it was, consuming her. If she had ever thought she was lost before, well then, better she had stayed that way.

He finished the song and reined Kriye in. She halted Myshla beside him, aware of an arch like ruby vaulting the avenue before them. The last rays of the sun illuminated his face.

Words rose unbidden, a scrap of a line from an ancient saga. She opened her mouth, had to touch her tongue to her lips to remind herself how to speak. Even so, her voice came out soft and a little hoarse from emotion. " 'They say that your eyes contain fire, that your face fills with light.' "

Expression flooded his face. She had seen that look before, after battle.

"Now," he said triumphantly, "now you are mine."

"Advance, travelers. I await you."

Tess stared at Ilya, frozen in shock, but already that betraying expression had vanished and he wrenched his atten-

tion away from her and stared past the ruby arch, up the
height of the stairs to the landing and the great doors beyond.

Following his gaze, she got an impression of a solitary
figure ridiculously small, robed in white, before her glance
caught on the last four signs carved into the stone archway.
She felt as though she could not breathe. Right to left she
traced the carvings, and they read:

*To the Sun's Child do all who enter here give Obeisance,
for these are His halls.*

The Sun's Child she knew to be the Emperor because this
writing was Chapalii. These gardens, these woods, these
statues, this avenue, this palace—it was impossible.

It was true.

"Ilya, we can't bring them here."

He still gazed upward. "Bring whom here?" he asked,
intent on the figure above.

"The khepelli. Ilya! The writing, do you know what it
says?"

That got his attention. His gaze leapt to her. "No one
knows what it says."

"I can read it. I know."

He stared at her, so devoid of expression that she thought
for a moment that he was confused.

Above, the figure spoke again, not impatient but firm, an
old woman's strong voice. "Advance, travelers. I await
you."

"We must finish the ceremony." He started Kriye forward under the arch. But his gaze searched the carvings for
the instant he could see them, and when he dismounted and
began to lead Kriye up the stairs, he said in an undertone,
"What do they say?"

She had fallen behind, but she had no trouble catching up
because Ilya was limping badly. Black pillars rose on either
side of them, like spears upraised to contain those who
thought to stray from right conduct. The sun slid beneath
the high dome. Shadows bathed their path.

" 'To the Sun's Child do all who enter here give Obeisance,' " she translated, " 'for these are His halls.' "

"But the Sun's Child is a girl," he objected.

"According to the jaran."

"According to whom was it a boy?" She looked away
from him. "What does this have to do with the khepelli?"

They came to the top of the stairs and halted. An old woman waited there. She held a clay bowl in her hands. Its interior gave off light by some agent Tess could not detect, illuminating the woman's lined face but shadowing her eyes.

"I am the guardian of the shrine." She examined each of them in turn. "You have ridden together at sunset up the sacred avenue." The quiet resonance of her voice made it seem almost threatening. "Do you know the penalty for sacrilege?"

"I know it," said Ilya.

Tess shut her eyes briefly. Opening them, she saw that the priestess's gaze was directed at her. "Ah, I know it," she answered hastily, sure some ritual was going on here that she did not understand.

"Do you know the Laws of the Avenue?" she asked Ilya.

"I know them."

"She is not your kin."

"No."

She inclined her head and looked at Tess. "Do you know the Laws of the Avenue?"

Tess hesitated. Ilya was looking at the priestess, not at her. He had a slight, satisfied smile on his face. "No," she said abruptly, suspicious, "no, I don't."

"You do not know the Laws of the Avenue?" she repeated, with a sharp glance at Bakhtiian.

"No."

"Is he your kin?"

"Yes," said Tess, on firmer ground here. "By his aunt's gifting, he is my cousin."

Ilya glanced at her and swiftly away, looking startled.

"This grows interesting," said the priestess, but she did not look amused. "By gift but not by birth?"

"No, not by birth."

"By two questions, young man," said the priestess sternly, "you have gambled with the Laws."

"Ah, but my name is known here." To Tess he sounded infuriatingly smug.

"I know very well what your name is, Ilyakoria Bakhtiian. Do not trifle with me when the stakes are so high. What is your name, child?"

"Terese Soerensen." Tess looked from one to the other, bewildered by this interchange.

"You see, Bakhtiian, her name is not known here. Thus am I forced to act rather than accede."

For a moment, silence reigned. Behind the priestess, the high walls of the palace rose up into the twilight sky. Fading reliefs embellished them, vague shapes that seemed to move in the failing light.

"No," said Ilya. "I have accepted responsibility for her under older laws than these."

"Do not correct me. Here there are no other laws but those of the Avenue. In this place, she alone accepts that responsibility." She paused. He stood utterly still, as if only now absorbing and measuring some threat. "That she does not know what this journey has brought her does not, I fear, release her from its consequences." They both looked at Tess. The priestess examined her with simple appraisal, but Ilya—Ilya looked afraid, and that dismayed her. "Consider what it is that you have done, Bakhtiian. Consider it well. Now, Terese Soerensen, you will come with me."

"No!" cried Ilya. His sudden movement up one step alarmed Tess, but the priestess did not move. The light in her hands shone full on his face. He seemed very pale.

"Do you threaten me?"

"She is not jaran," said Ilya hoarsely. "I am responsible. You can't take her."

"Do you presume to tell me what I can and cannot do? Your own aunt gifted her into your tribe. If you regret now whatever rashness led you here, it is too late. The ceremony is completed. But her name is not known here. Thus, she must be tested and then released, one way or the other."

"Take me in her place." He made it an order not a request.

"You are presumptuous." Her voice cracked over them with all the harshness of a person used to complete rule and utter obedience. She lifted a hand. A door opened in the wall, and four white-clad men came out. Before Tess could react, the men surrounded Ilya. She put a hand on her saber. Then she realized none of them was armed with so much as a knife.

"You know the penalty for violence in this shrine," continued the priestess. Ilya stood stock-still, rooted to the stone, as if he were too stunned to react. The old woman moved her light to shine equally on all of them. Tess saw that the lines on her face were gentle and much marked about the eyes and the mouth. "Give your horse to one of the priests, child. Then come with me."

"Oh, gods," whispered Ilya, shutting his eyes. "I didn't think—" He broke off. Tess had never seen him with his emotions so uncontrolled. When he opened his eyes, his expression was clearly one of desperation.

"Clearly you did not think," responded the priestess caustically. "A man of your reputation. Have you anything whatever to say for yourself?"

He looked like a wild animal at bay, gauging its trap, as he examined the four men surrounding him, each in turn. But the cage was firm. To break out, he would have to use force, and here, in this shrine. . . .

"The penalty is death," said Tess, without thinking. "Wait. I don't understand. Do you mean to harm him? Is this all because of the Laws of the Avenue?"

"No. No physical harm will come to you or to him because you rode together down the Avenue at sunset."

Tess handed Myshla's reins to one of the priests. "Well, then," she said, seeing that Ilya had been pushed to the edge and would in a moment do something—something very final, she feared. "I will go with you. Willingly. Freely." She looked at Ilya as she said it.

"Tess." He turned his head in one smooth movement to look at her. She stared at him, bereft of words.

"Yes," said the priestess. "The penance the gods have put upon you, Bakhtiian, will be far harsher than any punishment I could devise." Up beyond, a single faint light winked into life in one of the high towers, a sentinel to whatever beings dwelt in this valley. "We must go, child."

Tess found that she was grateful to the priestess for this command. Too many things happening at one time: the ride, his face, the sudden kindling of fierce love only to face those simple, awful words, the Chapalii writing, the priestess, Laws, penance, his face. . . .

"But we can't let the khepelli come here," she said, grasping at the one thing she did understand.

The priestess had already turned away, assured of Tess's obedience. Now she turned back, and her white robe swelled out briefly with the turn. "Khepelli? What is this, Bakhtiian? Are there others in your party?"

He turned his head slowly to look at the priestess. "My

jahar, and the pilgrims we escorted from the issledova tel
shore." His voice was so even that it betrayed his agony.

The priestess shrugged. "Do not worry for them, child.
They will come by the usual road."

Ilya shut his eyes and took in a deep, unsteady breath.

"This is not the usual road?" Tess gestured toward the
Avenue behind them, now faded into the obscurity of dusk.

"That is a most unusual road. Come." She turned and
with a marked limp made her way toward the great doors.

"Ilya," Tess began. He would not look at her. And she
remembered what he had said, there at the ruby arch, with
her whole heart revealed before him: *Now you are mine.*
"You bastard," she said, and she strode away after the
priestess.

On the level, Tess was a head taller, but the old woman's
authority diminished the disparity in height between them.
"How might I address you?" Tess asked, mindful that on
this occasion formality was called for.

The priestess smiled. "For now, child, you may simply
follow me. Later, if the gods say it is fit, you may ask questions." At the great doors, they halted, and she examined
Tess for a moment by the light of her bowl. "You are not
jaran, and yet you are. This is a strong wind that blows, your
being here." She touched a gnarled hand to a panel, pressed
it, and the door swung open onto a long, high hall.

A hall distinctly Chapalii in shape and decoration. Stark,
abstract patterns lined the walls. They seemed to form pictures, until you looked at them directly; then their form slid
away, revealing nothing. Torches lit the hall. Soot and ash
shadowed the floor although a wide path lay clear down the
center. There was not enough of the black grit to account
for long use. How could they keep such a huge place clean
without machines?

"Enter, child."

Tess glanced back to see Ilya staring after them as dusk
grew at his back. The horses shifted restlessly behind him.
The door shut behind them and she was within the shrine.

They walked down the hall in silence. Nothing disturbed
their progress. No doors shut, no feet sounded but their
own, no voices pierced the heavy air. Yet beneath her feet,
Tess felt that the stone itself was alive, a bewildering sensation after so long in the open. She walked on her toes,
cautious and ready, a hand on the hilt of her saber. It took

her almost the entire length of the hall to sort through her thoughts and let her old self emerge above half a year's journey with the jaran.

The answer was so simple it was laughable. The palace must still be alive: with machines. Hidden, of course. Silent. Meant, like servants, to do their work unobtrusively, successful only if they went entirely unseen. The jaran priests, having no such conception of technology, had almost certainly never noticed any machines, had probably felt this strange trembling life to be the touch of the gods on their greatest temple.

Shadows mottled the scalloped ceiling. Reliefs lined the upper walls. It was the epitome of Chapalii architecture: breathtaking, ornate, and utterly useless, built for the sole purpose of having people walk from one end to the other. To be wealthy enough to spend money on things that could only be used once was to be wealthy enough to matter in Chapalii society.

"If you push there, behind that niche," said the priestess, "the door will move." They passed through into an enormous chamber, its decorations too profuse to be distinguishable in the gloom. This chamber gave on to a second, and thence to a third.

A huge monument, this was, and after unknown years still in incredibly fine condition. But the Chapalii prized efficiency as much as wealth. The machines ought to work for centuries at full capacity. The palace would be cleaned by mobile scrubbers programmed to vanish into the walls before they could offend the fastidious Chapalii eye. Hadn't she and Dr. Hierakis once tried to catch the scrubbers at it, that time on Odys, and failed? Such a palace, heated by fluid mechanics, buffered from the elements by diamond coating or some more advanced technique, could exist for generations.

"Here," said the priestess with humor. "You have forgotten me, Terese Soerensen. We turn here. Those of us who live here live in the back rooms, which are less overwhelming."

Tess smiled slightly and followed her into a less ostentatious corridor that led to humbler spaces. Also, doubtless, to the quarters for the stewards and the ke. Apartments for the nobility would be on the second floor, but the main maintenance room would be down here—that was what she had to find.

And she knew that it was worth it, this entire journey. Everything else aside, all the other joys and sorrows, everything she had learned and lost and become, this knowledge would be of priceless value to Charles. If spy she must be, spy she would become. She would leave here knowing why this palace existed and what the Chapalii were trying to hide.

"If you will wait here." Tess sat obediently on a bench in a narrow hallway while the priestess disappeared inside a room. Two torches gave a glum light to the corridor, and she could see into several rooms, scarcely more than closets, that showed signs of habitation: A couch with an old stain on the cushions, a table with a cloth on it, a sandal forgotten in a corner.

The priestess returned and led Tess down a white-walled hallway into a bright room. Twelve white-robed men and women regarded her, unsmiling. Tess blinked, rubbing at her eyes. She could not make out the source of the light. Walls of luminous stone lined the chamber, and it was bare of furnishing or ornamentation except for a cylindrical fountain at the far end, about twelve meters from her. While the priests studied her, she studied the fountain. It was a clear, hollow structure, intricately carved to reveal six spouts curled within, releasing a fine spray of rainbows and water that trickled into a basin and thence into a drain in the floor.

"You have ridden down the Avenue at sunset, knowing but not knowing what the Laws are, with a man who is but is not your kin," said the priestess. "Because your name is not known here, at this shrine where the gods' breath still lies heavy over the earth, the gods must judge you. Drink from the fountain, child. Drink your fill."

Tess looked around the circle of faces. They were all serious, dispassionate, yet none was unsympathetic. This was a test, but she could not connect it with what she knew of this culture or with Ilya's distress. She walked up to the fountain and knelt, cupping her hands to get a handful of water from the basin, and sipped at it, a bare touch. Lowered her hands slightly to watch the priests. Lifted her hands. Before her lips touched the water again, her mouth stung.

She swore and jumped up. The water in her hands spilled

onto the stone. She rubbed her hands roughly on her trousers.

"It burns!" She sat down, screwing up her face, trying to rub the stinging off of her lips. But if this was the gods' drink, she had surely failed to meet with their approval. And the penalty for sacrilege—she stood up. They would not kill her without a fight.

But they were all smiling. And none of them was armed.

"You have a certain enthusiasm for the truth which is refreshing." The priestess walked forward. "May I show you to a room for the night now?"

Tess did not move. "That was all? That was the test? I'm safe?"

"My child," said the priestess, a little scoldingly, perhaps, "no violence is ever done in this shrine."

"But the drink?"

"The water is poisonous. A sip does no harm, but were you dishonest or frightened, or greedy enough, you would have drunk your fill."

"And died."

The priestess shrugged.

"Does everyone who enters here whose name is—not known—have to pass this test?" she asked, suddenly curious about the Chapalii.

"No, only those who have transgressed the Law in some fashion."

"But how did I—?"

"First, child, you may call me Mother Avdotya. Second, you may come with me to your room. There is much to do if pilgrims are expected, and no time for all of us to stay with you."

Tess submitted. The hallway seemed very dark after the bright intensity of the fountain chamber. The priestess led her with her bowl of light down another hall, up stairs, and along a narrower corridor until they reached a room furnished with a single bed, a table, a chair, and a small window. And Myshla's saddlebags.

"You may sleep here. Yeliana will come for you in the morning."

Tess sat on the bed, hands folded in her lap. "May I ask some questions, Mother Avdotya?"

"Yes. You have earned that right."

Tess sighed and decided to begin where the ground seemed safest. "How long has this shrine been here?"

"I do not know."

"Who built it?"

"I do not know."

"How does it stay so—clean? Are there many of you here?"

"Never more than twenty-seven. It remains pure by its own devices."

"How does it stay light?"

"We have torches. The other lights come, perhaps, from the stone. I do not know."

"Does anyone know?"

She chuckled. "Do you think I am the old half-wit they have sent to you to keep you ignorant?" Tess blushed. Out the window she saw only dark and stars and the skeletal outlines of trees. "No, child. I am Eldest here. That is why I went out to the Avenue, when it was seen that a sunset ride had begun."

Tess could not yet bring herself to speak of the Avenue. "What will Bakhtiian do tonight?"

"He will remain outside. I hope it proves a cold night. I know from experience that stone is hard ground on which to kneel for so many hours, especially when the penitent does not know whether he has brought about another person's death." Tess winced away from the merciless chill in the old woman's voice. "Now I will leave you. You have a great deal to think about."

Tess took in a breath and stood up. "You said that we rode together down the Avenue at sunset as if that meant something. That—the ceremony was completed. What is the Law of the Avenue?"

Mother Avdotya turned back calmly, as if she had expected this question all along and merely hastened its appearance by pretending to leave. She rested her right hand on the back of the chair. Her left still cupped the bowl of light. "The honored ceremony. It takes great presumption—that, certainly, Ilyakoria Bakhtiian does not lack—because this is a holy place. For a man and a woman to ride down the Avenue at sunset, if they are not kin, is to marry their souls in the sight of the gods."

Tess sat down. "But—but we're cousins."

"Cousins have been known to marry, although it is rare, and more rarely approved."

"But I thought a man married a woman by marking her with his saber and then there was a period of prohibitions laid on them, and if they passed through these without breaking any, they were married."

"Yes," Mother Avdotya agreed, "that is the way of the jaran, the way of the people. The Law of the Avenue is unique. I have served here forty years, and only once before, twenty-six years ago, did a man and a woman ride the avenue."

"What happened to them?"

"It was she who had instigated it, for no better reason than envy of another woman's husband. She was too afraid to be honest when it came time to approach the fountain. He lives here still as a priest, having dedicated himself to serve where she died."

"Oh," said Tess, amazed she could produce so profound an observation. "He didn't think I would be tested, did he?"

"That seems to be the only word to his credit in this entire business that I can find," replied Mother Avdotya, quite unsympathetically.

"After all," Tess muttered to herself, "he would have no victory if I were dead." Then, seeing that the priestess was watching her with unnerving keenness, she shook her head, trying to clear it of confusion. "Why is it that so few of the jaran marry this way? Because they might be killed?"

"I'm not sure you entirely understand. The mark weds a woman to a man as long as her flesh carries it, or he lives. And only that long. But those who marry by this road marry the other eternally, for as long as their souls are born back into this world."

"Do you mean he did it believing it would bind me to him *forever?*"

"You see, child, why it is such an unpardonable thing he has done, knowing as he did that you were ignorant of it."

"Oh, my God."

The light on the priestess' bowl cast a glow on her face, shadowing ridges, highlighting the white sheen of her hair. Tess pinched the coarse blanket up into little hummocks and smoothed it down again. What had Kirill said? Bakhtiian did not like to lose.

"Yuri tried to warn me that I was riding into an ambush."

"An unusual ambush."

"I didn't even know we were fighting a war." Suddenly exhausted, Tess sank her head to rest on her open hands. "Oh, God." She could see his face, that brilliant, passionate face. She felt overwhelmed and utterly bewildered. There burned like a safe beacon her love for Kirill, like a campfire or a hearth's fire, warm and welcoming and contained, no great blaze, but restful and heartwarming. Like her love for Yuri, whatever differences there might be in how she felt for each of them. But like a wildfire that rages over the grass, obliterating everything in its path, this had come to her.

"I will leave you now," said Mother Avdotya.

The old woman went so unobtrusively that Tess scarcely noticed her leaving: the scrape of a shoe, cloth brushing wood, the low *snick* of the closing door. It was very dim, the furniture only dark slabs. Tess raised her head and stared outside at the lines of trees moving in the wind, etched against the night sky and the dark mass of clouds gathering, hiding the stars. Oh, yes, she understood him very well now. Perhaps Yuri was right, perhaps there was no difference for him between love and conquest.

Now you are mine.

He had what he wanted. "A wife has certain obligations to her husband that he may demand if she is unwilling to give them to him freely." She had no doubt now what those obligations included. That she loved him—that he now knew that she loved him—well, that only added sweetness to the victory.

Outside, the moon emerged from a scattering of clouds. Tess rose and went to the window, staring out. *This is not my world,* she told herself. *If he has married himself to you under his laws, then what of it? It does not bind you.*

Only it was her world, in a sense. She was its heir. And the ties of love and hate, of desire and indifference, of loyalty and betrayal are the only and all of the ties that bind us. She paced the tiny room for half the night before she finally got herself to sleep.

CHAPTER TWENTY-TWO

"Well, but I do these things under compulsion."
—EPICHARMUS OF SYRACUSE

Yeliana was younger than Tess expected; she looked about fourteen, with her heart-shaped face and solemn eyes.

"Mother Avdotya sent me," she explained, surveying Tess from the doorway. "I will escort you first to bathe and then to our midday meal." Solemnity vanished for a moment and she grinned. "You slept very late. Once I was allowed to sleep so late, when I was quite ill."

Tess rubbed her eyes and glanced out the window, and rubbed her eyes again.

"And you may borrow a decent shift, if you wish," Yeliana added, seeing that Tess had slept in her clothes, "if you would like to wash your clothing as well."

"I would, thank you."

To Tess's delight, the bath consisted of a heated, circulating pool. Yeliana agreed that it was miraculous and informed Tess that Mother Avdotya thought hot springs whose source they had yet to find must lie under the palace. If Tess took a little too much time, seduced by this luxury, the girl did not complain. She even helped her wash her clothes and spread them out to dry. A white shift was produced, belted, and proclaimed decorous. Tess left her hair hanging loose to dry.

Yeliana led her to the eating hall, a wood-paneled room flooded with sunlight through four huge windows in one wall and furnished with long tables and benches. The priests had clustered at one end of the room, and they shifted as she entered, moving to sit. Amid all the white, she saw a brilliant spot of red. He sat between two men, head bowed.

As Yeliana guided Tess forward, Ilya glanced up toward them. His entire being froze.

Abruptly, he pushed himself up. The two priests on either side were on their feet, a hand on each of his shoulders, before he was halfway standing. He looked once to each side and sank back onto the bench. He did not look up again. The two men sat.

From another room, three men brought in platters of food. Tess ate earnestly, truly hungry, but she could not help but glance at Ilya at intervals. Like her, he had bathed; he had trimmed his hair and his beard, had probably washed at least his shirt, early enough so that it had had time to dry. He attended to his food with an assiduousness helped by the disapproval with which everyone treated him. It was a silent meal. When all had finished, three women took the dishes away. Everyone else stood.

"Mother Avdotya has asked that you stay here," Yeliana explained, "so that you do not unwittingly disturb any of us at our duties. The rest of your party will surely arrive soon."

Tess watched the priests leave. The hall was empty except for herself and Bakhtiian. He was gazing down at the table, one finger tracing patterns on the grain. Tess walked across the room to stare out one of the windows at the garden. But he followed her, stopping a few paces behind her.

"Tess." His voice was quiet, unsure.

"I have nothing to say to you."

"Tess, if I had known, if I had even suspected the risk to you, I would never—"

"Battles are not won by men who refuse to take risks."

"What do you mean by that?"

"I'd rather not turn around to answer that question if you're wearing your saber."

"You needn't address me in that tone, Tess. I'm perfectly aware that my actions yesterday were ill-advised."

"*Ill-advised!* They weren't advised by anyone but yourself. You could have gotten me killed!" She turned to see his expression but the light falling on his face only brought out that blend of radiance and severity that made him so striking.

"Gods," breathed Ilya, as if he could not help himself. "White suits you."

Warmth spread up her cheeks. "This almost gives me

sympathy for Vera Veselov. Is this how men of the jaran revenge themselves on women who don't want them? Forcing them to marry them? My God, I think it is. I know it is.'' He went pale with anger but that only made her reckless. ''What is it you really want, Ilya? Me, or Jeds?''

''How dare you. Whatever you may think of me, I have honor.''

''Do you mean that it would be wrong to deceive me into marrying you to gain what I possess but not wrong to deceive me in order to—to what? To humiliate me by forcing me to become your wife?''

''To *humiliate* you?''

''I suppose you thought I'd be flattered.''

He looked as if she had just slapped him. ''Yes,'' he said hoarsely, ''and why shouldn't I have thought that? How many women do you suppose wish they were standing where you are now?''

''If so many women want you, then why didn't you pick one of them?''

''Because I wanted *you.*''

Tess went white. Said so baldly, the words terrified her. ''It's all war to you, isn't it? You only wanted me because you thought I was something you couldn't have.''

Silence fell between them. ''I have heard enough,'' he said in a low, unsteady voice.

''You're afraid to hear any more.'' She walked past him to the far corner, her head held high, knowing that she could have said nothing that would have hurt him more. Where had she gained such knowledge of him? A single drop of damp slid from one eye down along her nose to dissolve on her lips. She sat down on a bench and stared into the corner, determined to wait in stony and forbidding silence.

A moment later she heard voices. The door opened and a rush of feet and conversation entered.

''Well,'' said Kirill's voice above the rest. ''It's certainly cold in here.''

Tess brushed at her face with the back of one hand, stood and turned. Before anything, she noticed the distance between them—Bakhtiian still by the window, she in the corner farthest from him. No words could have spoken so clearly.

''Tess, what you are wearing?'' Yuri asked, walking across the hall to her. Mikhal and Kirill followed him, leav-

ing their four companions—the youngest of the jahar riders—by the door. The rest of the jahar was evidently elsewhere. "You haven't given yourself into the service of the
gods, have you?"

Her cheeks felt hot. "No, I haven't. One of the priest-
esses lent this to me while my clothes dry." She kept her
gaze fastened on Yuri, afraid to look at the others, at Bakhtiian, especially afraid to look at Kirill. "They have hot
springs here."

"Hot springs!" Mikhal stepped up beside Yuri, and by
doing so the two men—her brother and her brother-in-law—
made almost a barrier between her and Kirill. "Are all of
us welcome to use them?"

Kirill chuckled and merely spoke to her over their shoulders. "My heart, whatever did he do?"

"How long ago did you get here?" asked Yuri suddenly.

"Yesterday."

"You can't have, Tess. You can't possibly have ridden fast
enough to swing all the way around west and not even Ilya
would be mad enough to risk that impossible trail at night,
down the west slope."

"The west slope? But we came—" She stopped dead.
What an idiot she was. There must be another path, the
usual path, that led down into the valley.

A swift, almost imperceptible glance passed between Yuri
and Mikhal. "The Avenue," muttered Mikhal.

"When did you get here?" asked Kirill, his face pale.

Tess sat down on the bench.

Kirill pushed past Yuri and Mikhal and rested his hands
on the table, staring at her. "It's true, isn't it? You came at
sunset."

"Kirill," said Yuri in an undertone. By the door, Konstans and Petre and Mitenka and Nikita whispered together,
watching them. Mikhal had turned to stare at Bakhtiian. Ilya
seemed frozen by the window, his back to them all. "Kirill," Yuri repeated. "Don't make a fool of yourself."

"Did you come willingly?" Kirill asked in an undertone.
He did not move. "Ought I to wish you happy?"

Tess stood up. "You have no right, Kirill, to play out
whatever old grudge you have against Bakhtiian over *me*.
You have no right to question me in that tone. I thought you
were different from *him*." As she spoke, she saw—felt—
Ilya move, like a shadow along the wall, noiseless as he

limped toward the door. The young men moved aside uneasily to let him pass. "No, I didn't go willingly. No, you ought not to wish me happy. But it was done. There, does that satisfy you?"

Kirill went red and then white again and pulled back from the table. "Forgive me. I never meant—" He faltered.

"I know," she said, softening. "You should have heard what I said."

He grinned. "By the gods, I wish I had. I haven't seen Ilya look that chastened since that day seven years ago when his aunt—"

"Kirill!" said Yuri.

"Well, never mind." His face changed expression suddenly. "But that means he's your husband."

"Yes. We had just finished discussing that interesting fact when you came in." But she saw by his face that he was connecting "husband" with "sunset" and leading them together to "night" and drawing a conclusion which he did not like at all. "Yes," she added, feeling a certain malicious satisfaction in allowing herself to pass on this one piece of information, "he spent all night kneeling outside by the great doors. Or so I was told."

Kirill smiled, but it was the ghost of his usual smile, more show than feeling. "I hope his knee hurts like fire today," he said with vindictiveness that was unusual for him.

"Come on, Kirill," said Mikhal abruptly. "Let's go see about those hot springs." He grabbed Kirill by the arm and dragged him away to the others and herded them all out.

Leaving her and Yuri. "Well?" Yuri asked.

"Well, what? Thank God I'm going back to Jeds."

"It really is true?"

"Yes. You warned me, Yuri, and I didn't listen. I never thought that he would go this far. I didn't even know until it was too late."

"He didn't tell you, did he? Gods!" He laughed. "Oh, I beg your pardon, Tess, but how like him to never give up that kind of advantage. Of course he wouldn't have told you, not until he was sure of his victory."

"An appropriate choice of words. *He* didn't tell me at all. Mother Avdotya told me about the Law of the Avenue, and what it means. I could have been killed!"

"Killed!" He hugged her. "What do you mean?"

She explained.

He pushed back to look at her. "Gods, you must be angry."

"Do you know, that's the funny thing. He really was sorry for that. It must have reminded him of his family. The one thing he thinks he did wrong is the one thing I can forgive him for. I can't believe I really would have died, or that they would have let me die. I don't know. Maybe we're all blind that way about our own deaths."

"Then you're not too angry with him? You are his wife now, after all."

Tess smiled sweetly. "I'm not angry with him, Yurinya. I'd happily kill him. But it wouldn't do any good, would it? He'd just come back to plague me in his next life. No, I'm furious. I just wish I had a better vocabulary because I can't think of any words bad enough in any of the languages I know that would truly express what I would like to call him."

Yuri whistled. "You are mad, aren't you? Khaja mud snuffler?"

"No, that's not comprehensive enough. There might be a few phrases in Chapalii—oh, God, the Chapalii. Where are they?"

"Being shown to their rooms. Why do you ask? They went all sorts of colors in the face, you know, when we came out of the trees and saw the shrine for the first time."

"I'll bet they did. Damn. Do you trust me?"

"Yes."

"Then go find out where their rooms are."

"Tess." He hesitated. "My duty to Ilya. . . ."

"No, you're right. I can't ask that of you. I'll have to do this myself."

"Tess. . . ."

"Yuri, I'm sorry. I have a duty to my brother that must now supersede my duty to your aunt, for gifting me into your tribe. Can you understand that?"

He sighed and looked unhappy, but he nodded. "I understand."

"Go enjoy the hot springs. I'll be all right here."

He grimaced, kissed her on the cheek, and left.

She paced over to the window and stared out onto the bare lines of the garden. One bush trembled in the chill air with a few last leaves and four white flowers.

Footsteps sounded behind her, a heavier, measured tread. "Tess."

She turned. "Niko. You're not coming to plague me, too, are you?"

He chuckled and sat down on the table nearest her, letting one leg dangle. Dust rimmed his boot top, pale against the black cloth of his trousers. "I'll be discreet. Now, Tess, since Ilyakoria is not inclined at present to be very talkative, I apply to you for the truth of a rumor that has spread through the entire jahar."

"It's true."

"You rode down the Avenue together, at sunset?" She nodded. "And you went unwillingly?"

"Not unwillingly precisely. I went in complete ignorance." Niko's eyes widened. "Surely that doesn't surprise you, Niko? Bakhtiian never gives up that sort of advantage."

"I'm not sure I like your sarcasm. I may deplore the method, but you know very well that women have no choice in marriage."

"You know very well that I am not a jaran woman, and that I am in any case leaving for Jeds when we get to the coast."

"But you will still be married to him."

"Yes, by the Law of the Avenue, by the law of the jaran, I will still be married to him. When I am in Jeds, I will still be married to him—by the law of the jaran. But I am not married to him by the laws of my land."

"What about the laws of the heart?"

She spun away from him and walked right up to one of the great windows, putting her palm on the glass—no, it couldn't be glass because it leaked no cold through it from outside—and stared at the white sheen of clouds above. "Hearts can be betrayed. I admit this much, that wherever I go, I will always be bound to him in some way." She turned back. "But I will not submit to treachery."

Niko considered her in silence. "Ah," he said. "I think I need to have a talk with Ilyakoria. If you will excuse me?"

He left. Only the muted tapping of her foot on the floor disturbed the quiet in the hall. She felt, suddenly, as if her ears had been stuffed with cotton. The door opened and Yeliana appeared.

"Here you are," she said brightly. "Just as you ought.

Yurinya Orzhekov spoke with Mother Avdotya and said you might like to be shown round the shrine. She is about to lead the pilgrims round. It was their first wish, even before being shown their rooms." She giggled, very like a girl and not a sober young priestess. "I suppose I've grown rather used to it, having never seen anywhere else. Would you like to come?"

Tess blinked and collected herself. "Why, yes," she said, trying to imitate Yeliana's careless tone. "I would. You were born here?"

"Yes. I don't know who my parents are though. They always say I am the child of the gods, and all of them raised me."

"Are many children born and raised here?"

"A few." She shrugged. "Women and men, after all, will have children."

"Do all of them stay to become priests?"

She smiled a rather secretive, knowing smile. "Where else have they to go? Being orphans. Not all of them, but most do. Here is Mother Avdotya, and the pilgrims."

Tess suddenly realized the advantage in appearing in robes while the Chapalii, even Ishii, still wore tunics and trousers. Stewards wore clothing suitable for work. Lords wore robes, for wealth and governing and leisure. She inclined her head to Ishii, and to Garii and Rakii second. Then, feeling generous, she acknowledged the stewards. Robed, she was confirmed in rank. Ishii bowed; the others bowed. Mother Avdotya watched without comment or expression, and then requested that they follow her.

The priestess led them at a leisurely pace. The palace was huge and bewildering, so that Tess soon lost a sense of where she was and concentrated on details: A panel, her height but tens of meters long, made of a substance as pale as ivory, hollowed and carved into a filigree of plant and animal shapes. A vast hall housing a floor mosaic that spread out in blazing colors from her feet in the unmistakable pattern of a star chart. The huge, empty cavern of the dome, its walls edged by pillars as thin and smooth as her waist but colored a translucent pink that caught and scattered the light in fragmented patterns across the marble floor. Their height was lost in shadow, dispersed into the overlap of the dark stone that circled the last broad ring of the dome before it sloped inward, a spray of colored crystal radiating in to the cool clear lens of the center.

Ishii deferred to the priestess with unnerving respect, made only the most polite of comments, and revealed nothing. The others followed him. Garii did not even look at Tess, not once. It grew dark at last, and Mother Avdotya led them back to the eating hall.

Torches flickered along the walls, throwing shadows everywhere. Candles stood at intervals on the tables, illuminating the close wood grain and the nearby faces. The hall seemed very full, with the priests and the jahar and now the Chapalii, though half the tables were empty. Yuri waved at her. She walked over to sit with him and Mikhal, but as they moved to make room for her, Kirill suddenly appeared and squeezed in between her and Yuri.

"Kirill," said Yuri.

Kirill grinned, unrepentant. He looked a little flushed, but he was obviously determined to be charming and inoffensive. It was a cheerful meal. The food seemed lavish: two meats, one salty, one spiced, dark, soft slices of bread, two vegetables, all washed down with a watery ale. The priests were animated. The Chapalii sat at another table, but there would be days here in which to spy on them. Right now, she just wanted to enjoy herself. Over the empty platters and bowls Mother Avdotya called for songs, and Tess forgot herself so much as to sing a very improper tune that Yuri had taught her. No one was sure which was funnier: Tess singing the song, or Yuri trying to slide under the table because everyone knew he had taught such a thing to a woman.

While three priests cleared the dishes, Niko called for tales. First the men told witty and amusing tales, but it was as Josef was telling the old story of Mother Sun's daughter come to earth that Tess noticed the old priestess rise and limp out of the room. She returned as Josef finished, carrying a painted beaker. The priests fell silent, and silence spread out from them until no one was speaking.

The dull light gave the woman the appearance of a shade, tenuous and insubstantial, but her voice was firm. "This is a rare wine, brought out only on such special occasions as this. But do not drink of it unless your heart is undisturbed, lest the disturbance therein take hold of your senses for the night."

Only the slip of shifting boots and a single, smothered cough sounded. Mother Avdotya went first to the Chapalii; in the half light, Tess could not make out the colors on their faces. Ishii accepted, and thus so did the others. She moved to the next table, offering to each person in turn. Many of the priests drank; some refused.

When she halted beside Yuri, he lifted his cup. The liquid fell in a clear stream from the beaker, sounding in the cup like the suggestion of a waterfall heard from a great distance. Now she stood between Tess and Kirill, leaning forward. Tess saw that the patterns on the vase were a story told in pictures: a woman leading a pale horse and a man with wings and black hands crouched on a rock before her. She leaned farther forward to see the next panel, saw, instead, Kirill's eyes as he, too, looked around the container, but at her. The candlelight made the blue in his eyes look like the depths of some incandescent flame.

"Oh, no, Mother," he said in a tone only loud enough for the three of them. "My heart is very disturbed tonight."

Tess laughed, a sound that echoed across the stillness. She clapped one hand over her mouth and quickly looked away from his grin, only to find her gaze catch on Ilya. His face seemed pale and disapproving. She coughed and choked back her laughter.

"And you, Terese Soerensen?" asked the priestess.

Tess simply laid her hand over her cup, not trusting her voice, and her other hand over her eyes, not trusting herself to look at Kirill or Yuri. Trust Kirill to make her laugh when everyone else was being so serious. The priestess went on to Mikhal. By the time Tess felt it safe to look up, the old woman had gone on to the next table. Kirill and Yuri looked as innocent as babes. Yuri sipped thoughtfully at his wine.

Vladimir was offered the drink, but he glanced at Ilya and refused. Niko smiled and accepted. Bakhtiian. He set his lips together, managing to look stubborn and defiant and failing to look composed, and asked for the wine, his gaze fixed on the flame of the nearest candle. Without comment, the priestess poured and went on.

When she had finished, people began to talk again. There was a wave of laughter around Tess's table and everyone demanded to know what Kirill had said. Tess refused to tell them. Another round of songs followed, and then everyone settled in to talk.

The Chapalii left first, all together, and with them a handful of priests. Tess only noticed it as movement at the edge of her vision; she was listening to the conversation.

"Mikhal," Kirill was saying, "you know very well that strength can't always assure a swift victory."

"Why is that, Kirill?"

Across from her, Niko slipped into the seat Konstans had vacated. The conversation expanded easily to include him. When two others left and Josef and Tasha joined them, there was scarcely a pause. She could have sat here forever, the candles half gone, wax trailing down their sides, spilling over their holders to lie across the tabletop like pale roots exposed in rich soil. The golden pool of light echoed dimly in the torches racked up behind them on the walls. Kirill's leg warmed hers. Gods, how easy it was to be with these people. She trusted them, and they had given her their trust in return, one simple exchange which was all the currency they knew. She followed this path down into their souls— not far, perhaps, for she had not known them *that* long— but far enough to see that the composition of the path was one suited to her feet. And if the tongues of the men who had drunk of the wine seemed a little better oiled, it did not matter, because nothing they said shattered the spell that lay over this late conversation.

At the other end of the table, more men stood and left, to be replaced a moment later with two more. It was Ilya, Vladimir with him. Could he never leave her alone to enjoy herself? She realized that if she skipped over his face when her gaze shifted that way, she could ignore him reasonably well.

"Yes," Tasha was saying, "but if visions are gifted us by the gods, then we must judge them as omens."

"But what if visions are only waking dreams? Or trances?" asked Kirill. "What about that old woman in Arkhanov's tribe who used to fall on the ground and speak nonsense? And then she would remember nothing of it when she woke." He grinned. "They said. I was too scared to stay and watch."

"Kirill," said Niko, "you are arguing for no reason but to argue."

"Someone has to."

"Well, then, explain to me why old Aunt Lubkhov did these things."

"Only the gods can explain that, Niko," Kirill objected, and then he laughed. "Which gives the point to Tasha, of course."

Tess thought the poor woman probably had some kind of epilepsy. Two younger men got up and left. Vladimir, who had fallen asleep once already, gave it up and went away.

"Ow!" said Yuri, starting. "Niko! Oh, what a twinge in my back. I think I'll go to bed. Are you coming, Kirill?" He stood up.

"I'm not tired," said Kirill.

Mikhal stood as well. "Good. Didn't you wager me, Kirill, that the very first night we got here you would find the marble pool that Josef claims is hidden in these woods?"

"So I did," said Kirill in a odd tone. He stood up and glanced down at Tess. "Sleep well, my heart," he said, mockingly. He smiled sweetly at her, taking the sting from the words, and walked away with Yuri and Mikhal.

Tess realized that there were only five of them left: herself, Niko, Josef, Tadheus, and—Ilya was watching her. She felt faint. Somehow he had moved next to Niko. He was very near.

"Perhaps I'll go—" she began, and then Josef slid in next to her, Tasha on her other side.

"You know," said Josef, "it was when I was stalking that great hunting cat in the forests south of here that I fell in with those khaja traders who taught me some of their tongue, the one called Taor. Even within the jaran the tribes speak khush each a little different from the others. But this Taor, whatever their accent might be, I never heard a word then or since from traders on the west or the east coast, no matter how far south or north I might roam, that was not exactly the same as that word in another place."

Tess felt obliged to explain the difference between a native language with dialects and a lingua franca. The talk drifted to weather, no desultory chatter but a complex examination of the year's weather and how it boded for the winter. In a peculiar way it became philosophical. Tess felt utterly out of her depth and she shifted on the bench, waiting for the right moment to excuse herself.

"Ah, well." Niko stood. "I'm off to bed."

Tasha rose as well. "Good night." They left together.

"Ilya says you can read the writing in this shrine," Josef said.

"A little. I really—"

"Oh, I'm well aware that you're modest about your accomplishments. I don't think I've met anyone who can speak as many languages as you can, and khush so well, after so short a time with us. My grandfather used to say—" Josef was at his most compelling when he was telling tales. This one wound on until Niko and Tasha were safely gone. Then Josef yawned abruptly and with no warning whatsoever excused himself and deserted her.

His footsteps faded away, leaving her with a few guttering candles and Bakhtiian. It took no great intelligence to see that she had been set up. The torches had gone out. The candlelight cast his shadow on the wall behind him like a huge, black, jagged tapestry. His shirt gleamed a dull red. The pallid light made his face look as gaunt as a starving man's. He stared at her with unnaturally bright eyes. Speech failed her. She stood up.

"It's so late," she said stupidly. "I guess I'll go."

Of course he came after her. She accidentally took the wrong corridor, one that led along the gardens, but she did not have the courage to turn back. Afraid to run, afraid to turn back—what damned use was she?

She stopped and turned to face him.

But when he caught up with her, he took her by the arm and stared, simply stared, at her. The moon lit them. She was trembling.

"Let go of me."

"Tess." He put his other hand on her other arm.

"Are you drunk?" she said, breathing hard. She strained away from him.

"Drunk?" His voice was low, intense. "I only now see things clearly." His pull was like the drag of the tide; she could not help but be drawn in.

"I don't know what you're talking about." She tried to twist her arms out of his grasp, but his hands were too strong.

"You rode down the Avenue with me," he whispered, his face lit by the moon and the wine. "You are my wife."

"You led me into it." He slipped his arms behind her back, enclosing her. The heat of his hands seared through the cloth into her flesh. His lips were parted, so that the line of his mouth seemed soft and yielding. "I didn't know." Her voice came out hoarse. "You know I didn't know. You knew then. You trapped me."

"Trapped you?" His voice was like the touch of soft fur. He held her so close that she could feel the beat of his heart. "Do I fill you with such aversion?"

He did not let her answer but kissed her. Such compulsion as this was impossible to resist. The world could have gone ablaze at that moment and she would never have noticed. All she felt was him. There was no cruelty in Ilya Bakhtiian—if she had not known that before, she knew it now when it could not possibly be disguised. But there was passion. Gods, yes, enough of that.

They were forced eventually to pause to catch their breath. Reason flooded back. She pushed away from him. His eyes opened, and his grip tightened.

"No," she said. "Let me go."

"No."

"Let me go, Ilya."

"I will not." They had reached an equilibrium of opposing forces, she retreating, he restraining. He let go of one wrist and with his free hand traced the hard ridge of her spine, all the way to her neck. He drew his hand over the swell of her shoulder and down, fingers a caress on her skin, around her collarbone to the hollow of her throat, and leaned forward to kiss her there, lightly. She couldn't control her breathing. She shut her eyes.

"Bakhtiian. I will not submit to treachery. Now let me go." She felt his breath brush her neck but she held herself rigid; clenched all her muscles like a fist. If she gave in now, she would never respect herself.

He drew away. Slowly, reluctantly, he relinquished his grip on her.

She spun away from him and ran. When she reached the little room the priests had given her, she flung herself on the bed and wept. Her throat still tingled where he had kissed her. Finally she fell into an uneasy sleep filled with vivid dreams in which Ilya Bakhtiian played all too large a part.

In the morning, as she walked down the hall before breakfast, he came out from a side hall. They both stopped.

"Forgive me." He looked pale and tired and subdued.

"It *was* no better than treachery, and I was wrong to force myself on you in that fashion when you were ignorant of the consequences. I cannot withdraw myself as your husband, not now, but I will no longer trouble you."

He bowed, as courtiers bowed in Jeds to the Prince, and limped away, leaving her to stare after him. She walked on in a daze to the eating hall. Yuri waved at her from his seat beside Mikhal. Kirill was sitting across from them, looking pale himself. She hesitated and then sat down beside Kirill and surveyed Yuri and Mikhal wearily.

"I thank you for your support last night."

"But Tess—" Yuri began.

"Spare me, please. Did Niko kick you or something?" Yuri flushed. "Well, it didn't work." She did not look at Kirill, but she felt him shift beside her. "I slept alone. Gods, I'm not even hungry. Excuse me." She rose.

"Do you want company?" asked Kirill in a low voice.

Mikhal began to object, but Yuri silenced him with a hand on his sleeve.

"If I wanted anyone's company, it would be yours, Kirill, but no, I—" She hesitated, seeing the Chapalii rise en masse and politely thank Mother Avdotya and then file out the door. She ought to go with them but she was not entirely sure it would be safe to go alone. She glanced at Kirill. His color was a little high but he looked composed and remarkably calm. Could she ask him to escort her? Would it be asking him to betray his loyalty to Bakhtiian? What if Cha Ishii took a jaran presence to mean that Bakhtiian was supporting her and not him and reneged on the payment for this journey? Whatever love existed between her and Kirill, his place in Bakhtiian's jahar was of far more value to him than her convenience.

"If you're going to spy on the khepellis," Kirill said suddenly, "then one of the jahar ought to go with you to make sure you don't do anything foolish enough to antagonize them. We can't afford to lose those horses, after all."

"I'll go," said Yuri. "No, I think you're right, Kirill, but I think Ilya would elect to send someone other than you."

"Bakhtiian knows the worth of my loyalty to him."

"I'm leaving," said Tess, and did so. Kirill caught up with her outside. "How was that settled?" she asked.

"I reminded Yuri that I am his senior and twice the scout he is as well."

"That was low of you."

"But true nevertheless. Tess, if you want to follow the pilgrims, they went that way not this way."

"Oh." She laughed. "Very lowering to think that Yuri is twice the scout I am. Yes, there they are. Cha Ishii."

Cha Ishii stopped, but he made a fleeting sign with his hand and the others went on while he waited. They vanished around a corner, leaving Tess to face him alone. Kirill stood silently at her back.

"Lady Terese." He bowed. She glanced at his belt and saw that he was not wearing his knife.

Dumb, my girl, that is what we play now. "The shrine is indeed beautiful, Cha Ishii," she continued in court Chapalii, "but I do not understand why you came so far under such brutal conditions merely to survey such an alien place." Humans had necessarily to learn to speak the language of their emperor but few had occasion or opportunity to master the complex symbology that made up the written tongue and governed the decorative arts. Few understood how interrelated they were. Perhaps he would actually believe she did not recognize this place as Chapalii.

Pink spread up his cheeks. "You could not be expected to, Lady Terese, though you had already discerned that we were not priests." He placed his hands in that arrangement known as Lord's Supplication. "If I may be allowed to acquaint you with our work?" She nodded, and he turned and conducted her into the most opulent sections of the palace. Kirill trailed three steps behind them. Ishii ignored him as thoroughly as he would ignore one of his own stewards. "We are, in fact, archaeologists." Color shifted in subtle patterns on his face.

"Indeed! Archaeologists. Why masquerade as priests, then?"

He clasped his hands behind his back. "In the Earth form I believe this word translates as 'the study of antiquity,' and it therefore demands some perspective of time and culture which these people cannot possess, being of a more primitive stamp. To their understanding, a religious expedition is comprehensible and not so far removed that our activities in systematic measurement cannot be construed as a form of worship."

"I understand your concern, but surely, Cha Ishii, you might have applied to the duke for permission to conduct your study." She smiled, enjoying this fencing, and glanced back at Kirill. He returned her gaze blandly since he could not understand a word they were saying.

"This did precipitate embarrassment, Lady Terese. It was deemed necessary to continue our investigations in secret because we feared that your brother would forbid the expedition."

"Was there such a pressing need to continue it?"

He directed her along a whitewashed hallway and thence into a magnificent salon decorated with a tile pattern on floor and ceiling and walls that, seeming to repeat, never quite repeated itself. "We have been investigating the relics of this particular civilization for many years now."

"On *this* planet?"

"No, indeed, Lady Terese. This is a star-faring civilization which predates our current Empire. We were greatly surprised to find traces of it here."

I'll just bet you were, she thought. This confession rang truer than anything he had ever told her before. They must have been dismayed to find relics of Chapalii provenance here on the planet of the human duke who, of all their enemies, would surely use any information he acquired against them. "I am intrigued. Perhaps you can enlighten me further."

Whether he believed that she had been misled by these confidences or whether he tacitly agreed to continue their little fencing match she could not be sure. Perhaps he hoped for the best. In any case, he began a vague discourse on the supposed attributes and history of this civilization, all of which sounded plausible, none of which sounded too betrayingly Chapalii. But it was when they were standing under the dome, staring upward, that Ishii said unexpectedly:

"You were right to wonder why I would conduct an expedition that my rank and birth ought to render repulsive to me. If my father's father had not precipitously died, leaving his affairs in the hands of his wife for one year before his heir could return to take things in order— There were grave losses. Our family was inevitably and immediately cast down from the status we had so long held. What could we expect, having left to us only five estates and two merchant fleets? And I, younger son of the youngest son—" Was there a trace of wry humor in his words? She could not tell. "— was chosen to accept this task. Much will be restored to us, Lady Terese. You see that I could not refuse my duty."

"Indeed, I see," replied Tess, quite shocked. They went on as if he had said nothing.

Coming out into a little courtyard of slender pillars engulfed in green vines, she saw a lone Chapalii disappear into the garden. Ishii was looking at the palace, examining some design on the wall, and had not seen him.

"I will walk alone now," said Tess, dismissing him. She waited for him to retreat inside. "Which way did he go, Kirill?" she asked in khush as soon as Ishii was gone.

"What, the other one? This way."

He led her into the garden. It was a clear day for autumn. A breeze cooled her cheeks, stirring the ends of her braided hair. He stopped on the edge of a grassy sward and gestured to a little fountain burbling merrily on the other side, up against a fringe of trees. Hon Garii stood there alone, one hand in the water.

"Stay here," said Tess in an undertone. She marched across the grass.

Garii turned. He flushed pink and bowed deeply. "Lady Terese."

"Hon Garii. We have created certain obligations between us. Is this not true?"

"You honor me with your acknowledgment, Lady Terese. I alone rashly instigated these obligations. That you have chosen to indulge me in this matter reflects only credit to you."

"Yet your family is pledged to Ishii's house."

"This is true. And to pledge myself to you, Lady Terese, must seem to a Tai-endi like yourself the grossest and most repugnant of behaviors. But I have observed and studied, and I have reflected on this man, Bakhtiian, and seen that by his own efforts he creates opportunity for himself. I am clever. I am industrious. Yet my emperor decrees that I must toil in the same position as my father's father's father, and suffer the consequences of an act committed by an ancestor I could not even know. Does this seem fair to you?"

"No, truly it does not. But Hon Garii, to work for me is to work for my brother, the duke. You must know what this means."

He bowed again. "I am yours, Lady Terese. Command me as you wish."

This was it, then. She took in a deep breath. "I must see the maintenance rooms. I must know the truth of this palace, why it is here, and why Cha Ishii was ordered to investigate. Will you meet me tonight in the eating hall after the rest are asleep?"

His skin remained white, colorless. So easily did he betray his emperor. "As you command, Lady Terese."

She nodded. "Then return to your duties now, and say nothing of this to anyone." He bowed and walked past her back to the shrine. She let out a long sigh and tested the water in the fountain with her finger. It stung. She wiped her finger on her sleeve and turned, hearing Kirill behind her.

"What an unmelodious language they speak," he said, looking after Garii's retreat. He hesitated and considered the grass, a peculiar expression on his face. "Tess, what does it mean that your brother is this *prince* in Jheds?"

Coming from Kirill, it seemed a puzzling question. "It means that he rules a great city and a great deal of farm and pasture and woodland lying all around it and supervises a port with many ships and rich trading from lands close by and lands far away across the seas."

"When you go back to Jheds, what will you do? If you are his heir, then—then you would become like an etsana, wouldn't you? You would have your own tent, and eventually children. You would need a husband, or a man to act as your husband—" He pulled his hand through his red-gold hair. "Tess, no one ever said—Bakhtiian can never go back there. He has given himself to this work now. Whatever he wants from you, he can't go with you." He looked at her finally, hope sparking in his eyes. "But—" He broke off, took in a deep breath, and went on. "But I could."

Foliage covered the verdant height of the surrounding hills, wreathed here and there with a curl of cloud, like some half-forgotten thought. An insect chirruped and fell silent. "Oh, Kirill," she said, and stopped.

He smiled a little wryly. "I know very well, my heart, that your brother probably already has some alliance arranged."

"No," she said in an undertone. "He doesn't. I won't lie to make that my excuse. I can't take you with me."

You can you can you can. Her thoughts raced wildly. His leaving would not alter anything; his knowing the truth about where she really came from would never matter. But what would life be like for him? She would be his only anchor in the bewildering confusion of space, of Earth, of the Empire. He would be utterly dependent on her. The kind of love they had was not strong enough to weather that sort of relationship, was not meant to. One or the other of them would soon fall out of love; one or the other would grow to resent their circumstances. And once he had left, Kirill could never return. She could not tear him apart from every seam that bound him to the fabric of life. Kirill loved her sincerely, she believed that, but she also believed that Kirill loved and had loved and would love other women as well. That was the real difference between Kirill and Ilya: Kirill was far more resilient.

"Gods, Kirill," she said, moved by his asking, by his offering. "Believe me, if I could, I would take you."

He hung his head, and she grimaced and went to hug him. He allowed this freedom, he put his arms around her, but after a moment he disengaged himself gently. "I believe you. Tess, I will always respect you most of all for your honesty." He kissed her chastely on the cheek, hesitated, and then walked away.

There was a stone bench beside the fountain. Tess sat on it and leaned her head back, letting the weak heat of the sun beat on her face.

And I used to think my life was complicated. Life as Charles's heir was beginning to seem like child's work now. She felt thoroughly exhausted and yet she had an uncanny feeling that she was waiting for someone else to accost her. *Get it all over with in one long, miserable scene. King Lear must have felt like this, battered by one storm after the next.* Then, because the comparison was so ludicrous, she chuckled.

Boots scuffed leaves. She looked around. "Hello, Vladimir. You startled me."

"You were here with one of the khepelli," he said accusingly. "Ilya has said all along you were a spy."

Tess examined Vladimir. His vanity was the vanity of the insecure. He had taken great pains with his appearance, had trimmed his hair, and shaved his face so no trace of beard or mustache showed. Jewelry weighed him down: rings, bracelets, necklaces—were all of them from lovers? He had a deft hand for embroidery but no taste at all, so that the design adorning his sleeves and collar was merely garish. The ornately-hilted saber that Ilya had gifted him, the legacy of the arenabekh, simply capped the whole absurd ensemble.

"So I am, Vladimir," she agreed amiably, "which is why I sent Kirill after him."

He blinked. "But—" He shrugged suddenly, a movement copied from Bakhtiian, and sat down carefully on the grass. "Why did you come here, then?"

"I'm traveling to Jeds. I thought you knew that."

"I know what you say. Josef told Niko that you can read the writing here. But no one can read that, not even Mother Avdotya."

"How do you know?"

"I was born here," he replied without visible emotion. "Or at least they say that I was."

"You must know Yeliana. You must have grown up with her."

"She was very young when I left." Behind him, through a ragged line of bushes, she saw the slender lines of a statue, something human, its features worn away so that there were only depressions for the eyes and a slight rise to mark the lips. "She is as much of a sister as I have ever had. But I did not want to become a priest."

"So what did you do?"

He shrugged again, that childlike copy of Bakhtiian. "I rode to join Kerchaniia Bakhalo's jahar-ledest. Ilya found me there." *So,* thought Tess, *your life began when Ilya found you.* "I'm very good with saber," he offered by way of explanation for this inexplicable action on the part of the great Bakhtiian. "And Ilya had lost his family."

Had lost a nephew, Tess reflected, *who might well have been around Vladimir's age now.* Perhaps this was one way of atoning.

"You knew about the shrine," said Vladimir abruptly. "You came here, planning all along to trick him down the Avenue."

The accusation was so preposterous that Tess laughed. "You think I sailed across wide seas from a far distant land, risked my life, all for the express purpose of marrying Bakhtiian? Whom I had, incidentally, never heard of."

"Everyone has heard of him," said Vladimir stiffly.

"But Vladimir," she said, deciding that the only fair
throw here would be one equally wild, "why should I want
to marry Bakhtiian? I am a great heir in my own right, and
anyway, everyone knows that Bakhtiian has never loved anyone since—"

"It's not true," he cried, jumping to his feet. "You'll
never make me believe that of him." He stalked away.

Since she had been about to say, "since his family died,"
she wondered what Vladimir had thought she was about to
say. By God, he was afraid that once Bakhtiian had a legitimate family, he, Vladi, would be cast off again. Poor child,
to have to live so dependent on one person's whim.

A flight of birds caught her eye as they wheeled and dove
about some far corner of the park. She heard their faint
calls, laughable things, like the protests of the vacillating.
A rustling sounded from a bush, and a small, rust-colored
animal, long-eared and short-legged, nosed past a crinkled
yellow leaf and scrambled out to the center of the sward,
huffing like a minute locomotive. It froze. The tufts of hair
in the inside of its ears were white, but its eyes were as
black as the void.

She felt inexplicably cheered. However hard it had been—
and still was—it had been right to tell Kirill that he could
not come with her. It had been honest, and it had been true.
She shifted on the bench. The little animal shrieked, a tiny
hiccup, and it fled back into the bush, precipitating a flood
of rustling around her and then silence. She smiled.

On Earth she had learned to walk without hearing, to look
without seeing. She had surrounded herself with a wall.
Here she listened: to the wind, to the horses, to the voices
of the jaran as they spoke, wanting to be heard, to hear. On
Earth she had taught herself to deal with people as if they
weren't there; only to protect herself, of course. Yet how
many times had she spoken to people, only to realize later
that she had never once looked them in the eye? In this land,
one saw, one looked, and the lowering of eyes was as elo-
quent as their meeting.

She ran one hand over the case that protected her mirror,
over the enameled clasps. In this land, the austerity of the
life demanded that every human exchange, however ambig-
uous, be thorough and complete. There was nothing to hide

behind. In this land, a mother's first gift to her daughter was a mirror in which the daughter could see her own self.

Of course, they didn't have showers. This was a considerable drawback. Or any kind of decent information network. That she missed. She had borrowed Sister Casiara's legal tract from Niko, and read it through twice now, and the second time it had bored her almost to tears. But there were other things and other ways to learn. Tasha was the most accurate meteorologist she had ever come across. Josef could analyze his surroundings with a precision and an accuracy that would make a physical scientist blush with envy, and he could follow a cold trail with astonishing skill. Yuri understood more about the subtle shadings of the human heart than he probably knew he did. And if she had felt more pain here, then she had also felt more joy, more simple happiness. It was a trade worth making. Here, in the open lands, where the spirit wandered as freely as the wind, it was hard to be miserable.

CHAPTER TWENTY-THREE

"An enemy is not he who injures,
but he who wishes to do so."
—Democritus of Abdera

That night after supper, Tess went back to her room and waited. When the moon had set, she strapped on her saber and both her knives and slipped out into the corridor, closing the door carefully behind her. The latch clicked softly into place.

She stood for a moment, one hand resting against the cool stone of the wall, until her eyes adjusted to the new blend of shadows. Then she set off.

In the eating hall, Garii waited for her in the shadows. A soft, dreaming silence lay over the shrine, lulled by the distant swell and ebb of a melodic chant sung over and over by a wakeful priest. Garii turned and, even in the darkness, he bowed, knowing it was she. He crossed the hall to her, bowed again, and led her into the maze of the palace.

Tess was soon lost. Had he abandoned her, she could not have retraced her path. For all she knew, he was leading her in circles. Then they passed through the entry hall, walked down a broad flight of steps, rounded a corner, and she found herself in a room she knew she had not seen before. A pale light washed it, the barest gleam. About the same size as the eating hall, the room had ebony floors and was ringed with two rectangular countertops, one inside the other, freestanding within the room. By this door and next to the door at the far end stood two tall megalithic structures that reminded her abruptly of the transmitter out on the plains.

Garii walked across the hall to the far door. She followed

him, and he slid the panel aside and waited for her to pass through first. She hesitated. Should she trust him? But what choice had she now?

She found herself in a blank, white-walled room that was unfurnished, empty. The walls were as smooth as glass, and it was bitterly cold. She rubbed her arms and turned, only to see Garii removing his knife from his belt. She grabbed for hers—but he pointed the knife at the far wall. A sigh shuddered through the air, and the far wall fell away before them.

A dark gap lay beyond. He gestured. She passed through into the tunnel, and he followed her. The gap shut seamlessly behind them.

The darkness hummed. Putting out her hands, one to each side, she felt walls on either side. Light winked on ahead. A brief chime startled her. She took ten steps forward, and the dark passage opened out into a room. Amazement stopped her in her tracks.

A bank of meter-high machines circled the walls, a gleam of metal in the dull light. By the scattering of red panels on their surface, she could guess they were some kind of computer and environment system for the palace. In front of her, above the bank, hung a huge screen, perhaps five meters square. The screen showed a three-dimensional star chart with a huge territorial area that she did not recognize demarked in red. But she recognized the placement of many of the stars.

Hon Garii crossed beside her and went forward to the counter. He examined a small screen set into the machinery. Leaning forward to press a long bar, he spoke at last.

"Lady Terese, I have done as you commanded and brought you here."

"What is that chart?" she asked.

Without looking up, he touched another bar. "The program now running will overlay the current territorial boundaries of the Empire onto the Mushai's chart."

The Mushai? The traitor? Garii straightened. The screen changed. In the second before he turned, she understood.

A second territory was now demarked in blue. This territory was much smaller than the first, was entirely contained within the first. This territory Tess recognized immediately: the Chapalii Empire, including its subject states. It was a map she knew very well, having seen it often enough in her brother's study when she was a child. But what territory did the first one—that huge expanse of red—demark?

"What information do you desire, Lady Terese?"

She stared as the screen scrolled forward through its data banks. "Leave this on."

A planet, twisting in the void. The continents of Rhui traced in brown. *Da-o Enti*, the screen displayed. Type 2.7.14. Subsector *Diaga 110101*. Property of *Tai-en Mushai*.

Tai-en Mushai. *The* Mushai, the mythical Chapalii traitor who had destroyed the legendary first empire of the Chapalii—an empire ten times the size and power of the one her brother battled. A legend, the Chapalii said, because of course *their* empire had never fallen, could not fall. A legend about the fall of a mythical Golden Age. So they said.

The screen scrolled forward: graphics, shipping charts, energy centers, trade and military tables, statistics, all in the same archaic but recognizable script she had seen on the arch. As the data fed across the screen, she knew it was no legend. Hundreds, perhaps thousands of years ago, the Chapalii Empire had been twice the size of the empire Earth and her League were subject to now. Tai-en Mushai had broken that empire, had gathered together the information necessary to destroy it. And that information was here, in this computer.

Garii stepped forward, full into the backlight generated by the screen. "Lady Terese. We must not linger here. If Cha Ishii should arrive, he will not be pleased to discover you here."

Tess drew her knife but kept it pressed hard against her thigh, hiding it from him. "Do you expect him?"

"No."

"I need a copy of everything in that data bank." Her grip tightened on the knife. This was the real, the final, test of his loyalty to her.

He did not answer for a moment. It was too dim to tell his color, but his face shadowed, as if something were passing above him. "As you will, Tai-endi," he said, so softly that she almost did not hear him.

He turned to the bank under the screen. She approached, close enough to watch him work but not too close. But he did not hesitate. He pressed a small cylinder into a round slot and two red bars on the counter shuddered and changed to orange. On the screen appeared the upright black cylinder that stood for "memory." In such a static culture, evidently some Chapalii standards had not changed over the centuries. Figures scrolled on beneath it. Garii stood silent, hands on the bank, neither looking at her nor speaking. She could not begin to guess what he was thinking.

When three chimes sounded in sequence, he lifted his head. A circle appeared around the cylinder sign on the screen: finished, saved.

"Take it out," Tess whispered, but he was already pulling the cylinder out of the slot. Four Chapalii glyphs had been burned in red onto the cylinder's shiny black surface, but the cylinder was too small and she was too far away to read what they said. In a few seconds, the letters faded to a dim outline, and at last to nothing, dissolved into black.

Garii lifted up the cylinder, pivoted, and, bowing, offered it to her as easily as if the information contained in that cylinder was nothing more than a ship's menu for the week. She resisted the temptation to snatch it out of his hand and instead stepped forward carefully and halted an arm's length from him.

Standing so long in one place, she had forgotten how cold the room was. The floor burned like ice on the soles of her feet. Garii watched her, his skin as pale as frost. He said nothing, but he blinked once, a thin membrane like an inner eyelid flicking down over his opaque eyes. She put out her hand. He gave her the cylinder. It was still warm.

"Now, erase the transaction."

He turned back to the bank and leaned forward to touch bars. She took a step away from him. Taking advantage of his attention being turned elsewhere, she slipped her hand down the neck of her tunic and tucked the cylinder securely into her understrap. Straightened her tunic. Garii continued keying bars in some complex configuration. Above, the screen scrolled more slowly now through its data. As she stood, taking slow breaths in and out, in and out, trying to calm her racing heart, she looked up and caught in her breath again.

Rhui was on the screen. An Imperial catalog number appeared below it. Obscure. So primitive that it would be expensive to exploit. The sector of space it lay in had been assigned to the ducal holdings of Tai-en Mushai. Except that the League Exploratory Survey had discovered Rhui. The Chapalii had never disputed the claim.

The Mushai's private records came up. Points of light appeared like lonely beacons at a few places on the planet. Building sites? Landing points? New figures appeared, humanoid figures, cross-screened with a second planet. Tess drew in her breath sharply. That second planet was as familiar to her as her own hand.

Sites, indeed. Dispersion sites. Seeding sites. The Tai-en Mushai had seeded this planet with human stock. Earth stock. An obscure, barbaric planet, unwanted by the First Empire. What better place to contemplate, breed, and commence rebellion? What better material to do it with?

But the Mushai had died, perhaps in battle. The First Empire must have fallen with him, leaving Rhui to the ancient cycles of human civilization. And his center of operations, well-hidden, had remained lost, untouched until the Second Chapalii Empire—centuries? millennia? later—had ceded this unimportant planet and system to the rebel they wished to placate. Until the Second Empire realized what it had overlooked. How long ago had it been?

Rhui's image turned. A bright rectangle flashed, the site of the great lord's palace: the shrine of Morava. Tess pressed her free hand to her chest, feeling the cylinder where it lay between her breasts. It was no longer than her fingers, not more than three centimeters in diameter. Garii still examined the counter, not watching her.

Tess raised her hand. With the flourish accorded only to those of the very highest rank, she bowed to the Mushai's screen, to the rebel, long dead. With respect, and with ironic gratitude for the gift he had given her, his human heir.

As if in answer, a chime rang from one of the consoles. A bar of white light over the screen clicked on then off. Garii straightened abruptly. Tess heard the scrape of a shoe on the hard floor.

She whirled. The passage behind was so dark that at first she could only see a dim shape against blackness. It stepped forward, thin, almost awkward in its delicate, long-limbed slenderness.

It was Cha Ishii. He held one of their laser-knives in his hand, its bores shining red. It was pointed at her. "This is indeed a surprise, Lady Terese." He inclined his head deferentially but the knife did not waver.

"Did you know I was here?" she asked.

"Yes." He took one step toward her, and his gaze flicked to Hon Garii and then back to her. "I was so informed." His face colored, but in the dimness she could not make out the shade. A moment later she was blinded by a flash of light.

She flung up one arm to cover her eyes. Behind her, something heavy fell to the floor. She felt its impact shudder through her feet. The barest wisp of burning touched her senses and then dissipated into the chill air. She lowered her arm and turned sluggishly, afraid of what she would see.

Garii lay crumpled on the floor in front of the console. A tiny hole pierced his tunic, low in the chest, ringed with an outline of black. Above him, the screen flashed a new image, and then another.

"Doubly a traitor," said Ishii in his flat monotone, startling her out of her stupor. "That he should attempt to better his station by breaking his pledge to my house and attaching himself to you is deplorable but such shameful actions are not, I fear, unknown among the lower classes. But that he should then betray you in turn." For the first time, she heard clear emotion in his voice. "Such infidelity must be so repugnant to any of our rank that I beg your pardon for mistaking his character so much as to allow him this expedition and thus force you into this unfortunate association. I am deeply ashamed."

Tess could only stare at the laser. The thin, dark opening, sparked with red, was now directed at her abdomen. Doroskayev's body had been laid open as if a butcher knife had sliced him wide—how had Garii been killed so neatly? Or was a clean death reserved for one's own kind? Ishii examined the body with a grimace of distaste, as if he had just eaten something offensive. Finally, she found her voice. "*He* alerted you?"

"Indeed, such behavior must be pathological in origin. I had begun to hope that we could perhaps conceal all from you, Lady Terese, and thus finish our journey with no further incident. I regret that you found this room."

"Why did you come to Rhui now, Cha Ishii? Why not earlier? Why did you ever give this system to my brother?"

He took another step toward her. His face reflected the light of the screen, a constant shifting as data scrolled out, the accumulation of a life's work. "I fear that was a significant oversight, which I was sent to rectify. We only recently learned that this palace existed. And now that the duke is conducting ethnographic surveys of the native populations, he is bound to find it eventually. It must not be here to be found. I am sure you understand.''

''But unless you blow it up, he'll find it someday.''

Ishii's lips twisted, as much of a smile as she had ever seen from a Chapalii. ''The Mushai himself encoded a false set of data so that it would appear that this was merely a hunting lodge, an eccentric noble's secret playhouse, seeded with species from other planets for his amusement. Your brother will find nothing to comment upon. The Emperor cannot control every lord's whim, or his far-flung travels. I am only sorry that the Mushai did not live to trigger the false codes into the system.''

Blue from the screen colored Ishii's face, then red, like a sweep of blood. ''How did the Mushai die? How long ago?''

''Time uncounted, years beyond years it was. His ship was blown up in battle. According to my best calculations, we passed its graveyard on our journey here. His death would have been instantaneous.'' He made a clicking noise with his tongue and took another step toward her. He was a body's length away. ''I will do my best, Lady Terese, to make yours painless as well.''

A low humming filled her ears, but it was only the undertone of the machinery, amplified by her fear. He held light that could slice through air, sear flesh. There was not even space here to roll aside.

''Cha Ishii, I outrank you. You cannot kill me.''

He sighed. ''Be assured that I and my family will do penance for your death. I regret its necessity deeply. But you have seen too much. Now, please drop the knife.''

She had been holding it back behind her leg, hoping he would not see it. Now she lifted it. ''We are at an impasse, Ishii. Both armed.''

''I hope you do not believe that I did not know of this dead one's offering to you? I am not so blind as that, Lady Terese. But only my weapon is programmed to kill one of my species.''

While he was talking, she slid her thumb over the hilt: light streaked out. Nothing happened but for a brief echo glittering off the screen.

''You see, Lady Terese, that I have always told you the

truth." He blinked, his inner eyelids flicking down and up.
The pistol lowered slightly, like a reprieve. "Violence is
such an inelegant transaction. Perhaps we could bribe you."
Was it her imagination or had his voice taken on a coaxing
tone? "Leave this palace, Lady Terese. Forget what you
have seen. Forget this journey. And we will take Bakhtiian
off planet with us. We will give him the treatments that will
make him live one hundred of your years, and you can have
him." He lowered the pistol even further, gaze hard on her
as if he was trying to measure some attribute in her character. "Does that tempt you?"

Tempt her? To have Ilya for a hundred years. To show
him the stars.

The stars, where the jaran, a name that could—that
would—resonate across a continent, meant nothing. *Lord,
it would kill him.*

The pistol rested at Ishii's side, but his finger still touched
the firing lever.

"I fear, Cha Ishii, that you will make me laugh. Of
course, he might make a sensation for a time, which would
be diverting enough, I suppose, but when it wore off, I
would have to dispose of him. That would be tiresome."
She took a step toward him and casually rested her hand on
her saber. His hand did not move. "But I think you will
find that there are other commodities that might persuade
me."

"Other commodities?" A flash of many lights on his face
as the screen changed, then a sick, brilliant white. "I do
regret this hasty, slovenly solution, Lady Terese, for you
would do so very well at court. But I am not a fool. The
sister of a mushai, a traitor, cannot be bribed." He raised
the pistol to point straight at her heart. "Please remove your
belt and the weapons."

Her hands shook. She slipped the tongue of her belt free
of the buckle and took another step toward him. The harsh
light had drained all color from his face. He looked as if
his skin were painted on. "The duke knows I am on this
planet. I left him a message. A letter." Her voice broke. It
was her last play. "You will be ruined."

"Unfortunately, the message to your brother was destroyed. The duke never received any letter from you. I
must assume that he believes you still on Earth. There is no
reason to trace you here." His finger—

She lashed out with her hand, the instantaneous reaction of cold fear. The buckle of the belt smashed into his hand. He cried out. The shot seared into a bulk of metal, a high, harmless crack. She whipped the belt back. The hard metal caught his fingers. His knife fell to the floor. Tess kicked it away. It skittered across the smooth surface and slid under Garii's slumped body.

The impetus of her kick brought her forward, and she plunged into Cha Ishii. Without even thinking, she knifed him in the abdomen. He screamed and fell.

Caught in his falling, she lost her balance and came down with her knees in his stomach. He made a sound, a cry. She scrambled forward, pulling out the knife, tripping on the belt, stumbling, getting up. Then she was in the passage, slipping on the smooth floor, hitting her knee hard as she went down, catching herself one-handed, pushing up. She got her balance and drew her saber, holding the belt in her other hand. Glanced back. Ishii was gasping as he struggled to get up. She ran.

Her hand, thrust in front of her, came up against sheer wall. It fell away. She tumbled out into the empty, white room. As the door slid back into place behind her, she stuck the knife into the crack. The door shut with a sharp grinding noise, not quite closed. She shoved at it. It did not move.

"Jammed. Please, God, jammed." She ran to the other door, paused there, trying to stop breathing so loudly. A tear snaked down her cheek to dissolve, warm and salty, on her lips. The door was shut. She gave it a gentle push, and it slid open a handsbreadth. She saw nothing, heard no sound at all from the chamber beyond. She slipped into the room with her saber preceding her. The two megaliths framed the doorway like sentinels at a tomb. A scraping noise sounded behind her. She ran.

She got no farther than six steps. A figure emerged from a megalith. Like the strike of a snake, a hand gripped her right wrist, twisting it so her saber fell, a brilliant clatter on the floor, and pulled her in. An arm closed around her back. Her hands were trapped, one in back, one in front of her, her legs constrained by space. Her hair rested against a head. Head. Neck. Throat. She ducked her head, got it under the chin, and pushed up; lunged with her teeth for the throat.

It happened so fast that she only knew that both her arms were jerked painfully up behind her back. A hand locked on her chin, holding her head bowed back, fingers pressed tight on her jaw. His face held a breath away from hers.

"Try that again," he said, his eyes two points of blackness, "and I'll have to—" Abruptly, he jerked her chin to one side, as if he could not stand to look at her. His beard tickled her cheek.

"Oh, God," said Tess. She would have fallen if he had not been holding her.

"By the gods." Bakhtiian looked past her to her saber, a gleam on the ebony floor. "I think it is time for you to tell me the truth."

CHAPTER TWENTY-FOUR

"To protect it within your silent bosom."
—EMPEDOCLES OF AGRAGAS

He did not let go of her until they were inside the room that the priests had given him to sleep in. She was panting, dizzy from the pace he had set, the sudden halts, the fear of every blind corner. Her wrist ached where he held her. When he released her, she staggered backward. The bed frame caught her knees and she half-fell to the hard mattress. All of her breath sighed out of her. She sank back against the wall and rested her face in her open hands. Light flickered. She lifted her head. He set a candle on the little table midway along the wall.

His stare was so hard that she looked down. "What, did he try to kill you?" he said finally, as if he had thought of doing it once or twice. 'If you will be caught spying, then you must expect to suffer the consequences."

She stared stupidly at him. Half a meter to the right and the shot would have burned through her.

"I could not sleep," said Ilya at last. "I saw you meet the pilgrim called Garii and go with him. He took you into the white room, but when I looked inside, you had vanished. Then Ishii came and went inside, yet the room remained empty—to my sight, at least. And you came out, running as if demons were after you. There is blood on your hand, by the way. Where did you go?"

There was blood on her hand. She wiped her face frantically but only the barest smear came off. There was not much, after all: a pale stripe across her knuckles and a few drops darkening her sleeve.

"You have done violence in the shrine," he said.

Her head snapped up. "No! He tried to kill me. It was self-defense, damn you. I didn't kill him. God, he killed Garii. He would have *killed* me!"

"Where did all this take place?"

"There's a secret room, a secret door. Don't you have anything I can clean this off with? It stings."

He took a step toward her. She jerked up, but he was only turning to open the door. He went out. She was suddenly seized by a paralyzing terror: what if he had gone to find Ishii? Or Mother Avdotya? A hand rattled at the door—but it was Ilya. He tossed her a damp cloth and resumed his stance against the door, regarding her with his unrelenting gaze. She scrubbed at her hand and her cheek and then sat, staring at the rag until finally she dropped it on the floor next to his bed.

"You have no farther to retreat," said Bakhtiian, "and I want an explanation." The candlelight threw his shadow high up on the wall, arching over onto the ceiling, so that it seemed to lower down on her like the approach of a storm. "You had better be honest with me, because I am—completely—out of patience with you."

"I can't tell you."

"You can't tell me! The penalty for violence—"

"You aren't listening to me!" She pushed up to her feet. "He tried to—" Inside her shirt, the cylinder slipped down. She grabbed at her side.

"Tess!" he cried, starting forward. "He hurt you—"

"No." She stepped back, half up onto the bed.

Ilya stopped short. "Let me see."

"No."

He walked forward. She backed up along the bed, standing on the mattress, until he had cornered her.

His shadow seemed to take up an entire wall. Under her hand, through her shirt, the cylinder felt hard and cold. He looked at her hand, cupped at her waist. Slowly he placed one foot up on the bed and, with a slight grimace, pushed up with the other, so that he, too, was standing on the bed. He placed a hand on either side of her, trapping her.

"What do you have?"

The implacability of his voice terrified her. "I can't show you."

"You will."

Finally, she lowered her head in acquiescence. He stepped

down. Too quickly, this time; he winced and with a marked limp moved back to the middle of the room.

"Oh, God," she said under her breath. This was it. All her efforts for nothing: now he would know, and she could not begin to imagine what the knowledge would do to him.

She turned into the corner and retrieved the cylinder. With it in her hand, she stepped down from the bed and handed it to him.

He took it to the candle. "I see no writing. Is this some holy relic?"

She felt impelled to smile, thinking of what Ishii had said about archaeology. "Yes, the relic of a prince who is long since dead."

He turned it in the light as if its black sheen fascinated him. "Whom ought this to belong to?"

"That depends on which one of us you talk to. Myself or Ishii."

"Why do you want it?"

"My brother wants it. It represents—I can't explain in a few words. Power and knowledge."

"Why should your brother have it? It is the pilgrims, after all, who have come on this journey for holy purposes."

"For *their* purposes."

"Which are?"

"Bad ones."

"While your brother's are good? That is very easy, my wife, but rarely true." She winced at his cutting tone. "Well?"

"How long do you want the explanation to be?" She rubbed at her eyes with her palms, then lowered them, taking in resolve with a deep breath. "Ilya. The khepellis will use that relic to enslave my people. Already they control most of the trade that enriches Jeds. And many other cities. But if my brother gets that relic, then he can work to free all those the khepelli have subjugated. Not just for his own sake. You have to believe me. He isn't—his work is for other people not for himself."

Her gaze on him worked like a fire. He took a step toward her, away from the table. Framed by light and shadow, he seemed to Tess a man in some half-remembered legend, a force in and of himself, caught between the new world and the old. "How could you read the inscription on the arch?"

"I have learned—" She broke off.

"You have learned the tongue the khepelli speak. You said it was their writing. Last night, after—" He jerked his gaze away from her suddenly, staring down at the lines of wax that laced a tangled pattern around the base of the candle.

"Last night," he began again, "I went to the sacred fountain to—to reflect. But two of the pilgrims were in the room. They did not see me, but I saw them drink from the basin. Deeply. It did not harm them, Tess. They aren't like us. I have always known that—only a blind man would not see it—but this. . . . The water did not poison them. They aren't—" He hesitated, as if once said, the words would alter his world forever.

Which they would. She could not look at him, stared instead at the candle burning down. Soon its flame would fail, having consumed everything that it could feed on. *They aren't from this planet.*

"They aren't human," he said. "There are old stories about the ancient ones who lived here long ago, who were driven away by war or drought or sickness, or by us—those who are women and men, jaran and khaja both—never to be seen again. I think those stories are true. I think they fled away across the seas and founded a kingdom in lands far from here. And now they've come back to find what they left behind. Am I right? Did their ancestors build this place?"

In the silence she heard the clack of twigs as the wind stirred in the garden outside. "Yes."

"And as they traded and grew strong, your brother must have sent you to watch them."

"Not precisely, but . . ." She trailed off, shaking her head.

"And you followed them here, to discover—you didn't know either, did you? That they had once lived and ruled here."

"No," she said, a hoarse whisper. "No. We did not know."

"They believe they have some right to this land?"

"I don't know." But the opening leapt full into her mind. "But if my brother gets this relic, then he will ensure that they never exploit these lands. Jaran lands. They will be forced into treaties. They will trade, or at least their trade will be circumscribed, that is—"

"You are either lying to me," he said, "or else you haven't the faintest idea what you're talking about. What will your brother do with this relic? How can his having it help him in his good purposes?"

"I don't know *how* he will use it, not to tell you details. Except that it will help him disrupt their trade. Help him keep them from ever claiming these lands, if that is their intent. Because it is proof entire that they did indeed once reside here."

He lifted the cylinder, extending his arm so that the black shape marked the distance between them. As it did. How could she not have seen it before? He was bound by his world, bound still to Newton's universe, which, like the idea of the Chapalii being *not* human, was wildly revolutionary to him. Farther than that—farther than that did not even exist for him. To him, Rhui *was* the universe.

"If I agree to help you," he said, "what guarantee do you offer me that your actions, and mine in aiding you, will not harm my people? Will not prevent them from fulfilling their destiny?"

She crossed to him, halting a bare arm's length away from him. He was not so much taller than she as she had at times thought. "Ilya," she began, and she faltered. Meeting his gaze, she knew without a doubt that if she kissed him now, used passion, used her love for him as her guarantee, he would help her. But it would be no better than a weapon used to get what she wanted. As he had used her ignorance to make her his wife.

"Ilya. We have clasped friends, and I have given my honor into your hands. That is *my* guarantee. And by the honor you gave into mine, my right to ask your aid and protection."

The room was still, like the hush before dawn, only two motionless figures in the fading glow of the candle.

"Damn you." He jerked his gaze away from her, staring into the shadowed corner. "By my honor," he murmured, as if to the gods themselves. As if he wished with all his heart that she had used any other argument but that.

She simply breathed, watching him, and the wind sighed and called outside. She could not read the expression on his face.

"Then you will help me?" she asked at last in a low voice.

He met her gaze. "I will not let them kill you," he said with such simplicity that she knew that it was true. "I will get you to the coast and safe on a ship for Jeds. Will you let me keep this until then?" He turned the cylinder so that it winked in the candlelight. "Only to keep it safe. By your honor and mine."

"Yes. By that guarantee, I trust you."

"By my honor," he said, so quietly that she scarcely heard it, "but not as my wife." The he shook his head, as if he had not meant to say it, or her to hear it. "You look exhausted. I think it would be best if you didn't go back to your room tonight." He hesitated, then gestured to his bed. "No one will remark on your sleeping in the same room as your husband."

She flushed, and her gaze strayed to the bed. She saw how neatly he had folded his blankets at the foot, how carefully he had hung his saddlebags over the endpost. Only a scrap of material sticking out from the opening suggested untidiness: a shirtsleeve, with a needle pierced through it, as if he had been interrupted in the middle of embroidery.

She simply nodded, afraid to venture words.

He picked up the candle. Darkness moved around him as he carried it to the door.

"But you must sleep—" she protested, seeing that he meant to leave.

"Someone must guard you."

"Ilya. . . ." She was not sure what she wanted to say to him. She was not sure what she wanted at all, except that, right now, she wanted him.

He blew out the candle abruptly, flooding her in darkness. The door opened and closed, and then the *snick* of the latch sounded as it fell into place outside.

She lay down on the bed and pulled the blankets up over her. The cloth felt coarse against her skin, scented of grass and the summer earth. He had lain under these blankets. She wrapped a corner of one under her, so that her cheek lay against it, and with that comfort, she slept.

* * *

Storm clouds raced in over the mud flats of Odys Massif. Charles Soerensen stood in the wind and the hard slap of rain, out on his balcony. Beyond, at the far towers of Odys Port, a ship had landed. Suzanne was on that ship, back from Paladia Major without Tess, without any indication that Tess had been on the *Oshaki* after it had left the Delta Pavonis system.

But Suzanne had not come back alone.

Charles turned and walked back inside. Jamsetji sat at Charles's desk, manipulating graphs in the air above the flat screen. On the flat surface, the net burrowers dredged deep into the datanet, seeking any scrap of information on Chapalii protocol in the matter of transfers of fealty. Almost every tunnel led back, like a blind maze, to the hand of the Yaochalii, the emperor. *By the emperor's hand, thus will it be granted.*

Jamsetji glanced up at Charles and shook his head but otherwise did not stir. A chime shattered their silence. The transparent wall sealed down across the balcony behind Charles. Jamsetji rose and moved aside so Charles could sit down at his desk.

A seam in the tiled wall peeled open, and Suzanne walked in, followed by four Chapalii. One was Hon Echido, flushed blue with distress. Two were also of the merchant class, by their robes, but they wore the wrist and neck torque of the Office of Protocol. And the fourth Chapalii—

Charles almost stood up. As quickly, he decided against it. "Tai-en," he said, and inclined his head the merest degree, acknowledging an equal.

"Tai Charles," said the duke. He was tall, awkwardly thin, and his skin was dead white.

Suzanne bowed to the precise degree. "Tai Charles," she said in Anglais, "this is the Tai-en Naroshi Toraokii. He has come from Chapal with these officers from Protocol to arraign this fugitive member of the family Keinaba, whose name has been stained with dishonor and so must vanish from the sight of the emperor."

Charles rose because he judged that it was now polite to do so, and answer enough to Suzanne's words.

The Tai-en Naroshi examined the chamber, the tiled wall, the sweep of balcony, the sheen of the desktop, and, briefly, the still, silent figure of Jamsetji, waiting quietly at Charles's right. Then he inclined his head toward Charles as to an equal, and spoke.

When he was finished, Suzanne translated. "The Tai-en states that if his honored peer desires a translation circuit to be installed, he can arrange for such, allowing the females of his house to return to their scholarly studies without having to waste their talents and valuable time translating mere words.''

''My honored peer is generous. I will consider his offer with great pleasure.''

Suzanne's mouth quirked up, not into a smile, not quite, and she repeated his words to Naroshi. What he thought of them it was impossible to tell. Colors tinted the skin of the two Protocol officers. Echido was still flushed blue. Naroshi remained as pale as ice. He spoke again.

''The Tai-en states that he wishes to relieve his honored peer of the burden of the presence of this ke, this low one.'' Suzanne glanced at Echido. The merchant clutched his hands together, saying nothing with them at all. ''The rite of extinction has been completed for all of the possessions of the princely house that no longer exists, except for Keinaba. The emperor is restless that this matter remains unresolved. Thus, peace cannot be achieved until this ke is returned and his name obliterated with his family's.''

''It is indeed benevolent of my honored peer to consider taking this burden from me.'' Charles waited while Suzanne translated, and then he looked directly at the two Protocol Officers. ''Did Keinaba take part in the offense that has tainted all who owed allegiance to that princely house?''

Naroshi blinked, but that was his only reaction.

Both officers bowed. One spoke at length, and Suzanne translated, but in Ophiuchi-Sei-ah-nai. ''Charles, he basically says that whatever breach of protocol, whatever conspiracy, the prince and dukes and lords were involved in went no lower than that. But, of course, the merchants and all of their stewards and artisans are dishonored by the association. Everything, all their wealth, all their holdings, will revert to the emperor to be dispensed back by him to whatever princes he favors right now.''

''I did a wee bit of checking,'' said Jamsetji in a low voice, in the same language. ''It cleared with what we thought. Given the information we have and our ability to calculate their markers of wealth, that princely house and holdings was the richest, or among the richest, in the empire.''

''Not least because of Keinaba,'' replied Charles, also in Ophiuchi-Sei. ''Yet I have a dispensation from the emperor's hand. Yes, I see. I wonder if this is a coincidence or a test?'' But his eyes had lit already. It had been too long since he had faced a real challenge.

In Anglais, he said, ''Tell my honored peer that I have taken in the loyalty of Keinaba.'' Suzanne translated.

The Protocol officers flushed a sickly hue of violet. Echido paled, and his hands rewove themselves into Merchant's Bounty.

Not a flicker of color tainted Naroshi's skin. His chin tilted the slightest degree before he spoke.

''The Tai-en states that he cannot act on this matter, merely do as his duty instructs: that is, return the merchant in question to the emperor. If his honored peer wishes to accompany him so as to bring this matter forward to the emperor's discretion, he would be pleased to offer him passage on his ship back to Chapal.''

''My honored peer is munificent. I accept and will be pleased to accompany him to Chapal.''

Naroshi inclined his head. He was gratified at the Tai-en's acceptance. His skin stayed white. They exchanged a few more compliments, a few last pleasantries, and then Naroshi took his leave. The Protocol officers begged leave to follow him, and Echido bowed as servant to master, to Charles, and accepted their escort. His skin was paler than theirs, as if he felt secure that he and his family would be spared. It was still not as dead pale as the duke's had been. They left the room to silence.

''Goddess in Heaven and Earth,'' swore Suzanne. ''What the hell did you do that for?''

''I think the time is right,'' said Charles softly. ''I think it is something I had better do. It gives us a foothold in the cliff, rather than that bare toe's width of ledge we're clinging to now. What do you make of Naroshi? Have I made an enemy or an ally in that one? My God, he had exceptional facial control. Jamsetji, dig up everything you can about the Toraokii dukedom.'' Charles moved to one side so that Jamsetji could sit down at his desk.

''But, Charles.'' Suzanne marched over to the desk and set her palms down on it, leaning on them, glaring up into his face. ''What about Tess?''

''Suzanne, what can I do? If she's on Rhui, Marco can find her.''

''What if she's in danger? If she's injured? Captured? Being held prisoner? What if she's dead?''

"Must I remind you that in bitter political terms Tess is expendable? Chapalii law allows for me to adopt an heir, who will then be as legal as an heir of my blood. It's been suggested by the emperor himself, in order that I might have a proper male heir."

"We're not talking political terms, Charles. We're talking about your sister."

"Suzanne, you may take it for granted that I love my sister." He kept his voice as even as a Chapalii voice, revealing nothing. "You may be sure that if she comes to harm through Chapalii machinations, those responsible will suffer for it. *If* I have the power to act against them. But I can do nothing for her here. We must grasp the opportunity that presents itself. Keinaba is rich. Through their shipping we will have ties and access to every port and every planet and every system, and, by God, every back door that merchants squeeze through, in imperial space. We can't afford to lose that chance."

Suzanne pushed herself up and spun away to walk out onto the balcony. The transparent wall peeled away to allow her access, and shut behind her, to protect the office from the beating rain and the skirling wind. The tide was out. The tules lay flat against the muddy shallows, pressed down by the gale. Clouds roiled above, dark and turbulent.

Charles watched her for a moment, and one moment only, and then he turned and walked to the side room to pack what few things he needed for the journey. The seal stood open between the office and the little chamber.

"Richard and Tomaszio can arrange whatever formal items I'll need," said Charles over his shoulder. "And a message to Cara, in Jeds, to let her know what's happened. She can forward anything to Marco. He'll have to act on his own for now."

Jamsetji snorted. "Always does, that one," he said to the air. "Rich and Tomas will go with you, as always. Who else?"

"Suzanne, of course. I need her. That's all. If this falls out as I hope, we'll have a whole Chapalii merchant house at our disposal. My God, think of it, Jamsetji. Think what we can do with that." He went in to the efficiency, and the wall sealed shut behind him.

Jamsetji grinned at the first trickle of information scrolling up on the desk. "Maybe the long haul ain't going to be so damned long."

Suzanne came in from the balcony, soaked and still angry. "Sweet Goddess, what a storm." She glared at Jamsetji. "What are you smiling about? What if Tess is down on Rhui in the middle of a storm like that?"

"You worry too much, young woman. And the truth is," he dropped his voice to a whisper, "you don't trust her any better than her own brother does. Not really. Not to take care of herself. But I'm betting she can."

"Can take care of herself, or find someone to take care of her? Well, I cursed well hope you're right." Suzanne cast one last, reproachful glance toward Charles, who emerged from the efficiency with his hands full of bottles and bits. "I'll go get ready," she said sourly, and stalked away to the far wall. The tiling peeled open to let her through.

* * *

A soft knock on the door woke Tess. She started up. Sun shone in through the window and she knew it was late, midmorning, perhaps. She grabbed for her saber as the door opened, but it was only Vladimir.

"Good morning," she said, suddenly embarrassed to be found sleeping in Ilya's bed.

He did not look at her. "Here's some food and water." He set a tray down on the table and retreated to the door.

"Thank you." His sullen expression did not alter. "Vladimir, where is Bakhtiian?"

His gaze roamed the chamber, coming to rest finally on Ilya's saddlebags, slung casually over the endpost. "He'll be back. I'll wait outside until you're ready to go wash." He left.

She straightened her clothing and put on her boots and then ate and drank a little, and went to the door. It opened before she reached it, and Vladimir gestured her outside.

She hesitated. "But—"

"It's safe. Mother Avdotya has taken the khepellis to the sacred pool, with ten of the jahar for escort. Come on." He sounded peevish as he said it.

Probably, Tess thought, as she followed him to the chamber with the hot springs, he wished that Ishii had managed to kill her. It was impossible to truly enjoy the luxury of the hot springs but equally impossible not to linger a little too long. Vladimir finally tapped impatiently on the door, and she dried off hurriedly and dressed.

Back in the room, Vladimir paused by the door. "Are you really going back to Jheds?" he asked.

"Yes."

He looked so comically relieved that she chuckled. "You may laugh," he said with unexpected fury. "You have family. You have a place given to you. Ilya is all I have. Do you think a girl like Elena wants an orphan for a husband?"

"I'm an orphan, too, Vladimir. My parents died over twelve years ago. But it's true, I do have a brother."

"Oh, the one in Jheds. What do I care about Jheds? I have been riding with the tribe for two years now. I'm still nothing but an orphan to them. Ilya's pet. But you—you were there ten days, and Mother Orzhekov gifted you her own daughter's tent."

Voices sounded from the hall. Vladimir had been red; now he turned white. The door opened, and Bakhtiian appeared.

"Leave us," he said. Vladimir stared straight into Tess's eyes, his mouth a bitter line. "Vladi," said Ilya.

The young man glanced at Ilya and stalked out of the room, shoulders taut. Ilya raised his eyebrows, shrugged, and walked over to the table to sit on its edge. One booted leg dangled elegantly.

Then his reinforcements arrived. The usual ones, of course: Josef promptly sat down on the floor, Niko sat beside Tess on the bed, and Tasha shut the door behind him and stood blocking it. Tess blushed.

"Well," said Ilya, and she realized that he was a little embarrassed by this situation as well.

Niko rescued them. "One of the khepelli is indeed missing. We can find no trace of him."

"The one missing," said Ilya, taking charge again, "is the one you met last night. The same one you met with in the garden yesterday."

"Ishii killed him." Tess felt the force of all their gazes on her.

"For betraying his own kind?"

"Yes. No. Yes, for breaking his loyalty to Ishii, but really, he killed him for then betraying me in turn. It was Garii who alerted Ishii that we had gone—" She shrugged.

"To this secret room which I could not find, even last

night when I returned there. I see. This gives me rather more respect for Lord Ishii. One betrayal might betoken a real change of heart, but two—'' All four men shook their heads. ''Mother Avdotya also noticed the missing pilgrim but she will not pursue those who are not bound by the laws of the jaran. There, it seems, the matter ends.''

''But what about Tess?'' asked Niko. ''If Ishii would murder one of his own men, then I must believe that she is truly in danger as well.''

''Oh, I don't doubt it.'' Ilya's tone was slightly mocking. ''I think we will have to seek Veselov's aid.''

''Veselov!'' This from Tasha.

''To separate Soerensen from the pilgrims means we must split the jahar. Obviously, with khaja lands to ride through, and Dmitri Mikhailov still somewhere behind us, that would be idiotic. I propose we leave Tess and a few of the riders here at the shrine, where it is safe, and with the rest ride to Veselov's tribe and ask Veselov to send a portion of his jahar to escort her to the coast. We will ride ahead with the khepellis, see them to their ship, collect our horses, and wait for the others there.''

''What if the khepelli decide to kill all of you?'' Tess asked.

''Is this relic, and your death, so valuable to them?''

''It might be.''

He smiled. ''That is why you will write a letter to your brother that explains—briefly—the situation. As soon as it is done, Josef will ride ahead. With three horses, he will make good time.''

''Won't that be dangerous?''

Josef grinned. ''I've done rasher things in my youth. I speak the khaja tongues well enough to get by. And I think I am a good judge of men's hearts.''

''I suppose that is why you joined up with Bakhtiian?''

All four men laughed.

''Did Yuri tell you that he is the only man in my jahar not born or married into our tribe?'' Ilya asked. ''Well, I cannot answer to that accusation.'' He tilted his head to one side, smiling, a surprisingly youthful, sweet expression. It made her so uncomfortable that she stood up and gazed out the window. He coughed. The other men shifted. ''In any case,'' he said finally, ''if we're all killed, at least your brother will know of it.''

Through the window she saw part of the garden, thick lines of bushes, a white statue half-hidden behind a tree. It was quiet. From somewhere in the distance she heard the sound of singing.

"Who will stay?" asked Niko.

"Yuri and Mikhal," said Ilya immediately. "Two more, I think. Konstans, perhaps."

"Kirill," said Josef. "That is my recommendation."

There was a silence. Tess could not bring herself to turn around.

"Mine, too," said Tasha. "You must leave someone who can take command of whichever part of Veselov's jahar will be sent."

"Then you, Tadheus," said Ilya stiffly.

"Ilya," said Niko, "you must eventually give Kirill the responsibility he deserves."

A longer silence. Outside, a man's voice shouted, a cheerful yell, followed by women's laughter.

"Very well. Kirill, Konstans, Yuri, and Mikhal."

"I'll go prepare, then," said Josef. Tasha made some similar excuse, and Niko left after them.

She turned. Ilya still sat on the table. He was looking at his hands. He glanced up at her.

"You'll need paper." He crossed the room to rummage in his saddlebags, lifting out a tube of soft cloth and the leather-bound Newton.

"Ilya—" she began, but he took them back to the table and set them down. Unwrapping the cloth, he revealed a quill and a tightly sealed pot of ink. Then he slipped his knife out of its sheath and turned the Newton open to the flyleaf. She could not bear to watch. In a moment, he said, "Would you like me to wait outside?"

"No." She came over to the table. He retreated to the bed with the precious book and sat cradling it in his hands while she bent down to compose the letter.

Charles. I am stranded on Rhui but am currently safe. The Chapalii have sent a clandestine expedition to Rhui which I stumbled across and followed: the Tai-en Mushai— yes, that one—once possessed this planet, and he left a palace and computer banks which contain all the information he gathered which led to the downfall of the First Empire. It really happened! I now possess in storage the contents of his files. I am traveling for Jeds now, but the Chapalii are

still a threat to me. If something should happen to me, if
you should receive this letter and I do not arrive in Jeds
from the north by ship within a month or at most two, then
look for the people called the jaran, *who live on the northern*
plains, and specifically for a man named Ilyakoria Bakh-
tiian. They have sheltered me. Here she hesitated, and then
simply signed her name.

She stood, blew on the fine, marbled paper now covered
with her scrawl, and offered it to him. He took it.

"I will keep the relic until we meet at the coast." He
gathered up his quill and ink, packed everything neatly away
into his saddlebags, and swung the packs onto the table. He
did not look at her. She did not look at him.

"What will you tell the pilgrims?" she asked finally.
"Won't they be suspicious? I don't want you to lose your
horses."

"I'll tell them—" He paused. An odd note to his voice
made her look up at him. Seeing her gaze, he smiled sardonically. "I'll tell them that you married me and are now
my wife and so will be staying here."

"Don't tell them that!" He blinked away from her vehemence, his expression shuttered. "I didn't mean. . . . "
How could she explain that the Chapalii would take such an
explanation very seriously indeed, and that it would cause
enormous, negative repercussions for Charles. "I just meant
because marriage is not a light thing for the khepellis, that—"

"Do you think it is a light thing for jaran?" he demanded. "Don't insult me above everything else."

"I only meant that *my* marriage, because of who I am,
would be taken very seriously. . . ." She broke off.

"And I am of so little importance to the Prince and these
khepellis that *my* marriage is of no account at all? Except,
of course, that I married *you.*"

Which was true, of course. She flushed. "Damn it, Ilya.
I never said that."

He smiled slightly. "Very well, then I will tell Lord Ishii
that I don't trust you, that you have broken the laws of our
tribe, and I have left you behind under guard until I can get
them safely onto ship and return to deal with you later."
He said it with great satisfaction.

"Very well," she echoed, and then, because there was
nothing more to say, said nothing. Neither did he speak.

They stood a body's length apart, the table between them. She dropped her gaze to stare at the tiny striations in the floorboards, flowing dark into light, some blending one into the next, some utterly separate. They stood in this manner for so long that she began to wish that he would do anything, anything but stand there silently and look at her.

At last he swung his saddlebags up onto his shoulders and moved to the door. She looked up. He paused with his hand on the latch. "Fare well, my wife," he said softly.

"Fare well," she murmured. Then he was gone. As if she had been pulled along behind, she went to the door and laid her head against the wood. What would she say to him when they met again at the coast? Twenty-five days seemed like an eternity.

From outside came the noise of horses, that familiar ring and call of leaving that she had grown so accustomed to, had even come to love. Leaving, traveling, arriving; always moving and yet, because your life and family journeyed with you, always staying in the same place. She hurried to the window and stood up on the bed to look out just in time to see riders, too far away to make out as individuals, mass and start forward away along a path that soon took them into the woods and out of her sight. But she stood still, long after sight and sound of them had faded, and stared out onto the cool of midday and the quiet oasis of the park.

A scratch at the door. She jumped down from the bed, but it was only Yuri.

"Tess." He hugged her. Pulling back, he examined her face. "Well," he said, "it's no use staying shut up in here. It's a beautiful day outside. Come on. Have you seen the sacred pool yet?"

She had not. So they rode there, the four riders, herself, and Yeliana, and had a little picnic. The sacred pool was really nothing more than a circular marble pool surrounded by pillars, sited in a lovely meadow. A few late-blooming bushes added romance to the setting. The men flirted charmingly with Yeliana, who was delighted to have so many good-looking young riders to practice on.

"There's only Andrey, who is young," she whispered to Tess, "and I've never liked him. He came here five years past to become a priest, but I think it was just because he's so ugly and sour-faced that none of the women wanted him. All the others are as old as the hills. I was sorry when Vladi left.'' Then she smiled at something Konstans said and asked him about his wife and baby.

Tess stood and walked over to the edge of the pool, where Kirill stood alone, watching the water ripple in the sunlight. ''You're very quiet today.''

''Did you ask Bakhtiian to leave me in charge?'' he asked.

''No. Josef and Tasha and Niko did.''

His face lit. ''Did they? By the gods.'' His posture shifted, and he looked very pleased with the world. He grinned. ''Meet me here tonight, my heart, and I will show you how this pool has captured the moon.''

''Kirill.'' She faltered, and set her lips for courage, and looked at him.

''You love him,'' he said.

''Yes.''

''So much.''

''Yes.''

His expression was hard to read, compounded half of resignation and half of—something else. ''But Tess, you won't even lie with him. Isn't that cruel?''

''For me or for him?''

''For him, of course. What you do to yourself is your own business, although I must say—''

''I don't believe that *you* would scold me for that.''

''I don't *hate* Ilya, Tess, or wish him ill. I never have, even if I might envy him now for winning your love.''

''But I love you, too, Kirill.''

''Yes. You gifted me with your love, but you gifted him with your heart.''

''Kirill.''

''Oh, Tess. Don't cry, my heart. It doesn't matter. It was a fair race. I don't begrudge him winning it, and I don't blame you for choosing him.''

''I'm not choosing him. I'm going back to Jeds. And would you stop being so damned noble?''

He laughed shakily. ''All right,'' he said violently. ''The truth is, I'd like to murder him. Slowly. Strangle him, maybe, or better yet—no, that's an ill-bred thing to say in front of a woman.''

She smiled and wiped a tear from her cheek. ''That's better.''

''I accept what I must, Tess. What other choice do I

have?'' He frowned and then left her to walk back to the others.

She remained by the pond. After a while Yuri came to join her. "What were you and Kirill talking about?"

She shrugged.

"You don't want to go back to Jeds, do you?"

"What other choice do I have?" she asked.

"Well, *I* think—"

"Yuri, do you want to get thrown in the pond?"

"Certainly I do. What do you think?" He grinned. "I want to go back to the shrine. It's getting dark, and I'm hungry. Are you coming?"

"Bakhtiian never accepts his circumstances," she said in a low voice. "He changes them."

"What did you say?"

"Nothing, Yuri. I'm coming."

The weather remained fair for the next six days. They achieved a kind of equilibrium: in the mornings, Kirill insisted on a grueling practice session with saber, with the permission of Mother Avdotya, of course, and many of the male priests and even Yeliana came to watch. In the afternoons, some combination, always Tess and Yuri, often Kirill, and sometimes Mikhal and Konstans, would go riding in the great park that surrounded the shrine. Every night, Tess and Yeliana took a torch and a few candles and sneaked down to the hot springs to luxuriate there for a lazy, glorious hour.

The fifth night, Yeliana said out of the dark waters: "I will go with you."

"Go with me? Where?" asked Tess.

"Go with you when you leave here."

"But I can't take you to Jeds."

"Oh, I don't want to go across the seas. But you rode with the men. Why shouldn't I? I always envied Vladi that he left here. I never went because there was no place for me to go. I have no tent, no mother or aunt to gift me one. It is easier for a man. If he distinguishes himself in battle, then a woman might not set her brothers on him if he marked her. And there, he has a place in a tribe. But if I could learn to fight—"

"But, Yeliana—"

"You did it. Are you saying other women cannot?"

"No, but—"

"I hate it here," she said without heat, simply as a fact. "I'm young enough. I can learn."

"Well," said Tess slowly, "you can go where Vladimir went—to Bakhalo's jahar-ledest. If he'll take you. I have an old saber I can give you. It isn't a very good one, but—"

"A saber!" Yeliana's excitement manifested itself in muffled splashing at her end of the baths. "My own saber!"

What have I started? Tess thought, and sighed.

The next morning, Yeliana appeared again at practice and Tess politely asked Kirill to show the girl the most basic strokes. Kirill raised his eyebrows, but he complied.

"Do you know what I think?" said Yuri at midday, when they sat resting under a tree. "I think she must be Vladi's sister by the same parents."

"Why? They don't look so much alike."

"No, but for the color of their hair and eyes. And she's rather tall for a girl. But did you see her with those cuts? Oh, she's very rough, and very new, but there's a certain grace, a certain touch for the blade. . . . I'll never have it, no matter how many years I practice."

"You're not the hardest worker at saber, Yuri."

"That's true, but even if I were—it's not in me."

"No." She smiled and settled her arm around his shoulders. "You have other gifts."

"Yes, and whenever women say that, it's never a compliment."

Movement erupted at the distant doors that led into the shrine. A moment later, Mikhal came running up to them.

"Riders, coming in," he said, and ran off again.

Tess and Yuri scrambled to their feet and followed him.

"Look!" cried Yuri. "It's Petya!"

It was a small group—only eight young riders—but merry as they greeted the four men from Bakhtiian's jahar. But Tess hung back. She could only watch, and after a few moments, even that was too much. She fled into the park and walked, just walked, out into the woods.

Midday slid into afternoon. Finally, she knew she had come far enough—except that nowhere would be far enough—and she turned back. The first shadings of dusk were beginning to color the park when she heard a horse blowing off to her right. She ran over and found herself looking out over the secluded meadow that sheltered the sacred pond. A man, leading two horses, stood by the pool, staring down into the water.

"Kirill."

He spun. "Don't ever go off like that! Anything could have happened to you! Damn it, what were you thinking? Yuri was half crazy, wondering where you had gone."

"But I . . . I. . . ." To her horror, she began to cry, and she collapsed onto her knees on the soft cushion of grass.

"Tess!" A moment later he enclosed her in his arms and held her to him. "What is it, my heart?"

"I don't want to go," she whispered into his shoulder. Tears stained his shirt.

"Then don't go."

"I have to."

"Why?"

The question struck her to silence. She rested against him, comforted and warm. He shifted on the grass and she looked up at him, so near. He sighed, a long exhalation of breath, and pulled her gently down to lie with him on the grass.

"It's cold," she murmured.

"I brought blankets."

"If Yuri is worried—"

"He knows where we are." He kissed away her tears, one by one.

"But, Kirill, did Veselov only send eight riders?"

"Here." He helped her up. "Your tent is over here. It will be warmer inside. Yes, for now. Petya says that Mikhailov's jahar came up a few days after we left, and Sergei Veselov sent out the main force of his jahar to stay between Mikhailov and the Veselov tribe. But they swung north, so it's no danger to us. But still, there were only a few riders left in camp when Ilya rode in. We'll ride to meet the tribe and then Veselov will lend us more men once Mikhailov has swung clear."

She crawled into her tent and found it rich with blankets. She laughed and nuzzled into them, then sobered. "But why should Mikhailov swing clear? What if he follows Ilya?"

Kirill shrugged. "Bakhtiian can solve his own problems. Do you want me to go?"

He sat so close to her that she could feel his breath on her cheek. Before she could answer, he embraced her suddenly and fervently. "Don't ask me to go, Tess," he said in a fierce whisper.

Tomorrow she would ask Yuri if it was really possible to love two men at the same time yet in such different ways. Tonight she simply pulled Kirill tight against her, not letting him go, because she knew that this was his way of saying farewell.

CHAPTER TWENTY-FIVE

"So far as depends on courage."
—CRITIAS OF ATHENS

The tents of the Veselov tribe lay along the river's bank in a haphazard line, strung out in clumps of family groups camped together. The two great tents, one belonging to the etsana and one to her niece, stood in the center of the long line. It was unusual this early to see a fire blazing in the fire pit dug between the two tents, but one was. Three scarlet-shirted men stood there, rubbing their hands by the warmth, watching the large kettle of water that rested over the flames. Dawn pinked the horizon but the sun was not yet up.

"Vladi," said Niko. "Go find Anton Veselov and ask him how she is doing." Vladimir nodded and walked away to the etsana's tent. "That woman," said Niko uncharitably, "never did a good thing in her life, and now with everything else, she has to fall ill. What if she dies? Little Arina ought to be etsana but that damned cousin of hers will wrest even that from her if she can."

Ilya blew on his hands and glanced toward Vera Veselov's tent, where nothing stirred. A woman emerged from the etsana's tent, glanced at them, and walked with Vladimir toward the river. "Arina is young, just eighteen, I believe. But I think you underestimate her, Niko. Only Vera and her father want Vera to take etsana. I think the rest of the tribe will support Arina, should it come to that."

"She is too young to become etsana."

"But they are the last of the family left. There is no older woman to take it unless they take it out of the family altogether. What that girl needs is a good, steady husband. If she is married, it will not seem so imprudent to make her etsana.''

Niko glanced at Ilya curiously. ''You sound as if you have someone in mind.''

''Kirill.''

''Kirill!''

''Yes. Kirill.''

''You're plotting, Ilya.''

''Niko. When Mother Sun sent her daughter to the earth, she sent with her ten sisters, and gifted them each a tent and a name. The eldest was Sakhalin, then Arkhanov, Suvorin, Velinya, Raevsky, Vershinin, Grekov, Fedoseyev, and last the twins, Veselov and Orzhekov. Each sister had ten daughters, and each daughter ten daughters in turn, and thus the tribes of the jaran were born. Next spring we will begin our ride against the khaja lands, and of the ten elder tribes, who will come without questioning me?''

''All of them,'' said Niko. He paused. ''All but Veselov.''

''Arina Veselov wants Kirill. She told her mother, and her mother told me.''

''What does Kirill want?''

''Kirill knows his duty,'' said Ilya stiffly. ''You said yourself that I ought to give him the responsibility he deserves.''

''I suggest,'' said Niko in a carefully calm voice, ''that you let Kirill make his own choice in this matter. You already mean for Yuri to mark Konstantina Sakhalin. . . .''

''How did you know about that?''

''I may be old, Ilya, but I am neither blind nor deaf to the way your mind works, or to the exaggerated sense of duty Yuri feels toward you. Not that he would make her a bad husband, mind you. Ilya, what happened that night at the shrine? Josef and Tasha and I gave you every opportunity.''

The fire popped and flamed, licking the base of the kettle. ''I do not wish to speak of it, Niko.''

''Ilyakoria, you *are* her husband.''

''Yes, I am her husband,'' he said, rounding on Niko, ''and when Lord Ishii tried to kill her and she was forced to ask for my protection, did she ask me because I am her husband and she is my wife? No, Sibirin, she asked me on the honor we gave each other as friends. She does not want me.''

"Doesn't she?"

"Very well," agreed Ilya sarcastically, "perhaps she desires me, perhaps she even loves me, but she will not have me because I trapped her."

"Trapped her?"

"Treachery, that is the other word she used."

"Well," said Niko, "Tess does not mince words."

"Gods," said Ilya.

"So what will you do now?"

Ilya stared away, out to where the wind drew ripples in the dark, coursing waters of the river. The sun breached the eastern horizon. "She is going back to Jeds. I will get my horses and then—you know what I mean to do."

"And what about Tess?"

"What about her?"

"Are you going to just let her leave?"

Ilya's gaze fixed abruptly on the older man. "I want her, Niko. I thought I would go to any length to get her, but now—now I see that if she does not want me, I must let her go."

Niko smiled, but gently, to take the sting out of the expression. "You are learning humility, Ilyakoria."

"Yes," he said fiercely. "And I hate it."

Light spilled out, dusting with brightness the brilliant patterns woven into the walls of the gathered tents. "My dear boy," said Niko slowly, "do you love her?"

"I *married* her!"

"Loving a woman and wanting a woman are not the same thing."

Ilya simply stared at him, perplexed. "Of course, to desire a woman only because she is pretty—"

"I am not speaking of anything so simple. Listen to me, my boy. When you came back from Jeds, you had found the path you were destined to ride, knowing that it would bring you fame that no other jaran had found before you. But the gods play this game with us, challenging us to strive for fame, and yet how many of us can ever hope to beat their players: the wind that never ceases, the deep earth, the rain that dissolves the ashes of the dead, the unbounded sky, and the silent stars. They play their game well. They have only to wait us out to win."

The rising sun laced his pale hair with silver. "Yet now and again, a man or a woman is born who has weapons against these opponents, one who can command quiet, who can see beyond death, one who can hold fire to the old ways and let them burn. You are such a man. You can change the jaran. You are changing them. You can leave this world with a name that will live forever. You can win that game.'' He fell silent. Two women spoke in low voices from the etsana's tent, too far away for words to be distinguishable. From the farther edge of camp, a man hallooed, and a child yelped and laughed.

''But you will die in any case, Ilyakoria. What good is everlasting fame to a man if he dies unloved?''

A wind had come up. It touched Ilya's hair, stirring it like a whisper.

''Love, Ilya. That is what we who are mortal have been gifted, a gift never given and never known by the undying. The wind cannot love the plain, but I can love the plain, and I can love much more than that and be loved in return. Fame is something you want. A woman is someone you love.''

''I don't know,'' said Ilya in a low voice, averting his gaze from Niko's keen one. ''I don't know what the difference is.''

Niko sighed and rested a hand on Ilya's shoulder. ''I don't envy you.''

Ilya laughed a little unsteadily, and then grinned at the older man. ''Was that meant to comfort me?''

''No, it was meant to keep you honest.''

''Then I will tell you this much.'' His voice shook as he went on. ''I don't want her to leave.'' He shut his eyes, struggling to keep his expression controlled. ''I don't want her to leave,'' he repeated in a whisper, and then, as if the only way to keep his control was to keep talking, he went on. ''I remember the first time I saw her, and she told me in that elegant Rhuian she speaks that she wasn't going to harm me. Harm me! She could barely stand. Gods, how I wanted to laugh. But when the gods exacted that life, when it was done, I went after her. I don't know—I was afraid that she would think I was a barbarian, and then I was offended that she did. It was months before I began to wonder why I cared what she thought. And Sonia and my aunt! She walked into camp, alone, starving, with nothing but the clothes on her back, and they took her into the family. Do you know how long Vladi has been riding with the jahar, and still not accepted?''

"Vladi," said Niko kindly, "does not have Tess's ability to make friends."

"Then my aunt gifted her with her own daughter's tent! And she rode out with us, and I knew it would be a day, two days, three days at most, before she gave up—and then those damned—they knew I wanted her gone and still Yuri and Mikhal and Kirill and the others helped her."

"Until she could do it herself. She beat you fairly, Ilya." Niko chuckled, seeing Ilya's expression. "What, you aren't still mad about that, are you?"

"Damn her," said Ilya with heat. "I hate losing. Gods, though, I was impressed. She barely knew how to ride when we started. Do you suppose you know anyone as stubborn as she is?"

"Yes," said Niko innocently. "I think I do."

For an instant, Bakhtiian looked offended, and then he called Niko a very unsavory name that had once started a feud between two tribes that lasted three generations.

Niko laughed heartily. "I like watching your face," he said. "But I'm curious. When did you decide that you had to marry her?"

"Do you know, I did something I had never done before—something I had never had to do before. I put myself in her way one evening, thinking—hoping—that she would ask me to lie with her. I thought she needed comfort. It was after we found those three butchered riders of Doroskayev's. That was when I discovered that she and Fedya—'' He shrugged.

"It took you that long?"

"Where a woman slept had never before concerned me. But I'm glad she chose Fedya. He began making songs again before he died. For her. And I didn't have time to learn them all.'' He shook his head. "When we were up in the hills on that damned ill-fated scouting expedition. . . . I know the exact moment. We were down, the hunter stalking us, and my fingers touched her neck."

He raised one hand to touch the single gold necklace at his throat. "I ran. I ran because it was so strong. But it wasn't until we reached Veselov's tribe, the night of the dance, that I could see it for what it really was. Tess came to talk to me because I couldn't dance. When I saw her, I finally understood that I loved her.''

A woman hurried up to the etsana's tent, spoke with someone inside, and hurried away again. Around them, the camp was waking up. Three children ran by, bound for the river.

Niko coughed. ''Excuse me for saying so much, Ilya, but then why did you go off with that—'' He glanced toward the other tent, still quiet. ''That awful woman.''

Bakhtiian flushed. ''Because Tess left me to go dance, just jumped up and left me, went straight to—'' He broke off.

''Ah,'' said Niko.

''And then in front of everyone she had the audacity to gift Petya with *that* necklace. And then, do you know what she said to me that day? She said, 'I wonder who got the beauty and who got the beast.' She said that. To me.''

''And that,'' said Niko with awe, ''is why you married her. By the gods.''

''Yes,'' said Ilya sardonically, ''how fortunate for me that the Avenue presented itself so conveniently. The gods have a strange humor, Niko. In trying to bind her, I bound only myself.''

''Oh, you bound her as well.''

''Perhaps. But in Jeds, our laws mean nothing.''

''Bitterness does not enhance you, Ilyakoria.''

''Here are Anton and Vladi,'' said Ilya. At the same moment, Vera emerged from her tent, dressed in a bright blue tunic with a chain of silver bells around each ankle. She arrived beside Niko and Ilya a few steps before the two men, but her attention was all for Bakhtiian.

''You did not come to my tent last night,'' she said in an undertone but not quietly enough that Niko could not overhear. ''Three nights you have refused me, Bakhtiian.''

''I beg your pardon,'' he said politely, and turned to greet Anton Veselov.

''There's news,'' said Veselov.

''Your mother?''

''No, she is the same. Arina will stay with her. But ten riders just came in. Mikhailov's jahar slipped away last night, and it looks as if they've ridden hard south. Sergei sent word that you may have the ten riders for your journey to the coast. That way,'' he added, looking thoughtful, ''you can leave today, since you ought to gain enough of a head start that Mikhailov cannot catch you now. With the ten riders, you'll have double his men, counting the pilgrims, that is.''

But Bakhtiian was frowning. ''What about the rest of Veselov's jahar?''

''They'll stay between Mikhailov and our camp. I don't think you need worry that Mikhailov will attack us, even if his riders outnumber ours.'' Anton grinned. ''He'll save his fighting for you, Bakhtiian.''

''But if Mikhailov has swung south, then my men, and yours, from the shrine, will ride straight into him because they're riding here.''

There was a moment of coiled silence.

''Petya is with them,'' said Vera, an odd, unsettling note in her voice. She looked sidewise at Ilya, but he was staring south.

The three men watched him, waiting.

''Niko! Tell Tasha to stay here. Choose ten of our riders to stay with him, to guard—to remain as escort for the khepellis. On no account are they to allow any of the pilgrims to wander out by themselves—just as we've set our guard these past nights. Anton, we're riding south. All the riders here and the rest of my men.''

''Very well, Bakhtiian. What will you tell Sergei, when we meet up with him?''

''What will I tell him?'' asked Bakhtiian. He shrugged off the question, energy taut through every line of his body. ''Vladi, come. They've already too many hours on us.'' He strode off, and even with his limp, Vladimir had to hurry to keep up with him.

''Does he think Sergei will simply hand command of his jahar over to him?'' Anton asked, more curious than anything else.

''Yes,'' said Niko. ''If you will excuse me.'' He inclined his head toward Vera and left, leaving the two cousins side by side at the fire.

''You may hope Petya is killed,'' said Anton suddenly, ''but you will never get him, Vera. Never.'' He smiled.

''I hope your mother dies,'' said Vera.

''So do I,'' replied Anton amiably. ''Then Arina won't have to be polite to you anymore just for Mother's sake. If you will excuse me.'' He inclined his head with exact courtesy and left her standing alone while the fire flamed and roared and the water bled steam into the chill morning air. Vera did not move for some minutes. Then, seeing several women approaching the etsana's tent, she tossed her golden hair back over her shoulder with a flourish and went to greet them.

They left the shrine at midmorning, delayed by a protracted argument with Yeliana, who wanted to come with them. There were extra horses, so the case was not utterly unthinkable, but Mother Avdotya remained firm: Yeliana could not be released that easily from her service to the gods.

"I don't know how well she'll serve the gods," said Yuri as they finally rode away, "if she's forced to do it."

Tess had waved once but Yeliana had only turned and run back into the shrine, weeping. "I think Mother Avdotya is only trying to protect her. She's very young. How would she fare, Yuri, riding out with us? Who would take her in? She'd be alone."

"You were alone."

"Yes, and I would have been dead very soon if Ilya hadn't found me. Yuri, why was your tribe so hospitable to me and not to Vladimir?"

Yuri frowned and rubbed his chin. "I meant to say because he's an orphan but now I think it was because you weren't jaran. You were different. Perhaps it is better that Yeliana stay at the shrine. And yet there must be a woman somewhere who has no daughters and would take her in." He shook his head. His fine hair shone in the sun. "But who is to know if the bond would hold, if times grew hard or the woman got sick, and they shared nothing between them but words."

"But you and I, Yuri, are not related by anything but the gifting of a tent."

"You and I, Tess," he said somberly, "have been related by something much stronger than words or a tent since the moment we met, and you know that is true. We shared a mother once, and died, and now we have found each other again."

"Yuri. I never thought of it like that. As if we were looking for each other. It was a strange enough path that led me to you."

"Poor thing," he said with a grin. "Now I feel responsible. If you hadn't come looking for me, you wouldn't have ridden into Ilya."

"Yuri," she said suddenly, "Yuri, have you ever thought—would you ever think—of coming back with me to Jeds?"

He flushed and then looked away from her for a moment before he met her gaze again. "I will miss you, Tess. I will miss you bitterly. But this is my home."

He went ahead, riding in front of her up the narrow trail that switchbacked up the hillside to lead them out of the valley of the shrine of Morava. Somewhere behind them lay Hon Garii's corpse—if Ishii had not already fed it to the recyclers. Tess shuddered.

"Are you cold?" Yuri asked when the trail spilled out onto the plain and they could ride side by side again.

"No, just thinking."

"I'm sorry, my sister, but I can't."

"No, you are true to yourself, Yuri. That's what I love you for."

He glanced ahead up to the front of the group, where Kirill rode with Mikhal. "Kirill asked you."

"I can't take him, Yuri."

"No. I suppose not. He would hate Jeds, and you would grow to hate him for hating it. And Ilya will never go back, unless, of course," he grinned, "we ride so far south that our army comes at last to the very gates of the city. If I may beg your pardon for suggesting it."

"You're forgetting one thing. I am the heir to Jeds, so by marrying me—"

"No, I won't believe that he married you for that—or at least, if he did, he didn't know he was—I mean, that part of him might have known, but not that he thought about it. Do you understand what I mean?"

"Yes, I think I'm beginning to understand Bakhtiian tolerably well."

Yuri laughed. "By which you mean that you think that Bakhtiian wants you for yourself alone, and yet, that your brother is Prince in Jeds is inseparable from who you are."

"What?"

"I'm being wise, Tess."

"Gods," she said, and laughed. "You're being completely incoherent. But perhaps there's some relation between being wise and being unintelligible.''

"Only to those," said Yuri with dignity, "who have not yet achieved wisdom." He paused, and then said in an altered tone: "Tess. I will only say this once. Stay with us. I know I ought not to ask it of you, that I have no right, but I have this—this feeling that you will outlive Ilya." He was speaking quickly, in an undertone, as if he had very little time to say what he thought. "Not that that would be any surprise; he's ten years older than you, and with us going to war against the khaja—but still, there would be time for you to go back to Jeds later, wouldn't there? Or if you must return now, couldn't you come back here after? Or better yet, stay here for a few years and then go. Does it have to be one *or* the other? Why must it all be so final, Tess?"

Because you can't understand the distance I have to travel. She did not say it. Instead, she smiled sadly at Yuri and glanced away without answering.

"Look," she said, "why is Petya riding in? Isn't he on scout—Yuri, what's wrong?"

Petya reined his horse aside by Kirill. A few words sufficed.

"Turn around, everyone!" Kirill shouted. "Back to the shrine. Mikhailov's jahar is ahead of us."

They had all pulled up their horses. Yuri suddenly grabbed Tess's reins and jerked Myshla's head around, kicking his horse.

"Yuri, what—?"

"He means it. Ride!"

Myshla broke into a canter. Tess glanced back. What she saw almost stopped her heart. First two, then four, then ten riders cleared the far swell of grass, pausing to survey the group below.

As one, the eleven riders turned to follow Tess and Yuri. Tess kicked and Myshla galloped. Gods, there could be nothing worse than this. If they could gain the shrine—

Then Konstans appeared from the south. His pace as he cleared the rise in front of her and galloped down toward them was fueled by fear. "Kirill!" he cried. "Mikhailov is behind us. He's blocked the trail down to the shrine—" Then he caught sight of the riders beyond. He jerked his horse to a mincing halt and stared, horrified.

"Cut loose the remounts," shouted Kirill. They turned

in their saddles, sabers out, and sliced through the leads that held their extra horses.

A second group of riders, too many to count in one glance, appeared from the direction of the shrine. Myshla fought against the tight rein. Beside her, Yuri cursed under his breath.

"Petya and Mikhal at point. Tess and Yuri right behind them, and the rest behind them, with me." Kirill's glance touched her for an instant, searing, before he looked past her to Mikhailov's jahar. Up beyond their scarlet-shirted figures, a lone bird circled. Kirill studied the movements and positions of the jahar with astonishing swiftness. "We'll break east. Wait."

Two men conferred on the forward rise, gesturing, staring down at them. Above, three feather-light clouds, high and white with a hint of blue, edged the sky.

"They've got men east already," said Mikhal. Tess was amazed at how calm his voice was.

"Damn them," said Kirill. Briefly, a cloud covered the sun. "West. Now!"

They broke.

It was a mad race. Immediately riders from the south and north galloped to cut them off. Tess gauged her speed and theirs, and guessed where they would converge.

"We'll make it," she gasped.

And then, from behind, Kirill shouted: "Let Yuri and Tess through! Petya, home!" Petya and Mikhal split off, and Myshla stretched out into a full gallop, Yuri's Khani easily keeping up. Tess threw a glance back over her shoulder. Gods, how could she not have known: Veselov's riders had no better horses than Mikhailov's men. Already two men were fighting, sabers flashing in the sun. All along, Kirill had meant to get her free if he could not save the others.

"Damn it, Tess!" Yuri shouted. "Ride! There's ten men headed straight for us."

Behind, the race had disintegrated into a ragged line of skirmishes, trailing after Tess and Yuri like so much flotsam. She was just leaving them behind.

"Tess!" Yuri cried.

She hunched down over Myshla's back and rode after him.

Except that Mikhailov had long since encircled them. She had a moment to reflect on that before Yuri whipped Myshla's rump with the end of his reins, causing her to shy left, while he veered right, straight into the oncoming clump of riders.

"Yuri!" she screamed. The others—oh, God, the others she could leave behind but not him. She jerked Myshla hard around and rode after him.

The ten riders scattered from his charge, but a few sliced at him as he plunged through. She saw him sway, and then she was on the first one.

He cut at her, and she parried. His eyes went wide with shock as he realized she was a woman, and she threw a wild sweeping backstroke that cut across his chest. Then he fell from his saddle, and she could see Yuri again. Yuri, parrying desperately against three men. Something struck her from behind, a stinging flash, but she kicked Myshla toward Yuri, drove up behind him, hard against one of the riders, jarring him off his stroke. She thrust her saber at him almost blindly. Another man closed beside her, shouting.

"Move off!" a man yelled.

Suddenly she and Yuri sat alone, side by side. His face was white. Silence had descended on the field. She had an instant's comprehension of every position within her sight: that was Mikhailov, not five meters from her, Vasil and Leotich on either side of him. Other riders she did not know flanked them, poised to advance. Farther on, she saw Kirill and Konstans and a few of Veselov's riders. Kirill was holding his saber in the wrong hand. His face was streaked with blood. Halfway between the two groups, a fair-haired man lay still upon the grass.

Yuri swayed in his saddle. His face looked as if all the blood had drained from it. "Damn you, Tess," he whispered. "What good is it if you don't get free?"

"By the gods," said Dmitri Mikhailov, "it *is* the same woman."

"Damned fools," snarled Leotich. "Doroskayev said Bakhtiian had a woman with him, but you wouldn't listen."

"No matter," said Mikhailov. "It's the cousin I want now. Kill him, Vasil."

"I won't," said Vasil. "He's never done you any harm. Let him go."

Far away a voice hailed them, shouting something about another jahar.

Yuri swayed again. His head lolled back, and blood trickled from his mouth. Slowly at first, then tumbling, he fell from his horse.

Wind stirred in her hair. From above, a bird called, a loud, raucous cry.

"Make sure he's dead," said Mikhailov, and began to turn his horse away.

Sheer, cold rage obliterated everything else. She drove Myshla forward. She would kill him—

Someone shouted a warning. He turned. She raised her saber and cut. Two things hit her at once. Myshla lurched and plunged beneath her, toppling. She fell hard on her side, breath expelled from her lungs, and scrambled to her feet.

Only she did not get there. A body slammed against her. Pain tore deep into her side. Far away, a man screamed her name.

"Khaja pig, I'll kill you!" cried Vasil, and the weight was dragged off her. "She's a woman, curse you to Hell."

"Veselov! Let him go!"

The flurry of movement confused her. When it cleared, she saw only Vasil, standing over her. His hair shone like spun gold in the sunlight.

Her vision blurred in a haze of light and shadow, and then darkened.

She breathed. Grass tickled her nose, and she sneezed. Pain lanced through her. The day was silent. Everyone was gone. She stared up at the white trail of a cloud far away, and the bright, high, solitary sun. A bird called, once, twice.

She forced herself up onto her hands and knees. Noise pounded in her ears, shouting and horses all mixed until it made no sense. She crawled, dragged herself forward because she knew he was here, somewhere close by.

Then she was there, kneeling, staring down at him.

"Yuri." Her voice sounded distant, detached. He lay utterly still. There was a transparent cast to his skin, to his pale lips, as if his purity were infusing his mortal form. The tears ran down her face, falling on his lips and on his cheek. His eyes fluttered and his lips moved, moved again.

"Tess." It was the barest whisper. She bent down close to him. The scent of blood and grass drowned her. He lifted one hand and held it, wavering, searching for her. She caught it before it could fall back, pressed the dry skin to her lips, kissing it again and again as if her kiss could heal him.

Suddenly, his gaze focused on her. He blinked once, slowly. "Don't cry," he said, puzzled. "Live."

"Yuri. Yuri." Even her tears did not wake him. She put her cheek against his lips but nothing stirred. "Yuri!"

"Tess! Oh, gods, Tess."

"Where is she?"

"There. There. Gods, look at the blood. Vladi, help her up."

A hand closed on her shoulder.

"Leave me alone!" she cried, and she swung wildly to dislodge it. Lost everything in the pain that ripped through her side. She slumped forward over Yuri's body.

"Leave her alone!" That voice she knew. She stirred weakly. "Make Kirill lie down. Gods, he'll die where he's standing. Petya says you were ambushed."

A few gasping breaths, and then Kirill's voice, weak and strained. "Mikhailov's jahar. We rode straight into them."

She felt a hand come to rest on her neck. By the way it felt, gentle and implacable at the same time, she knew it was *him*. "Come, my wife," he said in a voice so strangely cool that she wondered why he spoke so oddly to her, "you must move now." His hands shifted her, and she choked down a moan and was suddenly cradled in his arms, looking up at him.

"Ilya," she said. And then she knew what was the only important thing in the world. "Mikhailov."

"Tess, don't speak."

"No. Mikhailov. Wanted Yuri. Dead." His face changed. Looking into his eyes, she felt fiercely that what they shared now would always bind them.

"I'll kill him," he said. "I'll kill him myself."

"Thank you," she whispered, and because she felt safe, held by him, she let pain wash her into oblivion.

"You love her," said Kirill. His voice rasped with pain.

Bakhtiian simply sat, holding Tess against him as if he meant never to let her go. Blood leaked onto his fingers. He stared at her face, and if he had heard Kirill, he gave no sign.

"Vladimir," said Niko. "We need tents for the wounded.

We need fires and hot water. Send Anton Veselov here and send Sergei Veselov with riders to track Mikhailov.''

"But, Niko, shouldn't we carry the wounded back to Veselov's tribe?" Vladimir asked.

Niko glanced at Kirill, who stared white-faced at Ilya and Tess from where he lay on the ground, and then at Yuri's slack body, and farther, at the other riders strewn like so much wreckage across the field. "For those who can, yes. But some of these won't live so long. Now go." Vladimir nodded and ran off.

Niko knelt beside Kirill. "Let me see, boy," he said brusquely. "No, don't argue with me. This is a bad cut here but mostly blood." Kirill gasped and clutched at Niko's arm. "Yes, that one's to the bone but it's clean. But what happened to this shoulder?" Tears came to Kirill's eyes as Niko probed the wound, and his breathing grew so ragged that Niko pulled away.

"I can't feel my right arm," Kirill whispered hoarsely. "Nothing."

"Gods," Niko sighed under his breath. "Well, young fool," he said roughly, "if you're still alive so far, I think you'll live to regret it. Just lie still. I'll bind those two wounds and then I'll leave you until I can look to the others."

"Tess—" Kirill whispered.

"Don't you mind Tess. Anton!"

Anton Veselov knelt beside Kirill. "Let me bind those," he said. "I've cloth."

Niko moved to crouch beside Yuri. He laid a hand on Yuri's throat, searching for a pulse.

Anton worked on Kirill as he spoke. "Ivan Charnov is dead. Matvey Stassov and Mikhal Yakhov will be dead by morning. Three of Mikhailov's men are dead. Five others of both jahars badly wounded. The rest—" He gestured with his head. "As you see them. They'll live. Sergei has taken twelve riders after Mikhailov."

"So few?" Both men started round. It was Bakhtiian who had asked the question.

"Sergei," said Anton, "does not believe Mikhailov will attack him."

"She got Mikhailov," said Kirill in a low voice. "Tess, I mean. Damn." He shut his eyes. "I don't know how badly but, by the gods, she got him.'' He said it fiercely, with glee. ''Aren't you done yet, Veselov?''

''Let me bind that shoulder up,'' said the other man evenly. ''Then I'll let you rest.''

Niko sighed and moved away from Yuri. ''Ilya, I must look at Tess. Put her down. Ilyakoria.''

Niko's voice was sharp enough that it got Bakhtiian's attention. He hesitated, and then, carefully, expressionlessly, he laid her down on the grass.

''I don't want you watching me,'' said Niko severely.

Ilya stood and walked over to Kirill. For an instant, he stood above him, staring down as Anton Veselov bound Kirill's shoulder and arm into a sling.

Kirill opened his eyes and, with an effort, focused his gaze on Bakhtiian's. He grinned weakly. ''She may choose you in the end but, by the gods, she chose me first.''

''Yes, you won that fairly. But you were always too damned charming for your own good. I always envied you that, Kirill.''

Kirill's eyes widened. ''Did you! Gods. I never knew.''

''Anton,'' said Niko impassively, ''can you help me here?''

Anton glanced at Kirill, then at Bakhtiian, and retreated to assist Niko. Ilya so forcefully did not look after him that it was obvious that he wanted nothing more than to know what they were doing. Instead, he knelt beside Kirill.

''So Mikhailov is injured?''

''Yes. I don't know—let me—''

''Don't get up. That you've gone this long with those wounds astonishes me. He left five men for dead, and if he's wounded, he'll be forced to run and wait for now. Gods, I've got to get those khepellis to the coast before the winds change. Damn them. I'll deal with Mikhailov when we return.'' He hesitated. Beyond, a man began to scream in pain, and then, mercifully, the cries ceased. ''You did well, Kirill,'' he said softly.

''By the gods,'' said Kirill in a faint, mocking voice; it was all that was left him. ''Are you praising me, Bakhtiian?''

''Here is some water,'' said Ilya, giving him a few swallows from his pouch.

Suddenly, behind them, Tess moaned and shifted away from Niko's grasp, struggling toward Yuri's body.

"Don't burn him," she whispered. Niko captured her and shook his head roughly at Ilya to go back. "Don't burn him. Don't burn him." As abruptly, she fainted again.

"Damn you, Niko," said Ilya. "I'll wait no longer. Will she live?"

"It's a deep knife wound. We've staunched the bleeding as well as we can. She has other wounds but it's this one— I can't say, Ilya. It's low in the abdomen. We can only wait. I'm sorry."

Vladimir ran up. "Tents, blankets. Petya has gone back to the tribe to bring their healer. There'll be enough fuel for a small fire soon but the great fire will have to wait until nightfall."

"Vladi," said Ilya, "bring me Kriye."

Vladimir blinked and obeyed.

Ilya walked past the unconscious Tess and knelt beside Yuri. For a moment he simply rested his hand on Yuri's pale brow. He gazed at Yuri's face, so quiet in repose. A few tears slipped down his face to dissolve in his dark beard. Then he gathered his cousin into his arms and stood, and walked to his horse.

"Ilya," said Niko, glancing up. "What are you doing? The fire hasn't been built yet—"

Ilya winced as he put his weight full on his injured knee to swing Yuri's body over the horse and mount up behind him. Yuri's hair hung down, stirred into a semblance of life.

Anton and Vladimir stared at him, shocked. Kirill had his eyes shut.

"Ilyakoria," began Niko. "He has earned his release—"

"Only to be separated from her?" Ilya replied harshly. "Didn't you hear what she said?" Without waiting for Niko to reply, he reined Kriye away. "I'll be back." And rode out onto the plains, alone.

CHAPTER TWENTY-SIX

"Of night, lonely, blind-eyed."
—EMPEDOCLES OF AGRAGAS

Tess lived for a time in gray oblivion. Pain throbbed through her, as constant as the pulse of her blood. She lay on her back, aware only of darkness, a thick dry coarseness against her hands and lips, a heavy, hot, sharp ache in her side. She thought someone was with her but perhaps it was just a dream. She wanted to scream and thrash about, anything, if only it would dispel the pain.

"Tess." *His* voice, soft, uncertain.

Because she thought he was a hallucination, she lifted her hand to test his reality. Yes, he had a knee, a thigh, a hip, a chest—his hands caught hers, raising it to his face. His cheeks were damp. She moved her fingers on the soft coolness of his skin. He lowered her hand to his lips and kissed it repeatedly.

"You're taking advantage of me," she whispered.

"Tess! How do you feel?"

"Am I going to die?" she asked with a kind of vague hope.

"No, Tess. No. You must not die."

"Oh, well," she said, disappointed. She coughed, weakly, starting a spasm through her side so acute that gray surrounded her again.

"Tess. Don't leave me!" It was as much a command as a plea. One of his hands moved to rest on her cheek. His fingers, cool and light, traced the line of her jaw.

"Where are the khepelli?" she asked, when she could talk again.

"We're leaving this morning. I'm taking them to the coast. You won't see your brother this winter, I fear."

"But—" Memory came in fits and starts. "The letter I wrote—"

"It went with Josef. I have the relic. I'll write another letter, by my own hand, explaining—" He broke off. "I will find someone trustworthy to carry it to Jeds. I promise you, Tess."

"I believe you."

A man moved at the entrance. "Bakhtiian? Your horse is ready."

"A moment." He smoothed back her hair from her temple. "Tess. Promise me you will live."

"Why?" Bitter, this memory that overwhelmed her; more bitter than her pain. "Why should I live when Yuri died?" She began to cry, an agony, leaking from her like blood. She choked on a sob, and it hurt all through her, and she jerked, writhing, anything to free herself of it.

His hands pressed her shoulders down, and he held her there until she stopped fighting. "Because, my wife, you have other responsibilities," he said coldly.

She stared up at him. How close he was. She could smell the faint salt odor of his sweat. Her hands followed the smooth cloth up his arms to his back and settled on the curve of his neck, pulling down. His hands slipped off her shoulders to the bedding on either side so that, as they kissed, none of his weight rested on her. It was a light kiss but lingering.

"Gods, woman," he said unsteadily, breaking himself free gently and reluctantly, "if you use that kind of argument, you can persuade me to anything."

"Kill Mikhailov," she whispered.

"I have already promised to do that."

"Yes," she said, remembering, "you have. Oh, God. Yuri is gone."

And then he bent until his lips brushed her cheek. "No," he said, whispering, as if what he meant to impart to her was too important, or too sacrilegious, to say any louder, "he is not gone." He drew back.

"But he's dead—Ilya." For a moment she saw him very clearly, even in the dimness of the tent. "You didn't let them burn him."

"He will come back to us, Tess," he said simply.

She laughed, a weak, faint chuckle, because she did not believe him and yet she did.

"Tess, I must go. You have not yet promised me that you will live."

She drew a long, shuddering breath and lifted a hand to touch his face again. The flickering lantern light made him seem darker than usual, shadows playing between the occasional glimpse of a tear. "You'll plague me forever, won't you?"

"Forever," he promised.

"Gods, you will, too. I promise."

"My husband," he prompted.

"My husband," she echoed.

"No, the whole thing."

"I promise you, my husband. There, are you satisfied?"

"For now. Oh, Tess." He sighed, and leaned down to kiss her once, twice, then her hands, her eyes, her cheeks, her forehead and, last, her lips once again.

From outside: "Ilya!"

He kissed her again, and then, taking the lantern with him, he left her in darkness.

She lay in a stupor for an eternity. Light flashed at the entrance to the tent, and a man knelt next to her.

"Tess, it is Niko. Can you sleep, my child?" His weathered hands stroked her face gently.

"It hurts. It never stops."

"There, child. Let me tell you a story." His voice did eventually soothe her, and she slept.

It was only a short respite. Niko washed her, gave her water to drink, after a time fed her a warm gruel. Speaking made her cough, so she did not speak, and she was too weak to attempt anything else. She hurt constantly. For long periods she simply stared into the darkness, and all she could see was Yuri lying dead in the grass.

She woke once from a shallow sleep and lay for what seemed like hours before she recognized the familiar sound serenading her: rain. A man dozed beside her, a steady, rhythmic sound. She reached out, touching him with the tips of her fingers. He woke abruptly and sat up.

"Tess?"

"Who is it? Where is Ilya? Why hasn't Yuri come back?" She shook her head. "No. Don't answer that."

"Ilya has been gone three days, my child."

"It's raining."

"Yes." There was a note in his voice she could not recognize. "Yes, my child, it is. Are you warm enough?"

The rain sounded like pebbles being shaken in a distant tin. "My toes."

He moved around out of her sight. She fell into a long, dreamless sleep. When she woke, she was thirsty, and he gave her water; after that she was hungry, and he fed her. She slept again.

A cool breeze on her face woke her. Someone had thrown up the tent flap. Light caught the outlines of her feet under blankets. The sides of the tent stirred, brushed by the wind. A dark figure sat outside, engaged in mending a shirt.

"Niko?"

The hands stilled. "Tess." He crawled in to her. "How do you feel, my child?"

"I hurt. Where are we?"

"We are in your tent, here where—well, we will move you to Veselov's tribe when you are safe to be moved. You had a very deep wound, young woman."

"Am I lucky to be alive?"

"Yes, child. I should think you are. Now let me look at your wounds."

As he reached for the blanket, she felt down along her body. She wore only her shirt.

"Niko." He paused. "Niko, how long have I been lying here?"

"Five days."

"Five days," she said in a small voice. "You've had to do everything. . . . Oh God, Niko, I'm so . . ."

"Embarrassed?" he supplied. "My dear girl, if you're strong enough to feel embarrassed, then you are certainly going to recover. This is the best sign I could have looked for."

"Don't tease me."

"I'm not. I have tended both men and women in my time for any number of illnesses and injuries, some far more intimate than yours. And I had six children. The human body holds no surprises for me."

Tess laughed. "Damn, it hurts to laugh."

"Well, hold this. This will hurt more. Cry if you wish." He rolled her onto her side.

It did hurt more. She clutched at the belt he had given

her, squeezing it until her hand ached. At last, at last, he let her down, but then he pulled up her shirt and examined her abdomen with great care, pushing and probing with excruciating gentleness.

"Well. Not as bad as I feared. Not quite so good as I hoped. But you will do, my child. You will do."

"Can I move?"

"In a few days, we'll see."

"Unless I die of frustration before then. Niko, I don't even remember getting hit."

"You weren't hit. That is, you have two saber cuts, one on your back and one on your thigh, but they're healing neatly. No, you were stabbed with a knife. What man would do that to a woman, I cannot imagine."

She shut her eyes. She saw things in a haze, blurred by pain and grief and blessed oblivion. "I don't know. I don't know. It wasn't Mikhailov. And Vasil pulled him off me, whoever he was."

"*Vasil!*"

"Yes, Vasil. Vera's brother."

"I know who Vasil is. Was he party to Yuri's death?"

"No. No. He told Mikhailov to let Yuri go. It must have been Leotich."

"Leotich. One of Doroskayev's riders, I think. I might believe that he would—well, he's dead, Tess. We found him on the field."

"Who else?" she asked, not wanting to. "Who else died, Niko?"

"Come, child, let's not speak of that now."

"*Tell me.*"

"We had to put Myshla down, Tess. I'm sorry. Four riders from Mikhailov's jahar. I don't even know their names. Three from Veselov's: Ivan Charnov, Matvey Stassov, and Leonid Telyegin. But perhaps you didn't know them."

"Who else, Niko? Oh, God, not Kirill?"

"No, Tess, no. Last I saw Kirill, he was badly hurt but alive. Konstans, too."

"Not Mikhal? Oh, gods, what will I tell Sonia?" She began to cry.

"Tess. Tess. Don't cry. It wasn't your fault."

"Yes, it was my fault, damn you, and you know it. If I hadn't made Garii take me there, Ishii wouldn't have found us, and he wouldn't have killed Garii, and he wouldn't have

wanted to kill me, and then Ilya wouldn't have made us wait
and come after and we wouldn't have run into Mikhailov
and then Yuri wouldn't be dead. And now Mikhal. It is my
fault. It is my fault.'' She began to sob, noisy, awkward,
painful sobs that wracked her body.

Niko settled back and did nothing. Soon enough she exhausted herself and, with tears still seeping down her face,
she fell asleep.

When she woke again, she was alone. She called out Niko's
name once, softly, but he did not answer. Well, it was all
she deserved. As if the memory had been seared into her,
she could see Yuri falling from his horse, ever so slowly.
If she could only catch him, then perhaps he might live—
but Yuri was dead. Mikhal was dead. The ache of her wound
paled beside the ache of her loss.

Niko came then, but she would not speak to him and only
mechanically obeyed his injunctions to eat and drink. After
a while, having tried stories and songs and one-sided conversation, and even reading aloud from the volume of Casiara, he left.

It was better that way. Yuri would have cajoled her into
crying, teased her, laughed her into it. She hated herself for
not dying with him, hated herself more for wanting to live,
a coward afraid of the dark. How could she ever face Sonia?
Sonia, the one person with that same open confidence that
Yuri had, whom she had deprived of a brother and a husband in a single swift stroke. Sonia would never look at her
again with anything but loathing. And Ilya. He would know
very well whose fault this was. Her thoughts wound down
in this manner and left her in desolation.

It rained for hours, for days, perhaps; she neither knew
nor cared. She submitted listlessly to Niko's care.

''It's clearing,'' he said finally. She did not know whether
it was morning or afternoon, only that where the flap lay
askew a thin line of light lanced across the dark floor. She
refused to ask how many days it had been. ''Today we are
moving you to Veselov's tribe.''

She stared at the shadowed roof. Although he kept her
scrupulously clean, still her back itched, a constant, damp
prickling. Mold was surely growing in the blankets. The air
was overpowering, dank. Her legs chafed where they rubbed
the coarse bedding.

He sighed. ''Your wounds are showing some progress, girl, but your spirits aren't.''

He knelt close to her, filling all her space. Before his entrance she had been remembering Yuri demonstrating, to her immense delight, how *not* to use a saber, with Kirill acting as his willing and hilarious foil. ''Why can't you leave me alone?''

''To what? To die? I believe you promised Bakhtiian that you would live.''

''Did I?''

''Don't you remember?''

''I don't care.'' And then, perhaps because his words had triggered it, she did remember. She flung an arm across her eyes so that she wouldn't have to look at Niko. ''He doesn't care anyway. Why should he? I killed Yuri and Mikhal.''

''You are a difficult child. Why do you suppose Ilya wants you to live?''

''To torment me.''

''Tess, I am getting rather tired of you. I'm leaving now, and when I return, it will be to take you out of this tent and move you to Veselov's tribe. Do you understand?''

''I don't want to go.''

''You haven't a choice.'' He left.

She lowered her arm and stared at the canvas above her, recalling Ilya in all his moods and depressing herself further. Then, so soon it startled her, Niko threw the tent flap unceremoniously back. She had to cover her eyes with her hands until they could adjust to the unaccustomed light.

''Now. You are coming out. Here, Tasha, help me, please.''

They pulled her out on the blanket and bundled her onto one of the light wagons that the women used to transport their tents. It hurt, but not as much as the sight of Petya, with his damned beautiful face, without the slightest visible scar from the battle. And he was riding Yuri's Khani. Tess was filled with such a vicious, burning wish that Petya could have died instead of Yuri that she was horrified at the depth of her own hatred.

''Tess, I'm so glad you're alive.'' Tess glanced up to see that Arina Veselov was driving the wagon. Arina looked at Tess's expression, and looked away again, questioningly to Niko. Tasha and Vladimir were taking down her tent. No one spoke. When they finished and brought the tent and gear to put in beside her, she pulled the blanket up over her face and ignored them.

For three days, she ignored them. After the first day, only Niko and Arina spoke to her, both unfailingly kind. Tess grew sick of their kindness. She could not look at Petya without feeling that same sickening jealousy, that hatred, so she did not look at any of them. The jolting of the wagon hurt, every bump, every jar, but not enough, not enough to make up for everyone who had died.

When they rode into Veselov's camp, she hid herself, buried herself in blankets, and wished with all her strength that they would leave her alone. The wagon halted. Their voices spoke together, low, conspiring. She could hear in the distance the noises of the camp, and could gauge fairly enough that they had stopped some ways away. *Thank God.*

Then: "Ah, here you are," said Niko with relief. "I can do nothing with her. She has given up, I think. She blames herself for what happened."

Weight rocked the wagon. A moment later, a strong hand yanked the blanket away from her face. She shut her eyes.

"Tess, look at me."

Because his voice surprised her, she opened her eyes. "Kirill."

"Well?" he asked. He bore a pink scar on his forehead and past his ear, down to his jaw. His right arm and shoulder were swathed in a sling.

"Go away," Tess said, acutely embarrassed by his presence, staring at her with such knowing eyes.

He lifted his left hand, and the figures behind him moved away. "So, my heart, is this how you repay Yuri's sacrifice?"

She flushed, trapped here under his gaze because she could not move. "How dare you scold me!"

"How dare I? How dare you pretend you're the only one who loved Yuri? Who cared for Mikhal? Don't you think Petya hates himself, wondering why his best friend is dead and he's still alive? Don't you think the rest of us would give our own lives to bring them back? But we can't because we're alive and they're dead. Nothing will bring them back, Tess, and you might as well be dead, too, if all you care for is your own grief."

She stared at him. She felt stripped of words.

"Tomorrow Niko says he'll let you sit up," he added,

softer now. "By the gods, Tess, if you aren't walking by the time Bakhtiian gets back, you aren't the one who'll get the worst edge of Ilya's tongue. So think of the rest of us, if you please."

Then he walked away. Limped away. He favored one side, and his right arm and shoulder were stiff and lifeless. Arina Veselov met him twenty paces out, and he allowed her, small as she was, to support him with an arm at his elbow.

Tess began to cry, but silently. When Niko came up, she simply reached for his hand and held it tightly, while Tasha and Vladimir put up her tent, and Niko and Tasha carried her over to it.

"Might I lie outside for just a little bit?" she asked.

"Yes, child. Set her down here, Tasha."

It was afternoon. Beyond, she saw the tents of Veselov's camp. Women talked, but quietly, and children played, more quietly still. She saw a few riders, but not many, and most of them she did not recognize.

"Where is Petya?" she asked.

"Here. Petya!"

A moment later, Petya arrived, looking pale. He wore three necklaces, one of them the amber one she had given him.

"Petya," she said. "I'm sorry."

He ducked his head, paling even more. "Tess," he said, and then he turned away abruptly and she realized that he was crying. He strode away quickly, out into the grass.

"Inside now," said Niko. "Rain is coming on." They hauled her in, and Tasha retreated. "Well, child, have you decided to live?"

"I thought I made a promise. Oh, Niko, I remember the last thing he said to me. He said, 'Don't cry. Live.' Oh, Niko." The wind rustled the tent flap. A light spatter of rain fell. "Will it always be this painful?"

"Not always, child, but we will sit with you, those of us whom you care to see, as often as you wish, if that will comfort you."

"Please." She brought his hand to rest on her cheek. Presently, she fell asleep.

* * *

Sometimes, Marco Burckhardt reflected, your luck was out, and sometimes it was in. Sometimes things seemed too damned easy, given all the trouble and worry that had come before.

He sat in the cleanest inn in Abala Port, a filthy port town well up the inland sea, about thirty days' sailing north of Jeds. The winds had been good. His luck was in.

A Chapalii dressed in native-looking clothing, tattooed on his left jaw with the mark of the steward class, was haggling with the innkeeper. Just ten paces from Marco. Just as, right on the edge of town in an old barracks and corral, three more Chapalii stewards watched over a veritable fleet of the most beautiful Kuhaylan Arabians Marco had seen in a good long time. Right there, at the second of Karima's modeled landing points, he had—what was the old phrase—struck gold.

He had sent one scrambled analog burst back to Jeds to inform Dr. Hierakis of the situation. More than that, not knowing what kind of communications equipment the Chapalii had hidden in their gear, he dared not attempt.

A bearded man dressed in a silkily smooth scarlet shirt tucked into black trousers came down the stairs and paused, staying back in the shadows, watching the Chapalii. The steward counted out eleven copper coins and received in his turn five loaves of bread and a slab of cheese. With this bounty, he left. The man came in to the room and, with a nod toward the innkeeper, strolled over to Marco's table.

Marco eyed him with interest. This was the other foreigner in town, a man who had, so the innkeeper informed him, ridden in from the northeast some days before Marco's arrival.

"May I sit down?" asked the man in passable Taor.

Marco gestured. The man sat. He carried himself easily, confidently, yet warily, and he wore a saber at his belt.

"My name is Josef Raevsky. You are from Jeds, I think. I have been watching you these past few days."

"Yes, you have." Marco smiled. "And I you. You're also a foreigner in these parts."

"But you are from Jeds. A merchant, perhaps?"

"I have made no secret of who I am."

"No," said Raevsky. "You are *Marko Burkhhart,* an emissary from the Prince of Jeds. Seeking new trade. So you say. And you are interested in the *khepelli* and their horses. You are waiting to see what becomes of them."

The way he said the word alerted Marco instantly. Here,

the townsfolk called them *chepalis*. This was their name in a different tongue; this was a man who was interested in them as well. Of course, Marco had heard gossip: even in a port town, to have three entirely different foreign visitors—the Chapalii counting as a group of one—at one time was a marvel and much discussed at the inns and around the harbor. An emissary from the Prince of Jeds; strange-looking foreigners from over the seas with their cargo of fine horses; and this man, who was, said the old innkeep, a man from that people called the *zherawn,* savages from out in the wilderness.

"Say, lad," called the innkeeper, interrupting them. Over the last five days he had decided that he liked Marco, foreigner though he was. The quality of Marco's gold and Marco's gossip had won him over. "I laid that money you said down on them spices, and sure enough, when the *Queen Aireon* sailed in this morning, that was the first cargo they picked."

"I'm pleased for you, old man," replied Marco. The old man's very young wife came in from the back, carrying two buckets of water, and she smiled shyly and meaningfully at Marco and then slipped back outside. Marco turned back to the bearded man. "Why, Raevsky? Do you know what will become of them?" Then, on a sudden impulse, he went on. "The truth is, I'm also looking for a woman. A Jedan woman." He had already manufactured the story to give her importance but not too much importance. "A merchant's sister. Her ship was lost but the merchant believes she may still be alive."

Josef Raevsky examined him, and Marco felt abruptly that he was being measured and judged by a man whose judgments were worth something. "You mean," said Raevsky, "the sister of the Prince."

Marco was rarely too astonished to be at a loss for words. But the sudden euphoria that overwhelmed him now obliterated everything else. A moment later, he realized that he was grinning.

Josef Raevsky stood up. "Come with me." He went to the door without looking back, and walked outside.

Marco rose to follow him.

"Say, lad," said the innkeeper. "My wife heard a bit of interesting news last night from the captain." The old man's wife was not only young but unexpectedly good-looking, and Marco had quickly ascertained that her favors were for the asking, if one was willing to pay. It was the other reason the innkeeper liked him: that he had paid well and the young woman had enjoyed herself. "Yea. A warband of them damned *zherawn* rode into town late last night. We see them every second year or thereabouts, in here, trading and such like. But the captain said they've some of them *chepalis* with them as well." Then, either because Marco's expression betrayed him or because the old man was keener than he looked, he went on. "That's what you've been waiting here for, in't it? More of them foreigners. And it looks like now we know why all these strangers have come into our port this late in the year."

"Thank you," said Marco. He went outside. Josef Raevsky was waiting for him. "Where are we going?" Marco asked.

"There's someone who wishes to see you."

They walked to the outskirts of town. The rains had not come in great force yet, so the roads and tracks were still dry. But it was getting cold at night. Barefoot children stared at him from doorways. An old woman carded wool. Heat swelled out from a blacksmith's forge.

Within sight of the barracks, Josef halted. Marco stared. What had been a quiet outpost before was now bustling with activity. Scarlet-shirted men examined the horses while Chapalii, clearly more Chapalii than the four who had been here all along, spoke to each other and to a trio of red-shirted men over to one side.

"Have you seen enough?" Josef asked.

"What does this mean? Why are they here, and who are you?"

"We are *jaran*. We have escorted these pilgrims from the *issledova tel* shore to this port, where they will set sail for their own lands across the seas."

"The horses are for you," said Marco, suddenly understanding something the innkeeper had said. "You must be—" There was no word in Taor that he knew for nomads.

"We are not *khaja*, if that is what you mean. The ones who settle in one place. We ride."

One question answered, a million sprouting to take its place. "Who wants to talk with me?"

"Come. We will go down to the port to see the *khepelli* to their ship."

Marco followed and Josef led him down to the docks. As he waited, Marco chatted with the ship's master of the *Queen Aireon,* which was returning to Jeds the next day. The ship he had come in on eight days before had already sailed on northward. As he watched, a sail cleared the horizon and banked toward the harbor.

It took until midday for the ship to anchor within rowing distance from the docks. By that time, fifteen Chapalii with an escort of fifteen brilliantly clad riders arrived at the dock. Marco realized quickly enough that he himself was being escorted by Josef. Being watched so that he did not interfere with their leave-taking. The Chapalii were being sent home. Well, being put on the ship, at least. Marco was wild to know how they intended to get off-planet from here, but he had a healthy respect for the saber riding on Josef Raevsky's hip.

Boats came. The Chapalii loaded gear into them. In all this, Marco quickly discerned that two people—one Chapalii, one jaran—were being deferred to here. One Chapalii lord. The jaran man—from this distance, it was hard to tell, except that he was clearly in charge. The Chapalii clambered awkwardly into the boats. Final respects were paid, and the human sailors at the oars began the long stroke out to the ship.

And that was that.

Except, of course, it wasn't. Across a hundred meters' distance, a man turned to stare at Marco. Every alarm Marco had honed by instinct to its finest degree went off. Danger.

"Come," said Josef. A crowd had long since gathered to watch. An audience, of course. Somehow, Marco was no longer surprised at any twist this journey might take. He followed Josef meekly but cautiously.

The man waited for them as a prince waits. He was of middling height, but height never matters in the kind of man he was. On a whim, Marco bowed to him, with the flourish granted to the nobility in Jeds.

"You are the emissary from the Prince of Jeds," said the man in faultless Rhuian. His accent was slight but melodious. "I am Ilyakoria Bakhtiian. I have two letters and a holy relic for you to deliver to the prince." He gestured with a hand, and Raevsky extracted a leather pouch from the saddlebags of Bakhtiian's horse. "By the way." Bakhtiian said it offhandedly. "If I ever find out that you did not deliver the messages and the relic to the prince, I will hunt you down and kill you.'' He gave Marco the pouch.

Marco took it. For the first time in his life, he felt entirely out of his depth.

''Please,'' said Bakhtiian politely. ''Examine each item so that you know what you're carrying.''

Marco nodded, still not trusting himself to speak. He opened the pouch and pulled out the cylinder. Stared at it, knowing instantly that it was of Chapalii manufacture. And read Tess's letter. *Tess*.

''But I must come with you,'' he said, looking up. ''I must get to Tess.''

''Do I need to repeat myself? She said that this is important to her brother, that he needs it, not next season or the one after but now. Therefore, you will deliver it.''

His men flanked him, a scatter of brilliant color, all armed, most mounted. Josef Raevsky stood to one side. But it was clear to Marco that Bakhtiian was the most dangerous of these men. That he was a man who would, who could, who had killed, a man who would not hesitate to do so again if his will were crossed.

''I understand,'' said Marco finally.

''Good,'' said Bakhtiian.

''But is Tess safe? Where is she?''

Bakhtiian looked so angry in that instant that Marco took an involuntary step back. ''She is with my people,'' he said fiercely. He turned on his heel and began to walk away.

''Wait. Surely I can send a message to her. A gift.''

Bakhtiian spun back. He looked furious. ''What?'' he snapped. ''Write something, then.''

Marco always wore the emergency kit at his belt. He had an emergency transmitter he could send to her but he had nothing to write on here, had no parchment except back at the inn. Bakhtiian said a few words in a foreign tongue, and Raevsky rummaged again in the saddlebags and brought out a book—a book!—and a quill pen and ink.

''Here.'' Bakhtiian carefully tore a page out of the front of the book and handed it to Marco.

Marco stared. Newton's *Principia*, the title page. He felt disoriented; he felt like laughing. Newton in the hands of this barbarian. He glanced up to see Bakhtiian's unnerving stare focused on him. Crouching hastily, he set the page on his knee and wrote in Anglais.

My darling Tess, your dear old Uncle Marco wonders what the hell you're up to on Rhui, but most of all he hopes you are safe. I am sending an emergency transmitter by way of your escort. For God's sake, child, let us know where you are and that you're well. I am not going to endanger my life at this time by trying to follow your escort back to you. And I'm sure you understand that the Mushai's cylinder must get to Charles as soon as possible. As you must. I do not understand what your circumstances are. If you are being held against your will, though it does not seem so from your letter, you can merely activate the primary codes and we will come and pick you up in a shuttle and damn the Interdiction. If not against your will, then I will only say this: You have a duty to your brother. You also have a duty to yourself. Make of that what you will. I send my love. Marco Burckhardt

Marco fished the emergency transmitter from his pouch. It looked like a little dagger, snuggled into a leather sheath. He folded the letter carefully and slid it inside the sheath, and handed the dagger to Bakhtiian. Bakhtiian took it without a word and turned and walked back to his horse.

Should he follow them? Could he, without being killed; that was the real question. He judged it unlikely. He must hope that Tess would get the transmitter; it would keep track of her whereabouts, whatever she chose to do with it. He opened her letter to Charles and read it again. Unwound the cylinder from its fabric blanket and stared. *The Mushai. Goddess help them all.* He'd damned well better get this back to Charles. If Tess was not safe for now in the hands of Ilyakoria Bakhtiian, then she wasn't safe anywhere.

Bakhtiian mounted and turned to stare at Marco as if memorizing his features in case they met again and Bakhtiian discovered that Marco had indeed not fulfilled his duty. And Marco had a sudden flash of insight: if this barbarian prince ever decided that he wanted to conquer the civilized lands, then Goddess protect those lands that lay in his path.

They rode away, these *jaran*, much to the relief of the townspeople of Abala Port. But then again, it would give them something to talk about for the entire winter. Marco tied the leather pouch to his belt and went to talk to the ship's master of the *Queen Aireon* about getting passage with them back to Jeds.

CHAPTER TWENTY-SEVEN

"An eddy, of all manner of forms,
is separated off from the whole."
—DEMOCRITUS OF ABDERA

A formal delegation arrived the next morning. Niko had thrown the tent flap back, and Tess saw four women approach Niko where he sat outside: an older woman she vaguely recognized, Vera, Arina, and—she craned her neck to get a better look but she had not been mistaken: it was Yeliana, dressed in a knee-length green tunic with a pair of belled trousers bagging out below, tucked into her soft boots.

To Tess's surprise, it was Arina who stepped forward. "Nikolai Sibirin, we women have decided that it is improper that your patient be so isolated. If you choose the hospitality of this tribe, then we ask her to reside in my tent. As her healer, you will, of course, be given free access."

Niko had already stood. Now he simply bowed his head. "As you wish, Mother Veselov."

Tess tried to move enough to see Arina's mother but the older woman was nowhere in sight. Niko crawled into the tent.

"What did you mean, 'Mother Veselov'?" Tess whispered.

"Arina is etsana now. Didn't I tell you? Her mother died nine days ago and was taken out to the grass these six days past. Ah, but you were—I heard it from Vladimir, who rode messages between us and the tribe until you could be brought here."

"Arina is etsana! I'd have thought Vera would have demanded that honor—"

"Hush, child. They're outside. And you must not under-estimate Arina, or her brother."

"Well, I'm sick of this tent."

"Yes, you will be among women. Varia Telyegin is the healer here, and a very fine one, too."

"But you'll still stay with me, Niko."

"Of course, my child. Don't forget to thank Arina, for she must be treated with respect now."

But upon being eased outside, Tess found her whole position, lying flat on her back and staring up at pretty, petite little Arina, who was younger than herself, to be utterly absurd. "I can't call you 'Mother,' " she blurted.

Arina laughed. "I should hope not, Tess. I'm not even married." Then she blushed suddenly and quickly knelt beside Tess. "Come. You'll be much happier with us. Here, Yeliana, can you take this corner?" Yeliana obeyed, looking too shy to speak.

"I am so glad you are getting better, Tess," said Vera, taking another corner.

Tess smiled vaguely, not trusting her, but Vera looked and sounded sincere enough. Perhaps the shock of almost losing her husband would make her appreciate him more. Varia Telyegin was the fourth, and with Niko trailing meekly behind, they carried her on the blanket through a suddenly empty camp and installed her in what seemed glorious comfort in the outer room of Arina's great tent. The three older women left, leaving Yeliana to tuck pillows behind Tess and arrange her suitably while Niko watched.

"How did you get here?" Tess demanded.

Yeliana glanced up at Niko, then back at Tess. "I ran away. If you could ride with the men, then why shouldn't I do what Vladimir did and go to Bakhalo's jahar-ledest and train? And gain a place for myself in a jahar?"

"How did you come here then?"

"I found the—I found Sibirin, and I rode back here with Vladi. And—" She paled, looking almost scared. "She who was Mother Veselov had just died, and—well, Arina Veselov has only the one brother, and he is married into the Charnov kin, so she hadn't anybody to—" She faltered. When she spoke again her voice had dropped to the barest whisper. "She gifted me her tent, Tess. The one she had when her mother was alive. She says I am to be her sister." Yeliana put a hand to her cheek and wiped away tears. "She *trusts* me, that I will not break this bond. Even after I broke service with the gods and ran away from the shrine.''

"And will you break the bond? To go and train?''

"Never!'' She rose and turned to survey Niko, a slight, passionate girl arrayed with an adolescent's fierce loyalty. He smiled at her. "Sibirin. I cannot ask so much of my sister yet, but if in a year, when she is married and perhaps things are more settled, might I ask her about Vladimir? If he is my brother, then wouldn't he be welcome in my tent?''

"Yeliana, I cannot answer that question. I am not an Elder in this tribe, and in any case, Vladimir has a duty to his dyan. And, perhaps, an interest in a girl in the Orzhekov tribe.''

"But what woman would want an orphan for a husband?'' Yeliana asked.

"If he has made a place for himself, and hers is secure enough, then any woman, I think, who cares for such a man might allow him to mark her. Vladi cannot just mark whom he wishes, after all. Her brothers might well kill him for his trouble.''

"Oh,'' said Yeliana, looking quite as young as she was.

"Yeliana,'' said Tess. "Could you leave us for a moment?'' Yeliana nodded and hurried out. "Niko, why would Arina take her in?''

"Tess, Arina's position is not exactly strong. You must understand that. She is young and unmarried, and she also must contend with a cousin who is, may I say, the kind of relation with whom one's best dealings are done from a position of strength. As etsana, Arina has every right to gift Yeliana into the tribe, as Irena Orzhekov did with you, though many will consider such a gifting rash. As well it might be. But Vera is not well liked, and her only other relation is her father. And her husband, of course. I do not count Vasil because he is no longer welcome here. So Arina has gotten herself another pair of hands, one, incidentally, that will be utterly and personally loyal to her. Don't think Yeliana's life will be easy, though I don't think it will be harsh either.''

"When is Arina going to marry?'' Tess could not keep a certain roughness from her voice. "Soon, I suppose.''

"That, my girl, is none of our business. Do you understand me?''

"Yes, Niko,'' she said meekly. "When can I walk?''

"You can walk when I say you can and not sooner. But I think you will find your confinement less irksome here. By the way, Tess, I would not let anyone know about the Avenue. Yeliana has been spoken to, as have Konstans and Kirill and Vladi. Arina knows because she must. Otherwise, we won't speak of it until Ilya returns."

"What about Tasha?"

"Tasha does not need warning."

"Why must it be a secret? Are you ashamed?"

Niko laughed. "Ah, I'm beginning to hear that refreshingly brutal tone in your voice again. You must be getting better. We will wait for Ilya's return."

It was all he would say.

The days began to have a certain pattern to them. She was allowed to sit for longer periods of time each day, and while she was awake, there was always someone to sit with her: Yeliana most of all, Arina when she could, other young women; even, surprisingly often, Vera. Tess was forced to admit that Vera could be good company when she chose to be, and for whatever reason, Vera chose to entertain Tess. Occasionally Vladi was allowed into the tent in Yeliana's company, but he rarely had anything to say. Anton Veselov had ridden with Bakhtiian to the coast. Niko was the only other man she saw, until at last, seven days later, the damp weather ceased and she was moved out under the awning, where she was permitted to receive visitors.

Tasha came by, and Petya, and Vladi, and Konstans, and two young riders she did not know very well, who had been with them in the battle. Finally Kirill came by. Arina, seeing who it was, excused herself and reminded Yeliana that there was work to be done elsewhere.

Kirill sat down beside her. He glanced at her sidewise and blushed. "You are looking much better, Tess."

"How is your arm, Kirill?"

He shrugged, but the gesture was awkward and unbalanced. "I have a little movement in my shoulder again but I can feel nothing at all in my right arm. If I could not see it there with my eyes, I would think I had lost it. Niko says perhaps in time it will heal."

"You must exercise it. Keep moving it."

He glanced at her again, the briefest touch, and looked away. "Over fifty young men have ridden in to camp here over the last eighteen days. Already they speak of Bakhtiian's great ride beginning next spring. Twelve rode in this morning from Bakhalo's jahar-ledest, and they say that Bakhalo himself may bring the rest here. It's good land with enough water and forage and close to khaja lands. So,'' he paused, looking down at his hands, the picture of modesty, "all these young riders need someone to teach them. And I can't fight.''

"Oh, Kirill, I'm sorry.''

He lifted his gaze to look directly at her for an impetuous moment, and then wrenched his gaze away. Silence stretched out between them. At last, in a whisper, he spoke. "All I ever wanted was to be a rider. It would have been better if I'd died.''

She felt herself pale with fear. She grabbed his good hand. "Never say that, Kirill. Never!''

"We are in camp, Tess. Everyone can see us. I have my reputation to think of. Forgive me.''

"There is nothing to be forgiven,'' she said, but her voice shook and she let go of his hand. "So you will train them.'' They spoke on in this fashion until the subject was exhausted, and even then Kirill lingered, and they discussed whether Yeliana might teach her to spin so that she might have something to do with her hands. Niko arrived finally and chased Kirill off.

"You must be circumspect in your dealings with unmarried men,'' he said mildly, watching Kirill walk away.

"I think I'll ask Arina if she has any mending I can do,'' said Tess, ignoring his rebuke. "When do I get to walk?''

"Tomorrow.''

"Tomorrow!''

"Yes. I think twenty days is time enough. If you are not healed inside now, then—well, let me say that differently. I think resting has achieved as much as it can. Now we must work you again.''

"Oh, Niko, how kind you are.''

"One can only be as kind as one is willing to be ruthless.''

"Oh, God.'' She pressed her hands over her eyes and wiped hard along her cheeks. "That's exactly the kind of thing Yuri always said. I miss him so much.''

He knelt beside her and rested a hand on her hair. "As do we all, my child. Juli and I had six children, and three of them died very young. But I carry all of them in my heart, and I always will.''

Tess sighed and rested her head against his chest. They sat that way for some time.

But the next morning she felt ridiculously excited, so much so that Arina laughed at her. ''You can't *run* today, you know. Ah, here is Niko.''

''Now, Tess,'' said Niko, ''if it hurts badly, you must tell me. Some discomfort I expect.''

''Oh, thank you.'' She grinned. Niko took her on one side, Yeliana, being the taller of the two women, on the other, and they helped her stand up. She felt dizzy. When they let her go, she wondered for a moment if her legs would work, and then she took one step, and a second, and a third and all the way past Arina and pushed through the tent flap to go outside.

''Tess!'' Niko said from behind her, but she ignored him. But the bright light hit her like a wash of pain and she staggered. And fell right into Kirill.

He clasped her tight with his good arm, hesitated, and then lowered her to the rug and let her go, stepping back all the way to the edge of the awning. Arina and Niko and Yeliana hurried out of the tent.

''Tess! I *told* you—''

''Oh, Niko, your face. No, I feel fine. I just lost my balance—'' Then she saw that Kirill was looking anywhere but at her, and that Arina was staring at the rug. ''I'm sorry, Niko,'' she finished, suddenly contrite.

''You will walk when and as much as I allow, young woman.''

''Yes, Niko.''

''Well, then. I'll allow you to walk back into the tent, and I'll see to your wounds. Then we will see.'' But in the end he let her walk twice more that day, once all the way around the great tent.

''Well, girl,'' he said that night, sounding satisfied as he examined the knife wound, ''you'll keep this scar but I think you'll live.''

In five days he allowed her to walk as far as the camp growing up downstream from the Veselov camp, a huddle of small tents belonging to young riders, come to join Bakhtiian. She went there every morning with Yeliana to watch Kirill training the young men. He had learned to compen-

sate a little for his dead arm, but even so, he was clearly
never going to fight or ride in a jahar again. He looked to
her not so much older as more sober, as if his youth had
finally bled away into the grass with the blood he had lost
that terrible day. Every morning she walked, and watched,
and then walked back to Arina's tent at midday. In the afternoon, she would sit beneath the awning and visitors would
come. It embarrassed her, but she learned graciousness. It
reminded her of Charles, of the way he received embassies
and guests in Jeds, of the way conferences and media and
smaller, quieter planning sessions came to him on Odys and
Earth. Tasha brought her a pair of fine boots he had made
for her. Aleksia Charnov gave her her dead brother's finely
wrought dagger. Vera taught her how to lace beads together
into headpieces. While Tess practiced this intricate work,
Kirill and Arina would sit with her, and the three of them
would carry on excruciatingly pleasant and polite conver-
sations until Niko arrived to take her for her late afternoon
walk.

"How many days has it been?" Tess asked Niko one fine
winter afternoon, with the sun shining high in the sky. It
was chilly but not cold.

"Forty-one days. Tess, it is time you let him go—"

A shout came from the direction of the camp. He paused
and stared back, and she paused as well. Kirill was walking
after them.

He was flushed as he came up to them, and he kept his
gaze fixedly on Niko. "Sibirin, there is news. Let me walk
with Tess." Something communicated but not spoken
passed between the two men.

"With Tess's permission," said Niko.

"Given," said Tess. Niko inclined his head and walked
back to camp.

"What news, Kirill?" she asked, suddenly shy. *Oh, God.*
Her heart raced. *What if Ilya was back?*

"Will you walk with me, Tess?" he asked. He rested his
left hand on her elbow, as familiar with her now as he had
always been before. She walked with him until they got as
far as the river, and no one could see them.

"Do you want to sit down?" His color was high. He did
not look at her.

"No, I'm fine." She followed him along the river. Water
flowed and eddied along the bank.

"Tess. Tess. I can't say this."

"Kirill, I have always trusted you."

He sighed and stopped dead in his tracks to look directly at her. "I have to marry again, Tess. My mother has no daughters and no nieces to take care of her when she's old. And I only had one child."

"You have a child, Kirill?" She was astonished.

"Yes." He began walking again in silence, as if the subject was too painful to speak of. She waited him out, and at last he spoke again. "Little Jaroslav. His mother's kin took him, of course. I want children, Tess. Arina Veselov wants me." He stopped and turned to her. "I would be an etsana's husband. I can't fight anymore. What else am I to do?"

"Of course you must." Somehow she kept her voice steady. "I think you will be happy with her, Kirill. I like her very much."

"Yes, she has a good heart. But she is not you, Tess. Oh, gods, forgive me. I have no right to say that."

"Kirill, she will treat you better than I ever could." Then, because it was better than crying, she reached out and embraced him, burying her face in his hair.

He held her for a long moment with his one good arm. She felt his right arm, immobile in its sling, pressing against her chest like an inert object. The river ran heedlessly on behind them.

"Will you care, then," he asked softly, "if I love her?"

"Yes, I'll care. Kirill, I want you to love her. I want you to be happy."

He pushed her back. When he grinned, he looked almost like his old self again. "I daresay, my heart, that we will have a quieter life than you and Ilya."

She flushed. "What was your news, Kirill?"

"Didn't I tell you?" he asked innocently, and then he kissed her chastely on the cheek and turned to lead her back to camp. "No, it isn't what you think. Our tribe has come, Tess."

"Our tribe?"

"Yes."

It took her a long moment before his words developed meaning. *Our* tribe.

"Sonia!" she shrieked, and clapped her hands over her mouth.

"Don't run. Niko will have my other arm if I let you hurt yourself."

She halted abruptly. "I can't go back. How can I face her?"

"Because of Yuri and Mikhal? Tess, she will need another sister very badly now. And anyway, it was a scout brought the news. They won't be here until tomorrow. Come, Tess. You have more courage than this."

She was terrified suddenly at having to face Sonia after so long. And worse, at having to face Ilya. Forty-one days. Soon enough he would return. All too soon. What could she possibly say to him? He would take every advantage of her; he could not help it. She recalled very clearly now how he had gotten her to acknowledge their marriage: "I promise you, my husband." But with Yuri's death, she felt drained of all the life and all the energy that had ever allowed her to face Bakhtiian on equal terms. Soon enough, going on like this, there would be nothing left of her but ashes.

"I have to go back to Charles," she whispered.

"What?" Kirill asked.

"Nothing." But she mentally kept up the litany as they walked back to camp, cycling round and round: *I have to go back to Jeds. I have to go back to Charles.* And at each pause, she could hear Yuri's voice: "Why does everything have to be so final, Tess?" *Because things are final, Yuri,* she said to him. *Because people die and I don't want to go through this again.* She clutched Kirill's arm more tightly, and he glanced at her, but mercifully he said nothing. She wiped away tears with the back of her hand. *Because I'm afraid.*

"Gods, Kirill, I can't go back there crying."

"Why not? You're a woman. And you lost your brother. Why shouldn't you cry? It's nothing to be ashamed of."

She smiled through her tears. "My sweet Kirill," she said, and then they came to camp and she relinquished her grip on him. Arina Veselov came to greet them, looking sober but not unhappy, and led Tess back to her tent, repeating the news Kirill had told her. Kirill followed them, but he walked next to Arina now not next to Tess.

The evening dragged on. That night she could not sleep. Morning came too soon, and then, dragging on toward midday, lasted far, far too long.

"Look!" said Yeliana, standing up. "Look there. Wagons."

Tess scrambled to her feet. She could not help it, she ran—as well as she could run—out to the edge of camp and into the grass as the wagons and riders and the bleating flocks crested the rise and trundled down toward them in a cacophonous, chaotic mass. She halted, searching, staring, until—

"Sonia!" Oh, God, she looked the same; pale, maybe; and then they embraced. Tess burst into tears. Sonia burst into tears. They both cried, hanging on each other. Finally, as wagons lurched past them and children squealed with excitement and a horse brushed by so close its tail flicked Sonia's tunic, they separated.

"How did you know?" Tess asked.

"Niko rode out to us last night." Sonia had changed not at all. Her voice, her face, everything—like Yuri in so many ways, and yet utterly and only like herself. Except for the new lines of grief etched under her blue eyes. "He told Mama about—" she faltered—"about Yuri, and Mikhal, and Fedya."

Fedya. Fedya had died so long ago that to Tess it seemed almost a distant memory. Gods, would Yuri fade like that?

"Tess, what's wrong? You've gotten so thin and so pale. Niko says you almost died. Well, we'll take you to our tent and Mama will fatten you up."

And so, when the Orzhekov tribe set up its camp alongside the Veselov camp, Tess was taken politely but firmly back into Mother Orzhekov's domain. Her tent was set up next to Sonia's. Sonia's children—the baby, Kolia, grown quite tall, and walking—made free with her space and her blankets and her gear, and she ate every night under the awning of Mother Orzhekov's great tent, and took her daily walks to the training ground with Sonia.

"Why does that awful woman come here every day?" Sonia asked three days after their arrival. "Poor Petya. She can't love him."

"Oh, look, here she comes." They giggled a little and then controlled themselves.

"I do not think the khaja will be able to resist this army," said Vera, settling herself gracefully beside them. Her gaze took in the field but did not seem to dwell for longer than an instant on her own husband where he stood to one side with Konstans and a few other young men, watching Kirill talk with an old man.

"That is Kerchaniia Bakhalo, isn't it?" Tess asked.

"Yes," said Vera. "He arrived yesterday, and I'm sure he has sixty young men with him. I hear ten of them are orphans, and one is not only said to have killed his entire tribe with a plague but stolen a horse from the Mirsky tribe as well."

Sonia laughed. "What, and none of the Mirskys caught him and killed him for it? And they always bragging about what fine riders they are? He must be very terrible or else very clever. Which of them is he?"

"How am I to know?" Vera asked. "He is only an orphan, after all. I suppose if any riders from the Mirsky tribe come here, then they'll kill him." Her gaze drifted out to Bakhalo and Kirill, who were consulting with Tasha and two elderly men no longer dressed in the red and black of jahar riders. "Poor Arina." Vera smiled sweetly. "I think she thought Kirill Zvertkov would mark her but now I don't think he will. What do you think, Tess?"

Tess shrugged. "Oh, I suppose he is waiting for his mother to get to know her first."

"I thought he had other interests." Then, evidently tired of this game, Vera rose and excused herself.

"Does Kirill have other interests?" asked Sonia. "Tess, don't look away from me. You're blushing. We haven't talked much about your journey, you know. Only about Yuri and Mikhal—" A pause here, and she went on. "—and Fedya, and I am very glad you and Fedya—but, Tess, I know very well there are things you aren't telling me."

She could not talk about Ilya to Sonia. Not now, not when the only way she had to cope with her fear of his return was to not think of him as hard as she could. But her feelings for Kirill were true enough and still raw enough that they could serve as a smoke screen.

"Tess, I will make no secret now that I had hoped, when you left us, that you and Ilya—well, never mind that. What is it you want to tell me?"

"Kirill and I were lovers. But I can't—I can't marry him, and Arina Veselov has made it known that she wants him as her husband. I like Arina Veselov—"

"But you loved Kirill. Ah, well, he is charming in his own way. I've always preferred quieter men. If it is true that he can never use that arm again, then he's done very well to become an etsana's husband. But if he loves you, Tess, then what is to stop him marking you?''

"He won't mark me. No, we've resolved this between us, Sonia. He'll mark Arina. He's waiting—I don't know. I don't understand, sometimes, how Arina can like me.''

"Do you think she ought to hate you for loving Kirill and for Kirill's loving you? Why should she? He'll make her a good husband. And he'll have other lovers. Now Vera, Vera doesn't like you one bit, my sister, and that makes me think—'' She halted. On the field, Kirill had turned, and he looked up at them and lifted his good hand to wave.

"Do you think I could?'' asked Tess suddenly.

"What, marry him? But women have no choice in marriage, Tess, don't you know that?''

Tess flushed. "Practice saber a little. I'm much better, really.''

"Dressed in those clothes?''

"I'll ask him.'' Tess rose. Sonia chuckled and walked down with her. Kirill came to meet them, followed by Kerchaniia Bakhalo.

"Why shouldn't I fight?'' Tess asked. "I've already learned a great deal.''

"You've learned a little, Tess,'' said Kirill mildly, though he grinned at Bakhalo. "But you've been very well taught. Why not? That is, Sonia, if you think Mother Orzhekov will approve.''

"No,'' said Tess. "This is my choice. I'm going to fight. And I promise to stop when I get too tired.''

"I'll walk you back to your tent,'' said Sonia.

As they left, Tess turned to her. "You aren't going to try to talk me out of this, are you?''

"No, ought I to? Tess, however much you are jaran, you aren't jaran and you never will be. Why shouldn't you fight if you wish to? But I'd better tell Mama now because I'm sure malicious tongues will see the news gets to her in other ways.''

So every morning Tess wore her jahar clothes and her saber and went to the practice field. She had to rest frequently, but other than that, Kirill and Bakhalo made no concessions to her at all. Bakhalo was a dry old stick of a man who was unfailingly unkind to all his students, though scrupulously fair, and Kirill possessed the unlikely ability to treat her with the same cheerful ruthlessness as he did the others: they had been lovers, they had loved, but here on the field he could separate those feelings from his teaching even while Tess struggled to separate them from her learning.

As they paused one day, she to rest, he to survey two of Bakhalo's students fencing, she stood beside him casually and watched as well.

"He's very good," she said of one of the fencers. "He's one of the orphans."

"He's better than Vladimir," said Kirill. "But I won't put them together yet because while this fellow won't take it personally, Vladi will. You get along very well with all these orphans. Or have you taken them under your wing?"

"Kirill, I haven't any wings."

"Tess, you are Bakhtiian's wife. That gives you rather more—very well, I won't say anything further."

"The truth is, that except for Konstans and you and Tadheus, when he comes by, the ones who are orphans are the only ones who don't treat me strangely. The others aren't sure what to make of me, a woman wearing jahar clothes."

"Fairly earned."

"You know that, and those in Bakhtiian's jahar know it, but the rest don't. Aleksi there, and the other orphans, don't care because they're set apart, too."

"Well, it's true most of them treat you stiffly, but for all that, you're doing well. But you mustn't push yourself."

"Kirill, I want to tell you how much I respect that you've been able to teach me—that—" She hesitated. "Everything there's been between us—"

"There is between us," he said quietly.

"There *is* between us, and you never favor me or bully me."

"Bully you?" He laughed. "My heart, if ever Ilya tries to teach you fighting, he will bully you for fear he'd otherwise favor you."

"Ilya," said Tess, "will never teach me saber."

"What's going on over there? Boys, stop a moment." Kirill turned. "By the gods, how did he manage to ride in here with no more disturbance than that?"

Tess turned.

He stared straight at her. Of course. If there was anyone else on the practice field—and there were a good eighty or so young men out there—they might have been invisible for all he knew. From this distance, she could not tell if he was angry or amused. From this distance, she would know him anywhere. He walked out onto the field toward her, and instantly she saw one change: he was no longer limping. It lent a certain implacable purpose to his stride that had been lacking those weeks when he was injured. Niko walked beside him, and Josef and Tasha, and Anton and Sergei Veselov. But in a moment, Niko veered off to greet Bakhalo, towing Sergei Veselov in his wake, and then Kirill started forward, deserting her, to fall in with Josef and Tasha and Anton Veselov.

Ilya halted in front of her. *If I faint,* Tess thought, *then I don't have to say anything.* God, he was beautiful. The midday sun shone strong on his face. His black hair curled slightly at the ends but she could tell from its wave and thickness that he had just cut it, and his beard was neat and impeccably trimmed. He wore a second necklace around the curve of his throat, this one of finely polished black stones strung together. Tess glanced to either side. Most of the young men were staring at them. Bakhtiian broke his gaze from her and surveyed the field. Instantly, they retreated, and a moment later Bakhalo called for an assembly down at the other end of the field. Kirill had vanished.

"Walk with me," ordered Ilya.

Yes, definitely, he was angry. "I beg your pardon?" she asked.

"Will you walk with me, I beg you," he repeated in exactly the same tone of voice. She walked. As soon as they were out of earshot, he began. "Do you suppose I rode all that way only to return to find my wife wearing men's clothes standing out in the middle of the practice field with every unmarried man in camp?"

"You gave me this shirt."

He took ten steps before he answered. "It was fairly earned."

"And some of them are married."

"Arina Veselov isn't married."

"Don't you dare."

"I beg your pardon, Tess. I had no right to say that."

She stopped, emboldened by the softening of his voice. "When did you get here? Where is the jahar?"

"Josef and I, and Sergei and Anton, rode forward scout.

The rest will be here late this afternoon.'' His face lit suddenly. "And the horses! One hundred and twenty-four. Tess, they are beautiful.'' His expression changed, watching her, and he lifted a hand to touch her cheek. She stopped breathing. Then he glanced back toward camp. They still stood in full view of the field and of a fair portion of the tents of Veselov's camp. He dropped his hand as swiftly as if she had burned him.

Somewhere she found the ability to start breathing again, but her breaths came uneven and a little ragged.

"And the khepellis?" she asked, speaking quickly to cover her agitation. "Did they get on a ship? There was no problem? And the letter for my brother, and the relic?"

He began to walk again, but she did not move. He halted and came back to her. "Tess, do you want to stand here where everyone can see us?"

"Yes."

"Very well. Here is the letter."

She unrolled it. "But this is from Marco!"

"You know him?"

"Yes, he's part of Charles's—retinue. Ah, he travels a lot. He supervises trade agreements."

"Is that so?"

She flushed and, instead of looking at him, read the letter. Your dear old Uncle Marco, indeed. He had been at Charles's court in Jeds frequently when she was there as a child but he was not precisely the sort of man who enjoys children. Dr. Hierakis and Suzanne Elia Arevalo had spent more time with her than he ever had. Marco explored, and he had come from Earth to explore Rhui in the oldest way known, on foot, by horse, by sea, for Charles but mostly, she suspected, for the adventure. *Make of that what you will.* She read back through the letter.

"He sent something for me."

Ilya hesitated, then slipped a dagger from his belt and handed it to her. Tess held it in her palm. Such a tiny thing to be so important.

"Well," she said finally, for something to say. "Thank you."

"I told him I would kill him if I ever found out that he hadn't delivered either message or relic."

"Ilya!" She wanted to laugh but he looked so grim that

she smoothed the letter out instead. "I feel sure it will get there. And the khepellis?"

"I hope you will forgive me, Tess, but I lied to Lord Ishii. I told him—" His voice shook. "—that you were dead." He stopped. "Tess," he whispered. "I didn't even know, all that time, if when I came back, you would still be alive." The agony in his expression disturbed her so much that she found refuge in staring off toward the camp. Though a number of young men still worked on the practice field, in the camp itself some event had occurred to excite the interest of the tribe. Children ran, screaming and leaping, and adults walked quickly away from the periphery of the camp toward the hidden center.

"Niko took good care of me," she said in a voice not her own. "And anyway, Bakhtiian, as I recall, I promised you that I would live."

"Yes," he said in a steadier voice, "you did. Can you forgive me the lie?"

Startled, she looked up at him. "Of course, I forgive you. You probably saved my life." She faltered.

"You will never grant me anything simply because I am your husband, will you? Nothing, except when you were so ill that it was easier to agree than to argue. Nothing of your own will. Well, you told me yourself you did not want me. I ought to have listened."

"Ilya. . . . " Once, before everything had been shattered by Yuri's death, she would have yelled back at him. Now she simply felt faint. "I have to sit down," she said apologetically.

"Tess! Gods, you're pale." He closed the gap between them and picked her up in his arms. "I'll take you back to my aunt's tent."

"I can walk."

"You will not walk, my wife. You're exhausted and as pale as the winter grass. I think I may be allowed to carry you so far."

It was no use fighting, so she simply lay against him, cradling her head on his shoulder and shutting her eyes. She could not bear to see what kind of stares were surely being directed their way. She heard Niko.

"Ilya! What is wrong?"

"She is exhausted. You've been working her too hard. Is this how you take care of her?"

"She was fine until you came back," said Niko crossly. "But I was coming to get you in any case. You are wanted at your aunt's tent."

Tess kept her eyes clenched shut. He walked with her easily, as if the burden was gratifying to him. She heard a few whispers, a few broken comments, but nothing she could not ignore. For a little stretch, there was silence, as if no one was about. But when he halted, she felt a roiled hush surrounding them, as of many people whose attention was split among several momentous occurrences.

"Nephew." This in Irena Orzhekov's ringing tones. "I hope you will come forward and explain this immodest display. This woman may be your cousin but she is also unmarried."

"Unmarried! She is my wife."

The silence rang more loudly than shouts would have. Tess opened her eyes. Most of the members of the tribes of Orzhekov and Veselov had gathered here before the awning of Mother Orzhekov's tent. Beneath the awning, the two etsanas faced each other, seated respectably on pillows. Blood still wet Arina's cheek, seeping from the cut scored from her cheekbone diagonally down to the line of her jaw. Kirill stood behind her, looking pale but determined. His mother knelt in front of the two women, and whatever discussion Ilya's precipitous entrance had interrupted clearly involved her.

"Your wife?" demanded Mother Orzhekov. "I see no mark, Nephew."

Every gaze was fixed on them. Behind Irena Orzhekov sat her three daughters. Sonia stared transfixed, hands on her cheeks, lips parted, fighting back a grin. Behind Arina Veselov, behind Kirill, sat Vera, and behind her, Yeliana. Vera's face was white, her mouth a thin line.

"Let me down," Tess whispered fiercely.

"Ah, so you have come back to me," he murmured. "You were acting far too meek." He lowered her gently and set her on her feet beside him but he did not relinquish his grip around her waist. It would be undignified to struggle in so public a place and with such an audience. Doubtless he counted on it.

"Niko," he said, "I thought my aunt had been told."

"Bakhtiian, it was not my right to tell."

Ilya glanced at Tess. "With your permission?" he asked,

but he did not let go of her. She nodded mutely. "Mother Orzhekov," he said formally. "Terese Soerensen and I rode down the Avenue of the shrine of Morava at sunset. The ceremony was completed. The bond has been sealed. So she is indeed my wife. And I," he added, with a sardonic edge to his voice, "am her husband."

Silence could not contain their audience's astonishment. Exclamations, comments, every kind of noise broke out, and hushed to stillness when Irena Orzhekov rose. Arina sat with complete composure. Kirill, behind her, now looked strangely serene. Sonia had clapped her hands together, delighted. Vera—Vera was gone.

"I will have quiet," said Mother Orzhekov. "I think this assembly has ended. If you agree, Mother Veselov. And you, Elders?" More nods from various aged faces.

She had to say no more. The crowd dispersed quickly and with a great deal of noise.

"Come here, Ilyakoria," said Irena when only the etsanas and their families and five Elders from each tribe remained. She sounded displeased. He looked not the least bit cowed. "You will sit beside me until our business is finished here. Tess, sit with Sonia."

Sonia said nothing when Tess sat down next to her but squeezed her hand.

"Now, Olya Zvertkov, is it truly your wish to bind yourself over into the Veselov tribe?"

These negotiations went on for some time. The two etsanas haggled over tents and pots and how many of which flock ought to go to which tribe in recompense for the loss of Kirill's mother or the gain of Kirill himself. Tess rubbed her eyes and lay her head on Sonia's comforting shoulder, and Sonia put her arm around Tess to hold her steady.

At last they agreed, and Arina rose. Bakhtiian rose as well. "I have not yet released Kirill from my jahar," he said. "And while I claim the right to perform that release in private, I ask that he remain behind now."

The two women nodded, and Arina took her family and her Elders and left. Bakhtiian gave his aunt a curt nod and then walked away to where his tent was pitched some distance behind hers.

"Tess!" whispered Sonia. "Why didn't you tell me! Did Yuri know?"

"Yes."

"Well, the gods' blessing on that. It would have made him happy."

"Everything made Yuri happy," said Tess bitterly, and then she stopped, seeing what Bakhtiian had brought them from his tent. Two blankets, folded neatly, and on top of them, two red shirts, folded with equal neatness. A scrap of sleeve showed on one, a line of Yuri's distinctive embroidery.

"I bring these to you, his sisters." Ilya knelt before his cousins and held out his hands. Kira, the eldest, took them from him with reverence, but instead of turning to Stassia first, she turned to Tess.

"Which will you have, my sister?" she asked.

Tess started to cry silently. She took the topmost shirt gently from the pile and held it hard against her face. The silk was cool and soft. Sonia took the other shirt and cradled it against her chest. She, too, was weeping. Kira and Stassia each took a blanket.

"Because my kinsman Yurinya has neither brother nor father living, I return his saber to you, my aunt." He offered it to her.

Tears ran down Irena's face, but her expression remained composed. "You are his nearest male relation. It is yours, now, Ilyakoria."

He shut his eyes for an instant. "Thank you," he murmured, and he simply held it a moment before he remembered where he was. Then he turned to Kirill.

"Perhaps, Zvertkov, you will tell Yuri's sisters, and Mikhal's wife, how they died."

Kirill was very pale but his voice was steady, and the account he gave covered Yuri and Mikhal with so much glory that Tess could hardly believe it was true though she knew it was: that Mikhal had ridden back into the fight instead of riding for help, as he might well have done with no shame—as Petya had; that Yurinya had saved Tess's life. The children had crept up to listen, and Katerina and Ivan clutched their mother, faces solemn. Stassia held little Kolia.

"And were they burned," asked Irena when he had finished, "and released from the burdens of the earth, as was their right?"

Niko and Kirill both looked at Ilya. Tess hid her face in her hands.

"They were given," said Ilya with no expression in his voice, "what they most wished. Now, Aunt, if you will excuse me, I will ask Sibirin and Zvertkov to accompany me while I return what is theirs to Fedya's and Mikhal's families."

Irena inclined her head. "You are excused, Nephew. And Ilya." She paused. Tess looked up. "To marry cousins is dangerous. To marry them in the sight of the gods—well, we shall see. Certainly you have never lacked arrogance. But you have ridden a long way to return here, and with this I can sympathize. For this night, Nephew, my tent is yours." She rose and shook out her skirts, and then turned to address her family. "Come, children. You must take your blankets to your mothers' tents tonight."

Ilya simply stared at his aunt for a moment, as if this gesture bewildered him. But then, then he turned his head smoothly to give Tess so piercing a look that she felt as if they were already alone and she stripped utterly naked, far past such unimportant layers as clothing and skin, down, down to where the wind sweeps fire across the earth itself.

Then he turned and strode away, Niko and Kirill at his heels.

CHAPTER TWENTY-EIGHT

"If one does not hope
one will not find the unhoped for,
since there is no trail leading to it,
and no path."
—HERACLEITUS OF EPHESUS

Dusk, stars, evening.

Tess let Sonia help her dress in all the beautiful women's clothing gifted her by Nadezhda Martov, bracelets, the beaded headpiece. She felt empty, burned away until she was hollow.

"You're being very quiet," said Sonia. "I'll leave the lantern, and you can sit here on these pillows. Tess, it isn't as if you haven't lain with him before—" Abruptly, she sat down beside Tess and took her cold hands in her own. "You haven't?"

Tess could only shake her head numbly.

"But you rode down the Avenue together."

Tess found a whisper. "I didn't know."

"You didn't know!" Sonia was speechless for a moment. "I can only suppose that he didn't have the nerve to try to mark you, knowing you could use your saber, so he— Gods!" Tess glanced at her. The lantern light cast edges on the soft planes of Sonia's face. "Well, Tess, I'm sorry, but you're his wife now, and I can't interfere." She kissed her on the cheek and stood up, abandoning Tess in the middle of the silken mass of Irena Orzhekov's finest pillows. "But listen to me." Her voice was quiet but vehement. "Perhaps we do not know one another so well, you and I, but I can see into your heart, my sister, and I know you are strong enough for what has been given you."

"For Ilya?"

"Ilya is not the sum of your life, Tess. You forget that I have been to Jeds. I have seen the prince on progress through the city. I know there is more to you than these plains, and yet, there is Ilya as well. And you are the only woman—the only woman? no, the only person, truly—who has the courage to stand up to him on every ground. If there is no one to hold him in check, then what is to happen to him and to us?''

Tess stared down at her hands. ''You're asking too much of me,'' she murmured, but when she looked up, Sonia had gone. Every doubt she had ever carried flooded back in on her. All the burdens of being Charles's heir, the cold weight of duty, and now this. *Lord, to add this on top of it all.*

She heard from outside the sound, but not the words, of a brief conversation: a woman's voice, a man's. Then the rustle of the tent flap and his movement through the outer chamber. He pushed aside the curtains that separated the outer chamber from the inner one and halted, poised there.

''Gods,'' he said, staring at her, ''you are beautiful, my wife.''

She said nothing, but her gaze followed him as he let the curtains slip down behind him and crossed to her. He knelt in front of her.

''I brought this for you.'' He unclasped the black necklace and with the greatest tenderness clasped it around her throat. He let his hands settle on either side of the curve of her neck, warm hands, though she felt the slight tremble in them against her skin. He gazed at her as if the answer to every question he had ever asked rested in her face.

He was so close but she could move neither toward him nor away from him, caught in this eddy.

''I am lost,'' she whispered.

His eyes narrowed and his lips, slightly parted, closed tightly. ''You are afraid of me.'' He took his hands from her. ''You were never afraid of me before,'' he said accusingly.

She wrenched her gaze away from him. ''I don't know what I am.''

She felt him stand, and looked up to see him walk to the curtain. ''You are my wife. You are also, I believe, heir to the Prince. And Sonia's sister, and a daughter to Irena Orzhekov. But mostly you are Tess.'' He looked furiously angry and yet at the same time terribly upset. ''And if Tess ever decides she wants me, I will be waiting for her.''

He jerked the curtain aside and left. Tess sank back into

the pillows. She felt so utterly relieved that she could almost laugh at herself. She stared at the shadows dappling the soft ceiling of the tent. Footsteps stirred, and the curtain slipped aside.

"Tess?"

"Oh, hello, Sonia," said Tess in a voice that sounded almost normal.

"Tess. I—" She hesitated. "Do you— Perhaps— That is, I saw Ilya— But perhaps you'd rather I left you— I don't know—"

"I'm hungry," said Tess, sitting up.

"Well," said Sonia briskly, "you hardly ate a bite at supper so that doesn't surprise me."

"You aren't mad at me?"

"What occurs between you and Ilya is not any of my business, Tess."

Tess stood. "You and Yuri have been matchmaking since the day I got to your tribe. Admit it."

"No, in fact, it was several days before the thought occurred to me. It was at the dance, when you told him you were riding with them. And forced him to accept it and take you along."

"What's wrong with me?" Tess asked, remembering how brash she had been.

"You were almost killed, and you still haven't regained your strength. And you saw your brother killed. I grieve as much as you do but I didn't see him die. I can still imagine that he is simply out riding and will come back tomorrow. I don't envy you that knowledge or that memory."

"But, Sonia, I want that knowledge and that memory. For you, they rode out one day and never came back. I couldn't stand to live that way."

Sonia took her gently by the arm. "Perhaps that is why you still practice saber. Come, Tess. There's still meat, I think, or if you wish, a celebration at the Veselov camp. Arina has gone into seclusion for the next nine days but we women can visit her. I'm sure she would like to see you."

"Yes," said Tess, taking great comfort in the thought of the company of women, "I'd like that."

Sonia surveyed her critically. "And I want you to know how very much I hate you for being able to wear that particular shade of green. That is Nadezhda Martov's dye, is it not? Yes, we had some of her cloth once but it simply made me look ill, and it did nothing for Stassi or Kira or Anna either, so we had to trade it off. It made us sick to give it up. But it looks stunning on you." Tess blushed, remembering Ilya's voice as he called her "beautiful."

"Well? Are we going? Or are you going to stand there and gloat over your good looks all night?" Tess laughed and followed her out.

It was easy enough, in the morning, to go back to her old habits: in the mornings she would practice saber and fighting, and in the afternoons she would work and gossip with the women. Now that Bakhtiian's jahar had returned, she had plenty of company on the practice field, and their acceptance of her presence there did not go unnoticed by the others: especially the respect with which such noted riders as Josef and Tasha treated her. Bakhtiian, who observed and even participated out on the field at intervals, ignored her as he might ignore any other young rider whose presence was beneath his notice. If he did address her, it was always and only as "Cousin." He spent a great deal of time with his new horses, or speaking with the men who had come to join him, or taking reports from the scouts and parties of riders sent out to search for Mikhailov. Kirill continued to be a patient, fair, and shrewd teacher, and he carried himself with a new self-assurance to which even the older men deferred at the appropriate times. But Tess kept in general to the company of the orphans, feeling rather more comfortable with them, half in and half out of the tribes, than with anyone else.

With the women she felt entirely at home. Mother Orzhekov said nothing about her marriage. If anyone noticed that she slept in her tent and Ilya in his, no one mentioned it to her. At meals, Ilya was unfailingly polite to her. If she caught him staring at her now and again—well, then, could she blame him? If she caught herself staring at him—well, God knew how handsome he was.

"I am getting stronger," she said to Sonia one day. "I got through all morning without having to rest."

"Yes," said Sonia, "and we've worked all afternoon without you resting either. Tonight Arina comes out of seclusion. Poor Kirill has been hiding outside of camp all afternoon."

"Yes," said Tess with a grin, "he was looking rather nervous and pink at practice. I told him so."

"You *are* feeling better."

"Yes," said Tess, realizing it was true. "I am."

After supper, Tess went alone to her tent and pulled out the tiny dagger and stared at it. She slid her thumb up the blade, felt it hum. The hilt peeled away. Charles needed to know that she was alive. She lifted it to her eye level so the intricate machinery could take her retinal scan. Then, with decision, she triggered the codes. Not the primary codes, the emergency alert, but the secondary pulse, tuned to her signature code, that said merely, *I am safe.* For five minutes it pulsed, silent to her ears, and then it stopped. She slid the transmitter back into its sheath and left it with her saber and her jahar clothes, safe in her tent.

That evening the two tribes held a dance in honor of Mother Veselov's wedding. Arina was carried out to the great fire, weighed down with so much finery that she actually shone. Kirill, allowed to see her for the first time since the day he had marked her, greeted her with a kiss far more intimate than was proper for so public a place, and he was chastised good-naturedly all evening by women and men both.

"Really, Kirill," said Tess, standing aside with him while they watched the dancing, "such an immodest display astonishes me in you." He laughed. He was very happy. "Why don't you just leave early?"

"Oh, I would if I could, Tess, but you know it isn't right. We have to stay here until the very end."

"Poor Kirill. Hello, Sonia."

"You will dance with me, Kirill," Sonia said.

"Sonia, I can't—"

"Not as you used to, no. But you'd better learn."

"Tess," pleaded Kirill, "save me."

"Forgive me," said Tess, "but I have urgent business elsewhere." She left him to his fate.

She walked a ways around the periphery and there, like a beacon, she saw him. Except that he was speaking with Vera Veselov, and Vera was leaning very close, her body canted toward him in a most intimate fashion. Tess stopped dead. It took her a moment to recognize the emotion that had taken hold of her. Arina, of course, shone with joy at this celebration, but Vera was as always the most striking woman present. Tess drew herself up and marched over to them.

"Oh, I beg your pardon, Vera," she said sweetly, "but my husband has promised me this dance."

Ilya looked startled. Vera smiled, but it was probably the most vicious smile Tess had ever seen. "No, I beg *your* pardon, Tess. I hope you enjoy the celebration." She turned on her heel and strode swiftly away.

"Had I promised you this dance?" Ilya asked.

"No. You were behaving most improperly, Bakhtiian."

"Was I?"

"Flirting like that? Yes, you were."

"But this is a celebration. One can allow a little immodesty at a celebration."

"Not that much," Tess muttered. "What did she want, anyway?"

"What do you suppose she wanted?"

"Yes, I suppose it would be easy enough to slip away and return to her tent. Everyone is *here,* after all."

"Yes, it would be," he agreed.

"What are you smiling at?"

"Your temper."

She did not like the way he was looking at her. "Well," she demanded, "are we going to dance?"

Immediately, he drew back. "You know I prefer not to dance," he said stiffly.

"What, is it too undignified for you? But you dance very well, Bakhtiian, and I *love* to dance. Therefore, you will dance with me."

"As you command, my wife," he said meekly, and followed her out. He danced very well indeed, and she made him dance three dances with her before she agreed to pause. They walked off to the side, he with his hand lingering at her waist until, remembering himself, he shifted it self-consciously to his belt.

"You look very lovely tonight," he said, not looking at her.

"Thank you." She smiled. His sudden shyness made her feel bolder. "But you know, I'm more comfortable in jahar clothes. I only wear these to please Mother Orzhekov."

"As you should," he said in a constrained voice.

"You don't approve of me fighting, do you, Ilya?"

"I have no right to dictate what you do as long as my aunt approves it."

"Your aunt doesn't approve it. Or, that is, I did not ask her permission."

He rounded on her. "You didn't ask her permission! Tess, I remind you that—"

"Don't lecture me. Yes, I am beholden to her hospitality. Yes, she took me in, for which I will always be grateful. But I am not jaran, Ilya, and as long as my behavior does not offend your gods, I will do what I think is best for myself."

"Even if it displeases my aunt?"

"Even if it displeases *you.*"

"I suggest," he said coldly, "that we either end this conversation now, before we make a spectacle of ourselves, or continue it elsewhere, where the entire camp cannot hear and see us."

She began to walk away from the crowd and the fire and he walked beside her. Their silence was not as much antagonistic as measuring. "Teach me saber," she said.

"What, right now?"

"Yes, right now. No, of course not right now. Tomorrow. The next day."

"I can't teach you, Tess."

"Because you don't want to?"

"Because I can't. Give me credit, please, for so much self knowledge. I would not teach you well or fairly."

"Well," she admitted, a little mollified, "Kirill said as much. Then let me ride in your jahar."

"You are not adept enough yet, nor experienced enough yet. Not for my jahar or for any dyan's jahar."

"If I learn enough to become so?"

"Most of these young men have been fighting with saber since they were boys, I might remind you."

"Am I that bad?"

"No," he said reluctantly. "You're rather good, for how few months you've been practicing. You have a certain gift, you're strong, and you work very hard."

It was quiet in the Veselov camp. The great fire burned with a roar alongside the beaten ground of the practice field, where now the dancing was being held. A man passed them, hurrying toward the celebration, and they saw a shape slip into a tent out at the edge of camp.

"Where are we going?" Ilya asked finally.

"I'm not sure." She looked up at the brilliant cast of

stars above. Somewhere out there, worlds spun and ships traveled, spanning vast distances; Charles wove his plots, and the Chapalii wove other plots still. Her life, all of it, and yet this world was hers as well. She had done her duty to Charles—tracked the Chapalii and not only alerted him to their presence but discovered a relic of such value that she could not begin to measure it. "I'm not sure what I ought to do anymore, or what I can do, or whether or not Yuri was right."

"Right about what?" he asked softly.

She stopped. They had walked about halfway through the Veselov camp, and the two great tents, one belonging to Arina and one to Vera, lay some fifty paces behind them. A low fire burned in the fire pit that separated the tents, illuminating the wedding ribbons woven up the tent poles that supported the awning of Arina's tent. And, Tess saw, a small pile of gear deposited on one corner of the rug: her new husband's possessions, to be moved inside by him this night.

"Oh, damn," said Tess in a low voice. "Look, there's Vera."

Vera stood just outside the entrance to her own tent, talking with a man Tess could not recognize from this distance. By the way she was gesticulating with her arms, Tess could guess that it was poor Petya, and that he was being scolded for some illusory offense.

"Tess," said Ilya as softly as he had spoken before but in an utterly changed voice, "where is your saber?"

"In my tent."

"Damn. Walk back to the fire."

"Ilya."

"*That* is Vasil. How he got into this camp I do not know, why Vera is sheltering him I do not care to guess, but there is going to be trouble any moment now. Go alert Josef and Tasha."

"Where are you going?"

He put one hand on his saber hilt. "To talk with him."

She laid both hands on his chest. "No. Don't be a fool. Don't you remember when Doroskayev sent men into Sakhalin's camp to kill you? What if Vasil isn't alone? Let's walk back to the fire together, now."

But it was already too late. Vera's companion had stepped past her and it was obvious that, even over such distance and in the darkness, Vasil and Ilya were looking at each other. The flap leading into Vera's tent swept aside, and three men rushed out, sabers drawn.

"Stahar linaya!" Ilya cried. He drew his saber. "Tess! Back to the fire."

She stepped away from him. The three men closed, slowing now to split around him, and Ilya edged away from her. Vasil had not moved. Tess ran for Vera's tent.

"Damn you!" Vera was shrieking. "Go kill him! You coward, go kill him!"

Vasil backhanded her so hard she fell to the rug. She began to sob. "You're a fool, Vera. He will never love you. But who is this?" He sidestepped Tess's rush neatly, tripped her, and than pinned her to the ground. "The khaja pilgrim. How interesting."

Behind, she heard the ring of sabers and a distant—too distant—shout. "Give me your saber," she said to Vasil from the ground, "and I'll speak for you, and maybe they'll spare your life."

"He rode with her down the Avenue," Vera gasped out between sobs. "I want him dead."

"Vera. Shut up. Get the horses." Then, moving before she realized he meant to, Vasil lifted Tess up and pinned her to him. "They'll never spare my life, and I don't plan on giving it up. Retreat to me!" he cried.

Horses snorted and pawed beside them. Vera stood at their heads, clutching their reins. Tears streamed down her face. "You are a coward," she gasped. "You're afraid to kill him. You've always loved him more than you ever loved me."

"Forgive me," said Vasil, and in the instant before she realized he was speaking to *her,* Tess got her head turned enough to see Vasil's three men sprinting back toward them, Ilya at their heels. Farther, much farther back, cries of alarm and shouts and commotion stirred the camp. Then she saw the flash of Vasil's knife, and a hard knob struck her temple.

* * *

Charles Soerensen sat in an anteroom of the imperial palace. Indeed, the only city left on the homeworld of Chapal *was* the imperial palace.

It had taken him five days from his arrival on Paladia Major to get dispensation to enter imperial space, and five days on Chapal to get this far, seven doors away from au-

dience with the emperor. Suzanne sat next to him, decently
swathed in scholar's robes; she was his best interpreter—
best except for his own missing sister, of course—but very
few females were allowed into the imperial presence. Across
from them, on benches grown from crystal, sat Hon Echido
and two elder members of Keinaba, those who would par-
take of the rite of loyalty with Charles in the emperor's
presence.

If the emperor allowed it. Charles allowed himself a
smile, a brief one, secure that Chapalii did not interpret
facial tics as meaningful of emotion or thought. For all he
knew, it would take him five months to get past those last
seven doors, and even then he did not know if the Keinaba
dispensation would still be in force. But, like water working
past a dam in a stream, eventually he would find his way
past each obstacle. Eventually, one way or the other, he
would get the key that would allow the next rebellion to
succeed.

The far door—the door leading back away from the emperor's presence—opened, and Tai Naroshi Toraokii entered
with his retinue. The near door opened, revealing a lord in
the silver livery of the imperial house. Tai Naroshi paused
in front of Charles. Charles did not rise.

"Tai-en." Naroshi inclined his head.

"Tai-en." Charles inclined his head in turn. "The translation program works very well. Your artisans are efficient."

"I am gratified that you find them so. I express my grief
with your family at this time."

Charles glanced at Suzanne, wondering if the program
was not working. She blinked twice: the words were correct. "Your concern is generous, Tai-en," Charles replied.

"Perhaps you will adopt a proper male heir now. I would
be honored, Tai-en, if you would consider my sister, who
is an architect of great renown, for the design of your sister's mausoleum. She would certainly design a fitting and
magnificent structure of unparalleled beauty."

One of his retinue had flushed blue. Charles stared at
Naroshi, both of them equally impassive.

Suzanne pulled the loose drape of her hood over her face.
"Oh, Goddess," she said in a stifled voice.

"Tai-en," said Charles at last. "Are you telling me that
my sister is dead?"

If Naroshi was surprised by Charles's ignorance, or by his directness, he showed no sign of it. "This one of mine, who is named Cha Ishii Hokokul, has brought me this news. Are you telling me, Tai Charles, that you have not heard it yet?"

The far door swept aside and Tomaszio strode in, followed by a lord in imperial silver who was flushed green with disapproval. Charles stood up. The lord halted, facing two dukes, and let Tomaszio proceed alone.

"This is just in," said Tomaszio in Ophiuchi-Sei. "Goddess, I'm sorry to disturb you here, Charles, but it's code red from Odys."

Charles took the palm-sized bullet and just stood for a moment. Suzanne still held the cloth across her face. Keinaba watched. Naroshi and his retinue watched. The one called Cha Ishii watched, skin fading to a neutral white.

Charles pressed his thumb to the pad, and the bullet peeled open. It was not even scrambled, the message, just two bites. One bore Marco's signature code, and it read: *Tess found the key.* The other, the unique signature code of his only sibling, his heir, twined into the secondary pulse of an emergency transmitter's beacon and flatcoded to be sent on to him: *I am safe.*

Without a word Charles nodded to Tomaszio, dismissing him, and handed the bullet to Suzanne, who lowered the cloth enough to read it and then with a suppressed gasp pulled the cloth back over her face again. She pressed the fail-safe on the tube, and the casing and contents dissolved in her hand.

"Your sympathy is well-taken, Tai-en," said Charles. He sat down.

"Tai Naroshi Toraokii." The lord at the near door spoke, and he bowed to the precise degree. "I beg you to allow me to admit you into the next antechamber."

Naroshi inclined his head to Charles. "Tai-en."

"Tai-en."

Naroshi and his retinue went on, moving one step closer to the emperor's presence.

"Oh, Goddess," said Suzanne again.

Hon Echido had flushed blue. "I beg of you, Tai Charles, to indulge me in this. Has the Tai-endi Terese indeed died? I would be stricken to desolation were it so. She was kind to me."

Charles examined Hon Echido, examined the Keinaba elders. He glanced at Suzanne, who lowered the cloth from her face. Drying tears streaked her face. She lifted a hand and wiped them away.

"My servants," said Charles, and then he tapped off the translation program. "Hon Echido," he said in Anglais. "Do you understand what it means to be allied to my house?"

Hon Echido bent his head, subservient. "I understand. You are *daiga*, human, and will be always a barbarian, you and your kind." His skin faded to orange, the color of peace. "But we chose, we of Keinaba, to live rather than to die. Thus we have made our choice."

"Then I will tell you this. The Tai-endi lives but it is better that we alone, of my house, know this."

The three merchants studied him, knowing full well that such a declaration meant that their duke had chosen to enter the struggle, to vie for position within the emperor's sight, to begin the slow, intricate dance of time uncounted and years beyond years, the politic art, the only art granted to males: the art of intrigue.

* * *

"Oh dammit dammit my head hurts," Tess muttered. She opened her eyes and shut them immediately. "The light hurts. Ilya." She was cradled against his chest. "Why is everything moving so much?"

"Because we're riding," he said, sounding amused.

"Who the hell are you?" she demanded, trying to push away from him. Her wrists and ankles were bound, and she was seated sidesaddle on his horse, held against him. "Vasil!"

"I apologize for that blow to the head but there really was no way to get out of there without a hostage." He smiled.

"Good Lord," said Tess, getting a good look at him as her eyes adjusted to the light, "you really are the handsomest man I've ever met."

He laughed. "Thank you. I will take the compliment in the spirit in which it was offered."

"You bitch," said a second voice. "You aren't content with just one, are you?"

"Vera," said Vasil, "spite makes you ugly. Yevgeni, take her forward, please."

Yevgeni grinned and urged his horse into a gallop. Vera clutched at his belt and her face went white but she kept yelling back at them, the words lost in the wind.

"Poor Yevgeni," said Vasil. "Our family has always been cursed with loving its face more than its heart. You two, go and keep him company, if you will." The other men rode after Yevgeni. "I hope your head isn't hurting too much."

"I still have a headache. It seems to me that now that you're free of the camp, you can let me go."

"Oh, no, Terese Soerensen, we're not free yet. So Ilya married you, did he?" He looked thoughtful. "You rode down the Avenue together. He must love you very much."

"He *wants* me," said Tess, and then, because the tone of her voice reminded her of the venom in Vera's voice, she went on. "Yes, he does love me. It's just taken me this long to really understand that." She paused a moment, shading her eyes. All she could see was unending grass around them, and she had not the faintest idea where they might be or in what direction the camp lay. "Why am I telling you this?"

"Because we are alike, you and I," he said with perfect seriousness.

"Are we? In what way?"

"We both love Ilya. But he will never have me, and therefore he must die."

"How like your sister you are," she said bitterly, and suddenly wished he was not holding her so closely.

"Yes, I am," he said cheerfully. "It's a terrible thought, isn't it? I find her quite unbearable."

"You could have killed him last night."

Vasil shrugged. "The truth is, I am a coward. I'll never be able to kill him with my own hand. That's why I ride with Mikhailov, to let him do it. But I see this subject is upsetting you. Shall we speak of something else?"

She turned her head away from him, staring out at the men riding ahead of them. "I don't want to speak to you at all."

They rode on in silence for a time. Her head ached, but when he paused long enough to give her some water to drink, the pain dulled to a throb.

"Can't you at least untie my ankles so I can ride more comfortably?" she asked at last.

"Certainly. I'll untie your ankles and your wrists if you

will promise me on your husband's honor that you won't attempt to escape.''

''Damn you. I can't promise that.''

''I didn't think you would. Ilya holds his honor very high.''

She did not reply. They rode on, and she gauged by the sun that they were riding northeast. In early afternoon they rode into a hollow backed by a steep ridge. A copse of trees ringed a water hole at the base of the ridge, and beyond it lay a small, makeshift camp. One great tent was pitched on the far side, on a low rise above the others, twenty small tents scattered haphazardly below it. The inhabitants were mostly men, she saw as they paused on the crest of a rise to look down, but women and children were there as well.

Vasil and his companions made directly for the great tent. Dmitri Mikhailov stood outside, leaning on a crutch, watching them.

''Evidently you failed,'' he said. ''Who is this? The khaja pilgrim? Why?''

''I wouldn't have failed!'' Vera cried. ''I would have gotten him to come back with me but then *she* interrupted me!''

''He would never have gone with you,'' said Tess. Her ankles were bound loosely enough that she could stand next to Vasil.

''Do you think so? Everyone knows you sleep in separate tents. You couldn't even get your own husband to lie with you.''

Tess was suddenly struck with a feeling of great pity for Vera, who had nothing left to her now but her own gall to succor her through the months and the years. ''I'm sorry,'' she said.

Vera slapped her. Vasil grabbed his sister and wrenched her arm back so hard that Vera gasped with pain.

Mikhailov sighed. ''Must I put up with this? Karolla!''

A young woman about Tess's age emerged from the tent. ''Yes, Father?'' Her gaze settled on Tess, and she looked surprised and curious at the same time. She bore an old, white scar of marriage on her cheek.

''Take this Veselov woman somewhere, anywhere, that is out of my sight.''

''Yes, Father.'' Karolla looked at Vasil. Tess caught the infinitesimal nod that he gave her, as if it was *his* permission and not her father's that she sought. "Well, you must be Vera. I'm sure you'd like to wash and get some food. Will you come with me?"

Vera gathered together the last shreds of her dignity and with a final, parting glance of sheer hatred—not for Tess but for her brother—she walked away with Karolla.

"You three," said Mikhailov to the riders, "please follow them and see that she makes no mischief. Now, Vasil, what happened?"

"As Vera said. Vera got us into camp easily enough but Bakhtiian would not go with her to her tent. It was luck that this woman and Bakhtiian came walking through camp—well, there wasn't time to fight him fairly, so I took her as hostage."

"That is very well, Vasil, but how will this help us kill Bakhtiian? We are already driven into a corner, and now he will attack us with far superior forces."

"But, Dmitri, she is his wife."

"There is no mark."

"By the Avenue."

"Gods!" Dmitri looked at her for the first time as if her presence mattered to him. "Is that true?"

Tess did not reply. Her cheek still stung from Vera's slap.

"Yes," answered Vasil. "Given the brief moments we had to get out of the camp alive, I did as well as I could. I told Bakhtiian that if he did not leave us alone, I would let Vera kill her."

Mikhailov smiled, bitterly amused. "Did you? *Would* Vera kill her?"

"I think so. Gladly. Vera is not *all* show, Dmitri."

"But would you let Vera kill her?"

Vasil shrugged. "I don't know."

"Well, send Yevgeni with a message: Tell Bakhtiian that if he gives himself into our hands, we will free his wife."

"Will Bakhtiian believe you?"

"What is left us, Vasil? This is our last chance. We'll break camp and move, and when Bakhtiian comes, we must kill him. Put her in my tent."

Vasil picked Tess up and carried her inside, depositing her on two threadbare pillows in the outer chamber. Mikhailov followed them in.

"Leave us," he commanded. Vasil left without a word. Mikhailov lit a lantern and then twitched the entrance flap down with his free hand. The other hand still gripped his crutch. "Yes," he said, following her eyes to the crutch. "You nearly cut my leg off. I'll have this hurt for the rest of my life."

"Why do you want to kill him?" she asked. The lantern cast shadows high on the dim, sloping walls.

His mouth was an angled line, like the edge of shadow. "I don't know that you can understand the complexities of the jaran. His reputation hurts mine. His greatness lessens all. His peace enslaves us to his will. He has great notions, our Bakhtiian, but he will kill us as surely as he saves us."

"The old ways must give way before the new," said Tess quietly. She had a sudden, fierce vision of Charles's face, still and shadowed, knowing as he must that in time, whether years or centuries, whether in his lifetime or his descendants', this sanctuary that was Rhui would be breached and flooded, its culture obliterated by the wave of progress brought down from the stars. "But even if you kill Bakhtiian, it will still happen. You are a thousand tribes, and a thousand thousand families, and the lands of the khaja stretch all around you. Another man will come to the jaran, and he will lead them into war against the settled lands."

Mikhailov limped over to her, grabbed her shoulders, and jerked her to her feet. He was very strong, and he could stand quite well without the crutch. "Are you a prophet?" he asked, not mocking at all. "Is that why Bakhtiian married you, a holy woman?"

"Oh, I'm many things, but not a prophet, I don't think. Let me go, Mikhailov, let me go free, and I'll see that your family and your riders are forgiven all this."

"Not myself?" He smiled.

"No," she said even more softly. "You killed my brother."

His eyes were a deep blue, deeper than any she had seen, almost green, like the sea. He muttered an oath and let her go. She fell in a heap onto the pillows.

"Even if what you say is true, I will be dead and burned. But I swore by the gods and by my honor that I would not let Bakhtiian destroy my people while I yet lived. And if your brother died, then only remember, that is the price every sister will pay for Bakhtiian's dreams."

He blew out the lantern and left her in darkness. It was true, of course. Where Bakhtiian commanded, men died. It was true of Charles as well, and if he acted on the information she had given him in the Mushai's cylinder, many more, humans and Chapalii, would die. And, of course, he would act on that information. He had to.

"If there is no one to check him, then what will happen to him, and to us?" If she stayed, would Ilya return to the plains and live out his life in peace and quiet, for her? Almost she could laugh at the absurdity of it. Another man *would* come, another Bakhtiian, another Charles.

And yet together with them, fires would burn in the night and families would gather and bonds be forged based on duty and loyalty and love. A family would take in an orphan, friends would clasp hands, and a man and a woman would come to know and love one another. How could both these things, death and life, hatred and loyalty, killing and love, exist at the same time? There was no good answer. There never was.

She pulled up her knees and struggled to untie her ankles, but it was hard to see and her bonds were tight. A breath of wind stirred the tent, moving along the walls, and then abruptly light glared in on her and was as suddenly extinguished.

A hand caught her chin, and a man kissed her on the mouth. She rolled away from him. He laughed and lit a lantern.

"You have fire in you," said Vasil. "I can taste it."

"How dare you!"

"Because I am more a part of Ilya than you can understand, Tess." He knelt beside her and cut her loose with his knife. "Here are some jahar clothes. You can probably get out of camp without being noticed. You can take the knife but not my saber, I fear. I'll need it."

"Why? Turn around." Obediently, he turned his back to her, and she slipped into the inner chamber and changed quickly, hooking the curtain back just enough that she could see him. "Why?" she repeated, stripping off her tunic. "You brought me here."

"Yes, I brought you here. But now I see it was a mistake. I can't protect you. Mikhailov will let Vera kill you, or she will find a way to kill you in the confusion of the battle."

"That still doesn't explain why."

"You can't understand. So long as I thought Ilya had never and would never marry because he loved *me,* so long as I

thought that he banished me from his jahar only because he
wanted his war more than he wanted me and did it selfishly,
knowing the jaran would never follow him believing there
might be something between us, so long as that, I could
want him dead. But he rode with you down the Avenue.''
He laughed again. ''Why do you suppose it never occurred
to me that he never really loved me except when we were
boys, that he had simply not yet found a woman to match
him? That he banished me because I forced him to make
that choice?''

''I don't know. I don't think the answer is that easy.'' She
pulled on the black trousers. They fit her well enough, once
the red shirt was tucked in and belted. ''And he would never
give up his war for me either.''

''No, but you wouldn't ask him to.''

''Did you? My God, that took a lot of nerve.''

''Yes, but then, I'm very beautiful, you know.'' He
turned. ''Here is the knife.'' He tossed it to her casually
but not without malice. She caught it deftly. ''Cut out his
heart, if it hasn't all burnt away by now. But leave a corner
for me.''

''Thank you, Vasil.''

''Oh,'' he said with a smile that made him look uncannily
like his sister, ''I wish you joy of him. Go.''

She walked past him to the flap and thence out under the
awning, not looking back. Men and women moved below,
striking the camp. She walked swiftly over the crest of the
rise and turned back along it toward the high ridge. Then
she ran until she could break into the trees. She had no idea,
really, what she ought to do, except that once Mikhailov left
this camp, someone, some scout, even Bakhtiian's entire
force, would track him here. And find her waiting. She hiked
out of the trees, which gave scant cover, and scrambled up
along a ridge of rock to the top of the height.

There she turned to survey Mikhailov's camp. Far below,
Vasil walked through the camp. Karolla ran up to him and
took his arm. He shifted to answer her, then froze, and his
face lifted suddenly and he stared.

Beyond the hollow the sun spread like a flow of water
from the crests of hills. Looking out along Vasil's line of
sight, past the hill that marked the other end of the valley,
Tess saw a solitary rider emerge on the lit swell of a far rise.
He sat there for the space of ten heartbeats before a man

shouted off to her right, and the other sentry left his post, running into camp. The rider urged his horse forward.

"Oh, God," whispered Tess.

Men emerged from tents. Horses were saddled. Movement flooded toward the end of the valley where he was about to enter. Alone.

She should have stayed in the tent. At least she had a knife. She had never imagined he would ride in alone, just for her.

The sun illuminated Bakhtiian as he crested the last hill and came down the final slope. Men surrounded his horse. Four riders closed in around him. Mikhailov limped out from the crowd. Taking the horse's reins, he led Bakhtiian through the camp as if he were a king. It was very quiet.

Quietest of all when they drew up next to Vasil, who had not moved. Something communicated but not spoken passed between them, the dark man tall on his horse and the fair man staring up at him. Tess thought, *that is how it has always been between them.*

Vasil stepped forward. He had a hand on his saber but it was his other hand that lifted. He grasped Ilya's fingers, lifted the dark man's hand to his lips, and kissed it. Mikhailov said something. For a moment no one moved. Vasil let go of Bakhtiian's hand and Mikhailov led the horse on. Vasil did not follow. They were halfway through camp, people dropping away from the main escort, heading toward Mikhailov's tent, before Tess realized where they were going and that they would not find her there.

"You idiot," she said aloud. She pushed herself forward and slid along the loose rock. Pebbles slipped and tumbled out from under her boots, and she fell, sitting hard on the stones.

Out on the plain, riders came.

A jahar rode in. To its right, a second. To the left, more men rode, their shirts brilliant against the dull grass. In an instant she would hear their cries. In an instant they would reach the camp. But they would never find Ilya in time. She saw neither Bakhtiian nor Mikhailov below. She impelled herself forward, sliding and scrambling down the slope.

She reached the trees just as the first wave of riders hit. She pushed through, thrusting aside branches without care that they snapped back to whip her face. A woman screamed. Men shouted. Metal rang on metal. She burst out of the copse and ran for the camp—to be almost trampled by a knot of horses. She flung herself aside. A horse pulled up beside her, and she looked up to see Vasil. Blood painted his face, and stained his side and one leg.

"Veselov, come on. We're going," shouted one of the men ahead of him, reining in a half-wild horse.

"I told you I was a coward," said Vasil. "But I love my life too well."

"Vasil, where did he go?"

"To Mikhailov's tent." He offered her his saber. When she took it, he gave her a brief, bitter smile and rode on, away from the fight.

Tess ran. The world dissolved into confusion. She dove to one side to avoid the trampling hooves of a line of horses. One of the animals, pressed too close to a tent, caught a leg in the ropes. The horse stumbled, throwing the rider off its neck. The tent shuddered and collapsed. Tess scrambled past it and ran on.

Two horseless men dueled, an eddy in the current rushing around them. Three women, a child sheltered between them, huddled against the wall of a tent. A sudden shove pitched Tess to her knees, and she ducked her head, flinging up her saber, as a horse galloped past. No blow came. Ten steps from her a man lay groaning. Blood bubbled from his mouth.

She struggled on. She felt as if she were fighting upstream. Her lungs stung. Riders galloped past. Men ran in twos and threes. Mikhailov's daughter stared at her, pale-eyed, from the sanctity of a tent. She got a moment's glimpse of Vladimir, mounted, cutting through a clump of horsemen, his saber tracing an intricate pattern through their midst. Beneath the shouting and the cries of the wounded, she heard the constant, anguished sobbing of a woman. A man cursed, shrill and fluent. There was a confusion of shouting: "Break right; fall back; Tasha, to me, to me."

Then she was beyond the fighting. Mikhailov's tent stood alone before her. With her saber leading, she charged up the hill. She could hear voices from inside the tent. A shout. She was almost there. Her breath came in ragged gasps.

A man cried out. Something hit the side of the tent. Then a saber, thrust with murderous force, ripped through the tent to gleam for a single, dull moment in the afternoon sun.

They seemed to be there a year, she and the bloodstained saber, frozen together. It was withdrawn. The form of a body slid down the inside of the tent wall.

Dead.

Far below, a man screamed in agony.

Tess flung herself to the entrance, jerked aside the frayed tent flap, saber raised. Shadows obscured the body slumped against the tent wall. A dark stain spread out on the light rug beneath the limp, tumbled form. The killer stood with his back to her, stiff with tension, arm pulled back as if for another strike, his fingers gripped to whiteness around the hilt.

She took a step. The flap rustled down behind her. He turned and without a break lunged toward her.

His movement halted as suddenly as if rope had brought him up short. The saber fell from his hand. She froze.

He said in the barest whisper: "Tess."

She took a single step toward him. Another. With a slight, inarticulate cry, she dropped her saber and ran into him.

Even at this short distance, he had to take two steps backward to counterbalance the force of their meeting. He had no chance to say anything more because she was kissing him. At first randomly, a cheek, an eye, whatever presented itself, but when he regained his footing he pulled her tight against him and returned her kiss.

Reality existed where their bodies touched, and where they touched, it was as if they were melding, as earth dissolves into the sea and that, evaporating into air, kindles to fire. He murmured something indistinguishable and kissed her along the curve of her jaw to her neck, to her throat. She pulled his head back and kissed him on the mouth again. What other substance could there be in the world, at this moment, but him? And all of him fire.

She felt his attention shift away from her, and he broke away and grabbed for a saber. She dropped to her knees and picked up Vasil's saber and rose to stand beside him.

"Bakhtiian!"

They both relaxed. "Niko," he said. "I'm safe." His gaze returned to her face, a look comprised of equal parts hunger and disbelief. From outside came a muffled command and the sound of horses riding away.

The tent flap was swept aside. Niko strode in, halting just past the entrance. Josef and Tasha screened the daylight behind him. "Ilya. Tess! Thank the gods!" His eyes shifted to the slumped form. "So Mikhailov didn't get away."

"Get rid of it," said Ilya. Without a word, Josef and Tasha carried the body out.

"The battle is won, Mikhailov's riders are dead or wounded. A few got away. We need some decision. There's wounded to be considered, and the camp is already half struck. Anton Veselov thinks—"

"We'll stay the night," said Ilya. "There's a fire to be built."

"Yes," agreed Niko, "but we can leave a few riders to watch over the pyre while the rest—"

"Niko," said Tess. "Go away."

An infinitesimal pause. Niko's gaze came to rest on Tess. He began to speak, looking back at Ilya, but only a meaningless syllable came out. A longer pause as he watched Ilya, whose gaze had not strayed from Tess, some invisible line connecting them down which their gazes were impelled to travel.

"Yes," said Niko. "I can see that I have overstayed my welcome." Then he grinned and retreated quickly, pulling the tent flap shut as he left.

Outside, men called out, horses neighed, a woman sobbed. Already the first faint smell of ulyan reached them, but it was something far outside her, the sun seen from a brightly lit room. She felt *him*, a presence palpable as heat.

Into their silence, he said smoothly, "Where *did* you get that imperious tone of voice?"

"From you." She set down the saber, picked up the lantern, and walked into the inner chamber. He followed her, halting where his boot came to rest against a pillow. The lantern limned him in light where he stood facing her.

"Tess," he said softly. "You're trembling."

"How could you have been so stupid? I thought he killed you. You idiot. Why did you ride in here alone?"

"I took the chance that once they saw me, they would forget for just long enough that I had a jahar behind me."

"My God, you're arrogant."

Even shaded as he was, she could see the intensity of his eyes. "Is that what you think of me?" he asked.

She felt an intangible swelling within her, a tangle of anger, of wild-eyed hope, of exultation. And she felt despair, knowing he would someday far too soon die. "You know what I think of you, damn you."

If laughter could be noiseless, could be the set of a body changing, a stance, an arm shifted sideways, she would have said he laughed. At the same moment she became acutely aware of his body, of its sensuality of line, of the curve of his jaw, the cut of his trousers over his hips, the slight caressing lift of the fingers of the hand nearest her, like an enticement. One side of his mouth tugged up into a half-smile. "Gods, Tess," he said, and everything about him changed. "How you hate it when I'm right."

Four steps took him into her arms.

He was asleep when she woke, The lantern still burned. It was as silent as death outside. The dim glow on his face gave him a luminous tinge, as if their lovemaking had sparked some smoldering center within him that now flamed forth, investing him in light. She shifted to pillow her head on his shoulder. He woke.

"You're all lit," he murmured, gazing raptly at her. His hand brushed up to her cheek, tracing the line of her jaw, and then as if with a will of its own slid down to the soft rise of her breasts. "I love you."

Tess smiled.

He kissed her.

They rolled, and their legs got tangled in a blanket. As he sat up to free them, he paused. With the swiftness of intimacy, she felt his attention focus away from her. From outside, she heard a cough and the murmur of words exchanged.

"Let me go check outside," he said, standing. Divested of clothing, his body had a simplicity of line that illuminated the grace and slender power of his build.

Tess watched him walk, entirely unself-conscious of his own beauty, to the curtain. "You're a very pleasing sight, my husband, but don't you think you should put something on?"

He laughed and let her toss him a pair of trousers, which he slipped on. The cloth partition swayed as he pushed past it. She heard his footfalls on the rugs beyond.

Alone, she became suddenly aware that they were in Mikhailov's tent—or his daughter's tent, or his wife's—did Mikhailov even have a wife? She sat up, pushing the blankets aside, and sorted through the clothing strewn in their haste across the rug, folding what she recognized and stacking it to one side. A sleeping pallet and pillows, and along one wall a pair of boots neither hers nor Ilya's, together with a stoppered leather flask, a wooden bowl and two cups inlaid with bone and silver, and an old, faded weaving folded into a neat square; that was all. No other possessions, nothing marking what woman lived here, or why this tent had come into Mikhailov's keeping.

Ilya was speaking with someone—two people now, she could tell by the voices. Each time *he* spoke, she turned toward the sound without at first realizing what she was doing. She shook her head, chuckling, and wrapped a blanket around herself and waited. Soon enough she heard him move across the outer chamber, heard him pause, and when he pushed aside the curtain it was with both sabers in one hand. He looked preoccupied. Then he saw her, and his entire expression changed. He sighed, set the sabers down, and embraced her. They fell back onto the pillows.

"Tess." He shifted. "That was Niko. He tells me that—"

"Ilyakoria. I don't care what Niko told you."

He laughed, his lips cool on her skin. His hair, so lush and so dark, brushed her mouth. It smelled as if it had been freshened in rain, touched with the scent of almonds. "It's true. I don't either." She kissed him, pressed her face against his neck, breathing him in.

Suddenly he drew back, cupping her face in his hands. "Tess. I know who you must be." His eyes were brilliant with longing as he gazed at her, his expression so vulnerable that her heart ached with love for him. "You are the Sun's Child." She shook her head, not understanding him. "The Sun's daughter, come from the heavens to visit the earth."

Tears welled in her eyes, and she hugged him fiercely. "No, my love, no," she whispered. "I'm just Tess. Oh, Ilya, I love you."

He kissed the tears away, each one, carefully, thoroughly. "No more of those. I will stop complimenting you."

"Oh?"

He smiled. "We don't need words, Tess." He kissed her. And again.

CHAPTER TWENTY-NINE

"Now let life proceed,
and let him desire marriage and a wife."
—ANTIPHON THE SOPHIST

Ilya kissed her awake. She put her hands up to embrace him, and realized that he had dressed. She sat up. Outside, a man sang in a rich tenor about a fair sweet girl who had kissed him by the river.

Ilya had pulled the curtain back just enough to let in the light that illuminated the outer chamber. She looked down at herself, naked, and then at him. "Somehow, I feel that you have me at a profound disadvantage."

"Not at all." He slid one hand smoothly and searchingly from her hip to her shoulder, letting it come to rest at last on the curve of her neck alongside the black necklace. He kissed her. "Who is more distracting?"

"You are. *I* was asleep."

He laughed and stood up. "Come, my wife, it is late, and time to strike camp so we can leave." He pulled her up to her feet. She kept hold of one of the blankets and let it drape around her, feeling a little shy, here in the morning. "If you don't mind his help, Vladimir will assist you in striking the tent."

"I don't mind his help, but Ilya, who does it belong to now that Mikhailov is dead? Or is it his daughter's?"

Ilya picked up the weaving and shook it out. "This is a Mikhailov pattern, and Mikhailov's mother was a famous weaver. He had no other kin, and his daughter is an Arkhanov, I believe." He shrugged. "It is mine now."

"Yours!"

He folded the weaving with reverence and lifted his gaze

to her with perfect serenity. "Fairly won. In any case, Bakhtiian's wife must have as great a tent as every etsana."

"Perhaps you ought to consult with Bakhtiian's wife first to see what she wants."

"No, Tess. In this matter I will not compromise. I will no longer be compelled to take my meals at my aunt's tent. And you, my wife, must be given the consequence you deserve."

"What? As the only woman in the tribes whose consequence derives from her husband? What will your aunt say?"

"My aunt will say nothing. The jaran are mine now. Don't you understand? Mikhailov was the last one who rode against me." He crossed swiftly to her and embraced her, holding her. He sighed against her hair. "Forgive me, but I must ride out now. Vladimir will stay with you."

"Stay with me?" But he kissed her and left, leaving her to stare as the curtain swayed from his passing and then stilled. She dressed in the jahar clothes Vasil had given her, belted on his saber, and went out. Vladimir sat with his back to the tent. She walked past him and ran to look down into the hollow, but even as she searched, she saw a group of about thirty riders start away, Ilya in their midst. Even though she might have shouted and gotten his attention, she refused to do anything so undignified. Below, women loaded the few wagons left to Mikhailov's people. Children sat quietly on bundled pillows. Wounded men lay on the ground. Farther, beyond the hollow, lay a circle of wood and other fuel within which lay the bodies of the slain. Mercifully, it was too far away for her to recognize any of them.

"I thought they would have lit that already," she said, turning back to Vladimir.

He shrugged, that peculiarly immature copy of Ilya. "It took them this long to gather it. They had to break up a few of the wagons, too." He blinked. "That isn't the shirt Ilya gave you."

"No," she said absently, watching.

The jahar had paused by the pyre. A single woman stood alone there, and it was she who threw on the torch. Flames caught, smoldered, and then licked and grew. Smoke rose. The riders reined their horses away and disappeared out onto the plains. The woman turned and trudged back into camp. The other women ignored the pyre, except perhaps to pause and glance its way. As if, Tess thought, their pain was already too much to bear.

She recognized now who the woman was, walking back through the hollow and still walking, up toward Tess and her father's tent: It was Karolla.

"Vladi," said Tess, wanting support, and Vladimir came and stood beside her.

Karolla stopped before her. For an instant she stared at Tess as if the sight of a woman in jahar clothing shocked her. She put a hand to her eyes, caught back a sob, then lowered her hand.

"I beg your pardon," she said in her soft voice. "Do you need help with the tent?"

"Thank you," Tess stammered. "But surely it is *your* tent."

"I would not want it even if it was mine," said Karolla fiercely. "It is Bakhtiian's now." She hesitated. "Perhaps you do not understand. This was my father's mother's tent, not my mother's. In any case, I left the Arkhanov tribe and my mother when my father left them to ride against Ilya, so even if it were her tent, I would have no right to it. Those of us who left are no longer welcome there."

There was a kind of bitter but practical fatalism about Karolla Arkhanov that made Tess very sad. "You must have loved your father very much," she said softly. She found she could not look at Karolla, knowing she had made Ilya promise her that he would kill Mikhailov.

"I loved him," said Karolla simply, "but I left because Vasil Veselov marked me."

"Vasil marked you!"

Karolla's smile was bittersweet. "Oh, I know I'm not a handsome woman. He only marked me to force my father to take him into his jahar. I knew he never loved me, but he has always been kind to me." She flushed, and Tess could see very well that she loved her husband. She paused, and the color rose even higher in her cheeks, as if she was struggling. "Do you—do you know what happened to him?"

My God, she doesn't even know, and she's almost too proud to ask. "Yes. I saw him. He was wounded but alive. He got away safely, Karolla."

"Thank you," said Karolla. "There is one wagon left, for this tent. Shall we take it down?"

Tess could only obey. Vladimir remained silent, standing

at her side, and then helping them strike the tent. He seemed less sullen, if not more thoughtful. After her own small tent, this one seemed huge and unwieldy, but she soon discovered how cunningly it was constructed, so that three people could strike it without difficulty.

As she was rolling up the last rug, Vladimir paused beside her. "Tess," he said in a low, warning voice. She stood up.

Vera came up the rise toward them, holding a child in her arms and another by the hand. Golden-haired, gorgeous children: as soon as they came close enough, Tess knew whose they must be. The girl detached herself from Vera and ran to Karolla.

"Mama," she said, and her face was streaked with tears, "when is Papa coming back?"

"Hush, child. Help me with these pillows, if you please. Can you throw them in the wagon?" The little girl did so, and Vera deposited the other child, younger and not obviously boy or girl, into the back of the wagon.

"Karolla," said Vera, ignoring Tess and Vladimir completely, "Mother Yermolov says she will drive this wagon. I am going with the wounded."

"As you wish, Vera," said Karolla. Vera descended back to the line of wagons forming with its escort of riders. The familiar, acrid scent of ulyan wafted over them, borne by the breeze. "Well," said Karolla, "if you do not mind, Terese Soerensen, may my children ride in this wagon?" The little girl had climbed in and sat huddled next to her sibling.

"No. I mean, you needn't ask my permission." The last thing she wanted was to have poor Karolla begging her for favors. "It isn't as if—" She halted suddenly. "Vladi, how am I getting back to camp?"

Vladimir looked at her, puzzled. "What do you mean, Tess?"

"Did Ilya leave a horse for me?"

"Why would Ilya leave you a horse? There are women here, after all."

"Ah," said Tess. "Of course. Certainly I would go with the women. Naturally you must ride in the wagon as well, Karolla. I am sure Mother Orzhekov and Mother Veselov will treat you kindly when we reach camp, and make some place for you."

Karolla glanced behind at her children—at Vasil's children. "Do you think so?" she asked, suddenly looking far more tired than a woman so young ought to look. "Here is Mother Yermolov."

Mother Yermolov trudged up the hill with a child and an adolecent girl in tow. She was old and wiry but hale, and she had the look of a woman who has outlived all of her children. She stopped and inclined her head respectfully to Tess, and then inspected the animals in the traces before climbing into the seat. Karolla and the adolescent helped the child into the wagon and got in after her.

"Well, Tess," said Vladimir, "I'll ride close by, in case you—well, Ilya said to stay close by you."

"Thank you, Vladi," she said, and was left standing, watching him go, while the women waited for her.

"Perhaps you will sit next to me," said Mother Yermolov. "The rest are ready to go, and we must lead, of course."

Given no choice, Tess climbed up beside her. "Thank you," she said, determined to be gracious.

"I don't envy you, my dear," said Mother Yermolov, almost gruffly, and they started forward.

By the time they had gone over the second hill, Tess hated the wagon. It was slow and clumsy, and every bump jolted horribly. Perhaps, just perhaps, it was better back among the pillows, but she could not bring herself to look back at Karolla or her beautiful children. She stared enviously at the riders, free as they ranged along the line. True to his word, Vladimir stayed beside her but it was impossible to talk to him, and she had nothing to say to him in any case. Vasil's saber, stuck awkwardly to one side, rubbed into her thigh. The wagon lurched. Tess grabbed at the side and got a splinter thrust deep in her hand. Cursing, she pulled it out with her teeth.

"You are not accustomed to traveling this way," said Mother Yermolov mildly. "Put your hands—yes, there, and there. That's right."

Behind, the adolescent girl was talking to Karolla.

"But Yevgeni wasn't found, so he must have gotten away. He'll find me again!"

Karolla murmured something indistinguishable.

"But is it true that she is Bakhtiian's wife? That they lay together yesterday?"

"Valye, where are your manners?"

Valye lowered her voice but kept on. "It's just it seems cruel to love with death all around."

"Better to be loving than mourning."

A pause, and then a whisper: "They say she comes from a great khaja city in the south, but she can't. She's so clean, and khaja are always filthy. Is it true she rode with Bakhtiian's jahar? That's what I'm going to do, Karolla. I'm going to learn how to fight, and then I can ride in jahar with my brother. When he comes back. I won't go back to my aunt's tribe. I hate her."

"Valye," said Karolla in a weary voice, "what choice do you have? She is your kin, your mother is dead, and though Yevgeni protected you this long, he is gone now. You've no one else."

"I won't," said Valye, and subsided into silence.

The wagon lurched on.

"What will all these women do?" Tess asked Mother Yermolov finally.

"As Karolla said. They will go to their kinswomen."

"They must all of them have lost fathers or brothers or husbands."

"Or sons." The old woman shrugged. "The men make war. We can do nothing about that. We have our own lives."

Tess turned to stare at the column behind. Women and children sat in the wagons, many with wounded men cushioned in their laps or on pillows beside them. Somewhere a woman sang, a pure soprano—as sweet as Fedya's voice and just as sorrowful. The escort rode alongside, up and down the line.

"And in the spring," said Tess, "Bakhtiian will lead the jaran against the khaja and the settled lands."

Mother Yermolov's eyes had a glint about them, a spark, as if at some old joke only she knew. "Then I pity the khaja women who are mothers and sisters and wives."

"But you were with Mikhailov. Do you now support Bakhtiian?"

"Mikhailov is dead. Bakhtiian killed him fairly. I hold no grudge against him. It is men's business, after all."

The wagons halted briefly at midday. Tess climbed down and decided, as soon as she felt earth beneath her boots, that she would walk the rest of the way. But though she had thought the wagons slow-moving, once they started again, she found them passing her. Even knowing who she was, women offered her a seat as their wagons passed her, but she shook her head and plodded grimly forward. The wagons passed her one by one until at last the final wagon rolled alongside and, gaining, moved ahead of her. Four blood-stained, unconscious men lay among pillows. One, young and black-haired, looked dead. Vera sat with them. Her gaze met Tess's for an unmeasurable instant. Her face was white. Then Vera looked away as if she had not seen her. Tess walked on, letting the gap widen bit by bit in front of her. But then, it was impossible to lose their track in the grass, and in any case, Vladimir still rode over to the side, not too close now but never losing her from his sight.

A shout came from far ahead. Riders crested a distant ridge and poured down toward them. The lead wagon lurched over an intervening rise and was lost to Tess's view. The others followed, one by one. A single rider cantered down the line.

"Niko!"

He pulled up beside her. "Tess! Why are you walking here?"

"Have you ever tried to ride in one of those things?"

"Ah, no." He dismounted. "Well, I suppose when I was a child."

"I can't ride in those wagons."

"Look. We've fallen behind." He waved at Vladimir, and Vladi reined his horse forward and cantered away. "I'll walk with you." The grass brushed at their boots. Tess plucked a stem, peeling back the brittle leaves that embraced it. "Tess," he said in an odd voice, "how did you get that shirt? Weren't you in women's clothing when you were taken from the camp? Oh, damn." He led his horse away from her and moved the reins so that he could mount.

The comment was not directed to her. About a dozen riders had crested the near rise and rode down toward them. Ilya was riding Kriye. Tess had to look away from them because together they looked so handsome.

He dismounted. "Tess!" He was so transparently ecstatic that she couldn't help smiling. "Tess. Why are you walking back here?" He stopped in front of her, so close that if she leaned forward she would touch him. His red shirt had a pungent, fresh scent, and his hair was slightly wild, mussed by the wind. She reached up and brushed a lock of hair away from his eyes. He seemed about to say something. Instead, he swayed into her, slid his hands up her arms, and kissed her fiercely.

After a bit, Tess opened her eyes. She broke off the kiss. "Ilya, everybody is watching."

He whirled, separating himself from her so abruptly that she had to take a step back to maintain her balance. Yes, twelve men, with Niko; men from his jahar. They were all grinning. Only a few attempted to look away. Ilya took three steps toward them, halted, and fixed his stare on Niko.

"Sibirin! Don't these men have anything to do?"

Niko swung up on his horse. "Yes, Bakhtiian. Of course they do."

"Gods! Then *see* that they make themselves busy. Do you understand me?"

"Certainly, Ilya. Of course. We were just leaving." They rode away.

Ilya muttered under his breath.

"Does that mean what I think it does?"

"Forgive me. Oh, Tess, it's been such a long day." He took a step back toward her, halted. His mouth thinned, and his voice dropped until it was so low she could barely hear him. "Where did you get those clothes?" He closed the distance between them and reached to touch the embroidery on the sleeve of the shirt. "This is Vasil's. Where did you get this?"

"Vasil gave them to me. He cut me free when I was tied up in Mikhailov's tent, and he gave me his saber."

"What happened to him?" She could not interpret the expression in his voice.

"He—he was badly wounded and had no choice but to retreat."

"You are lying to me. If I know Vasil, he ran."

"He was wounded."

"Are you defending him? What happened to the clothing Nadezhda Martov gifted you?"

"It's in the wagon. With *your* tent."

If he noticed her emphasis, he ignored it. "Is that how you treat things given you in friendship? Cloth of Martov's dye and weave is precious, and I expect you to remember that. As soon as we get to camp you will take those clothes off. And that saber. Give them to Vera. I don't care what you do with them but I will not have them in my tent."

"You have no right to order me in this way. Whatever happened between you and Vasil has nothing to do with me."

He was furious now. "It has everything to do with you. Why do you suppose he gave you that, knowing you would wear it? Knowing you are my wife? You *will* obey me in this."

"I will not—" she began, enraged. And then she saw that she had plunged into a morass far beyond her knowledge, that her anger was solely for the way in which he so blithely and unthinkingly ordered her to do as he wished, while his—his anger spilled out from some old wound that had never healed. "I will not," she said again, lowering her voice abruptly, "give anything to Vera. But I will ask his wife if she wants them."

"His *wife!*" His expression changed so swiftly, through so many competing emotions, that she could put a name to no one of them.

"Yes. Perhaps you did not know. He marked Mikhailov's daughter some years past. There are two children as well, a little girl and a younger one. A boy, I think."

He controlled himself, and now she could not interpret his expression at all. "Why are you walking back here?" he asked again. "Mother Yermolov said you rode some distance in the wagon with her and then got out."

"Ilya, you never asked me how I wanted to return to camp. You simply left."

"But, of course—"

"—I would travel with the women? With Vera? With Karolla Arkhanov, whose father I begged you to kill? With children whose fathers and brothers are dead? Killed by *your* men? And them all knowing me as your wife. You never asked me."

He regarded her in silence. His face was still. "Well, Tess," he said finally, a little awkwardly, "will you ride with me back to camp?"

"I accept your apology," said Tess. He swung onto Kriye and offered her his hand gravely. She laughed suddenly, unsteadily.

"Tess," he said, immediately concerned. "What's wrong?"

"Don't you remember? When you found me on the hillside. Gods, it seems long ago."

Though she expected him to, he did not smile. "I will never forget it."

She took his hand and mounted behind him, wrapped her arms around his waist, and leaned her head against him. Then, smiling, she kissed him on the neck, once, twice.

"Stop that."

Wind moved in the grass. She laughed into his hair. "Is something wrong, my husband?"

He urged Kriye forward and did not reply for a long while. She simply rested against him, content for now.

"There is one mare," he said at last. "A beautiful creature though rather bad-tempered. But I think you can handle her."

"Bad-tempered?"

"No, I chose the wrong word. She is high-spirited. She has mettle. Rather like—well, she's a fine horse. She will be yours, if you wish her."

"Rather like me, were you going to say? Thank you, Ilya. I thought you were going to stop complimenting me."

"I will never stop complimenting you. And if you continue to complain about it, I will simply compliment you twice as often."

"That sounds like a threat."

"It is. Tess, two days ago you were about to tell me whether Yuri was right. Right about what?"

Tess shut her eyes, leaning against him, and thought of Yuri. Her sweet Yuri, gone now, but not lost to her as long as she remembered him. Though memory could never be a substitute for his presence. She tightened her arms around Ilya. "It was the last thing he said to me, almost. He said that if I left for Jeds in the spring, I could still choose to come back, or I could stay a few years here and then go. He said that it didn't have to be so final."

They rode so long in silence that they came into sight of the line of wagons, and farther, the first outlying tents of the great camp ahead and the thin line of trees that marked the river.

He pulled Kriye up. She dismounted, and he swung down next to her. First he simply looked at her. The gods knew, she understood him well enough by now to know how difficult it was for him to accept that the world did not simply bend to his will, that what he chose might not always come to pass, that some decisions were not his to make.

Then he sighed. "Does it have to be final, Tess? Will you go and never come back?"

Tess just shook her head. She rested her hand on his cheek a moment, and then reached up to dishevel his hair. "You are, you know."

"I am what?" he asked, suspicious.

"*Diarin*. I'm not leaving in the spring, Ilya. Though that doesn't mean I can stay here forever."

Something flashed in his eyes. "Well, then." He drew his saber. "I'm tired of having to explain how it is you are my wife."

Tess raised her chin. His blade came to rest on her cheekbone. With the lightest of movements he pulled it across her cheek. The cut stung. A thin line of blood welled up, and a few drops flowed like tears down her skin.

She drew Vasil's saber.

"Tess." He took a step backward. Slowly, deliberately, his eyes on her hand, he lowered his saber.

The brilliance of the sun lit his face. With her eyes fixed on the blade, her wrist unaccountably steady, she marked him swiftly and lightly, leaving a cut scarcely deeper than the one on her own cheek. He touched the mark with his free hand, staring down at the blood on his fingertips. Then he lifted his hand to brush his lips, tasting the blood.

"Well, my wife," he said in a voice so calm that she could tell it covered some extreme emotion, "now we are doubly bound." Then he smiled.

"You smug bastard, you're pleased with yourself."

"Of course I am. I have what I wanted."

Tess could not help but laugh because he said it without the slightest conceit but rather as a simple statement of fact. "But I feel it only fair to warn you, Bakhtiian, that I am going to continue to practice saber."

"If Bakhalo and Zvertkov agree to take you on, then I will not interfere. Tess, you're laughing at me."

"Only because you do not like it."

"Don't like you training for jahar?"

"No, don't like it when people laugh at you. Shall we go into camp?"

"As you wish," he replied, a little reserved, but then, Tess reflected, he would probably never truly grow used to people laughing at him, and he would certainly never like it.

As they approached the camp, Sonia came running to meet them. "Tess! Tess! she called, bridging the distance by shouting. "You'll never believe what happened! Vladimir just rode in and straight up to Elena's mother's tent, and marked her."

"Marked Elena's mother?"

"No, no, you fool, marked—" Sonia stopped short some ten strides from them. "Tess!" She stared. Her gaze shifted to Ilya and her entire expression underwent such an unmistakable change, she looked so utterly dumbfounded, that Tess laughed and Ilya actually smiled. Sonia found her voice. *"Ilya!"* Then lost it again.

"Come, Tess," said Ilya coolly. "We have our tent to set up."

They walked some ten paces before Sonia came to life. "Yes, you will need to set up your tent," she said in the exact same tone her cousin had used, "because you'll have to go into seclusion now. Elena will be furious, having to share her celebration with you."

"Well," said Tess apologetically, "I hope Elena won't be too disappointed."

"Then we can delay ours for a day," said Ilya, "so she and Vladi can have a celebration for themselves. After all, *we* are already married."

"Yes, but it isn't the same as being marked." Sonia blinked innocently. "Is it, Ilya?"

"Certainly not," he agreed, but the glance he flashed Sonia bore a warning.

She grinned at him, unrepentant. "Don't worry, Cousin. It won't hurt your looks. I'm sure women will think you're twice as handsome with a scar."

He carried it off coolly enough, though, walking through the sprawl of the camp to his aunt's tent, where Mother Yermolov had driven the wagon containing his tent. A number of people clustered here: the two *etsanas,* seated on their pillows beneath the awning of Mother Orzhekov's tent, and some part of their families as well as a few of the refugees from Mikhailov's camp.

There was a long moment of silence as everyone turned to stare. Mother Orzhekov raised one eyebrow eloquently. Arina hid her mouth behind her hand, trying not to look as young as she was. But Kirill, standing behind his wife, spoke first, of course. "Well, Tess," he said, "are you trying to start a new fashion?" Most of the crowd laughed.

"Aunt," said Ilya, "perhaps you will grant permission for my wife to pitch her tent next to yours."

Irena nodded. "Of course, Nephew. Sonia, Stassi, Pavel, you may assist them." Then she went back to her consultation with Arina, which clearly involved Mother Yermolov, Karolla Arkhanov and her children, and Vera, who stood beside her cousin, staring at nothing. Petya hovered nervously in the background.

Stassia's husband Pavel led Kriye away. Ilya allowed Sonia and Stassia to help pitch the tent, and he even permitted them to help Tess strike her tent and carry her belongings to the rugs under their awning. No farther would he let them, and he and Tess spent what little time remained until supper arranging the interior of the great tent. It took rather longer than it might have, interrupted frequently by kisses.

Supper proved rather lively. He sat through it without speaking unless he was spoken to. Tess enjoyed herself thoroughly, and she could not help but laugh with Sonia when an unusually large number of men, including his entire jahar and others who had enough standing to invite themselves, came to watch him bid the ritual farewell to his newly-marked wife and then be escorted away.

"Sonia. Stassia. Kira. I charge you with Tess's retreat."

Tess's seclusion was restrictive only in that she could not leave the tent. Lanterns were lit. Children ran in and out, jumping on the pillows and throwing the blankets around. Women filtered in, bringing gifts of food and drink for the coming days, and then left again. Arina arrived, kissed her, and left. Karolla Arkhanov came in, looking wary.

"I wish you blessings," she said.

"I have something for you," said Tess, and gave her Vasil's clothing.

Karolla flushed and clutched these gifts against her chest. Then she looked down at her children. "Here, little one," she said to the girl. "Here is your Papa's shirt for you to keep until he comes back."

Tess hesitated. "The baby, is that a boy?"

"Yes." She flushed and hugged the little boy to her side.

"I think this will go to him, then, when he is old enough." And she offered Karolla the saber. Karolla looked stunned, and she quickly took herself off.

"Well," said Sonia, offering Tess some little sweet cakes that Arina had brought. "But I won't ask."

"Children." Irena Orzhekov appeared at the entrance. "Tess and I will speak alone for a moment."

Sonia and Stassia shepherded the children out. Mother Orzhekov sat on a pillow next to Tess, and Tess suddenly felt self-conscious, sitting here in a tent as large as the etsana's, placed on a pillow beside her as an equal.

"I hope," she said tentatively, "that you don't think it presumptuous of me to have this tent, Mother Orzhekov."

"My child," said Irena, "that Bakhtiian has gifted you with this tent is his right, given what he has become. And in any case, I believe from what Sonia has told me that you come from an important family in your own right, in khaja lands."

"That's true," Tess admitted. "But I feel a little overwhelmed here."

"With my nephew?"

Tess smiled. "That wasn't actually what I meant. I mean, having this tent, and everything that means. I don't have any idea how to—except that I've worked beside your daughters, but to have my own tent—well, I've lived in a city all my life. I don't know what to do."

"You are still my daughter. I have daughters enough and grandchildren enough and other kin to share with you the work and the responsibility that this tent gives you. But you understand, Tess, that this is *his* tent, truly."

"Oh, yes. I understand that."

"Yet it *must* be yours as well. I trust that you have the strength to make it so."

Tess thought about this a while. Irena allowed her the silence to do so. "Yes," she said finally. "I do. Will you have some cakes?"

Irena smiled and took one. "You and I will deal very well together, Tess."

They sampled the sweets for a little while, commenting on their flavor.

"What will happen to Vera?" Tess asked at last. "And to Karolla Arkhanov?"

"Arina is willing to take Vera back but that is a question that must go before the assembled Elders of both tribes. There will have to be some punishment." She frowned. "Arina is also willing to take in Karolla Arkhanov and her two children. I don't like it. I suspect Arina of harboring a fondness for her cousin Vasil which is impairing her judgment.''

"Oh.'' Tess examined Irena Orzhekov thoughtfully. "Didn't you like Vasil?''

"Yes, I liked him. He was utterly charming, as of course he knew he was. But I would never trust him. And should it come to that, Tess,'' she said severely, "neither should you.''

Tess wisely did not respond to this bait.

"Well, Karolla was no different than the rest of us, to fall in love with a handsome face, and she has obviously been loyal to him, so perhaps their children will inherit her heart to make up for having his looks.''

"Ilya is handsome,'' Tess pointed out.

"My nephew,'' said his aunt, "is arrogant, ambitious, impulsive, and even vain, but he is not, I think, conceited, Tess. If you have a duty to your kin in this far-off city, you must not let Ilya bully you into staying here. I love my nephew but I am not blind to his faults.''

"It is true, Mother Orzhekov, that I have a duty to my brother. But I also—'' She hesitated, twining her fingers together. *But you also have a duty to yourself. And sometimes you cannot understand how to serve a greater cause until you understand yourself.*

"I also have time—'' time enough, that the jaran could not comprehend— "to fulfill my duty to him in years to come. But I will write him a letter.'' Tess paused and smiled, remembering the letter she had left him on the *Oshaki* that he had never received. "I will write Charles a letter that explains honestly what has happened and the choice I have made.'' *Because,* she thought, *I am no longer afraid to be honest with him or to make choices that he might not approve of.*

Irena nodded, as if Tess's unspoken thought had spoken to her as clearly as her words. "You must be tired, my daughter. I'll leave you now.'' She gave Tess a brief but warm kiss on the cheek and left.

As soon as Irena had gone, Tess took Marco's letter out, unrolled it, and began to write a letter to Charles on the blank side. The words came swiftly and with confidence. Just as she finished, Katerina and Ivan tore into the tent and leapt on the pillow vacated by their grandmother. Kolia toddled in after them and immediately grabbed a cake in each hand.

"Vania!" Sonia called from outside. "I told you not to bother Tess. Katerina!"

"Out."

Tess started around. "Ilya!"

He stood in the curtained entrance that partitioned off the inner chamber. "Ivan. Katerina. Out. Your mother is calling. Yes, here's a kiss." They accepted their kisses and then ran out, giggling. Kolia lifted his arms, and Ilya sighed, but he picked him up. "You're a nuisance, kriye," he said, and kissed him on each fat cheek. "Now." He took him over to the entrance and with a firm shove propelled him outside.

"There you are, Kolia," they heard Sonia say. "Tess?"

"I'm fine," she replied. In a lower voice, "Ilya, are you mad? I'm not supposed to see you for nine days."

"Why did I mark you, damn it?" He sat down beside her and absently ate the last cake. "I forgot all about those damned restrictions."

"You'd better leave."

"Oh, no, my wife. It is from dawn tomorrow that I may not see you, and I'll, by the gods, stay in this tent until dawn."

"Yes, my husband," she said mildly.

He put his arm around her and they sat for a time in silence.

"I want children, Tess," he said suddenly.

"Yes, Ilya," she agreed.

He glanced at her. "I don't trust you when you're in this mood."

"Which mood?"

"You're being very agreeable."

"Oh, I'm sure it won't last."

He sighed, content, and gathered her closer to him.

The two lanterns cast a warm glow across them, the blending of two shifting, impatient fires that, never still, were yet constant. Their light burned on through the night, long since forgotten. Outside, the wind stirred the grass, and the river ran on, and a fire smoldered between tents, ready to take flame again in the morning.

DAW

Coming in HARDCOVER in August 1992:

CHANUR'S LEGACY
by C.J. Cherryh

Ten years have passed since the events of CHANUR'S HOME-COMING, and Pyanfar, captain of *The Pride*, has become the most important personage in the Compact, while her niece Hilfy is now captain of her own vessel, *Chanur's Legacy*. Hard-pressed to take care of the business of the *Legacy*, Hilfy accepts a million credits from Meetpoint's stsho stationmaster to transport a small, mysterious "religious" object to another stsho on Urtur Station. Despite the warnings of those around her, and her own misgivings, Hilfy feels it's a commission she just can't turn down. But as complications begin to unfold, Hilfy and her crew are caught in an ever tightening web of intrigue, and only time will tell whether the young captain can determine who is truly her ally and who is her enemy in this deadly game of interstellar politics.

☐ **Hardcover Edition** UE2519—$20.00

DAW
Science Fiction at Its Best

W. Michael Gear

Forbidden Borders

He was the most hated and feared power in human-controlled space—
and only he could become the means of his own destruction. . . .
☐ **REQUIEM FOR THE CONQUEROR (#1)** UE2477—$4.99
☐ **RELIC OF EMPIRE (#2)** UE2492—$5.99

Cheryl J. Franklin

The Network/Consortium Novels:

☐ **THE INQUISITOR** (UE2512—$5.99)
Would an entire race be destroyed by one man's ambitions— and one
woman's thirst for vengeance?

Betty Anne Crawford

☐ **THE BUSHIDO INCIDENT** (UE2517—$4.99)

In the future in which Japan economically dominates the Earth, the
past and the present are constantly being "rewritten" by their paid
Historians. But So Pak, son of Earth's finest Historian, seeks another
path—the path of "freedom." Seeking to learn the truth about two lost
mining expeditions, he launches a mission on the starship *Bushido*. But
someone is determined that neither So Pak nor the *Bushido* will ever
return to Earth.
